Songs of the Dying Earth

Songs of the Dying Earth

Stories in honor of Jack Vance

Edited by

George R. R. Martin and Gardner Dozois

TOR®

A Tom Doherty Associates Book
New York

This is a work of fiction. All of the characters, organizations, and events portrayed in these stories are either products of the authors' imaginations or are used fictitiously.

SONGS OF THE DYING EARTH

First published in the United States by Subterranean Press

A Tor Book
Published by Tom Doherty Associates, LLC
175 Fifth Avenue
New York, NY 10010

www.tor-forge.com

Library of Congress Cataloging-in-Publication Data

Songs of the Dying Earth / [edited by] George R. R. Martin and Gardner Dozois.—1st ed.
p. cm.
"A Tom Doherty Associates book."
A tribute anthology to Jack Vance's seminal Dying Earth series.
ISBN 978-0-7653-2086-5
1. Science fiction, American. 2. Fantasy fiction, American. I. Martin, George R. R. II. Dozois, Gardner R.
PS648.S3S49 2010
813'.0876208—dc22

2010035742

First Tor Edition: December 2010

Printed in the United States of America

0 9 8 7 6 5 4 3 2 1

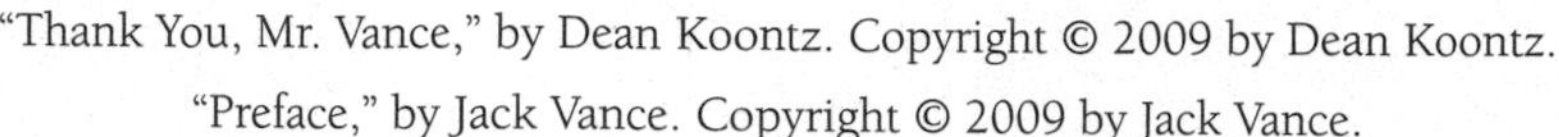

COPYRIGHT NOTICES:

To Jack Vance, the maestro,
with thanks for all the great tales,
and for letting us play with your toys.

Table of Contents

THANK YOU, MR. VANCE

By Dean Koontz

IN 1966, at 21, fresh from college, I was a fool and possibly deranged, although not seriously dangerous. I was a well-read fool, especially in science fiction. For twelve years, I pored through at least a book a week in that genre. I felt that I belonged in one of the other worlds or far futures of those tales more than I did in the world and time in which I'd been born, less because I had a wide romantic streak than because I had low self-esteem and longed to shed the son-of-the-town-drunk identity that fate had given me.

During the first five years that I wrote for a living, I produced mostly science fiction. I was not good at it. I sold what I wrote—twenty novels, twenty-eight short stories—but little of that work was memorable, and some was execrable. All these years later, only two of those novels and four or five of those stories might not raise in me a suicidal urge if I reread them.

As a reader, I could tell the difference between great science fiction and the mediocre stuff, and I was drawn to the best, which I often reread. Considering that I was inspired by quality, I should not have turned out so many dreary tales. I was driven to write fast by economic necessity; Gerda and I had been married with $150 and a used car, and though bill collectors were not breaking down the door, the specter of destitution haunted me. A need for money, however, is an insufficient excuse.

In November of 1971, as I moved toward suspense and comic fiction and away from writing SF, I discovered Jack Vance. Considering the hundreds of science fiction novels I had read, I am amazed that I had not until then sampled Mr. Vance's work. With the intention of reading him, I bought numerous paperbacks of his novels but never opened one, partly because the covers gave me a wrong impression of the contents. On my shelves today is an Ace edition of *The Eyes of the Overworld*, with a cover price of 45 cents, featuring Cugel the Clever in a flaring pink cape against a background of cartoonish mushrooms like giant genitalia. A 50-cent Ace edition of *Big Planet* features well-rendered men with ray guns riding badly drawn alien beasts of dubious anatomy. The first book I read by Jack Vance, in November 1971, was *Emphyrio*, published at the budget-busting price of 75 cents. The cover illustration—perhaps by Jeff Jones—was sophisticated and mystical.

Every writer has a short list of novels that electrified him, that inspired him to try new narrative techniques and fresh stylistic devices. For me, *Emphyrio* and *The Dying Earth* are such books. Enthralled with the former, I finished the entire novel without getting up from my armchair, and the same day I read the latter. Between November of 1971 and March of 1972, I read every Jack Vance novel and every piece of his short fiction published to that time—and although many more books were to come, even then he had a long bibliography. Only two other authors have so captivated me that for a time I became immersed in their work to the exclusion of all other reading: on discovering John D. MacDonald, I read thirty-four of his novels in thirty days; and after stubbornly avoiding the fiction of Charles Dickens through high school and college, I read *A Tale of Two Cities* in 1974 and, over the next three months, every word of fiction Dickens published.

Three things in particular fascinate me about Mr. Vance's work, the first being a vivid sense of place. Far planets and distant future Earths are so well portrayed that they expand like real and fully colored vistas in the mind's eye. This is achieved by many means, but primarily by close attention to architecture, first the architecture of key buildings; and in architecture I include interior design. The opening chapters of *The Last Castle* or *The Dragon Masters* contain excellent examples of this. Furthermore, when Jack Vance describes the natural world, he does so in the manner neither of a geologist nor a naturalist, nor even as a poet might describe it, but again with an eye for the architecture of nature, not merely of its geological features but also of its flora and fauna. The appearance of things does not intrigue him as much as does their *structure*. Consequently, his descriptions have depth and complexity from which images arise in the reader's mind that are in fact poetic. This fascination with structures is evident in every aspect of his fiction, whether it is the structure of languages in *The Languages of Pao* or the structure of a system of magic in *The Dying Earth*; and in every novel and novelette he has written, alien cultures and far-future human societies ring true because he gives us the matrix and the lattice, the foundation and the framing on which the visible walls are stood and hung.

The second quality of Mr. Vance's fiction that fascinates me is his masterly evocation of mood. Each of his works features a subtly modified syntax, scheme of imagery, and coherent system of figures of speech unique to that tale, usually in the service of the implicit meaning but *always* in the service of mood, which itself grows from his subtext, as it should. I am a sucker for mood. I can forgive a writer many faults if he has the capacity to weave a warp and weft of mood from page one to the end of his story. One of the great things about Jack Vance is that the reader is enthralled by the mood of each piece without having to overlook any faults.

Third, although the people in a Vance science-fiction novel are less real than those in the few mystery novels that he wrote, and are constricted by the conventions of a genre that for many decades valued color and action and cool ideas above characters with depth, they are memorable and, over the body of his work, reveal that the author puts much of himself in the cast members of his tales. The recognition of the author intimately threaded through the tapestry of key characters exposed to me, back there in 1971 and '72, a primary reason why my science fiction often failed: as a child raised in poverty and always-pending violence, I had read science fiction largely for escape; therefore, as a writer, I was loath to draw upon my most intense life experiences when writing SF, but instead usually wrote it as sheer escapism.

In spite of the exotic and hypercolorful nature of Jack Vance's work, reading so much of his fiction in such a short time led me to the realization that I was withholding my soul from the stories that I wrote. If I had remained in science fiction after this moment of enlightenment, I would have written books radically different from those that I had produced between 1967 and 1971. But I immersed myself in the Vance universe as I was moving on to suspense novels like *Chase* and comic novels like *Hanging On*; consequently, the lesson I learned from him was applied to everything I wrote after leaving his preferred genre.

I know nothing about Jack Vance's life, only the fiction that he has written. During those five months in 1971 and '72, however, and every time I have read a Vance novel in the years since, I have known I am reading the work of someone who enjoyed a largely happy childhood and perhaps an idyllic one. If I'm wrong about this, I don't want to be corrected. When I settle into a Vance story, I see the sense of wonder and the confidence and the generous spirit of someone who was given a childhood and adolescence free from fear and without want, who used those years to explore the world and, through that exploration, came to embrace it with exuberance. Although my journey to a happy adulthood followed a dark and sometimes desperate path, I do not envy Jack Vance if his route was sunnier; instead, I delight in the worlds of wonder that his experiences made it possible for him to create, and not least of all in that singular world that awaits its end under a fading sun.

The Dying Earth and its sequels comprise one of the most powerful fantasy/science-fiction concepts in the history of the genre. They are packed with adventure but also with ideas, and the vision of uncounted human civilizations stacked one atop another like layers in a phyllo pastry thrills even as it induces a sense of awe—awe in the purest sense of the word—the irresistible yielding of the mind to something so grand in character that it cannot be entirely grasped in all its ramifications but necessarily harbors an ineffable mystery at its heart. The fragility and transience of all things, the nobility of humanity's struggle against the certainty of an entropic resolution, gives *The Dying Earth* a poignancy rare in novels of fantastic romance.

Thank you, Mr. Vance, for so much pleasure over the years and for an important moment of enlightenment that made my writing better than it would have been if I had never read *Emphyrio*, *The Dying Earth*, and all your other marvelous stories.

PREFACE

By Jack Vance

I WAS happily surprised when I learned that so many high-echelon, top-drawer writers had undertaken to produce a set of stories based upon some of my early work. Here I must insert a caveat: some may regard the above sentiment as the usual boilerplate. In no way! For a fact, I am properly flattered by this sort of recognition.

I wrote *The Dying Earth* while working as an able seaman aboard cargo ships, cruising, for the most part, back and forth across the Pacific. I would take my clipboard and fountain pen out on deck, find a place to sit, look out over the long rolling blue swells: ideal circumstances in which to let the imagination wander.

The influences which underlie these stories go back to when I was ten or eleven years old and subscribed to *Weird Tales* magazine. My favorite writer was C. L. Moore, whom to this day I revere. My mother had a taste for romantic fantasy, and she collected books by an Edwardian writer called Robert Chambers, who is now all but forgotten. He wrote such novels as *The King in Yellow*, *The Maker of Moons*, *The Tracer of Lost Persons* and many others. Also on our bookshelves were the Oz books of L. Frank Baum, as well as *Tarzan of the Apes* and the Barsoom sequences of Edgar Rice Burroughs. Around this same time Hugo Gernsback began publishing *Amazing Stories Monthly* and *Amazing Stories Quarterly*; I devoured both on a regular basis. The fairy tales of Lord Dunsany, an Irish peer, were also a substantial influence; and I cannot ignore the great Jeffery Farnol, another forgotten author, who wrote romantic swashbucklers. In short, it is fair to say that almost everything I read in my early years became transmuted into some aspect of my own style.

Many years after the first publication of *The Dying Earth*, I used the same setting for the adventures of Cugel and Rhialto, although these books are quite different from the original tales in mood and atmosphere. It is nice to hear that these stories continue to live in the minds of readers and writers alike. To both, and to everyone concerned with the production of this collection, I tip my hat in thanks and appreciation. And to the reader specifically, I promise that you, upon turning the page, will be much entertained.

—Jack Vance
Oakland, 2008

ROBERT SILVERBERG

The True Vintage of Erzuine Thale

ROBERT SILVERBERG is one of the most famous SF writers of modern times, with dozens of novels, anthologies, and collections to his credit. As both writer and editor (he was editor of the original anthology series New Dimensions, perhaps the most acclaimed anthology series of its era), Silverberg was one of the most influential figures of the Post New Wave era of the '70s, and continues to be at the forefront of the field to this very day, having won a total of five Nebula Awards and four Hugo Awards, plus SFWA's prestigious Grandmaster Award.

His novels include the acclaimed *Dying Inside*, *Lord Valentine's Castle*, *The Book of Skulls*, *Downward to the Earth*, *Tower of Glass*, *Son of Man*, *Nightwings*, *The World Inside*, *Born With The Dead*, *Shadrack In The Furnace*, *Thorns*, *Up the Line*, *The Man in the Maze*, *Tom O' Bedlam*, *Star of Gypsies*, *At Winter's End*, *The Face of the Waters*, *Kingdoms of the Wall*, *Hot Sky at Morning*, *The Alien Years*, *Lord Prestimion*, *Mountains of Majipoor*, two novel-length expansions of famous Isaac Asimov stories, *Nightfall* and *The Ugly Little Boy*, *The Longest Way Home*, and the mosaic novel *Roma Eterna*. His collections include *Unfamiliar Territory*, *Capricorn Games*, *Majipoor Chronicles*, *The Best of Robert Silverberg*, *The Conglomeroid Cocktail Party*, *Beyond the Safe Zone*, and the ongoing program from Subterranean Press to publish his collected stories, which now runs to four volumes, and *Phases of the Moon: Stories from Six Decades*, and a collection of early work, *In the Beginning*. His reprint anthologies are far too numerous to list here, but include *The Science Fiction Hall of Fame, Volume One* and the distinguished *Alpha* series, among dozens of others. He lives with his wife, writer Karen Haber, in Oakland, California.

Here he takes us south of Almery to languid Ghiusz on the Claritant Peninsula adjoining the Klorpentine Sea, a place as balmy as it gets on The Dying Earth, to meet a poet and philosopher who takes to heart the ancient adage, Eat, drink, and be merry, for tomorrow we die. Especially *drink*.

The True Vintage of Erzuine Thale

ROBERT SILVERBERG

Puillayne of Ghiusz was a man born to every advantage life offers, for his father was the master of great estates along the favored southern shore of the Claritant Peninsula, his mother was descended from a long line of wizards who held hereditary possession of many great magics, and he himself had been granted a fine strong-thewed body, robust health, and great intellectual power.

Yet despite these gifts, Puillayne, unaccountably, was a man of deep and ineradicable melancholic bent. He lived alone in a splendid sprawling manse overlooking the Klorpentine Sea, a place of parapets and barbicans, loggias and pavilions, embrasures and turrets and sweeping pilasters, admitting only a few intimates to his solitary life. His soul was ever clouded over by a dark depressive miasma, which Puillayne was able to mitigate only through the steady intake of strong drink. For the world was old, nearing its end, its very rocks rounded and smoothed by time, every blade of grass invested with the essence of a long antiquity, and he knew from his earliest days that futurity was an empty vessel and only the long

past supported the fragile present. This was a source of extreme infestivity to him. By assiduous use of drink, and only by such use of it, he could succeed from time to time in lifting his gloom, not through the drink itself but through the practice of his art, which was that of poetry: his wine was his gateway to his verse, and his verse, pouring from him in unstoppable superiloquent abundance, gave him transient release from despond. The verse forms of every era were at his fingertips, be they the sonnet or the sestina or the villanelle or the free chansonette so greatly beloved by the rhyme-loathing poets of Sheptun-Am, and in each of them he displayed ineffable mastery. It was typical of Puillayne, however, that the gayest of his lyrics was invariably tinged with ebon despair. Even in his cups, he could not escape the fundamental truth that the world's day was done, that the sun was a heat-begrudging red cinder in the darkening sky, that all striving had been in vain for Earth and its denizens; and those ironies contaminated his every thought.

And so, and so, cloistered in his rambling chambers on the heights above the metropole of Ghiusz, the capital city of the happy Claritant that jutted far out into the golden Klorpentine, sitting amidst his collection of rare wines, his treasures of exotic gems and unusual woods, his garden of extraordinary horticultural marvels, he would regale his little circle of friends with verses such as these:

The night is dark. The air is chill.
Silver wine sparkles in my amber goblet.
But it is too soon to drink. First let me sing.

Joy is done! The shadows gather!
Darkness comes, and gladness ends!
Yet though the sun grows dim,
My soul takes flight in drink.

What care I for the crumbling walls?
What care I for the withering leaves?
Here is wine!

Who knows? This could be the world's last night.
Morning, perhaps, will bring a day without dawn.
The end is near. Therefore, friends, let us drink!

Darkness…darkness…
The night is dark. The air is chill.
Therefore, friends, let us drink!
Let us drink!

"How beautiful those verses are," said Gimbiter Soleptan, a lithe, playful man given to the wearing of green damask pantaloons and scarlet sea-silk blouses. He was, perhaps, the closest of Puillayne's little band of companions, antithetical though he was to him in the valence of his nature. "They make me wish to dance, to sing—and also…" Gimbiter let the thought trail off, but glanced meaningfully to the sideboard at the farther end of the room.

"Yes, I know. And to drink."

Puillayne rose and went to the great sideboard of black candana overpainted with jagged lines of orpiment and gambodge and flake blue in which he kept the wines he had chosen for the present week. For a moment, he hesitated among the tight-packed row of flasks. Then his hand closed on the neck of one fashioned from pale-violet crystal, through which a wine of radiant crimson glowed with cheery insistence.

"One of my best," he announced. "A claret, it is, of the Scaumside vineyard in Ascolais, waiting forty years for this night. But why let it wait longer? There may be no later chances."

"As you have said, Puillayne. 'This could be the world's last night.' But why, then, do you still disdain to open Erzuine Thale's True Vintage? By your own argument, you should seize upon it while opportunity yet remains. And yet you refuse."

"Because," Puillayne said, smiling gravely, and glancing toward the cabinet of embossed doors where that greatest of all wines slept behind barriers of impenetrable spells, "This may, after all, *not* be the world's last night, for none of the fatal signs have made themselves apparent yet. The True Vintage deserves only the grandest of occasions. I shall wait a while longer to broach it. But the wine I have here is itself no trifle. Observe me now."

He set out a pair of steep transparent goblets rimmed with purple gold, murmured the word to the wine-flask that unsealed its stopper, and held it aloft to pour. As the wine descended into the goblet it passed through a glorious spectrum of transformation, now a wild scarlet, now deep crimson, now carmine, mauve, heliotrope shot through with lines of topaz,

and, as it settled to its final hue, a magnificent coppery gold. "Come," said Puillayne, and led his friend to the viewing-platform overlooking the bay, where they stood side by side, separated by the great vase of black porcelain that was one of Puillane's most cherished treasures, in which a porcelain fish of the same glossy black swam insolently in the air.

Night had just begun to fall. The feeble red sun hovered precariously over the western sea. Fierce eye-stabbing stars already blazed furiously out of the dusky sky to north and south of it, arranging themselves in the familiar constellations: the Hoary Nimbus, the Panoply of Swords, the Cloak of Cantenax, the Claw. The twilight air was cooling swiftly. Even here in this land of the far south, sheltered by the towering Kelpusar range from the harsh winds that raked Almery and the rest of Grand Motholam, there was no escape from the chill of the night. Everywhere, even here, such modest daily warmth as the sun afforded fled upward through the thinning air the moment that faint light was withdrawn.

Puillayne and Gimbiter were silent a time, savoring the power of the wine, which penetrated subtly, reaching from one region of their souls to the next until it fastened on the heart. For Puillayne, it was the fifth wine of the day, and he was well along in the daily defeat of his innate somberness of spirit, having brought himself to the outer borderlands of the realm of sobriety. A delightful gyroscopic instability now befuddled his mind. He had begun with a silver wine of Kauchique flecked with molecules of gold, then had proceeded to a light ruby wine of the moorlands, a sprightly sprezzogranito from Cape Thaumissa, and, finally, a smooth but compelling dry Harpundium as a prelude to this venerable grandissimus that he currently was sharing with his friend. That progression was a typical one for him. Since early manhood he had rarely passed a waking hour without a goblet in his hand.

"How beautiful this wine is," said Gimbiter finally.

"How dark the night," said Puillayne. For even now he could not escape the essentially rueful cast of his thoughts.

"Forget the darkness, dear friend, and enjoy the beauty of the wine. But no: they are forever mingled for you, are they not, the darkness and the wine. The one encircles the other in ceaseless chase."

This far south, the sun plunged swiftly below the horizon. The ferocity of the starlight was remorseless now. The two men sipped thoughtfully.

Gimbiter said, after a further span of silence, "Do you know, Puillayne, that strangers are in town asking after you?"

"Strangers, indeed? And asking for me?"

"Three men from the north. Uncouth-looking ones. I have this from my gardener, who tells me that they have been making inquiries of *your* gardener."

"Indeed," said Puillayne, with no great show of interest.

"They are a nest of rogues, these gardeners. They all spy on us, and sell our secrets to any substantial bidder."

"You tell me no news here, Gimbiter."

"Does it not concern you that rough-hewn strangers are asking questions?"

Puillayne shrugged. "Perhaps they are admirers of my verses, come to hear me recite."

"Perhaps they are thieves, come from afar to despoil you of some of your fabled treasures."

"Perhaps they are both. In that case, they must hear my verses before I permit any despoiling."

"You are very casual, Puillayne."

"Friend, the sun itself is dying as we stand here. Shall I lose sleep over the possibility that strangers may take some of my trinkets from me? With such talk you distract us from this unforgettable wine. I beg you, drink, Gimbiter, and put these strangers out of your mind."

"I can put them from mine," said Gimbiter, "but I wish you would devote some part of yours to them." And then he ceased to belabor the point, for he knew that Puillayne was a man utterly without fear. The profound bleakness that lay at the core of his spirit insulated him from ordinary cares. He lived without hope and therefore without uneasiness. And by this time of day, Gimbiter understood, Puillayne had further reinforced himself within an unbreachable palisade of wine.

The three strangers, though, were troublesome to Gimbiter. He had gone to the effort of inspecting them himself earlier that day. They had taken lodgings, said his head gardener, at the old hostelry called the Blue Wyvern, between the former ironmongers' bazaar and the bazaar of silk and spices, and it was easy enough for Gimbiter to locate them as they moved along the boulevard that ran down the spine of the bazaar quarter. One was a squat, husky man garbed in heavy brown furs, with purple leather leggings and boots, and a cap of black bearskin trimmed with a fillet of gold. Another, tall and loose-limbed, sported a leopardskin tarboosh, a robe of yellow muslin, and red boots ostentatiously spurred with

the spines of the roseate urchin. The third, clad unpretentiously in a simple gray tunic and a quilted green mantle of some coarse heavy fabric, was of unremarkable stature and seemed all but invisible beside his two baroque confederates, until one noticed the look of smouldering menace in his deep-set, resolute, reptilian eyes, set like obsidian ellipsoids against his chalky-hued face.

Gimbiter made such inquiries about them at the hostelry as were feasible, but all he could learn was that they were mercantile travelers from Hither Almery or even farther north, come to the southlands on some enterprise of profit. But even the innkeeper knew that they were aware of the fame of the metropole's great poet Puillayne, and were eager to achieve an audience with him. And therefore Gimbiter had duly provided his friend with a warning; but he was sadly aware that he could do no more than that.

Nor was Puillayne's air of unconcern an affectation. One who has visited the mephitic shores of the Sea of Nothingness and returned is truly beyond all dismay. He knows that the world is an illusion built upon a foundation of mist and wind, and that it is great folly to attach oneself in any serious way to any contrary belief. During his more sober moments, of course, Puillayne of Ghiusz was as vulnerable to despair and anxiety as anyone else; but he took care to reach with great speed for his beloved antidote the instant that he felt tendrils of reality making poisonous incursions through his being. But for wine, he would have had no escape from his eternally sepulchral attitudinizing.

So the next day, and the next, days that were solitary by choice for him, Puillayne moved steadfastly through his palace of antiquarian treasures on his usual diurnal rounds, rising at day-break to bathe in the spring that ran through his gardens, then breakfasting on his customary sparse fare, then devoting an hour to the choice of the day's wines and sampling the first of them.

In mid-morning, as the glow of the first flask of wine still lingered in him, he sat sipping the second of the day and reading awhile from some volume of his collected verse. There were fifty or sixty of them by now, bound identically in the black vellum made from the skin of fiendish Deodands that had been slaughtered for the bounty placed upon such fell creatures; and these were merely the poems that he had had sufficient sobriety to remember to indite and preserve, out of the scores that poured from him so freely. Puillayne constantly read and reread them with keen pleasure. Though he affected modesty with others, within the shelter of his own soul he had an unabashed admiration for his poems, which the second wine of the day invariably amplified.

Afterward, before the second wine's effect had completely faded, it was his daily practice to stroll through the rooms that held his cabinet of wonders, inspecting with ever-fresh delight the collection of artifacts and oddities that he had gathered during youthful travels that had taken him as far north as the grim wastes of Fer Aquila, as far to the east as the monster-infested deadlands beyond the Land of the Falling Wall, where ghouls and deadly grues swarmed and thrived, as far west as ruined Ampridatvir and sullen Azederach on the sunset side of the black Supostimon Sea. In each of these places, the young Puillayne had acquired curios, not because the assembling of them had given him any particular pleasure in and of itself, but because the doing of it turned his attention for the moment, as did the drinking of wine, from the otherwise inescapable encroachment of gloom that from boyhood on had perpetually assailed his consciousness. He drew somber amusement now from fondling these things, which recalled to him some remote place he had visited, summoning up memories of great beauty and enchanting peace, or arduous struggle and biting discomfort, it being a matter of no importance to him which it might have been, so long as the act of remembering carried him away from the here and now.

Then he would take his lunch, a repast scarcely less austere than his morning meal had been, always accompanying it by some third wine chosen for its soporific qualities. A period of dozing invariably followed, and then a second cooling plunge in the garden spring, and then—it was a highlight of the day—the ceremonial opening of the fourth flask of wine, the one that set free his spirit and allowed the composition of that day's verses. He scribbled down his lines with haste, never pausing to revise, until the fervor of creation had left him. Once more, then, he read, or uttered the simple spell that filled his bayside audifactorium with music. Then came dinner, a more notable meal than the earlier two, one that would do justice to the fifth and grandest wine of the day, in the choosing of which he had devoted the greatest of care; and then, hoping as ever that the dying sun might perish in the night and release him at last from his funereal anticipations, he gave himself to forlorn dreamless sleep.

So it passed for the next day, and the next, and, on the third day after Gimbiter Soleptan's visit, the three strangers of whom Gimbiter had warned him presented themselves at last at the gates of his manse.

They selected for their unsolicited intrusion the hour of the second wine, arriving just as he had taken one of the vellum-bound volumes of his verse from its shelf. Puillayne maintained a small staff of wraiths and revenants for his household needs, disliking as he did the use of living beings as domestic subordinates, and one of these pallid eidolons came to him with news of the visitors.

Puillayne regarded the ghostly creature, which just then was hovering annoyingly at the borders of transparency as though attempting to communicate its own distress, with indifference. "Tell them they are welcome. Admit them upon the half hour."

It was far from his usual custom to entertain visitors during the morning hours. The revenant was plainly discommoded by this surprising departure from habit. "Lordship, if one may venture to express an opinion—"

"One may not. Admit them upon the half hour."

Puillayne used the interval until then to deck himself in formal morning garb: a thin tunic of light color, a violet mantle, laced trousers of the same color worn over underdrawers of deep red, and, above all the rest, a stiff unlined garment of a brilliant white. He had already selected a chilled wine from the Bay of Sanreale, a brisk vintage of a shimmering metallic-gray hue, for his second wine; now he drew forth a second flask of it and placed it beside the first. The house-wraith returned, precisely upon the half hour, with Puillayne's mysterious guests.

They were, exactly as Gimibiter Soleptan had opined, a rough-hewn, uncouth lot. "I am Kesztrel Tsaye," announced the shortest of the three, who seemed to be the dominant figure: a burly person wrapped in the thick shaggy fur of some wild beast, and topped with a gold-trimmed cap of a different, glossier fur. His dense black beard encroached almost completely on his blunt, unappealing features, like an additional shroud of fur. "This is Unthan Vyorn"—a nod toward a lanky, insolent-looking fellow in a yellow robe, flamboyantly baroque red boots, and an absurd betasseled bit of headgear that displayed a leopard's spots—"and this," he said, glancing toward a third man, pale and unremarkably garbed, notable mainly for an appearance of extreme inconsequence bordering on nonpresence, but for his eyes, which were cold and brooding, "is Malion Gainthrust. We three are profound admirers of your great art, and have come from our homes in the Maurenron foothills to express our homage."

"I can barely find words to convey the extreme delight I experience now, as I stand in the very presence of Puillayne of Ghiusz," said lanky Unthan Vyorn in a disingenuously silken voice with just the merest hint of sibilance.

"It seems to me that you are capable of finding words readily enough," Puillayne observed. "But perhaps you mean only a conventional abnegation. Will you share my wine with me? At this hour of the morning, I customarily enjoy something simple, and I have selected this Sanreale."

He indicated the pair of rounded gray flasks. But from the depths of his furs, Kesztrel Tsaye drew two globular green flasks of his own and set them on the nearby table. "No doubt your choice is superb, master. But we are well aware of your love of the grape, and among the gifts we bring to you are these carboys of our own finest vintage, the celebrated azure ambrosia of the Maurenrons, with which you are, perhaps, unfamiliar, and which will prove an interesting novelty to your palate."

Puillaine had not, in truth, ever tasted the so-called ambrosia of the Maurenrons, but he understood it to be an acrid and deplorable stuff, fit only for massaging cramped limbs. Yet he maintained an affable cordiality, studiously examining the nearer of the two carboys, holding it to the light, hefting it as though to determine the specific gravity of its contents. "The repute of your wines is not unknown to me," he said diplomatically. "But I propose we set these aside for later in the day, since, as I have explained, I prefer only a light wine before my midday meal, and perhaps the same is true of you." He gave them an inquisitive look. They made no objection; and so he murmured the spell of opening and poured out a ration of the Sanreale for each of them and himself.

By way of salute, Unthan Vyorn offered a quotation from one of Puillayne's best-known little pieces:

What is our world? It is but a boat
That breaks free at sunset, and drifts away
Without a trace.

His intonation was vile, his rhythm was uncertain, but at least he had managed the words accurately, and Puillayne supposed that his intentions were kindly. As he sipped his wine, he studied this odd trio with detached curiosity. They seemed like crude ruffians, but perhaps their unpolished manner was merely the typical style of the people of the Maurenrons, a locality to which his far-flung travels had never taken him. For all he knew, they were dukes or princes or high ministers of that northern place. He wondered in an almost incurious way what it was that they wanted with him. Merely to quote his own poetry to him was an insufficient motive for traveling such a distance. Gimbiter believed that they were malevolent; and it might well be that Gimbiter, a shrewd observer of mankind, was correct in that. For the nonce, however, his day's intake of wine had fortified him against anxiety on that score. To Puillayne, they were at the moment merely a puzzling novelty. He would wait to see more.

"Your journey," he said politely, "was it a taxing one?"

"We know some small magics, and we had a few useful spells to guide us. Going through the Kelpusars, there was only one truly difficult passage for us," said Unthan Vyorn, "which was the crossing of the Mountain of the Eleven Uncertainties."

"Ah," said Puillayne. "I know it well." It was a place of bewildering confusion, where a swarm of identical peaks confronted the traveler and all roads seemed alike, though only one was correct and the others led into dire unpleasantness. "But you found your way through, evidently, and coped with equal deftness with the Gate of Ghosts just beyond, and the perilous Pillars of Yan Sfou."

"The hope of attaining the very place where now we find ourselves drew us onward through all obstacles," Unthan Vyorn said, outdoing even himself in unctuosity of tone. And again he quoted Puillayne:

The mountain roads we traveled rose ten thousand cilavers high.
The rivers we crossed were more turbulent than a hundred demons.
And our voices were lost in the thunder of the cataracts.
We cut through brambles that few swords could slash.
And then beyond the mists we saw the golden Klorpentine
And it was as if we had never known hardship at all.

How barbarously he attacked the delicate lines! How flat was his tone as he came to the ecstatic final couplet! But Puillayne masked his scorn. These were foreigners; they were his guests, however self-invited they might be; his responsibility was to maintain them at their ease. And he found them diverting, in their way. His life in these latter years had slipped into inflexible routine. The advent of poetry-quoting northern barbarians was an amusing interlude in his otherwise constricted days. He doubted more than ever, now, Gimbiter's hypothesis that they meant him harm. There seemed nothing dangerous about these three except, perhaps, the chilly eyes of the one who did not seem to speak. His friend Gimbiter evidently had mistaken bumptiousness for malversation and malefic intent.

Fur-swathed Kesztrel Tsaye said, "We know, too, that you are a collector of exotica. Therefore we bring some humble gifts for your delight." And he, too, offered a brief quotation:

Let me have pleasures in this life
For the next is a dark abyss!

"If you will, Malion Gainthrust—"

Kesztrel Tsaye nodded to the icy-eyed silent man, who produced from somewhere a sack that Puillayne had not previously noticed, and drew from it a drum of red candana covered with taut-stretched thaupin-hide, atop which nine red-eyed homunculi performed an obscene dance. This was followed by a little sphere of green chalcedony out of which a trapped and weeping demon peered, and that by a beaker which overflowed with a tempting aromatic yellow liquid that tumbled to the floor and rose again to return to the vessel from which it had come. Other small toys succeeded those, until gifts to the number of ten or twelve sat arrayed before Puillayne.

During this time, Puillayne had consumed nearly all the wine from the flask he had reserved for himself, and he felt a cheering dizziness beginning to steal over him. The three visitors, though he had offered them only a third as much apiece, had barely taken any. Were they simply abstemious? Or was the shimmering wine of Sanreale too subtle for their jackanapes palates?

He said, when it appeared that they had exhausted their display of gewgaws for him, "If this wine gives you little gratification, I can select another and perhaps superior one for you, or we could open that which you have brought me."

"It is superb wine, master," Unthan Vyorn said, "and we would expect no less from you. We know, after all, that your cellar is incomparable, that it is a storehouse of the most treasured wines of all the world, that in fact it contains even the unobtainable wine prized beyond all others, the True Vintage of Erzuine Thale. This Sanreale wine you have offered us is surely not in a class with that; but it has much merit in its own way and if we

drink it slowly, it is because we cherish every swallow we take. Simply to be drinking the wine of Puillayne of Ghiusz in the veritable home of Puillayne of Ghiusz is an a honor so extreme that it constringes our throats with joy, and compels us to drink more slowly than otherwise we might."

"You know of the True Vintage, do you?" Puillayne asked.

"Is there anyone who does not? The legendary wine of the Nolwaynes who have reigned in Gammelcor since the days when the sun had the brightness of gold—the wine of miracles, the wine that offers the keenest of ecstasies that it is possible to experience—the wine that opens all doors to one with a single sip—" Unshielded covetousness now gleamed in the lanky man's eyes. "If only we could enjoy that sip! Ah, if only we could merely have a glimpse of the container that holds that wondrous elixir!"

"I rarely bring it forth, even to look at it," said Puillayne. "I fear that if I were to take it from its place of safekeeping, I would be tempted to consume it prematurely, and that is not a temptation to which I am ready to yield."

"A man of iron!" marveled Kesztrel Tsaye. "To possess the True Vintage of Erzuine Thale, and to hold off from sampling it! And why, may I ask, do you scruple to deny yourself that joy of joys?"

It was a question Puillayne had heard many times before, for his ownership of the True Vintage was not something he had concealed from his friends. "I am, you know, a prodigious scribbler of minor verse. Yes," he said, over their indignant protests, "minor verse, such a torrent of it that it would fill this manse a dozen times over if I preserved it all. I keep only a small part." He gestured moodily at the fifty volumes bound in Deodand vellum. "But somewhere within me lurks the one great poem that will recapitulate all the striving of earthly history, the epic that will be the sum and testament of us who live as we do on the precipice at the edge of the end of days. Someday I will feel that poem brimming at the perimeters of my brain and demanding release. That feeling will come, I think, when our sun is in its ultimate extremity, and the encroaching darkness is about to arrive. And then, only then, will I broach the seal on the True Vintage, and quaff the legendary wine, which indeed opens all doors, including the door of creation, so that its essence will liberate the real poet within me, and in my final drunken joy I will be permitted to set down that one great poem that I yearn to write."

"You do us all an injustice, master, if you wait to write that epic until the very eve of our doom," said Unthan Vyorn in a tone of what might almost have been sorrow sincerely framed. "For how will we be able to read it, when all has turned to ice and darkness? No poems will circulate among us as we lie there perishing in the final cold. You deny us your greatness! You withhold your gift!"

"Be that as it may," Puillayne said, "the time is not yet for opening that bottle. But I can offer you others."

From his cabinet, he selected a generous magnum of ancient Falernian, which bore a frayed label, yellowed and parched by time. The great rounded flask lacked its seal and it was obvious to all that the container was empty save for random crusts of desiccated dregs scattered about its interior. His visitors regarded it with puzzlement. "Fear not," said Puillayne. "A mage of my acquaintance made certain of my bottles subject to the Spell of Recrudescent Fluescence, among them this one. It is inexhaustibly renewable."

He turned his head aside and gave voice to the words, and, within moments, miraculous liquefaction commenced. While the magnum was filling, he summoned a new set of goblets, which he filled near to brimming for his guests and himself.

"It is a wondrous wine," said Kesztrel Tsaye after a sip or two. "Your hospitality knows no bounds, master." Indeed, such parts of his heavily bearded face that were visible were beginning to show a ruddy radiance. Unthan Vyorn likewise displayed the effects of the potent stuff, and even the taciturn Malion Gainthrust, sitting somewhat apart as though he had no business in this room, seemed to evince some reduction of his habitual glower.

Puillayne smiled benignly, sat back, let tranquility steal over him. He had not expected to be drinking the Falernian today, for it was a forceful wine, especially at this early hour. But he saw no harm in somewhat greater midday intoxication than he habitually practiced. Why, he might even find himself producing verse some hours earlier than usual. These uncouth disciples of his would probably derive some pleasure from witnessing the actual act of creation. Meanwhile, sipping steadily, he felt the walls around him beginning to sway and glide, and he ascended within himself in a gradual way until he felt himself to be floating slightly outside and above himself, a spectator of his own self, with something of a pleasant haze enveloping his mind.

Somewhat surprisingly, his guests, gathered now in a circle about him, appeared to be indulging in a disquisition on the philosophy of criminality.

Kesztrel Tsaye offered the thought that the imminence of the world's demise freed one from all the restraints of law, for it mattered very little how one behaved if shortly all accounts were to be settled with equal finality. "I disagree," said Unthan Vyorn. "We remain responsible for our acts, since, if they transgress against statute and custom, they may in truth hasten the end that threatens us."

Interposing himself in their conversation, Puillayne said dreamily, "How so?"

"The misdeeds of individuals," Unthan Vyorn replied, "are not so much offenses against human law as they are ominous disturbances in a complex filament of cause and effect by which mankind is connected on all sides with surrounding nature. I believe that our cruelties, our sins, our violations, all drain vitality from our diminishing sun."

Malion Gainthrust stirred restlessly at that notion, as though he planned at last to speak, but he controlled himself with visible effort and subsided once more into remoteness.

Puillayne said, "An interesting theory: the cumulative infamies and iniquities of our species, do you say, have taken a toll on the sun itself over the many millennia, and so we are the architects of our own extinction?"

"It could be, yes."

"Then it is too late to embrace virtue, I suspect," said Puillayne dolefully. "Through our incorrigible miscreancy we have undone ourselves beyond repair. The damage is surely irreversible in this late epoch of the world's long existence." And he sighed a great sigh of unconsolable grief. To his consternation, he found the effects of the long morning's drinking abruptly weakening: the circular gyration of the walls had lessened and that agreeable haze had cleared, and he felt almost sober again, defenseless against the fundamental blackness of his intellective processes. It was a familiar event. No quantity of wine was sufficient to stave off the darkness indefinitely.

"You look suddenly troubled, master," Kesztrel Tsaye observed. "Despite the splendor of this wine, or perhaps even because of it, I see that some alteration of mood has overtaken you."

"I am reminded of my mortality. Our dim and shriveled sun—the certainty of imminent oblivion—"

"Ah, master, consider that you should be cheered by contemplation of the catastrophe that is soon to overcome us, rather than being thrust, as you say, into despond."

"Cheered?"

"Most truly. For we each must have death come unto us in our time—it is the law of the universe—and what pain it is as we lie dying to know that others will survive after we depart! But if all are to meet their end at once, then there is no reason to feel the bite of envy, and we can go easily as equals into our common destruction."

Puillayne shook his head obstinately. "I see merit in this argument, but little cheer. My death inexorably approaches, and that would be a cause of despair to me whether or not others might survive. Envy of those who survive is not a matter of any moment to me. For me, it will be as though all the cosmos dies when I do, and the dying of our sun adds only an additional layer of regret to what is already an infinitely regrettable outcome."

"You permit yourself to sink into needless brooding, master," said Unthan Vyorn airily. "You should have another goblet of wine."

"Yes. These present thoughts of mine are pathetically insipid, and I shame myself by giving rein to them. Even in the heyday of the world, when the bright yellow sun blazed forth in full intensity, the concept of death was one that every mature person was compelled to face, and only cowards and fools looked toward it with terror or rage or anything else but acceptance and detachment. One must not lament the inevitable. But it is my flaw that I am unable to escape such feelings. Wine, I have found, is my sole anodyne against them. And even that is not fully satisfactory."

He reached again for the Falernian. But Kesztrel Tsaye, interposing himself quickly, said, "That is the very wine that has brought this adverse effect upon you, master. Let us open, instead, the wine of our country that was our gift to you. You may not be aware that it is famed for its quality of soothing the troubled heart." He signalled to Malion Gainthrust, who sprang to his feet, deftly unsealed the two green carboys of Maurenron ambrosia, and, taking fresh goblets from Puillayne's cabinet, poured a tall serving of the pale bluish wine from one carboy for Puillayne and lesser quantities from the other for himself and his two companions.

"To your health, master. Your renewed happiness. Your long life."

Puillayne found their wine unexpectedly fresh and vigorous, with none of the rough and sour flavor he had led himself to anticipate. He followed his first tentative sip with a deeper one, and then with a third. In very fact, it had a distinctly calmative effect, speedily lifting him out of the fresh slough of dejection into which he had let himself topple.

But another moment more and he detected a strange unwelcome furriness coating his tongue, and it began to seem to him that beneath the

superficial exuberance and openheartedness of the wine lay some less appetizing tinge of flavor, something almost alkaline that crept upward on his palate and negated the immediately pleasing effect of the initial taste. Then he noticed a heaviness of the mind overtaking him, and a weakness of the limbs, and it occurred to him, first, that they had been serving themselves out of one carboy and him out of another, and then, that he was unable to move, so that it became clear to him that the wine had been drugged. Fierce-eyed Malion Gainthrust stood directly before him, and he was speaking at last, declaiming a rhythmic chant which even in his drugged state Puillayne recognized as a simple binding spell that left him trussed and helpless.

Like any householder of some affluence, Puillayne had caused his manse to be protected by an assortment of defensive charms, which the magus of his family had assured him would defend him against many sorts of immical events. The most obvious was theft: there were treasures here that others might have reasons to crave. In addition, one must guard one's house against fire, subterranean tremors, the fall of heavy stones from the sky, and other risks of the natural world. But, also, Puillayne was given to drunkenness, which could well lead to irresponsibility of behavior or mere clumsiness of movement, and he had bought himself a panoply of spells against the consequences of excessive intoxication.

In this moment of danger, it seemed to him that Citrathanda's Punctilious Sentinel was the appropriate spirit to invoke, and in a dull thick-tongued way Puillayne began to recite the incantation. But over the years, his general indifference to jeopardy had led to incaution, and he had not taken the steps that were needful to maintain the potency of his guardian spirits, which had dimmed with time so that his spell had no effect. Nor would his household revenants be of the slightest use in this predicament. Their barely corporeal forms could exert no force against tangible life. Only his gardeners were incarnate beings, and they, even if they had been on the premises this late in the day, would have been unlikely to heed his call. Puillayne realized that he was altogether without protection now. Gently his guests, who now were his captors, were prodding him upward out of his couch. Kesztrel Tsaye said, "You will kindly accompany us, please, as we make our tour of your widely reputed treasury of priceless prizes."

All capacity for resistance was gone from him. Though they had left him with the power of locomotion, his arms were bound by invisible but unbreakable withes, and his spirit itself was captive to their wishes. He could do no other than let himself be led through one hall after another of his museum, staggering a little under the effect of their wine, and when they asked him of the nature of this artifact or that, he had no choice but to tell them. Whatever object caught their fancy, they removed from its case, with Malion Gainthrust serving as the means by which it was carried back to the great central room and added to a growing heap of plunder.

Thus they selected the Crystal Pillow of Carsephone Zorn, within which scenes from the daily life of any of seven subworlds could be viewed at ease, and the brocaded underrobe of some forgotten monarch of the Pharials, whose virility was enhanced twentyfold by an hour's wearing of it, and the Key of Sarpanigondar, a surgical tool by which any diseased organ of the body could be reached and healed without a breaching of the skin. They took also the Infinitely Replenishable Casket of Jade, once the utmost glory of the turban-wearing marauders of the frigid valleys of the Lesser Ghalur, and Sangaal's Remarkable Phoenix, from whose feathers fluttered a constant shower of gold dust, and the Heptachromatic Carpet of Kypard Segung, and the carbuncle-encrusted casket that contained the Incense of the Emerald Sky, and many another extraordinary object that had been part of Puillayne's hoard of fabulosities for decade upon decade.

He watched in mounting chagrin. "So you have come all this way merely to rob me, then?"

"It is not so simple," said Kesztrel Tsaye. "You must believe us when we say that we revere your poetry, and were primarily motivated to endure the difficulties of the journey by the hope of attaining your actual presence."

"You choose an odd way to demonstrate your esteem for my art, then, for you would strip me of those things which I love even while claiming to express your regard for my work."

"Does it matter who owns these things for the upcoming interim?" the bearded man asked. "In a short while, the concept of ownership itself will be a moot one. You have stressed that point frequently in your verse."

There was a certain logic to that, Puillayne admitted. As the mound of loot grew, he attempted to assuage himself by bringing himself to accept Kesztrel Tsaye's argument that the sun would soon enough reach its last moment, smothering Earth in unending darkness and burying him and all his possessions under an obdurate coating of ice twenty marasangs thick, so what significance was there in the fact that these thieves were denuding him today of these trifles? All would be lost tomorrow or the day after, whether or not he had ever admitted the caitiff trio to his door.

But that species of sophistry brought him no surcease. Realistic appraisal of the probabilities told him that the dying of the sun might yet be a thousand years away, or even more, for although its inevitability was assured, its imminence was not so certain. Though ultimately he would be bereft of everything, as would everyone else, including these three villains, Puillayne came now to the realization that, all other things being equal, he preferred to await the end of all things amidst the presence of his collected keepsakes rather than without them. In that moment, he resolved to adopt a defensive posture.

Therefore, he attempted once more to recite the Efficacious Sentinel of Citrathanda, emphasizing each syllable with a precision that he hoped might enhance the power of the spell. But his captors were so confident that there would be no result that they merely laughed as he spoke the verses, rather than making any effort to muffle his voice, and, in this, they were correct: as before, no guardian spirit came to his aid. Puillayne sensed that unless he found some more effective step to take, he was about to lose all that they had already selected, and, for all he knew, his life as well; and in that moment, facing the real possibility of personal extinction this very day, he understood quite clearly that his lifelong courtship of death had been merely a pose, that he was in no way actually prepared to take his leave of existence.

One possibility of saving himself remained.

"If you will set me free," Puillayne said, pausing an instant or two to focus their attention, "I will locate and share with you the True Vintage of Erzuine Thale."

The impact of that statement upon them was immediate and unmistakable. Their eyes brightened; their faces grew flushed and glossy; they exchanged excited glances of frank concupiscence.

Puillayne believed he understood this febrile response. They had been so overcome with an access of trivial greed, apparently, once they had had Puillayne in their power and knew themselves free to help themselves at will to the rich and varied contents of his halls, that they had forgotten for the moment that his manse contained not only such baubles as the Heptochromatic Carpet and the Infinitely Replenishable Casket, but also, hidden away somewhere in his enormous accumulation of rare wines, something vastly more desirable, the veritable wine of wines itself, the bringer of infinitely ecstatic fulfillment, the elixir of ineffable rapture, the True Vintage of Erzuine Thale. Now he had reminded them of it and all its delights; and now they craved it with an immediate and uncontrollable desire.

"A splendid suggestion," said Unthan Vyorn, betraying by his thickness of voice the intensity of his craving. "Summon the wine from its place of hiding, and we will partake."

"The bottle yields to no one's beck," Puillayne declared. "I must fetch it myself."

"Fetch it, then."

"You must first release me."

"You are capable of walking, are you not? Lead us to the wine, and we will do the rest."

"Impossible," said Puillayne. "How do you think this famed wine has survived so long? It is protected by a network of highly serviceable spells, such as Thampyron's Charm of Impartial Security, which insures that the flask will yield only to the volition of its inscribed owner, who at present is myself. If the flask senses that my volition is impaired, it will refuse to permit opening. Indeed, if it becomes aware that I am placed under extreme duress, the wine itself will be destroyed."

"What do you request of us, then?"

"Free my arms. I will bring the bottle from its nest and open it for you, and you may partake of it, and I wish you much joy of it."

"And then?"

"You will have had the rarest experience known to the soul of man, and I will have been cheated of the opportunity to give the world the epic poem that you claim so dearly to crave; and then, I hope, we will be quits, and you will leave me my little trinkets and take yourselves back to your dreary northern caves. Are we agreed?"

They looked at one another, coming quickly and wordlessly to an agreement, and Kesztrel Tsaye, with a grunt of assent, signalled to Malion Gainthrust to intone the counterspell. Puillayne felt the bonds that had embraced his arms melting away. He extended them in a lavish stretching gesture, flexed his fingers, looked expectantly at his captors.

"Now fetch the celebrated wine," said Kesztrel Tsaye.

They accompanied him back through chamber after chamber until they reached the hall where his finest wines were stored. Puillayne made a great show of searching through rack after rack, muttering to himself, shaking his head. "I have hidden it very securely," he reported after a time. "Not so much as a precaution against theft, you realize, but as a way of

making it more difficult for me to seize upon it myself in a moment of drunken impulsiveness."

"We understand," Unthan Vyorn said. "But find it, if you please. We grow impatient."

"Let me think. If I were hiding such a miraculous wine from myself, where would I put it? The Cabinet of Meritorious Theriacs? Hardly. The Cinnabar Vestibule? The Chrysochlorous Benefice? The Tabulature? The Trogonic Chamber?"

As he pondered, he could see their restiveness mounting from one instant to the next. They tapped their fingers against their thighs, they moved their feet from side to side, they ran their hands inside their garments as though weapons were hidden there. Unheeding, Puillayne continued to frown and mutter. But then he brightened. "Ah, yes, yes, of course!" And he crossed the room, threw open a low door in the wall at its farther side, reached into the dusty interior of a service aperture.

"Here," he said jubilantly. "The True Vintage of Erzuine Thale!"

"This?" said Kesztrel Tsaye, with some skepticism.

The bottle Puillayne held forth to them was a gray tapering one, dust-encrusted and unprepossessing, bearing only a single small label inscribed with barely legible runes in faint grayish ink. They crowded around like snorting basilisks inflamed with lust.

Each in turn puzzled over the writing; but none could decipher it.

"What language is that?" asked Unthan Vyorn.

"These are Nolwaynish runes," answered Puillayne. "See, see, here is the name of the maker, the famed vintner Erzuine Thale, and here is the date of the wine's manufacture, in a chronology that I fear will mean nothing to you, and this emblem here is the seal of the king of Gammelcore who was reigning at the time of the bottling."

"You would not deceive us?" said Kesztrel Thale. "You would not fob some lesser wine off on us, taking advantage of our inability to read these scrawls?"

Puillayne laughed jovially. "Put all your suspicions aside! I will not conceal the fact that I bitterly resent the imposition you are enforcing on me here, but that does not mean I can shunt aside thirty generations of family honor. Surely you must know that on my father's side I am the Eighteenth Maghada of Nalanda, and there is a geas upon me as hereditary leader of that sacred order that bans me from all acts of deceit. This is, I assure you, the True Vintage of Erzuine Thale, and nothing else. Stand a bit aside, if you will, so that I can open the flask without activating

Thampyron's Charm, for, may I remind you, any hint that I act under duress will destroy its contents. It would be a pity to have preserved this wine for so long a time only to have it become worthless vinegar in the moment of unsealing."

"You act now of your own free will," Unthan Vyorn said. "It was your choice to offer us this wine, nor was it done at our insistence."

"This is true," Puillayne responded. He set out four goblets and, contemplating the flask thoughtfully, spoke the words that would breach its seal.

"Three goblets will suffice," said Kesztrel Tsaye.

"I am not to partake?

"If you do, it will leave that much less for us."

"You are cruel indeed, depriving me even of a fourth share of this wine, which I obtained at such expense and after negotiations so prolonged I can scarcely bear to think of them. But so be it. I will have none. As you pointed out, what does it matter, or anything else, when the hour of everlasting night grows ineluctably near?"

He put one goblet aside and filled the other three. Malion Gainthrust was the first to seize his, clutching it with berserk intensity and gulping it to its depths in a single crazed ingurgitation. Instantly, his strange chilly eyes grew bright as blazing coals. The other two men drank more judiciously, frowning a bit at the first sip as though they had expected some more immediate ebullition, sipping again, frowning again, now trembling. Puillayne refilled the goblets. "Drink deep," he abjured them. "How I envy you this ecstasy of ecstasies!"

Malion Gainthrust now fell to the floor, thrashing about oddly, and, a moment later, Kesztrel Tsaye did the same, toppling like a felled tree and slapping his hands against the tiles as though to indicate some extreme inward spasm. Long-legged Unthan Vyorn, suddenly looking deathly pale, swayed erratically, clutched at his throat, and gasped, "But this is some poison, is it not? By the Thodiarch, you have betrayed us!"

"Indeed," said Puillayne blandly, as Unthan Vyorn joined his writhing fellows on the floor. "I have given you not the True Vintage of Erzuine Thale, but the Efficacious Solvent of Gibrak Lahinne. The strictures of honor placed upon me in my capacity as Eighteenth Maghada of Nalanda do not extend to a requirement that I ignore the need for self-defense. Already, I believe, the bony frame of your bodies has begun to dissolve. Your internal organs must also be under attack. You will shortly lose consciousness, I suspect, which will spare you from whatever agonies you

may at the moment be experiencing. But do you wonder that I took so harsh a step? You thought I was a helpless idle fool, and quite likely that scornful assessment was correct up until this hour, but by entering my sanctum and attempting to part me from the things I hold precious, you awakened me from my detachment and restored me to the love of life that had long ago fled from me. No longer did the impending doom of the world enfold me in paralysis. Indeed, I chose to take action against your depredations, and so—"

But he realized that there was no reason for further statements. His visitors had been reduced to puddles of yellow slime, leaving just their caps and boots and other garments, which he would add to his collection of memorabilia. The rest required only the services of his corps of revenants to remove, and then he was able to proceed with a clear mind to the remaining enterprises of a normal afternoon.

"But will you not now at last permit yourself to enjoy the True Vintage?" Gimbiter Soleptan asked him two nights later, when he and several other of Puillayne's closest friends had gathered in a tent of sky-blue silk in the garden of the poet's manse for a celebratory dinner. The intoxicating scent of the calavindra blossoms was in the air, and the pungent odor of sweet nargiise. "They might so easily have deprived you of it, and who knows but some subsequent miscreant might have more success? Best to drink it now, say I, and have the enjoyment of it before that is made impossible for you. Yes, drink it now!"

"Not quite yet," said Puillayne in a steadfast tone. "I understand the burden of your thought: seize the moment, guarantee the consumption while I can. By that reasoning, I should have guzzled it the instant those scoundrels had fallen. But you must remember that I have reserved a higher use for that wine. And the time for that use has not yet arrived."

"Yes," said Immiter of Glosz, a white-haired sage who was of all the members of Puillayne's circle the closest student of his work. "The great epic that you propose to indite in the hour of the sun's end—"

"Yes. And I must have the unbroached True Vintage to spur my hand, when that hour comes. Meanwhile, though, there are many wines here of not quite so notable a puissance that are worthy of our attention, and I propose that we ingest more than a few flasks this evening." Puillayne gestured broadly at the array of wines he had previously set out, and beckoned to his friends to help themselves. "And as you drink," he said, drawing from his brocaded sleeve a scrap of parchment, "I offer you the verses of this afternoon."

The night is coming, but what of that?
Do I not glow with pleasure still, and glow, and glow?
There is no darkness, there is no misery
So long as my flask is near!

The flower-picking maidens sing their lovely song by the jade pavilion.
The winged red khotemnas flutter brightly in the trees.
I laugh and lift my glass and drain it to the dregs.
O golden wine! O glorious day!

Surely we are still only in the springtime of our winter
And I know that death is merely a dream
When I have my flask!

AFTERWORD:

I BOUGHT the first edition of *The Dying Earth* late in 1950, and finding it was no easy matter, either, because the short-lived paperback house that brought it out published it in virtual secrecy. I read it and loved it, and I've been re-reading it with increasing pleasure in the succeeding decades and now and then writing essays about its many excellences, but it never occurred to me in all that time that I would have the privilege of writing a story of my own using the setting and tone of the Vance originals. But now I have; and it was with great reluctance that I got to its final page and had to usher myself out of that rare and wondrous world. Gladly would I have remained for another three or four sequences, but for the troublesome little fact that the world of *The Dying Earth* belongs to someone else. What a delight it was to share it, if only for a little while.

—Robert Silverberg

MATTHEW HUGHES

Grolion of Almery

ALLOWING A stranger to take refuge from the dangers of a dark and demon-haunted night in your house always involves a certain amount of risk for both stranger and householder. Particularly on the Dying Earth, where nothing is as it seems—including the householder and the stranger!

Matthew Hughes was born in Liverpool, England, but spent most of his adult life in Canada before moving back to England last year. He's worked as a journalist, as a staff speechwriter for the Canadian Ministers of Justice and Environment, and as a freelance corporate and political speechwriter in British Columbia before settling down to write fiction full-time. Clearly strongly influenced by Vance, as an author Hughes has made his reputation detailing the adventures of rogues like Henghis Hapthorn, Guth Bandar, and Luff Imbry who live in the era just *before* that of *The Dying Earth*, in a series of popular stories and novels that include *Fools Errant, Fool Me Twice*, *Black Brillion*, and *Majestrum*, with his stories being collected in *The Gist Hunter and Other Stories*. His most recent books are the novels *Hespira*, *The Spiral Labyrinth*, *Template*, and *The Commons*.

Grolion of Almery

MATTHEW HUGHES

When next I found a place to insert myself, I discovered the resident in the manse's foyer, in conversation with a traveler. Keeping myself out of his sightlines, I flew to a spot high in a corner where a roof beam passed through the stone of the outer wall, and settled myself to watch and listen. The resident received almost no visitors—only the invigilant, he of the prodigious belly and eight varieties of scowl, and the steagle knife.

I rarely bothered to attend when the invigilant visited, conserving my energies for whenever my opportunity should come. But this stranger was unusual. He moved animatedly about the room in a peculiar bent-kneed, splay-footed lope, frequently twitching aside the curtain of the window beside the door to peer into the darkness, then checking that the beam that barred the portal was well seated.

"The creature cannot enter," the resident said. "Doorstep and lintel, indeed the entire house and walled garden, are charged with Phandaal's Discriminating Boundary. Do you know the spell?"

The stranger's tone was offhand. "I am familiar with the variant used in Almery. It may be different here."

"It keeps out what must be kept out; your pursuer's first footfall across the threshold would draw an agonizing penalty."

"Does the lurker know this?" said the visitor, peering again out the window.

The resident joined him. "Look," he said, "see how its nostrils flare, dark against the paleness of its countenance. It scents the magic and hangs back."

"But not far back." The dark thatch of the stranger's hair, which drew down to a point low on his forehead, moved as his scalp twitched in response to the almost constant motion of his features. "It pursued me avidly as I neared the village, growing bolder as the sun sank behind the hills. If you had not opened..."

"You are safe now," said the resident. "Eventually, the ghoul will go to seek other prey." He invited the man into the parlor and bade him sit by the fire. I fluttered after them and found a spot on a high shelf. "Have you dined?"

"Only forest foods plucked along the way," was the man's answer as he took the offered chair. But though he no longer strode about the room, his eyes went hither and thither, rifling the many shelves and glass-fronted cupboards, as if he cataloged their contents, assigning each item a value and closely calculating the sum of them all.

"I have a stew of morels grown in the inner garden, along with the remnants of yesterday's steagle," said the resident. "There is also half a loaf of bannock and a small keg of brown ale."

The stranger's pointed chin lifted in a display of fortitude. "We will make the best of it."

They had apparently exchanged names before I had arrived, for when they were seated with bowls of stew upon their knees and spoons in their hands, the resident said, "So, Grolion, what is your tale?"

The foxfaced fellow arranged his features into an image of nobility beset by unmerited trials. "I am heir to a title and lands in Almery, though I am temporarily despoiled of my inheritance by plotters and schemers. I travel the world, biding my moment, until I return to set matters forcefully aright."

The resident said, "I have heard it argued that the world as it is now arranged must be the right order of things, for a competent Creator would not allow disequilibrium."

Grolion found the concept jejeune. "My view is that the world is an arena in which men of deeds and courage drive the flow of events."

"And you are such?"

"I am," said the stranger, cramming a lump of steagle into his mouth. He tasted it then began chewing with eye-squinting zest.

Meanwhile, I considered what I had heard, drawing two conclusions: first, that though this fellow who styled himself a grandee of Almery might have sojourned in that well-worn land, he was no scion of its aristocracy—he did not double-strike his tees and dees in the stutter that was affected by Almery's highest-bred; second, that his name was not Grolion—for if it had been, I would not have been able to recall it, just as I could never retain a memory of the resident's name,nor the invigilant's. In my present condition, not enough of me survived to be able to handle true names—nor any of the magics that required memory—else I would have long since exacted a grim revenge.

The resident tipped up his bowl to scoop into his mouth the last sups of stew. His upturned glance fell upon my hiding place. I drew back, but too late. He took from within the neck of his garment a small wooden whistle that hung from a cord about his neck and blew a sonorous note. I heard the flap of leathery wings from the corridor and threw myself into the air in a bid to escape. But the little creature that guarded his bedchamber—the room that had formerly been mine—caught me in its handlike paws. A cruel smile spread across its almost-human face as it tore away my wings and carried me back to its perch above the bedchamber door, where it thrust me into its maw. I withdrew before its stained teeth crushed the life from my borrowed form.

WHEN NEXT I returned, morning light was filtering through gaps in the curtains, throwing a roseate blush onto the gray stone floors. I went from room to room, though I gave a wide berth to the resident's bedchamber. I found Grolion on the ground floor, in the workroom that overlooks the inner garden, where I had formerly spent my days with my treacherous assistants. He was examining the complex starburst design laid out in colors both vibrant and subtle on the great tray that covered most of the floor. I hovered outside the window that overlooked the inner garden; I could see that the pattern was not far from completion.

Grolion knelt and stretched a fingertip toward an elaborate figure composed in several hues: twin arabesques, intertwined with each other and

ornamented with fillips of stylized acaranja leaves and lightning bolts. Just before his cracked and untended fingernail could disarrange the thousand tiny motes, each ashimmer with its own aura of greens and golds, sapphire and amethyst, flaming reds and blazing yellows, a sharp intake of breath from the doorway arrested all motion.

"Back away," said the resident. "To disturb the pattern before it is completed is highly dangerous."

Grolion rocked back onto his heels and rose to a standing position. His eyes flitted about the pattern, trying to see it as a whole, but, of course, his effort was defeated. "What is its purpose?" he said.

The resident came into the room and drew him away. "The previous occupant of the manse began it. Regrettably, he was never entirely forthcoming about its hows and how-comes. It has to do with an interplanar anomaly. Apparently, the house sits on a node where several dimensions intersect. Their conjunction creates a weakness in the membranes that separate the planes."

"Where is this 'previous occupant?' Why has he left his work dangerously unfinished?"

The resident made a casual gesture. "These are matters of history, of which our old Earth has already far too much. We need not consider them."

"True," said Grolion, "we have only now. But some 'nows' are connected to particularly pertinent 'thens,' and the prudent man takes note of the connections."

But the resident had departed the area while he was still talking. The traveler followed and found him in the refectory, only to be caught up in a new topic.

"A gentleman of your discernment will understand," said the resident, "that my resources are constrained. Much as I delight in your company, I cannot offer unlimited hospitality. I have already overstepped my authority by feeding and sheltering you for a night."

Grolion looked about him. The manse was well appointed, the furnishings neither spare nor purely utilitarian. The walls of its many chambers were hung with art, the floors lushly carpeted, the lighting soft and shadowless. "As constraints go," he said, "these seem less oppressive than most."

"Oh," said the resident, "none of this is mine own. I am but a humble servant of the village council, paid to tend the premises until the owner's affairs are ultimately settled. My stipend is scant, and mostly paid in ale and steagle."

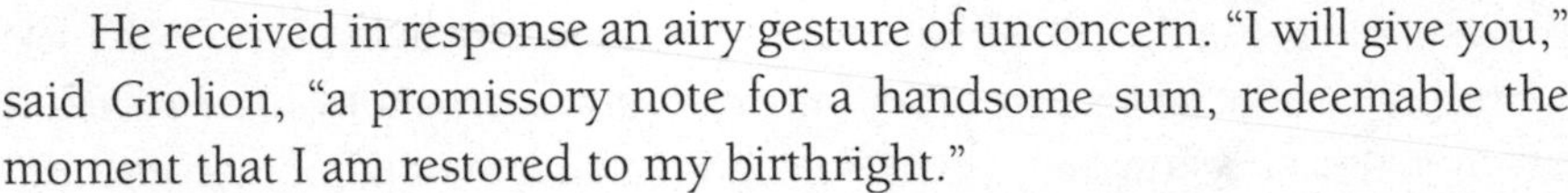

He received in response an airy gesture of unconcern. "I will give you," said Grolion, "a promissory note for a handsome sum, redeemable the moment that I am restored to my birthright."

"The restoration of your fortunes, though no doubt inevitable, is not guaranteed to arrive before the sun goes out."

Grolion had more to say, but the resident spoke over his remarks. "The invigilant comes every other day to deliver my stipend. I expect him soon. I will ask him to let me engage you as my assistant."

"Better yet," said Grolion, his face brightening as he was struck by an original idea, "I might assume a supervisory role. I have a talent for inspiring others to maximum effort."

The resident offered him a dry eye and an even drier tone. "I require no inspiration. Some small assistance, however, would be welcome. The difficulty will be in swaying the invigilant, who is a notorious groat-squeezer."

"I am electrified by the challenge." Grolion rubbed his hands briskly and added, "In the meantime, let us make a good breakfast. I find I argue best on a full stomach."

The resident sniffed. "I can spare a crust of bannock and half a pot of stark tea. Then we must to work."

"Would it not be better to establish terms and conditions? I would not want to transgress the local labor code."

"Have no fear on that score. The village values a willing worker. Show the invigilant that you have already made an energetic contribution, and your argument is half-made before he crosses the doorstep."

Grolion looked less than fully convinced, but the resident had the advantage of possessing what the other hungered for—be it only a crust and a sup of brackish tea—and thus his views prevailed.

I knew what use the resident would make of the new man. I withdrew to the inner garden and secreted myself in a deep crack in the enclosing wall, from which I could watch without imposing my presence upon the scene. It was not long before, their skimpy repast having been taken, the two men came again under my view.

As I expected, the resident drew the visitor's attention to the towering barbthorn that dominated one end of the garden. Its dozens of limbs, festooned in trailing succulents, constantly moved as it sampled the air. Several were already lifted and questing in the direction of the two men as it caught their scent even across the full length of the garden.

Sunk as I was in a crack in the wall, I was too distant to hear their conversation, but I could follow the substance of the discussion by the emotions that passed across Grolion's expressive face and by his gestures of protest. But his complaints were not recognized. With shoulders aslump and reluctance slowing his steps, the traveler trudged to the base of the tree, batting aside two of the creepers that instantly reached for him. He peered into the close-knit branches, seeking the least painful route of ascent. The resident repaired to his workroom, a window of which looked out on the court, enabling him to take note of the new employee's progress while he worked on the starburst.

I left my hiding place and angled across the wall, meaning to spring onto the man's shoulder before he ascended the tree. The way he had studied the contents of the parlor showed perspicacity coupled with unbridled greed; I might contrive some means to communicate with him. But so intent on my aims was I that I let myself cross a patch of red sunlight without full care and attention; a fat-bellied spider dropped upon me from its lurking post on the wall above. It swiftly spun a confining mesh of adhesive silk to bind my wings, then deftly flipped me over and pressed its piercing mouthparts against my abdomen. I felt the searing intrusion of its digestive juices dissolving my innards, and withdrew to the place that was both my sanctuary and my prison.

WHEN I was able to observe once more, Grolion and the resident had ceased work to receive the invigilant. I found them in the foyer, in animated discussion. The resident was insistent, arguing that the extra cost of Grolion's sustenance was well worth the increased productivity that would ensue. The invigilant was pretending to be not easily convinced, noting that a number of previous assistants had been tried and all found wanting.

The resident conceded the point, but added, "The others were unsuitable, vagabonds and wayfarers of poor character. But Grolion is of finer stuff, a scion of Almery's aristocracy."

The invigilant turned his belly in the direction of Grolion, who at that point in the proceedings had made his way to the partly open outer door so that he could examine the road outside and the forest across the way. "Are you indeed of gentle birth?"

"What? Oh, yes," was the answer, then, "Did you see a ghoul lurking

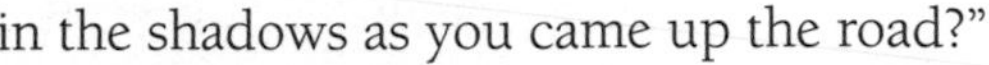

in the shadows as you came up the road?"

"We noticed it this morning and drove it off with braghounds and torches," said the invigilant.

"Indeed?" said Grolion. He edged closer to the door, used the backs of one hand's fingers to brush it further ajar, craned his neck to regard the road outside from different angles. I saw a surmise take possession of his mobile features.

"Now," said the invigilant, "let us discuss terms—"

Grolion had turned his head toward the speaker as if intent on hearing his proposal. But as the official began to speak, the traveler threw the door wide, then himself through it. To his evident surprise, the doorway caught him and threw him back into the foyer. He sat on the floor, dazed, then moaned and put his hands to his head as his face showed that his skull had suddenly become home to thunderous pain.

"Phandaal's Discriminating Boundary," said the resident. "Besides keeping out what must be kept out, it keeps *in* what must be kept in."

"Unspeak the spell," Grolion said, pain distorting his voice. "The ghoul is gone."

"He cannot," said the invigilant. "It can only be removed by he who laid it."

"The previous occupant?"

"Just so."

"Then I am trapped here?"

The resident spoke. "As am I, until the work is done. The flux of interplanar energies that will then be released will undo all magics."

Grolion indicated the invigilant. "He comes and goes."

"The spell discriminates. Hence the name."

"Come," said the invigilant, nudging Grolion with the heel of his staff, "I cannot stand here while you prattle. Rise and pay attention."

The discussion moved on. The resident's plan was approved: Grolion would be granted his own allowance of ale, bannock, and steagle, contingent upon his giving satisfaction until the work was finished. Failure to give satisfaction would see a curtailment of the stipend; aggravated failure would lead to punitive confinement in the house's dank and malodorous crypt.

Grolion proposed several amendments to these terms, though none of them were carried. The invigilant then took from his wallet a folding knife that, when opened, revealed a blade of black stone. He cut the air above the refectory table with it, and from the incisions fell a slab of steagle.

He then repeated the process, yielding another slab. Grolion saw what appeared to be two wounds, seemingly in the open air, weeping a liquid like pale blood. Then, in a matter of moments, the gashes closed and he saw only the walls and cupboards of the refectory.

The invigilant left. The resident gave brisk instructions as to the culinary portion of Grolion's duties—the preparation of steagle involved several arduous steps. Then he went back to the design in the workroom. I sought an opportunity to make contact with Grolion. He was at the preparation table, a heavy wooden mallet in hand, beating at a slab of steagle as if it had offended him by more than the sinewy toughness of its texture and its musty odor. He muttered dire imprecations under his breath. I hovered in front of him, flitting from side to side rhythmically. If I could gain his attention, it would be the first step toward opening a discourse between us.

He looked up and noticed me. I began to fly up and down and at an angle, meaning to trace the first character of the Almery syllabary—it seemed a reasonable opening gambit. He regarded me sourly, still muttering threats and maledictions against the resident. I moved on to the second letter, but as I executed an acute angle, Grolion's head reared back then shot forward; at the same time, his lips propelled a gobbet of spittle at high speed. The globule caught me in midflight, gluing my wings together and causing me to spiral down to land on the half-beaten steagle. I looked up to see the mallet descending, and then I was gone away again.

BY THE time I had found another carrier, a heavy-bodied rumblebee, several hours had passed. The resident was in the workroom, extending the design with tweezers and templates. The last arm of the sunburst was nearing completion. Once it was done, the triple helix at the center could be laid in, and the work would finally be finished.

Grolion was halfway up the barbthorn, his feet braced against one of its several trunks, a hand gripping an arm-thick branch, fingers carefully spread among the densely sprouting thorns, many of which held the desiccated corpses of small birds and flying lizards that had come to feed on the butterfly larvae that crawled and inched throughout the foliage. The man had not yet noticed that a slim, green tubule, its open end rimmed by tooth-like thorns, had found its way to the flesh between two of his knuckles and was preparing to attach itself and feed; his full attention was on his other hand, carefully cupped around a gold-and-crimson almiranth newly emerged from its cocoon. The insect was drying its translucent wings in the dim sunlight that filtered through the interlaced limbs of the tree.

Grolion breathed gently on the little creature, the warmth of his breath accelerating the drying process. Then, as the almiranth bent and flexed its legs, preparing to spring into first flight, he deftly enclosed it and transferred it to a wide-necked glass bottle that hung from a thong about his neck. The container's stopper had been gripped in his teeth, but now he pulled the wooden plug free and fixed it into the bottle's mouth. Laboriously, he began his descent, tearing his pierced hand free of the tubule's bite. The barbthorn sluggishly pinked and stabbed at him, trying to hold him in place as his shifting weight triggered its feeding response. From time to time, he had to pause to pull loose thorns that snagged his clothing; one or two even managed to pierce his flesh deeply enough that he had to stop and worry them free before he could resume his descent.

Through all of this, Grolion issued a comprehensive commentary on the stark injustice of his situation and on those responsible for it, expressing heartfelt wishes as to events in their futures. The resident and the invigilant featured prominently in these scenarios, as well as others I took to be former acquaintances in Almery. So busy was he with his aspersions that I could find no way to attract his attention. I withdrew to a chink in the garden wall to spy on the resident through the workroom window.

He was kneeling at the edge of the starburst, outlining in silver a frieze of intertwined rings of cerulean blue that traced the edge of one arm. The silver, like all the other pigments of the design, was applied as a fine powder tapped gently from the end of a hollow reed. The resident's forefinger struck the tube three more times as I watched, then he took up a small brush that bore a single bristle at its end, and nudged an errant flake into alignment.

Grolion appeared in the doorway, grumbling and cursing, to proffer the stoppered jar. The resident shooed him back with a flurry of agitated hand motions, lest any of the blood that dripped from his elbows fall upon the pattern, then he rose and came around the tray to receive the container.

"Watch and remember," he said, taking the jar to a bench and beckoning Grolion to follow. "If I promote you to senior assistant, this task could be yours."

"Does that mean someone else will climb the barbthorn?"

The resident regarded him from a great height. "A senior assistant's duties enfold and amplify those of a junior assistant."

"So it is merely more work."

"Your perspective requires modification. The proper understanding is that you command more trust and win more esteem."

"But my days still consist of 'Do this,' and 'Bring that,' and nothing to eat but mushrooms from the garden and steagle."

"The ale is good," countered the resident. "You must admit that."

"Somehow it fails to compensate," said Grolion.

"Pah!" said the resident. "I had hopes for you, but you are no better than the others!"

"What others?"

But the question was waved away. "Enough chatter! Watch and learn." The resident removed the stopper from the container, inserted two fingers and deftly caught a fragile leg. He drew the fluttering creature out, laid it on a mat of spongewood atop the workbench, then found a scalpel with a tiny half-moon blade. With a precise and practiced stroke, he severed the almiranth's triangular head from its thorax.

While the wings and legs were still moving in reflexive death throes, the resident donned a mask of fine gauze and bid Grolion do the same. "A loose breath can cost us many scales," he said, picking up a miniature strigil. Delicately, he stroked the wings, detaching a fine dust of gold and crimson, demonstrating the technique of moving the instrument to the left to pile up a pinch of gold on one side, and to the right to accumulate a minuscule heap of the other hue. When each of the four wings was stripped to the pale underflesh, he produced two hollow reeds, and, using the gentlest of suction through the gauze, drew the pigments from the table.

"There," he said, "a productive morning. Grolion, you have earned your ale and steagle."

Grolion did not respond. He had not been attending to the demonstration, his eye having instead been caught by the shelves of librams and grimoires on the opposite wall. One of them was bound in the blue chamois characteristic of Phandaal's works.

The resident saw the direction of his assistant's gaze and spoke sharply. "Back to your duties! Already I can see a green-and-orange banded chrysalis on that branch that hangs like a limp hand—there on the left, near the top! I don't doubt that's about to provide us with a magnificent nighttorch!"

"I must tend my wounds," said Grolion. "They may fester."

"Pah! I have salves and specifics. You can apply them tonight. Now get yourself aloft. If the nighttorch escapes, neither ale nor steagle shall pass your lips."

"This is a sudden change of attitude," Grolion said. "But a moment ago, I was being congratulated and promised promotion."

"I am of a mutable disposition," said the resident. "Many have tried to change me, but mine is a character that does not yield. You must fit yourself around my little idiosyncracies. Now go."

The set of his shoulders an unspoken reproach, the assistant went back to the barbthorn. With the resident watching his progress, I thought it ill-judged to follow. But Grolion did not reascend the tree. Instead, as he neared its wide base, where the thick roots delved into the ground, he suddenly stopped then stepped sharply back, as if some dire threat blocked his path.

The resident noticed. "What is it?" he cried.

Grolion did not turn but peered intently at the tangle of roots, as if in mingled fear and fascination. "I do not know," he said, then bent gingerly forward. "I have never seen the like."

The resident came forward, but stopped a little behind the traveler. "Where is it?" he said.

A feeler reached out for Grolion. He batted it away and crouched, leaning forward. "It went behind that root, the thick one."

The resident edged forward. "I see nothing."

"There!" said Grolion. "It moves!"

The resident was bent double at the waist, his attention fixed downward. "I still don't—"

Grolion came up from his crouch, moving fast. One blood-smeared hand took the resident by the throat, the other covered his mouth, and both worked in concert to achieve the assistant's goal, which was to spin the resident around and force his back against the lower reaches of the tree, where the thorns and barbs were thick and long.

Stray tendrils darted at Grolion's arms, but he ignored the sucking mouths and held the resident fast against the trunk. Now heavier tubers leaned in from the sides, sensing the flesh pressed against the carpet of fine hairs on the tree's bark. In moments, the man was a prisoner of more than Grolion's grasp. The assistant took his hands from the resident's throat and lips, but warned as he did so, "One syllable of a cantrip, and I will stop up your mouth with earth and leave you to the tree."

"No new spells can be cast here," the prisoner gasped. "Interplanar weakness creates too great a flux. Results, even of a minor spell, can be surprising."

"Very well," said Grolion, "now the tale. All of it."

The telling took a while. Grolion considerately pulled away creepers and feeders, keeping the resident only loosely held and only slightly drained. I steeled myself to hear the sordid history of the resident's treachery and the village council's complicity, though I knew the tale intimately: how they had bridled at my innocent researches, conspiring to usurp my authority, finally using cruel violence against me.

"He was obsessed with the colors of the overworld," the resident said. "I was his senior assistant, with two others under me. We were just village lads, though quick to learn. He established himself here because, he said, the conditions were unusually propitious—a unique quatrefoliate intersection of planes, a node from which it was possible to reach deep into two adjacent dimensions of the upper world, and one of the infernal."

A tooth-rimmed sucker, sensing the flavor of his breath, probed for his mouth, but Grolion knocked it aside. The resident spoke on. "He particularly craved to see a color known in the overworld as refulgent ombre. It cannot exist in our milieu; what we call light is but a poor imitation of what reigns there.

"But our village sits on the site of Fallume the Ept's demesne, long ago in the Seventeenth Aeon. So potent were the forces Fallume employed that he permanently frayed the membranes between the planes. My master's researches had shown him that, here and here alone, he could create a facsimile of the upper realm and maintain it indefinitely. Within that sphere he could bask in the glow of refulgent ombre and other supernal radiances. To do so would confer upon him benefits he was eager to enjoy."

The details followed. The microcosm of the overworld sphere would spontaneously self-generate upon completion of a complex design made from unique materials: the pigmented scales of four kinds of butterflies whose larval forms fed only on the sap and leaves of a unique tree, with which the insects lived in symbiosis—predators drawn to consume the insects were led into its maze of branches, where they impaled themselves on barbed thorns and thus became food for the vegetative partner.

The tree had a unique property, being able to exist in more than one plane at the same time, though it presented a different form in each milieu: in the first level of the overworld, it was a kind of animal, a multilimbed hunter of the transmigrated souls of small creatures that evanesced up from our plane; in the underworld, it was a spined serpent whose feeding habits were obscure, though distasteful. The attributes of all three realms co-existed in the tree's inner juices. Eaten and digested by the worms that crawled the branches, the ichor was transmuted by the process that turned the larvae into butterflies, and was precipitated out in the scales of their viridescent wings. Taken while fresh, the colors of the scales could be arranged, at this precise location, into the design that would cause the facsimile of the overworld to appear. Within that sphere, refulgent ombre would shine.

Grolion halted the resident at this point. I saw his energetic face in motion as he sorted through the information. Then he asked the question I had hoped he would: "This refulgent ombre, is it valuable?"

"Priceless," said the resident, and I saw avarice's flame akindle in the assistant's eyes, only to be doused as his prisoner continued, "and utterly worthless."

Grolion's heavy brows contracted. "How so?"

"It can only exist in the facsimile, and the facsimile can only exist here, where the planes converge."

Grolion turned to regard the workroom. "So the starburst cannot be moved? Or taken apart and reformed elsewhere?"

"Disturb a grain of its substance, and it will depart through the breach, taking you and me, the house, and probably the village, with it."

A scowl pulled down the vulpine face. "Tell the rest."

"The master erected this manse, laid the garden, planted the tree. The village council welcomed him; in recent years traffic along the road has become scant; wealth no longer flows our way. They made an accommodation: the village would provide him with assistants and sundry necessities; he, in return, would perform small magics and provide the benefit of steagle."

"And what is this steagle?"

"It is an immense beast that swims through endless ocean in an adjacent plane—you will understand that the terms "ocean" and "swim" are only approximations. He gave the village the knife that cuts only steagle; slice the air with it, and a slab of meat appears. With each cut, a new piece arrives, dripping with lifejuices. We would never know hunger again."

"A useful instrument."

"Alas," said the resident, "it, too, only works where interplanar membranes are weak. A mile beyond the village, it is just another knife."

Grolion scratched his coarse thatch. "Does the steagle not resent the theft of its flesh?"

"We have never given the matter any thought."

The villagers had taken the bargain. And all was as it should have been, except that the tree flourished more boisterously than anticipated. Birds and lizards had to be augmented by occasional wanderers who had taken the wrong fork and who were impressed as "assistants." Even they were not enough. Thick creepers began to prowl the village at night, entering open windows or even forcing the less sturdy doors. Householders would arise in the morning to find pets shriveled and livestock desiccated, drained to the least drop. Then the tree started in on the children.

"The council came to my master, but found him consumed by his own ambitions. What were a few children—easily replaceable, after all—compared to the fulfillment of his noble dream? He counseled them to install stronger doors.

"But the village threatened to withdraw support, including we who assisted. My master begrudgingly invoked Phandaal's Discriminating Boundary, to keep the tree in bounds. But the spell also confined us."

Hearing this, I was saddened anew at the thought of the council's shortsightedness, when I had been making such good progress in my work. I tried not to listen as the resident told the rest: how, while I slept, my assistants had fed my watcher a posset of drugged honey, then stolen into my chamber with knives.

The dastardly attack came, coordinated and from three directions at once, catching me unawares in the midst of my sleep-wanderings. I awoke and defended myself, though without magic, I was in a poor situation. However, I had not become a wielder of three colors of magic without learning caution. The traitors were surprised to discover that I had long since created for myself an impregnable refuge in the fourth plane, to which I fled when the struggle went against me. Unfortunately, they had done such damage to my physical form that only my essence won through.

"He left behind his physical attributes," my former assistant was telling Grolion, "and these we sealed into a coffin of lead lined with antimony. Thus he cannot reach out to repair himself; instead, he projects himself from his hiding place, riding the sensoria of passing insects, seeking to spy on me." He swallowed and continued, "Something is boring into my ankle. If you release me from the tree's grasp, I swear to do you no harm."

Grolion tugged away the tuber that was feeding on the resident's leg and batted away another that was seeking to insert itself into the prisoner's ear. He pulled free the creepers that had been thickening around the resident's torso, then yanked the man loose. The resident gasped in pain; scraps of bloody cloth and small pieces of flesh showed where barbed thorns had worked their way into his back and buttocks.

Grolion tore the man's robe into strips and bound his wrists and ankles. But he considerately hauled the bound man out of the tree's reach before going to reinspect the workroom and the design. He reached for the Phandaal libram, but as his fingers almost touched its blue chamois, a blinding spark of white light leapt across the gap, accompanied by a sharp crack of sound. Grolion yelped and quickly withdrew his hand, shook it energetically, then put the tips of two fingers into his mouth and sucked them.

He left the room, took himself out to a bench along one side of the garden, equidistant between the tree and the workroom. Here he sat, one leg crossed over another, his pointed chin in the grip of one hand's forefinger and thumb, and gave himself over to thought. From time to time, he looked up at the barbthorn, or over to the workroom window, and occasionally he considered the tied-up resident.

After a few minutes, he called over to the resident, "There were three of you. Where are the other two?"

The resident's upturned glance at the tree made for a mutely eloquent answer.

"I see," said Grolion. "And, ultimately, what would have happened to me?"

The resident's eyes looked at anything but the questioner.

"I see," Grolion said again, and returned to thought. After a while, he said, "The lead coffin?"

"In the crypt," said the resident, "below the garden. The steps are behind the fountain in the pool of singing fish. But if you open it, he will reanimate. I don't doubt he would then feed us all to the tree. He used to care only for refulgent ombre; his murder, followed by several incarnations as various insects, most of which die horribly, may have developed in him an instinct for cruelty."

Grolion went to look. There was a wide stone flag, square in shape, inset with an iron ring at one side. He seized and pulled, and, with a grating of granite on granite, the trapdoor came up, assisted by unseen counterweights on pulleys beneath. A flight of steps led down.

I did not follow. The glyphs and symbols cut into my coffin's sides and top would pain me, as they were intended to do. I flew over to a crack in the wall above the resident, and, having established than nothing lurked therein, I settled down to wait.

I knew what Grolion would be seeing: the much-cracked walls and damp, uneven floor of the crypt, the blackness only partly relieved by two narrow airshafts that descended from small grates set in the garden wall above; the several bundles of cloth near the bottom of the steps, containing the shriveled remains of my former junior and intermediate assistants, as well as the wayfarers who had, individually, sought shelter from the invigilant's ghoul and found themselves pressed into service; and one end wall, fractured and riven by the barbthorn's roots as they had grown down through the ceiling and the soil above it.

And, of course, on a raised dais at the opposite end of the crypt, the coffin that held my physical attributes. They were neither dead nor alive, but in that state known as "indeterminate." I did not think that Grolion would be curious enough to lift the lid to look within; that is, I was sure he possessed the curiosity, but doubted he was foolish enough to let it possess him, down there in the ill-smelling dark.

When he came back up into the red sunlight, his brows were down-drawn in concentration. "No more work today," he told the resident. "I wish to think."

The tree had been stimulated by its tastes of the resident. Its branches stirred without a wind to move them. A thick tubule, its toothed end open to catch his scent, was extending itself along the ground toward where he sat, still bound but struggling to inch away. Grolion stamped on the feeder and kicked it back the way it had come, then hauled the resident by his collar farther toward the workroom end of the garden. He turned and stared up at the tree for a moment, then went to look at the starburst again. Thinking himself unobserved, he did not bother to prevent his thoughts from showing in his face. The tree was a problem without an opportunity attached; the design was valueless, even when completed, since it had to remain where it was; the Phandaal on the shelf was precious, but painfully defended.

He came back to the resident. "What happens when the design is completed?"

"A microcosm of the overworld will appear above it, and it will be absorbed."

"Could we enter the microcosm?"

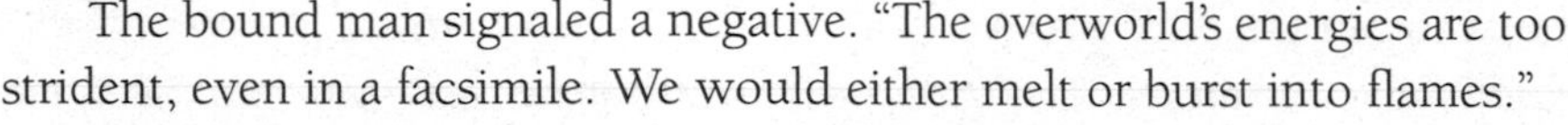

The bound man signaled a negative. "The overworld's energies are too strident, even in a facsimile. We would either melt or burst into flames."

"Yet your master intended to enter it."

"He spent years toughening himself to endure the climate. That was what made him hard to kill."

Grolion strode about with the energy of frustration. "So we are locked in with a vampirous plant and a magical design that will destroy us if it is not completed. Only your master truly understands what needs to be done, but if I revive him, he will probably feed me to the plant to gain the wherewithal with which to finish his project and achieve his life's goal."

"That is the situation."

Grolion abused the air with his fist. "I reject it," he said. "My experience is that unhelpful situations will always yield to a man of guile and resource. I will exert myself."

"In what direction?"

"I will eliminate the middleman."

The resident was framing a new question when a voice called from the corridor. A moment later, the invigilant's belly passed through the archway, followed shortly after by the man himself. He took in the scene, noting the resident's bonds, but said only, "How goes the work?"

The resident made to answer but Grolion cut him off. "A new administration has taken charge. The situation as it stands is unsatisfactory. It will now be invested with a new dynamic." He moved toward the invigilant with an air of dire intent.

"What's this?" said the invigilant, a look of alarm making its way to the surface of his face through the rolls of fat beneath it. His plump hands rose to defend himself, but Grolion treated them as he had the tree's creepers; he pulled up the flap that closed the invigilant's wallet and seized the knife that cut steagle. A flick of his wrist caused the blade to spring free with a sharp click.

"You cannot threaten with that," said the invigilant. "It cuts only steagle."

"Indeed," said Grolion. He made for the tree, in his peculiar bent-kneed stride. The invigilant bent and undid the resident's bonds, but both stayed well clear of the barbthorn. My rumblebee was tired, but I drove it to follow the traveler.

Grolion marched to the base of the barbthorn. Several wriggling tubers reached for him, the tree having not fed well for many days. He slashed at the air with the black-bladed knife, a long horizontal cut at head height. Lifejuices spurted, bedewing the hairs of his arms with pink droplets. He ignored them and made two vertical cuts, one each from the ends of the first gash. Now he cut a fourth incision in the air, at knee height and parallel to the first. Then he gripped the knife between his teeth and thrust his hands into the top cut. He seized, tugged, and ripped until, with a gush of lifejuices, a slab of steagle the size of a sleeping pallet fell out with a splat onto the stone paving.

Grolion stepped back. The barbthorn's feeders sampled the air above the dripping flesh, then, as one, they plunged down and fastened multifanged mouths onto the meat. The tubules pulsed rhythmically as the tree fed. Grolion paused to watch only a moment then, wielding the knife again, he stepped to the side and repeated the exercise. Another weighty slab of steagle slapped the pavement, and the tree sent fresh feeders to drain it.

"Now," said Grolion, "for the design." He folded the steagle knife and pocketed it then, with the tree occupied with steagle, he threw himself up and into the barbthorn. Ever higher he climbed, ignoring the wounds his passage through the thorns inflicted on him, while he methodically stripped every branch of its chrysalises, be they mature, middling, or newly spun. These he tucked into his shirt, until it bulged.

When he had them all, he dropped swiftly down through the foliage, paused at the base to cut another wedge of steagle for the tree, then strode to the workroom. "Follow me!" he called over his shoulder.

The invigilant and the resident did so, though not without exchanging freighted glances. I flew to where I could get a view of the proceedings. There was Grolion at the work bench, pulling handfuls of chrysalises from his shirt. He found a scalpel and sliced one open, as the resident looked on open-mouthed.

An almost-made almiranth appeared. With surprising deftness, Grolion teased it free of its split cocoon, laid the feebly wriggling creature on the benchtop, and, with a pair of fine tweezers, spread its wings. He breathed gently on the wet membranes to dry them. Then he turned to the resident and said, "Now you collect the scales."

Wordlessly, the resident did as he was told, while Grolion informed the invigilant that his task was to sort the chrysalises by species and apparent maturity. The official's mouth formed an almost hemispherical frown and he said, "I do not—"

Grolion dealt him a buffet to the side of the head that laid the invigilant on the floor. He then stood on one foot, the other poised for a belly-kick, and invited the prostrate man to change his views. Trembling, the invigilant got to his feet and did as he was told.

Time passed. The tree fed, the men worked, and the supply of scales for the starburst grew. When Grolion had extracted the last moth mature enough to have harvestable scales, he asked the resident, "Have we enough?"

The resident looked at the several reeds, each loaded with pigment and said, with mild amazement, "I believe we do."

"Then get to work." To the invigilant, he said, "You will act as assistant, handing him the reeds as he asks for them."

They set to. Meanwhile, their new supervisor went out to the tree. The barbthorn, having sensed the availability of a rich and ample source of food, had sent forth its primary feeder; this was a strong tube, as thick as Grolion's thigh and rimmed by barbed thorn-teeth as long as his thumb. It had fastened onto the second of the two slabs of steagle, which it was rapidly draining of substance. The operation was accompanied by loud slurps and obscene pulsations of the fleshy conduit. The first slab was but a shrunken mat of dried meat.

"Let us keep you occupied," said Grolion, deploying the black blade. He cut a fresh segment of steagle from the air, twice the size of the others, and let it fall beside the now almost-shriveled piece. Tubules strained toward the new sustenance, and, in a moment, the thick feeder left off from the slab it was draining and drove its thorns into the more recent supply. The tree shivered and a sound very like a moan of pleasure came from somewhere in the matrix of branches.

Grolion loped back to the workroom. The two men, on their knees beside the design, looked up with apprehension, but he waved them to continue. "All is as it should be," he said, almost genially. "Soon we will be able to put this unpleasantness behind us. Continue your work while I inspect the premises."

He left the area and I could hear clinks and clatters as he rummaged through other rooms. After a while, he came back to the garden, a bulging cloth sack in his hand. Leaving the bag near the workroom door, he went to the tree again, saw that it had fully drained the latest steagle. Its tubules were again sampling the air. An expression that I took to be simple curiosity formed on the man's foxlike face. Unfolding the knife once more, he cut again, standing on tiptoe to make the upper incision, stooping almost to

the ground for the lower, and thrusting the blade arm-deep into the cuts. Out fell a huge block of steagle and Grolion stood drenched in viscous pink. He brushed at himself, then went to immerse himself among the singing fish, which gave out an excited music as the flavor of their water changed. The tree, meanwhile, was writhing in vegetative ecstasy, sending up new shoots in all directions.

The resident and the invigilant were now finishing the starburst. The former laid a line of deep vermilion against a wedge of scintillating white nacre, then bid the latter hand him a reed filled with stygian black. This he used to trace a spiral at the heart of the pattern, delicately tapping out the pigment a few scales at a time.

He finished with the black, then called for old gold and basilisk's-eye green, two of the rarest colors from the barbthorn's palette. The invigilant passed him the reeds just as Grolion hove into view through the doorway, dripping wet and bending to retrieve his bag of loot. "How now?" he said, his unburdened hand indicating the design.

The resident appeared startled to hear himself declare, "I am about to finish."

"Then do so," said Grolion. "I have wasted enough time in this place."

Now came the moment. I flew close, but my rumbling buzz annoyed Grolion; he brushed me aside with a brusque motion that sent me tumbling. I fetched up hard against the side of the doorway, damaging one of my wings so that I fell, spiraling, to the floor. I looked up to see him frowning down at me, then his huge foot lifted.

"Look!" said the invigilant and the crushing blow did not come. All eyes turned toward the space just above the center of the starburst where, as the final iridescent flakes of color fell from the end of the reed, a spark had kindled in mid-air. In a moment, like a flamelet fed by inrushing air, it grew and spread, becoming a glowing orb that was at first the size of a pea, then the width of a fist, now of a head, then larger, and still larger. And as it grew, the starburst that had been so carefully laid upon the workroom floor was drawn up in a reverse cascade of sparkling colors, to merge with the globe of light, now scintillating with scores of rare hues, having grown as large as a wine cask, and still waxing.

The three men watched in fascination, for playing across their eyes were colors, singly and in combination, such as few mortals have ever seen. But I had no thought for them now, not even for my betrayal and the unjust abuse I had suffered. I flexed my injured wing, told myself

that it would bear the rumblebee's weight long enough. I bent my six legs and threw myself toward the light, willing my three good, and one bad, membranes to carry me forward.

Instead, I drifted to one side, away from the prize. And now the resident noticed me. At once, he knew me. He came around the edge of the tray, from which the last trickles of the intricate design were flowing up into the orb of light, and struck at me with the hand that still held the final reed. I jinked awkwardly to one side, a last few ashy flakes of nacre dusting the hairs on my back, and the blow did not fall. But my passage had brought me close to Grolion again, and his hand made the same sharp stroke as before, so that the backs of his hairy fingers caught me once more and sent me spinning, helpless—but straight into the globe!

I passed through the glowing wall, heard within me the rumblebee's tiny last cry as its solid flesh melted in the rarified conditions of this little exemplar of the overworld that had now appeared in our middling plane. Freed from corporeality, I experienced the full, ineffable *isness* of the upper realm, the colors that ravished even as they healed the wounds. Refulgent ombre was mine, and with it ten thousand hues and shades that mortal eyes could never have seen. I languished, limp with bliss, enervated by rapture.

Somewhere beyond the globe of light, the resident, the invigilant, and the wanderer went about their mundane business. I cared nothing for them and their gross doings, nor for the parcel of flesh, bone, and cartilage that had once housed my essence and was now itself confined in a coffin of lead and antimony.

They had feared my retribution. But there would be no revenge. Then was then, now was now, and I was above it all, in the overworld. I exulted. I reveled. I swilled the wine of ecstasy.

THE MAN who called himself Grolion stared at the multicolored orb. It had stopped growing after the bee had entered it. All of the starburst was now absorbed and the globe hung in the air above the empty tray, complete and self-sufficient. Curious, he reached a hand toward it, but Shalmetz, the man who had finished the design, struck away his arm.

Grolion turned with a scowl, fist raised, but subsided when Shalmetz said, "A sliver of ice thrown on a roaring fire would last longer than your flesh in contact with that."

Groblens, the fat village officer, pulled back his own hand, that he had been hesitantly stretching toward the microcosm. Grunting, straining, he levered himself to his feet. "Is it over?" he said.

Shalmetz observed the globe. "It seems so."

"Test it," said the traveler, aiming his chin toward the blue book on the shelf. Shalmetz touched a finger to the book's spine. "No spark."

Grolion gestured meaningfully. Shalmetz made no objection but with a rueful quirk of his lips, passed across the Phandaal. "You are welcome to it," he said. "I will return to my job at the fish farm."

"Give me back the steagle knife," the fat man said. "It is of no use beyond this eldritch intersection of planes."

"It will have value as a curio," the foxfaced man said.

Shalmetz looked through the window. "The village may need it to keep the tree content. It seems to have developed a fondness for steagle." And more than a fondness. The barbthorn had been growing, and was now half again as tall as it had been that morning, and substantially fuller. Moreover, it had grown more active.

"I will cut it one more portion," he said, "to keep it occupied while we depart. After that, it becomes part of my past and therefore none of my concern. You must deal with it as you can. I recommend fire."

To Shalmetz and Groblens, the plan had obvious shortcomings, but before they could address them, the traveler was loping to the base of the tree. Again, he cut deep, wide, and long, and in moments another block of steagle dropped before the questing feeders. The tree fell upon the new food with an eagerness that, when displayed by a vegetative lifeform, must always be disturbing.

But there was an even more troublesome coda to its behavior: even as its smaller tubules fixed themselves to the slab of steagle, the main feeder, now grown as thick as a man's body, darted toward the still closing gap in the air from which the pink flesh had come. Before the opening could close, the thorn-toothed orifice thrust itself through. The end disappeared. But it had connected, for immediately the tube began to pump and swallow, passing larger and larger volumes along the feeder's length, as if a great serpent was dining on an endless litter of piglets.

A deep thrumming came from the plant, a sound of mingled satisfaction and insatiable gluttony. It visibly swelled in height and girth, while a new complexity of bethorned twigs and branches erupted from its larger limbs. The man with the knife stepped back, as the tree's roots writhed

and grew in harmony with the rest of it, cracking the wall against which it had grown, tearing up the stone pavement in all directions, upturning the fountain and sending the singing fish out into the inhospitable air to gasp and croak their final performance.

The man turned and ran, stumbling over broken flagstones and squirming roots that sprang from the earth beneath his feet. Shalmetz and Groblens fled the workroom just as the tree's new growth met the foundation of its wall at the garden's inner end. In an instant, the wall was riven from floor to ceiling. The room collapsed, bringing down the second story above it, though when the debris settled, the kaleidoscopic orb that held a facsimile of the overworld, which in turn held the blissful essence of the house's builder, remained unscathed, shining through the billows of dust.

The bag of loot was beneath a fallen roof timber. Its collector reached for it, found it held fast. He addressed himself to one end of the beam, and by dint of prodigious effort was able to lift and shift the weight aside. But as he stooped and seized his prize, he heard Shalmetz's wavering cry of fear and dismay.

The man stood and turned in the direction of the other's gaze. He saw the barbthorn, now grown even huger, looming over the ravaged garden, roiling like a storm cloud come down to earth. Its main feeder, now wide enough to have swallowed a horse, continued to pump great gobbets of steagle from beyond this plane. A constant bass note thrummed the air and the ground shook unceasingly as the roots drove ever outward.

But it was not the tree that had frightened Shalmetz or that now caused both him and the invigilant to turn and flee through the corridor that led to the foyer and the outer door. It was the vertical slit that was rending the air above and below the place at which the feeder left this plane and entered another. The fissure rose higher and lower at the same time, cleaving stone and earth as easily as it cut the air. And through the rent appeared a dark shape.

The traveler stood and watched, his bag of loot loose in his grasp. A thing like a great rounded snout, but ringed about its end with tentacles, was forcing its way through the gap, splitting it higher and lower as it came, throwing a bow wave of earth and stone in either direction. More and more of the creature came through, and now it could be seen that, at the place where it would have had a chin if it had had a face, the barbthorn's feeder was fastened to its flesh. Around the spot where the thorns were sunk out of sight was a network of small scars, and three fresh wounds, still dripping pink juice.

The tentacled snout was now all the way through the gap. Behind it, the body narrowed then swelled again, displaying a ring of limb-like flukes all around its circumference that beat at the air, propelling the creature forward. It showed no eyes, but its tentacles—four large ones and more than a dozen minor specimens—groped toward the tree as if they could sense its presence.

Now two of the steagle's larger members seized the feeder tube, and, with an audible rip of tearing flesh, detached it from its face. Pink lifejuices gushed from the deep wound left behind, and one of the smaller tendrils bent to place its flattened, leaf-shaped end over the injury.

As the feeder came loose, the tree roared, a sound like an orchestra of bass organ tubes. The main feeder writhed in the steagle's grasp and the barbthorn's every creeper, branch, and tubule strained and flailed toward the source of combined nourishment and threat. The steagle met the assault with equal vigor, and now a kind of mouth appeared at the center of the ring of tentacles, from which issued a hiss like that of a steam geyser long denied release, followed by a long, thick tongue coated with a corrugation of rasping hooks and serrated, triangular teeth.

The tentacles pulled the barbthorn toward the steagle, even as the tree wrapped its assailant in a matrix of writhing, thorned vegetation. The traveler heard cracks and snaps, roars and moans, hisses and indefinable sounds. He felt the ground quake anew as the impetus of the steagle's thrust tore the barbthorn's new roots from the ground.

Time to go, he told himself, and turned toward the passageway through which the others had fled. But he found himself in the midst of a wriggling, seething mass of roots, erupting from the earth amid volleys of flying clods and pebbles that stung and bruised him. Though he stepped carefully, finding firm footing was impossible; the entire floor of the garden was in constant, violent motion. Worse, some of the roots had snapped, and their ends flailed the air like whips and cudgels. One dealt his thigh a hard blow, knocking him off balance, and as he spun around, a root the thickness of his thumb struck his wrist.

The impact numbed the hand that held the bag. It fell between two roots, and, though he feared his arm might be trapped if the two came together, he reached for the prize. But as his fingers touched the cloth, the floor of the garden collapsed into the crypt below, taking the loot with it, and leaving the man teetering on the brink of the cavity.

He threw himself backward, ignoring the slashing, flailing blows that came from all sides, then turned and scrambled for the corridor that led out. *I will come back for the bag*, he told himself.

Behind him, the rest of the steagle emerged from the rent between the planes: a segmented tail that ended in a pair of sharp-edged pincers. These now joined the front of the creature in its attack on the barbthorn, and their reinforcement proved decisive. Though the tree's thorned limbs continued to beat and tear at the steagle's hide, raising a spray of pink ichor and gouging away wedges of flesh, the unequal battle was moving toward a conclusion. The tentacles and pincers tore the limbs from the tree and severed its roots from the stem, flinging the remnants into the hole that had been the crypt. The barbthorn's roars became cries that became whimpers.

And then it was done. The steagle snapped and cut and broke the great tree into pieces, filled the hole in the earth with them. At the last, with discernible contempt, it arched its tail and, from an orifice beneath that appendage, directed a stream of red liquid at the wreckage. The wood and greenery burst instantly into strangely colored flames, and a column of oily smoke rose to the sky.

The steagle, somehow airborne, floated around the pyre, viewing it from several angles. Its passage brought it within range of the multicolored microcosm of the overworld, which hung in the air, untroubled by the violence wrought nearby. The steagle paused before the orb. Its eyeless face seemed to regard the kaleidoscopic play of colors that moved constantly across the globe's surface. One of its minor tentacles reached out and stroked the object, paused for a moment as if deciding whether or not it fully approved of the thing's taste, then curled around it and popped it whole into the steagle's maw.

The mouth closed, the creature turned toward the rent in the membrane between the planes, and in less time than the man who called himself Grolion would have credited, it was through and gone. The air healed itself, and there was only the burning devastation of the tree and the shattered garden to indicate that anything had happened here,

The man had watched the final act from atop a rise some distance down the road. Here he had found Shalmetz and Groblens. The latter was too winded by the combination of pell-mell flight and a life-long fondness for beebleberry tarts, but the former had greeted him thusly: "Well, Grolion—if that is even an approximation of your name—you certainly invested that situation with a new dynamic."

The traveler was in no mood to accept criticism; he answered the remark with a blow that sat Shalmetz down on the roadway, from where he offered no further comments. After a while, he and Groblens made their way back to the village. The other man waited until the eerie flames subsided. Toward evening, when all was still, he crept back to the manse.

The house had collapsed. The hole that had been the crypt was full of stinking char. Of his bag and its contents, he could find no trace. The only object left unscathed was the lead coffin, whose incised runes and symbols had somehow protected it from the otherworldly fire. It was not even warm.

The man used ropes and pulleys to haul the object from the pit. In the same outbuilding that had held the tackle, he found a two-wheeled cart. He lowered the coffin onto the vehicle and pushed it away from the stink and soot of the burned-out fire. He admired the emblems and sigils that decorated its sides and top; he was sure that they were of powerful effect.

When he had wheeled the cart out to the road, he set his fingers to the coffin's lid and pried it loose. He had hoped for jewels or precious metals; he found only fast-rotting flesh and wet bones, with not even a thumb-ring or an ivory torc to reward his labors. He said a harsh word and threw death's detritus into a roadside ditch.

Only the coffin itself remained. It might prove useful, if only for the figures carved into it. But now he saw that with the removal of the contents, the signs and characters were fading to nothing.

Still, he believed he could remember most of them. Tomorrow he would carve them into the lead, then cut the soft metal into plaques and amulets. These he could sell at Azenomei Fair, and who knows what possibilities might then arise?

AFTERWORD:

BACK IN the early sixties, when I was busy becoming a teenager, my eldest brother was into science fiction. He would leave paperbacks and pulp mags around the house, and I would take them up and devour them. One was an issue of *Galaxy* with a story called "The Dragon Masters" by someone named Jack Vance. I read it and was transported. As I moved toward my twenties, whenever I had nickels and dimes enough, I would haunt used bookstores, vacuuming up sf as fast as I could. Any day that I came across a new Vance book or a mag with a new Vance story was a good day.

By my mid-thirties, I had pretty much stopped reading sf in favor of crime fiction. But I still bought and read anything new by Vance; once, when I was supposed to be on vacation, I lay on a hotel bed and did nothing all day but read *Suldrun's Garden*, the first Lyonesse book. Now, forty-five years after I first encountered him, Jack Vance is the only author I reread, and I never cease to fall under the spell.

In a well run world, prominent geographical features and wide, impressive plazas and boulevards would bear his name.

—Matthew Hughes

TERRY DOWLING

The Copsy Door

ONE OF the best-known and most celebrated of Australian writers in any genre, winner of eleven Ditmar awards, four Aurealis Awards and the International Horror Guild Award, Terry Dowling made his first sale in 1982, and has since made an international reputation for himself as a writer of science fiction, dark fantasy and horror. Primarily a short story writer, he is the author of the linked collections *Rynosseros*, *Blue Tyson*, *Twilight Beach* and *Wormwood*, as well as other collections such as *Antique Futures: The Best of Terry Dowling*, *The Man Who Lost Red*, *An Intimate Knowledge of the Night*, *Blackwater Days* and *Basic Black: Tales of Appropriate Fear*. He has also written three computer adventures: *Schizm: Mysterious Journey*, *Schizm II: Chameleon* and *Sentinel: Descendants in Time*, and, as editor, produced *The Essential Ellison*, *Mortal Fire: Best Australian SF* (with Van Ikin) and *The Jack Vance Treasury* and *The Jack Vance Reader* (both with Jonathan Strahan). His most recent book is the fourth and final Tom Rynosseros collection, *Rynemonn*. Born in Sydney, he lives in Hunters Hill, New South Wales, Australia (www.terrydowling.com).

In the mordant tale that follows, one that takes us through an enigmatic doorway to a place outside of space and time, he shows us that the race isn't always to the swift or the victory to the strong…

The Copsy Door

TERRY DOWLING

When Amberlin the Lesser stepped into his workroom that spring morning, he found his manservant Diffin staring out of the Clever Window again. The workroom was in the uppermost chamber of the east tower of the manse Furness and looked out over a silvery broadwater of the Scaum, then across the Robber Woods to far Ascolais. It was where Diffin was always to be found when his chores were more or less done, watching the old red sun made young and golden again by the special properties of the glass.

Not for the first time that morning, Amberlin wondered if the strange lanky creature had found a new way to slip his holding spell.

"Diffin, I was clear in every particular. You were to consult the Anto brothers about the state of the Copsy Door and bring word at once."

The loose-limbed creature trembled with what the ageing wizard hoped was appropriate contrition, but which he suspected was more likely suppressed mirth, then swung his long face reluctantly from the window.

"No, master. You were most specific. I wrote it down on my little slate, see? You said to fetch word and bring it to you *here* at once. Since here is here, I did precisely as you instructed and hurried right back."

"But I was out in the garden. Someone had neglected to water the lillobays and quentians again. Did you not hear them weeping?"

"Not at all. My mind was firmly on my task. And since you were not *here* any longer—"

Amberlin raised his hand. "As you say. Well, now I am here and I am dreaming of penalties. What word from the brothers?"

"The Copsy Door has formed, true and sure, as you predicted, master, and will no doubt last the day before slipping off again. The brothers have been hiding it behind the baffle screen as you instructed and will continue to honor their agreement in every respect. Once you find a way inside, then it's a full quarter for them of whatever is within."

"To which their response was?"

"Nothing but the happiest of smiles, master, and an idle remark that perhaps a third share would mark you as a benefactor to watch. They are actually stalwart, good-natured fellows, clearly maligned in the tales of those who do not know them as well as you or I."

"Indeed. You told them I am wary of any of the tricks for which they are also known?"

"Just so, master. They are not too sure of what 'wary' means in the sense you use it, but they said that it was always good to have the full measure of one's skills appreciated."

"You said nothing else?"

Diffin shook his loose-jowled head. "Only that my name was Diffin, in the event they had forgotten and there was a gratuity on offer."

"*They* said nothing else?"

"Nothing. I would have written it on my slate. Ah, wait. Now I remember. That they would hope to expect you at mid-morning."

"What! It is that now! Diffin, you are far too lax!"

The creature pulled at his long chin as if deep in thought. "Perhaps I wrote it down and the slate is faulty. That would explain much."

"Perhaps you will benefit from fetching my Holding Book so we can refresh our memories on the more instructive aspects of Genial Compliance."

"But, master, there is no time! While tidying up, I took the opportunity of placing that least kind of books safely in the west tower library to give it a change of outlook. Also, as you well know, the book is so heavy and now resides at the top of a very tall bookcase. Would it not be better if I saved you the trouble and made recompense by staying here and keeping a sharp and dutiful watch for strangers and vagabonds approaching?"

Amberlin turned, regarded the wonder of a golden sun in the clear blue sky of aeons past. "Through the Clever Window, of course?"

"Oh yes, master. There are erbs reported out by Callow Tree. If they dare come this way, then they will look so much friendlier under a *yellow* sun."

CLOSE BY the confluence of the Scaum and the River Tywy, the archmage Eunepheos the Darke had once built the splendid shadow-manse of Venta-Valu, an edifice of cunning pentavaults and intricate schattencrofts, the whole set under six fine dormers crowned with ghost-chasers and spin-alofts in one of the classic styles of Grand Motholam.

The centuries had been kind to the structure, all things considered, but following Eunepheos untimely vanishment into the Estervoid, supposedly at the hands of his great rival Shastermon, steadily, inevitably, the cohesion spells had spoiled and Venta-Valu had fallen into ruin. The intricate shadowforms were soon plundered by visiting adepts and shadow-factors, and much of what remained was leached away by shadow-wights and other creatures drawn to compressed darkness, so that, by the 21st Aeon, the residence was little more than a handful of glooms and hollows scattered along the riverbank, too insubstantial to bother with.

Except for whatever lay behind the Copsy Door. Eunepheos had been as wily as any of his fellows, and had installed what appeared to be a particular cellar or basement that remained both sufficiently corporeal and yet resistant to all attempts at entry. Sealed by a here-again, gone-again Copsy Door calibrated to the protracted time-values of its maker's favourite requiem, it was set into the embankment well above the Scaum, as if left as a deliberate taunt to the greedy and the curious.

Amberlin believed he finally knew the way in.

Now, studying his reflection in the Safe Mirror as he prepared himself for his journey, he was by and large pleased with what he saw. He was in his final years, no doubt, like the old sun itself, but was still impressively tall and certainly formidable-looking in his dark green robe set with old-gold frogging, maiden-thread serentaps, and gilt curlicues. His long grey hair and stylish tripartite beard held by its three opal clasps still had enough flecks of black, and he liked to think his eyes were bright with resolve and old-world cunning rather than an excess of brandywine, rheum, and too many late nights spent reading in front of the fire. He felt as ready for the

Door and the brothers with their interminable schemes as he could ever hope to be.

And while Amberlin knew better than to let the Copsy Door be the sole answer to his troubles, hope remained the only meal worth having these last few decades. If not this, then what else was there? Nearly a century before, at the full blush of his powers, he had known upwards of fifty spells and cantraps. He could recite them from memory—the intricate syllables and pronunciations uttered just so—even the most exacting convolutes, glossolades, and prattelays, with no need of spell books or prompt lists, no reliance on the often fractious, sometimes duplicitous sandestins and daihaks in his employ to whisper embarrassing reminders.

But then, even as years and failing memory had worn those fifty-plus spells down to a zealously guarded twelve, Amberlin had experienced his worst of days.

In the workings of an ancient feud, specifically a longstanding dispute over the ownership of a particularly fine gossawary tree in the Robber Woods, that spiteful parvenu Sarimance the Aspurge had blighted him with Stilfer's Prolexic Inflect, so that the syllable patterns of every spell Amberlin then uttered, every conjuration that he *could* still remember, were tweaked, spoiled, and sent awry in some way or other: by a lengthened vowel here, a protracted consonant there, a sudden diaresis shift or interogative. Something once as trivial as renewing the Genial Compliance on Diffin—an utterance of seconds—now required an hour of careful concentration, while only rarely did a spontaneous conjuration prove effective in any way.

What an embarrassment to engage in that trifling exchange with Tralques at the Iron Star Inn that day and then, having invoked his greatest display spell, Aspalin's Fond Retrieval, being left to explain why he had countered the upstart's dazzling conjuration of a troupe of performing silver dryads with nothing more than a lowly earthenware teapot reciting bawdy ballads from the Land of the Falling Wall. What an agony to escape the deodand at Wayly Corners, then from his refuge in the tossing heights of a lamplight tree see his Astemic Sunderblast turn an entire hillside into yellow flowers with softly chiming wind-bells. The deodand had either been discouraged by the sheer novelty of the display, or had more likely wandered off out of boredom, but Amberlin had been left to justify to neighbors and curious passers-by why he had preferred to stay aloft swaying in the breeze for four hours instead of simply blasting the creature outright.

The whole affair had given Amberlin a not altogether unwelcome reputation for subtlety, capriciousness, and new-found stoicism. Some even called him, and never entirely in jest, Amberlin the Philosophe, and drew pleasing if somewhat off-handed parallels with his fabulous namesakes, Amberlins I and II, two of the mightiest after Phandaal in all the long history of Grand Motholam. It could have been worse.

But Amberlin knew it was only a matter of time before the spiteful Sarimance, that upstart Tralques, the Anto brothers themselves, or even that wilful mooncalf Diffin brought forth the various bits and pieces they knew and saw how it truly was, and he found himself the laughing-stock of Almery, Ascolais, and beyond, the punch-line of the season's joke.

Amberlin glanced at the antique chronometer floating above his desk. It was well past time to be on his way. Fortunately, the housekeeping and protection spells for Furness required but a single one-syllable word, and today took merely fifteen subvocalized attempts before luck had it safely in place. Amberlin strode briskly down the path, then, with a single glance up at Diffin gazing at a sun that no longer was, he gripped his staff firmly and set off across the water-meadow to where the remains of Venta-Valu stood in the roseate morning light.

THOUGH AMBERLIN'S few remaining spells had become ordeals of frustration and dismay, with even a text as fundamental to sound wizardry as Killiclaw's Primer of Practical Magic hardly worth the trouble of opening, he possessed other adjuncts borrowed, bought or bequeathed to him through a long lifetime that required no utterances at all. If he were reasonably careful, he could still present as someone to be approached with caution and crossed at great peril.

One such possession was the antique baffle screen the Anto brothers now used to hide both themselves and the cellar Eunepheos had wrought so long ago. As Amberlin strode along the riverbank, he fitted the yellow key-glass coin to his left eye and revealed both the Copsy Door and the brothers wilfully hiding amid the more substantial of the old manse footings.

It was hard to know what passed for humor or wit in those sly, self-serving minds. Now, by remaining quiet, it seemed as if they wanted to make Amberlin lose face by having to ask that they reveal themselves.

"Let us be about it then!" he called, taking care to direct his gaze precisely at where each was concealed, and was pleased at how swiftly the grins left the startled, moony faces. Now both scrambled to their feet and stood, burly, copper-skinned and practically hairless in their humble village work-smocks and thick leather aprons, giving silly grins again.

"Kept it safe, your magnificence," Joanto said, brushing the grass from his apron. "Did all you said exactly to the letter."

Boanto wiped his chin with the back of a hand. "Ready and eager to uncover what's within, your mightiness."

The Copsy Door itself was a smooth milk-glass lid set at forty-five degrees into the hillside. About it, merging with the grassy bank, were the schattendross relics of old wall and arch footings, a sad handful looming up to become twists and tendrils before fading into nothing. Through them, the old red sun cast a purple light that made the day seem further along than it was. Not for the first time, Amberlin wondered what had possessed Eunepheos to create such a place. There was gloom and shadow enough in these latter days.

Amberlin pushed back his sleeves in the sort of theatrical flourish all wizards practiced in the privacy of their innermost sanctoria, and made as if to study the milky lid. "Joanto, take your water-bucket and fetch fresh water—mind now, free from any impurities. Boanto, go find five red wildflowers from that meadow there. Flawless, you understand. Not a blemish or this will not work."

The brothers exchanged glances, clearly displeased at having to miss any part of what the wizard now did, but dared not linger.

Amberlin watched as they hurried off muttering and casting backward glances. Then, even as Joanto stooped to fill his bucket and Boanto discarded one flower after another in his quest for perfect blooms, Amberlin took the green operating coin for the baffle screen in one hand and the yellow eye-coin in the other and slammed them together. The result was a rather spectacular and very satisfactory flash complete with a thunderclap that echoed in the hills and sent reed-birds rising along the Scaum.

The brothers, of course, saw it as a fine conjuration rather than the pyrotechnics accompanying ancient science at work. Even as the thunder faded, they came scrambling back, Joanto discarding his bucket, Boanto throwing aside his fistfuls of flowers along the way.

"No matter! No matter!" Amberlin called. "My simplest Sunderblast has brought Eunepheos' door undone. Light the torches and let us proceed."

Boanto wiped his chin again and studied the perfectly round hole where the Copsy Door had been. Its blackness was absolute. "Surely a fine magical glow would be more convenient, your magnificence."

"Surely it would," Amberlin countered loftily. "But think on it further, Boanto. You fine robust fellows must continue to play some modest part in this to warrant as much as a *quarter* share."

Joanto gave a shrewd sideways look. "But we were the ones who found the old requiem manuscript in that trunk in Solver's attic while—er—visiting his poor, ill—er—now deceased mother that day, then immediately brought it to you."

"True, but you brought it to me knowing I valued old manuscripts and syllabaries and was a likely buyer, nothing more. It was I who spent the hours researching Eunepheos and finally learned how to apply that scrap of melody to this fine Copsy Door so we could plot its comings and goings."

"As you say, master," said Joanto. "And I like that word 'we'. 'We' is so much friendlier than 'I'."

"You've been talking to Diffin, I can tell. For now, be satisfied with the generous quarter 'we' agreed upon."

Boanto rubbed his chin. "But what if yonder hole is empty? A quarter of nothing is nothing at all."

"Indeed. But who knows? Prospective apprentices in training for Furness must seize any opportunity to demonstrate appropriate skills."

The brothers eyed one another at the thought of access to the impressive and well-appointed manse their informant Diffin had long boasted about.

Joanto quickly set to lighting the torches. "Right you are, master. You conserve your fine magic. Bo and I will light the way to unstinting generosity and open-handed remuneration."

"To the bottom of a mysterious hole in a riverbank at the very least. But well said, Joanto. In fact, surprisingly said. You will make a fine factotum someday. On you go, brave lads."

Warily, reluctantly, the brothers stepped one after the other into the hole. Amberlin followed, relieved to find conventional stone steps leading down to an ordinary enough stone-lined corridor cut into the hillside. Whatever Venta-Valu had been above ground, here in the underhill more conventional methods were at work. More importantly, ordinary corridors usually signified ordinary destinations and conventional rewards like treasure troves and prized collectibles.

But while the brothers no doubt thought of gold and gems, perhaps a few of the easier glamors to ease their way in the world, Amberlin longed for spell books and periapts, something, anything, to free him from the debilitating nightmare of Stilfer's Prolexic Inflect.

He said nothing of this, of course, simply continued by torchlight along a corridor flagged and walled with slabs of finely set teracite, with darkness stretching before and a more unsettling darkness closing in behind.

What had this place been? Amberlin wondered. Not a tomb, surely. Many wizards preferred to self-immolate in a blaze of scintillance before a suitable audience at an exact day and hour, as if in answer to some higher calling only they had cognizance of. Others chose to exit in the solemn pursuance of some marvelous interdimensional quest, so they claimed, something that would ensure a legacy of bafflement and wonder and become the stuff of legends.

Amberlin may have fallen a long way to his present desperate straits, but never for a moment did he forget that any adept's reputation depended on one part magic to five parts showmanship. As the great Phandaal himself was purported to have said, "A good exit makes up for a good deal." If the showmanship far outweighed the magic in these days since Sarimance's curse, then so be it. That too took considerable skill.

At last, the corridor opened into a large stone tholos chamber, completely empty save for a single black mirror set against the far wall. The glass stood in an ornate gilt frame and was nearly the size of a door.

Even without his long years of experience with mirrors, Amberlin would have allowed that a spread of reflective darkness in that particular configuration did not bode well. The brothers clearly agreed. Finding the tholos empty, they had begun muttering to one another. Before Amberlin could reassure them, a voice called from behind.

"Our heartfelt thanks, Amberlin. Tralques and myself agreed that you were the one to get us inside."

Amberlin turned and barely controlled the rush of anger and dismay he felt. At the mouth of the entry corridor, casting illumination with the milkfire globe set in the end of his staff, stood his old adversary, Sarimance the Aspurge. The formidable mage looked as self-assured and resplendant as ever in his rich vermilion day-robe, with tight black curls framing his round face and, yes, the familiar maddening grin Amberlin remembered from that worst of days.

Beside him, with a more conventional lantern raised high, stood Tralques, the smirking upstart from the Iron Star Inn, as thin and nervous-looking in his dark blue travelling robe as Sarimance was round and supremely confident in his dazzling red.

"You have caused me many miserable hours, Sarimance," was all Amberlin could think to say. He knew he had been careless, that no spell now uttered in his defence could possibly turn out right.

"No doubt, old friend," Sarimance replied, clearly enjoying the moment. "But then you would have inconvenienced me with equal sang-froid, I'm sure, had the circumstances permitted. You seem surprised that our fine lads here have been so forthcoming in inviting us to your party."

Amberlin put on his bravest face. "Joanto, Boanto, you must put any hopes of employment at Furness out of your mind. All such offers are henceforth rescinded. You are to consider them null and void."

The brothers stood chuckling to one side.

Joanto went further and spat on the floor. "As you see, magnificence, three quarters of something can quickly become nothing as well."

Amberlin maintained as much aplomb as he could manage. "Furthermore, you may inform Diffin that his services are no longer required. He can join you in the employment queue in Azenomei."

"Now, now, Amberlin," Sarimance remonstrated, stepping further into the room. "Do not blame the lobster for being a lobster. More to the point, remember that some husbands have more than one wife and service all fairly. Best accept that your erstwhile employees already had employment before entering your service and simply saw a way to get two jobs done. But since we are all here, bold wayfarers together, what do you make of this glass?"

Amberlin knew that the immediate barbs and retorts that sprang to mind would serve no useful purpose. "It is undoubtedly a door. Eunepheos the Darke is reputed to have had several mirror doors at Venta-Valu in his salad days."

Sarimance stepped forward to examine the ominous black shape. "How then do we open it? Do your books tell?"

From behind him, Tralques peered at the glossy surface. "The question is, do we really wish to know?"

"Be easy, Tralques," Sarimance said, smiling all the while. "Our redoubtable colleague here has all manner of tricks and competencies. Provided uttering them is not required, of course."

Tralques and the brothers chuckled at the barb.

Amberlin pretended not to hear. "May I suggest that Joanto and Boanto earn their way in this by first polishing the mirror? Dust and other blemishes mar the surface and could well affect its operation, rather in the same way that a particular inconvenient conjuration presently afflicts me."

Sarimance smiled, but the brothers protested.

"We are holding our torches!" Joanto said. "A vital task that requires all our attention, as brother Bo will affirm."

Boanto nodded vigorously. "Moreover, the glass looks especially smooth and clear from where we stand."

Amberlin made a sound of impatience. "Then you must stand closer. Pass your torches to Tralques and he will be our light-bearer and illuminate the glass while you polish it with your kerchiefs."

"We possess no kerchiefs!" Joanto cried.

Boanto put on a thoughtful expression. "But perhaps we could go and buy some at the fair in Azenomei and hurry right back."

Sarimance gestured and uttered a pronouncement. "Do not trouble yourselves. You will now find excellent kerchiefs in the pockets of your work aprons."

"But we have no pockets either!" Boanto protested. "Perhaps we had best go and—" then found he had both pockets and kerchiefs to spare, a half-dozen of each, and that Joanto had the same.

"Bah," muttered Joanto, pulling forth a fine lace kerchief. "Sometimes lofty folk take all the fun out of finding a bargain."

With no other choice, the brothers reluctantly approached the black mirror. Joanto gave a tentative rub with his cloth, then, when nothing untoward happened, Boanto did the same.

"It seems very well behaved for a magic glass," Boanto said.

"Aye, Bo," Joanto agreed. "Perhaps it appreciates the attention and will reward us for such kindly treatment."

Encouraged, they began polishing and cleaning in earnest while the magicians looked on.

Becoming ever more zealous, Joanto finally spat on the glass as a prelude to removing an especially stubborn spot. The mirror gave a deep sigh, then, in a flash of glittering darkness, its surface heaved forward in a great pseudopodium, snatched up the brothers, and carried them off into the frame and out of sight. A distant wail could be heard from the other side, then absolute silence.

Before any of the wizards could remark on the occurrence, a figure stepped through the golden frame: a shapely young woman wearing a form-fitting costume of black and yellow diaper. Only her face remained uncovered, showing clear blue eyes and a radiant smile. She gestured towards the mirror door.

"Gentlemen, if you will. Eunepheos awaits."

"Eunepheos!" cried Tralques. Though shrewd and ambitious, the young mage had come by his magic through paternal largesse from Ildefonse the Preceptor, and was still new to matters of decorum and proper conduct.

"Then take us to him at once!" Sarimance demanded. "We are important dignitaries and most eager to meet him."

Amberlin said nothing, just waited as the winsome creature—human, sandestin, some even rarer kind of eldritch wunderwaif, it was impossible to tell—stood to one side of the frame and gestured for them to enter.

Sarimance thought on it and hesitated. "Amberlin, as this is still officially your expedition, please be so good as to lead the way."

"With pleasure," Amberlin said, and approached the frame. What was there to lose? Since Eunepheos could as easily have snatched them all away as he had the brothers, there was no reason to hesitate. In a moment, and with nothing more than an odd tingling sensation along his arms and legs, he was through the doorway and standing in a vast pillared hall lit by a wash of balmy golden light. Overhead blazed a million scintillants; out through the flanking colonnades were great gulfs of shadow. So, too, darkness filled the high windows.

Amberlin suspected the answer. Just as Venta-Valu had been a demesne of shadow in the failing light of Old Earth, this was its shadow-side equivalent: a manse of rich sunlight and colour in the midst of eternal shadowlands.

In moments, Sarimance, Tralques, and the maiden were beside him. Of the Anto brothers, there was no sign.

"Come forward!" cried a great voice from a dais at the far end of the hall, and the magicians moved forward to meet their host.

It was a fascinating sight that greeted them. On the dais, a long-legged, silver-haired figure in black and gold lounged on a great throne, his sharp face and hawklike gaze turned on them as they approached. At the foot of the dais were all manner of wondrous oddities from the forgotten heraldries of Grand Motholam: armored heridinks and plymays, glinting scarfades and lizard-skinned holimores—creatures either born in various

undervoids and overworlds or raised in flasks, vats, and home-made vivaria. The fabulous entourage fidgeted, muttered, and groomed themselves as Amberlin, Sarimance, and Tralques followed their lovely guide to the four wide steps before the throne.

"Great Eunepheos," the lovely woman said, her voice filling the golden chamber. "I bring you, first, Amberlin the Lesser, leader of these three grand explorers into the underhill, then Sarimance the Aspurge from Azenomei, and Tralques Iron Star, illegitimate son of Ildefonse the Preceptor. They alone possessed the skill and ingenuity to defeat your Copsy Door at Venta-Valu and so accepted your invitation; then, against all better judgement, summoned up sufficient courage and daring to enter your most hallowed tholos in the underhill."

Eunepheos gazed at each as he was named. "Thank you, lovely Asari," he said. "You may take your place." He waited while the maiden in black and yellow bowed and went to stand between two blue-enamelled heridinks, then turned his dark eyes back to his visitors.

"I am pleased, gentlemen, that you chose to accept our invitation, and am complimented by your attention. It was good of you to come."

Amberlin noted the finality in the word 'was,' but said nothing. Sarimance, however, felt the need to speak.

"Great Eunepheos. A codicil to the proceedings, if I may. I must point out that my companion Tralques and I are not necessarily part of our colleague's expedition. It was Amberlin who first conceived it, then found a way to defeat your Copsy Door by way of diligent scholarship. It was he who, without consulting sympathetic colleagues, chose to intrude in your domain. Tralques and I, concerned for his welfare in such an unknown, mysterious place, thought to keep an eye on how he fared and perhaps persuade him to re-consider his venture. Our commitment to the enterprise may be more apparent than real."

"I grasp your meaning in every regard," Eunepheos said. "And it is always heartening to see friends come to each other's aid in such matters. Still, you are here now, and, since three wizards are the stipulated minimum, the contest can proceed."

"The contest, noble Eunepheos?" Tralques asked.

"All will be explained. But first, allow me to present our judges."

Eunepheos gestured and three great niches formed in the wall above the throne. In each rested a man-sized glass case. Two were of shimmering silver shot with veins of old rose and flashing indigo. They flanked a case of rich buttery gold filled with arcs of scintillating red and burnt orange. At first, the dazzling cases sizzled with all manner of roiling energies, but soon settled down to a quiet, almost predatory watchfulness.

"Gentlemen," Eunepheos continued. "Before you are the remembrance chambers of the greatest of us. At the centre, beyond equals, eternally first, stands that of Phandaal the Great. To left and right in flashing silver, you see those of Amberlin the First and Amberlin the Second. They will be our judges."

Eunepheos left a pause for dramatic effect, but Tralques could not remain silent.

"These are not their bodies, surely?"

"That is not for me to say," Eunepheos answered, as courtly as ever. "Who knows where these great ones went upon withdrawing from our midst so long ago? What is death and extinction to the likes of such ascendants? Be satisfied that there is a residual link between our world and theirs, a vital connection spanning the ages, and that it pleases them enormously to have watched me set my little trap at Venta-Valu. Think of how it delights them that I test their successors in these latter days, some of whom are wise and generous like yourselves, others vain and grasping and interested only in self-advancement. Imagine their pleasure as I lured three legitimate inheritors like yourselves, ingenious enough, brave enough, and sufficiently determined to make the crossing through the shadow glass into Dessinga to compete in their contest. The less charitable might see it as culling, weeding out the dross, but paragons like yourselves no doubt see it for the appropriate duty of care that it is."

Tralques took a step forward. "As my illustrious friend and colleague just now explained, great Eunepheos, Sarimance and I are merely here in a supernumerary capacity to Amberlin's original group—"

"Nonsense, Master Tralques," Eunepheos countered. "You are far too modest and it does you credit. Your resolve is as strong as his, I'm sure. Our contest is to be one of magic, here, now, in this great hall. Each of you will take turns conjuring up your finest. In three rounds, three attempts, each bout strictly limited to no more than two minutes, you will present a display worthy of our mighty judges. Three rounds, three chances to win. The winner goes free, of course. The Copsy Door will open to him alone. The others will stay and add their fine energies to Dessinga to help maintain this golden place."

"I must cry foul!" Sarimance said. "There is an unforgivable bias. Our friend Amberlin here is the namesake of two of the judges. They will surely

be predisposed. I suggest the contest be abandoned until two new judges can be appointed. Tralques, Amberlin, and I will return, say, a year from now to see if—"

Eunepheos raised a hand. "Sarimance, listen well. You cannot imagine what shame, scorn and disgust our noble Silver Adepts here would normally feel because a sorry pretender persists in bearing their name. You see no latter-day Phandaals, do you? No surfeit of Llorios, no glut of Dibarcas Maiors? Who would dare? Who would risk the possibility of reprisal? But the leader of your fearless expedition has been bold enough to take the name of his betters without regret or contrition. No doubt he will say it is to honor his ancestors rather than simply out of pride and hubris, or because his parents were careless. So be it. We will soon see, one way or the other. But if there is a bias, then surely it is in *your* favor, not his. So let the contest proceed! Tralques, you look so dignified in your fine blue robe, you will go first, then you, Sarimance, then your expedition leader, Amberlin."

Without further hesitation, Tralques strode purposefully out into the hall, spun about and gestured magnificently.

"Great Eunepheos, illustrious judges, respectful spectators and brother wizards, I greet you and present for your diversion and edification the Wholly Self-Made Mankin!"

There was a moment's hesitation, then a floating head appeared in the hall before them, its broad moon-face grinning amiably, peering this way and that, regarding its surroundings with what could only be happiness and wonder. For twenty seconds it regarded the dais, the three shimmering remembrance cases, the wizards, and the assembled underlings, then, from below the chin, a body formed, legs extending down till the creature stood on the floor at last.

No sooner had the feet settled than the head sprouted antlers, each tine tipped with a glowing red bulb. The apparition glanced up in wonder as more nodules formed along the tines, each one swelling till it fell away like ripe fruit and was caught by the creature, who immediately began juggling them. The hands were soon lost in a blur as ten, twenty, soon hundreds of the coloured orbs went soaring into the air. In a final flourish, the orbs were all sent aloft together, first to transform into gorgeously plumed songbirds that gave a single plangent cry, then to explode in a cascade of dazzling colors.

When the dazzle subsided, the head, body and accessories were nowhere to be seen. Tralques stood alone, bowing before Eunepheos and the judges.

Eunepheos, Sarimance and Amberlin applauded with gusto. The underlings, however, stood rapt in silent attention as if not sure how to act. The three radiant cases stood without comment.

"Splendid, Tralques!" Sarimance cried. "It is nice to see that old routine done so briskly."

"Splendid indeed," Eunepheos said. "Most impressive, Tralques Iron Star. Sarimance, to the floor if you will!"

Sarimance strode forth like a blood-red demon of yore, staff flashing with its brilliant white tip. He too spun about in fine style, arms flung wide as if for applause, though none was yet forthcoming. Sarimance, Amberlin observed, clearly valued the niceties of showmanship as much as he did.

"Great Eunepheos, mighty Remembrances, colleagues and friends, I bring you the Penultimate Callestine Redoubt, as first performed in far-off Sarmatica before the Nine."

Waves of bright blue light, like mighty ocean swells, rushed through the arches at the sides of the hall and began clashing and heaving against one another in the middle of the vast space. Gulls cried. The smell of brine filled the air. Then, emerging from the toss of spray and luminous foam, came a galleas in full sail, its oars striking the waves, complete with flags snapping in a strong head-wind and mariners calling.

While the wizards watched, the ship began to swing about in the beginnings of a terrible maelstrom, turning faster and faster until, at last, it sank beneath the ethereal waves and was lost. But even as those waves closed over the hapless craft, a great tower lifted from where it had been, a lighthouse looming up out of the swells to stand strong and unassailable, its tapered length striped with the heraldic colors of Grand Motholam, its great beacon pulsing out across the angry seas.

Then it was gone: lighthouse, wind and waves, and the silence in the hall was in itself spectacular after all that had been.

"I have never seen the Redoubt done better," Eunepheos confessed. "Sarimance, you are undoubtedly a master of the first rank. I dare not try to guess what you will give us for your final offering."

"I thank you, great lord," the Red Wizard replied, and returned to the others.

"Now you, noble Amberlin," Eunepheos said. "The one with the skill and courage to defeat my Copsy Door, who judged intrusion into Dessinga worth all risk and danger and even now welcomes all consequences. Your first offering please."

Amberlin stepped forth, feigning a confidence he did not feel. He did a magnificent spin-about and flourish with his staff that, he liked to think, surely had the plymays, heridinks, and holimores wide-eyed with amazement, if such a concept had any purchase in those antic minds.

But what could he try? What might he invoke that the Inflect would not ruin? Dare he attempt the Absolute Cardantian Triflex? The intonations were clear, the words mostly monosyllables. But he dared not hesitate. Even as he began speaking the words, he resolved to show no consternation at the result. Whatever happened was to be treated as exactly what was intended.

He concluded the pronouncement and gestured magnificently.

Twenty-six chickens sat on a large Alazeen rug, blinking and pecking at bits of dust in the weave.

There was silence in the hall except for some idle clucking. Some in the audience of adepts and underlings may have thought to admire the wonderful patterns in the old rug, others the interesting fact that every third chicken was either cross-eyed or had but a single eye. Certainly there was much to ponder on.

Amberlin himself was dumbfounded by the sheer bathos of the result, but made himself smile as if at some subtlety no-one else could see. He then chuckled and, as a desperate but possibly ingenious improvisation, wagged a finger at the nearest chicken as if in reproach at some inappropriate, possibly scurrilous, remark it had just now made. The chicken blinked its single eye and went back to picking at dust-mites in the rug.

Forty-two seconds from the moment of their appearance, both rug and chickens vanished in an equally anticlimactic pop, and the room was as before. Amberlin strode as decisively as he could back to his place before the dais.

"Most unexpected!" Eunepheos said. "Either there are subtleties here only the most refined sensibilities can discern or you are so confident of your final performance that you are trifling with us and saving your best till last."

"Though it was a very fine rug," Tralques admitted, clearly nonplussed by the whole thing.

"And most singular chickens," Sarimance remarked, barely able to contain his amusement.

"Indeed," said Eunepheos. "And contrast always has its place. But let us continue. Tralques, to the floor!"

"Great lord," Tralques temporized. "Would not some small refreshment be in order? I know for a fact that the Iron Star Inn has the best—"

"Nonsense, Master Tralques. We have hardly begun. To the floor, I say. After such wonders, our judges are keen to see more!"

Tralques again stepped forth into the great room. Without preamble, he flung his arms wide and uttered another spell from his repertoire.

Out in the hall, a giant child lay sleeping face-down on the paving. On the infant's broad back stood twenty silver dryads playing musical instruments: fantiphones and asponades, twizzle-horns, fukes, and quarter-drums. As they executed a most jolly jig from the hills beyond Kaspara Vitatus, the child's dreams curled up in spirals of fanciful imagery, so that clowns and eagles tipped into castles and cottages, with glimpses of monarchs and djinn vying with hints of dragonry, all in the most wonderful melange.

At the minute-forty mark, the seemingly random elements came surging together to form a single face: that of Eunepheos himself, smiling and benign.

"It is often well done when well enough done," the image intoned cryptically, and the whole fascinating ensemble vanished, leaving Tralques bowing respectfully to those on the dais.

This time, the underlings in the entourage applauded along with the wizards, rattling their armour, weapons, chains and fine jewelry according to their various stations and condition in the Dessinga hierarchy.

"Elegantly and grandly done!" Eunepheos cried with obvious approval.

"The Fine Silver Dalliance," Sarimance said. "I remember it fondly. And there wasn't a single chicken, one-eyed, cross-eyed or otherwise to mar the proceedings."

Amberlin smiled and applauded too, but carefully said nothing, though he did note in passing that Tralques had refined his conjuration considerably since their meeting at the Iron Star Inn that day. Sarimance had obviously been providing lessons in embellishment and framing effect.

Amberlin's thoughts returned at once to his remaining eleven spell patterns. He ran through the sequences, trying to settle on two that would see him through the contest with some chance of acquitting himself. His three punitive conjurations automatically disqualified themselves, of course, leaving eight to choose from, only two of which were in any way suitable for display purposes. Then again, who could say, the Inflect might work in his favor and serve up something truly marvelous. It was a possibility.

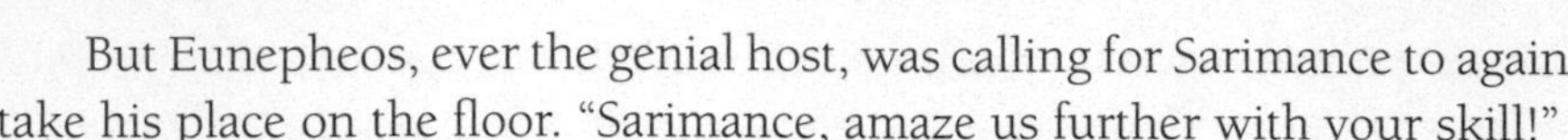

But Eunepheos, ever the genial host, was calling for Sarimance to again take his place on the floor. "Sarimance, amaze us further with your skill!"

"If I may, great Eunepheos, I would ask that the beautiful Asari be permitted to assist."

Eunepheos looked to where Asari stood among his entourage and nodded, and the lovely maiden in black and yellow diaper moved out to join the Red Wizard.

Even as she turned to regard those at the dais, the vermilion-clad mage gestured hieratically. Asari immediately lifted into the air in a smooth and graceful motion. Apart from a momentary widening of her eyes in surprise, she retained her composure, rising up until her lithe form was suspended twenty feet in the air.

Sarimance's staff then projected a beam of white light that struck the maiden's body and lanced through it in a multitude of colors as if through a prism. The colorforms spiraled out from her, creating struts, pinions, and articulations, then vibrant membranes, finally forming the wings of a vast butterfly that extended out to fill the entire hall. On those spread wings of light and color suddenly appeared forms and faces, identities from history and legend who came forth to peer through Asari's wing-lenses and regard the throng watching below.

Eunepheos actually gasped as the faces of his own father and mother looked down upon him with benign regard.

At the minute-thirty mark, the wings began to close around Asari until they were fully furled, wrapping her in shimmering light so that she was like a fabulous cocoon. At one minute-fifty, the vestiges cleared completely and the girl descended to the floor again, none the worse for her brief transformation.

The audience of wizards and magicals applauded enthusiastically.

"Most impressive and most tasteful," Eunepheos said, his severe hawk-like face again softened with what seemed genuine pleasure.

Neither Tralques and Amberlin deigned to speak. It was the second round, and the knowledge that only one of them would make it back through the Copsy Door was sobering.

"Amberlin the Lesser," Eunepheos cried, and the appropriate formality seemed to contain a touch of wry humor. "Please regale us with your next confection!"

"Gladly, noble sir!" Amberlin said, moving out onto the floor with new determination. Having considered his few appropriate spells, whatever havoc the Inflect now wrought would likely be better than anything his correct utterances could deliver.

He turned, gave a smile he hoped seemed part mischief, part conspiratorial delight, then subvocalized his utterance and gestured with raised arms as before.

A child's red balloon floated into the hall accompanied by tinkling from an unseen music box. For all of forty seconds it drifted back and forth while the melody played, then its knotted end suddenly released and it went jetting about the chamber, making a distinctly risque sound as it deflated. Before it could fall to the floor, it vanished with a final distinct raspberry.

Tralques was doubled over with laughter.

Sarimance stood with tears rolling down his cheeks.

Eunepheos sat with a grin of wonder and perplexity fixed on his sharp face.

It was Tralques Iron Star who first managed to speak. "Perhaps the rest of the carnival is on the other side of the mirror door and can't remember the password." He collapsed with laughter again.

Sarimance fought for composure. "At least, dear Amberlin, you have saved yourself the expense of hiring a rug and chickens! You might at least have showed us the music box, since its off-stage presence smacks of a certain degree of parsimony on your part and, for a fact, the melody did become a bit tiresome."

"Enough!" Eunepheos cried. "We take the bad with the good, the great with the small. Some of us may simply relish the prospect of remaining in Dessinga more than others. Tralques, be so good as to honor us with your final presentation!"

"Gladly, great lord!" Tralques replied, the seriousness of the occasion finally giving him control of his mirth. Yet again he strode forth, took his place, and muttered the words of a new conjuration.

The hall immediately darkened and a great single eye opened in the wall above the entry glass. Each time it blinked, a small spot-lit table appeared at which sat a dining couple, youths and maidens for the most part, happily discussing their private affairs. Then, blink by blink of the great eye, older couples appeared as dinner guests as well, then fabulous creatures, winged and horned and wearing the tabards of ancient bestiaries. An agreeable hubbub filled the vast hall, the words in human languages and other tongues rising up as intricate streamers of light and color to form an incredible braid overhead.

Even as the braid began turning, drawing the streamers into an ever-lengthening maypole knot, a beautiful music filled the hall, both stately and yet at the same time achingly poignant to hear, a melody for absent friends, precious things lost and times out of mind.

At precisely the one minute fifty mark, the eye gave a final blink and the chamber was empty again.

"The Bayate Knot," Sarimance said, giving his insufferable smile. "And never done better."

"Astounding! Impressive! Delightful!" cried Eunepheos. "Tralques, your star is clearly on the ascendant! Now, Sarimance, give us your very best!"

Sarimance levitated, spiralled up into the air like a vermilion torch, then slowly descended to the floor, an overture that Amberlin judged needlessly excessive, even ostentatious.

As Sarimance gestured, two great golden doorways formed to the left and right of the chamber. Through the left-hand portal came a procession of the greatest wizards Grand Motholam had ever known.

First there was Calanctus the Calm, resplendent in the purple, green, and orange robe he wore at the Alancthon Festival so long ago when he defeated Conamas the Sophist. The magician walked smiling past the dais and inclined his head once in courteous greeting.

Close behind came Dibarcas Maior, wearing the intricate fire-weave robe for which he had been celebrated across the lands, and with two fire-demons dancing upon his shoulders. He raised an arm in greeting and moved on through the right-hand portal. Zinqzin the Encyclopaedist followed, holding in his arms the two great wonder-books that had ensured his place in the annals of the truly great. He too inclined his head to the assembled fellowship and passed beyond the door.

Then appeared Amberlin I in an emerald green gown streaked with gold, with Amberlin II close behind, masked and robed in luminous yellow. Both seemed overly solemn compared to the others; their nods to Eunepheos and his companions were measured and respectful, but their manner was somewhat aloof. One after the other they stepped through the right-hand door and disappeared.

The Vapurials appeared next, all three laughing and saluting the spectators with their eternally replenishing goblets of wine from far Pergolay. As they reached the right-hand exit, they flung down their goblets, which exploded in their personal color sprays of cobalt, saffron, and umber.

Then Llorio the Sorceress entered the great room in a sedan chair carried by a dozen liveried lizard-heads. If the rumors were true, they were former suitors, each one giving up their lives for a single night each year with their splendid mistress. Llorio smiled and regarded the watching wizards as if, even now, she might consider their eligibility for a place in her service. It was an unnerving moment.

Members of the Green and Purple College came next, three dazzling wizards and three beautiful sorceresses wearing their fabulous turbans and College regalia, striding forth and waving at the spectators, clearly enjoying the occasion. No sooner had they passed by the dais and reached the exit than the Arch-Mage Mael Lel Laio swept into the room, nodded at Eunepheos and the judges, rather perfunctorily it seemed, almost as if he preferred to be somewhere else, then proceeded on his way.

Kyrol of Porphyrhyncos followed, and it seemed he was to complete the display, for no sooner had that powerful black-skinned wizard moved past in his robes of silver assantine than there was a pause.

Then came a swelling fanfare of destiny-horns and the room glowed with a wash of blue-white radiance as, first among them, Phandaal the Great appeared, smiling and magnificent. He actually paused before the dais and raised his arms in a brotherly salute before continuing on his way, the destiny horns playing all the while. As he entered the golden exit door, he gestured behind him, and the portal vanished in a final burst of radiance.

How the hosts of Dessinga applauded! No doubt they had been carefully schooled to recognize each member of that fabulous procession.

"You honor us indeed, Master Sarimance," Eunepheos said. "The greatest ones are well known for both their acute sense of protocol and for their restive natures in matters of place, so that often even the manifestations we have seen today are not always easy together. You have managed to bring us a most harmonious and well-behaved display under the circumstances. I commend and thank you."

"I aimed only to please," Sarimance said, and returned to his place before the dais.

"Amberlin, to the floor!" Eunepheos cried. "Now we see what you have been holding back! I, for one, can hardly wait."

Amberlin gave a smart half-bow, just langorous enough, then took his place and turned. It was his final chance. He would risk everything.

Without further thought, he invoked Aspalin's Fond Retrieval, once his greatest display spell, hoping that this time the vowels and articulations held true, or that some new skewing by the Inflect delivered an improvement in scale and majesty.

The air was split with a resounding thunderclap and lit all over with great stabs of lightning, then a very fine and wholly unexpected vortex began spiralling out in the hall, churning and roaring.

It boded well and Amberlin dared to feel hope. He watched as the mighty cone of air finally narrowed and funneled down on a single lighted spot.

The anomaly then vanished in a final clap of thunder, leaving complete silence.

A lowly earthenware teapot sat upon the paving. It gave a tentative, "Me-Me-Me!" in a broken, throaty voice, then began reciting a bawdy ballad from the Land of the Falling Wall. It had just finished the chorus and was starting on the second verse when the contest time limit was reached and both kitchen utensil and song vanished in a puff of crimson smoke.

"Great Eunepheos, I can explain everything—" Amberlin began to say, but Eunepheos interrupted.

"It is after the event," he said, rising from his throne. "Explain nothing! Now it is time for our judges to deliver their decision. Noble magicians, step out upon the floor one last time, if you will, and face your adjudicators."

The three wizards did so, watching as the glass cases behind Eunepheos buzzed and crackled with renewed energies. Finally, when sufficient discussion had transpired, a single thread of force projected from each to penetrate Eunepheos' body. When he now spoke, his eyes glowed with a lambent white light and his voice was an overlay of three voices made into one.

"By the order of presentation, we appraise you," the composite voice said. Eunepheos the Darke stood frozen, only his mouth and jaw moving. "Tralques Iron Star, wonderfully done. You use magic borrowed from your betters, but inheritance is always difficult in magical affairs and you acquitted yourself superbly."

Tralques bowed. "Thank you, noble sirs. Your example will inspire me to do better next time, I'm sure."

Eunepheos seemed not to hear. "Sarimance the Aspurge, your invocations showed imagination and a truly commendable degree of respect to those who are your betters. You are skilful, strategic and inspiring, if somewhat unforgiving."

Sarimance bowed. "Great lords, my relentlessness is inspired by your own discipline and dedication. We can only dream of the time when you were among us and thank you for gifting us with your presence here today."

Again there was no acknowledgment from Eunepheos or the remembrance cases.

"Amberlin the Lesser," the triple voice said. "Today you have surprised us with the selections you chose for such an important occasion. But you have shown a sense of novelty and the unruly, and there is about you an insouciance and irreverence that we like. In short, you have remembered that since we too are wizards of great power, if only as remembrances, for us magic and magical display are easy and second nature. What is missing from our lives are the elements of absurdity and genuine surprise. You have provided these things in ample measure—and are therefore our winner!"

Sarimance immediately cried out. "What! Great lords, I protest—!"

He vanished in a puff of smoke.

Tralques actually thought to flee, but only managed two steps before he too disappeared, this time in a twist of light.

Two new scintillants appeared among the thousands on the ceiling of the chamber.

Amberlin, utterly dumbfounded, went to give thanks, but instead found himself on the riverbank outside the Copsy Door at Venta-Valu with Diffin standing to one side, visibly trembling with what seemed a mixture of relief and fear.

"Oh, master, it is so good to see you," the lanky creature said.

Amberlin managed to regain his composure. "Diffin, why are you here?"

"Master, I was looking out through the Clever Window as I promised I would when, just like that, it darkened over and a sharp, very frightening face appeared. It said that you had won a great contest of wizards and that the Anto brothers were never to be seen again. Nor were the wizards Sarimance or Tralques to be relied upon as referees in any future employment that I might care to seek."

"I see. Anything more?"

"Nothing, great one. Though I might add that the lillobays and quentians have been freshly watered and that the Holding Book is back in the east tower and seems much happier, so far as books of power can indicate such things, with how the new Diffin comports himself."

"Very well," Amberlin said, adjusting his robes. "Let us take a day or two to see how the new Diffin comports himself."

And together they set off to where the towers of the manse Furness stood glinting in the light of the old red sun.

AFTERWORD:

JACK'S WORK had an enormous impact on me as a teenager. I first encountered it when I was fifteen with "The Dragon Masters" in the August 1962 issue of *Galaxy* magazine, and thereafter quickly tried to find everything by him that I could. He went straight to the top of a small list of distinctive SF and fantasy voices I was discovering at the time, among them Ray Bradbury, J.G. Ballard, Cordwainer Smith and Philip K. Dick. He seemed to be doing something very special, or, perhaps more to the point, seemed to be doing familiar things in a very special way.

While I didn't discover *The Dying Earth* until ten years later, that linked collection confirmed everything I already loved and admired about Jack's work: the elegance and euphony of the writing, the distinctive cadences and rhythms, the sheer inventiveness and antiquarian caste, the way less was so often more and how the standard writing corollary of 'Show Don't Tell' effectively became: 'Don't Just Show, Suggest.'

Being introduced to Jack and his family by Tim Underwood at the end of 1980 meant the world to me, and led to the start of a very special friendship, one which has never ceased to be a source of great pleasure. One moment I'm a soldier sitting on a doorstep at the 3TB army base in 1968 reading *Star King* and *The Killing Machine*, then thirty years later I'm drifting off to sleep to the words of *Night Lamp*, *Ports of Call*, and *Lurulu* coming through the walls as Jack 'reads' through his current work in progress using his talking computer program. One moment I'm a steadfast fan, a fledgling storyteller refining my craft in faraway Sydney, trying to land my first sale, then I've become "The Smuggler" and one of Jack's closest friends, making annual visits to the wonderful house in the Oakland hills, switching on the navigation lights in the bar whenever he announces that the sun is well and truly over the yard-arm, making sure there's not a trace of zucchini to spoil a meal, taking enormous pains when playing washboard to Jack's banjo, ukelele, and kazoo always to finish at the same time. As Jack has said on many occasions, usually when several glasses of tipple have come and gone: "Vance deposes, Dowling disposes!" Neither of us is sure what it means, but it makes for a fine toast.

As well as sharing many unforgettable adventures with Jack and Norma over the years, among them our momentous road trip to Three Rivers in January 1984 where we visited a genuine (we insist!) haunted house, we've spent hours discussing projects, process and storytelling in general. In a special sense, "The Copsy Door" is the result of years of rich and sustained exposure to Jack's work, and of countless hours chatting before the fire, working at the kiln, listening to the Black Eagle Jazz Band, and choosing who, among friends and notables, would make the wholly imaginary voyage from Oakland down to Sydney on the fine Vance ketch, *Hinano*.

On a more specific note, I once unwittingly "borrowed" the name Amberlin from Jack's *Rhialto the Marvelous* as a name for a café in my Tom Rynosseros stories. Jack in turn took my coining "shatterwrack" for the extinct volcano Shattorak in *Ecce and Old Earth* (unwittingly, he insists!). It seemed fitting that my contribution to this book had to concern a particular wizard named Amberlin.

How did the story come about? Why, it was very much a case of painting myself into a corner. I simply had Amberlin step into his workroom one fine morning to deal with something called a Copsy Door, then saw where it went from there. I like to think that, in more ways than one, Jack himself helped with the writing.

—Terry Dowling

LIZ WILLIAMS

Caulk the Witch-Chaser

BRITISH WRITER Liz Williams has had work appear in *Interzone*, *Asimov's*, *Visionary Tongue*, *Terra Incognita*, *The New Jules Verne Adventures*, *Strange Horizons*, *Realms of Fantasy*, and elsewhere, and her stories have been collected in *Banquet of the Lords of Night and Other Stories*. Her books include the critically acclaimed novels *The Ghost Sister*, *Empire of Bones*, *The Poison Master*, *Nine Layers of Sky*, *Snake Agent*, *The Demon and the City*.and *Darkland*. Her most recent novels are *The Shadow Pavillion* and *Winterstrike*. She lives in Brighton, England.

Here she takes us along with a witch-chaser as he leaves Azenomei and heads down the river Scaum to the open sea, away from Almery and toward the bleak shores of Alster—and also toward, for better or worse, a change of professions…

Caulk the Witch-chaser

LIZ WILLIAMS

Caulk the witch-chaser came out of Almery on a rising tide, sailing first the brief distance down the Xzan, then the Scaum, towards the coast. Occasionally, he took the strand of hair out of the pouch and studied it: it lay silver in his palm, like the light of the long-lost moon, but he knew that if he looked at it under the sun, it would be the dull scarlet of old blood. Caulk smiled thinly at this thought, opening his coat and adjusting first his thirty nine daggers, then the scalps. The smell of the Scaum rose up, salty and brackish, redolent of unsuccessful poison.

By midnight, he had reached the mouth of the estuary. He anchored the boat for a few minutes, sent down a fluke-loaded line, then brought it back up writhing with glass eels. He cooked them in a mess in a pan, ate absently, and headed for open sea.

This had all come about in Azenomei, a month ago, when Caulk had first met the owl-killer. Normally, he would not have bothered with such a person: Caulk had standards of fastidiousness which the owl-killer

unfortunately failed to meet. The man—small, balding, with huge pale eyes—had lurched against him in a tavern, spilling cheap ale over Caulk's high black boots. Caulk clucked in exasperation and the owl-killer leered at him.

"Bit fussy, aren't we, for someone who drinks in hovels?"

"I am here on business," Caulk replied icily, wiping ale off his boots.

"Aren't we all?" The owl-killer cackled and broke into a small capering dance, the feathery pelts flapping at his waist in a manner that was somehow lewd. Caulk blinked, and the owl-killer was gone. Dismissing the matter, Caulk waited for his own appointment, which failed to materialise. In disgust, for it was now twilight and too late to return from Azenomei, Caulk purchased a bowl of leeks, then arranged a room in the inn above and stalked up the stairs to his new residence: a low room, black beamed, with panels of a russet wood. Caulk deemed it acceptable enough, though the bed was lumpy, and, on investigation, the mattress bore faint stains of a suspicious nature. Caulk wrapped himself in the coarse blanket and fell into an uneasy sleep, punctuated by leek-fuelled dreams.

He woke under attack. A harsh voice assaulted him; something brushed roughly across his face. Throwing the blanket aside, Caulk snatched one of his daggers from beneath the pillow and thrust it in the direction of his assailant. It struck something yielding: there was a startled squawk. An owl dropped dead to the floor, yellow beak gaping. Caulk hissed with annoyance; he was certain he'd left the window closed. On investigation, this proved still to be the case. The owl must have been crouching in the rafters.

Moments later, someone banged on the door.

"Be silent!" Caulk commanded. "Do you wish to wake the whole household?"

"I demand entry!" said a voice that was somehow familiar. "You have trespassed upon my province, I require redress."

Irritated, Caulk threw open the door, daggers at the ready, but was immediately rendered nerveless by a bolt of jade light. The daggers dropped from his hands and clattered to the floor. Caulk strove to speak but a muttered pervulsion caused the spell to choke in his throat. Caulk stared in outrage at the owl-killer, who ran into the room, gathered up the round, feathery corpse, and stashed it in a bag.

"Now," the owl-killer said, fixing Caulk with a beady glare. "*About* redress."

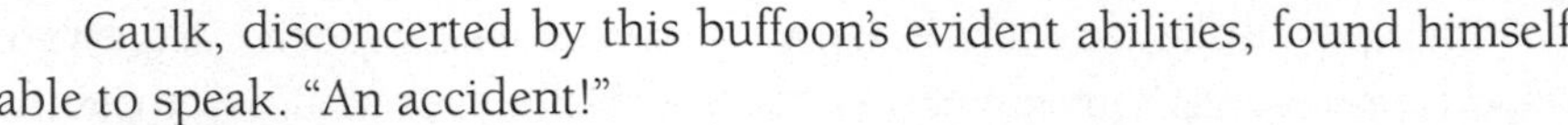

Caulk, disconcerted by this buffoon's evident abilities, found himself able to speak. "An accident!"

"Nevertheless."

"I intended no harm! The thing attacked me!"

"Doubtless you startled it."

"I was asleep!"

"The authorities in Azenomei take a dim view of folk who trample and stamp over the purlieus of others," the owl-killer mused. "I know of one such who, only last week, was hoisted onto a gibbet of pettish-wood and lambasted by the populace, before being transported to the midst of the Old Forest and obliged to find his own way home. He has not yet succeeded in this endeavour, that I am aware of."

"But—"

"It is doubly unfortunate that my brother, Pardua Mott, happens to be the head of the Azenomei Board of Fair Trading. A man of the most upright and correct rectitude, a respectability so pronounced that he had his own daughter exhibited in the Hall of Reproachable Conduct minus her undergarments, after her branding."

"I—"

"I am, however, a fair man," the owl-killer Mott went on judiciously. "I am prepared to concede a measure of inadvertency in your actions."

"That's very—"

"Rather than have you hauled in irons before my relative, which admits little other than a mild form of personal satisfaction, I shall demand an alternative form of reparation. You see," the owl-killer said, beadily, "I need a *particular* owl…"

AS HE passed the distant humps of the erg-barrows along the upper shore of the estuary, Caulk relived this unfortunate course of events and grew exceedingly sour. White Alster was known to be a dismal place, with little to recommend it, unless one happened to be a connoisseur of remote rocky spars, ruined fortresses, and black sucking bogs. Moreover, Mott had been unreassuringly vague as to the whereabouts of his quarry.

"Besides," Caulk had protested, still beneath the unnerving dictates of the pervulsion, "I am a witch-chaser, not an owl-finder. Surely that's *your* remit."

The owl-killer gave an avian blink. "Indeed, and I am, of course, aware of your profession. Your high boots, the enfoldments of your hat, the multiple hems of your coat, all speak of your calling. However, lamentable circumstances entail that should I set foot on the shores of White Alster, I will activate a locater spell and a vast shrieking will alert the hags to my presence. Besides, all that you are likely to encounter is largely within your own area of expertise. Sea-hags and tarn-wights *are* witches, after all, not to mention shape shifters."

Bitterly, Caulk conceded this to be true.

"I shall give you an aid—a strand of owl-witch hair. Watch it closely. It will twitch you in the required direction."

Steal a witch's hair and you stole a piece of her power. Even novices knew that. Caulk looked narrowly at the strand and asked, "And if I refuse?"

He did not care to recall what came next: the indignities of a further pervulsion and the contortions it entailed. Mott's merry laughter still stung his ears. Now here he was, sailing towards White Alster on a following wind and leaving Almery and its manses far behind. Caulk was aware of a pang, from more than the spell, that prodded him onward.

He sailed for several days, becoming increasingly bored by the dull expanse of choppy sea. Occasionally, bloat-fish rose up from the depths and regarded him with bland white eyes, whereupon Caulk was forced to summon a frothing conjuration and drive them off. Once, a great flapping bird moved ponderously from horizon to horizon, but otherwise there was little sign of life. It was with a relief mingled with apprehension that Caulk saw a broken shore rise up in the far reaches of the sea: White Alster.

It was not immediately obvious how to approach a suitable landing site, if any existed. What initially appeared to be a range of shattered turrets resolved itself into mere rock; a squat cylinder of stone that had seemed only an outcrop bore windows on its far side, but there was no sign of jetty or pier, and when Caulk looked back, the windows themselves were gone.

A bleak place, overlain with a sanguine glow in the last light of the dying sun. Caulk had seen worse, but also better. He thought with a shudder of the Land of Falling Wall, its ergs and leucomances. But White Alster, too, was said to have forests: who knew what lay within? Tempting to simply turn back towards Almery—but the pervulsion snagged at his neuronal pathways and Caulk grimaced.

At last, when he was beginning to fear that he would be obliged to sail fruitlessly along the coast forever, a flat plateau of rock became apparent, slimed with black weed and underlying a stump of castle. With renewed enthusiasm, Caulk drove the boat forward, sending out a spine of rope which clung relentlessly to the weed-decked stone. By degrees, Caulk hauled the boat inward until it was possible to make it secure by means of an ancient bronze ring and for him to step out onto the rock.

Once upon the shore of White Alster, Caulk became aware of a plangent sensation, comprised of subtle melancholy and longing. At once, the lowering sky above him, with its shades of grey and rose, and the foam lashed coast, appeared less forbidding, more appealing. He turned his face to the castle, to find that a face was watching him in return.

Caulk took an involuntary step back and narrowly missed tumbling off the dock. The face—little more than a pallid oval with black slits of eyes—had withdrawn into the shadows of the castle. A sea-hag? Caulk was too far away to tell. A bell-like note filled the air, and Caulk stumbled forward.

No. He must leave, at once. Memories of a wight burrow in Falling Water beset him, he had met this kind of thing before. Caulk muttered a spell and all was as before: the cold coast, the churning sea. Then the spell drained away like bathwater and Caulk was once more pulled forward.

As he reached the edge of the dock furthest from the sea, he realised that an eroded stair led upwards. The bell sounded again, sweet and plaintive amid the crash and spray of the waves. Caulk blinked, trying to remember why he'd come. Something about owls...But the bell once more rang out and Caulk staggered up the stair, protest ringing inside his head.

It was close to dark. A mauve twilight hung over the coast and the world was suddenly calm and hushed, the boom of the sea muted by the thick rock walls between which he now stood. The bell came again and it wasn't a bell, not quite, but contained faint notes amongst the main strike, a fading, ancient tune. Caulk smiled, now striding eagerly upward.

She sat in the middle of her chamber, wearing violet and grey. Black hair fell down her back, bound with silver. The white face was the same, and the long dark gaze. She sat before a complex thing, an ebony instrument that almost hid her from his view, comprised of many dangling pegs and latches which she struck with a small hammer.

Caulk hesitated at last, but it was too late. The song had already reached out and snared him in silver webs of sound. He snatched at a dagger but

his hand fell uselessly to his side. The sea-hag began to whistle, louder and louder, until the noise wove itself into the echoes of the instrument and Caulk dropped to the floor.

The sea-hag rose and poked him with a long toe.

"Well, well, well," she said. "A witch-chaser, eh? From Almery, by the fashion of your hat." She licked white lips. "I think a tea party is called for."

CAULK LAY enveloped in coils of writhing noise. It made it difficult to think. He was still cursing himself at having fallen for the sea-hag's lure.

The sea-hag herself stood a little distance away, in the company of her sisters. There were three of them, all cast from a similar mould, though one had hair the colour of willow leaves, and the eyes of another were a whiteless jade. They murmured and smiled and whispered behind their long hands whenever they looked in Caulk's direction. But mostly they were occupied with admiring his daggers.

The tea set sat on a nearby table, next to the curious instrument. Caulk could see lamplight through the thin china cups, which were embellished with roses. He strained at the bonds of sound, but they were as tight as ropes and his struggles only constrained him further. The sea-hags gave little glinting laughs.

"Not long now," one of them said. She bent and drew a fingernail down Caulk's cheek. He felt a trickle of wetness in its wake, followed by the familiar tang of iron.

"We want you to choose," another sea-hag said. "Which one of us is the fairest? Whoever you choose shall take the longest knife."

Death, to touch the daggers of a witch-chaser. They'd have to be cleansed, if he got out of here. Caulk took a long breath, storing it up.

"Shall we?" the willow-haired hag simpered. The sisters sat down at the table, arranging their tattered garments with fastidious care. The black-haired hag poured tea, which descended in a steaming dark stream into the cups. It did not look like tea, thought Caulk, squinting up from the floor. It didn't smell like it, either. He took another breath, judging the moment. The sound writhed around him, holding him fast.

"So," the black-haired hag said, taking a bite of a small mossy cake. "Which one of us, then?"

Caulk clamped his mouth shut and glared at her.

"Oh," green-hair whispered, "he doesn't want to play!"

"We'll *make* him play!" Black-hair rose, taking one of Caulk's daggers, thin as a pin, from its holster. Caulk sucked in another breath.

"Speak!"

Caulk did not speak. He thought he had it now. He pursed his lips and whistled, emitting a high-pitched stream of sound. He heard it mesh with the bonds that held him, throwing them outward. The sea-hags screamed, clapping their hands to their ears. Caulk took a frantic breath and whistled louder, feeling his face grow redder with the effort, but the bonds held, and held...He felt the break a second before it happened, sensing the shift in tone which signified that the sound-web was about to snap. Then it shattered. In an instant Caulk was on his feet, snatching at the dagger as thin as a pin with his left hand, and a dagger as white as bone with his right. Two sea-hags went down in a rush of greenish blood over the tea cups, struck through the throat. That left the willow-haired woman, whom Caulk killed with the black dagger, up under the ribs. She cursed him as she died, but Caulk laughed and whistled it away.

Gasping, he lent on the wall to get his breath back. The stone felt rough and wet beneath his hand. At the end of the chamber, a little arched window looked out onto darkness. Caulk peered through it and saw the glint of the heaving sea far below. Salt water is always a power: Caulk, with a remaining scrap of a spell, called up an arch of foam and cleansed the daggers. The bodies of the sea-hags were already rotting down into kelp and slime.

His head clearing somewhat, he remembered the instructions given to him by the owl-killer.

They frequent a tarn called Llantow, to the north, between two hills, not far from the coast. I cannot provide you with a map. You will have to watch the hair.

Not very helpful, Caulk had thought at the time, with the pervulsion twinging inside his head. He thought the same now, but perhaps the sea-hag's fortress contained a map? Gently, he tried the door and it swung open. Caulk stepped out, into a shadowy corridor. The sea wind blew through, a thin, eldritch whistling. Caulk looked right and left. The corridor appeared to be empty. For the next hour or so, he would have no magic to conjure up a light. He slipped down the passage, hearing the sea boom and crash through the holes in the ruin. Caulk ran through a maze of passages, seeing nothing except huge pale moths, floating about the ruin like ghosts. The eyes of the sea-hag? Possibly. But they did not seem to be paying any attention to him.

He sprinted down a staircase, hearing his own footsteps echoing like the tap-tap of a bone xylophone, scanning side rooms. But there was nothing and no-one. Outside, it seemed a cleaner, purer world. He had done someone a service, at least, in ridding White Alster of the hag-nest above him. Hopefully, he'd done it before the hags had had time to spawn, sending their jelly out into the stagnant pools and waiting for it to fruit. But he had no illusions: more hags would scent the deaths and move into the ruin. It might not take very long, so Caulk, temporarily magic-less, resolved to stay clear. He headed weakly out across the moor, away from the coast, and made an uneasy bed for the night under a bush. Over the moors, a cromlech was dimly visible: best avoided, to Caulk's mind, as the likely home of visps and leucomances.

The next day dawned with a pallid grey sky. Caulk looked out across a landscape of black moss, tarns like obsidian eyes, low hills. Against the grey morning, the vista was sombre. Caulk sighed and made a bleak meal of dried posset. Then he studied the strands of hair: they twitched in his hand, pointing north. He started walking, hopefully in the direction of Llantow tarn.

He had heard no owls overnight. He was not sure whether to be encouraged by this or not. If there were owl-witches, then perhaps they were keeping to their hunting grounds of Llantow. Or perhaps the owl-killer's information was out of date and there *were* no owl-witches. Caulk gave another sigh, this time of frustration. He did not think 'I couldn't find any' would be a satisfactory explanation, in which case an enforced holiday from Almery would prove necessary, assuming that the pervulsion allowed him that option. Caulk was reluctant to test its limits.

He kept walking, following the hair, which twitched and writhed like a worm. Towards late afternoon, a shimmering dark expanse that might, or might not, be Llantow tarn came into view, lying under a glowering range of hills. A rainbow glinted in its depths, swirls of rose and jade, and Caulk was immediately wary: he'd seen such things before, in Falling Water. Marsh-sprites and tarn-frits used them as a lure; Caulk looked pointedly away.

Around the tarn were clusters of small trees, with white bark and dark green foliage. A peppery scent filled the air—this must be what passed for spring in White Alster. Caulk's nose began to itch, not good news, for someone needing to remain surreptitious. He took a determined breath and headed, via a circuitous route, toward the tarn.

If any owl-witches were in residence, it would be in the crags on the hillside, rather than around the tarn itself; apart from the trees, there was no adequate shelter. Caulk crouched low behind a thicket of juniper, dined off posset, waited for twilight.

Nothing. Still nothing—and then, just as the pitiful sprinkle of remaining stars pricked out, there was the rustle of wings overhead, and an owl soared out across the rippling face of the tarn. Caulk, stiff and cold in the juniper, saw through amplifying glasses the tell-tale extra limbs tucked underneath the wing span: little atrophied arms and legs that, when the shifting magic occurred, would flesh out into human shape.

Elation and relief were rapidly followed by adrenalin. The actual existence of an owl-witch now necessitated planning and capture, rather than a sorry return to Almery with a tale of failure. On the other hand, the attempted capture of a witch might result in no return to Almery at all. Caulk watched, wrestling with professional misgivings, as the owl-witch swooped down on something at the far end of the tarn. A thin shrieking filled the twilight, followed by sounds of bones being crunched. Caulk gave careful attention to the skies, and, seeing nothing, backed up the hillside. The best time to catch a witch would be during daylight, but, at the moment, he was too close to the hunting ground. He crawled up towards a pile of boulders, then hid. More witches flew out from the crags. Caulk counted five, including the initial sighting. He was so intent on the witches that he failed to smell the leucomance until it was almost upon him. Caulk turned at the last instant, to glimpse a narrow head, glowing eyes, bared teeth. The leucomance crouched and twittered at a pitch that made Caulk's ears bleed. He threw a dagger, but the leucomance bounded up onto one of the boulders, where it sat grinning at him. Caulk cursed and the leucomance put a hand behind one pointed ear, grinning harder. Its genitals twitched, repulsing Caulk, who threw another dagger out of sheer irritation. The leucomance leaped high, there was the beat of wings in the darkness and the leucomance was gone with a sudden cry. All well and good, except that the commotion had attracted the attention of the remaining witches, who now came to perch on the boulder and watch Caulk with shining, intrigued eyes.

"Hold!" Caulk shouted, as the last witch came in to land and dropped the dead leucomance with a heavy thud. "I am Caulk the Witch-chaser!" He brandished two of the daggers, letting his coat fall open so that the others were clearly visible. "I have slain a nest of sea-hags on the coast of White Alster! I have hunted tarn-wights in the Tsombol Marsh, and weasel-witches in the polders of Taum!" He twitched the coat open further, displaying the scalps. "See these?"

"All too clearly," an owl-witch said. She quivered, the little limbs extending and fleshing out, her round head elongating, until a woman wearing nothing but a feather cloak stood in front of Caulk. Vestigial breasts and a hooked nose did little for him, and the witch's skin was a faint grey, reflecting the light from a patch of luminous moss. She smiled, displaying teeth as sharp as the leucomance's. She preened before Caulk, who forced a look of reluctant admiration to cross his features.

"All those dead sisters," the owl-witch said. Beside her, the others also metamorphosed. Two were clearly older than the others, but, like the sea-hags, they had a similar range of appearance. Another damned nest, Caulk thought, but kept the admiring expression in place.

"Do not try to make me feel guilt, madam," Caulk said. "No witch loves another."

"But we love witch-chasers *less*," the witch said, and smiled.

He could not take all of them down, and he knew it. "How do you feel about owl-killers?" Caulk asked.

A hissing, spitting moment of frenzy, during which Caulk stepped rapidly back and reached for longer knives. The first witch made a rattling noise in her throat and brought up a bony, bristling pellet, which she spat out at Caulk's feet.

"What talk is this?"

"I was hired—no, *compelled*—by one such to come here," Caulk told her. "An owl-killer of Almery, named Mott."

More hissing. Caulk again moved back.

"We know of Mott," one of the older witches said. Her small mouth curled in disdain. "A wicked man."

"No argument from me," Caulk said quickly.

"Mott cannot come to White Alster," the old witch said. She shrugged her shoulders and the cloak ruffled up. "He would die. He stole my hair."

"Aha!" said Caulk. He held out the strand and snatched it back as she clawed towards it. "Would this be it, by any chance?"

"My hair!" The witch's face was avid.

"You spoke of a compulsion," another witch murmured.

Caulk laughed. "What benefit is there for me, in killing owl-witches?" He hefted the strand of hair higher, keeping it out of reach. "Your pelts

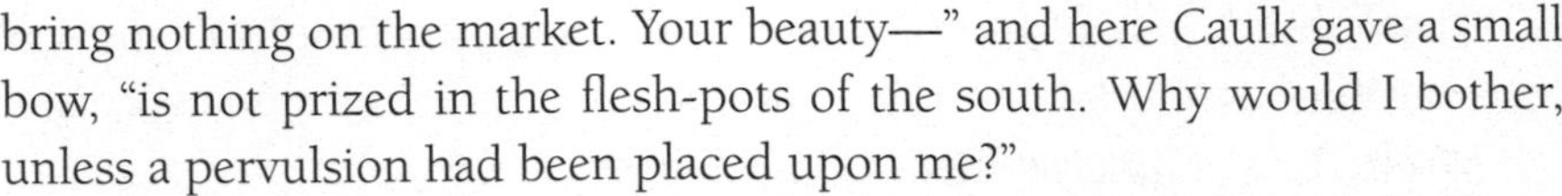

bring nothing on the market. Your beauty—" and here Caulk gave a small bow, "is not prized in the flesh-pots of the south. Why would I bother, unless a pervulsion had been placed upon me?"

"I would kill you," the eldest witch said, considering. "But I have a score to settle with Mott."

Caulk looked towards the moss, conjured a small bolt of heat. The moss sizzled and fried.

"No more sting than a nettle," a witch said, with scorn.

"Maybe not. But enough to fry a strand of hair," replied Caulk. There was a moment of silence.

"A witch-chaser is not the best person to enlist," the younger witch said.

The older one put her head on one side, regarded Caulk. "Not even for a price?"

"What kind of price?" Caulk said, very wary.

"Tell me," the old witch said, "how happy are you, with your life?"

Caulk thought. *Not very*, was the answer to that. He'd chased witches the length and breadth of old Earth, watched the stars start to go out, made enough to survive, little more. Plus there was the constant annoyance of folk like Mott. When younger, the work had afforded a degree of satisfaction, but of late, that had begun dangerously to pall…

The young witch rustled her cloak, revealing hints of skin that were starting to become more appealing.

"Then I have an idea…" the old witch began.

CAULK'S BOAT put back into Almenomei harbour on a rising tide. He stepped out onto the dock, seeing the ancient town with different eyes, evaluating turrets and gables and eaves. Absently, he rubbed the sore place on his wrist: the old witch had not been gentle, but then, that wasn't the way of owls, as Caulk now more fully appreciated. Yet, it was a small enough price to pay for the quietening of the pervulsion, which now lay still within his head.

He had been told to send word by courier to Mott, using a certain combination of digits and letters which, the owl-killer had assured him, would be comprehended by any reputable messaging company. Caulk located a courier at the inn, and then waited in the same upstairs chamber in which he had met Mott. It brought back memories, none of them pleasant. And yet, it had led to changes that were intriguing…

There was a knock on the door; Caulk opened it, to find an eager Mott outside.

"Well, did you find my owl-witch, Caulk?"

"I did."

"Where is it?"

"Within."

Mott took care to keep out of immediate dagger thrust, Caulk observed, but that hardly mattered. He fingered the bite on his wrist. The owl-killer glanced impatiently around the chamber. "It looks empty. I see no pelt, no hangings. Where is my owl-witch?"

"Here," Caulk said and felt the wrench as bone turned, skin turned, soul turned. He swept up on broad black wings to the height of the chamber, then down, as Mott's pale eyes widened for the last time.

Some while later, Caulk hoicked up a pellet and spat it onto what was left of Mott's body. Then he soared up and out of the chamber, over the roofs of Azenomei, heading first down the Xzan and then the Scaum towards the open sea. He'd told the girls that there would be a recently empty turret—much nicer than the boulders of Llantow, with plenty of room and a nice view. It would, he thought as he flew, prove eminently suitable for a new home.

AFTERWORD:

I WAS eleven years old. It was the mid 1970s and I lived in a small, bucolic city in the West of England. I longed to travel to the Gobi desert, to Siberia, to South America, but options for doing so were…limited. So I voyaged through books instead, and by the time I was eleven, I was already widely travelled—to Narnia, Prydain, Green Knowe, Prince Edward Island. Then one day my mother grew bored with the Gothic novels she'd been reading and brought back something different from the local library—a novel called *City of the Chasch*. I read it, very quickly. Then I read it again. After that, we went back to the library and returned, over time, with *Planet of Adventure* and the *Demon Princes* books, and with *The Dying Earth*.

Since then I have been to the Gobi, and to Siberia. I've never taken a spacecraft or a time-machine to Tschai, or the Dying Earth, but I know they're real places—I've been there, too, after all. And when I was eleven, I started writing the novel that would, years later, become *Ghost Sister*. I was nominated for the Philip K Dick Award, some years ago in Seattle, for that book. And, during the convention, I interviewed Jack Vance. I told him it was all his fault. 'Godammit,' he growled. 'You gotta be so careful with stuff like that.'

—Liz Williams

MIKE RESNICK

Inescapable

SOMETIMES YOU'RE better off if your heart's desire is out of reach…

Mike Resnick is one of the best-selling authors in science fiction, and one of the most prolific. His many novels include *Santiago*, *The Dark Lady*, *Stalking The Unicorn*, *Birthright: The Book of Man*, *Paradise*, *Ivory*, *Soothsayer*, *Oracle*, *Lucifer Jones*, *Purgatory*, *Inferno*, *A Miracle of Rare Design*, *The Widowmaker*, *The Soul Eater*, and *A Hunger in the Soul*. His award-winning short fiction has been gathered in the collections *Will the Last Person to Leave the Planet Please Turn Off the Sun?*, *An Alien Land*, *Kirinyaga*, *New Dreams for Old*, and *Hunting the Snark and Other Short Novels*. In the last decade or so, he has become almost as prolific as an anthologist, producing, as editor, *Inside the Funhouse: 17 SF stories about SF*, *Whatdunits*, *More Whatdunits*, and *Shaggy B.E.M Stories*, a long string of anthologies co-edited with Martin H. Greenberg—*Alternate Presidents*, *Alternate Kennedys*, *Alternate Warriors*, *Aladdin: Master of the Lamp*, *Dinosaur Fantastic*, *By Any Other Fame*, *Alternate Outlaws*, and *Sherlock Holmes in Orbit*, among others—as well as two anthologies co-edited with Gardner Dozois. He won the Hugo Award in 1989 for "Kirinyaga," the story that follows. He won another Hugo Award in 1991 for another story in the Kirinyaga series, "The Manumouki," plus the Hugo and Nebula in 1995 for his novella "Seven Views of Olduvai Gorge", the 1998 Hugo for "The 43 Antanean Dynasties", and the 2005 Hugo for "Travels With My Cats". His most recent books include the novel *The Return of Santiago*, and the anthologies *Stars: Original Stories Based on the Songs of Janis Ian* (edited with Janis Ian), and *New Voices in Science Fiction*. His most recent books are the collection *The Other Teddy Roosevelts*, the novels *Starship: Mercenary*, *Starship: Rebel*, and *Stalking the Vampire*, and a "Kirinyaga" related novella, *Kilimanjaro: a Fable of Utopia.* He lives with his wife, Carol, in Cincinnati, Ohio.

Inescapable

MIKE RESNICK

His name was Pelmundo, and he was the son of Riloh, Chief Curator of the Great Archive in the distant city of Zhule. Like all fathers, Riloh wanted a son who followed in his footsteps, but like many sons, Pelmundo was determined to make his own way in the world.

He had been a soldier, and then a mercenary, and finally he became a Watchman of the city of Maloth, which nestled alongside the River Scaum. He wore a shining silver medallion, his pride and joy, full five inches across, as a token of his office, and a plain sword that had tasted blood more than once rested in a well-worn scabbard at his side. His leather garments bore the mark of not only his station, but the horned bat that showed him to be favored by the city's true protector, Umbassario of the Glowing Eyes. It was Pelmundo's job to keep the streets safe from drunks and rowdies, and the homes safe from thieves. The greater dangers, the other-worldly and nether-worldly, were the province of Umbassario.

It was a symbiotic relationship, reflected Pelmundo; Umbassario protected the town against all other magicks, and in turn the town turned a blind eye toward his own.

But it was not Umbassario and his creatures that dominated Pelmundo's thoughts. No, it was a golden creature that played havoc with his mind and his dreams. Her name was Lith, perfect in form and movement, golden of skin and hair, a youthful witch, still in her teens, but already with a woman's body and a woman's power to enchant even without magic.

Pelmundo was totally captivated by the young golden witch. She had left her village and never spoke of her parents, dividing her time between her home in a hollow tree in the Old Forest, and, when she had business in the city, Laja's House of Golden Flowers, and of all the golden flowers who plied their ancient trade there, her blossoms were the sweetest.

Time and again, Pelmundo would approach her, awed and tongue-tied by her sensuous beauty, but determined to plead his cause. Time and again, she would laugh in amusement.

"You are but a Watchman," she would say. "What can you possibly offer in exchange for my love?"

He would speak of honor, and she would speak of trinkets. He would promise love, and she would snicker and point out that the poorest jewel lasted longer than the greatest love. He would beg just to be with her, and the golden witch would vanish, only the echo of her amused laughter lingering in the empty air.

Pelmundo sought out Umbassario, who lived in a snake-filled cave high in the rocky outcroppings beyond Maloth. It was lit by black candles, and the light flickered off a thousand bats that slept their days away hanging upside down between the stalagmites before being sent off on their unholy errands.

"I have come to—" he began.

"I know why you have come, Watchman," replied the mage. "Am I not Umbassario of the Glowing Eyes?"

"Will you help me, then?" asked Pelmundo. "Will you enchant her so that she can see only me?"

"And be blind to the rest of the world?" asked Umbassario with an amused smile. "That would almost be fitting."

"No, I don't mean that," protested the Watchman. "But I burn for her. Can you not instill the same fire within her?"

"It is there."

"But she teases and ignores me!"

"The fire is there, but it does not burn for *you*, son of Riloh," continued the mage. "It burns only for Lith. She is a physically perfect woman, so she seeks only physical perfection—in jewels, in clothes, in men."

"But you can change that!" urged Pelmindo. "You are the greatest of all the magicians who ply their trade up and down the River Scaum. You can *make* her love me!"

"I could," acknowledged Umbassario. "But I will not. There once was a woman, almost as young and almost as perfect as the golden witch of your heart's desire. I made her fall in love with me when I was younger and more foolish. Every night on the silken mat, she was the most responsive female that has ever lived, I truly believe that. But each time I would look into her eyes, even as her body jerked and spasmed in ecstasy, I would see the repugnance that my magic had banished to some secret inner part of her, and the taste of our erotic bliss turned to dust in my mouth. Finally, I removed the spell, and she was gone within an hour. Is that what you would want with Lith?"

"I truly do not know," answered Pelmundo. "If I just had the chance, I know I could make her love me."

The old mage sighed. "I don't believe you have heard a word I have said. The golden witch loves only herself."

"She will love me, with or without your spells," said Pelmundo with iron determination.

"Without, I should think," replied Umbassario as the Watchman left his cave.

Pelmundo walked back to Maloth in a foul mood that was apparent to one and all. People stayed out of his sight, and even the curs that scoured the street for scraps remained hidden until he passed by. Finally he entered the Place of the Seven Nectars, glared at the innkeeper and ordered the nonexistent Eighth Nectar, and, a moment later, was given a flagon filled to the brim. It tasted, he thought, exactly like the Seventh Nectar, but as it eased its way down his throat and warmed his insides, his temper began to improve and he decided not to protest.

He left the tavern and headed across the street to Laja's House of Golden Flowers, where he found Taj the Malingerer standing in the street, staring at the front door.

"Greetings," said Taj. "You can tell she is here today. She attracts men as honey attracts bees."

"Who do you mean?" asked Pelmundo, feigning ignorance.

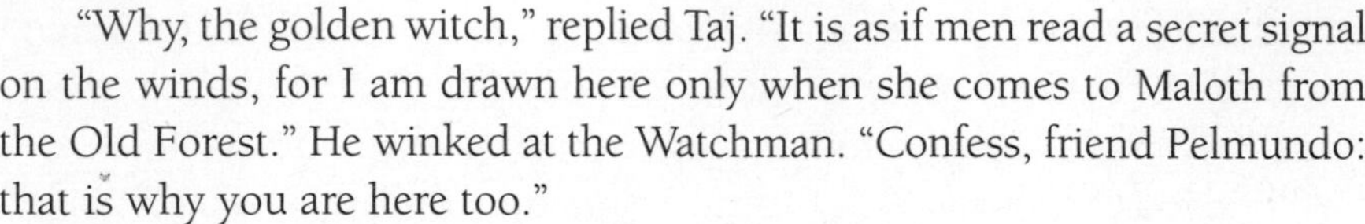

"Why, the golden witch," replied Taj. "It is as if men read a secret signal on the winds, for I am drawn here only when she comes to Maloth from the Old Forest." He winked at the Watchman. "Confess, friend Pelmundo: that is why you are here too."

The Watchman glared at him and said nothing.

"My only question," continued Taj, "is why she is here at all. Probably she is not yet skilled enough to pay her way as a witch." Another wink. "Or perhaps *this* is the kind of witchcraft and enchantment at which she excels, for I love and honor my wife except on days Lith has come to town, and I have never seen you so much as look at any other woman."

"You talk too much," said Pelmundo irritably, because he disliked hearing the uncomfortable truths that rolled so easily off Taj's tongue.

"I am almost through talking," answered Taj. "For when the next man is escorted out of the house by Leja, it is my turn to pay my respects—and my tribute—to Lith."

As the words left his mouth, Leja, old wrinkled crone who had once been almost as beautiful as the golden witch—some said two hundred years ago—led Metoxos the silk merchant to the door and bade him farewell. Suddenly, both men became aware that Lith herself was standing next to Leja—slender, with an animal grace, full ripe breasts, golden skin, hair that seemed to be made of spin gold, full red lips, and laughing eyes that seemed like sparkling embers.

"Prepare yourself, golden one," said Taj, "for you are about to meet a *real* man, not a used-up walking wrinkle like that pathetic Metoxos."

Leja reached out with her walking stick and cracked Taj across the shin.

He yelped in surprise. "What was *that* for?" he demanded.

"Be careful what you say about us walking wrinkles," she answered.

"Come," said Taj, taking Lith roughly by her bare arm. "Let us leave this crazy old woman behind and let me feast my eyes upon you in private."

"You eyes have become bloated by the feast," said Lith. "I do not like bloated eyes." She turned to Pelmundo. "You are the Watchman. This person is annoying me."

"He is a braggart and a boor, but he has every right to be here," said Pelmundo unhappily. "This is, after all, the House of Golden Flowers."

"Get rid of him and I will give you a kiss," said Lith.

"He is my friend," said Taj. "He laughs at your offer."

"Look at him," said Lith, obviously amused. "Is he laughing?"

Taj turned to face Pelmundo, who was clearly not laughing.

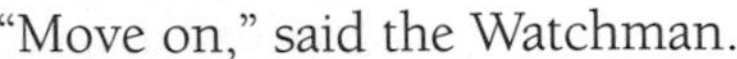

"Move on," said the Watchman.

"No!" shouted Taj. "I have the tribute. I have waited my turn!"

"You have waited in the wrong line for the wrong flower," said Pelmundo. "Move on."

He lay his hand on the hilt of his sword. Taj looked at the sword. It was not new, did not shine, bore no jewels, no mystic inscriptions; it was the workmanlike tool of a man who used it with bad intentions.

"We are no longer friends, son of Riloh!" snapped Taj, starting to walk away.

"We never were," replied Pelmundo.

He waited until Taj had gone one hundred paces, and then turned back to the doorway. Leja had returned to the dimly-lit interior of the structure, but Lith remained.

"And now your reward," she said softly.

He stepped forward. "You have never let me touch you before," he noted.

"And you shall not touch me now," she said. "*I* shall touch *you*."

"But—"

"Be quiet, step forward, and receive your reward," said Lith.

Muscles tensed with excitement, loins bursting with lust, Pelmundo stepped forward.

"And here is your prize," said Lith, kissing him chastely on the forehead.

He stepped back and shook his head as if he could not believe it. Lith smiled slyly.

"That is *it*?" he said, dumbfounded.

"That's all Taj was worth," she replied, her eyes bright with amusement. "For a greater reward, you must perform a greater deed."

"And for the greatest reward you have to offer?" he asked eagerly.

"Why, for that, you must perform the greatest deed," said the golden witch with a roguish smile.

"Name it, and it shall be done!"

"When I am not here, I live in a hollow tree in the Old Forest," began Lith.

"I know. I have looked for your tree, but I have never found it."

She smiled. "It is protected by my magic. I think perhaps even Umbassario of the Glowing Eyes could not find it."

"The deed!" he said passionately. "Get to the deed!"

"Whenever I come to Maloth, or return from here to my forest, I must pass through Modavna Moor," continued Lith.

Suddenly Pelmundo felt the muscles in his stomach tighten, for he knew what she would say next.

"Something lives on that moor, something evil and malignant, something that frightens and threatens me whenever I walk through it, a creature from some domain that is not of this world. It is known only as Graebe the Inevitable. Rid the earth of Graebe and the ultimate reward is yours, Watchman."

"Graebe the Inevitable," he repeated dully.

She struck a pose, with the moonlight highlighting her bare breasts and naked hips. "Is not the prize worth it?" she asked, smiling at his discomfiture. "Send him back to the hell he comes from, and I shall let you ascend to a heaven that only I can provide."

Pelmundo stared at her for a brief moment.

"He is as good as dead," he vowed.

Pelmundo knew that he could not face the creature without enchantments and protections, so he headed to the high outcroppings beyond Maloth and sought out Umbassario in his candle-lit cave.

"Greetings, Mage of the Glowing Eyes," he said when he was finally facing the old man.

"Greetings, son of Riloh."

"I have come—" began Pelmundo.

"I know why you have come," said Umbassario. "Am I not the greatest magician in the world?"

"Except for Iucounu," hissed a long green snake in a sibilant tongue.

Umbassario pointed a bony forefinger at the snake. A crackling bolt of lightning shot out of it and turned the snake to ashes.

"Does anyone else care to voice an opinion?" he asked mildly, staring at his various pets. The snakes slithered into darkened corners, and the bats closed their eyes tightly. "Then, with your kind indulgence, let me speak to this foolish young Watchman."

"Not foolish," Pelmundo corrected him. "Impassioned."

Umbassario sighed deeply. "Does no one listen to me even in the sanctity of my own cave?" His glowing eyes focused on Pelmundo. "Listen to me, son of Riloh. The golden witch has bewitched you, not with magic, but with what women have been bewitching men with since Time began."

"Whatever the reason, I must have her," said Pelmundo. "And I will need protections and spells against such a creature as Graebe the Inevitable."

"Graebe is *mine*!" shouted the magician. "You will not touch him!"

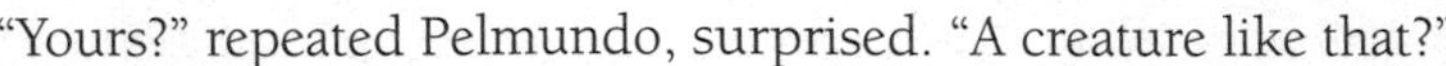

"Yours?" repeated Pelmundo, surprised. "A creature like that?"

"You protect the city against thieves and ruffians. I protect it against greater evil, and Graebe is the weapon I use."

"But he sucks out men's souls with those great prehensile lips and feasts upon them!"

"He sucks out diseased souls that no one else would have," said Umbassario.

"He dismembers his victims while they still live."

"*You* seek a reward, do you not?" said the magician. "The dismemberment is *his*."

"He threatens the golden witch."

Umbassario smiled. "Then why is she still alive? After all, he is Graebe the Inevitable."

Pelmundo frowned. It was not a question he was prepared for.

"Then I shall tell you," continued Umbassario. "If you were to enter the hollow tree in which she lives, you would find a golden loom, upon which your witch is weaving a tapestry of the Magic Valley of Ariventa." He paused. "The tapestry is hers, but the loom is Graebe's, made from the bones of a golden creature he killed in the netherworld. Your witch does not want you to perform a heroic deed to prove yourself worthy of her. She wants you to eliminate a creature that only seeks what belongs to him. And if she was as helpless as you seem to believe, he would long since have obtained it."

"If he is Graebe the Inevitable, why has he not?" asked Pelmundo.

"Because he is drawn to souls like a moth to flame, and she has none."

"You must not say such things about her," admonished Pelmundo.

"Is your love of life so fleeting that you dare say such things to me in my own cave?" demanded Umbassario. "Did you not just see what happened to my favorite snake?"

"I meant no offense," said Pelmundo quickly. Then his spirit stiffened. "But I will have the golden witch, and if that means I must slay your creature, then I will do so."

"Despite what I have told you?" said the magician.

"I must," replied Pelmundo. "She is everything I have ever wished for, everything I have ever dreamed of."

"Be careful what you wish for," said Umbassario with a secret smile, "and of what invades your dreams."

"I am sorry it has come to this," said Pelmundo. "I do not wish us to be enemies."

"We shall never be enemies, son of Riloh," the magician assured him. "We shall just not be friends." A final smile. "Do what you must do, if you can—and remember, you have been warned."

"Warned?" said Pelmundo, frowning. "But you have told me nothing about Graebe the Inevitable."

"I was not talking about Graebe," replied Umbassario.

Pelmundo turned and left the cave, and began climbing down over the rocky outcroppings. When he was finally on level ground, he considered going to a lesser mage, but he knew that if Graebe was truly Umbassario's creature, only a magician of equal power could supply him with the charms and spells he needed.

"Then I shall have to defeat you as I have defeated all other foes," muttered Pelmundo, staring off toward Modavna Moor, which separated Maloth from the Old Forest. "Be on your guard, monster, for Pelmundo, son of Riloh, is on your trail."

And so saying, he began his march around the village and into the foreboding darkness of Modavna Moor. The mud seemed to grab his foot with each step, and to hold it tight, as if to say, "Foolish man, did you think to run from Graebe the Inevitable?"

Suddenly he saw a Twk-man mounted on a dragonfly. The dragonfly circled his head twice, then perched lightly on a leaf.

"You are far from your stomping grounds, Watchman," said the Twk-man. "Are you lost?"

"No," answered Pelmundo.

"Then beware lest you be found," said the Twk-man, "for Graebe the Inevitable is abroad this day."

"You have seen him?" said Pelmundo. "Is he near?"

"If he were near, I would be elsewhere," said the Twk-man. "Endlessly he searches, both for his loom and the witch who took it."

"Then you have nothing to fear," said Pelmundo.

"I have a life and a soul, and I wish to keep them both," said the Twk-man. "You would do well to preserve yours while you still can."

"But you tell me he wants Lith."

"He *searches* for her," corrected the Twk-man. "But he sucks the souls of whatever crosses his path."

"Fly ahead, Twk-man," said Pelmundo, "and tell him that his fate is approaching him inexorably."

"Approach Graebe the Inevitable?" gasped the Twk-man, clearly shocked.

"Then fly away—but know that after today there will be no more cause for fear or alarm."

The Twk-man tapped his dragonfly, and circled Pelmundo twice more. "I have never seen such suicidal madness before," he announced. "I must burn it in my memory, for surely no one will ever go searching for Graebe again."

"Not after I slay him, they won't," promised Pelmundo.

"It is very odd," said the Twk-man. "You do not look like a man who wishes to race into the gaping maw of his death."

"Or his destiny," said Pelmundo, visions of Lith's undulating golden body dancing in his mind.

"She must have promised you much, Watchman," said the Twk-man.

"She?" repeated Pelmundo.

"Did you really think that you were the first?" said the Twk-man with a laugh. Then he was gone, and Pelmundo was alone once more.

"Father," said Pelmundo softly, "I pledge the coming battle to you, for after I have slain the Umbassario's nightmare creature my triumph shall be written up in song and story, and the day will come when as Chief Curator you file it in a place of honor in the Great Archive of Zhule." Then, looking forward, he said in a steady voice: "Creature, beware, for your doom is approaching you!"

Deeper and deeper into the moor he went, the mud grabbing at his feet, his sweat cascading down his body. "Here I am, creature," he said again and again. "You have but to show yourself." But there was no sign of Graebe the Inevitable.

Pelmundo trod through the moor for an hour, then another, with no sign of any other living thing.

"The Twk-man was wrong," he said aloud. "There is no monster abroad today. I must find the wherewithal to pay a mage for a spell to draw him to me, for without him there can be no ultimate reward from the golden witch."

He plodded ahead, and finally reached the edge of the moor. The trees were less closely clustered now, and narrow rays of sunlight finally penetrated through the dense foliage. Birds chirped, crickets sang, even the frogs seemed at peace with their surroundings.

And then, suddenly, there was silence—an almost tangible silence. Pelmundo lay his hand on the hilt of his sword and peered ahead, but could see nothing—no shape, no movement, nothing at all.

He looked to the right and the left. Not a thing. His hand moved to his medallion, which he touched for luck and moved slightly to cover his heart."Fear not, beasts of the moor," he said at last. "My quarry has fled."

"But your inevitable doom has found you," growled an inhuman voice from behind him.

Pelmundo whirled around and found himself face to face with a creature out of his worst nightmares. The bullet-shaped head boasted coal-black eyes slit like a cat's at high noon, nostrils that were uniquely shaped for sniffing out souls, gross misshapen lips whose only function was to suck the souls from its prey. It was shaggy, covered with coarse black hair. Its hands had but a single function: to grab souls and hold them up to its mouth. Its feet served but one purpose: to carry it to its prey, on dry land, on mud, even on water.

"I am Graebe the Inevitable," it growled, stepping forward as Pelmundo retreated step by step, the mud feeling like more of Graebe's hands, grasping at his ankles, holding tight to his feet.

"No," said Pelmundo. "You are my tribute to Lith, the golden witch."

"She has taken what does not belong to her," said Graebe. "Now she tempts you with what does not belong to you."

"I have nothing against you, monster," said Pelmundo, "but you stand between my and my heart's desire, and I must slay you."

"Your heart has nothing to do with the desire you feel," said Graebe contemptuously. Suddenly, the creature smiled. "This is a most fortuitous meeting. I have not dined all day."

Pelmundo tried to step back as Graebe the Inevitable approached him, but his feet were mired in the mud, and he knew he would not be able to fight on a firm terrain of his own choosing. He withdrew his sword, grasping the hilt with both hands, holding it upright before him, prepared to slash in any direction—

—and at that instant a shaft of sunlight struck the Watchman's medallion.

Graebe stared at the shining medallian, the smile frozen on his misshapen, soul-sucking lips. Suddenly he emitted a howl of anguish that echoed through the moor, and held his hands up to shield his eyes from the vision he saw.

Finally, he lowered his hands and stared once more at his image in the medallion.

"Can that be *me*?" he whispered in shock.

Pelmundo, puzzled, held the sword motionless.

"I was a man once," continued Graebe, still barely whispering. "I made a bargain, but not to become...*this!* It is more than I can bear."

"Have you never seen your reflection before?" asked Pelmundo.

"A very long time ago. When I was...as you." Graebe stared hypnotically at his face in the medallion. "The rest of me," he said, "is it the same?"

"Worse," said Pelmundo.

"Then do what you must do," said Graebe, lowering his hideous hands to his side. "I cannot go on. Do your worst, and claim your golden reward, little joy may it bring you."

The creature lowered its head and closed its eyes, and Pelmundo raised his sword high and brought it down swiftly. A moment later, the head of Graebe the Inevitable rolled on the ground, but when Pelmundo looked at it, it was the head of a man, not handsome, not especially ugly, but a man, not a creature of darkness and horror.

Pelmundo squatted down next to the severed head, frowning. He felt no regret about having killed the thing that had become Graebe the Inevitable. He felt no guilt about the fact that in death it had metamorphosed into a man. But he felt outrage that he could not prove to Lith that he had indeed slain the creature of the moor and should be given that most coveted reward.

"It is Umbassario's doing," he growled, and he made the decision to confront the mage, and either get him to change the human head back into the hideous Graebe, or at least testify to Lith that he had performed the task she set for him.

But when he stood up he felt somehow strange, not as if he had drunk too much at the Place of the Seven Nectars, but as if the world had somehow changed in indefinable ways. The colors seemed different, darker; the birds and insects louder; the mud weaker, as if it had finally decided to relinquish its hold on him; and he could sense the unseen presence of three Twk-men, two mounted on dragonflies, a third sitting on a branch high above the ground.

He began the trek to Umbassario's cave, finding himself strangely unwinded as he climbed over the rocky outcroppings that led up to it. He reached up, gaining purchase on a rock, and his hand seemed to be a claw.

"A trick of the light," he growled, blinking his eyes rapidly. But the hand did not change.

"Come in," said Umbassario's voice from within the cave, and he entered.

"I have come—" he began.

"I know why you think you have come," said Umbassario of the Glowing Eyes. "But you have come because I called to you."

"I heard nothing," he said.

"Not with your ears," agreed Umbassario. "You have killed my pet, my servant, he who did my bidding, and I demand reparation."

"I have no money. You know that."

"I said reparation, not tribute," said the mage. "And you shall supply it. I warned you not to harm my creature, and you ignored me. I must have a servant. It shall be you."

"I cannot," he said. "I have my duties as the Watchman—and I have a reward to claim."

"You shall never claim it," said Umbassario. "The golden witch will shrink from your touch as she shrinks from no other. As for you, no-longer-Watchman, your servitude to me has already begun, and will last until the sun finally burns itself out. Study your hands well—and your feet. Place your fingers to your face, a face that would have frightened even Graebe. You are mine now."

He felt his face. The contours were strange, inhuman. He screamed, but it came out as an inhuman howl.

"And because the golden witch is the reason you disobeyed my orders and killed my creature, she shall serve you as you must serve me. You will never touch her, but you will use her. Her beauty, her sensuality, will attract an endless stream of admirers. Men will come from as far away as Erze Damath and Cil and Sfere to gaze upon her, and I will allow you this one freedom, this one happiness: in your rage and jealousy, I will allow you to kill these men that she attracts. You will thread their unseeing dead eyes upon a cloak, and when the cloak is full, when it cannot accommodate one more eyeball, then perhaps we shall talk about restoring you." A crooked smile. "But I suspect by then you will not want to return the weak, puny thing of flesh and blood that you once were."

He tried to speak, but words felt strange in his mouth.

"I intuit that your name tastes of guilt and shame upon your tongue," said Umbassario. "You shall need a new sobriquet."

"I am…I am…" He tried to pronounce "Pelmundo," and the word died on his tongue.

"I am…" He fought to force the words out. "I am…the…son of…" He stopped again.

"Once more," said the mage.

"I am..." His tongue felt thick and alien. "I am chun of..."

"So be it," replied Umbassario, who knew his creature's name all along. "You are Chun."

"Chun," he repeated.

"You are Chun the Unavoidable. You have one day to put your affairs in order. Then you will do my bidding. Now begone!"

And Chun found himself standing in the darkened street between the Place of the Seven Nectars and Leja's House of Golden Flowers.

At first, he was disoriented. Then he saw a figure lurching drunkenly down the street, and he knew that his cloak would soon begin.

An instant later, Taj the Malingerer felt a presence beside him in the night.

"I am Chun the Unavoidable," said a deep, inhuman voice. "And you have something I need."

AFTERWORD:

ONE OF the very first science fiction books I bought as a kid was Jack Vance's *The Dying Earth*, in its original paperback edition published by Hillman. (It cost me a quarter; it goes well over $100.00 on eBay these days.) I became an immediate fan, picking up *Big Planet* and all the other Vance titles—but then, as now, I had a special love for his tales of the last days of a dying Earth in a worn-out solar system. (So did a lot of other writers—not just the ones in this tribute volume, but dozens of writers over the years have emulated his style and borrowed some of his concepts, not as plagiarists, but as a loving tribute to his skills and his enormous influence throughout the field.)

When Carol and I decided, back in the 1970s, to enter a few Worldcon masquerades, the very first costume we chose to make was Chun the Unavoidable and his shill, Lith the Golden Witch. We won at Torcon, the 1973 Worldcon in Toronto...and now, thirty-six years later, it's a pleasure to go back and offer my literary thanks to Chun and Lith, two of Jack's more unforgettable characters.

—Mike Resnick

WALTER JON WILLIAMS

Abrizonde

WALTER JON Williams was born in Minnesota and now lives near Albuquerque, New Mexico. His short fiction has appeared frequently in *Asimov's Science Fiction*, as well as in *The Magazine of Fantasy and Science Fiction*, *Wheel of Fortune*, *Global Dispatches*, *Alternate Outlaws*, and in other markets, and has been gathered in the collections *Facets* and *Frankensteins and Other Foreign Devils*. His novels include *Ambassador of Progress*, *Knight Moves*, *Hardwired*, *The Crown Jewels*, *Voice Of The Whirlwind. House Of Shards*, *Days of Atonement*, *Aristoi*, *Metropolitan*, *City on Fire*, a huge disaster thriller, *The Rift*, a *Star Wars* novel, *Destiny's Way*, and the three novels in his acclaimed Modern Space Opera epic, "Dread Empire's Fall," *Dread Empire's Fall: The Praxis*, *Dread Empire's Fall: The Sundering* and *Dread Empire's Fall: Conventions of War*. His most recent books are *Implied Spaces* and *This Is Not a Game*. He won a long-overdue Nebula Award in 2001 for his story "Daddy's World," and took another Nebula in 2005 with his story "The Green Leopard Plague." He also scripted the online game "Spore."

In the fast-moving and suspenseful story that follows, we journey with a student architect headed through the mountainous Cleft of Abrizonde to the school in distant Occul, who inadvertently gets caught up in a war between the Protostrator of Abrizonde and the rulers of Pex and Calabrande, and who finds that opportunity can come along at the most unexpected of times—and that you'd better seize it when it does!

Abrizonde

WALTER JON WILLIAMS

The student architect Vespanus of Roë, eager to travel to the city of Occul in the country of Calabrande, left Escani early in the season for an ascent of the Dimwer, the deep river that passes through the Cleft of Abrizonde on its way to the watery meads of Pex, the land where Vespanus, waiting for the pass to open, had passed a dreary winter in the insipid flat callow-fields of the brownlands.

The local bargemen claimed an early ascent was too hazardous for their craft, so Vespanus traveled upriver on a mule, a placid cream-colored animal named Twest. The Dimwer roared in a frigid torrent on the left as Twest made her serene ascent. There was still snow in the shadows of the rocks, but the trail itself was passable enough. The river bore on its peat-colored waters large cakes of ice that, Vespanus was forced to admit, would in fact have posed something of a danger to barge traffic.

Though nights were frigid, Vespanus employed his architectural talents and his madling Hegadil, who each night built him a warm, snug little home, with a stable attached for the mule, and who disassembled both the next morning. Vespanus thus spent the nights in relative comfort, reclining on purfled sheets, smoking Flume, and perusing a grimoire when he was not experiencing the pleasing fantasies brought on by the narcotic smoke.

On the third day of his ascent, Vespanus perceived the turrets and battlements of a castle on the horizon, and knew himself to be in the domain of the Protostrator of Abrizonde. Against this lord he had been warned by the bargemen—"a robber, boorish and rapacious, and yet strangely fashionable, who extorts unconscionable tolls from any wayfarer traveling through the Cleft." Vespanus had inquired if there were routes available that did not involve traversing lands menaced by the Protostrator, but these would have involved weeks of extra travel, and so Vespanus resigned himself to a severe reduction in his available funds.

In any case,the Protostrator proved a pleasant surprise. A balding man whose round face protruded from a tissue-like lacy collar of extravagant design, and whose personal name was Ambius, the Protostrator offered several nights of pleasant hospitality, and never asked for a single coin in payment. All that he desired was news of Pex, and gossip concerning the voivodes of Escani, of whose affairs he seemed to know a great deal. He also wished to know of the latest fashions, hear the latest songs, receive word of new plays or theatrical extravaganzas, and hear recitations of the latest poetry. Vespanus did his best to oblige his host: he sang in his light tenor while accompanying himself on the osmiande; he discussed the illicit loves of the voivodes with a completely spurious authority; and he described the sumptuous wardrobe of the Despoina of Chose, who he had glimpsed in procession to Escani's Guild of Diabolists, to which she was obliged by ancient custom to resort every nine hundred and ninety-nine days.

"Alas," said Ambius, "I am a cultured man. Were I a mere robber and brute, I would rejoice on my perch above the Dimwer, and gloat as the contents of my strongrooms grew and glittered. But here in the Cleft, I find myself longing for the finer things of civilization—for silks, and songs, and cities. And never a city have I seen for the last thirteen years, since I assumed my present position—for if I traveled either to Pex or to Calabrande, I would instantly lose my head for violation of the state's unjust and unreasonable monopoly on taxation. So I must content myself with such elements of culture as I am able to import." He gestured modestly toward the paintings on the wall, to the curtains of mank fur, and to his own opulent, if rather eccentric, clothing. "Thus I am doomed to remain here, and to exact tolls from travelers in the manner as the Protostratoi before me, and dream of distant cities."

Vespanus, who was not entirely in sympathy with the Protostrator's dilemma, murmured a few words of consolation.

Ambius brightened.

"Still," he said, "I am known for my hospitality. Any poet, or performer, or troupe of players will find me a kind host. For these are immune to my tolls, provided that they bring civilization with them, and are willing to provide entertainment. And gentlemen such as yourself," with a nod toward Vespanus, "are of course always welcome."

Vespanus thanked his host, but mentioned that he would be leaving for Calabrande in the morning. Ambius returned a sly look.

"I think not," he said. "There will be a storm."

The storm came as predicted, dropping snow in the courtyard and sending storms of hailstones that rattled on the roof-plates, and Vespanus spent another two nights, not unpleasantly, beneath the Protostrator's roof. On the third day, thanking again his host, he mounted Twest and began once again his ascent of the Cleft.

He traveled but half a day when, examining the track ahead, he saw through a notch in a looming ridge the red glint of sunlight on metal. Indeed, he saw, there was a good deal of glinting ahead—on snaffle irons, on erb spears, on the crystalline tips of fire-darts, and on banners bearing the device of the Exarch of the Calabrande Marches.

Vespanus turned Twest about and raced as quickly as the irregular terrain permitted to the Protostrator's castle. Once there, he informed the surprised Ambius that the Exarch was advancing down the Cleft with a large armed force.

Ambius bit his upper lip. "I don't suppose," he said, "that you would care to remain and ennoble my defense?"

"Greatly though it would enhance my name to die in defense of the Protostrator of Abrizonde," Vespanus said, "I fear I would prove useless in a siege. Alas, just another mouth to feed."

"In that case," Ambius said, "would you bear a message to my agent in Pex instructing him to recruit a force of mercenaries? I confess that I have few warriors here at present."

"So I had observed," said Vespanus, "though it seemed graceless to remark on it."

"It is my custom to recruit the garrison up to strength in the spring," said Ambius, "and dismiss most of them in late autumn. Aside from the expense of maintaining troops over the winter, there is always the danger that the soldiers, confined to their barracks and subject to the tedium and monotony of the season, would seek to remedy their ennui by means of a mutiny, in which I would be killed and one of their captains made the new lord. Therefore I keep about me in the winter only those soldiers whose absence of ambition has been proven by years of prosaic and lackluster service."

"I congratulate you on this sensible policy," said Vespanus, "ill-timed though it is in the present circumstances."

Again, Ambius chewed his upper lip. "It was hard experience that drove me to this custom," he said, "for thirteen years ago it was I, an ambitious captain, who killed the previous Protostrator on the eve of the New Year, and hurled his body from the Onyx Tower into the Dimwer."

"No doubt it was a change for the better," Vespanus said tactfully. "But if you are to give me a letter, by all means do so at once—for I have no desire to be caught by the army of the Exarch."

Ambius provided the letter, and, once again, Vespanus set out on Twest, nor did he employ his madling to build his shelter until full darkness had fallen and the dim stars of the Leucomorph had risen in the East. In the morning, fearful of aerial spies, he glanced about carefully from the structure's windows before leaving the shelter and readying Twest for the day's ride. He had traveled only a hundred yards before he saw, emerging from the Dimwer's mists two or more leagues below, the coils of an army looping back and forth on the trail. Amid the glint of weapons, he saw the blue and callow-yellow banners of Pex.

Cursing his ill luck and worse timing, Vespanus goaded his mule uphill again, and managed to reach Abrizonde Castle just as the scouts of Calabrande advanced into sight from the other direction. He was granted admittance to the castle, and observed at once that the fortress had been put on a war footing. Boom-rocks were laid by to be hurled on the heads of attackers. Arrow guns and fire sticks were seen on the walls, manned by soldiers who seemed competent, if uninspired and inclining toward the middle-aged. Spikes on the roof- and tower-tops, newly anointed with poisons, were prepared to impale flying attackers. Servants, splendidly equipped from the castle's spacious magazines, were receiving hasty instruction in the use of their weapons.

Vespanus joined Ambius at his observation point in the Onyx Tower, and found the Protostrator in elaborate full armor of a deep azure color, the helmet topped by the rearing, fanged likeness of a lank-lizard. Vespanus reported the advance of the second army, and watched Ambius stalk about the room in thought.

"I suppose that Pex and Calabrande may be at war," he said, "and, each attempting to invade the other by means of the Cleft, they meet here by sheer chance."

"Do you think that's likely?" Vespanus asked hopefully.

"No," said Ambius, "I don't." He gave Vespanus a searching look. "I believe you are acquainted with the thaumaturgical arts?" he asked.

"I know some of the lesser magics," Vespanus said, "and indeed was en route to Occul in order to further my studies when the army of Calabrande barred my way."

"Know you any spells or cantrips that might be of use in our present circumstance?"

"I equipped myself with spells suitable for besting the occasional highwayman or Deodand, but I had not anticipated fighting whole armies. And in any case, I have already told you, as I enjoyed your kind hospitality, that my chief specialty is architecture."

Ambius frowned. "Architecture," he repeated, his voice dour.

"I create buildings of a fantastic nature—following the wishes of my client, I first generate a phantasm, a perfect visualization of the completed building. After which I employ one of the minor sandestins, of the type called 'madlings,' who builds the structure in a matter of hours, flying in the materials from anywhere in the chronosphere wherein they may be found. It remains but for the client to furnish the place, and even this I can arrange for a suitable fee."

Ambius narrowed his eyes. "Can your madling also demolish structures—siege works, for example?"

"Any sandestin could. But I fear that, if I used my Hegadil against anything as formidable as a well-equipped army, any competent wizard would banish or kill the creature before it could accomplish its task."

Ambius nodded. "My study contains a small library of grimoires, left behind by the many Protostrators who lived, and died, here before me. The spells and cantrips are of a nature that would be of use to a military man, though I confess that their contents largely elude me. I am not particularly gifted in matters of magic, and depend strongly on countercharms, amulets, and other defensive incunabula."

"Perhaps I had best view these grimoires," Vespanus said.

"You anticipate my wish precisely," said Ambius.

Ambius took Vespanus to his private quarters, which involved the de-activation of a number of traps—only now was Vespanus beginning to understand the true scope of his host's paranoia—after which Vespanus was taken to a small, snug room carpeted with the skin of an ursial loper, and lined with bookshelves.

Vespanus looked with interest at the narrow windowsill, in which he found a crystal bottle in which a dark-haired miniature woman gestured urgently.

"You have a minikin?" he asked. "Does she do tricks?"

"My wife," said Ambius, with a casualness too obviously feigned. "Hoping to supplant me, she attempted to shrink me six years ago, but I managed to nudge her into the trap before she could maneuver me into it. As long as the bottle exists, she will remain her current size, and also her considerable sorcerous powers will be completely suppressed."

"Help me!" cried the little woman in a tiny voice.

"The grimoires," said Ambius, pointing, "wait on yonder shelf."

Vespanus affected not to notice the trio of Nymphic Icons standing on the shelf in front of the row of grimoires—bronze statues of fetching ladies, they were capable of being transformed into full-sized, lively, and sweet-natured women, and explained a great deal about how Ambius had solaced himself in the absence, or rather the reduction, of his spouse. Vespanus studied the grimoires, most of which purported to be the work of the great Phandaal, but were almost certainly by lesser hands. He glanced briefly at the contents of several, and chose three.

"If I may…?" he asked.

"Indeed," said Ambius.

They made their way out of the Protostrator's private quarters, Ambius re-setting the traps behind him, and began their walk across the courtyard toward the Onyx Tower. It was at this moment that a brilliant yellow blaze began to flare above the castle, as radiant as the Sun in its vigorous youth. Vespanus raised a hand against the glare and mentally reviewed his small store of spells in hopes of finding something that might apply in the current situation.

The soldiers of the castle immediately swung their weapons around and opened fire, flaming darts whirring through the radiance overhead, arcing high, and landing well beyond the castle walls.

"Cease fire, you imbeciles!" roared Ambius. "Cease fire! This is a phantasm, not an enemy you can shoot through the heart!"

Vespanus looked at his host in surprise. Despite his elaborate wardrobe and affectations of culture, Ambius had shouted out his orders like a born

commander. Vespanus was reminded that Ambius had, before his present elevation, been a professional military man.

In response to the shouted orders, the soldiers on the battlements gradually checked their enthusiasm for violence. The radiant blaze diminished in intensity, enough to reveal the figures of two men floating in what looked like a brilliant crystal sphere. The vigorous white-haired man, by the fact that his robe contained the blue-and-yellow of Pex quartered with the red-and-white of its ruling family, Vespanus judged to be that country's Basileopater. He did in fact bear some resemblance to his image on coins. The other, more angular man, by the devices on his cloak, Vespanus assumed to be the Exarch.

The two gazed down at Ambius with expressions of superiority mingled with contempt.

"Ambius the Usurper," said the Exarch, "you are proclaimed outlaw. If you do not surrender your fortress, your person, and your unnecessarily trigger-happy garrison, you will face the wrath of our united armies."

"I see no reason why I should give you these things," said Ambius, "when I might offer you instead the pleasure of trying to take them."

The Basileopater of Pex smiled. "I rather thought that would be your attitude."

Ambius sketched a bow. "I endeavor to provide satisfaction to my guests," he said. He bowed again. "Perhaps you worthies would honor me by joining me for dinner tonight, here in the castle. I flatter myself that I set a good table."

"Out of sensible caution," said the Basileopater, "I fear we must decline. You gained your present position through treachery to a superior, and we cannot suppose that a usurper's morals will have improved in the time since."

Ambius shrugged. "You were so fond of my precursor that you waited a mere thirteen years to avenge him?"

The Exarch inclined his shaved head. "We assumed you would last no longer than your predecessors," he said. "Though we deplore the efficiency with which you collect tolls that rightfully belong to us, we nevertheless congratulate you on your tenacity."

"Your mention of tolls brings up an interesting question," said Ambius. "Assuming that you manage to capture my stronghold, which of you will then occupy it? To whom will the tolls belong, and which of you will have to march home empty-handed? Which of you, in short, will succeed me?"

Ambius, Vespanus knew, had put his finger on the critical point. Whoever controlled the castle would be able to rake wealth out of the Cleft, while whoever did not would have to suffer the loss. Though it was possible that the two commanders had agreed to a joint occupation and a sharing of the wealth, Vespanus couldn't imagine that two such ambitious rulers would keep such an agreement for very long.

As Ambius asked his question, the Basileopater and the Exarch exchanged glances, then looked down at the Protostrator, their faces again displaying those annoyingly superior smiles.

"Neither of us will occupy the fortress," the Exarch said.

"You will appoint some third party?" Ambius asked. "How would you guarantee his loyalty?"

"There will be no third party," the Exarch said. "Once the castle is ours, we will demolish it to the last stone. Each of us shall retire to our toll stations on our respective ends of the Cleft, which shall then be patrolled in order to make certain that Castle Abrizonde is not rebuilt by any new interloper."

Ambius made no reply to this, but Vespanus could tell by the way he chewed his upper lip that this answer was both unexpected and vexing in the extreme. He could well believe that Ambius understood that he, his fortress, and his fortunes were doomed.

That being the case, Vespanus took the opportunity to secure his own safety.

"My lords!" he called. "May I address you?"

The two rulers looked at him without expression, and made no reply.

"I am Vespanus of Roë, a student of architecture," Vespanus said. "I was on my way to Occul to further my studies when I passed a night here, and now by chance I find myself under siege. As I have nothing to do with this war one way or another, I wonder if it might be possible to pass the lines and go about my affairs, leaving the quarrel to those whose business it remains."

The co-belligerents seemed sublimely uninterested in the problems of such as Vespanus.

"You may pass the lines," the Exarch said, "if you agree to furnish us with complete intelligence of the castle and its defense."

Vespenus tasted bitter despair. "I can hardly promise such a betrayal of hospitality," he said, "not in public! The Protostrator would then have every reason to detain me, or indeed to cause me injury."

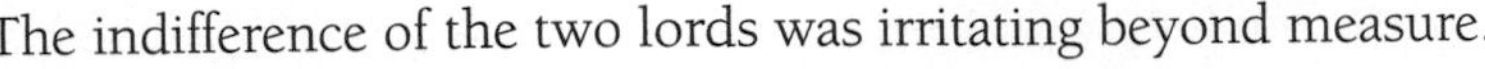

The indifference of the two lords was irritating beyond measure.

"That is hardly our problem," said the Basileopater.

Fury raged through Vespanus. He was tempted to spit at the two rulers, and only refrained because he could scarcely imagine his spittle rising so high.

They had *discounted* him! In the brief moment in which he had held their interest, they had both derogated him as worthy of no consideration whatever—no threat to their power, no help to the Protostrator, nothing worthy of their attention. Never in his life had he been so insulted.

The two floating lords returned their attention to Ambius.

"You have not taken advantage of our offer of surrender," said the Basileopater. "We shall therefore commence the entertainment at once."

At that instant, an ice-blue bolt descended from the sky, aimed directly at Ambius. Without indication of surprise, Ambius raised an arm to display an ideograph graven on an ornate bracelet, and the bolt was deflected into the ground near Vespanus. Vespanus was thrown fifteen feet and landed in an indignified manner, but otherwise suffered no injury. He jumped to his feet, brushed muck from his robes, and directed a look of fury at the two placid lords.

"I note only for the record," said Ambius, "that it was you who accused me of treachery, but were the first to employ it. I also remark that the employment of an aerial assassin, equipped with Aetherial Boots and a Spell of Azure Curtailment, is scarcely unanticipated."

The Exarch scowled. "Farewell," he said. "I trust we shall have no more occasion to speak."

"I agree that further negotiations would be redundant," said Ambius.

The illusory sphere brightened again, more brilliant than the old Earth's dull red sun, and then vanished completely. Ambius searched the sky for a moment, perhaps in anticipation of another flying assassin, then shrugged and walked toward the Onyx Tower. Vespanus scrambled after, anxious to retrieve his lost dignity…

"I hope you are not offended," he said, "that I attempted to remove myself from the scene of conflict."

Ambius gave him a cursory glance.

"In our decayed and dying world," he said, "no one can be expected to act with any motive other than self-interest."

"You analyze my motives correctly," said Vespanus. "My interest is in remaining alive—and in repaying those two dolts for their dismissal

of me. Therefore I shall throw myself immediately into the defense of the fortress."

"I await your contribution with breathless anticipation," Ambius said, and the two ascended the tower.

No further attacks took place that day. Through the tower's windows, which had the power of adjustment, so that they could view a subject from close range or far away, Ambius and Vespanus watched the two armies as they deployed into their camps. No enemy soldier approached within range of the castle, and, in fact, most seemed to remain out of sight, behind the crests and pinnacles of nearby ridges. Vespanus spent the afternoon trying to cram useful spells into his brain, but found that most were far beyond his art.

As the great bloated sun drifted toward its union with the western horizon, and as the first stars of the Leucomorph began to glimmer faintly in the somber east, Vespanus opened the compartment on his bezeled thumb-ring and summoned his madling, Hegadil.

Hegadil appeared as a dwarfish version of Ambius, clad in the same extravagant blue armor, with a round, vapid face gazing out from beneath the crested helm. Vespanus apologized at once.

"Hegadil has a tendency toward inappropriate satire," he concluded.

"In fact," Ambius said, "I had no idea the armor looked to well on me." He looked at the creature with a critical aspect. "Do you send him to fight the enemy?"

"Hegadil is not a warlike creature," Vespanus said. "His specialties are construction, and, of course, its obverse, demolition."

"But if the army is guarded by sorcery…?"

"Hegadil willl not attack the army itself," said Vespanus, "but rather its immediate environment."

"I shall look forward to a demonstration," Ambius said.

Vespanus first sent Hegadil on a whirlwind tour of the enemy camps, and within an hour the madling—reappearing as a caricature of the Basileopater of Pex, a tiny white-haired man dwarfed by his voluminous robes with their blazons and quarterings—gave a complete report as to the enemy's numbers and deployment. Both armies proved to be larger than Ambius had suspected, and it was with a doomed, distracted air that he suggested Hegadil's next errand.

Thus it was that, shortly after midnight, a peak overhanging part of the Exarch's army, having been completely undermined, gave way and buried several companies beneath a landslide. The army leapt to arms and let fly in all directions, a truly spectacular exhibition of firepower that put to shame the morning's demonstration by the castle defenders.

At the alarm, the army of Pex likewise stood to its arms, though in silence until, a few hours later, a bank of the river gave way and precipitated a part of the baggage train into the ice-laden river, along with all the memrils that had drawn the supplies up the trail. Then the camp of Pex, too, fell into disorder, as soldiers tried to get themselves and their remaining supplies as far from the river as possible. Scores got lost in the dark and fell into hidden ditches and canyons, and some into the river itself.

Pleased with the results, Vespanus complimented Hegadil and promised him three months off his indenture.

In the morning, the besiegers attempted revenge, the armies' spellcasters hurling one deadly spell after another at the castle. The air was filled with hoops of fire, with viridian rays, with scarlet needles, and with the thunder of prismatic wings. All was without effect.

"Countercharms are woven into the very fabric of this place," Ambius said with great satisfaction, and then—thinking doubtless of Hegadil and others like him—added, "and into the rock on which it stands."

Hegadil's next nightly excursion was less profitable. The enemy were encamped with more care, and magical alarms placed in vulnerable areas that would alert enemy sorcerers to Hegadil's arrival. The madling managed to brain a few sentries with rocks spirited from out of time and dropped from above, but on the whole, the evening's venture had to be scored a failure. It was with a dispirited tread that Vespanus took himself to his quarters for a rest.

He awoke mid-afternoon, broke his fast, and joined Ambius in the Onyx Tower. There he found the Protostrator talking to a green twk-man, even smaller than the miniaturized wife in Ambius' quarters, who had flown to the castle on a dragonfly.

"My friend brings news that an army from Pex has come to attack the castle," Ambius reported.

"The news seems somewhat delayed."

"It came as soon as the dragonfly permitted," Ambius said. "Insects do not fare well at altitude, and in a chilly spring."

"I should like to have salt now," said the twk-man, in a firm voice.

Ambius provided the necessary nourishment.

"In summer," he said, "there are never less than a dozen twk-men here at any one time. I see to their needs, and they provide perfect intelligence of the movements of armies and traffic on the Dimwer."

And, Vespanus thought, gossip about the voivodes of Escani and the Despoina of Chose.

"Our enemies seem to have anticipated this," Vespanus said.

"True. They came ahead of the dragonflies and their news."

"And behind *me*," Vespanus muttered in anger.

Vespanus peered out of the tower's windows and saw that the enemy deployments had not changed.

"They're waiting for something," Ambius said. "I wish I knew what it was."

Vespanus stroked his unshaven chin. "The two lords are proud. Can we cause discord between them, do you think?"

"In this," said Ambius, "lies our greatest hope."

"Allow me to stimulate their rivalry."

At sunset, he summoned Hegadil from his resting-place in the architect's thumb-ring. The madling was instructed to level the top of a small hill to the east of the castle, beyond the range of any of its weapons, and equidistant between the two armies. A small fortress was there constructed. And, when the red sun made its sluggish climb above the horizon, it illuminated not only the battlements and miniature towers of the fortress, but the long banner that curled in the wind like a snake's forked tongue, the banner that read, "*For the Bravest*."

From the tower, Vespanus perceived a stir among the besieging soldiers, pointing arms and waggling lips. Officers were summoned. These summoned bannermen. The bannermen summoned generals. And eventually the Exarch and the Basileopater of Pex were observed on their individual knolls, studying the fortress by means of far-seeing devices.

After that, a patrol was seen heading toward the fortress from the army of Calabrande. Perceiving this, the army of Pex sent its own patrol. The patrols surrounded the fortress and sent scouts inside. These returned to their units with the news that the fortress contained only a single long couch, suitable for a single person to take his rest.

Both patrols returned to their respective armies. Then, for several hours, nothing happened. The officers retired to their luncheon. The sentries returned to their drowsy patrols. The dull red sun crawled across the dark sky like a blood-bloated spider.

Vespanus cursed his useless scheme, and went to bed.

Just before nightfall, another patrol came from each army, soldiers accompanied by enchanters, and they set up a camp on the flat country in the shadow of the fortress. One designated champion of each army, armed to the teeth, walked into the fortress, where they presumably spent the night, like shy virgins, perched on either end of the couch.

Certainly, they expected to be attacked. And just as certainly, they were not—the castle's defenders lacked even that much power. In the morning, the champions strutted out to polite applause from their followers, and then made their way to their respective armies.

"We have made a beginning," Vespanus said.

"Not now," said Ambius.

He was in his morning conference with the twk-men. Four more had arrived, a small squadron, and he gave them instructions to carry messages and to observe the enemy.

"My friends tell me that five barges are coming down the Dimwer from Calabrande," Ambius said. "Each contains a large object, but these items are shrouded by canvas."

"I mislike this attempt at concealment," said Vespanus.

"I also," said Ambius. "I also recall, with a certain foreboding, our speculation that the enemy forces were waiting for something, and now wonder if this might be the arrival that will precipitate their grand assault. I will sent one of the twk-men to view these barges in greater detail."

The twk-man scout had not returned by the afternoon. Ambius chewed his upper lip.

"Perhaps," he said, "Hegadil might be of use."

Hegadil was sent to view the barges, and returned some moments later. He reported that each barge contained a cradle that held a bottle-shaped object some eight paces in length, each made of dark metal chased with elaborate silver Flower-and-Thorn designs. Some of these he traced on the tower walls with a finger.

"Projectors of the Halcyon Detonation!" Ambius exclaimed. "Our cause is lost!"

Vespanus attempted to stifle his alarm. "How so?" he said. "Did you not say that the fortress was proof against any form of magic?"

"Magic, yes!" Ambius said. "But the Projectors do not employ magic, but rather an ancient form of mechanics no more magical than a fire-arrow. The Halcyon Detonation can blast our walls to bits!"

Vespanus turned to Hegadil. "How long before the barges arrive at the enemy camp?"

The madling—he had appeared today in the form of Austeri-Pranz, one of Vespanus' instructors at Roë, an intimidating man with bulging, rolling eyes and a formidable overbite—gave the question his consideration.

"Two more days, perhaps," he judged.

"Two more days!" Ambius echoed. "And then the end!"

"Don't despair," Vespanus said, though with the sense that he was speaking more to himself than to his companion. "I shall send Hegadil to sink the barges!"

"They will be prepared for such an attempt," Ambius said.

"Nevertheless…" Vespanus turned to Hegadil.

"May I complete my report?" Hegadil said.

"Yes. There is more?"

"Each of the barges contains between seven and ten bargemen. There are also a dozen soldiers on each craft, one officer, and an enchanter. Pinned to the prow of the first barge, with a silver needle, is the corpse of a twk-man."

"When you sink the barges," Vespanus said, "you must avoid being run through with a needle, or indeed with anything else."

The madling rolled Austeri-Pranz's eyes at him.

"How do you wish me to proceed?" he asked.

"Rip the bottoms out of the craft. Undermine the rivernbank and sent it crashing into them. Drop large stones from above. Whatever best suits your talents and imagination."

"Very well," the madling said dubiously, and vanished, only to return moments later.

"The barges have magical protections," he said. "I was unable to sink them, or to drop anything upon them. They travel in the middle of the river, and are not vulnerable to collapsing banks."

"Build a mound in the center of the river, beneath the waters," Vespanus said. "Make its height such that the barges can just clear it. Then take some of the spikes from the castle roofs, and plant them in the mound." He looked at Ambius in triumph. "We will tear out the bottoms of the barges."

Ambius waved a hand. "Let the attempt be made."

Hegadil was sent forth again, only to have the barges detour neatly around the obstacle. The attempt was made again, with like result.

Ambius looked bleakly out of the window.

"Continue your plan to sow distrust among our enemies," he said. "It is all we can hope for."

"I wonder," Vespanus said, "if the promise of liberty would motivate your wife into fighting in defense of Castle Abrizonde?"

Ambius considered this for a moment, then shook his head.

"Not yet," he said.

That night, Hegadil demolished the fortress in which the enemy champions had waited, and built instead a golden-domed structure ornamented at the corners by allegorical figures representing Knowledge, Truth, Sapience, and Insight. The banner overhead said, "*For the Wisest*."

Again scouts trooped out, again parties left the armies at sunset. Two magicians, magnificently bearded respectively in copper and midnight-black, approached the structure with their guards, and entered.

In the morning, they marched out again, their beards unruffled, their expressions a little puzzled.

"What next?" asked Ambius. "*For the Cleanest? For the Most Fashionable?*"

"You shall see," said Vespanus.

During the day, a wide-ranging, ingenious assortment of ruses were employed to effect the destruction of the barges, but with no success. The barges and their deadly cargo were expected within the day. Hegadil reported that the enemy magicians on the barges now bore identical superior smirks on their faces.

That night, the madling demolished the mansion of the magicians and built instead a palace faced with veined marble, crowned with lacy towers, and with a great flag proclaiming *For the Greatest Ruler*. Ambius paced the tower room in unsettled silence, chewing his upper lip. Vespanus did his best to sleep.

Shortly before nightfall, the Exarch and the Basileopater, each commanding a battalion of elite troops, crossed to the palace and took their places in what they must have known was a trap. Vespanus rejoiced that their vanity did not permit them to behave otherwise.

Once again, Vespanus had no intention of attacking those in the palace directly. He, and Castle Abrizonde, entirely lacked the means.

Instead, he instructed Hegadil to seal the palace from the outside, and then to plate the palace with enormous sheets of adamantine metal. If Vespanus could not actually kill the inhabitants, he would do his best to seal them inside, after which he would fill the interior with a poisonous vapor.

After he sent Hegadil on his errand, Vespanus paced back and forth on the battlements as he awaited the outcome of his scheme. The field was silent, the night cold. In his mind, Vespanus pictured vast sheets of armor being lowered silently into place, all along the distant palace.

Then there was a sudden flare of light that limned the marble towers of the palace, followed by a rush and a clap of thunder. More flashes followed, red, yellow, and blazing orange, and the air was filled with shrieks, war cries, and the beating of invisible wings.

Vespanus cursed his luck, his ancestors, and every human being for fifty leagues round. Before he was quite finished, Hegadil appeared by his side—once again in the form of Austeri-Pranz, a sight alarming enough without the addition, in this case, of charred, smoking clothing and a singed beard.

"Alas," Hegadil croaked, "they were prepared. I barely escaped annihilation."

Disgusted by the turn of events, Vespanus opened his thumb-ring and let Hegadil take his healing rest there. He then took himself to bed.

In the morning, he awoke to the sounds of acclamation, as the two enemy lords left the palace to the cheers of their armies. Vespanus bent his mind entirely to the subject of escape. In the confusion of the final assault, he thought, he might be able to swim the river, possibly with Hegadil's assistance, and then take refuge in a shelter created by the madling while the enemy armies went about their business…

It was a wretched, dangerous plan, but it was the only one that occurred to him.

He rose, broke his fast, and went to the Onyx Tower. A pair of twk-men orbited the Protostrator's head in gay silence, as out-of-place as a cheerful red cap on the statue of a Deodand. Ambius, his round face by now set in an expression of permanent dolor, gestured toward the armies of Calabrande. Looking from the window, Vespanus saw that a ridge-top, out of range of any of the castle's weapons, had been perfectly leveled.

"A platform for the Projectors of Halcyon Detonation," Ambius said. "The twk-men inform me that the barges will arrive at the enemy camp later this morning. Afterwards, it will take the army most or all of the day to drag the weapons from the landing-stage to their position. We may expect the grand assault at dawn tomorrow."

"It would take a sandestin, or a madling like Hegadil, to level that ridge overnight," Vespanus said.

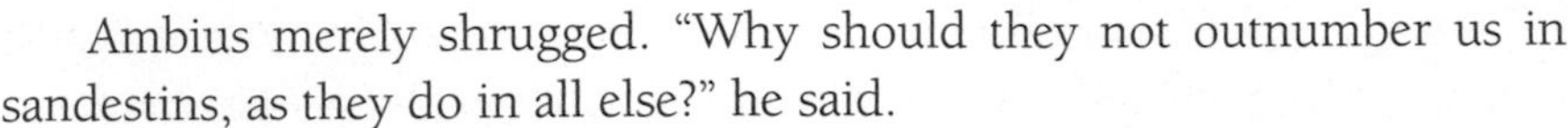

Ambius merely shrugged. "Why should they not outnumber us in sandestins, as they do in all else?" he said.

"Perhaps we should find out."

Vespanus opened his thumb-ring and summoned Hegadil. The creature appeared in the form of a dead twk-man, green skin turned gray, a needle thrust like a spear through his abdomen.

"Abandon this distasteful form," Vespanus said, "go to the ridge yonder, and discover if you can undermine it and drop the Projectors into a pit of your own creation."

Hegadil was gone for three or four minutes, and then returned, this time as a dwarfed Exarch, the lord's habitual superior smile now turned to a deranged leer.

"A sandestin named Quaad guards the platform," he reported. "He is far stronger than I, and informed me that he would tear me to bits if I attempted any digging."

Vespanus opended the thumb-ring.

"You may return to your rest."

When Hegadil was bottled up, Vespanus went to the windows and manipulated their adjustable properties to give himself a closer view of the ridge.

"Those are engineers on the site," he said. "They employ instruments familiar to me from their uses in architecture and surveying—tripods and alidades, chains and rods, altazimuths and dividing engines. Are they proposing to build something there?"

"The opposite," said Ambius. "They intend destruction. They measure precisely the distance and angle to the castle, so that the Projectors may be better aimed so as to blast us to ruin."

Vespanus paused for a moment to absorb the melancholy implications of this revelation. Suddenly, diving into the Dimwer did not seem so dreadful a plan. Ambius, who now seemed very diminished in his grand array, slowly rose to his feet.

"I fear it is time to visit my wife," he said.

Curious, Vespanus followed Ambius to his quarters. Ambius either did not mind his presence, or was unaware of it. The Protostrator disarmed the various traps on his door, then led Vespanus again into his study.

This time he found himself with a better view of the Protostrate—she was a buxom woman, with wiry hair, and, even at her current size, a piercing voice. From the Protostrator's attempts to communicate with her, Vespanus gathered her name was Amay.

Amay began abusing Ambius as soon as he entered the room and continued throughout the interview. The gist of her comments—leaving aside the personal references to Ambius, his person, and his habits—was that she would delight in the destruction of the castle, and would not prevent it if she could.

Perceiving that his arguments were futile, Ambius shrugged and walked to a shelf, where he found a vial filled with an amber liquid. Loosening the stopper, he poured a single drop into the neck of the crystal bottle, whereupon Amay staggered, spat, and collapsed into unconsciousness.

"Sometimes it is necessary to think in silence," he said, as he returned the vial to its shelf, "and this narcotic will guarantee my peace for some hours."

"Very effective," Vespanus observed.

Ambius contemplated the supine figure of his wife. "I fear that six years in a glass bowl has given her an unshakable prejudice against me," he said.

"That would appear to be the case," Vespanus said. "Would it help if I conducted a private conversation with her?"

Ambius gave him a doleful look. "Do you think it would help?" he asked.

Vespanus shrugged his most hopeless shrug. "Truth to tell, I believe it would not."

Vespanus went to the buttery and helped himself to bread, cheese, and liquor. He wondered if he might, that evening, hurl himself from the Onyx Tower into the Dimwer and survive, perhaps with the help of Hegadil, and then be carried to freedom by the current.

Unlikely, he thought. The defenders of the castle would only be the first to shoot at him.

He considered those Calabrandene engineers with their alidades and dividing engines, and the smug smiles that had been reported on the faces of the Exarch's magicians. He considered how the Basileopater and the Exarch had dismissed him as insignificant, and how all his schemes for the defense of the castle had come to nothing.

"Even their sandestins are stronger than mine," he muttered, which led his thoughts to consideration of the nature of the sandestins, their ability to travel freely in the chronosphere, to visit Earth in any eon from its fiery birth to its long icy sleep beneath the dim stars and dead sun. Then he considered how this ability to travel in time had affected their psychology, had made the sandestins and their lesser cousins, the madlings, extraordinarily accepting of whatever environment in which they found themselves. So different, so wildly diverse, were the scenes which a sandestin could view during the course of its existence, that Vespanus supposed they had no choice but to accept the world with a literalness that, in a human, would prove a serious handicap…

As he considered this, along with thoughts of the engineers and the smug smiles of the enchanters, his mind alighted upon an idea that had him sitting up with a start. He spat out his mouthful of cheese, then liberated Hegadil from his thumb-ring.

"I desire you to visit again the sandestin beneath the platform," he said, "and inquire if it has been instructed to prevent you from adding to, rather than subtracting from, the structure."

"I will ask," Hegadil said.

He was back a moment later.

"Quaad has not been so instructed," Hegadil said.

"Into the ring, now!" Vespanus said. "For I must visit the Protostrator."

From the Onyx Tower, Ambius was watching the enemy platform, where the first of the Projectors, still in its cradle, was being dragged into position.

"I have an idea," he said.

At Vespanus' instruction, Hegadil slowly added to the substance of the platform, raising the side facing the castle until the platform sloped, very slightly, with the muzzles of the Projectors raised somewhat above their intended angle. The sandestin Quaad observed these actions and—as Hegadil was not undermining anything—did not act.

When the sickly sun began its daily crawl above the eastern horizon, Vespanus and Ambius saw that both armies had been fully deployed, ready to storm the castle once it had been sufficiently reduced. The Exarch's banner floated above the platform, amid his great Projectors. On the other side of the castle, the Basileopater of Pex stood before a snow-white pavilion, his elite guard ranked before him.

"Any moment now," Ambius said, and before the last word had passed his lips, the Projectors fired, and the Halcyon Detonation soared over the castle's towers to explode amid their allies of Pex. The Basileopater's pavilion vanished in a great sheet of flame and dust. Salvo followed salvo, one enormous thunderclap detonation after another. The Basileopater's army dissolved beneath a brilliant series of flame-flowers.

Nor did the Exarch or his forces observe this, for Vespanus, utilizing the magics that had served him as an architect, had built an illusory castle wall in front of the genuine wall, one identical to the original. As the Projectors fired round after round, Vespanus created illusory explosions against the wall, along with encouraging floods of debris. To the Exarch, it would look as if he was slowly but surely blasting Castle Abrizonde into the dust.

Vespanus delighted in this glorious demonstration of his art. Let them disregard him *again*, he thought, and he would serve them likewise!

It was nearly half an hour before word at last reached the Exarch that his plan had miscarried. The Projectors ceased their fire. The Exarch was seen storming about on the platform, lambasting his magicians and thrashing his engineers with his wand of office.

From the army of Pex, nothing was heard except the sounds of cries and wailing.

Thus it stood for the balance of the day. At midafternoon, a twk-man flew to Ambius.

"I bring a message from the Logothete Terrinoor, who now commands the army of Pex," said the new arrival. "The Logothete and the army of Pex burn with a desire to avenge the death of their lord at the hands of the treacherous Calabrandene,"

"I am interested in any proposal the Logothete may offer," said Ambius.

"The Logothete proposes to attack the Exarch in the middle of the night," said the twk-man, "but in order to accomplish this, he will have to pass the army beneath the walls of the castle. May he have your permission?"

Ambius could not conceal his expression of grim triumph. "He may," he said. "But if there is treachery, we will defend ourselves."

The twk-man, refreshed with a gift of salt, carried this message back to the Logothete. Thus it was that, in the dead of night, Ambius and Vespanus watched the army of Pex move in silence past the castle and march in silence toward the army of Calabrande. The Calabrandene had scouts and sentries on the perimeter of their camp, so they were not caught entirely unawares, but the soldiers of Pex were filled with fury at the death of their lord, and their charge carried far into the enemy works. The night was filled with the ferocious sound of snaffle-irons and swords, and brilliant with the flashes of deadly spells.

"Look!" said Ambius. "They carry away the Projectors!"

The attackers had detailed soldiers and beasts of burden to drag the Projectors from their platform to their own camp. These great objects were carried off with great labor as the army of Pex was driven slowly

back from the enemy works, and as the great weapons passed the castle, a Calabrandene counterattack drove the army of Pex back, and suddenly there was fighting in front of the very gates of Castle Abrizonde.

"Shoot!" Ambius cried to his soldiers. He drew his sword. "Drive them all away! If we can mount the Projectors on the walls of the castles, we will be invulnerable!"

The soldiers of the Protostrator fired from the castle walls into the mass of warriors below, boom-rocks and poisoned arrows raining down at the two armies locked in their own desperate combat. The invaders reeled in confusion.

"To me, soldiers!" Ambius cried. He drew his sword. "We must sally!"

Again, Vespanus was surprised at the martial vigor of Ambius. His orders were prompt, vigorous, and effective—and they were obeyed. The gates of the castle were flung open, and the Protostrator led out the greater part of his garrison. This attack, being unexpected, drove away the forces of both Pex and Calabrande, and left the Projectors abandoned on the field. Ambius did his best to organize his forces to drag at least one of the Projectors into the fortress, but both Calabrande and Pex constantly counterattacked, and the fighting waxed and waned beneath the walls. Vespanus, lacking any skills that would be of use, watched from the battlements, and heard at last a cry of dismay from the defenders of Abrizonde.

Back through the gate came the garrison, much reduced, bearing the body of Ambius, the Protostrator, who had been severely wounded. Now Vespanus, in the absence of any other authority, began to call out orders. Soldiers on the walls poured down a fire that kept the plain clear.

Gradually the fighting died away. The morning revealed the five Projectors abandoned beneath the walls of the castle, some toppled from their cradles, the others with their muzzles pointed in random directions. It was clear that the castle's defenders could prevent either army from claiming these prizes.

As the morning wore on, Vespanus from the Onyx Tower observed the two armies, now at enmity, begin their mutual, miserable retreat to their homelands.

At noon, one of the soldiers reported to him.

"The Protostrator is dead," he said.

"On the contrary," said Vespanus. "The Protostrator is alive, for I am he."

The soldier—one of those, Vespanus recalled, chosen for his lack of ambition and general subservience—merely bowed, and then withdrew.

Vespanus gazed over the battlements for a moment, considering his next action, and then descended to the courtyard on his way to the quarters of the Protostrator. Word of his elevation had preceded him, and Vespanus was gratified that the soldiers he passed saluted him as their commander. Once at Ambius's door, Vespanus tried to disengage the traps that Ambius had left behind—and managed to dodge a bolt of orange fire at only the last second. Having finally got the door open at the cost of a singed sleeve, he advanced to the Protostrator's study and approached the Protostrate in her crystal bottle. He took a chair to a place near the shelf and sat. For a moment, he and Amay contemplated each other through the gleaming crystal. At length, he began to speak.

"You will rejoice with me, I'm sure, in the defeat of the enemy and the safety of the castle," he said, "as you will mourn with me the death of your husband."

She bowed her head, then raised her chin and said, "While hysterical laughter and bitter tears are both reasonable options in the current situation, I believe I shall decline both."

"As you think best," Vespanus said gravely.

"I wonder if I may beg of you a favor," said Amay. "Could you take one of those bronze nymphs from the shelf yonder and give this bowl a sharp rap?"

"To what end?"

"Is it not obvious? I desire to be liberated."

"I find that possibility problematical." Carefully he regarded her. "Were you at liberty, you would attempt to install yourself as the ruler of Abrizonde, and as I have just declared myself the new Protostrator, we would find ourselves in immediate conflict."

Amay received this news with surprise. Her miniature face contorted as she considered her response.

"On the contrary," she said. "I would be your help, support, and guide. You will need my aid to find your feet as the new lord of the Cleft."

"I propose to err on the side of caution," Vespanus said, and as Amay took in a breath to begin reviling him in the same terms with which she had abused her husband, Vespanus held up a hand.

"The late lord Ambius spoke to me of his isolation here, of the absence of polite society and the arts. One might conclude he regretted his decision to make himself the lord."

"Don't you believe it," Amay said. "His ambition was great."

"And my ambition is not," said Vespanus. "While I desire material comfort, I have no inclination to hold an isolated fortress in an empty country for all the years of my youth, nor to battle the armies of entire nations."

"In that case," said Amay, "you should liberate me to become the new ruler, and trust me to reward you amply for your service."

"I have a somewhat different plan," Vespanus said. "I shall remain the lord but for a single season, and skim the profits of the bargemen and merchants of the Dimwer. After which, I shall become a mere student once more, and carry myself and my gains away on a hired barge. Once I have gone a safe distance, you will be liberated by one of the soldiers acting on my orders, and immediately take your place as the greatest lady in the history of Abrizonde."

Amay, blinking, contemplated this for a moment.

"I believe that is fair," she judged, "much though I mislike remaining in this bottle for any length of time whatever."

Vespanus bowed at her politely. "What is unfair," he said, "is that I must pay the soldiers, and hire the summer force, without the means to do so. Therefore I must have access to the late lord's strong rooms—and as in the course of our acquaintance I noted the Protostrator's suspicious mind, and his cunning facility with traps that has just cost me the sleeve of my robe, I assume that the strong rooms are protected. I apply to you, therefore, for any knowledge you may have concerning these traps, and how to disarm them."

Amay's eyes narrowed in suspicion.

"Surely you may pay the soldiers with money extracted from tolls."

"The late war may cause a bad season for commerce on the Dimwer, and, in that event, I would be left with nothing. And in any case, I wish to offer the current garrison a bonus for their brave defense."

"The money in those rooms should be mine!" Amay said. "I have earned it, with six long years as a puppet in this little globe!"

"Consider the many years you will remain here in Abrizonde," said Vespanus. "The endless flow of money and commerce up and down the Dimwer, and the great fortune that you can build for yourself. Whereas I will have to live for the rest of my life only on such money as I can carry away."

"You shall *never* have my money! Never!" And then Amay, shaking her fist, began to berate Vespanus in much the same style with which she had earlier addressed her husband.

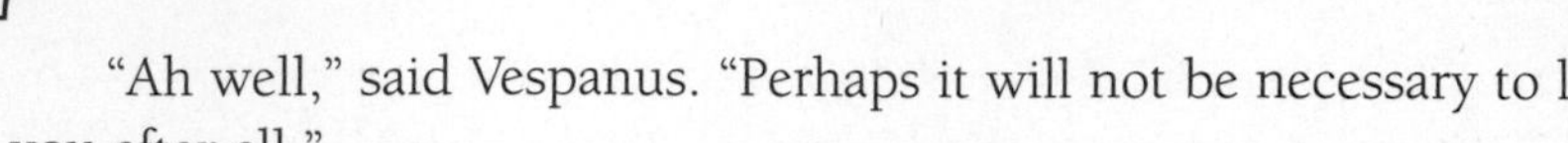

"Ah well," said Vespanus. "Perhaps it will not be necessary to liberate you after all."

He took from the shelf the vial that he had seen Ambius employ, and opened the stopper to pour a single drop into the neck of the crystal bottle. Spluttering a few last curses, Amay immediately fell into profound slumber.

When she awoke, she found herself reclining on a coverlet of pale samite, and cradled in a bed of carved ebony. The room was small but exquisitely appointed, with many mirrors, furniture inlaid with mother-of-pearl, and carpets of intricate design and brilliant hue.

She gave a start of surprise, and sat up. Facing her, languid on a settee, was the figure of Vespanus of Roë.

"This is my room!" said Amay.

"Your late husband preserved it much as you left it," said her interlocutor. "If you like, you may consider it evidence of some lingering fondness on his part."

"Or lack of imagination!" said Amay. She glanced over the room. "I seem to have been set at liberty."

The figure of Vespanus bowed gravely. "I reconsidered my earlier position. The garrison, drunk with victory, is ill-inclined to obey my orders, twk-men bring news that the army of the Exarch seems prepared to renew the contest, and under the circumstances I begin to find the watery meads of Pex strangely attractive." He rose.

"I have taken passage on the first barge of the season," he said, "and I have also taken the liberty of placing upon it exactly half the contents of the late Protostrator's strong rooms, which I hope you will agree is fair. I tarry but for any messages you may wish me to carry, and for any sums that you may wish to entrust to me for the purpose of hiring soldiers to augment your garrison."

Amay swung her legs from the bed and rose, a little carefully, to her feet.

"Half?" she said. "You have taken half?"

"Surely I deserve some reward for preserving your place here, and for liberating you."

Amay's eyes glittered. "*Some* reward, yes—but half?"

He cleared his throat. "If you have no messages for me to carry, then I shall leave you to your business." He bowed, and in haste stepped toward the door.

"Stay!" she called. When he hesitated, she took a firm step toward him.

"It was bad enough," Amay said, "that I spent six years confined in that wretched globe, deprived of honor and my sorcerous powers. It was bad enough that I was forced to endure the presence of my husband, and watch him consort with those bronze nymphs—and bad enough that I could see him adding to his fortune day by day, counting the coins and gems that he extorted from the bargemen before storing them in his strong rooms." She glared at him, showing even white teeth. "And is it not bad enough that I am expected to endure a *thief*, a thief who takes half my substance and offers in recompense to *carry my messages!*"

He bowed again, and put a hand to his chest.

"Bear in mind," he said, "that I set you free. Do I not deserve anything for this favor?"

"Indeed you do," Amay said. "I shall kill you now, and quickly, rather than string you by your heels from the Onyx Tower!" With a ferocious gesture, she spoke the words that called forth the Spell of Azure Curtailment.

Nothing occurred. Amay stared into the face of Vespanus, which stared back, an expression of wide-eyed surprise on his face.

"So you have a charm proof against that spell," Amay said. "But nothing can stand against the Excellent Prismatic Spray!"

Again she spoke the words of a spell, enhancing its affect with ferocious gestures. Again nothing happened, and her companion blinked at her in surprise.

"I think we have learned enough," said the voice of Vespanus, and Amay glanced about uneasily, for the voice had seemed to come from the air, and not from her companion. Then she started and drew back as the figure of Vespanus shifted and changed into that of a leering figure with rolling eyes, a full beard, and a prominent overbite.

Then there was a scene of frantic motion, as the leering man began to dash around the room with incredible speed. He laid hands upon the very room itself and took it apart piece by piece, the whole disassembly taking place in just a few seconds, after which there was nothing left but the figure of the leering man and walls of transparent crystal.

"Allow me," said Vespanus, peering into the crystal bottle, "to introduce my madling, Hegadil."

Hegadil bowed elaborately as Amay stared first at the madling, and then at Vespanus, standing in her husband's study.

"I thought it best to discover whether you were trustworthy," Vespanus said. "While you were asleep, I had Hegadil construct a duplicate of your

bedchamber inside the bottle. As he has a talent for impersonation, I also ordered him to adopt my form and see whether you would attack me once you found yourself at liberty. Alas, my lady, you failed that test…"

"I am chastened!" Amay said quickly. "I reconsider!"

"I am not so foolish as to trust you again," Vespanus said. "Come, Hegadil!"

Hegadil stepped through the wall of the crystal bottle, and flew to the ring on Vespanus' finger.

"Farewell, my lady," Vespanus said. "I leave you to contemplate your long and doubtless tedious future."

He left the study before she could speak. In truth, he had not expected any great success with the lady Amay, but he had thought the ploy worth trying. In any case, he would have all summer to puzzle out any traps on the strong room doors—and, of course, he would have the help of Hegadil, which would be considerable.

Pondering thus his own prospects, the Protostrator Vespanus walked to the Onyx Tower, and from its highest room contemplated his new domain.

AFTERWORD:

I SEEM to be fairly unique in acquiring my taste for Jack Vance's fiction as an adult.

Most Vance readers seem to have encountered him when they were young. I did, too, but I must have read the wrong stuff, or I read it badly, or maybe I just didn't get it.

But then I kept hearing from my writer friends about what a terrific writer Jack Vance was, and how much they admired him. And these were writers whose taste I trusted.

So off I went to read *The Demon Princes* series. Then the *Alastor* books, and the *Tschai* series, *Big Planet*, and—by and by—*The Dying Earth*.

And so I developed a grownup's appreciation for Vance's glorious high style, his psychological acuity, and for the breadth of his invention.

In the *Dying Earth* novels and stories, I very much enjoyed the scheming of Vance's sophisticated, amoral wizards, obsessed with politesse, possessions, and prestige, and I thought to tell a story of a character who had not yet earned a place among the elite. Vespanus is young, insufficiently schooled, and possibly second-rate. In order to take his place among the rulers of the Dying Earth, he must employ his limited powers with subtlety and finesse.

Abrizonde, Pex, and Calabrande are countries of my own invention, though I hope I have invented them in the Vance style. They are populated by Vancean creations such as sendestins and twk-men, callow-fields and miniaturized sorcerers, as well as some of my own inventions such as the Halcyon Detonation.

I was delighted to include such Vancean objects as alidades, altazimuths, and dividing engines, which though used in the story by Calabrandene engineers are actual implements used in our actual world by actual surveyors.

Perhaps reality itself pays occasional homage to Jack Vance.

—Walter Jon Williams

PAULA VOLSKY

The Traditions of Karzh

HERE'S THE story of a lazy and languid lothario who receives the keenest of incentives to apply himself to his studies—the imminent threat of death.

Paula Volsky is the author of the popular *The Sorcerer's Lady* series, consisting of *The Sorcerer's Lady*, *The Sorcerer's Heir*, and *The Sorcerer's Curse*. Her other books include *The Grand Ellipse*, *The White Tribunal*, *The Gates of Twilight*, *The Curse of the Witch Queen*, *Illusion*, *The Luck of Rohan Kru*, and *The Wolf of Winter*. Born in Fanwood, New Jersey, she now lives in Basking Ridge, New Jersey.

The Traditions of Karzh

PAULA VOLSKY

Dhruzen of Karzh, long-time acting master of the manse, surveyed his nephew at length. He beheld a spare and elegantly-clad young man, with black hair framing a pale, lean face, and dark eyes heedlessly content. The sight appeared to please him. His round face pinkened with gratification, his round eyes beamed benevolence.

"Nephew Farnol," Dhruzen observed, "I wish you a happy birthday. Today you attain the age of one-and-twenty. Let us drink to that accomplishment."

"Gladly, Uncle." Farnol of Karzh angled a dutiful inclination of the head.

The two kinsmen touched goblets and drank.

"The wine is to your liking?" Dhruzen inquired with solicitude.

"Excellent."

"I am glad, for it is yours, as of this day. Indeed, the manse and all of its contents are yours, now that you have come of age. Tell me, Nephew—now that you are master here, what do you intend to do?"

"Do? Why, busy myself with management of the estate, I suppose, and other pursuits. Kaiin offers no end of occupation. My swordplay falls short of perfection; I shall continue the practice bouts. There is the theatre, always in want of patrons; the declamatory competitions, the

Vringel Attitudes, the Perambulating Rocks, the Scaum Scullers, the quest to replicate the ancient Golden Light of the Sun—"

"Occupation?" Dhruzen's lids drooped. "Say rather, diversions, frivolities. Nephew, you squander your force upon trifles. Always you evade the issue of true importance. You speak nothing of magic, whose power measures the eminence of our line. The patriarchs of Karzh all possess some measure of magic. Where is yours?"

"Oh, I have not the aptitude. I cannot hold the simplest of spells in my head, they fly from me like timid birds." Farnol flexed a careless shrug. "What matter? There are other pursuits equally meritorious."

"Oh, Nephew—Nephew—Nephew." Dhruzen shook his curled head in smiling sorrow. "Far be it from me to criticize, but you refuse to acknowledge the essential verity. The master of this manse must possess some measure of thaumaturgical skill. It is a tradition of Karzh. For years, you have neglected your studies, and I—shame upon me—I have indulged your idleness. Now that you have come of age, matters must alter."

"It is a little late for alteration. Uncle, pray do not trouble yourself," Farnol counseled easily. "I have not turned out so badly, and no doubt all is for the best."

"Brave philosophy. I am not without hope, however, that I may yet persuade you to my point of view." So saying, Dhruzen struck the small gong on the table beside him, and a brazen note resounded.

Into the chamber stepped Gwyllis, household fixture for years beyond count, dry and brittle as an abandoned chrysalis.

"Bring it in," commanded Dhruzen.

Gwyllis bowed and retired. Moments later, he was back, tottering beneath the weight of a sizable object that he placed with care at the center of the table.

Farnol leaned forward in his chair. He beheld a swirling complexity of interlaced vitreous coils, colorless for the most part, but marked with occasional touches of crimson. At first, the great glass knot appeared randomly formed, but closer inspection revealed elements of structure and design. Here, a subtle pattern of glinting scales. There, the suggestion of a talon. The hint of a snout, the wink of a fang. And visible at the center of the gleaming mass, a compact dark heart, its nature open to conjecture.

"Beguiling, is it not?"

"Indeed." Farnol looked up to meet his uncle's happy gaze. A nameless pang assailed him.

"Nephew, you will observe the small leaden casket reposing at the center of the glass knot. Its contents are not without interest to you, but will not be reached save by way of sorcerous art. I invite you to open the casket."

"Sorcery is quite beyond me. An iron hammer of good weight, fit to shatter the glass impedimenta, should serve just as well." Farnol spoke with a lighthearted air designed to conceal growing uneasiness.

"Impractical. The importunate blows of a hammer would serve only to reinforce the resolve of the defenders."

"Defenders?"

"The glass reptiles, Nephew. They appear lifeless, but do not deceive yourself. They brim with righteous defensive zeal. Once roused, their tempers are short and their venom swift."

"Indeed?" Farnol took a closer look, and now discerned the intricately interlaced, transparent saurians. Crimson color marked their eyes, their claws, and their bulging poison ampoules. Their number was impossible to gauge. "Well. They seem stout guardians. Let them protect their treasure, whatever it may be. I will not disturb them."

"I urge you to reconsider. The casket at the center of the reptilian knot recommends itself to your attention, for it contains the sole known antidote."

"Antidote?"

"To the bane that you have just swallowed. It was in the excellent wine. I had feared that you might note the addition of a foreign substance, but your mind seemed set on other things. Perambulating Rocks, perhaps. Or Vringel Attitudes."

"Poison! Then you have murdered me, Uncle?"

"My dear lad, you must not think it. Do you take me for an ogre? What I have done reflects pure avuncular affection. I offer you an opportunity to honor the traditions of Karzh. If the conditions I impose appear extreme, you may take it as an expression of my absolute confidence in your abilities. Now attend, if you please. The draft that you have swallowed is trifling in its effect, scarcely more than an inconvenience. Three or four days must elapse before internal desiccation occasions anything beyond passing discomfort. Another two or three before desiccation gives way to conflagration, and a full ten days before the inner fires consume heart, mind, and life. But why speak of such unpleasantness? Surely it is irrelevant. You need only apply the most rudimentary of magical spells to loosen the knot, open the casket, and swallow the antidote. No doubt you will complete the task within

hours, if not minutes, for how could the legitimate master of the manse fail? Nephew, I know that you will make me proud." Rising from his chair, Dhruzen clapped his kinsman's shoulder, and departed.

For some seconds, Farnol of Karzh sat motionless, studying the tangle, then spoke without turning his head. "Gwyllis. Fetch me a hammer, an ax, or a crowbar."

"Useless, Master Farnol," returned the ancient servant, in tones treble and tweetling. "Be certain that it is magic alone will serve your purpose. Master Dhruzen has ordered it so."

"I shall summon a magician from the city."

"The adept will not be admitted. Master Dhruzen has ordered it so."

"I shall carry the glass knot into Kaiin, then."

"The knot may not leave the manse. Master Dhruzen—"

"I shall order otherwise, and the servants must obey. I have come of age."

"An alteration in status perhaps unrecognized by the duller among the household menials."

"Ah, Gwyllis—my uncle has planned it well. I fear I am a dead man. There is but one course left. I must kill Dhruzen before the poison takes me. It is a small consolation, but it is better than nothing."

"Permit me to suggest an alternative. While it is true that your uncle's methods and motives appear questionable, there can be no denying the validity of his argument. It is more than probable that you possess a certain measure of sorcerous ability. You have been given considerable incentive to discover it. You must now apply yourself."

"Impractical. My mind is not constructed to encompass magical spells. My measure of natural ability expresses itself as a negativity."

"Here is neither the time nor place for negativity. As for the construction of your mind and the quality or quantity of your abilities, such things are perhaps less immutable than you imagine. Tcheruke the Vivisectionist, who dwells among the hives at the edge of Xence Moraine, is just the man to sift your brain for hidden talent."

"Vivisectionist?"

"A courtesy title, I believe. Tcheruke is a magician of much erudition, paired with intermittent and unpredictable philanthropy. If your plight interests him—and I would advise you to make certain that it does—then he may undertake to repair all deficiencies. Seek out Tcheruke, and do so without delay."

Farnol nodded. Deep inside him, a point of heat glowed into being.

THE SUN stood near its low zenith when Farnol rode away from Manse Karzh. The weary star glowed through a veil of purple haze. The warmer tones faded out of existence at the horizon, where the indigo skies deepened to the color of ink. To the south rose Kaiin, its white walls reflecting faintly violet light. The burnished dome of Prince Kandive the Golden's palace dominated the skyline, and beyond glinted the waters of the Bay of Sanreale. The narrow track before him circled the northern extremity of the city, winding through the quiet hamlets and leading by leisurely degrees to the Old Town, a silent wilderness of tumbled ruins, broken walls and prostrate columns, fallen turrets and shattered towers, all worn smooth and rounded of contour by the passage of uncounted ages. Past a broken obelisk he rode, beyond which spread a wide court, and now he found his way littered with eyeless corpses—here a great warrior in cloison armor, there a young man in a green cloak, and others, many others. Their cavernous regard chilled him to the heart, but could not extinguish the little fire burning hot at the pit of his stomach. He nudged his horse and rode on.

The senescent red sun limped across the sky, and now the Old Town lay behind him. The grade of the path steepened as the land began to undulate. Shaggy fields of Foun's dalespread clothed the hillocks and hollows in patinated bronze, sparked with the bright rose-gold of vessileaf. Another hour of riding brought him to the verge of Xence Moraine.

FARNOL DREW rein and gazed about him. The land dipped and rolled like the waves of a petrified sea. Everywhere bulked the great boulders and mounds of debris deposited in the lost ages of the past; all of them polished to satiny sheen. The long rays of the westering sun warmed multifarious crowns and summits to crimson. Shadows pooled purple and charcoal in the hollows. Among the hills wound a slow brown stream, its banks lined with tall, narrow, emphatic mounds, whose regularity of size and shape suggested intelligent construction. He studied them for a time, but caught no hint of motion or life. At length, he urged his horse forward at a cautious pace.

The deserted mounds rose twice the height of a man. Closer inspection revealed them to be formed of rock, mortared with glinting crystalline adhesive and plastered over with a black substance whose even luster suggested porcelain. For the most part, the outer coverings were intact and unblemished. Here and there, however, the force of some ancient assault had ripped away chunks of matter to reveal interiors comprising countless compact polyhedral chambers strung like beads upon narrow corridors and galleries. Farnol resisted the impulse to halt and inspect. The sun was sagging toward the horizon, and the shadows rose like spectres from the depths of the ancient earth. He rode on, following the curves of the listless stream until he encountered a gigantic mound, towering above its companions, rising five times the height of a man. The featureless structure communicated nothing beyond assertiveness, yet instinct pushed him toward it. Twice he circled the mound, discerning no gleam of light, no evidence of habitation. Dismounting, he approached and rapped upon the hard surface. No response, but now at last he glimpsed life. A sinuous form slipped along the edge of his vision, and was not there when he turned to look. The wind sighed in regret. His heartbeat quickened, and the spot of heat at the bottom of his stomach seemed to pulse. Farnol drew a deep breath, tried to moisten dry lips, and rapped again.

A nearby tuft of rewswolley shuddered in response. The bristling stalks parted to reveal a hole. A lean figure thrust its head, shoulders, and torso up into the dying light. Farnol glimpsed grey garments; a narrow face partially concealed by a mask fitted with bulging, faceted eyepieces; bony white hands with long, curved fingernails; and a cloak of diaphanous, transparent stuff.

"Well, and what do you seek?" asked the stranger.

"I seek Tcheruke the Vivisectionist."

"What do you want of Tcheruke?"

"His assistance, for which I am willing to pay well."

"And what does he care for your terces? Shall he bury them on the Xence Moraine, and wait to see if they sprout?"

"I can offer him an interesting tale—the story of a foolish young heir to a fine estate, a treacherous uncle, and a murder taking place slowly, over the course of ten days."

"I state with assurance that Tcheruke will hear it, for I am he. Enter." Head and torso vanished into the hole.

Farnol hesitated. The sinuous form slithered nearly into view for a moment, or he thought that it did. When he turned, there was nothing. Delaying no longer, he tethered his horse, then slid feet first through the rewswolley down into the hole. He found himself in a barrel-vaulted passageway, its curving walls composed of neatly mortared stone, its low arch dictating a crawling progress. For a time, he advanced on hands and knees, his way barely lit by the weak rays trickling into the hole behind him, and a flickering glow somewhere ahead. Then, quite abruptly, he emerged from the passage into a six-walled chamber whose peaked hexagonal ceiling permitted upright posture. The room was austerely furnished with a pallet, low table, mats and floor coverings of woven and twisted grasses. A modest fire crackled on the hearth. An open case of many shelves contained books, folios, scrolls, and assorted small curiosities. Bunches of dried herbs, crystal whorls, and faintly luminescent bone fragments hung suspended from the ceiling.

Tcheruke the Vivisectionist turned to survey his visitor through faceted eyepieces. "Ah, you marvel at the nature of my home," he observed. "Know that I have built in accordance with the tastes of the Xence Xord, the race inhabiting this locale in ages past. Hybrid of man, shrew, knuve, and winged white ant, the Xence Xord constructed their hives of simple, functional beauty, inscribed verses in praise of Nature's wonders upon tablets of wax, developed the finest set of aesthetic standards ever known to this world, and at last solved the deepest mysteries of philosophy and morality. Their greatest writings they enclosed in spheres consigned to one of the countless voids between worlds. Then, the Xence Xord died, perhaps unequal to the burden of their own perfection. The wax tablets melted, and the location of the void between worlds was forgotten. But the philosophical treasures yet exist, awaiting rediscovery. To that end, Tcheruke dwells in this place, embracing the ways of the Xence Xord and entreating their small winged ghosts to return and enlighten him."

"And have they ever done so?"

"Once, ten years ago, a transparent form—something akin to rodent and termite—flitted through this hive, illuminating the recesses with its eer-light. I pursued it with my pleas, but it vanished. I am not without hope that it will one day return, and hold myself in perpetual readiness."

"A wise precaution." Farnol nodded gravely.

"I have spoken of myself, and now it is time for you to do likewise. Young man, state your name and tell your story. Should you engage my interest, you may sup here."

"My name is Farnol of Karzh, and I ask more than a meal of Tcheruke. Here are my circumstances." Farnol related his story concisely, but with animation.

Tcheruke listened in silence. His expression, if any, vanished behind the mask. The cock of his head communicated attentiveness. When he had heard all, he stood mute and motionless for the space of a meditative minute, then spoke.

"Your story is all that you promised. Were the Xence Xord present to hear it, they would doubtless offer you assistance. In good conscience, I can do no less. What would you have of me?"

"An antidote to the poison presently corroding my internal organs."

"Easily supplied, once the offending substance has been identified. To the best of my recollection, the world harbors some nine hundred sixty-eight thousand, four hundred seven elements and compounds of proven toxicity. Perhaps nine hundred sixty-eight thousand, four hundred eight, if you count grizamine, but I would regard its inclusion as redundant. Which of these poisons have you ingested?"

"I have no idea."

"Unfortunate. We shall commence testing without delay, but success is likely to demand some years of continuous effort."

"I have no more than ten days. No, they have already dwindled to nine and a half. Could you not furnish me with a talisman or rune fit to loosen the knot of glass reptiles?"

"Indeed not. Such intricacies demand recourse to a spell, and my librams contain many. I shall locate the appropriate incantation, you will encompass the syllables of power, and all will be well, as the Xence Xord themselves might desire. Now seat yourself and wait while I consult the writings."

"I will use the time to tend to my horse." Farnol crawled back along the low passageway, pushed through the rewswolley, and emerged into the open air.

The sun was setting. The last low rays bled over the quiet land. He cast his eyes this way and that, but caught no sight of his horse. He had left the animal tethered near the hidden entrance to Tcheruke's hive, reins wrapped about the central stalk of a tall moorsmere. And here was the same moorsmere, which he approached with trepidation. The torn remnants of leather reins wrapped the central stalk. A few long strands of chestnut hair had caught in the branches, and the leaves were spotted with blood.

The air seemed suddenly colder. He went back inside at once, where he found his host seated upon a mat at the low table, perusing a folio bound in moldering maroon leather.

"My horse has been taken," Farnol reported, "and I suspect the worst."

"No doubt you are right to do so. The great worms inhabiting this region are voracious of appetite and devoid of morality. Do not mourn the loss, but cultivate a philosophical detachment. It may be justly argued and supported by logic that the missing horse never truly existed. Now attend. You have done well in seeking my counsel. I have already discovered the requisite spell, a verbal concatenate of no great complexity known as the Swift Mutual Revulsion. You need only commit the syllables to memory, loose them at the appropriate moment—taking care to avoid mispronunciation, misplaced emphasis, transposition, inversion of pervulsion, or indelicacy of locution—and your difficulty is resolved. There before you lie the words. Learn them."

"I thank you, sir." Seating himself, Farnol regarded the folio. The yellowing page before him displayed the Swift Mutual Revulsion. The handwriting was faded, but legible, the diacritics plentiful and clear. The lines were ponderous, but not inordinately numerous. Encompassing the whole was no impossible feat. What signified his own unbroken history of failed sorcerous attempts? He had been an inattentive youth, a mere skipjack. This time, he would apply himself as never before, and this time he would succeed.

Accordingly, he focused his attention and set to work. The silent minutes passed. Deeply immersed in his studies, he failed to note his host's departure from the table. The syllables of power were bent on defying his efforts. Almost, they seemed to jig and hop on the page, as if to evade his vision—a familiar yet disconcerting manifestation. In the past, such calligraphic acrobatics had defeated him. Today, he persevered, plodding on to capture and store the phrases one by one. Presently, a voice impinged upon his consciousness.

"No doubt you completed your task long ago, and now sit musing. Attention, if you please. It is time to put your knowledge to the test."

Farnol blinked and looked up. Tcheruke had returned, bearing a fist-sized globular object which he deposited upon the table.

"Observe." The magician swept an inviting gesture. "I offer you a modest involution, comprising five separate lengths of twine. No doubt you might eventually pick it apart without recourse to magic, but let us imagine for the sake of argument that your time is limited, by something or other. You will employ the Swift Mutual Revulsion, and the five strands, suddenly imbued with intense detestation of one another, will pull apart with great vehemence, thus eliminating the knot. You are ready?"

"I am." Farnol strove to believe that it was true. He had wrestled long and hard with the lines. Surely they were his. Thus assured, he sang forth the spell. The weight and bulk of the syllables that he had crammed into his mind vanished in an instant, leaving nothing of themselves behind. For a moment, he sat almost bewildered, then recovered and looked to the knot.

It sat before him unchanged, tight and dense as ever. A small chitter of surprise escaped Tcheruke the Vivisectionist, and he shivered his cloak of membranous stuff in the manner of an insect fluttering its wings.

"Remarkable," observed the magician. "Never have I witnessed such profound inefficacy. I marvel."

"Ah." Farnol was sadly conscious of the void in his mind wherein knowledge had lately resided. "Indelicacy?"

"By no means. There is the wonder of it all. Your performance revealed inexperience, but I noted no distinct error, and thus no obvious source of failure. Intriguing. Additional observation is indicated. You must try again."

"Very well." Swallowing disappointment, Farnol resumed his studies. This time, memorization came more easily, and at the end of an hour's effort, he deemed himself master of the Swift Mutual Revulsion. A second attempt to employ the spell revealed the fallacy of this belief. Once again, the tangle of twine proved resistant, lying motionless as befit an inanimate object.

"Again, no apparent error. Interesting. Interesting." Tcheruke clicked thoughtful fingernails upon his eyepieces. "I must reflect. Set aside the folio, young man—it is useless. Later, perhaps. Well, well, we shall see." Thereafter the magician fell silent, ignoring all questions and comments.

Farnol followed his host's advice and set the book aside, but the syllables of the Swift Mutual Revulsion danced maddeningly across his mind. Should Tcheruke the Vivisectionist prove unable to assist him, where then could he go—what could he do? As if in response to a mental poke, the fire inside him flared. Farnol's lips tightened, and he pressed a hand to his stomach. The syllables of power went up in mental smoke.

The mute minutes expired. At last, his host placed a meal on the table—a simple dinner of stewed roots, spiced seed paste, wild gerufion, and fried grass cakes. Together they ate in silence. Upon finishing the last of his gerufion, Tcheruke finally spoke.

"I have pondered at length and formulated a theory. It is my belief that your difficulty roots itself in some congenital defect."

"I think not. Prior to my ingestion of an unidentifiable poison, I enjoyed excellent health."

"An infirmity so subtle in nature may well have escaped your attention. It may be no more than a minute glandular malfunction. An invisible occlusion, a sneaking sclerosis, a dangling ganglion. Once I have discovered the cause, the cure will doubtless suggest itself. To this end, I require the index finger of your right hand for purposes of testing and analysis. Come, let us perform the amputation. You will find that my title is not unearned."

Farnol blinked. "Does no practical alternative exist?"

Tcheruke considered. "A half gill of your blood might perhaps suffice, but only at cost of efficiency. Confirmation of results is likely to be delayed by the term of two hours, if not more."

"I will sacrifice the hours."

"As you will."

The blood was drawn, and Tcheruke commenced an examination. Farnol withdrew to a sleeping niche no larger than a coffin, where the small internal flame kept him wakeful for hours.

He emerged in the morning to discover his host again or still seated cross-legged at the low table in the main chamber.

"Ah, young man, be happy." Tcheruke radiated dignified triumph. "I have solved the mystery, and your troubles are at an end."

"Indeed?" Farnol's hopes bounded.

"It is as I surmised. A small chemical imbalance of the blood prevents your complete assimilation of sorcerous spells. This matter is easily resolved. Ingestion of a certain elixir corrects the flaw. The elixir is readily prepared, and I am willing to do so, for I tread the Path of the Xence Xord. The only contribution I ask of you is your assistance in obtaining the last of the necessary ingredients. Only one is wanting."

"Name it. I will supply the lack."

"You must bring me the headstone of a pelgrane."

"A pelgrane." Farnol repressed a shudder. "I see. Where is such an item to be purchased?"

"Nowhere on this earth, so far as I know."

"It is possible to kill a pelgrane, but scarcely without benefit of magic, or at least a squadron of heavily armed assistants. I have neither."

"Do not look so chapfallen. There is another possibility. Why think of confronting a live pelgrane, when you need only locate a dead one?"

"Not easily accomplished. If I am not mistaken, the pelgrane are believed to devour their own dead."

"Unverified, and irrelevant. The pelgrane's headstone is indigestible. If consumed, it will eventually reappear. There is a beautiful inevitability about it."

"Then I must discreetly scour the known haunts of these winged gluttons."

"Very discreetly, I would advise. A modest self-effacement is never inappropriate. To this end, I will invest you with a magical appurtenance whose use requires no skill—the Chameleon Mask, affording matchless excellence in protective coloration."

"How shall I recognize the headstone that I seek?"

"It is the size of a bean, mottled ultramarine and ocher, marked with points of black glow that drift restlessly about its surface. A colony of pelgrane is known to infest the region north of Porphiron Scar, and it is there I suggest that you search."

"That is a distance demanding of some time." Almost unconsciously, as had become his habit of late, Farnol pressed a hand to his stomach, and the heat from within reached his palm.

"Ah." Tcheruke the Vivisectionist shivered his cloak in sympathy. "There again, I can assist. I will give you a vial of the Stolen Repose. One sip of the soporific oil compresses eight hours of sleep into the space of twenty minutes. Beware, however. Two sips, and you are likely to sleep for a month. In this wise, you may vastly increase your waking hours of travel."

"But if my body enjoys eight stolen hours of sleep, will not the poison within likewise enjoy eight stolen hours in which to continue its work?"

"That is an interesting question. You must experiment, and inform me of the results. Come, time presses."

Farnol breakfasted upon boiled pods, leftover grass cakes, and tart stringeberry juice. His host presented him with the promised magical articles, which he placed in his pouch, and a small sack of provisions. There was little else to carry, for the bulk of his belongings, stowed in his saddle bags, had vanished along with his horse. At the last, he paused to address the magician. "I shall return as swiftly as may be. Should I fail in the search, and we do not meet again, allow me to thank you for your hospitality and generosity alike. You have done honor to the Xence Xord."

"No thanks are necessary. I relish the opportunity to acquire the pelgrane's headstone. In all truth, I have wanted one for years."

He crawled along the passageway and up through the rewswolley into the open air. It was dawn. A rim of deepest red, drowning in purple ink, edged above the eastern horizon. The great expanse of dark blue sky overhead verged upon black, but faint ruddy light silhouetted the tall hives of the vanished Xence Xord. Before him dipped and flowed the rounded irregularities of the Xence Moraine; protrusions brushed with reddish haze, the hollows lost in blackness. Beyond them, invisible as yet, loomed the naked bulk of Porphiron Scar.

He cast a wary glance around him, but glimpsed no undulant forms. The giant worms of the vicinity had presumably fled the rising sun. Drawing a deep draft of chill morning air, Farnol set off across the Xence Moraine.

For hours he hiked north, pausing briefly at midday to consume a lunch of grasscake, dried stringeberries, and black sausage skinny and shriveled as a mummy's finger. He encountered no man, no predatory beast, hardly a sign of animal life beyond the occasional bird or winged reptile gliding overhead. Neither incident nor recognizable landmark marked his progress across the Moraine, but certain interior changes signaled the passage of time. The warmth in his belly was spreading. As the hours and miles passed, the formerly compact spark expanded, infusing his core with heat too pronounced for comfort, but as yet no source of real pain; less disturbing for what it was than for what it promised.

There was little profit in the contemplation of imperiled viscera. He fixed his attention instead upon the surrounding terrain, with its soft swells and dips, its rocky debris lustrous as palace statuary, its subtly-shaded mantle of grey-green scourvale. Before him the land ascended by degrees to a distant ridge crowned with thick vegetation, black against the indigo sky. There rose the High Boscage that clothed the steep bluffs overlooking the River Derna, and toward the forest Farnol directed his steps.

He walked on for the rest of the day, pausing along the way only as often as need dictated. By sunset, the High Boscage had drawn appreciably nearer. Darkness fell, and progress halted. He ate, allowing his thoughts to dwell upon the lost pleasures of Kaiin, while devoting a corner of his mind and a measure of his senses to vigilance. No sinister presence made itself known, but for safety's sake, he donned the Chameleon Mask. The heavy fabric of the magical appurtenance wafted an evocative odor. A sense of powerful alteration rippled his perceptions. The world about him vanished in darkness, but he sensed a twisting of reality, and knew upon instinct that he was well hidden. He slept.

In the morning, the ineffably alien weight of the Chameleon Mask woke him. He rose and gazed about. Early light played dim and tranquil upon the Xence Moraine. No danger manifested itself, and he stripped the mask away with a sense of relief. His journey resumed.

Afternoon, and he walked the quiet shade of the High Boscage. Presently, he came to the summit of a steep bluff, where he stood gazing down upon the River Derna, its impetuous waters the rich color of rusted iron. Then on along the bluff, following the course of the river channel, until the tingling of his nerves told him that he was nearing his destination. *A colony of pelgrane is known to infest the region north of Porphiron Scar*, Tcheruke had told him, and the creatures might be anywhere. He kept a wary eye on the sky as he walked, while often scanning the ground for bones or remnants capable of housing the headstone that he sought.

Hours devoid of discovery passed until, at the close of the day, the sight of an airborne form threw him to the ground. There he crouched motionless, jaw clenched. From that vantage point, he studied the winged creature above, noting the batlike form, the curved snout, the ponderously adroit flight; a pelgrane, unmistakably. Fear welled, its ice momentarily quelling the heat of Uncle Dhruzen's poison.

The pelgrane passed across the face of the sun and vanished. Farnol's breath eased, and his hopes stirred. He had come to the right place. Here the pelgrane lived, and here presumably died. Where they died, their headstones must lie.

He searched the forest floor without success until darkness fell. He slept masked beneath the trees, and the weight upon his face, together with the smoldering heat in his vitals, woke him to a dawn sky alive with soaring pelgrane. He watched, fascinated and fearful, until the black company dispersed. Then he moved on through the forest, footsteps careful, eyes darting everywhere. Once, he caught a gleam of ultramarine under a bush, but found there nothing more than an ancient glazed sherd. Later, he discovered a spread of old bones moldering amid the shadows, but the horned tri-lobed skull did not belong to the species that he sought. Along a faint trail he wandered, and, as he went, the heat in his belly sharpened and expanded to fill assorted organs.

At last, he came upon a corpse—putrescent, half devoured—and his pulses quickened. Approaching with caution, he spied great leathern wings, an elongated head of black horn, fanged snout, gargoyle face. A dead pelgrane—potential key to his salvation. Drawing the knife from his belt, he knelt beside the corpse. The tough black substance of the head was resistant, but the eyes might offer ingress, or perhaps a rock would serve to crush the skull. Farnol sawed away with a will. So absorbed was he in his work that he failed to note a shifting shadow, a puff of breeze. A voice rasped at his back.

"*My mate, my meat.*"

He twisted in time to meet the leering eyes of a second pelgrane. The hook of a black wing slammed his head, and the world went dim. He did not entirely lose consciousness. He was aware but unable to resist as he felt himself seized and borne aloft. The cold wind on his face revived him. He heard the rusty creak of the pelgrane's wings, he saw the woods and the river far below, his last sight of the world. Presently his captor would let him fall upon some rocky outcropping, and then devour him at leisure.

The pelgrane did not drop him. On it flew along the Derna, until the bluffs heightened and steepened, and the vegetation clothing their rock dwindled. The bare shelves and ledges were dotted with massive nests of wood, river reed, and bone, cemented with clay. Toward one such spiky haven, Farnol was borne, and deposited on the shelf beside it. Over his protests, his captor deftly stripped the garments from his body, then tossed him into the nest. He shared the space with three hideous infant pelgrane, all of them asleep. At once, he attempted to climb out, and the powerful thrust of a great hatchet beak propelled him backward.

"Stay." The pelgrane's voice, while deep and harsh, was recognizably female.

"Madam, do your worst. I defy you."

"Ah, the meat is well spiced." She cocked her misshapen head. "Just as I would have it."

"Allow me to depart unharmed, else I visit destruction upon your young."

"Excellent. I encourage you to try." The pelgrane uttered a distinctive croak, and her repulsive progeny awoke.

Three sets of leathern wings unfurled. Three pairs of reddish eyes opened to fasten upon Farnol of Karzh.

"Observe, my little ones," the mother instructed. "I have brought you a specimen upon which to sharpen your skills. This creature is known as a man. Repeat after me. Man."

"*Man,*" the nestlings squeaked in unison.

"Do not be lulled into carelessness by the comical appearance. These bipeds display a certain low cunning, and some of them possess magic. Now, then. Who will show us how to bring him down?"

"*I! I! I!*" offered the nestlings.

"You, then." The mother gestured.

Wings spread eagerly wide, the designated infant hurled itself across the nest, half hopping, half gliding. Farnol deflected the attack with a blow of his fist. The pelgrane bounced off the wall and hit the floor, to the tootling merriment of its siblings and the full-bellied mirth of its dam.

"Can you do better?" Another winged gesture.

A second juvenile launched itself at Farnol's legs. He kicked it aside, and fresh guffaws arose around him. A third flapping attempt was similarly thwarted.

"Children, I am saddened," the mother pelgrane observed with patent untruth, for she still shook with laughter. "Your predatory performance leaves much to be desired. Now, attend. It is always best to take the prey unawares, but when that is impossible, you must take care to seek the points of vulnerability." Perching herself upon the edge of the nest, she leaned forward to point a precise wing tip. "Here—the neck. Here—the belly. The groin. And finally, never underestimate the utility of the knees, when approached from the rear. Thus and so." Her powerful wing smote the specified joints, buckling Farnol's legs. A shrewdly angled shove toppled him onto his back.

At once, the three nestlings were upon him, their combined weight pinning him to the floor, their abominable odor foul in his nostrils. In vain he struggled to dislodge them. Their baby fangs scored his limbs, and he felt the wet warmth of blood. Little squeals of joy escaped the infant pelgrane.

Farnol's desperate eyes sought out the mother, who sat watching with an air of serene domestic contentment. "A warning, madam!" he exclaimed. "Know that I have swallowed a potent bane, no doubt deadly to your kind as it is to my own. Would you allow your offspring to gorge upon poisonous provender? Think well!"

"Indeed. I think that I have never before heard this particular tale, and be certain that I have heard many. How gratifying to discover this old world offering fresh experience. You are correct, however, in noting the children's need of guidance." She raised her rasping voice. "Little ones, desist! Do not consume the man before you have had full use of him. Further practice is indicated. Desist, I say."

A protesting din arose. *Oh, Mother, the savor*! The maternal pelgrane remained obdurate, and the three nestlings withdrew, grumbling. The weight pressing Farnol's body vanished. His breath eased, and he sat up slowly. His flesh was crisscrossed with scratches and blotched with punctures. Fire licked his vitals, and fear chilled his mind.

"Again," said Mother.

This time, the three of them worked together, launching themselves simultaneously at his face, his abdomen, and the back of his neck. He beat them off at the cost of much effort and considerable blood, then slumped against the wall, exhausted. When the energetic youngsters launched a renewed, well-coordinated attack seconds later, they pulled him down with ease, and would surely have devoured him then and there, but for their mother's intervention.

"Not yet, children," she admonished. "But it should not be long. Your progress is noteworthy, and you have made your mother proud!"

Night fell, and the nestlings composed themselves for slumber, huddled in a malodorous heap. Mother seemed likewise to sleep, but evidently retained some awareness. Three times during the course of the night, Farnol attempted to climb from the nest, and each time she roused herself to forestall him. At last, he fell into a miserable, fitful slumber, filled with dreams of inner fire. He woke at dawn to find that his dreams reflected reality. The heat had spread from his midsection to scorch its way along his limbs.

The pelgrane were awake, infants bouncing, mother flexing her great wings.

"I go forth to forage," she informed her brood. "Today, it is easy. There is still plenty of meat left on your good father."

"Meat! Meat! Meat!" the gleeful infants shrieked.

"What—you feed upon the flesh of your own family?" asked Farnol, startled into speech.

"It would be a pity to let it go to waste. What, shall I demonstrate ingratitude, even incivility, in refusing the most beautiful sacrifice that any male can offer on behalf of his mate and his children?"

"And this beautiful sacrifice—was it altogether voluntary in nature?"

"Such a query can only be regarded as unseemly." Mother reproved. Her attention returned to her young. "For now, I leave you alone with the—what, sweet ones?"

"MAN!" chorused the nestlings.

"Just so. You may play with him, but take care, for he is not readily replaced. When I return, I expect to find the—"

"MAN!"

"Alive and free of major damage. Otherwise, I shall be cross." So saying, she launched herself into the air and flapped away, wings creaking.

No sooner was she out of sight than Farnol commenced climbing the nest wall. When one of the juveniles seized his ankle, he kicked the creature aside and hoisted himself to the rim, whence he caught sight of his belongings—garments, pouch, sword and scabbard—scattered about the ledge. As he swung one leg over the edge, the three small pelgrane set upon him. Their skills and coordination were improving by the hour. Farnol resisted with vigor, but they swiftly dragged him back, threw him down, and seated themselves respectively upon his chest, his stomach, and his thighs.

One of them took a small nip out of his shoulder, swallowed, and squeaked in pleasure. Another bit a similar morsel out of his leg.

"Enough, pernicious vermin!" Farnol cried out in desperation. "Devour me at your own peril—my flesh is toxic."

"Pah, we are not afraid!"

"We are pelgrane, we can digest anything!"

"You will see!" The speaker tore a small shred of skin from his back.

"Your mother will be cross," Farnol essayed between gasps of pain.

This consideration gave the infants pause. A doubtful colloquy ensued, at the close of which, the largest of them decreed, "Play now, eat later. The Man will run to and fro, and we shall bring him down."

"Play, play!"

The nestlings hopped from Farnol's body. He lay motionless.

"Come, get up and run about!" they exhorted.

"No." He did not stir. "The three of you will only knock me down again."

"Yes, that is what we intend. Come, play!"

"I will not. Shall I tell you the reason? Your game is too easy, fit only for feeble babes. It presents no challenge to fine, well-grown youngsters such as yourselves. Would you like to play a game demanding of skill, a game worthy of future hunters? One of the most prized accomplishments of the adult pelgrane resides in his ability to drop rocks, clods, bricks, and the like upon his quarry from above, stunning the prey at a distance and thus facilitating capture. It requires a keen eye, a steady talon, coolness, and precision. I wonder if you three are ready?"

"Ready, ready, READY!"

"Very well, then. You will drop or fling objects, while I seek to evade. The items must be light in weight, however, lest I be crushed, and your lady mother correspondingly vexed. I noted a number of suitable items lying scattered about the ledge, outside of the nest."

"We shall secure them—make ready to commence fruitless evasive action!"

The infants were capable of brief, low flight. They flapped and glided from nest to ledge with ease. For some moments, Farnol heard their voices racketing on the other side of the wall, and then they were back, clutching assorted objects; a stone, one of his shoes, his pouch. Briefly they swooped overhead, then simultaneously released their burdens. He took particular care to dodge the stone. The shoe grazed his shoulder in falling, and the pouch hit his head squarely.

"I win, I win!" One of the nestlings squalled in triumph.

"I shall win next time!"

"No, I!"

They vanished, and reappeared moments later. Two rocks and his other shoe rained down upon him. He evaded all. Clods of comparatively soft mud followed, and now he judged it wise to let them hit. Mud spattered his shoulders, face, and hair. High-pitched squawks of victory resounded.

"I concede." Farnol lifted both hands in good-humored defeat. "Had they been rocks, I must have succumbed. You have demonstrated your prowess." Retrieving his pouch, he opened it and found Tcheruke the Vivisectionist's vial of Stolen Repose intact. He pulled the cork and applied the oily contents to his naked body.

"What do you do?" The juveniles, perched on the rim of the nest, watched bright-eyed.

"I prepare a new game. I shall run to and fro, you will try to take me down. But it will not be so easy, this time. Observe, I anoint my flesh with

an oleaginous substance, allowing me to slide from your grasp as terces slip through the fingers of a profligate. You will not hold me."

"Yes we will, yes we will!"

"Prove it."

They flung themselves at him. Farnol jigged and dodged with vigor, eluding them for a time, but presently found himself prone, the nestlings perched on his back.

"We have won again!" A razor nip underscored the announcement.

Four or five nips followed, and a happy gabble arose among the pelgrane.

"The meat is sweet!"

"The new sauce is to my liking!"

"The sauce is tasty and delicious!"

He felt their avid tongues upon him; another bite or two, and then the animated voices slowed and slurred as the Stolen Repose took effect. The nestlings fell silent. One by one, they slumped to the floor and slept.

Farnol stood up, mind racing. He tossed his shoes and pouch from nest. Turning to the nearest infant, he stooped, strained, and succeeded in slinging the limp creature over his shoulder. Thus encumbered, he climbed the nest wall, tumbled the pelgrane out onto the rocky shelf, and jumped down, landing safely. His belongings still littered the shelf. Locating his sword, he drew the blade, and, with a sense of simple satisfaction, sliced off the slumbering infant's head.

The skull had not yet acquired the firmness of maturity. A few blows of a rock sufficed to smash it open. Investigation of the wreckage proved distasteful, but rewarding. At the base of the brain he discovered the headstone that he sought; an object no larger than a pea, hard as a pebble, pied blue and ocher, dusted with wandering motes of black glow. He wiped the headstone clean and placed it in his pouch, then dressed himself with all haste, for instinct warned him that Mother's return was imminent.

Quitting the ledge, he hurried away across the stony slopes, making for the shelter of the High Boscage. He took great care to skirt the numerous nests dotting the region, and as he went, he frequently looked to the sky. The thickets appeared immeasurably distant. Centuries seemed to elapse before he slipped into the welcoming gloom beneath the aged trees. From that shaded refuge, he cast another glance skyward, and now spied a winged form swooping low over the nest on the ledge.

Mother had come home to her abbreviated brood.

She alighted. Some moments of silence ensued. Then a scream rang forth, perhaps the most terrible cry ever to echo among those bluffs; an elemental blast of grief and ultimate rage. Farnol of Karzh cringed at the sound. Without conscious thought, he pressed the Chameleon Mask to his face, froze into immobility, and blended with his surroundings.

The scream resounded far and wide, carrying passionate promises along the River Derna. Its last reverberations died away, and its author took to the air, sailing in widening circles characteristic of a methodical hunt.

For some moments, Farnol stood petrified. Eventually, a sense of purpose heightened by inner heat set him in motion again. He looked up into an empty purpling sky. For now, Mother was nowhere in evidence. He removed the mask. Its tingle was maddening and its benefits belonged solely to a stationary wearer. He walked on beneath the concealing boughs.

The forest was quiet and dim, the path clear and firm, but his way was far from easy. Internal disruptions had become impossible to ignore. The toxic heat burned along every nerve, insolently proclaiming its own advance. It worsened by the day, in accordance with Uncle Dhruzen's predictions.

Some distraction from poisonous progress was furnished by hunger, for the provisions donated by Tcheruke the Vivisectionist had been lost, and the High Boscage offered little refreshment. More compelling yet was the distraction afforded by the dark figure periodically glimpsed patrolling the skies overhead. The broad wings, globular abdomen, and hatchet profile were unmistakable. Mother continued the hunt.

He pushed on at his best speed across a stretch of woodland entirely unfamiliar; he must have been carried high above it upon the occasion of his previous passage. Here, the tree trunks were curved like bows and crowned with tufts of long, transparent, membranous leaves. Rich growths of black renullta blanketed the ground, nourished by the tears of the Puling Jinnarool. The branches of the Puling Jinnarool supported a population of iridescent, large-headed insects with the sweet voices of grieving women. The air trembled with whispering plaints and reproaches.

Driven by hunger, Farnol plucked an insect from a branch and examined it closely. The creature possessed an exaggerated hammer head graced with feathery antennae, bulging purple eyes, and a meager tripartite body sheathed in chitin. Its appearance was not appetizing, but his need was great.

As if it divined his intent, the captive insect lifted its melodious voice in mournfully unintelligible plea. Its companions took up the cry, and a sorrowing, faintly accusing chorus arose, accompanied by a vast, urgent fluttering of countless wings. The trees and bushes quivered. The tiny voices harmonized. The uproar drew the attention of a dark figure wheeling above upon outstretched wing.

A rush of displaced air, a swift shadow, and Mother descended. There was time only to grab for the Chameleon Mask, to clap it across his face, and then she was there.

Farnol lay motionless under the trees. The ground was wet and black beneath him, springy with renullta and glinting with fallen leaves. Presumably, his own form appeared equally black, springy, and glinting. Before him, Mother paced the grove, long head turning from side to side, red eyes stabbing everywhere. He dared not gaze directly upon her lest she sense the pressure of his regard, and therefore kept his eyes low, watching her feet pass back and forth. Her burning glances discovered nothing, and the fervent vociferation of the insects was evidently incomprehensible. Thrice, she paused to sort odors, but the fragrance of the Puling Jinnarool masked all, and she clashed her fangs in frustration. A bitter hoot escaped her, and she took wing.

Farnol lay still for some minutes following her departure. When he judged the sky thoroughly clear, he rose and went his way. As he walked, he scanned the sky, and for an hour or more spied nothing untoward. Then she was back, skimming low over the trees, so close that he caught the wink of a jeweled ornament upon her crest; so close that she might easily have glimpsed motion. Perhaps she had done so, for she glided in tightening loops above his hiding place, passing close over his head half a dozen times before veering off with a petulant hitch of her wing.

Mother disappeared into the sun, and Farnol's trek resumed. For hours, he advanced slowly, his progress retarded by hunger, thirst, and internal conflagration. Around midday, he paused to feed upon handfuls of pearly fungi ripped from a fallen tree. Thereafter, the fire in his belly seemed to intensify, perhaps stoked by inedible fare.

An hour later, he reached a gap in the High Boscage; a broad, bare swath of ground, devoid of vegetation, black with the ancient marks of some forgotten disaster. At its center rose a polished dome, its walls a gleaming black touched with the polychrome highlights of a soap bubble. Prudence would ordinarily have dictated discretion. Today, hunger drove him.

A quick glance skyward detected no threat. Stepping forth from the shelter of the trees, Farnol made for the dome at a smart pace. He had not covered more than half the distance before a black form materialized overhead. No time for the mask; Mother had spied him. Down she came like a well-aimed cannonball.

The buffet of a leathern wing slammed him to the ground. Mother alighted beside him.

"Now, monstrous infanticide, my vengeance finds you!" the pelgrane declared.

"Not so, omnivorous hag!" Farnol dodged the stab of a lethal beak. Drawing his sword, he thrust, and a spot of blood splotched the other's breast. She fell back with a plangent cry. Springing to his feet, he fled for the dome. Mother followed.

He reached the glinting structure. A barely visible seam in its otherwise flawless surface suggested a doorway, upon which he pounded hard. A rounded entry presented itself, and he slid through. Behind him rose a scream of furious frustration, sharply diminished as the door closed.

Farnol blinked. He stood in utter darkness and bitter cold. Sheathing his sword, he stood listening, but heard nothing. At length, he inquired in civil tones, "Is anyone present? Or do I address myself alone?"

"You are not alone," spoke a soft, slow voice near at hand, its owner's gender and species impossible to judge. "No one need be alone. We are a family. I am Nefune. You are welcome among us."

"I thank you. I am Farnol of Karzh, a traveler. I come here pursued by the pelgrane, and the shelter that you offer is most welcome."

"The pelgrane is misguided. Its transgressions reflect simple ignorance. Perhaps, at some point in the future, great Vusq will be moved to vouchsafe insight."

"Great Vusq?"

"Our deity, the blind god of future things, who teaches His worshippers how to live in the world that is coming, the world that is ours when the sun embraces death. It will be an abode of illimitable darkness," Nefune continued in tones of intense fervor touched with exaltation, "of darkness without end, and immeasurable chill. We, the children of Vusq, prepare ourselves for the future reality. To this end, we live without light. The substance of our home excludes the vulgar rays and transient warmth of the doomed sun. When we must venture forth, we go blindfolded and sightless, in accordance with the will of Vusq. The more devout among us excise our eyeballs, and crush them to jelly upon the altar of Vusq. Those who perform this sacrifice are deemed blessed."

"Admirable." Farnol nodded invisibly. "Thus your sightlessness embodies foresight. A pretty paradox, but perhaps—"

His remark was interrupted by a ferocious thud that rocked the dome. A series of violent blows followed, punctuated by savage cries.

"It is the pelgrane," Farnol observed uneasily. "She tries her strength upon your house."

"Unhappy, benighted creature. She squanders time and vitality. The substance of our dome enjoys Vusq's blessing. You are safe here, Farnol of Karzh. You may stay as long as you wish. In fact, I urge you to abide here among us, and learn the ways of Vusq."

"*Stay. Stay. Stay.*"

The voices—multiple voices, their number indeterminate—hissed softly in the dark. Unseen hands patted his shoulders, his back. The light, corpse-cold, almost caressing touches raised gooseflesh along his forearms. He did not allow himself to recoil.

"But stay, we fail in hospitality," came the voice of Nefune. "No doubt you are hungry and weary, Farnol of Karzh. Will it please you to share our meal?"

"It will, and I thank you," returned Farnol, with feeling.

"Let us then repair to table, where we shall refresh ourselves and extol the greatness of Vusq. This way."

Nefune took his arm and led him forward. He saw nothing, but heard the light footsteps of others clustering close about him, and often he felt their icy hands patting his limbs and face. They seemed to walk a considerable distance, their path winding and twisting through a frigid void.

"Your home is remarkably generous in extent," observed Farnol.

"Ah, the darkness has a way of expanding space. It is a glorious thing, the darkness—comforting, profound, and holy. Those who seek the way of the future soon recognize the beauty of their chosen existence."

"*A glorious thing,*" whispered the unseen faithful.

"Those who tender the greatest gift in turn receive the greatest reward," Nefune continued. "Great Vusq delights in the sacrifice of devoted eyes. It is a matter worthy of thought, Farnol of Karzh. Here is our table. You may seat yourself."

Farnol obeyed. Exploratory groping soon taught him that the table consisted of nothing more than a mat of rough woven stuff spread out on the floor. He detected neither plate nor utensil.

"Reach out and avail yourself of Vusq's bounty," Nefune urged. "It is His gift to His servants."

Extending his hand, Farnol encountered the lip of a metal trough containing quantities of heavy, chilly porridge or gruel. Tentatively he tasted, and found the porridge innocent of flavor. It possessed weight, volume, exceptional density, and coldness; nothing more. Such was his hunger that he wolfed handful after handful; and such the cold mudslide power of the meal that the fires within were quelled, for the moment.

All around him in the dark, he heard the discreet sucking and smacking of polite ingestion. He heard too a plenitude of prayers, praise, invocations, and intense exhortations, the last of which he deflected as gracefully as he knew how.

The meal concluded, and Nefune spoke again. "Farnol of Karzh, the devout among us go now to the altar, there to perform our ritual ablutions and tender our offerings to Vusq. For all his greatness, the Lord of the Dark Future despises not the heartfelt gifts of His servants. Will you come now to the altar? There you may learn its size, contour, and feel, and thus grow accustomed."

"I thank you, but no," Farnol returned politely. "You have offered me every kindness, but it is time for me to take my leave. I've a task to complete, and time presses."

"Leave? By no means!" Nefune's hushed tones conveyed exclamatory ardor. "Come, reflect. Doubtless the pelgrane awaits without. Will you deliver yourself freely unto her hunger?"

Farnol had no answer.

"Better by far to tarry among us. Come, it is time for the evening rest. Sleep here tonight, and perhaps the dreams that Vusq sends will touch your heart."

"*Here tonight.*" The whispers shivered through the black air.

"Very well. Here tonight." He strove to conceal his reluctance. "Great Vusq's devotees are generous." Cold, weightless hands upon him again, and they conducted him to a sleeping mat too flat and thin to be called a pallet. He stretched himself out upon the mat, fully expecting to lie awake for comfortless hours, but sleep found him at once.

He woke blind and chilled to the bone. He had no idea how long he had slept, no idea whether it was day or night in the world outside the dome; the darkness confused such issues. The cold space around him was quiet. He caught a faint hiss of breathing, a soft rustle of movement, an unidentifiable vibration, nothing more. Very carefully, in nearly perfect silence, he rose to

his feet. Arms outstretched before him, advancing with hesitant steps, he groped in search of the curving exterior wall. When he found it, he would feel his way along the circumference until he located the exit. The pelgrane might or might not await him; at that moment, he did not care. Every instinct bade him depart the house of Vusq's faithful without delay.

Once his foot encountered a hard object that thrummed under the impact. Once he felt a slippery surface beneath him, and once he brushed something flabby and yielding that gurgled softly. Then his palm met a very smooth, seemingly glasslike barrier, and he knew that he had found the wall. Noiselessly he followed its curving course, fingers questing for a seam or indentation disclosing the location of a door.

The darkness breathed, and dozens of light, cold hands closed upon him. Soft voices spoke.

"Ah, it is our new brother, Farnol of Karzh."

"He has not yet acquired the ways of darkness. He is confused."

"Perhaps he wishes to tender an offering unto divine Vusq. He seeks the altar, but cannot find his way."

"Let us guide him. Fear not, Farnol of Karzh. We shall lead you to the altar, where change awaits. We are happy to assist a convert."

"You misunderstand," Farnol informed them. "I seek only the exit. I wish to resume my journey."

"We go now to the altar."

In vain Farnol argued and struggled. They lovingly dragged and propelled him through the dark until his knees bumped a solid, flat-sided structure, and his palm descended upon a level surface caked with some substance suggestive of desiccated jelly. Jerking his hand back, he exclaimed, "Understand that I am not temperamentally suited to the monastic life, and release me!"

"Peace, Farnol of Karzh. Know that divine Vusq cherishes you."

Farnol's desperate reply was lost. A great crash resounded overhead, and the dome shuddered. He looked up to behold a sliver of warm-colored light, visible through a freshly formed crack in the ceiling. As he watched, the crack widened to a fissure, the light strengthened, and chirping cries of consternation arose on all sides. A series of violent blows battered the roof, and a great rent opened, through which was visible the form of a pelgrane, assaulting the structure with a sharp-edged rock of estimable size.

Wrenching himself free of the astounded faithful, Farnol cast a quick glance around him. He beheld a company of fungus-white, hairless beings, with tiny countenances dominated by the enormous, palely protuberant eyes of night creatures. Many of the peaked little faces offered empty sockets. All seemed paralyzed, incredulous attention fixed on the crumbling ceiling. His glance traveled the curving wall, to fasten upon the outline of a rounded door. Dodging hairless white obstacles, he made for the exit. As he reached it, a broad section of the ceiling fell away, and Mother descended screeching into the dome.

Through the door and into the ruddy light of morning, dazzling for a moment or two, and then indescribably welcome. Farnol sprinted for the far edge of the clearing. As he ran, he cast a glance behind him, to see a trickle of demoralized faithful staggering out of the dome. Behind them, audible through the open door, arose the sounds of carnage.

He reached the shelter of the trees. The screaming died away behind him, and presently he heard it no more.

Hours of hiking brought him back to the bluffs that he remembered wandering days earlier. His way now led him downhill, and he made good progress despite a sense of scorching, shriveling internal activity, accompanied by growing weakness. He walked all day, and sunset found him back upon the Xence Moraine. He slept in the open, the Chameleon Mask heavy on his face. The night was cool, but he burned. He had not supped, there was nothing to eat, but he suffered little hunger.

Throughout the following day, he plodded the hills and hollows. His steps lagged, and his mind seemed similarly slow. He took little note of his surroundings, but managed to maintain awareness of the sky and its potential peril. Twice he spied a black, high-flying form, and each time hid behind the Chameleon Mask until the danger passed.

As the sun collapsed toward the horizon, he was dully surprised to find himself walking beside a listless stream, among familiar hives. An anomalously lofty structure reared itself before him—the hive of Tcheruke the Vivisectionist. The sight drove the mists from his mind. Recalling the location of the hidden entrance, he hastened to the tuft of rewswolley that concealed the passageway, and there found the way blocked by an immovable stone barrier.

Perhaps Tcheruke had departed. Perhaps Tcheruke was dead. Alarm filled Farnol. Striding to the silent hive, he pounded the wall with his

clenched fist, while calling aloud, "Tcheruke, come forth! Farnol of Karzh has returned, bearing the pelgrane's headstone, obtained at no little cost! Come forth!"

He heard the snap of a lock behind him, a whimper of hinges, and turned to behold the hooded head and skinny grey figure of the magician emerging from the hole.

"Who calls so peremptorily?" Tcheruke's faceted eyepieces glinted in the low red rays of the sinking sun. "Is it you, Farnol of Karzh? Welcome, welcome! You do not look well."

"My uncle's poison advances and my time dwindles, but I have not abandoned hope."

"*Abandon it now.*" A flutter of leathern wings, and Mother alighted before them. Her glowing gaze shifted from face to face. "Ah, a double prize."

At once Tcheruke the Vivisectionist began to chant the syllables of that formidable spell known as the Excellent Prismatic Spray. Without undue haste or apparent effort, the pelgrane struck the magician to the ground and placed her clawed foot on the back of his neck, pressing his face into the dirt and stifling his utterance.

"You may wait your turn and watch as I kill him," Mother advised Farnol. "Or you may attempt an entertaining flight. Such are your two choices."

"There is a third, madam." Drawing his sword, Farnol lunged.

Almost casually, she deflected the thrust. Catching the blade in her beak, she tore it from his hand and tossed it aside.

"My surviving young conceived a keen appetite for your flesh," she confided. "They have been clamoring for it. This evening, they will relish their dinner."

Farnol stared at her, aghast. Flight and resistance were equally hopeless. He might perhaps seek refuge in the hive while she busied herself with Tcheruke—there to wait for Uncle Dhruzen's poison to finish its work. No alternative possibilities presented themselves.

Pinned beneath the pelgrane's foot, Tcheruke wriggled uselessly. Deprived of coherent speech, he could express himself only by means of a thin, almost insectile shrilling. The razor notes seemed to carry a note of plea. Mother was little susceptible to emotional appeals, yet the plea did not go unanswered.

The dimming twilight air sang, and a band of ghostly winged visitants glimmered into being. They were small, reminiscent at once of rodent and termite; transparent, weightless, and glowing with eer-light.

Humming and chittering in tiny voices, the winged beings dove and darted about Mother's head. Affronted, she snapped her great beak, which passed harmlessly through luminous insubstantiality. Loosing an irritable hoot, she advanced a pace or two, crested head turning this way and that, fangs clashing. Relieved of her weight, Tcheruke sat up, rubbing the back of his neck. He caught sight of the ghostly troupe, and his face lit with a wondering rapture.

"The spell!" Farnol urged.

Tcheruke seemed not to hear. His ecstatic faceted gaze anchored upon the flitting ghosts. One hand rose, reaching out to them.

Despite their apparent ethereality, the visitants possessed a measure of force. Such revealed itself as the band clustered about the pelgrane, pressing so thick and close that she seemed clothed from head to foot in a lambent garment. For a moment, they hovered there, light pulsing, then the glow intensified to a blast of brilliance too great to endure.

Farnol threw an arm across his eyes. When he lowered it, the light had faded, and the pelgrane was nowhere to be seen. He blinked, and surveyed his surroundings swiftly. Mother was gone.

For a few seconds longer, the small ghosts hovered, humming, their cool eer-light playing upon the rapt face of Tcheruke the Vivisectionist. Then the transparent winged forms retreated, lost themselves among the hives, and so passed from view.

"Ah—the Xence Xord have recognized my existence!" Tcheruke rose to his feet, glowing with an internal light of his own. "I have beheld them in their perfection, and the hope of a lifetime is fulfilled!"

"Perhaps they will come back to you, and reveal the location of the void between worlds."

"I will entreat them incessantly. Their condescension upon this occasion renews my resolve. They have not heard the last of me! But come, young Farnol, come inside. The sun sets, and the worms will soon be crawling!"

Tcheruke vanished into his hole, and Farnol followed. Once within, he handed the pelgrane's headstone over to his host, who immediately commenced grinding, measuring, and mixing. While the magician labored, Farnol gulped beaker after beaker of cool bitterrush tea, in a vain effort to quench the inner fires that now roared. He consumed nothing solid. The mere thought of food now revolted him. Time passed. At length, Tcheruke handed him a cup containing a concoction of evil appearance

and vile odor, its surface dented with small whirlpools. He drank without hesitation, felt his nerves twist and his veins scream, and then lost consciousness.

In the morning, he woke sick and languid, but clear-headed. He drank cool tea, and refused food.

"And now, young Farnol, it is time to exert your mind," Tcheruke the Vivisectionist advised.

"Has your elixir transformed me? Have I now the power to assimilate?"

"We shall see. My folio lies upon the table, open to the Swift Mutual Revulsion. Apply yourself."

Farnol obeyed. Inner miseries impeded study, but he persevered, and presently encompassed the syllables, which settled into his brain with a conclusive mental click.

"And now, the knot?" he inquired, ready to test the efficacy of the magician's nauseous remedy.

"No. Forgive what may appear as a poor-spirited dearth of optimism, but I must observe that your present wretched condition admits of no delay. In short, you cannot afford time to experiment. You must proceed to Karzh with all alacrity, there to claim the antidote, which may or may not prove effective. To this end, I am prepared to transfer you, in token of my appreciation of the role you have played in securing my encounter with the Xence Xord. So, then!" Tcheruke clapped his hands briskly. "Stand here upon the clay square. Hold out your hands. Draw a deep breath, and hold it. Young man, I bid you farewell, and wish you fair fortune."

Tcheruke drew back and sang out a spell. Farnol was jerked up in a rush of whirling ether. An instant later, his feet touched the ground. He staggered, but retained his balance. Before him rose Manse Karzh, its ancient walls of pale stone draped in lush blue-green climber, its gables and turrets peak-roofed in tile weathered to a soft umber hue. For a moment, he stood staring as if amazed; then rubbed a recently-acquired reddish rheum from his stinging eyes, and advanced upon unsteady legs to enter his house.

A concerned-looking household servant intercepted him.

"Bid my uncle meet me at once in the dining hall," he commanded. The servant bowed and retired.

Farnol tottered through fire to reach the dining hall. The great glass knot still sat on the table. At its center, the leaden casket offering life—provided his uncle had spoken the truth; with Uncle Dhruzen, always open to question.

As if on cue, Dhruzen of Karzh walked into the room, closely attended by old Gwyllis. He checked at sight of his nephew, and a smirk of soft benevolence creased his face.

"My dear lad, such a joyous happening! Here you are, back home again, and looking so well!"

A grim smile twisted Farnol's lips. He said nothing.

"You have come home, no doubt, fully prepared to honor the sorcerous traditions of House Karzh. Eh, Nephew?"

"Yes," said Farnol.

"Really." Unpleasant surprise flashed across Dhruzen's countenance, dissolving swiftly into avuncular affection. "Well. I expected no less. Justify my confidence in you, Nephew. Display your sorcerous mastery."

"*I will,*" returned Farnol, with some persistent hope that he spoke the truth. Marshalling the last of his strength, he breathed deep and called out the Swift Mutual Revulsion. The syllables flew like arrows, and an inner certainty that he had never before experienced dawned. Expectantly, he regarded the knot.

The glassy coils began to writhe. A hissing chorus of inexpressible detestation arose. The undulations waxed in vigor, the hissing swelled to a hysterical crescendo, and the knot tore itself apart, its five component glass reptiles flinging themselves from the table top and shooting off in all directions. Farnol scarcely noted the vitreous lizards. Their disengagement exposed a small leaden casket. He opened it and discovered a flask. Drawing the cork, he drained the contents at a gulp. Dizziness assailed him, a weakness in his limbs, and a profound internal chill. Shuddering, he dropped into the nearest chair. He could hardly stir, and his vision was clouded, but not extinguished. He could watch.

The five glass reptiles, desperate to flee one another, were hurling themselves about the dining hall in mounting frenzy. Overturning furniture, caroming off walls, clawing woodwork, spraying venom, and hissing wildly, they had transformed the room into an arena. With a spryness exceptional in one of his years, Gwyllis had sought refuge atop the table. Dhruzen of Karzh's corpulence precluded similar prudence. As one of the lizards sped straight toward him, crimson eyes glittering and tail lashing, Dhruzen seized the nearest chair, raised it, and brought it down with force. Easily evading the blow, the lizard launched itself in a prodigious spring,

struck Dhruzen's chest like a missile from a catapult, knocked him to the floor, and drove little venomous fangs into his neck.

Dhruzen of Karzh commenced to jerk, twitch, and spasm. His back arched, his slippered heels drummed the floor, a froth bubbled upon his lips. His face turned an ominous shade of green, and presently he expired. All this Farnol watched with interest and mild compunction.

His own internal fires were abating. The heat and pain were dwindling, and a cool, fresh sense of renewal was stealing along his veins. He felt his strength returning, and he managed to rise from his chair. Catching Gwyllis' eye, he gestured, and the old servant understood at once. Gwyllis gingerly climbed down from the table. Together, the two of them flung the dining hall casements wide.

Perceiving escape from intolerable propinquity, the glass reptiles sprinted for the open windows. One after another, they leaped from the second story, shattering themselves to fragments upon the marble terrace below.

"You have recovered, Master Farnol?" Gwyllis tweetled.

Farnol considered. "Yes," he decided, "I believe I have. It would seem that Uncle Dhruzen spoke truly of that antidote. When you have fully recovered your own equanimity, Gwyllis, please effect Uncle Dhruzen's removal."

"Gladly. And then, sir? May I take the liberty of asking what you will do next?"

"Do?" The answer came with ease, as if it had been waiting a lifetime. "I shall continue working to build my sorcerous knowledge. I seem to have acquired the knack, and it is, after all, a tradition of Karzh."

"Welcome home, Master Farnol."

"Thank you, Gwyllis."

AFTERWORD:

MANY YEARS ago, when I was a youngster growing up in New Jersey, my parents often exchanged grocery bags full of used paperback books with friends and fellow-readers. Whenever a new bagful entered the house, I would sift through the contents in search of anything and everything interesting. One such scan turned up a few old issues of *The Magazine* *of Fantasy and Science Fiction.* I had never before encountered that magazine. I looked through an issue, and was quickly caught up in a story by a writer that I had likewise never before encountered. The story was "The Overworld," and the writer was Jack Vance. I read, and my tender young imagination was promptly caught in a bear trap. What a world was Vance's Dying Earth! I was enthralled with the exoticism, the color, the glamour, the magic, adventure, and danger. I loved the astonishing language, the matchless descriptive passages, the eccentric characters, baroque dialogue, the wit, style, inventiveness, and above all, the writer's deliciously evil sense of humor. Of course, I quickly discovered that "The Overworld" was only the first adventure of that reprobate Cugel the Clever—there were several more. The other issues of *Fantasy and Science Fiction* in that brown paper bag contained some of them. For the others, I spent months scrounging through used bookstores. It was not for another several years that I stumbled upon a copy of *The Eyes of the Overworld*, and finally acquired the entire Cugel narrative, as it existed at that time.

Much time has passed. There have been many other fantasy and science fiction writers to enjoy, admire (and envy!) My judgment has matured. But the sense of amazement and delight that Vance's stories awoke in me remains intact, as strong now as it was decades ago. And when I am asked (as writers invariably are) who influenced me, there are several names on the list, but the name that always pops out fast and first is Jack Vance.

—Paula Volsky

JEFF VANDERMEER

The Final Quest of the Wizard Sarnod

WORLD FANTASY Award-winning writer and editor Jeff VanderMeer is the author of such novels as *Dradin in Love*, *Veniss Underground*, and *Shriek: An Afterword*. His many stories have been collected in *The Book of Frog*, *The Book of Lost Places*, *Secret Life*, *Secret Lives*, and *City of Saints and Madmen: The Book of Ambergris*. As editor, he has produced *Leviathan 2*, with Rose Secrest, *Leviathan 3*, with Forrest Aguirre, which won the World Fantasy Award in 2003, *The Thackery T. Lambshead Pocket Guide to Eccentric and Discredited Diseases*, with Mark Roberts, and *Best American Fantasy*, with wife Ann VanderMeer, the start of a new "Best of the Year" series. He won another World Fantasy Award for his novella "The Transformation of Martin Lake," and has also published a book of non-fiction essays, reviews, and interviews, *Why Should I Cut Your Throat?*. His most recent books are a new collection, *The Surgeon's Tale*, co-written with Cat Rambo; a chapbook novella, *The Situation*; a collaborative anthology with Ann VanderMeer, *Fast Ships, Black Sails*; and the anthology *Mapping the Beast: The Best of Leviathan*. With Ann VanderMeer, he has co-edited the anthologies *Steampunk* and *The New Weird*, and *Best American Fantasy 2*.

They live in Tallahassee, Florida.

In the ornate story that follows, the wizard Sarnod, who has dwelt for untold ages in a lonely stone tower on an island in Lake Bakeel, imperiously dispatches two of his most potent servants on a hair-raisingly dangerous mission to the fabulous realms of the Under Earth, with the odds of success stacked dramatically against them—although if they *do* succeed, their victory may have consequences that no one could ever have expected.

The Final Quest of the Wizard Sarnod

JEFF VANDERMEER

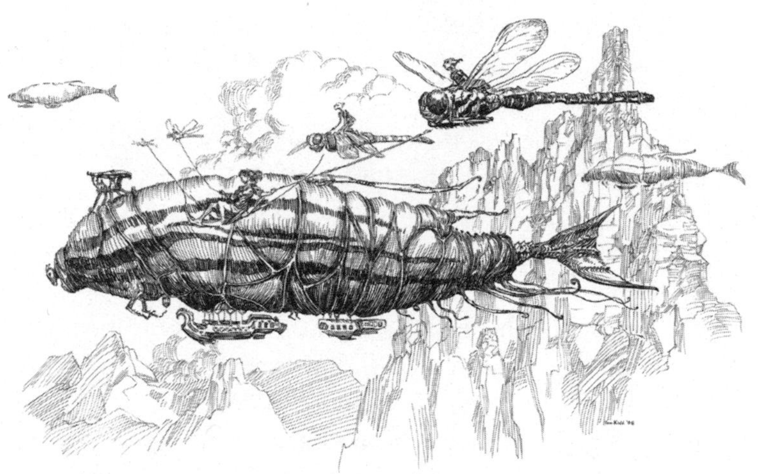

The morning the Nose of Memory arrived to destroy his calm, the Wizard Sarnod rose as on any other day late in the life of the Dying Earth. He donned his sea-green robes woven from the scales of a monstrous fish and stared out the window that graced the top of his tower. Soon, he would descend for his daily breakfast of salamanders—one served cold for memory, one served hot for his heart, and one served living for his brain—but first he sought the selfish comfort of surveying his lands.

The tower stood upon an island that lay at the center of Lake Bakeel, fed by a lingering finger of the Derna River. Beyond the lake lay the gnarled forests and baleful grasslands through which none, not even erb or Deodand, traveled without his knowledge or permission. Despite this mastery, Sarnod found that each new morning for more than a year had brought an unease, like a hook in his heart, accompanied by a strange thirst. He seemed always dry, his skin itchy and taut. The bowl of water he kept in his chambers did not help. The fresh, moist smell of the lake beyond came through the window like a thing physical, more threatening than the giant fish that roamed beneath its dark surface.

Sarnod lived alone in the tower but for the companionship of his two servants, both of whom he had ensorcelled to his need, using in part his own blood to bind or build them. The first was named Whisper Bird Oblique Beak, and the creature was always somewhere in the room with him, a subtle guardian of his person. The life of Whisper Bird had a poetry to it beyond Sarnod's ken, the poetry of silence. Whisper Bird lived invisible and remote, Sarnod's conversation with him ever terse yet ethereal.

At that moment, Whisper Bird spoke in Sarnod's ear, startling him. Whisper Bird said, "On the golden dais beneath The Mouth a creature has appeared from Below."

"A creature from the UNDERHIND? Impossible," Sarnod said.

"And yet…probable," Whisper Bird replied.

Just as there was an Over Earth, so too there were various Under Earths, one of which, nameless or unspeakable, Sarnod had found and harnessed to his will. He called it simply UNDERHIND, in the Speech of De-emphasis, because it was tiny, and there all the enemies he had punished lived miniaturized amid honeycombs of tunnels and caverns in the full knowledge, as Sarnod liked to think, of the enormity of their defeat.

"I will investigate," Sarnod said, and as if in response Whisper Bird passed through him to the door in a wave of cold and heat that made him shudder—*what manner of ghost, what manner of being, had he harnessed?*

Together, man visible and creature invisible, they went to see what had thus intruded on their daily ritual.

EVERY MORNING, Sarnod's other servant, T'sais Prime, prepared his breakfast of salamanders. But this morning, Sarnod's salamanders—green-glowing, plucked from the rich mud of the lake—lay forgotten on the kitchen counter, eyeless (for Sarnod did not like to see his food staring at him). The sounds of breathing came from the Seeing Hall beyond, where stood The Mouth and the golden dais.

The Mouth had been part of the tower long before Sarnod had taken up residence there. The two unblinking eyes above its inscrutable lips Sarnod himself had created—each a portal to a section of the UNDERHIND. Just as he did not like his food staring at him, he did not like a mouth without eyes. Under Sarnod's thaumaturgies, The Mouth now functioned also as a secret portal back from the UNDERHIND.

The Mouth had spoken only three times.

The first time it had said, "Beware the falsehood of memory."

The second time it had said, "What man can truly know but you?"

The third time it had said, "The fish rots from the head."

Little else had ever come out of it but stenches and perfumes. Until now.

IN THE ancient Seeing Hall, The Mouth and golden dais lay at the far end. To the left hung the huge circle of a shimmering window, through which the lake and sky reflected against the white marble in a myriad shades of blue.

Near the dais, T'sais Prime watched over the intruder. Her pale, dark-haired presence both loosened the hook in his heart and sent it mercilessly deep. Arms folded, she stared down at the dais with a blank look. T'sais Prime was the reflection of a woman created in the vats from tales and potions brought from far-distant Embelyon. Nothing of that reflection had ever been his, for she did not want him, and he chose not to coerce her, nor even inform her as to her true nature. She seemed to have none of the passion and fire of the original—some aspect of the formula he'd failed to master and which continued to elude him.

As guarded in her way as Whisper Bird was in his, T'sais only raised one eyebrow upon Sarnod's approach. That her expression was always half wistful, half sullen, pained him. She was the last from the now-cold vats; frustrated by his failures, Sarnod had turned his energies elsewhere.

"What is this thing that has come to us?" Sarnod asked.

"It has no head and yet it lives," T'sais said. "It lives, but why?"

"It entered with a blast of cold yet hot air," Whisper Bird said from somewhere to Sarnod's left.

Sarnod drew nearer. What T'sais had caught was trapped under a large bell jar upon the gold dais.

Sarnod took out a magnifying glass from his robes. He had found it in the tower, and like everything in the tower it had its own mind. As he trained the glass on the creature, the oval grew cloudy, then clear, the handle suddenly hot. The thing indeed had no head. It had no eyes. It had no mouth. Although Sarnod looked square upon it, the thing seemed to lose focus, move to the corner of his vision. He thought it was curled up, then longer, like a stretching cat.

A strange thought came to him, from memories far distant, almost not his own: of a dusty book, turned to a certain page.

Sarnod said the thought aloud: "It is called the Nose of Memory. It brings a message of a kind."

"Shall we destroy it?" Whisper Bird breathed from near Sarnod and then far away.

But Sarnod held up a hand in abeyance. "Let us see what it may offer, first. I will protect us from any harm it might bring." The unease in Sarnod's heart beat as steady as ever, but he realized he shared T'sais' malaise. This intrusion made him curious.

"Are you ready, Whisper Bird?" The animating principle behind Whisper Bird, Sarnod believed, had been both owl and heron—one watchful, one motionless, both deadly when called upon.

As T'sais stood back, Whisper Bird said, "Yesssss" from over Sarnod's left shoulder. For once, he did not flinch.

Sarnod put away the magnifying glass and surrounded the bell jar with a Spell of True Sizing.

Up, up, up came the Nose of Memory in all of its headless glory, rising and rising until it lay lolling over the sides of the dais, squat and grey and placid, about the size of a worry dog and wearing the bell jar as an awkward, teetering hat. It smelled in an unsatisfactory way of milk and herbs and brine.

Now the Nose of Memory at least resembled its name: a huge nose with five nostrils, completing, in a way, the face on the wall. It lay there for a moment, long enough for Sarnod to step forward. Then it snorted in such a thunderous fashion that even Sarnod flinched.

"Do nothing, Whisper Bird," Sarnod said, readying a spell of No Effect for what might come after.

Through one nostril and then the next and the next, until all five had ruptured, the Nose of Memory sent messages in a brittle blue smoke, writ in curling letters that, once smelled by Sarnod, blossomed into images in his mind. As the tendrils of smoke grew in length, came together, and began to form clouds, the Nose of Memory grew smaller and smaller until it resided somewhere between its unexpected largeness and its former smallness, and then became just a limp, lifeless deformity.

The smoke brought with it such severe memories that Sarnod forgot his readied spell, and wept, though his countenance remained stern. For he saw Vendra, created to be his lover, and his brother Gandreel, who had betrayed Sarnod with her. The memory lay like a crush of sour fruit in his mouth: intense, clear, and yet fast-fading.

Sarnod had cherished them both, had welcomed Gandreel to his tower after long absence in the service of Rathkar the Lizard King, only to find the two, several weeks later, by the shores of the lake, amid a grove of trees, locked in a carnal embrace. His wrath had turned the surface of the lake to flame. His sadness had changed it to ice, and then the numbness in his heart had restored all to what it had been before.

After, against their pleading, their weeping, Sarnod had banished them to the levels of the UNDERHIND. As with all of his enemies, he used his spells of Being Small, Pretending Small, Staying There, and Forgetting the Past for a Time. Into the UNDERHIND they had gone, and there they had now remained for many years.

Eruptions of hatred had scarred his heart ever since, had disturbed his sleep, made him lash out at every living thing that moved across plains and forest, many a traveler finding himself taken up by a vast, invisible hand and set down several leagues hence, usually in a much worsened condition.

But now, with the vapor of the past so vividly renewing the sharpness of his former love, his former joy, two pains massaged the hook in his heart. The pain physical presaged death. The pain mental presaged the birth of regret, for he had performed many terrible and vengeful deeds throughout his life, even if some seemed to have been committed by another self.

It had been, he realized, a long and lonely time without Vendra and Gandreel, the vats cold and useless, the world outside become stranger and more dangerous. With his desire for the one and his love for the other rose again a parched feeling—a burning need for the cleansing water of the lake. For a moment, he wanted to dive through the great window of the Seeing Hall and into the lake, there to be free.

"You are Sarnod the mighty wizard. That is not in your nature," he said, aloud.

"This we have now heard," Whisper Bird replied, with a hint of warning. "After many minutes of peculiar silence."

"Who could have sent this?" Sarnod asked. A sense of helplessness came over him with the voicing of the question.

"Master, shall we be spared the extent of your not-knowing?" Whisper Bird said, almost apologetically.

T'sais Prime sighed, said, "I am working on a tapestry that requires my attention. May I leave now?"

"Enough!" Sarnod said, rallying his resolve. "It matters not how it was sent or why, just what we should *send back* to the UNDERHIND."

"What can we send back?" T'sais Prime asked in a dull voice.

"*You*," he said, pointing at her. "And *you*," he continued, pointing in the vicinity of where he thought Whisper Bird might be lurking. "Each of you I shall send to the place that best suits your nature. You will find and bring back the woman Vendra and the man who is my brother, Gandreel, long-banished to the UNDERHIND." Then added, in warning: "*Them and them alone*—any other brought back shall perish in the journey! A prison the UNDERHIND is and a prison it shall remain."

Whisper Bird said only, "You will have to make us small."

"I have always liked the size I am," T'sais Prime said, "and the work I have been doing." Sarnod knew she labored solely on tapestries, which she created only because he had placed a spell of Fascination with Detail upon her.

Whisper Bird said something resigned in a language so ancient that Sarnod could not understand it, but it sounded like a creaking gate on a desolate plain.

Sarnod ignored them both equally and, using the half-senile machines that lived in the skin of the tower, made them see the images of Vendra and Gandreel, gone long before he had made T'sais and ensorcelled Whisper Bird. Then he gave them the power to project those images into the minds of any they might meet in their journeys. Then he made T'sais small. Whisper Bird had already reduced himself, and, in that form, was almost visible: a sunspot floating in the corner of the eye.

As they stood tiny on the golden dais looking up at him, Sarnod gave Whisper Bird and T'sais each three spells to use.

"Be wary of my brother Gandreel," he told them, "for he too was once a sorcerer, if of a minor sort, and he will have found ways to harness those around him to his will. As for Vendra, beware her guile.

"Know too that the minutes may pass differently for you in the UNDERHIND. What is a half-hour for me here may be a year for you, and thus you may return after much adventure to find it has been but a single day for me." Miniaturization was an uncertain thaumaturgy and it made mischievous play with time.

Sarnod levitated each in turn, and spun each without protest into one of the two open eyes—and thus into the UNDERHIND.

After they were gone, The Mouth grimaced and said, "Much may be lost in the seeking."

The hook in Sarnod's heart drove deeper.

The Nose of Memory, now akin to a canvas sack filled with soggy bones, expelled one last sigh.

WHISPER BIRD neither felt nor cared to feel the foetid closeness of the level of the UNDERHIND known to some as the Place of Mushrooms and Silence—this continuous cave with its monstrous bone-white lobsters waiting in dank water for the unwary; its thick canopy of green-and-purple-and-gray fungus that listened and watched; its bats and rats and blind carnivorous pigs; its huge and rapacious worms like wingless dragons, all of it boiled in a pervasive stench of decay, all lit by a pale emerald luminescence that seemed more akin to the bottom of the sea.

Invisible he might be otherwise, but not soundless, not smell-less, and thus his nerves were on edge. Even his invisibility itself was an illusion, an effect of the spell that had robbed him of his human form and condemned him to live not just on the Dying Earth but in far Embelyon simultaneously—so that he walked forever in two places at once, neither here nor there, his body like an image seen in twinned rows of mirrors facing each other down a long corridor. Even now, as he searched for the man and woman Sarnod had so ruthlessly banished from his life, a part of Whisper Bird explored the plains and forests of Embelyon.

Surrounded by so many watchful ears attached to dangerous bodies, Whisper Bird slowed his thoughts and stretched out his fear so thin that he could barely feel it. Thus fortifie, he continued on until, finally, he became uncomfortably aware of a rising hum, a distant sound that trembled through the ground carried by the uncanny whispers of the creatures around him. The sound marched closer and closer, resolved into the words "*bloat toad*," repeated again and again like a warning or chant.

Around him now floated great white fungal boweries that laid down lines like jellyfish trawling for the unwary and wounded. *A cloud of whipping mushroom tendrils. A pyramid of screaming flesh.* Moving within their poison sting unharmed were horrible visps and also corpse-white gaun: long-limbed, strong, be-fanged, stalking through the perpetual night.

Invoking his first spell, Phandaal's Litany of Silent Coercion, he brought a gaun close and projected the images of Gandreel and Vendra into it.

Have you seen either one?

The gaun's thoughts—like spiders with tiny moist bodies and long, barbed legs—made him shudder: *I will rend you limb-from-limb. I will call my brothers and sisters, and we will feast on your flesh.*

Whisper Bird repeated his question and felt the gaun's brain constrict from the force of the spell.

Beyond this cavern, beyond the corridor that follows, beyond the Bloat Toad, in the village there, you will find what you seek.

What is the Bloat Toad? Whisper Bird asked.

It is both your riddle and your answer, the gaun replied.

What does this mean?

But the gaun just laughed, and Whisper Bird, not wishing to suffer the retaliation of its fast-approaching brethren, Suggested that the creature batter its head against the corridor wall until it was dead, and then moved on through the darkness.

All around him now came the vibration of a discordant music fashioned from muttered thoughts, rising full-throated and deep from the dark: *bloattoad bloattoad bloattoad.*

IF WHISPER Bird must go slow and silent, so T'sais Prime must go fast and quick, and if never a bird had she been, it would have been to her benefit to be one. She arrived in the UNDERHIND known as The Place of Maddening Glass after "nightfall," when only the faint green glow from far above signaled the ceiling of this place, the light bleeding off from the level above, where Whisper Bird labored in his quest as she in hers. She was surrounded by a hundred thousand jagged gleaming surfaces—cracked sheets of mirror, giant purple-tinged cusps—reflecting such a welter of images that she could not tell what was real and what was not.

Ghoul bears and Deodands were fast-approaching, hot to her scent. Not built for the adventure of close combat, T'sais used her first spell, of Flying Travel, to summon Twk-Men. They descended from the sky on their dragonflies, here as large as small dragons.

Four bore her upward upon a raft of twigs lashed together and set between them, the space between the flickering dance of the dragonflies' wings so slight that T'sais thought they must surely overlap, and, out of rhythm, plummet to the jagged surface. But they did not.

At first, the Twk-Men seemed so solicitous and friendly that she wondered aloud why they had been banished to this place.

"I dared to ask for a thimbleful more of sugar for giving Sarnod information on his enemies," said one.

"I dared to fly over the lake while he watched," said the second. "It was summer and I was feeling lazy and desired to skim the surface, dip my dragonfly's wings into the water."

"I cannot remember why I am here," said the third. "But it seems not that much different than being on the surface. We die here and we die there, and though we cannot see the true sun, we know it dies, too."

The fourth Twk-Man, the leader of them all, would have none of her questions, though, and asked, "Whither do you go, and why, and do you have a pinch of salt for us?"

"I am seeking these two exiles," T'sais Prime replied, and projected the images of Vendra and Gandreel into all four minds of the Twk-Men, which set them to talking amongst themselves in the lightning-fast speech typical of their kind.

"We know one of them. The woman," the lead Twk-Man said. "How much salt will you give us to be led to her?"

T'sais' heart leapt, for she did not wish to spend longer in this place than necessary.

"A pinch of salt here is either a boulder, or, if it came with me, too small even for you to barter for," T'sais Prime said. "You will have to content yourself with the compulsion of the spell."

"Fair enough," the Twk-Man said, although he did not sound happy, and the buzz of his dragonfly's wings became louder.

"Where can I find her, Twk-Man?"

The Twk-Man laughed. "She lies upon a raft carried through the air by four unfortunate Twk-Men."

"Surely this is some form of joke," T'sais Prime said.

"Perhaps the joke is played on you," the Twk-Man said grimly. "Perhaps your quest is different than you think."

"Tend to your flying, and take me somewhere safe, lest I unleash another spell," T'sais said, although she needed to hoard all that Sarnod had given her.

Smiling savagely, the Twk-Man turned in his saddle and held up a mirror to T'sais' face. "In this place Sarnod has banished us to, we all see each others' faces everywhere. But perhaps in your world, you cannot see yourself?"

And it was true, she saw with shock—how could she not have realized it before?—Sarnod's former lover shared every element and description of her own face. Was she sent, then, by trickery into her own oblivion, or was there truly a quest for a Vendra, for a Gandreel?

"I do not like your tricks, Twk-Man," T'sais said. "I do not like them at all."

"It is a dark night," the Twk-Man said, "to fall so far, should your spell fade before we leave you."

THE ILL-FATED gaun proved truthful in his directions. No bigger than a man's fist, the Bloat Toad sat in the middle of a vast and empty cavern that was covered with dull red splotches and smelled vaguely of spoiled meat. In Whisper Bird's imagination, the Bloat Toad had been as large as a brontotaubus and twice as deadly. In fact, except for its glowing gold eyes and the prism of blue-and-green that strobed over its be-pimpled skin, the Bloat Toad looked ordinary.

Whisper Bird stood in front of the creature in that cathedral of dust motes and dry air: invisible shadow confronting placable foe.

It stared back at him.

Was it oddly larger now?

Or was Whisper Bird smaller?

Whisper Bird took a step to the side of the Bloat Toad, and as his foot came down—

KRAAAOOCK

—was lifted up by the leathery skin of an amphibian suddenly rendered enormous—and smashed against the side of the cavern. All the breath went out of Whisper Bird's delicate chest. Even though he existed in two places at once, it still hurt like a hundred knives. The Bloat Toad's tough but doughy flesh, which stank of long-forgotten swamps, held him in place for several horrible moments.

Then the pressure went away. Whisper Bird fell limply to the ground.

When he had recovered, Whisper Bird saw that the Bloat Toad sat once more in the center of the room. The toad was again small, strobing green-blue, blue-green.

Now Whisper Bird understood the nature of the splotches on the walls. Had he existed in just this one world, he would already be dead.

After many minutes of reflection and recovery, twice more Whisper Bird tried to pass the Bloat Toad—once creeping stealthy, once running fast without guile. Twice more, impervious to accompanying spells and with croak victorious, the Bloat Toad filled the cavern, re-crushing Whisper Bird. Until it felt to him as though he were a bag of sand, and the sand was all sliding out of a hole.

Bent at a wretched angle, hobbling, and badly shaken, he eventually stood once more before the Bloat Toad.

Now, in the extremity of his pain, Whisper Bird turned as much of his attention as he could to his second self in Embelyon, experiencing its forests, its rippling fields that changed color to reflect the sky. There, his family, wife and infant son, had lived in a cottage in a glade deep in the forest where they grew food in a garden and counted themselves lucky to be beneath the notice of the mighty princes and wizards who struggled for dominion over all. They did not care that the Earth was dying, but only that they were living. Who knew now how old his son was, whether there were streaks of gray in his wife's hair? Nor whether either would recognize him as human.

At some future moment, Whisper Bird might be whole and be once more with them, but for that he must move past this moment *now.*

As before, Whisper Bird stared at the Bloat Toad and the Bloat Toad stared at Whisper Bird.

"Do you talk, I wonder, Bloat Toad? Are you mindless or mind-full? Is there nothing that will move you?" Whisper Bird said, already flinching in anticipation of his words activating the toad's power.

But Bloat Toad cared no more for words than for the particulars of Whisper Bird's servitude. The creature stared up at Whisper Bird and made a smug croaking sound. *Kraaoock…*

A more direct soul would have tried to smash the Bloat Toad to death with a hammer and danced on his pulped remains. But Whisper Bird had no such weapon; all he had as a tool was his ghostly assassin-like *absence*.

And this gave him an idea, for Whisper Bird *could* split himself again if he so chose, an act of will only possible because he held the knowledge of his Essential Sundering within him like a half-healed wound.

Thus decided, Whisper Bird stood in front of the Bloat Toad—and leapt to both sides at once, like two identical wings with no body between them. It felt like deciding to die.

Bloat Toad, rising with incredible speed, gave out a confused croak—each eye following a different Whisper Bird—and *winked out of existence*.

OVER THE plains of broken glass, the Twk-Men took T'sais Prime. Soon, she understood the true nature of the glass, and why none lived amongst it for very long. Each shard had captured and now reflected the light of some more ancient time, which played out in an insanity of fractured prisms. As they traveled, she saw laid out below her, and identified for her by the Twk-Men, the Gardens of Mazirian, a raging Thrang the Ghoul Bear, impossibly large, and Sadlark in battle against the demon Underherd. She saw Kutt the Mad King leading his menagerie of magically created monsters, Kolghut's Tower of Frozen Blood, and, most terribly, a forever-replicating scene over many leagues, of Golickan Kodek the Conqueror's infamous pillaging of the people of Bautiku and subsequent creation of a squirming pyramid of human flesh five hundred feet tall. And, yes, eventually, though she chose to ignore them, many reflections of her own self, some tiny, some huge and monstrous, bestriding the landscape below, brought out from the crazed glass. After awhile, T'sais' initial horror gave way to such fascination that she could not bear to look down, as if her interest was unwholesome.

"What happens to those who walk the surface?" she asked the Twk-Men as they struggled with their burden. They were headed for what looked like a series of dull, irregular clouds on the horizon.

"They go mad," one replied.

"They become what they see," another said.

"They forget to eat or drink."

"They perish, believing all the time that they dine in the banquet hall of Kandive the Golden or are whispering in the ear of Turjan the Sorcerer."

"How did Sarnod create the glass?"

The lead Twk-Man laughed in an unpleasant way. "That is beyond Sarnod's ken. The glass is all that remains of the all-seeing Orb of Parassis, shattered in the War of the Underhinds. Sarnod's luck is that it inhabits his prison, making the lives of vanquished enemies worse by far than without."

"And yet," T'sais replied, "the glass illumines the UNDERHIND."

Day and night had no meaning in a world with no sun, dying or otherwise. Everything around them existed in a state of perpetual dawn or dusk, depending on the brilliance of the broken glass. The bright flashes of gold and green beneath them as ancient wars were fought, courtly dances re-enacted, and ghost-galleys sailed long dry oceans, now created a kind of weak sunrise.

Soon, T'sais saw that ahead of them the clouds had become strange oblong balloons that moved, their tan hides pulsing, tiny limbs sticking out from the sides, heads mere dots. "Floating mermelants," the Twk-Men called them, and, strapped to these creatures by means of ropes and cables and pulleys, were the frames of ships, canisters, balconies, and baskets. Even more peculiar, a vast tangled garden of flowers, vines, and vegetables hung from the moist moss-lined hull of each airship.

"Who are they, the people who live here?" T'sais asked.

"Raiders and builders and gardeners," the head Twk-Man replied. "Murderers and bandits and farmers and sky sailors."

"How can they be all of these things?"

The Twk-Man smiled grimly. "To be sent here, you must be a rogue of some kind, but to live here you must become something else."

"What if I do not desire to be taken there?" A sudden sense of helplessness overwhelmed her, despite her spells. To be beholden to the Twk-Men irked her, but to be dependent on strangers not bound to her will would be worse.

"You have no choice. We will not take you by air raft across this entire world; we will risk your already weakening spell if you do not free us. Besides, these people roam everywhere."

So saying, they increased their speed and soon left her on the deck of one of the ships, the living balloon above snorting and expelling strong yet sweet-smelling gasses.

The ship's captain waited for her, his crew of ruffians hanging back, although whether from respect or caution, T'sais did not know.

The Captain had two eye patches over his left eye, as if whatever lay hidden there had need of further restraint. The remaining light blue eye made him look younger than his years. A thick black beard covered much of his face. He had the wide, muscular build she favored in a man, and he smelled not unpleasantly of pipe tobacco.

Just as T'sais found it difficult to forget that the living creature above her was all that kept the ship from plummeting to the broken glass below, so too it was difficult to forget that in her world the Captain was smaller than a thimble.

"Welcome to hell," he said, unsmiling.

"Welcome to a spell," T'sais replied, with a passion that surprised her—and cast Panguirre's Triumphant Displasms, meaning to bind him to her.

But the Captain merely chuckled and removed one of his eye patches, whereupon the spell bounced back upon her and she felt an overwhelming urge to obey the Captain's every desire.

"Do not make me remove the other eye patch," he told her, although not without a certain humor.

Looking him in his one good eye, fighting the spell even as it mastered her, she asked, "Why? Will I die?"

"No," the Captain said, "but you would be so revolted by what lives in my eye that you would not sit down to dinner with me."

SOON, BEYOND the cavern guarded by the now curiously absent Bloat Toad, Whisper Bird came upon the outskirts of the village where the gaun had said he would find his quarry. The space above extended so far that the distant rock ceiling, glowing green from vast and mindless lichens, was little more than a conjecture. Things, though, could be seen moving there, in shapes that made Whisper Bird wary.

The village itself he at first thought had been built among the old bones of long-dead monsters. But he soon came to understand that it was built *from* those bones. For this site had clearly seen much violence, if violence distant in time. Amid teetering bone houses traveled such inhabitants as dared leave shelter. Too pale they were, and most so long remaining there that through the generations they had become blind, their eye sockets sunken, their ears batlike, their nostrils huge with secret scenting. They walked slowly and made no noise in doing so, trembling with each step in a way Whisper Bird could not decipher, whether from inbreeding or a terror from anticipation at every step of some unknown predator.

In the middle of the village square, an old man sat sightless atop the skull of some grotesque beast with three eyes and oversized fangs. He wore a beard of pale purple lichen, and the hair on his head swayed, made from tendrils of thin white mushrooms. His robes rippled, and Whisper Bird, shuddering, did not like to look upon them for long.

Whisper Bird came up beside him and said, "Do not be afraid. I seek only a man or a woman." He projected the images into the old man's mind. "Do you know them?"

The old man laughed. "Do you know who and what I am? With a flick of my fingers I could kill you. With a thought, your life extinguished."

"Then proceed, certainly, if that is your desire," Whisper Bird said. "But while we are exchanging useless threats: I could relieve you of the burden you call a life with the same effort it requires to stand here asking, again, *do you know this man, this woman*?"

"I am adept at sensing the invisible by now, creature," the man replied, ignoring Whisper Bird. "I can see your outline in my mind, and you are neither man nor bird but some combination of both."

"Do not call me creature," Whisper Bird said.

"Well, then, Not-Creature," the old man said, "did you know that you are a door?'

"Do not call me that, either," Whisper Bird said. He was tired. His body feasted on sunlight and sunlight existed only in the other world, not here. Here there was only a dull, thick soup of almost-light. His thoughts had become slow and looping on the one half, fast and bright on the other.

"But you *are* a door, Not-Creature," the old man said, laughing. "You have forgotten that. Even without my sight, I can see it: Embelyon, shining through you. As whither the Bloat Toad went, until recently the protector of this village."

"You know of the Bloat Toad?" Whisper Bird asked, caught by surprise.

"A wise man might suspect I am the one who positioned him there as a watchdog against our enemies."

"My belief in you is not strong," Whisper Bird said. "In any part of your story."

The old man ignored Whisper Bird, and said: "If you were to hold still long enough, I could escape this place through you. Leap through your body to the other side and come out breathing Embelyon's air."

"Even if what you say is true, old man," Whisper Bird said, "you would arrive the same size as an ant, and with the same fate. Would you escape only to be stepped on by the first mouse that crossed your path?"

The old man laughed again. "True words. Ah, but for that glimpse of sunlight, for that glimpse of the surface, perhaps a few moments would be enough."

"I will not hold still long enough, I promise you," Whisper Bird said. The thought of his body as a door disturbed him more than he could express.

"Is it not painful to live thusly?" the old man asked.

"Next you will see a barbed feather through your heart if you are not careful."

A fierce chuckle from the old man. "With such unkindly talk as that to spur me on, what choice have I but to use you as a door and then *close* you."

Whisper Bird felt a pressure in his head, a ringing and an echo, and though neither he nor the man moved, a great battle went on between their minds. More than usual, he bridged two sides of a widening divide, being forced opened against his will. Armies of thought met on dark plains and the frenzied, purifying fire of war erupted in the space between them.

DINNER DID not much resemble T'sais's expectations of it. Two lieutenants escorted her, still spell-dazed and trapped in thoughts of deep obedience to the Captain, to a cabin lined with shelves of ancient parchments and books. The books had an unkind legacy, having been scavenged from exiled travelers trapped, mad, and dead, upon the broken glass below. (Much later, she would say to him, "You must have knowledge of many spells," only for him to reply, "not all books are filled with spells, my love. Nor is a man wise to rely overmuch on them.")

Thick round windows on the left side of the cabin revealed the sky in flashes of deep greens, blues, and purples. There was a hint of spice in the air that came from the moss growing through the hulls. Always, too, there came from above and through the timbers a sound both slow and calm: the measured hum that was the breathing of the mermelant.

Worn tables and chairs that had seen long and constant service stood in the middle of the cabin. A map of the dying Earth lay upon one such table, and next to that, another map with much of its surface blank, sketches and notes in the margin. This was a map of the UNDERHIND as the Captain knew it, she would later discover.

A third table held evidence of much industry and preparation in the form of a feast of strange fowl, along with vegetables and mushrooms grown in the ship's hull. The savory smell nearly distracted her from the object of her unnatural adoration.

Once seated at this third table, the two lieutenants disappearing through an oval wooden door, the Captain released her from the reversed spell. Her heartbeat slowed and she could gaze upon the books, the chairs, the windows, without the need to always return her attention to the Captain.

Replacing his eye patch, the Captain said, "I will not take it off again so long as you never cast a second spell. Should you break this rule, I will have you thrown over the side. It is a long way to fall."

"So I have been told," T'sais said, utterly defeated. "I am thankful to you for that kindness."

To which the Captain nodded, then replied, "And I am thankful you have accepted my invitation to this simple dinner, which now demands my full attention."

Tucking a napkin into his shirt, the Captain said no more for a time as he availed himself of the pleasures of moist drumsticks and steaming potatoes, of crispy skin and boiled mushrooms. T'sais had to admit to herself that despite being plain it was delicious.

As to what else she should admit, T'sais was unsure. She knew not if she were all prisoner, part prisoner and part guest, or all guest—nor knew how much to tell of her purpose, especially with just one spell left to her name. So instead, she sipped from a wine both bitter and pleasant and watched the Captain unleash the force of his passions upon his meal. He was as different from Sarnod as anyone could be, and having had only knowledge of Sarnod for many years, the Captain both puzzled and fascinated her. That his men respected him was certain, and yet she had also seen that he laid no hand upon them nor spoke harshly to them.

Finally, the Captain finished to his satisfaction, wiping his mouth and allowing the plates to be cleared away.

"It is not often that we find such a stranger in our midst," the Captain said. "Those not native to this place are sent here by the wizard Sarnod and driven mad by the glass long before we ever find them. So I am curious, you who have given your name as T'sais Prime, through what manner of intent do you come to us? Armed with spells, upon a sky raft, escorted by no less than four Twk Men. There is much in this that puzzles me. Puzzlement is sometimes my lot, but puzzlement that puts this fleet in danger I do not tolerate. Should I be concerned?"

During this speech, the Captain held her gaze much longer than necessary, in a manner she would come to desire. But in that moment, at that first dinner, she felt under assault. Should she lie? And yet, if she withheld the truth now, what was left for her?

She stared back into the Captain's good eye and told him, "I seek Vendra, a woman whose appearance I share, and a man named Gandreel.

I would show them to you by projecting both into your mind, but this you might believe to be a spell cast upon you."

A smile from the Captain, a clear need to suppress greater mirth. "This is true—I might indeed consider such an unnatural intrusion to be a spell. Let us leave aside this question of what you seek. *Why* do you seek? Who, if anyone, *compels* you to seek?"

Now his regard had become so serious that T'sais, even released from the spell, gave herself over to the full truth.

"Sarnod," she admitted.

Did his demeanor darken? She could not tell.

"And what will you do when you have found either or both?"

"I am to bring them with me and leave this place."

"What if I asked you to take me instead?"

The Captain's presence across the table from her seemed suddenly to have more weight, more need, and she was terrified.

"I could not do so, even if I wished," she replied. "Any other would die on the journey. Sarnod has said it is so."

What now would he do to her? And yet the Captain did nothing, except recede into his seat a little, visibly diminished. He sighed. "It is of no import. I could not leave my crew behind; I am all but wedded to them now."

Her fear revealed as foolish, T'sais became angry, said, "As for questions, how then did you come to lose your eye?"

"Eh?" the Captain said. "I did not *lose* it. It was *taken* from me."

"What replaced it?"

He ignored her, said, "Sarnod *took* my eye. And banished me with my crew to this place. Over long years now, we have birthed more mermelants and added to the fleet. Sought escape. Although it never comes." For a moment, he looked old to her.

But she had her answer. Or thought she did. "Then I am now your prisoner."

The Captain replied with no small amount of weariness. "Revenge is for fools—and revenge by proxy worse foolishness still. You are a tool, T'sais. I am more concerned by the thought of what this *means*. This life is already dangerous, and we know not where we are or where it ends, though I have pledged the rest of my days to an answer. Perhaps you are part of that answer...or merely more of Sarnod's trickery."

Something in those words brought T'sais close to tears, although she fought them.

"I did not mean to distress you without cause," he said.

"My distress comes entirely from this place," she said. "Have you not seen all of the likenesses of me in the broken glass?"

"They are difficult to dismiss."

"They trouble me. I am just a reflection of a reflection, and not truly my self."

"And yet," the Captain said with sudden softness, his voice like a silken glove, "they have only made me more curious to encounter the image in the flesh."

"The kindness of that does not make me the least less troubled," she said. "But knowledge might. Do you know my lineage?'

"As it happens, I do," the Captain said, "from the books that surround us." He thus proceeded to tell her the story of T'sais and T'sain and all that had happened to them, of Turjan too, and his quest. He was a good storyteller, she thought as she listened, to be horrified and enthralled all at once, to want to know and yet not to know.

When he had finished and they sat once again across from each other and not within the ancient and mysterious world of Embelyon conjured up by the Captain, T'sais said in rising protest, "but I am *nothing* like what you describe."

"Are you sure?" That one light-blue eye seemed determined to lay bare her very core with its intensity.

"Certain enough."

Whereupon the Captain drew a blade from his boot and tossed it past her left ear. To her surprise, she caught it by the hilt as if born to it.

"That was luck," she said.

Whereupon he hurled an apple at her, which she impaled upon the blade, felt the weight of it held there, red and wounded.

"Yes," the Captain said. "Luck. If that word has some meaning other than the one I know."

She frowned. "This I do not want. It is not me," she said, and realizing it was true dropped the blade, apple bouncing across the floor.

The Captain reached across the table and took her hand in his. He had a callused hand, a rough hand, and she liked the feel of it.

"Sometimes," he said, "it is enough to *know* what one has hidden within them. It need not be *used* to be of use."

T'sais Prime stared at him as if he had said the one true thing in all the world.

The Captain rose, releasing her.

"Tomorrow," he said, "you will join our crew and I will assist you in your quest. As you will assist in ours. For, alas, I know where the one you seek can be found."

AS BATTLE raged, ebbed and flowed, the pressure in Whisper Bird's mind an intolerable weight, something inside of him began to burn where nothing had burned before, and he flung his voice into the void and cried out in anguish, and wrenched away the man's influence.

"*I am a door for no one*!"

The sound of Whisper Bird's voice was so loud that it made the slow folk around them seek shelter amid the discolored bones.

Before him, the old man slumped forward, sighed, and admitted to defeat. "I have studied much, I have studied long, for what else is there to do here, and yet it is not enough, I think."

Whisper Bird saw that the conflict had burned off the man's beard. The cloudy film had left his eyes, and he was staring right at and into Whisper Bird. Only now did Whisper Bird recognize the depth of the disguise.

"How could I not know earlier?"

Gandreel smiled. "Even you sometimes see only that which is visible."

"Apparently. Or I am not myself."

"What is it like now, in the tower?" Gandreel asked. "I remember it as a happy place, at times. When Sarnod was gone visiting the far reaches of his domain, Vendra and I would feast with the people of nearby villages. The tower conjured up for us never-ending food and wine. The music was most joyful."

"It is as it ever was."

"How is my brother?"

"Your brother has suffered a change of heart. He wishes for you to return with me."

"Ha, how you jest!" Gandreel said. "I have lost Vendra because of him and been reduced to bending my sad environs to my will. My brother is vengeful and banishment is the least of his trespasses upon the Dying

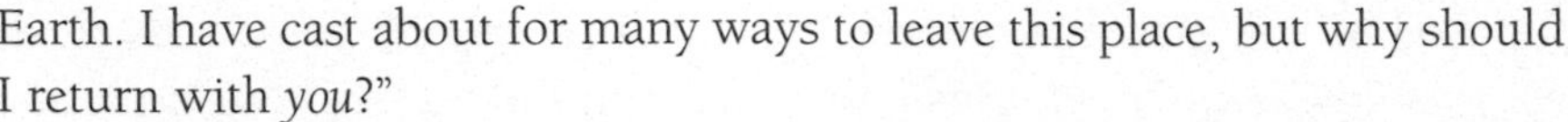

Earth. I have cast about for many ways to leave this place, but why should I return with *you*?"

Whisper Bird sighed. "I am but an unwilling servant with no special affection for Sarnod, who would avaunt to Embelyon and be whole and reunited with his family."

"Will your family recognize you now?" Gandreel whispered, although all attempt at stealth seemed foolish after Whisper Bird's great cry.

"I will make them recognize me," Whisper Bird said, and shuddered, for he realized that they might never recognize him, not in the way he wished, or that they might already be dead.

Gandreel looked away, as if Whisper Bird had said something impossibly sad. "I will come with you," Gandreel said. "And we will meet our fates together. I can see the portal leading back to Sarnod, but am only able to send *things* through it, not myself. This will not change"

"Was it you then who sent the Nose of Memory?" Whisper Bird asked.

Gandreel nodded. "Yes, in my stead, that it might change Sarnod's mind. And, perhaps, from what you say, with success."

"Be that as it may, we must now leave swiftly," Whisper Bird said, who heard disturbing sounds fast approaching. "I have awakened much from slumber."

"Yes, this is undeniably true, and more reason still to leave."

Lurching toward them, from the far-above ceiling, came all the deadly creatures of that place, to which Whisper Bird's cry had been as loud as the sound of a cliff falling into the sea.

Whisper Bird said the Spell of Unassailable Speed and led Gandreel out of that place.

FOR THREE months, two of them as lovers, T'sais Prime and the Captain, who one night whispered his true name to her, traveled across the land of Maddening Glass. For three months, they sought yet never found, with no hint of the woman Vendra but of her essential self always too many; she had only to look down to be aware of ghosts. For three months, she did not guess that the Captain might be delaying their arrival at her destination. There was much to distract her.

Alone together in bed after a frenzied conjoining, her head upon the Captain's hairy belly, T'sais Prime would ask him, "Why should you have me when there are so many other me's?"

And he would whisper more quietly than Whisper Bird, "Because you are the only T'sais Prime. This little fuzz upon the back of your neck that I like to kiss is yours alone. That look upon your face of amused puzzlement is yours alone. And this. And this," and after awhile, again aroused and again satisfied, she would fall into deep sleep contented with the truth of his answers.

Finally, though, they had traveled so far and for so long that, even with the distraction of many daily perils, T'sais Prime could not ignore that whenever they began to approach the far eastern cliffs that lined the edge of their world, the Captain would murmur to his first mate, and by the next day those cliffs would be more distant, not less so.

Thus, eventually she asked that terrible yet tiny question, *why?*, and from the look in the Captain's eye, she knew that now the Captain would take her there rather than risk lying to her again.

A week later—alone together in a small ship strapped to an infant mermelant—they came to a place where the broken glass below met a cliff that jutted out toward them. Carved upon the crumbling stone, obscured in part by vines, was a face mirroring T'sais Prime's own.

"What is the meaning of this?" T'sais asked, turning to the Captain.

"She you seek lives here, within the stone house atop the cliff. Know what is real and what is not," the Captain said.

"Why do you say that?" she asked as she embraced him.

"Some lives are illusion. Some places are more real than others," the Captain replied. Thus saying, he took off his second eye patch and placed it upon her face. "Use it as you will."

T'sais understood that he was talking past the cliff, past the stone house.

"You have twenty-seven freckles on your back," the Captain said sadly as she left the ship for the cliff. "Your left wrist has a scar from where you broke it, bucked from a horse. Your hair smells like lavender in the mornings. You do not like the sound of bees but love the taste of honey."

IN THE stone house, T'sais Prime found a woman who looked remarkably like her but for the graying of her hair. She sat upon a flaking gold throne in the middle of a great hall made entirely of starkest marble. Surrounding her were the remains of many skeletons sunken in amid many skulls, some

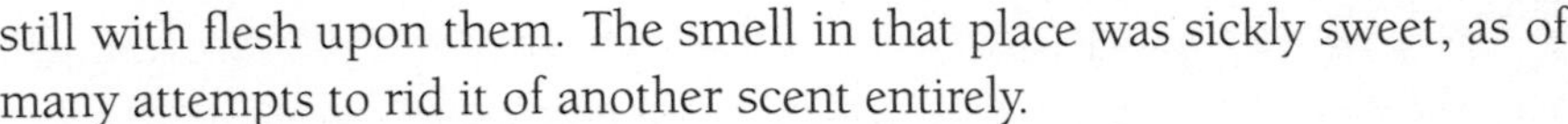

still with flesh upon them. The smell in that place was sickly sweet, as of many attempts to rid it of another scent entirely.

With caution, T'sais Prime approached.

The woman looked up and gave her a wicked smile.

"I see myself approach," she said, "and wonder why the mirror always moves, though I wish it to be still."

"Are you Vendra?" T'sais asked as she threaded her way through the bones.

"And lo!, the mirror talks," the woman said. "It tells me my chosen name, not that given to me, although in truth I am always and forever my own reflection. There is no escape for that."

"Why are there so many bodies here?" T'sais asked of Vendra. She hated the smothering silence, the sense of arriving in the aftermath of something gone terribly wrong.

"Them?" Vendra asked, with a wave of a be-ringed hand. "They escaped the broken glass to worship me—climbed up the cliff—but they bring the glass with them in their minds and they forget to eat and drink and they die all the same."

"But why?" T'sais asked.

A hungry smile. "Because to look upon me is to look upon the glass itself—I am a memory of the Dying Earth, a living reflection, just like you. But no matter that they die; others follow. That is the way of shadows."

"A spell?"

Vendra shrugged. "I cannot leave this hell of my own volition, but I have learned a few spells of my own from those who adore me. Spells built this stone mansion. Spells made the face in the cliff: a beacon, a lighthouse. *A beacon, a lighthouse. A beacon, a lighthouse. A beacon, a lighthouse...*"

But T'sais had sensed the sting behind the nectar and removed the eye patch, so that after several moment T'sais' urge to lie down and sleep among the corpses faded.

Vendra sighed, and her voice and intonations became normal again, and her gaze directed itself upon T'sais with unnatural intensity.

"I release you from your own spell, and willingly," T'sais said, "but if you attempt a second, I swear I will throw you off the cliff. It is a long way to fall."

Vendra took a long and shuddering breath. "Not that I'd kill a man willingly," Vendra continued as if nothing had happened, unable to look

at T'sais. "But you are not a double of a double in your purpose. Why are you here?"

T'sais almost did not tell her. "Sarnod has sent me to bring you back," she said, although in truth, Vendra horrified her almost as much as the thought of returning to Sarnod as one of his servants.

Vendra laughed bitterly, her amusement like salt upon a wound. "Sarnod is a cruel man, but I suppose he had one kindness within him: he let me choose a name that did not remind me I was a reflection, even if I am now required by my ambition to embrace it."

"And yet when he created me," T'sais said, "he named me a reflection but told me naught of my origins, that I might think myself original."

"One kindness," Vendra repeated. "One kindness amid so much else."

"He is much saddened by your absence," T'sais added, although she did not know the truth of this. In truth, though, Vendra did not seem much like her. This observation made her heart beat faster, made her think of the Captain waiting in his ship. *"What will you do?" he had said, and she had replied, "I do not know."*

Vendra's gaze narrowed. "And Gandreel?" For a moment, Vendra looked younger and without guile.

"Sarnod forgives all. I am here to take you back. Gandreel is also sought."

Vendra stirred on her rotting throne like something coming back to life. "I would like that," she said, managing to sound weary and hopeful at the same time. "Even if it is untrue."

"I have been given the power to send you back," T'sais Prime said, "but I will not return with you. You can tell Sarnod he would have to kill me first."

Vendra laughed. "My sad reflection, he wouldn't kill you. He would just punish you by sending you *here*."

AFTER VENDRA was gone, T'sais used her last spell to bring the stone house roaring down into dust, to release her own likeness upon the cliff face into faceless oblivion upon the broken glass below.

Then she rejoined the Captain on their ship.

"What does this mean?" he asked.

T'sais Prime smiled, and, handing him his eye patch, said, "You have seventeen scars on your body, four on your left arm, three on your right, two on your chest, three on your back, and the rest on your legs. Seven are from knives, the rest from all manner of spells and other weapons. You wear a beard to disguise your weak chin. You snore in your sleep like a wounded soul. You are as loyal and good as you are stubborn and pig-headed. There is nothing behind your second eye patch but a puckered scar."

This answer seemed to satisfy the Captain deeply.

THE BELLOWING of The Mouth brought Sarnod startled from a nap on his divan at the top of the tower. He had been dreaming of the cool, deep lake, a vision enhanced by allowing one dry hand to float within the ever-present bowl of water set upon the table next to him.

"*They return from the* UNDERHIND! *They return!*"

His heart a nervous patter, Sarnod rose quickly, gathered his green-blue robes about him, and descended to the Seeing Hall, there to stand, waiting, before the two eyes and now-silent Mouth. The sun through the great oval window shed unwelcome heat across the marble floor. The room, so large, felt small and stuffy as a trap.

The Mouth said, "Soon there will be an end to all of this," in no way reassuring Sarnod.

A sound came as of a screaming across the world.

Up popped his brother Gandreel, looking spry and healthy in white robes, despite the spots on his hands, the wrinkles at the corners of his eyes.

Gandreel stared at Sarnod with a puzzlement that Sarnod knew must be mirrored on his own face. For now, seeing his brother, Sarnod felt no outpouring of familial love, no lessening of the discomfort from the hook in his heart. Instead, he felt worse, his sense of unease deepening.

And yet, perhaps this was just the shock of first impressions, made worse by the manner in which they had parted company. Thus thinking, Sarnod stepped forward to greet his brother, saying, "Welcome home, dear brother, after what I know has been a time of much sadness, confusion, and long exile."

Gandreel's frown deepened, and he flinched away from Sarnod's embrace, saying, "Difficult enough to now meet the brother who *was* my brother, but you are not even Sarnod. Who are you then?" His tone hardened, and in his expression, Sarnod saw no hint of even a friend. "By what right do you come to be here?"

From off to Sarnod's left came Whisper Bird's voice, infused with unexpected emotion. "If not Sarnod, then to whom have I been enslaved all these long years?"

"Are you both mad?" Sarnod said, "Has the UNDERHIND robbed you of your senses? I *am* Sarnod. And you, Gandreel, you are my brother, who I admit I wrongly exiled. And, you, Whisper Bird, you must attend me *now* or risk great harm, for I am your master."

"I will attend you, but what would you have me do?" Whisper Bird said, suddenly very close to Sarnod.

Before Sarnod could respond, The Mouth said, "Sometimes reflections become shadows."

"This may be true," Whisper Bird said, "but, how then is it relevant?"

The sound of shrieking came again. Up popped Vendra from The Mouth, as old now as Gandreel, but still somehow youthful. No familiar trailed behind.

"Now my attendance is doubled in complexity," Whisper Bird said to Sarnod, who in Vendra's presence ignored both him and the fading thought of Gandreel's insult.

"Perfect, perfect Vendra," he said, to test the effect of these words from his lips. A surge of panic overtook him, for he still felt nothing, *nothing at all*. No passion. No hatred.

Vendra, for her part, stared only at Gandreel, whose gaze toward her was as deep and loving as Sarnod's was not. He took Vendra in his arms, his back to Sarnod, and they became reacquainted while Sarnod watched, hesitating in his intent.

"You are more beautiful than ever," Gandreel told her.

"You are less handsome than before," Vendra admitted, "but still more handsome than your brother by far. What shall we do, now that we are free?"

"I can play the lute," Gandreel replied, with mischief in his eyes. "You can sing. We will return to the court of the lizard king, if he and it still exist."

Vendra laughed, though she had missed his humor. "My love, would you rather perform for coins or rise powerful with our sorceries? I have learned much in the UNDERHIND, and I would put it to good use."

Gandreel stared at her for a long moment, as if unsure what to make of her, then said, "What does it matter, so long as we are alive, together, and in the wider world?", and although she seemed to agree, Sarnod could intuit her unhappiness with this question.

Now Vendra turned her attention to Sarnod, her lips curling into a kind of sneer as she stared at him from Gandreel's shoulder, her arms wrapped around her lover as if they would never again be apart.

"Sarnod's servant did not tell me that a stranger now ruled the tower," she said. "*Who are you?* You are not *Sarnod*."

To hear this denial from Vendra, even as he felt so little for her somehow, terrified Sarnod. He shouted at her, at Gandreel, who had also turned to look at him, "I *am* Sarnod, and this is my tower, and you will obey me!" Yet even with this said, Sarnod felt like an actor in a play, and underlying his anger was an odd, slippery confusion. As if each time he claimed Sarnod's name, it became less and less his own.

He would have made to bring a spell down upon them both, but The Mouth said, "There is little use in arguing with one whose mind is already made up."

"Nor in serving one whose mind is not made up," Whisper Bird said, to Sarnod's annoyance.

A shrieking scream announced a third arrival.

Up came a tall and shadowy figure, wreathed in smoke. As the figure walked forward, the smoke fell away, the face was revealed to Sarnod as… *Sarnod's own*!

Sarnod felt a lurch and dislocation deep inside. "What manner of trickery is this? Whisper Bird—is this your doing?"

"The only trickery in me is the doubling life I lead," Whisper Bird replied. "I am not responsible for this."

"Trickery?" Gandreel said. "Worse than that, to be lured here under promises from one who had no authority to honor them."

This new Sarnod glanced at Gandreel, then turned burning eyes and an unpleasant flash of sharp white teeth upon old Sarnod. "Oh, there is nothing of trickery here. I am Sarnod and this is just the giant fish I hooked, ensorcelled, and left here in my stead, armed with nearly all my spells and memories, that none might take undue advantage of my absence. A fish. Nothing more. Or less."

"Still your tongue!" Sarnod cried out. "You are an imposter!"

But this new Sarnod held up his hand, snapped, "Let your own tongue be still, fish, along with the rest of you! Did you think I would allow my own sorcery to be used against me? Or that you would keep your powers upon my return? Now that you have failed me as both guardian and guard, I decree this misspent year of Fish Misrule at an end!"

Sounds died in old Sarnod's throat, and there he stood motionless, wordless, before them all, observer and observed only. His panic had no voice, his distress no mannerisms. A kind of madness rose up in him, with no release. Desperate searching: *What memory is real and which imposed?*

Said Whisper Bird, "I am unsure who to now attend, nor why."

New Sarnod, turning to wary Gandreel and Vendra, now winced with a pain not physical. "I leave to consult on the subject of my errors in creation with others of my ilk, to correct the defects and deviations that led to *her*, for example"—and he pointed at Vendra—"and yet here I am, summoned back by knowledge of your presence in my domain, confronted once again by villains thought long exiled. Brother betrayer. Lover unconscionable. By what *right* do you think to escape exile?"

"Bring forth a spell," Vendra warned, "and I shall condemn you to a worse hell, I swear it. I am not now released only to return to that place."

Sarnod sneered. "Idle threat from an idle mind."

"Brother," Gandreel said, "let it not be this way."

"The choice is not yours," Sarnod said, taking a threatening step forward.

"Gandreel, steel yourself. We must kill Sarnod to be free," Vendra said. "Both of them." Even through his alarm, not-Sarnod saw how Gandreel extended to her a look as if she were as a stranger.

"We cannot kill them," Gandreel said. "Sarnod, even in this state, is my brother."

"Sometimes it's a better mercy," Vendra said.

"Enough!" Sarnod said. "Your betrayal is as fresh in my mind as if it were yesterday, and if the fish has one hook in his heart, I've two. The punishment for your betrayal," Sarnod said, turning his full regard upon Gandreel and Vendra as not-Sarnod looked on powerless, "is *death*, as exile is clearly not permanent enough."

So saying, Sarnod spoke the spell of Revolving Until Force Destroys and attempted to lift Gandreel into the air at great speed. But Gandreel met the spell with four words and an effort that made the veins in his neck bulge. The force of the spell disappeared through The Mouth, released Elsewhere. Gandreel dropped back to the ground from no small distance.

"Your petty sorceries shall not be enough to save you for long," Sarnod promised Gandreel, who was ashen and bent to one knee.

Sarnod brought forth the spell of Internal Dissolution, to induce great writhing agony in both Gandreel and Vendra.

Even in the midst of her distress, however, Vendra made a sign, spoke words in a tongue unknown to not-Sarnod, and deflected Sarnod's malice. The aftershock flung her into a pillar. She rose unsteadily with blood spackling her forehead.

"Stay your hand, brother!" Gandreel pleaded. "For the sake of mercy."

"Mercy? May Kraan hold your living brains in acid!" Sarnod shrieked. "May dark Thial spike your eyes!" If ever his countenance had been imperious, now it was beyond imperial. "My mercy is that you should be carrion together, not apart, for animals to feast upon." If there was any sadness in the look Sarnod gave Gandreel, the fish did not glimpse it.

Thus saying, Sarnod brought forth a third and more terrible spell, the spell of the Prismatic Spring, which would send many-colored stabbing lines at them, and deliver to them a cruel death. The stabbing lines coalesced above Sarnod's head at the behest of his raised right arm, and began to glow and brighten, Gandreel and Vendra in desperation bringing forth weaker spells that together suspended but could not abate the formation of the lines.

The wizard laughed like a creature long deranged. "Alas, that you are bereft of allies here. For Whisper Bird is mine and so is the fish. And both while you fend off my spell shall I send against you to break this stalemate."

So saying, Sarnod turned to not-Sarnod and, with a swift-curling motion of his left hand, cried out, "*Let this foolish fish return to what it once was*!" The hook left the heart of not-Sarnod, a release beyond imagining. He felt his human flesh melt away, replaced and bulwarked and expanded until he was again, as before, a gigantic fish with blue-green scales, balanced on its tail and fins, with gills that, tortured by air, longed for water. Fading human thoughts met old needs. He gasped and thrashed and tried to speak while the others, dwarfed, looked up at him in amazement.

"Now, fish, devour my enemies," Sarnod said, "and you, Whisper Bird, employ your invisible weapons, and between you both, bring this struggle to a close."

"As you wish, Sarnod," Whisper Bird said, "but it may take some time for me to cross the floor from fish to reach the foe."

Fish-Sarnod, meanwhile, propelled by ever-fading thoughts of life as the mighty wizard, confused and frightened and enraged, bellowed, "*I am Sarnod!*"

These words startled one and all in the Seeing Hall, even Sarnod. The stabbing lines faltered over his head. Gandreel stared at the fish from one knee. Vendra's glassy, pain-filled gaze affixed him.

"The fish believes it's you, my brother," Gandreel said. "Thus perhaps you are truly an imposter of a kind."

"Perhaps these thoughts can be enhanced," Vendra said, concentrating strangely upon the fish. "For surely Sarnod's spell is too far along for him to simply end it to confront new danger."

Whereupon the fish, staring at these apparitions with their strange sounds, insisted one final time "*I am Sarnod!*" although it no longer knew the meaning of the words, and, thus saying, concluded all conflict and discussion with a mighty leap forward toward the dimly perceived source of its affliction. In two gulps, it swallowed surprised, protesting Sarnod, the half-formed stabbing lines above him lashing out in blind confusion, then lunged for the huge window, smashed through, and plunged into the cool, deep, sad-dark lake beyond, the waters like a second skin, while from behind it sensed the shock in its wake, all of Sarnod's spells broken with his last smothered scream—Whisper Bird with a long sigh already returning to Embelyon, and, somewhere far-distant, T'sais sensing some fundamental change—and The Mouth's further exultations and wisdoms muffled as the fish dove deeper and deeper still, into the thick silt of the lake bed, and as Sarnod's final quest ended, sought only the oblivion of no-thought, no-dominion, and a feast of salamanders, in that place where the light from the dying sun could not penetrate except as a pale, fast-fading memory.

AFTERWORD:

I FIRST encountered Jack Vance through his "The Dragon Masters" novella. I found it during a school fieldtrip to the library when I was twelve, and it so dazzled me that I sought out Vance's Dying Earth tales. As a kid, I loved the adventure aspects and the outlandish imagination.

As an adult, my affection for Vance only deepened, because there was so much in the stories that I hadn't seen earlier. Cugel, for example, is the kind of person who does whatever is necessary to survive in what is a very harsh world. This makes him more of an anti-hero than a hero, because his actions can be morally suspect. Sometimes he is even driven to unnecessary cruelty. What saves him from being repugnant often has to do with the rogues around him: there's always someone worse than him that we're rooting against.

I also appreciated the genius quality of imagination even more as an adult. There's something about reading as a teenager that levels out these qualities—you see through the text to what it's trying to be rather than what it is, and you're much more forgiving of stylistic flaws. So, back in the day, I didn't think of Vance as being necessarily any more brilliant than anything else I was reading. But, coming back to Vance, I can really appreciate the high quality of the writing and of his rather black sense of humor.

In terms of my own writing, the idea of Vance creating or refining "scientifantasy," or far-future SF that read like fantasy, really resonated. I don't have much of a scientific background, but I liked the idea of the reader having to interpret the text in that way—to see past a "spell" and think that it might be some advanced form of nanotechnology or some other science incomprehensible to us today. As a result, Vance, along with Cordwainer Smith, had a huge influence on my *Veniss Underground* novel and related short stories. Without Vance, or Smith, I would never have even tried to write science fiction.

Vance's overall influence seems to me to have been vast. Some writers have long, productive careers and their sheer longevity makes them iconic. With Vance, there's a different sense—the idea that he was very much an innovator to whom the rest of the world eventually caught up. I doubt that some of the approaches in my work, or in any number of other writers' work, could or would exist without Vance. That there's such a wide Vance influence across many different kinds of writers strikes me as important, too. That's because a reader can interpret the Dying Earth in different ways: you can read them as straight-on fantasy stories; you can read through them to the far-future aspects; you can read through them in a postmodern way, because there's so much subtext. This, for me, is what has made them classics, and made them last for writers and readers alike.

—Jeff VanderMeer

KAGE BAKER

The Green Bird

ONE OF the most prolific new writers to appear in the late '90s, Kage Baker made her first sale in 1997, to *Asimov's Science Fiction*, and has since become one of that magazine's most frequent and popular contributors with her sly and compelling stories of the adventures and misadventures of the time-traveling agents of the Company; of late, she's started two other linked sequences of stories there as well, one of them set in as lush and eccentric a High Fantasy milieu as any we've ever seen. Her stories have also appeared in *Realms of Fantasy*, *Sci Fiction*, *Amazing*, and elsewhere. Her first Company novel, *In the Garden of Iden*, was also published in 1997 and immediately became one of the most acclaimed and widely reviewed first novels of the year. More Company novels quickly followed, including *Sky Coyote*, *Mendoza in Hollywood*, *The Graveyard Game*, *The Life of the World to Come*, *The Machine's Child*, and *Sons of Heaven*, and her first fantasy novel, *The Anvil of the World*. Her many stories have been collected in *Black Projects, White Knights*, *Mother Aegypt and Other Stories*, *The Children of the Company*, and *Dark Mondays*. Her most recent books are three new novels, *Or Else My Lady Keeps the Key*, about some of the real pirates of the Caribbean, the new fantasy novel *The House of the Stag*, and a full-length version of *The Empress of Mars*. In addition to her writing, Baker has been an artist, actor, and director at the Living History Center, and has taught Elizabethan English as a second language. She lives in Pismo Beach, California.

Here, she follows the infamous Cugel the Clever on a visit to the white-walled city of Kaiin, where he's soon embroiled in an intricate plot to steal a fabulous pet...a plot that proves to have unfortunate consequences for all concerned.

The Green Bird

KAGE BAKER

It amused Justice Rhabdion of Kaiin to dispose of malefactors by dropping them down a certain chasm located at the edge of his palace gardens.

Deep and steep-sided the chasm was, bottomed with soft sand, so that more often than not the objects of Justice Rhabdion's displeasure survived the fall. This was all to the good, as far as Rhabdion was concerned, since it provided him with further subject for mirth. On claret-colored summer afternoons, he used to have his Chair of Office moved out on the balcony that overlooked his garden pleasaunce, and which, incidentally, gave him an excellent view into the chasm as well. There he would smile to watch the antics of the enchasmates, as they fruitlessly sought to escape or quarreled with one another.

To further tease those unfortunates who had been so consigned, Justice Rhabdion had had vines of Saskervoy planted all along the chasm's rim, prodigious black creepers, with scarlet leaves in shape and function like razors, save for their motility and the small voracious mouths set just above each stem. Each enchasmed newcomer attempted to depart by means of seizing and scrambling up the vines, generally at the cost of

a finger or nose and never farther than the first third of the way before having to let go and fall.

Rhabdion's gardeners stinted the vines' feeding, to keep them keen; and this in time diminished their effect, for the enchasmates quickly learned better than to grasp at the vines. Therefore in their impatience to feed, the vines took to hunting for themselves, snapping out to catch any bird or bat so unwise as to fly within their reach.

The enchasmates, having made slings out of sandal-laces, would then fire small stones, striking the vines and causing them to drop their prey, upon which the slingers themselves would then gladly fasten, bearing the small tattered flesh back to the shelters built under the more concave angles of the chasm's walls. So were they provided with sustenance.

Then it chanced that a mining engineer from Erze Damath displeased Justice Rhabdion in some wise, and was inadequately searched before being thrown down the chasm. Certain tools he had concealed in his boots, and, once resigned to his misfortune, he retreated under the most acute of the leaning walls and there excavated, patiently chipping away at strata of porous aggregate to make yet deeper shelter from winter hail and the melancholy red light of the sun.

In time, his work provided the enchasmates with water, for he broke into a subterranean spring, relieving them thereby of the need to collect the bloody dewfall that dripped from the vines in early mornings—and with currency, for he struck upon a vein of purest gold, which was pounded into roundels and traded amongst them all in exchange for certain favors.

So a kind of society grew up at the bottom of the chasm, with its own customs and pleasures, all unnoticed by Justice Rhabdion, whose eyesight had waned as he grew older. Still he sat on his balcony through the fine purple evenings, chuckling at the occasional howls of despair that rose to his hearing from below.

CUGEL, SOMETIMES known as Cugel the Clever, became an enchasmate on the first day of spring, and the boom of the ice floes breaking on the river Scaum echoed off the upper walls of the chasm as he came pin-wheeling downward. He struck the sandy floor with a crash, and awhile lay stunned, long enough for the other inhabitants of that place to come creeping out to see whether he lived or no, and, if dead were the case, whether he had been a well-nourished and sedentary man. Alas for their hopes, Cugel detected their stealthy approach and sat up sharply.

Seeing him alive and whole, the foremost of the unfortunates smiled at Cugel. "Welcome, stranger! How have you offended, to end here?

Cugel scrambled to his feet and looked about him. He saw a score of wretches, some in the rags in which they had arrived, others in coverings of bat or mouse skins torturously pieced together by the use of bird-bone needles and short lengths of dried gut.

"Offended?" said Cugel. "Not in the least. There was a trifling misunderstanding, which was, sadly, blown out of all proportion by a jealous suitor. My advocate was astonished that the matter even came before the Dais of Adjudication. 'Friend Cugel,' he said to me, just before I was cast down here, 'Do not let your fiery spirits dampen! I will appeal your case and these baseless charges shall melt away, even as the ice upon great Scaum.' So much he said, and I am confident in his powers of persuasion."

"No doubt," said the nearest enchasmate, a splay-footed man with red hair, that hung to his shoulders in tangled ringlets. "And what, pray, is the name of your excellent friend?"

"Pestary Yoloss of Cutz is the man," said Cugel. The massed enchasmates smiled amongst themselves.

"Why, Pestary was *my* advocate too," said the red-haired man.

"And mine," said a swarthy man of Sfere.

"And mine," echoed many others. They laughed, then, at Cugel's pale face, and, for the most part turned away to their own affairs. The red-haired man approached more closely, and, drawing a small pouch from his loincloth, opened it with two fingers and worked forth three flattened nuggets of gold, looking less like coins than pieces of trodden farlock dung. These he offered to Cugel, would Cugel but grant him certain privileges of Cugel's person.

Cugel declined the transaction, though he looked thoughtfully at the gold.

He beat the sand from his clothing and made a slow circuit of the bottom of the chasm, gazing up at the vines of Saskervoy and noting how they twitched at the passing flight of a bird, sometimes lashing out to snap one from midair. He saw, too, how expert certain of the enchasmates were at knocking down the vines' prey. All the life of the community Cugel observed with shrewd eyes, before settling down with his long back against the chasm's wall and his long legs stretched out before him. He had

been wearing a liripipe hood when he had been thrown into the chasm, sewn with a pattern of red and green diamonds, and he removed it now and delved into the recesses of its long point. At his arm's length, he found what he sought, drawing forth in his nimble fingers a pair of spotted cubes of bone.

Thereafter, Cugel won himself many a succulent lizard or wren, and accrued a considerable store of gold, in games of chance with the other enchasmates. Seeing, however, that an unpopular man was unlikely to last long in that society, Cugel was at pains to distribute largesse of marrow-bone and pelts to his fellow prisoners, and made himself pleasant in divers other ways, primarily conversation. He found, to his irritation, that none were especially interested in hearing his traveler's tales; but each man, once encouraged to speak of his own life, went on at great length and seemed to relish having someone to listen.

Some were sycophantic courtiers whose flattery had failed them; some were petty murderers; some had disputed the amount of taxes they owed. Kroshod, the engineer from Erze Damath, had been a visitor unaware of local custom when he had most unwisely failed to tie three lengths of red string to the handle of his innroom door before retiring. To all these, Cugel listened with well-concealed boredom, nodding and occasionally tapping the side of his long nose and murmuring "Ha! What injustice!" or "Monstrous! How I do condole with you, sir!".

At last, he made the acquaintance of a certain elderly man in rags of velvet, who sat alone, wreathed in violet melancholy. Him Cugel approached with bland affability, inviting a wager on the cast of a single die. The elder looked at him sidelong and chewed his yellowed mustache a moment before replying.

"I thank you, sir, but no. I have never gambled, and have learned, to my grief, to avoid straying outside my field of expertise."

"And pray, sir, what would that be?" inquired Cugel, seating himself beside the other.

"You see before you Meternales, a Sage, erstwhile master of a thousand librams and codices. Had I been content with what I held for mine own, I would even now be stretched at mine ease, in far Cil; but I yielded to greed and curiosity, and see to what extremity I am brought for my treasure-hunting!"

"Perhaps you would elucidate," said Cugel, scenting useful information. Meternales rolled a wet eye at him.

"Hast ever heard of Daratello the Psitticist? He was a mage, and a pupil of none less than great Phandaal. Deep and subtle was his power, and prudent his employment of it; yet he was hunted to his death long ago, for reasons which he ought to have foreseen."

"I do not believe I know the name. Was he slain by thieves? And did they, perhaps, fail nevertheless to obtain his fortune? Which is, by chance, somewhere still concealed for some fortunate wayfarer to find?" said Cugel, hitching himself a little closer to Meternales, in the hope that he would lower his voice and thereby exclude other listeners.

"So it happened," said Meternales. "But the fortune was not, as you might imagine, in brassbound chests or bags of impermeable silk. His fortune was in spells. I, myself, once owned librams containing one hundred and six spells surviving from the age of Phandaal. Daratello, they say, had preserved double that number, in volumes borne away in stealth from Grand Motholam. Yet Daratello was only a man, as you or I, though a passing clever man. I have spent a life in study and austerities, and still can commit to memory no more than five spells of reasonable puissance at any one time. Daratello could memorize as much, it is said, but no more. His genius lay in the shifts he devised to circumvent his limits.

"There was a merchant traveled from the Land of the Falling Wall, who brought with him a pair of bright-feathered birdlings, and said they could be taught the speech of men. Daratello purchased them from the merchant, and took them away to his isolate redoubt, and there in seclusion taught each one half the spells he had preserved.

"Our human minds cannot contain so much. I hold my five spells after a lifetime's training; any attempt to memorize more would twist the matter of my brain to madness. Any common man would find his nose running and his eyes crossing were he to fill the hollow of his skull with more than one cantrap, and as many as three would break him in seizures and incontinence. Yet a bird's mind is bright and empty, heedless of human care or ambition; and it is the delight of green-feathered birds of that sort to memorize and store what they hear.

"Daratello carried the birds one on either shoulder. He had only to prompt one or the other, and the bird would murmur the spell of his choice into his ear, for his instant use.

"Such brilliance awoke envy wherever Daratello went. Attempts were made to steal his green birds; he withdrew to his far manse. Caravans full of petitioner-thaumaturges braved the miles to his door, offering chests of

gems and ensorcelled wares in exchange for the birds. Fruitless were their efforts, for he refused to admit them nor even to raise his portcullis.

"In the end, they grew importunate. Daratello was driven forth, with his birds; Daratello was hunted across Ascolais, Almery, even across the sea and the Silver Desert. He was besieged at last in a high tower of timber, and, most unwisely, his pursuers set it afire. So Daratello and his birds perished. And yet…there were some who claimed to see a single bird escape, flying free of the writhing smoke.

"Having read so much in an ancient tome of Pompodouros, I read more, and learned that others had claimed to have seen, and even briefly possessed, Daratello's surviving pet. I traced the green bird's whereabouts across five lands, and five ages. When I found no further references in books, I went forth myself, though I am but a scholar and ill-equipped for travel, and sought rumor of the marvelous bird in those places in which it had been last recorded as possibly having been known. I will not tell you what I spent in bribes to consult certain forbidden oracles, or with what pain the syllables of disclosure were wrenched forth from those who dealt in revelatory ambiguities.

"It must suffice to say that in the ninetieth year of my life, I came here, to white-walled Kaiin, and sought the yellow-eyed daughters of Deviaticus Lert."

"And who would these be?" Cugel arched one eyebrow. "Nubile sirens? Exotic beauties from Prince Kandive's pleasure pavilions?

"Not in any sense," said Meternales with a sigh. "Though Vaissa was reputed to have been a beauty in her youth. Wealthy and respected old dames, the sisters, as unalike as two children of one father might be, and 'tis said they hate each other dearly. It is said further that Deviaticus Lert scolded them often for their quarreling, and at last exerted his peace with a dead hand, for he made it a condition of their inheritance that they must dwell together in the family home, and on no account might either of them remove therefrom, on pain of being cut off from his fortune.

"And so they made a truce. Lert Hall is a squat townhouse horned with two towers, one to the east and one to the west. In the westernmost, Vaissa resides, with her jewels and her gowns and her rare perfumes. In the easternmost dwells Trunadora, with her books, her alembics, her vials and athenors."

"H'm! Is she a witch?"

"They are both sorceresses, though neither is inclined to active practice. Trunadora is of a retiring and studious nature, and Vaissa employed

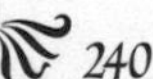

her charms to get her lovers, when she could still entertain them. Now she traffics in court gossip and meddles in the affairs of the young, dispensing love-philtres and advice. Trunadora remains aloof in her tower.

"At one point only do their lives intersect, these sisters, and that is in their affection for a certain green bird. How they came by him, I was never able to learn, but all my researches persuade me that he is the surviving one of the two once owned by Daratello. I attempted to buy him from the daughters of Lert, and was rejected in no uncertain terms."

"I should think so!" said Cugel, stroking his long chin. "They must find him remarkably useful, if he is in truth a repository for ancient spells."

"Yet it is otherwise!" said Meternales, clenching his fists in an agony of recollection. "They have no least suspicion of what they have, and the green bird—perhaps valuing a peaceful life—has apparently declined to enlighten them! He is as their child. They love him fondly, foolishly, as only a pair of ancient spinsters may love a pet. If the house of Lert went up in flames, Vaissa would cheerfully leave Trunadora to roast amid the coals, but she would heave aside burning beams to rescue Pippy; and you may guess that her sister would do likewise."

"'Pippy'? queried Cugel.

"That is the name they have given the bird," said Meternales sadly. "Well. Frustrated as I was in my repeated efforts to purchase the bird, I at last resolved to steal him. I am no burglar, I fear; I was caught attempting to scale the house wall. The city guard brought me before Justice Rhabdion, and the rest you may imagine."

"How very sad," said Cugel. "You ought to have employed a professional, you know."

"I thought of that," said Meternales, pulling at his beard in fretful wise. "Afterward."

THEREAFTER, CUGEL was observed to gaze often at the high walls of the chasm, pacing out distances and doing sums in the sand. His fellow enchasmates thought he had taken leave of his senses when he began trading gold for their rags, and dicing to win more rags still, but madness was a common condition in the chasm and no one thought the less of him for that.

When he had a great heap of rags, Cugel busied himself unweaving them, and plaiting the fibers together with his slender fingers into a rope of

considerable length. Having produced a coil of many ells, he wound it around his arm one fine morning and stood to harangue his fellow prisoners.

"Gentlemen! Who among you would escape this dismal confinement?"

The answer was so patently obvious that his audience merely gaped at him, until the man with red curls said: "Every wretch here desires his freedom. But what remedy?"

"I propose," said Cugel, with a brilliant smile, "a plan! Saving the very elderly, we are all lean as whipcord and reasonably fit, since the one advantage we have in this hellish place is that we are free from any diseases of surfeit. Have you ever been so fortunate as to watch acrobats making a human pyramid? Let us do likewise! Regard this fine rope I have made. By my calculations, if you are able to construct a pyramid thirty feet in height, and if I mount upon your backs and whirl my rope after the fashion of the herders of Grodz, I may cast it out and catch the arm of the statue of the goddess Ethodea, which you may have noticed on the edge of Justice Rhabdion's garden. I may then swing across and anchor it fast, and the rest of you may pull it taut and clear of the vines, and so follow me along it to freedom. What say you?"

Cugel's voice rang out like a trumpet, and the enchasmates were inspired. "Why have we never thought of this before?" cried the man with red curls. "Oh, to be free again!"

"There is only one thing needful," said Cugel. "I require a bar of metal, with which to weight the end of my rope, and which will happily catch in the crook of the goddess's arm. Has any among you such a thing? All heads turned to the engineer Kroshod, who carried a crow-chisel. He lifted it, looking dubious.

"This is good iron," he said, "But if it should be lost—" The impatience of his fellows would not permit him to finish his statement. The crow-chisel was snatched from his hands and passed to Cugel.

Thereafter, the strongest of the men linked arms and formed the first storey of the pyramid, under Cugel's direction. Other men removed their sandals and scrambled up to stand on their shoulders, linking arms likewise, and more scrambled up to make a third storey, and two more made a fourth. Swaying, trembling, sweating, they stood, as Cugel swarmed up them with his boots prudently tied about his neck.

"Make haste!" cried the man with red curls, who was in the bottom tier.

"Never fear," Cugel assured him, uncoiling his rope and swinging the weighted end in an ever-widening circle about his head. Once, twice, thrice, and he let it fly, straight for the goddess of mercy. The crow-chisel caught in the angle of her arm, the rope pulled tight. Taking firm hold, Cugel leaped and swung in a short arc, landing a full three-quarters of the way up among the vines of Saskervoy. Cugel swarmed up the rope in frantic haste, as the vines bit at him.

He lost a toe before managing to pull himself over the top, and ran limping to the base of the statue. There he stanched the bleeding with a hank of dried grasses before pulling his boots on once more. Swiftly he pulled the rope up after him and dislodged the crow-chisel from the statue. He examined the crow-chisel critically a moment, judging that it would undoubtedly prove useful in future endeavors, and tucked it into his belt before setting off through the garden of Justice Rhabdion, whistling through his teeth.

A FORTNIGHT'S dicing sufficed for Cugel to possess himself of funds for enough substantial meals to restore his person, a suit of fine clothing, and a few hours' worth of titivation in a tonsorial parlor. He preened before the barber's glass, pleased to imagine that whoever beheld him, in his present state, would judge him a debonair hero, dashing yet eminently trustworthy.

Cugel then betook himself to the vicinity wherein stood the residence of the yellow-eyed daughters of Deviaticus Lert. Their townhouse was easily enough found, with its pair of towers rearing against the sky like a dowager's horned headdress. He secured a room in an inn across the street, and for some few days observed carefully who came and went by the sisters' gate. Their door was kept by an immense old gogmagog, in his sand-colored skin so like to the color of the wall that he seemed like a guardian statue.

Regularly, in the early afternoon, an open palanquin would be carried forth past him by four gasping and staggering servants. In the palanquin rode a monstrously fat old creature, swathed in veils of white and powder-blue silk, with blue paint emphasizing the bright and brass-colored eyes wherewith she kept a sharp regard on the passing traffic.

Her habits were most regular. Cugel followed the palanquin at a respectful distance, and learned that Dame Vaissa was invariably borne off to the vicinity of Prince Kandive's palace. There she remained, engaged,

as far as Cugel could learn, in bibulous merriment, elephantine flirtation, and the adjudication of young lovers' quarrels. Generally, she was carried home in the early hours of the morning, a time—as Cugel was pleased to note—when the streets of Kaiin were dark, the haunt of footpads and other persons intent on mischief.

BUT THREE faint stars were visible when Cugel, waiting in the deep shadow of an alley, heard the uneven tramping footfall of Dame Vaissa's bearers returning to the house of Lert. He drew a white handkerchief from his pocket and waved it, a brief ghostly flash in the shadows but clearly visible to the hired bullies who waited in the doorway of the tenement opposite.

When the palanquin came abreast of the tenement, the bullies poured forth, brandishing clubs, with which they proceeded to break the kneecaps of Dame Vaissa's bearers. These crumpled to the ground with screams of pain, unable to so much as raise a hand in protest as Dame Vaissa was spilled from her palanquin into the street. Their screams were as nothing to Dame Vaissa's.

"Ho! Brigands! Murderers! Avaunt!" roared Cugel, bounding from the shadows with drawn sword. "How dare you! Fly, you worthless sons of Deodands! Oh, cowards, to attack a helpless lady!" He beat the nearest of the bullies with the flat of his sword, far more vigorously than had been agreed on, with the result that the man snarled and went for him in earnest with his club. Cugel's cheap blade was shattered. There had been murder done, but for the fact that Dame Vaissa rose ponderously on hands and knees and extended one beringed hand. She uttered a phrase of excoriation and the bullies were instantly alight as torches, burning to puffs of ash too quickly to shriek. Cugel, singed by proximity, danced backward.

"Fair madam, speak!" he cried, wondering whether his eyebrows had been crisped away. "Did the varlets hurt you? Allow me!" he added, hastening to lend an arm as Dame Vaissa endeavored to rise to her feet. Cugel winced in pain, for her weight was fair to pull his arm from its socket and her nails dug into his flesh; but the darkness hid his expression.

"I thank you, kind gallant, I am only a little bruised," said Dame Vaissa, in a voice husky and breathless. "Alack! Your sword has been broken."

"It was my father's," said Cugel, with an artful catch in his voice, "But no matter! It perished in the best of causes. Madam, we must not linger here; there may be others yet lurking. Pray allow me to escort you to your house. I will return with some of your household to collect the bearers. Where do you reside?"

Dame Vaissa permitted herself to be led, teetering on four-inch heels, to the house of Lert, and prudently resisted swooning from shock until she had charmed them past the door-warden and was comfortably seated in her own front hall. She revived long enough to waddle to the front door and murmur an incantation, in order that the gogmagog might permit Cugel egress; for it was so ensorceled as to permit entry only grudgingly, but was even less inclined to allow departure. Cugel led the gardener and scullery-boy back to the injured chair-bearers, who were still groaning and rolling in the street. There he left them to manage recovering their fellows, and wasted no time in running back to the house of Lert, cheerily giving the gogmagog the entry-password.

Dame Vaissa had been revived with a brandy posset, and was sitting up to receive Cugel when he returned. She bestowed upon him many coquett-ish expressions of gratitude, and would have pressed a purse of gold upon him as well, had Cugel not refused with a perfect imitation of chivalry. She saw him to the door, once again interceding for him with the door-warden; she implored Cugel to return by daylight, that she might converse with him at greater length during more respectable hours, and this Cugel gladly agreed to do. As he departed, he noted a staircase opening off the left of the hall, as one also opened off the right. He cast his gaze up there, hoping to spy a cage, but none was in evidence. Rather, from the top of the leftmost stair, a gaunt wraith peered down, a lean-chopped harpy in an old dressing gown, hair in curling papers, watching him with sunken yellow eyes.

Bowing and kissing Dame Vaissa's plump hand, he made his exit.

"IT IS so rare to find a brave *and* kind-hearted gentleman of breeding, nowadays," said Dame Vaissa, pouring out a cup of thin grey wine of Cil. Cugel accepted it and smiled at her across the cup's brim. She wore, today, an ensemble of mustard-colored sarcenet trimmed in a pattern of gold wire, with a choker and earrings of jet beads, and was liberally powdered and rouged.

"Dear madam, I merely did what any true man would do. Would, indeed, that I had been able to act more effectively! Would that I had been

able to carry away arms and armor from our estates at Kauchique, before I was sent into exile! Sadly, the fallen fortunes of my house have left me barely able to defend a fair lady's honor."

"How you do flatter an old woman," said Dame Vaissa, with a titter. "Am I correct, then, in assuming that you have presently no occupation?"

"A gentleman never has an occupation, dear lady. He has only pastimes." Cugel affected a lofty sneer into the distance. 'Nonetheless, it is true that I am, at the moment, without funds or prospects. Yes."

"Then I do wish you would allow me to offer you a position in my household," said Dame Vaissa, leaning forward to place her hand upon Cugel's knee. "The duties would be nominal, of course. And you would be doing *such* a favor for a poor old frightened creature living alone!"

"Why, madam, you place me in a delicate position as regards mine honor," said Cugel, making a gesture as though he were about to clap his hand to the pommel of his sword and then looking down with a well-acted rueful glance, as though remembering that it had broken. "How can I refuse my protection to a woman alone?...Though I had heard you have a sister."

"Oh, her!" Dame Vaissa made a dismissive gesture. "Poor creature's a recluse. Never came out in society at all, and now she's half-mad. Lives upstairs among her books. And, whereas I have a robust constitution and a healthy appetite, she has withered away like an old spider. You wouldn't find it worthwhile making her acquaintance, I can assure you. However," and her amber eyes brightened, "I can think of one person you ought to meet, if you would reside here with us. Assist me to rise, kind sir."

She extended a coy hand. Cugel hauled her to her feet from the chaise-lounge upholstered in lavender plush that was her customary receiving-seat, and she took a few rolling steps before muttering Phandaal's Hovering Platform. At once a disc, not quite a yard across, appeared before her, floating some three inches above the floor. A black rod, seemingly made of onyx, extended upward from one side, and curved at the end into a sort of tiller. Dame Vaissa stepped up on the disc and it moved forward at her command.

"There! Much more convenient. Let us proceed, dear Cugel."

She drifted before him like a great untethered balloon, up a flight of stairs and into a conservatory on the second floor of the main house. Cugel felt sweat prickling his forehead from the moment he entered the room, for it was disagreeably warm within. The upper walls and domed ceiling were all of glass, admitting the dull red light of the sun, but no breath of wind. He saw every variety of fruit tree growing in immense pots, and ferns, and orchids, and flowering vines that festooned the walls like tapestries. A fountain in the form of a Deodand urinating gushed quietly near the room's center, adding a further degree of moistness to the air.

Near the fountain, a ring of iron depended on a long chain from the ceiling, and small cups were set at either side of the ring. Perched between them was a green bird, with a long trailing tail of scarlet and a nutcracker beak. As Cugel approached, it cocked its head to regard him, with an ancient reptilian eye; then returned its attention to the woman, no less ancient and reptilian, who was offering it a slice of some pink fruit.

"Won't he have his sweet ripe breakfast? Look! It's the very first of the season, so it is, and Trunadora cut it up specially for her little precious Pippy. Won't he have some?" She placed the slice between her withered lips and leaned close to offer it to the bird, who took it diffidently.

"What are *you* doing here?" demanded Dame Vaissa. Dame Trunadora turned, indignant. Cugel recognized the old woman he'd seen peering from the staircase on the previous evening. Now she wore a pleated gown of gray velvet, with a long strand of white corals about her neck. Her face was severely clean, innocent of powder or mascara; but if it had not been, and if the aquiline bones of her face had been well-padded with fat, rather than protruding as shoal rock protrudes from sand at low tide, Cugel might have been able to discern some resemblance to her sister.

"What am I doing here? What are *you* doing here? Why aren't you in your boudoir, sleeping off another night of disgusting excess, as you customarily are at this hour of the day? *I* am the one who sees to it that darling Pippy gets his little breakfast. If it was left to you, he'd starve! And who is this? Have you started bringing your entertainments home again? I wonder you aren't ashamed, at your age!"

"You cold-hearted old stick!" Dame Vaissa gripped the tiller of her flying platform in a passion of rage. "You haven't an ounce of feeling, you haven't indeed! For your information, I was set upon by murderers and rapists last night on my way home, and had it not been for the timely appearance of this noble virtuous gentleman, anything might have happened! And how dare you imply that I neglect my little Pippy!"

"It's true!" Dame Trunadora addressed Cugel. "She never remembers to change the water in his drinking-cup!"

"You foul old liar!"

"And look here!" Dame Trunadora gestured at a green and calcined stalagmite of droppings directly under the bird's hanging ring, rising from the floor to a height of seven or eight inches. "This is *her* responsibility! I've waited for days to see if she even noticed it hadn't been cleaned. You never did it yourself, did you, you lazy sybarite? You had that manservant doing it, didn't you? The one I caught stealing the spoons."

Dame Vaissa opened and shut her mouth, words temporarily choked by outrage. Cugel, noting that Meternales had not understated matters, wondered how he might play the sisters against each other.

"She's been this way her whole life," Dame Trunadora told Cugel. "Always careless, always shirking her duties. She doesn't love our little sweeting the way I do."

"I do so!" Dame Vaissa's voice bellowed forth at last. "Is it my fault that my health is too delicate to get down on my poor hands and knees and scrub the tiles? And if you truly loved dearest Pippy, you'd have cleaned up the mess yourself, rather than let it mount on a matter of principle. Look! His poor little eyes are watering from the fumes! And poor Leodopoif never stole the spoons. You only dismissed him because you were jealous of his affection for me! But as it happens, dear Cugel of Kauchique has graciously accepted a position in my service. *His* delight it shall be, hereafter, to keep the floor beneath Pippy as spotless as new-loomed samite."

"Indeed, dear lady, I am eagerly anticipating the duty," said Cugel, happy to have a chance to speak for himself at last. "There was a great aviary on my father's estate, and many a time I assisted the keeper in caring for our dear feathered companions." He bowed to Dame Trunadora, in a close imitation of the elaborate reverences of the courtiers of Prince Kandive. Dame Trunadora regarded him with a chilly lemon-colored stare. She sniffed.

"Very likely," she said. "But if it is so, then you may as well begin at once. See the cabinet yonder, under the flowering sispitola? You'll find there a steel brush and a dustpan. Clean away the guano, and make certain you carry it over to the compost-pile afterward. Then wash down the floor with perfumed water, and dry it with chamois cloth."

"At once," said Cugel, bowing once again. "Please, concern yourselves no further! Only leave me here, to improve my acquaintance with little Pippy as I work."

"I should say not!" Dame Trunadora extended an arm thin as a broom-handle within its velvet sleeve. The green bird leaned down, and, steadying itself with its formidable beak, clambered onto her wrist. "Leave our adorable baby alone with a stranger? Really, Vaissa, what can you have been thinking?"

Dame Vaissa twisted her red mouth in a moue of disgust. "Look at his poor little claws! You haven't bothered to trim them in a month, obviously. Never mind, Pippy darling! You shall come with me now, and I shall show dear Cugel how we trim your little toenails."

She thrust out her arm and the green bird stepped readily across, flexing its gray and scaled feet for pleasure at the well-padded surface. Grimacing, she swung her arm around to Cugel. "Put out your arm, sir. Step up, Pippy! There now! You see, Trunadora? Pippy knows a gentleman when he sees one."

"You are too kind, madam," said Cugel, barely managing not to gasp as the needle-pricking talons punched through his sleeve and into his wrist. The green bird sidled up Cugel's arm to his shoulder, where he had an excellent view of its hooked, sharp-edged beak.

Cugel had further occasion to note the beak when it bit him, some three or four times during the process of learning to trim avian toenails. There were special silver clippers to be used, and a special diamond-dust file, and a special ointment to be painted on the creature's feet afterward. Dame Vaissa sat with her hands well within her sleeves, patiently instructing Cugel in the painful process, though he could barely hear her over the creature's deafening screams. Now and then, she remonstrated gently with Pippy, in the fond language mothers use to infants, when he removed yet another half-moon divot of Cugel's flesh from knuckle or fingertip or ear.

"Perhaps it has been awhile since you handled birds," Dame Vaissa remarked, extending a forefinger. She made kissing noises and Pippy leaped from Cugel's shoulder, leaving a mound of chrysoprase excrement there as it came and buffeting his head soundly with wingbeats. The green bird lighted on Dame Vaissa's hand and proceeded to preen itself, as Cugel, fingering the bleeding notch in his left ear, smiled through clenched teeth.

"Some few years, madam. And, of course, he isn't used to me yet. I trust we shall become great friends, if I am allowed to spend a little time alone with him."

"No doubt," said Dame Vaissa, with a yawn. "Well. We mustn't idle! Do please clean up the mess under the dear baby's perch, won't you? And, when you've finished, you might just step out to the porters' agency and fetch me a new set of chair-bearers. Tell them I wish for strapping fellows of matched height, preferably with chestnut hair. Protective greaves wouldn't be a bad idea, either. And I expect you'll want to bring your things here—were you staying at a lodging-house? You can have Leodopoif's old room, it's quite nicely appointed. Oh, and could you stop by Madame Vitronella's shop and ask her to make up five bottles of my personal cologne? Have her deliver it. And then, of course, I'll require you to attend me when I go out this evening. The dear Prince has appointed me principal judge in a contest of amateur efforts at love-poetry! *So* amusing!"

"TIRESOME OLD baggage!" Cugel grumbled, throwing himself down on the narrow bed that had been furnished him. He stretched out his long legs and folded his hands behind his head. It was past the hour of midnight, and he had spent most of the long day on his feet in the service of Dame Vaissa. Firstly, running the thousand little errands she had found for him, each one of which took him a substantial distance from the house and the green bird, and though he strained his ears to hear the incantation with which Dame Vaissa enabled him to get past the gogmagog, yet he was unable to make out so much as one clear syllable. His second annoyance lay in accompanying her to the court of Prince Kandive the Golden.

While this latter also kept Cugel far from the object of his design, nevertheless he had looked forward to swaggering and cutting a fine figure before the ladies at court. He had been disappointed to learn, therefore, that while at Prince Kandive's palace, he was expected to remain in the forecourt with the flunkeys and footmen of other nobles, partaking of orange-flower-water and small biscuits and listening to below-stairs gossip.

"Regardless," he told himself, "I am still Cugel the Clever! Already I have progressed farther than Meternales, whose wisdom was undoubted. He never got so far as I. Have I not already penetrated the house, and won the sisters' trust? I know where the bird is kept. All I require now is a chance to be alone with him, and a means by which to quiet him while I spirit him out of the house, and to learn the egression spell with which to pass the door-warden."

He considered the first requirement, scowling to himself. There was no hope of managing the theft during the hours in which he was expected to dance attendance on Dame Vaissa; for that was every hour in which she was awake. She generally rose sometime in the early afternoon. In the hours beforehand, Dame Trunadora kept close watch over the green bird.

Cugel's scowl darkened as he considered the vinegary charms of Dame Trunadora. At last, he shrugged. "What though, Cugel! Have you not an unfailing way with the female sex? If you cannot ingratiate yourself with the old witch, you are not your father's child."

SO, ON scant hours' sleep, Cugel made his way to the solarium. As he neared the door, he spotted a kitchen drudge toiling ahead of him, carrying a pair of buckets full of something that steamed.

"Ho, there! What is it you carry?"

The drudge turned dull eyes to him. "Hot water from the kitchen boiler. My lord must have his bath."

"Your lord? Do you mean the green bird?"

"Even he. My mistress requires it brought fresh every morning. I will be beaten if I deliver it late," she added pointedly. Cugel looked in vain for a curve of flesh he might pinch or swat, and settled for wresting the buckets from the drudge's hands.

"I will deliver the water today. Back to your dishpan!"

Muttering, the drudge left him. Cugel bore the water onward to the solarium, and shouldered his way through the doorway. At once, he spotted Dame Trunadora with the green bird on her shoulder, murmuring tender nonsense as she fed the creature sugared tapioca balls.

"Good morning, dear lady," said Cugel, setting down the buckets. "See! I have brought fresh water for little Pippy's bath."

"On whose orders?" Dame Trunadora demanded.

"Why—that is to say—your lady sister requested that I see to the bird's comfort in all respects. Therefore here am I, ready to serve in whatever manner you require."

Dame Trunadora narrowed her yellow eyes. Impatiently, she gestured at a wide silver basin, set beside a tall silver pitcher on a tabletop of green serpentine. "Pour the water, then!"

Cugel brought forward the buckets and obeyed, humble and deferential as any slavey. "What am I to do next, madam?

"Prepare the bath, fool." Dame Trunadora seized the pitcher herself, and poured forth a little chilled water perfumed with attar of flowers of

'Ood. She cast in also a measure of rose petals. "Put your hand in the water! It should be of a mild and pleasant temperature, not so cool as to give my adorable a chill, but by no means so hot as to scald him."

"Then I think perhaps you had better add more cold water," said Cugel, resisting the urge to cram his burned fingers into his mouth.

The water's temperature was adjusted to Dame Trunadora's satisfaction; only then did she hand the green bird down to the rim of the silver basin. He hopped in readily and began to splash about at once, throwing water in all directions but more often than not managing to wet Cugel.

"Watch Pippy closely," said Dame Trunadora. "Don't let him get water up his sweet little nostrils."

"Of course not, madam."

Dame Trunadora went to a cabinet in the wall and opened it, disclosing therein a mask of Shandaloon, the god of the south wind worshipped by the people of Falgunto. She raised her hands before it and uttered an imploration, and straightaway warm air came gusting forth from the god-mask's open mouth. Cugel meanwhile kept his gaze steadfast on the green bird, whose wet feathers had shrunk in an appalling manner to the gray under-down, giving it the appearance of some unwholesome hybrid of bird and drowned rat. All the while, he meditated on how he might win over Dame Trunadora, since his person had failed to please her.

"Madam," said Cugel at last, "I have a concern."

"Regarding my tiny beloved?" Dame Trunadora turned at once, to see that all was well with the green bird.

"No, madam, a personal concern of mine own."

"And why should it be mine?"

"I thought perhaps you might offer advice, since you know your sister well." Cugel twisted his countenance to express, as far as he was able, that he was in the grip of acute chagrin while still possessed of a fundamental chivalric impulse.

"Whatever can you be babbling about, man? Vaissa is easily known; all vanity and self-indulgence," said Dame Trunadora, with a sharp laugh. "And in her younger days, very well *known* by any handsome male who cared to apply to her."

"That is the matter of my concern," said Cugel, looking down as though abashed. A gout of bathwater hit his face, and he concealed a sidelong glare at the green bird with the hand that flicked the water away. "The lady is of reverend years. When she was beset, I rushed to her aid, as I

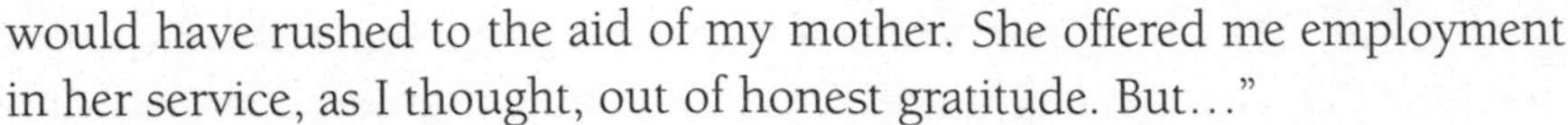

would have rushed to the aid of my mother. She offered me employment in her service, as I thought, out of honest gratitude. But…"

"Well?"

Cugel bit his lip. "How shall I say it without giving offense? Last night, she made certain…overtures, of an indiscreet nature."

Dame Trunadora looked him up and down. "What! To *you?*"

"Even I, madam."

She began to laugh, heartily. "Now by all the gods, she *has* grown desperate!"

"Needless to say, I am at a loss," Cugel went on, noticing that a certain glint of good temper, as of new-minted gold, had come into the old woman's eyes. "I would not for the world disoblige the good lady in any honorable request—so far as flesh will perform to a man's requirement, which it will not always do—but if nothing else, there is the lady's good name to consider."

Dame Trunadora whooped with merriment. "Her reputation was ruined years ago! There was a tavern in Kandive Court that was open 'round the clock, the *Princes' Arms*, and the youths at court took to calling it *Vaissa's Legs*!"

"I fear they speak with even less respect now," said Cugel, in nearly-believable sorrow.

"Oh, what do they say? Tell me!" cried Dame Trunadora. She arranged a plush towel on the table before the stream of warm air. "And bring my heart's little master from his bath."

The green bird was disinclined to leave the warm scented water, and Cugel sustained three minor and two considerable flesh wounds from its beak before managing to close his hands around the horrible-looking thing. Resisting the urge to dash its brains out, he brought it to the towel and set it down. "They say, madam, that Dame Vaissa is a pitiable old creature, who lost her beauty long since and now loses her wits."

"Do they really?" Dame Trunadora smiled as she bent down to watch the green bird lolling about on the towel, beating its wings to dry them. "What else?"

"Why, they say her beauty was never noteworthy to begin with. Also, that so voracious and predatory she was, young men oftimes climbed from her chamber window to get away, and thought a broken leg a reasonable risk if only they might escape," Cugel improvised. He wrapped his fingers in his jerkin, hoping the bleeding would stop.

"So they did," said Dame Trunadora, holding out a sugar-stick to Pippy. The bird snapped it in half with its beak. "Such a clever poppet! They did, until I showed them the secret passage in the wine cellar, that leads down to the river. They'd offer to go downstairs to fetch a bottle of fine old Cobalt Mountain vintage, to make sweet dalliance the sweeter, and how they'd run once she'd let them out of her sight! Three hours later she'd still be panting in impatience, and they well on their way to East Almery, to take their chances with barbarian women."

"Oh, dear," said Cugel, unable to believe his luck. "With respect, madam, were I not indebted to your sister for a position here—and the chance to make Pippy's delightful acquaintance—all this might cause Dame Vaissa to be lowered somewhat in my estimation."

"Call her a dreadful old trollop, if you like," said Dame Trunadora cheerfully. She eyed the bloodstains seeping through Cugel's jerkin. "Did Pippy nip you? You'll find a lavatory yonder, two doors down the corridor on the left. In the red chest in the corner are gauze and styptic."

"You are as gracious and virtuous as your sister is, lamentably, not," said Cugel. "But to return to the point, madam: what am I to do, should Dame Vaissa grow importunate again? I fear to refuse her, for I blush to admit I cannot afford to lose my position in your household, and yet the very thought—"

"Why, refuse her, man," said Dame Trunadora, grinning through chapped and colorless lips. "Then I shall retain your services myself. That will annoy her to apoplexy."

OVER THE next week, Cugel got very little sleep, studiously cultivating his acquaintance with Dame Trunadora by day and dancing attendance on Dame Vaissa by night. Though the latter beldam was, in truth, innocent of any attempt on Cugel's virtue—which strangely abraded his sense of pride—nonetheless she wearied him with her constant errands, sending him into a hundred pink and lace-trimmed hells to fetch new shoes of seven-inch heels, or sweetmeats, or unguents, or wigs. So envenomed, he improvised hours of malicious court gossip for Dame Trunadora's delight, regaling her as he chipped away at Pippy's ammoniac feces, or prepared dainty morsels for Pippy's delectation, or played the zithar (badly, his fingers being bandaged) in order that Pippy might be lulled to pleasant sleep by gentle melodies.

Though Cugel won Dame Trunadora's good opinion, none of his ministrations seemed to improve Pippy's opinion of him. The bird continued to bite him savagely, whenever it got the chance. Nor did it display any sorcerous abilities, not even to recite minor spells; its vocal repertoire was limited to ear-shattering shrieks and the single word "Hello", upon which it descanted in varying pitch and with monomaniacal persistence for hours at a time, until Cugel wanted to beat his own head against the wall, if not Pippy's.

Nor might Cugel steal much sleep in the three bare hours between waiting on either lady; for there was still the wine-cellar to be explored, until he was able to locate the secret exit. Three hours' covert search, over as many days, by the light of a candle-stub, found it for him at last: a cobwebbed door behind a stack of empty crates, with its antique and curiously wrought key hanging beside. Another hour it took to lubricate the lock and hinges with kitchen-grease procured from the drudge; another hour to coax the lock into opening. Cugel peered down the dank passage beyond and smelt the air of the river, and congratulated himself.

Next afternoon, while on an errand to procure for Dame Vaissa three ells of checkered bombazine of Saponce, Cugel deviated from his duty long enough to visit the river-wharf where he judged the other end of the tunnel must lead. There he saw many little boats unattended, and smiled to himself. Having learned so much, he briefly visited a minor wizard's stall in the marketplace, where, amongst the dubious potions and rank deceptions, he found what he sought, and purchased it with Dame Vaissa's silver.

"**WAY, THERE!** Make way for the most noble and gracious daughter of Deviaticus Lert!" roared Cugel, striding along before her slipping and puffing bearers. Dame Vaissa simpered from her high palanquin, and waved graciously at the other great folk being borne down the long aisle to Prince Kandive's palace, where flambeaux set between the cypress trees illumined the way. Two great pink-flowered magnolias bloomed at either side of the forecourt's entrance, and scattered lush petals on those entering through the immense gates that bore Kandive's armorial crest cunningly worked thereupon.

Orange lights streamed from the high windows of the palace, so that the white gravel of the forecourt seemed a bed of red coals, darkened here and there by the shadows of the bearers who jostled for room before the several dismounting blocks. Cugel bounded up to the block nearest the palace doors, and bowed to extend his hand to Dame Vaissa. Bracing his heels against the brickwork, he hauled her forth from her palanquin, and the bearers groaned in relief.

So far, the night had proceeded as any other night since Cugel had entered Dame Vaissa's service, but now, as Dame Vaissa swept toward the grand staircase on Cugel's arm, there came a faint yet distinct note, like the cracking of an iron cauldron left too long dry over a fire. Dame Vaissa faltered in her progress, and lurched, so that she would have fallen but for Cugel's solicitous arm.

"Oh, what is it? she cried. "Something's the matter with my shoe!"

"Let faithful Cugel see, my lady," he replied, seating her on the back of one of the stone wolves that guarded Prince Kandive's doors. "Alas! It's the left one. It would seem the heel has broken." Yet Cugel knew well it did not *seem*, but verily *had* broken, for had he not spent a careful quarter-hour with a jeweler's saw cutting through it on an oblique angle?

Dame Vaissa exclaimed in annoyance. "And on the night when Sciliand the Cross-eyed was to stand trial in the court of Love and Beauty! Now I shall be late. Oh, it's too unfair!"

"Too unfair to come to pass," said Cugel, with a knowing smile. "See, dear lady, what I have for you here, brought against just such an occurrence? Your second-best banqueting shoes. You may wear these now and miss not a moment of the fun."

"But, good Cugel, they are the wrong color," fretted Dame Vaissa. "These are scarlet, and do not suit my gown." And this was true; she wore an ensemble of turquoise green trimmed with moonstones. Cugel, having planned for this complaint, replied:

"Ah! Then wear them only an hour, while your faithful slave runs back and fetches something more suitable. So you will miss none of your amusements. You have a pea-green pair with diamond heels, have you not?"

"The very thing!" said Dame Vaissa. "Yes, Cugel, do be a dear and fetch them for me. Wake Trunadora. She'll let you out." She giggled and added, "She needs no beauty sleep, that's certain!"

Cugel fitted the red shoes on Dame Vaissa's plump feet, and assisted her up the grand staircase and through the doors. Then he was off and running through the moonless night, with the broken shoes in his hand and laughter in his heart.

The gogmagog at the door eyed him in a surly manner, but admitted him to the house of Lert readily enough on hearing the entry password. Once within, Cugel cast the broken shoes on a divan in the hallway. One bounced off a satin cushion, clattering to the floor.

"Who's there? cried a sharp voice. Dame Trunadora peered down her staircase, clutching her dressing-gown to her narrow bosom.

"Only I, madam, poor Cugel. I have a headache; your sister was so kind as to permit me to retire early."

"Very well, then," said Dame Trunadora, all suspicion melting from her voice. "Good night, worthy Cugel."

"Pleasant dreams, madam."

Cugel hurried deeper into the house, but failed to climb the stair to Dame Vaissa's tower; rather he went straight up to the solarium, pausing only to dart into the lavatory for the stout sack he had hidden there.

Within the solarium all was silence and darkness, for the daughters of Lert would suffer no lamp to disturb Pippy's slumbers. Cugel found his way between the potted orchids nonetheless, chuckling to himself as he made out the dark form of the green bird, silhouetted against the glass wall.

"Now, Pippy dearest," he said, drawing forth the Spancel of Submission he had purchased at the wizard's stall, "Bid farewell to your pampered life. From this day forth, you have a new master, and you shall see how he rewards insults to his person!"

Making a loop with the spancel, Cugel cast it over the green bird's head, and drew it tight. "Now! Come to my hand, docile!"

He held up one wrist, with the other hand shaking open the sack into which he meant to fling the bird, that it might not escape as he fled with it down the tunnel to the river. Pippy lifted its head, opening glowing eyes. A moment it regarded Cugel, as though in wonderment. Then its hackles rose, a sure sign of bad temper.

"I bid you come—" Cugel broke off in horror as he saw the hackles still rising, as the bird increased in size and leaped from its iron ring. It landed on the tiles before Cugel, who backed rapidly away to the length of the spancel. He gave it a futile tug.

"I said I bid—" But the creature raised a hand—a hand!—and, with a diffident gesture, lifted away the spancel and cast it to the floor. It stood a head taller than Cugel now, its eyes burning like twin fires. The flickering witch-light of a spell's dissolution showed Cugel the naked form and lineaments of a powerful man in early middle age.

Cugel would have taken to his heels then, but the mage made a peremptory gesture and Cugel found himself locked as in ice, barely able to breathe. An illumination filled the room. The mage spoke, in a voice like low thunder.

"Thief, you have sorely inconvenienced me! You have cost me a life of sweet and easy retirement. Shall I deprive you of yours? Or shall I devise some worse punishment?"

The mage summoned purple robes, which materialized to swathe his person. Then he clapped his hands and called, a sharp summoning cry. There came a scream from high within the house, changing in pitch as it continued, coming nearer, until the door to the solarium burst open. A bird flew in, a green bird with a yellow head, golden-eyed. It settled on the mage's left shoulder. A moment later came another scream, a squawking commotion in the night. One of the glass panes shattered and admitted another bird, as like the first as might be in every respect save that it trailed a string of moonstones about its neck. Trembling, panting with exertion, it settled on the mage's right shoulder.

"My dears, my poor little dears, we must move on," said Daratello the Psitticist, in a voice of tender regret. "This was a most excellent hiding place, and you have been brave little girls, but this two-legged weasel has penetrated our long refuge. What shall we do with him? Shall I allow you to peck out his eyes? But then he'd still have his tongue, to tell of what he's seen here. And I can't ask you to pull out his tongue, darlings; the nasty creature might bite one of you. No...Daddy will deal with him, after all."

Daratello extended his hand. "Felojun's Spell of Delusion, little Vaissa, if you please."

The last thing Cugel heard was the shrill metallic voice of one of the green birds, reciting dread words, before Daratello's voice repeated them and the universe shattered into meaningless color and sound.

THE KITCHEN drudge waited an hour past the usual time for Cugel to come for the hot water, before deciding she'd better carry it in herself. Two paces inside the solarium door, she stopped and stared openmouthed, to see Cugel the Clever perched inside the iron ring, his knees drawn up about his ears, his elbows held stiffly back. He cocked his head, observing her with a blank inhuman eye; then bent awkwardly and dug about in the seed-cup with his long nose, searching for millet seeds.

AFTERWORD:

IN THE early Sixties, just after Tolkien's books had made their initial tremendous splash in the American market, stateside anthologists were scurrying to cash in on the renewed interest in fantastical tales. I was home from school with bronchitis and my mother picked up a paperback anthology for me from Ferguson's Drugstore, *The Young Magicians*, edited by Lin Carter. The anthology's cover copy implied that if I loved Tolkien, I'd love the anthology because it was chock-full of similar fanciful goodness. The actual contents were garnered mostly from American pulps; there was a Robert E. Howard story, there were a couple of Lovecraft pieces, there was some Clark Ashton Smith, and "Turjan of Miir" by Jack Vance. Vance's story made the strongest impression on me, with its depiction of the decadent court of Prince Kandive the Golden and the perpetually furious anti-heroine T'sais. I loved the way Vance used language, dangling archaic words through his tale like clusters of ripe grapes, throwing out references to other places and people of the Dying Earth without explaining them, so that my imagination scrambled feverishly to color them in.

Many years later I encountered the tales of Cugel the Clever, a liar and thief in a doomed world of liars and thieves, as hapless as Wile E. Coyote and by several degrees less moral than Harry Flashman. Probably the least attractive hero it would be possible to find, struggling through a universe like a Hieronymus Bosch painting, a hero only in that nearly everyone else he encounters in that universe is on the make too; and yet the Cugel stories are howlingly funny. If I'd contributed a story to this anthology much earlier in my life, it might have been about T'sais, a girl raging at an imperfect universe. Having made it to midlife, though, and knowing now the value of a good pratfall, I was instead inspired to write about Cugel.

—Kage Baker

PHYLLIS EISENSTEIN

The Last Golden Thread

EVEN IF you come from a rich and successful family, the life of a mushroom merchant is not an exciting one. When the scion of such a family decides to spurn the mushroom business and pursue instead the difficult and dangerous trade of magician, he'll need all of his courage and all of his wits and resources...and yes, a few mushrooms as well!

Phyllis Eisenstein's short fiction has appeared in *The Magazine of Fantasy & Science Fiction*, *Asimov's*, *Analog*, *Amazing*, and elsewhere. She's probably best-known for her series of fantasy stories about the adventures of Alaric the Minstrel, which were later melded into two novels, *Born to Exile* and *In the Red Lord's Reach*. Her other books include the two novels in *The Book of Elementals*, *Sorcerer's Son* and *The Crystal Palace*, as well as stand-alone novels *Shadow of Earth* and *In the Hands of Glory*. Some of her short fiction, including several stories written with husband Alex Eisenstein, has been collected in *Night Lives: Nine Stories of the Dark Fantastic*. For twenty years she has taught creative writing at Columbia College Chicago, where she and her husband created and edited *Spec-Lit*, a trade paper anthology showcasing work by her students. Currently, she is employed full-time as Manager of copy editors at a major Chicago ad agency. Phyllis holds a degree in Anthropology from the University of Illinois, where she studied archaeology and traditional societies with arcane belief systems. She and her husband were born in Chicago, and have lived there together for the last forty years.

The Last Golden Thread

PHYLLIS EISENSTEIN

As the elder son of the house—by half an hour—it was Bosk Septentrion's privilege to sit beside his father at dinner. Generally, he avoided that privilege, having long since lost interest in his father's unending supply of advice, but this night they had a guest, and it was only common courtesy to share a meal with a traveler bound home to Ascolais. He knew his father's only concern was to create another mercantile connection with the south; Bosk's concern was the sapling that Turjan of Miir had caused to sprout from their dining table.

"A charming gift," said Bosk's father, passing Turjan another serving of succulent three-mushroom stew.

"A bagatelle," said Turjan. "It will live on the scraps of your meals and bear fruit in a year."

Bosk could not keep his eyes from the tree, its graceful bole and nodding leaves like a dancer with feathery hair waiting for the music to begin. He had never desired to be a merchant, though for ten generations that had been the fate of every Septentrion son. Now, fifteen winters into his life, he finally knew what he did desire. He looked at his father, speaking earnestly to Turjan of business. He looked at his younger brother Fluvio, at the other end of the table, stabbing the mushrooms in his stew as if they were small animals that might escape. Fluvio, he knew, enjoyed sitting next to their father; Fluvio was the true Septentrion heir.

Bosk reached out to touch the tree. The pale bark was as smooth as the timeworn surface from which it had sprung. Under the table, his father's buskined foot nudged his ankle, and he drew his hand back to take up his crystalline goblet and sip at the aromatic infusion of fermented mushrooms which was the culmination of the meal as well as the current topic of conversation.

"It may be an acquired taste," said Turjan.

"As so many things are," said Bosk's father. He lifted his own goblet high to show the warm bronze color. "We've also found it a useful anodyne for the headaches of overindulgence." He smiled at Turjan. "You'll take a flask home with you."

Turjan set his goblet down and lounged back in his chair. "You've laden me with gifts enough already, Master Septentrion."

Bosk's father waved that aside. "Dried mushrooms weigh nearly nothing. I merely wish you to remember the friendship you know here." He inclined his head toward Bosk, though his eyes remained on Turjan. "You have made an impression upon my boys that they will not soon forget."

Bosk noted that he did not even glance in Fluvio's direction.

With scarcely a pause, he went on. "Perhaps my eldest can show you around the estate. It has a few vistas worthy of attention. The gorge, of course."

"Of course," said Turjan. "And the mines themselves, possibly?"

Bosk's father shook his head with every evidence of regret. "Much too long a ride for an afternoon, I fear, and the miners are not eager for strangers. They barely tolerate our own visits."

"A shame," murmured Turjan. "Well, the gorge then, young Bosk?" He turned to the boy. "I think I would enjoy some exercise after such a satisfying meal." He pushed his chair away from the table, rose, and gave a small bow to his host.

Outside, they rambled the meticulously manicured grounds, and Turjan praised the lawn, the hedges, and even the ornamental rocks that flanked the long, eastward-curving path.

"The miners care for the grounds," Bosk told him. "That's part of our pact with them."

Turjan nodded. "I trust that, in return, they live well. Your delicacies certainly fetch high enough prices in the south."

"They live well," said Bosk. "Better in some ways than we do. Their halls never echo hollow in the night, and their fires warm their chambers better than ours."

Turjan looked back to the manse, which sprawled, wing upon wing, over a series of eminences. "Your halls are impressive. Your family has wealth that many would envy."

Bosk clasped his hands behind his back. "We have gained it all through serving our customers," he said, and he could hear his father's voice in the words.

"A fine merchant's attitude," observed Turjan.

They passed through a scatter of trees, and beyond, abruptly, lay the gorge of the River Derna, nearly a mile deep. At the bottom, the river was a narrow bronze ribbon, its flow glinting dully in the ruddy afternoon sunlight.

"Ah," said Turjan, and like other visitors, he paused with one leg closer to the chasm, the knee bent as if to push off backward, his whole weight swaying uncertainly from front leg to back. "At Miir, the river is bounded by heights, but none like this." He peered downward. "Not a sight for the faint of heart."

Bosk stood a single pace from the brink. He could not recall being afraid of the gorge, so early in life had his father brought him here. He watched Turjan flirt with it, fear showing in the damp sheen of his forehead, and he did not smile, though he knew Fluvio would have done so.

"Was there never a bridge nearby?" Turjan wondered.

Bosk pointed to the south. "They say there was, in the old days, and great conveyances crossed on a frequent schedule. A few stones still marked the approach on this side when my father was a boy, but they have crumbled away since."

Turjan drew back, leaving a comfortable margin between himself and the chasm. He motioned for Bosk to join him. "Has anyone ever fallen?"

The answer his father always insisted upon was negative, but Bosk had decided he would not lie to Turjan. "My mother," he said. "She fell, or perhaps jumped."

Turjan laid a hand on the boy's shoulder. "I am sorry to have asked such a painful question. I beg your forgiveness."

Bosk shook his head. "I don't remember her. It was soon after Fluvio and I were born."

"Hard to grow up without a mother," Turjan murmured.

Bosk took a deep breath. "Hard to grow up a Septentrion." Knowing only two ways to ask for anything—to beg, as he did with his father, or to negotiate, as he did with the miners—he chose to beg. He dropped to one knee. "Sir, whatever you require, I will do it with my whole heart. Only let me apprentice to you and learn the lore of sorcery."

Turjan crossed his arms over his chest and gazed at the boy for a long moment. "It seems exciting, doesn't it? To conjure a tree out of a table."

"I know there is more," said Bosk. "There is wisdom beyond measure and a thousand miracles to be wrought. How can any trade in mushrooms compare?"

Turjan shook his head. "None who practice sorcery today know more than a fraction of the edifice Phandaal once commanded. We spend our lives in frustration, trying to retrieve so much that has been lost. Better to be a traveling acrobat, young Bosk, than commit yourself to the lore we seek."

Bosk swallowed hard. "I ask only a small corner of the whole, sir. I would not presume to think myself capable of more than that."

Turjan glanced back toward the manse. "Why would you give up a soft life with a firm future for a world of endless questions?"

"Sir..."

"Bosk." He turned to the boy once more. "You are young to make such an important change."

"Is your answer no, then?"

"Your father would surely say so. I would guess that you have not discussed this with him."

The boy shook his head.

"Do so, then," said Turjan. "And if he approves, we can speak again someday. Possibly next year, when you have had time to consider this matter further."

Bosk felt his shoulders sag. "You doubt he will approve."

"As do you, or you would never have asked me first." Turjan gripped the boy's shoulder and urged him to rise. "Come, let's walk a little closer to the manse and speak of mushrooms. That's the lore you know already, after all."

Bosk sighed and nodded.

For ten generations, the Septentrions had dealt in mushrooms from Boreal Verge, and their knowledge of their wares was as deep as the gorge itself. Countless times, Bosk had gone with his father and brother on the day-long journey to the north, where the western face of the gorge was pocked by tunnel openings, and perilous trails of green serpentine, cut by centuries of miners, slanted down to those entrances. In the tunnels, the miners nourished their pale bounty and dried a dozen varieties that could only thus survive the journey to the south. Twice a year, the Septentrions transported this produce and returned with golden coins and foodstuffs that southerners took for granted but which were delicacies in the north—flour, dried fruit, vegetables preserved in oil.

It was a commerce that made Bosk feel trapped.

Turjan had been gone almost a month when the boy finally broached the subject of sorcery.

"What nonsense is this?" thundered his father. The family was at dinner with a newly carpentered table, the one with the tree having been consigned to a windowed alcove. "You will do as we all have done, and there's an end to it!"

Bosk pushed his plate of gratineed mushrooms away. "Father, please. Fluvio can serve the family as well as I can."

"Let him go, Father," said Fluvio.

"Be silent!" said their father. "We will not discuss this further."

Two nights later, after family and servants had retired, Bosk tucked a few coins into his waistband, packed panniers with clothing, provisions, a handful of fresh mushrooms for himself, and a sack of dried mushrooms for trade, and crept out of the manse. He was in the stable, saddling his favorite horse, when he heard a step behind him. A chill ran up his spine as he turned to face his father's wrath, but instead, there was his brother, in robe and slippers.

"He'll never change his mind," said Bosk.

"I'll tell him you went to the mines. That should be good for at least three days."

Bosk nodded. "You're welcome to every part of it."

Fluvio smiled slowly. "I was wondering when you would finally say that."

"He'll be as hard on you as he has been on me."

"I doubt that. He doesn't have another child waiting behind me."

Bosk turned back to the horse and sealed the pannier on the near side of the saddle. "I'm sorry it's been that way."

"I doubt that, too. But it won't matter once you're gone." Without another word, he turned and left the stable.

Bosk moved south by starlight, following the familiar route toward the markets of Ascolais. There was a road of sorts, and with dawn its

fragmentary pavement was occasionally visible beneath the vigorous undergrowth. Bosk knew that road, knew the isolated dwellings that dotted it, some in ruins, some still inhabited. He stopped at a few of the latter and traded mushrooms for hospitality, a long-established custom. The householders would tell his father he had passed, but that mattered little, for his father would surely guess his destination. He was surprised to see that the last of the ruins, which, in his memory, was a crumbling hovel half hidden by tall grass, had been transformed. It was whole now, the grass trimmed back into a broad esplanade.

The door was open a hand's breadth, and someone was peering out.

"Good afternoon!" Bosk shouted.

The door closed.

He glanced at the low sun. He had planned on camping in the shelter of the ruins. There was a brook nearby where he could fill his water bottle and catch a fish for his supper, and dry wood in plenty within a dozen paces of the road. Now he hoped he could still stop here, set his camp on the mown grass and sleep in the open on a night that promised to be fine. He led his horse to the water, then looped the reins over a low branch a respectful distance from the hut and removed the saddle to serve as his pillow.

The door opened again, not far enough to let him see inside, and a woman's voice called out, "Go away!"

He drew a fishing line from one of his panniers, baited it with a fragment of yesterday's supper, and soon had a fish, which he filleted with his dagger and set aside while he kindled his fire. He had a slick-surfaced pan for the fish, and a few fresh mushrooms left for adding to it, and soon the scent of supper wreathed him. When it was ready, he carried the pan to the door of the hut, knocked once, and said loudly, "You're welcome to join me."

Suddenly, the pan was wrested from him, and hard hands swept him off his feet and slung him over a surface as solid as a fence rail, knocking the breath from him. As he hung head downward, gasping, he realized he was doubled over the naked, muscular shoulder of a Deodand. His sheathed dagger was pinned between their bodies, unreachable; but the miners, who fought often for sport, had taught him a few things, and he managed to lodge one hand in the creature's armpit for leverage and hook his other arm around its neck. He wrenched fiercely. The Deodand made a guttural sound and clawed at his legs, and Bosk fought to curl his knees into its chest and use that purchase to increase the pressure on its head.

The creature was strong, but Bosk's desire to avoid being eaten was strong as well, and the contest continued until, abruptly, the two of them were on the grass. The Deodand's grip relaxed, and Bosk scrambled away from it, pulling his knife.

There was a golden arrow lodged in the creature's back.

"No need to run," said the woman's voice. "It's dead."

He looked up and saw her standing in the doorway of the hut, a golden bow in her hands, and for a moment he could not speak. She was a woman such as he had never seen before, beautiful, slender, and graceful, her hair and eyes as golden as the coins in his waistband, her skin a paler, creamy gold. Still breathing raggedly, he said, "I wasn't running," and he sheathed the blade once more.

"I see you were not," she said. And more softly, "You're just a child."

He straightened and felt the throb of strained muscles in his arms, shoulders, and thighs. "I am the heir of Boreal Verge," he said, though after saying it he remembered it was no longer exactly true.

"I don't know that land."

"To the north." He waved vaguely in that direction. He was surprised, when his hand passed before his eyes, to see it shaking. He swayed a little.

"You're injured," said the woman.

"Battered," he admitted.

She seemed to consider the matter. "Come inside," she said at last. "You would have shared your supper with me." She bent to retrieve his pan. The fish was nowhere to be seen. "I have enough for two."

"That is kind of you. But I should do something about that first." He nodded at the Deodand. "Before the scavengers come."

"I'll deal with it."

He shook his head. "I'll dig a trench for it over that way." He pointed down the road.

She circled the corpse and caught his arm. "Come."

At her touch, a thrill surged through him. She was a trifle shorter than he was, and her eyes, looking up at him, were wide and slightly tilted, and her bright hair brushed his skin like silken thread. He let her help him to the hut.

Inside, four globes shed yellow light from the corners of the room, showing a round table flanked by two armless chairs, a small cupboard against the near wall, and a narrow couch beyond. She pressed him into one of the chairs and set his pan and her bow on the table beside him. At the cupboard, she selected a small jar and took it outside, where she opened it and spilled perhaps a thimbleful of dark, heavy dust over the Deodand's body. The dust expanded to a cloud cloaking the corpse entirely, and a few heartbeats later, it dissipated, leaving nothing behind but a faintly depressed spot on the grass, and the golden arrow.

Bosk stared, open-mouthed, as she returned to the hut.

"It has no effect on the living," she said. She put the jar away and took a loaf and a plate of sliced cheese from a higher shelf and set them on the table. "Are you afraid to stay for supper?"

He shook his head and with awe in his voice said, "That was powerful sorcery."

She inclined her head. "I have some small knowledge." She took the other chair and tore a chunk of bread for herself.

"I am Bosk," he said.

"And I am Lith." She smiled the faintest of smiles and raised one finger beside her cheek. The lowest door of the cupboard opened of its own accord, and a carafe and two golden goblets floated out and settled on the table beside the loaf. She curled her finger, and the carafe poured pale, golden wine into the goblets.

Bosk picked up the nearer goblet. "I am bound to Ascolais to apprentice to a sorcerer," he said. "I hope to learn such things." The aroma of the wine was light, fruity, and appealing. Still, he waited for her to drink before he tried it, waited for her to eat before choosing from the plate himself. He did not want to think ill of her, but he was his merchant father's son, and he knew that no gift was without its price. He had wanted campfire space on her lawn in exchange for a fish supper. Now he was in her debt not only for a meal but for his life, and her golden beauty did not cause him to forget that.

"There is no poison in the food or wine," she said. She sipped from her goblet. "But suspicion can be a healthy habit. You would have done well to keep a better watch a little while ago."

"This was a safe enough place a few months past."

"There are very few truly safe places," she said, and she glanced over her shoulder, toward the far wall of the hut.

He followed her gaze. Above the couch hung a tapestry that shone in the light of the globes, a tapestry worked of every possible shade of golden thread, the tones rich and subtle, making a landscape of a broad river valley, a small village, and boundary mountains so real-seeming that they might almost have existed under some impossibly golden sun. The bottom of the tapestry was frayed, as if someone had torn it from the loom just before it could be finished. Perhaps, he thought, she was still working on it.

She turned away from it and drank from her goblet again.

"That's a beautiful piece," he said. "Your own work?"

She nodded. "A powerful piece of sorcery."

"Sorcery," he said with interest. "Of what sort?"

"A doorway to Ariventa. Or it would be if it were undamaged."

"Ariventa?"

"My home." She blinked a few times, and he could see the wetness of tears on her golden lashes. She took a deep breath. "But that's in the past, as so many things are." She drank again.

"A doorway?" he asked.

She lowered her eyes. "When I was very young, I had a great desire to travel to exotic lands. I studied the art, and finally I was able to create the tapestry and step through it to a place you might visit on your horse, but remote for me. And I had my travel. Oh, I had my fill of it. And then someone hacked the tapestry and stole away the finishing thread, and Ariventa became much too far away..." Now the tears began to trickle down her cheeks, and she wiped them away with the back of one hand. "Sorry," she whispered. "It's just so long since I've been home."

He glanced at the tapestry again. "Is there no other way to make the journey?"

She sighed deeply. "None that I know. None that anyone I've met here knows."

He wanted to reach out and stroke her hair reassuringly. "Will mending the tapestry allow you to return?"

"With the original thread, it will."

"And the thief—do you know anything about him?"

"Oh yes." She set her elbows on the table and leaned her forehead against her clasped hands. "It is Chun the Unavoidable."

He frowned. "Who?"

"He lives in the ruins north of Kaiin and keeps the finishing thread wrapped about the neck of an antique tourmaline vase. He finds amusement in withholding it from me. We are not friends, you see. He is...an unpleasant creature."

Hesitantly, Bosk touched her arm. "Is there some way I can get it back for you? If he loves mushrooms, I carry a supply of the north's finest, worth more than any golden thread."

She shook her head. "He has other tastes in food. I prefer not to think of them."

He took a deep breath, drawing strength from the feel of her smooth skin under his fingers. "I will find a potent weapon and force this Chun."

She shook her head again and eased her arm away from him. "You are a dreamer, young Bosk. Chun is much more dangerous than any Deodand. You won't even be able to enter his hall. Powerful spells keep out all but the golden-eyed, and your eyes are blue as the sky."

"I will hire a cadre of bravos, all golden-eyed, to enter for me."

One of her eyebrows rose a trifle. "You carry more mushrooms than I would have guessed."

He thought of his waistband, his panniers, and realized his assets were woefully deficient for that plan. "Well, perhaps not," he murmured.

"Never mind. I will be no worse off when you leave than I am now." She leaned back in her chair. "You have a long journey still ahead of you. You should rest. There is a mat stored under my couch, not uncomfortable, and the night promises fair. Take the bread and cheese with you."

He knew a dismissal when he heard it. Outside, the darkness was profound, but he traced his horse by its welcoming nicker and bedded down with Lith's mat and his own blanket beside his saddle. As he closed his eyes, he thought of the silken skin of her arm and the brightness of her hair, and his waking merged with a dream of her bending over him, smiling that faint smile.

In the morning, the hut was a ruin once more, and there was no trace of Lith, not even the mat upon which he had slept. Only the grassy esplanade remained to show that the place had been recently occupied. The pan, scrubbed clean, lay beside his saddle.

Bosk thought of her often during the remainder of his journey—when he lay down four nights later at an inn, the harbinger of more settled territory, when he asked at a farmyard for directions to Miir, as he rode down the causeway that led to the castle gate. His heart quickened in his chest as the gate responded to his knock, opening of its own accord, for he knew at that moment there must be something he could learn in sorcery to help her.

Turjan himself stood within the arched entry. "I wondered how soon you would undertake the journey."

Bosk descended from his mount. "My father forbade it."

"He will forgive you when you return home."

"Will I return?"

"We all return, someday," said Turjan. "Exactly when will be your own decision." He gestured for Bosk to enter.

The stable was near the gate and housed several fine horses and a groom who took over Bosk's own.

"An uneventful journey, I trust." Turjan guided his guest across a small courtyard to the main hall, a high-ceilinged chamber of marble floors and rich hangings, of tables inlaid with precious woods and chairs cushioned in crimson velvet.

"There was one event," the boy said. "A somewhat strenuous encounter with a Deodand, followed by a pleasant meal with a beautiful golden-haired witch named Lith. She had a magical dwelling that vanished in the night. Perhaps you know the lady?"

Turjan studied the boy's face. "You were lucky to be born with blue eyes. Were they golden, I doubt we'd be speaking now. Lith has a habit of sending golden-eyed men to an unpleasant fate in the home of Chun the Unavoidable. I believe she has quite depleted the golden-eyed population of Ascolais."

Bosk weighed that information against his own experience of her. "She seemed very unhappy."

"She has been unhappy for some time. A wise man would leave her to it. Ah, here is a much happier lady, and a sweeter one, too."

A child had emerged from a doorway on one side of the hall, a girl of perhaps nine years, wearing long, raven-dark braids and a tunic and hose that mimicked Turjan's. She strode up to Bosk with a cordial smile, and offered him her hand. The top of her head was barely higher than his waist.

"Welcome to Miir, Master Bosk. I am Rianna."

"My daughter," said Turjan.

Bosk bowed deeply and kissed her hand.

"We shall apprentice together," said Rianna.

"I consider that a privilege," said Bosk.

"You'll meet her mother at supper," said Turjan. "But first we'll show you your quarters."

His room was reached by climbing the broad staircase at the rear of the hall, and it was nearly as large as his bedchamber at Boreal Verge, with a lush carpet, a soft bed, and a window that looked out onto the courtyard. His belongings had been delivered already and the contents tucked into

one corner of a wardrobe that occupied most of a wall. New clothes were laid out on the bed, and in an alcove at the far end of the room lay a private bath, with steaming water waiting.

"One of the servants will escort you to dinner," said Rianna, and she and her father closed the door as they left.

The hot bath was welcome after so many days of cold brook water or none at all. He tried not to dawdle, but by the time he was dressed, the servant was already tapping at the door. In the main hall, the table was set for four, with three places occupied. The woman opposite Turjan was obviously the child's mother.

"My dear, this is the new apprentice," Turjan said to her. "Bosk, this is T'sain, my wife."

She was dark-haired and pale-skinned, as beautiful in her way as Lith, but completely different, for she had a quick, full smile. Turjan and Rianna were smiling as well, and Bosk nodded to all of them, feeling faintly jealous that there had been so few smiles at Boreal Verge's table. The meal, which included no mushrooms of any variety, was excellent, and the conversation flowed easily from one topic to another, from gardening to sorcery to the latest addition to Rianna's dollhouse.

"You shall see it later. You won't be disappointed," she promised.

The tale of the Deodand was drawn from him, and appropriate exclamations were forthcoming from the distaff sides of the table.

"She knew about it," said Rianna, with blunt indignation. "She should have killed it before it could attack an innocent traveler. I would have."

Turjan patted her hand. "I don't doubt you would have tried. But they are dangerous creatures. I suppose she thought an innocent traveler would distract it enough to provide an opportunity for the bow."

"It was a magical bow, wasn't it, Father?"

"Probably. But even with magic, a Deodand is a formidable adversary." He looked at Bosk. "That's the first lesson of apprenticeship—that you cannot escape unscathed every time."

"I won't forget it," said the boy. As he spoke, he felt himself beginning to yawn, and he tried to stifle it, but with little success.

Turjan pushed his chair back from the table. "The second lesson will be tomorrow." He gestured to the servant who had scurried forward to clear the table. "This can wait. Show Master Bosk back to his bedchamber."

In the morning, there was fruit and porridge at the same table, and then Turjan took him to the library where he would be studying. Rianna was there already, sitting at a long table, reading from a book as thick as her fist. She had a pad of vellum under her right hand and was copying a diagram to it in a meticulous hand. There were many tomes in the bookcases lining the walls, and a variety of pads and writing implements on the table.

"There is considerable wisdom in this room," said Turjan. "For now, you will spend your mornings investigating it, and after the midday meal each day, we will test what you have absorbed and determine what other techniques may enhance it. The collection has been laid out to begin with the simplest principles, here." He pointed to the highest shelf closest to the door. "You will work your way to the right on this first bookcase, and when you reach the end of the shelf, you will begin on the next lower. The first case should require approximately a year."

Bosk looked around the room with some dismay. He counted twelve cases.

"Did you think an apprenticeship in sorcery would be brief, young Bosk?" said Turjan.

Bosk straightened his shoulders and went to the first shelf to take down the initial volume. It was heavy. He set it on the table. "I see from the vacant place that your daughter is more than a year ahead of me."

"So she is. That is one of the advantages of being born to sorcery."

"Then, with your permission, I will endeavor to learn from her as well as from yourself."

Rianna looked up from her book, but said nothing.

Turjan smiled. "Well, we'll see what sort of teacher she makes." At the door, he said, "The midday meal will be in the tower garden. Rianna will show you. And Bosk—the books are by many different authors, and after a time you will find a certain repetition in them, though with variation. That, too, will be important to you." Then he was gone.

Bosk settled at the opposite end of the table from Rianna and ran his hands over the leather tooling of his book's cover. The script was so ornate that at first he could not read it, but by following its curves with a finger, he managed to spell out "Laccodel." He opened it to the first page. It was handwritten, but readable enough, and proved to be a history of Laccodel's attempts to reproduce the work of an older mage, part diary, part exercise book. Bosk chose a pad and stylus and made a few notes, though he did not at all understand what the notes meant. After a time, he looked at Rianna, who was annotating her diagrams with arcane sigils and tinted inks. She seemed so intent on her work that he hesitated to disturb her.

Yet soon enough she glanced up at him, and he thought he might offer a bit of polite conversation.

"What are you studying?" he said.

She added a stroke to the top of her drawing. "The Third Evolution of Mazirian's Diminution."

"Ah," he said, not knowing what else might be appropriate.

"My goal is to perfect it before my tenth birthday."

"And that will be…?

"Not long. Has Laccodel bored you already? His prose is turgid in the extreme."

"Not bored. Merely mystified," said Bosk.

She smiled with pursed lips. "He is a foundation of sorcery. He knew Phandaal himself."

"Your father spoke of Phandaal when he was at Boreal Verge. Who was he?"

"One cannot study sorcery without studying Phandaal." She turned to her book once more. "You'll learn about him and the rest of the great ones if you keep reading."

He took a deep breath and opened his book at the beginning. Instead of notes, this time he wrote queries on his pad. When he had filled three pages with them, he heard Rianna close her book with a thump. He looked up and saw her gazing at him with her chin cupped in one hand.

"Hungry?" she said.

Only then did he realize that his stomach was clamoring.

The tower garden was at the highest extremity of the castle, a place of multicolored flowers that tilted their petals to face Bosk as he passed, as if they were curious about their visitor. The view from their midst was impressive—the Derna green within its steep banks, the forest stretching north and west, the towers of Kaiin gleaming like a pale mirage on the southern horizon. The meal was set out on a trestle table—cold meats, jellied broths, vegetables steamed with four distinct spices. Bosk sampled them all, pleased that not a single mushroom appeared on any platter.

"We do eat mushrooms," said Rianna, "but Father thought they would bore you even more than Laccodel."

Turjan arrived after they finished and asked Bosk what he had learned that morning. Bosk offered his queries, and the three spent the afternoon discussing them, Turjan deftly leading Bosk through concepts he had not quite comprehended and calling on Rianna to expand upon them. Bosk found his zest for the lore of sorcery increasing as every answer provoked new questions. He scarcely noticed the ruddy sun sinking toward the west until it shone in his eyes.

Turjan leaned back from the table. "You'll do well enough, young Bosk. You have the desire, without which learning is mere rote." He gazed out at the shadowed landscape. "Have you had enough for today?"

Bosk considered the length of the evening that lay before him. "If you'll allow it, I'll look at the book again before supper."

Turjan smiled at him. "I think you'll be better served just now by something else." He turned to his daughter. "You've been chafing to show him the doll house."

She rose eagerly.

"An introduction only," her father said. "As we decided."

She was already gesturing for Bosk to follow her.

One flight below was a high-ceilinged chamber that occupied the whole breadth of the tower, with tall windows and glowing sconces alternating on every wall. The center of the space was occupied by a duplicate in miniature of Castle Miir, complete to the roof garden paved with tiny replica flowers. At his first sight of it, Bosk was astonished by the detail of architecture, and even more astonished when, at Rianna's touch, the outer wall split and swung open to reveal an interior as meticulously executed as the exterior. He knelt to peer at elaborately furnished cubicles, tapestries no larger than kerchiefs covering their walls, delicate chandeliers dangling from their ceilings. He found his own quarters, the bed and wardrobe and even the bath reproduced in toy size, a manikin no larger than his littlest finger standing at the door.

"Two years work," said Rianna, pride in her voice. "Every bit of it crafted by my hands. I even wove the linens. And watch." She spoke a phrase that Bosk could not quite make out, and draperies pulled themselves over the windows and the sconces went out, leaving a darkness so profound that he dared not move for fear of damaging something, possibly even himself. Then she spoke another phrase, and hundreds of tiny yellow-green lights, like so many fireflies, sprang into being in chandeliers and candelabra all through the doll house and in tiny lanterns outlining the gate, the courtyard, and the crenellations. There was light enough to allow Bosk to rise from his knees and walk surefooted all around the structure.

"How beautiful," he said. "And after it is all complete…?"

She crossed her arms and smiled. "Then I'll learn to make dolls that walk. And perhaps even talk." She plucked the manikin from his room and showed it to him. It had yielding skin and limbs that flexed, and it could be bent into a sitting position and perched in a tiny chair. Rianna left it so in the main hall, where three other dolls sat at a table much like the one where last night's meal had been served. One of the dolls was smaller than the others and had long black braids. She straightened that one and set it on a bed in another room. "I tried to convince some of the Twk people to live here. It's much more comfortable than their gourds." She took the two remaining original figures from the dining table and set them on a bed on the opposite side of the building. "But they refused."

"The Twk people?"

"You'll meet them." She stepped back and touched the gate, and the miniature castle swung shut.

"You left me at the table," Bosk remarked.

Rianna laughed softly. "They're only dolls, Bosk." A phrase made the wall sconces spring to life, and another extinguished the miniature lights.

He followed her downstairs to supper, which again included no mushrooms.

Laccodel's book occupied Bosk for many days, and then there was a second volume of Laccodel, and a third. By the time he had finished them and discussed their contents with Turjan and Rianna countless times, he felt he would know and hate Laccodel's prose style any time he encountered it. Yet his first magical effort arose from Laccodel, a transformation of citrine dust into amethyst, and he could not help feeling triumph at the simple change from yellow to purple.

"Well done," said Turjan. "And now back again."

It took Bosk two weeks to manage that.

"Sometimes undoing is the more important of the two," said Turjan.

"I prefer the purple," said Bosk, and he changed the dust again and stored it in a vial to remind himself that he had learned something. It seemed very little for the many weeks he had been studying,

The next day, a Twk-man arrived during the midday meal. He was a tiny creature, no larger than Bosk's littlest finger, greenish of skin, wearing a gauzy smock, and mounted on a dragonfly. As she did occasionally, Rianna's mother had joined the apprentices in the roof garden, and all the flowers had turned their petals to her, but when the Twk-man alighted, they tilted to him instead. T'sain offered her hand, the dragonfly leaped to it, and she held it close to her ear and nodded at something its rider said in a soft, buzzing voice. Then steed and rider flashed to the flowers, where the tiny man gathered pollen from a dozen blossoms and stowed it in two sacks behind his legs.

"Dandanflores," T'sain explained to Bosk. "Chieftain of the Twk people. They know all of the news of Ascolais."

"The last time he visited," said Rianna, "he told us you were coming."

The Twk chieftain made a circle around Bosk's head and flew off.

"Do they range far north?" Bosk asked.

"Not as far as Boreal Verge," said T'sain.

"Ah."

"Your family is too far away, Bosk."

"Oh, I was just curious." He did feel a twinge of disappointment, though.

"If you ever do want news from the Twk," said Rianna, "you must pay for it."

T'sain nodded. "They are as much merchants as your family, though their goods are less tangible."

He considered that. "What sort of payment would be appropriate for such a small creature?"

"They like our pollen," said T'sain, "as you saw."

"And I make them clothes of spider silk, the softest in the world," said her daughter. She frowned. "Now that you've seen one, don't you think they would enjoy living in my doll house?"

"If I were one of them, I would."

"We have discussed this before," Rianna's mother said, and her words were directed at Bosk rather than at her daughter. "The Twk have their own lives, and what they choose must be respected. They are neither toys nor slaves."

Rianna bent her head over her food. "You're right, of course. It's just that…creating living toys is so difficult."

Later, in the library, where both of them spent far more than the mornings Turjan required, Rianna said to Bosk, "Would you like to visit my doll house again?"

"Perhaps this evening. Just now, I'm trying to unravel one of Phandaal's simpler spells."

"Which?" She craned to see his book.

"The Insinuating Eye."

"That is advanced for your stage of knowledge."

"I've been reading ahead, trying to discern some overall structure to sorcery."

"Father says there is no overall structure, that all is haphazard."

"Phandaal thought there was structure."

"Laccodel says Phandaal thought there was structure, which is not at all the same."

Bosk sighed. "There are principles."

"I see no great connections among them."

"You are not even ten years old!" Bosk exclaimed. And then, at her injured expression, he said, "Forgive me. We are both very young in sorcery. What can we know?"

"You are younger than I," she said in a low voice, and she slammed her book shut and left the room.

When she did not return, he descended to the doll house chamber and found her sitting cross-legged on the floor, the miniature castle open before her. She was arranging tiny platters in the drawers of a tiny sideboard. She did not look up at him.

He sat down beside her. "I truly am sorry."

She did not speak.

He shifted to one knee. "I beg your forgiveness, Lady Rianna."

After a long moment, she said, "I know a great deal more than you do."

"Of course you do. It's why I depend upon you to help me." He eased back to a sitting position and gestured toward the sideboard. "Can I help you with this?"

She shook her head. "Your hands are too clumsy."

"I wish they were not."

She shut the last drawer with the tip of one finger. "Do you really want to do something for me?"

"I'll do whatever you ask."

She looked at him at last, sullenness fading from her lips. "I'll teach you a spell if you'll promise not to tell Father. He'd say you're not ready for it."

"You have my promise," said Bosk.

"It's Mazirian's Diminution."

"The one you are studying."

"Yes. I'll teach you the First and Second Evolutions, and you must commit both to memory. Both."

"And they will accomplish...?"

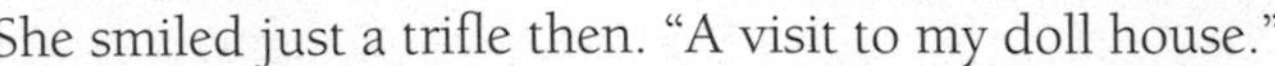

She smiled just a trifle then. "A visit to my doll house."

"Ah," he said. "Diminution. Of course."

"Will you do it?"

He thought of the amethyst dust he had taken such pride in creating. It seemed like nothing now. "Yes!"

The spells were complex, requiring certain pauses, certain intonations, and a few sounds that did not quite seem human. Memorizing them was by no means simple. Yet after little more than an hour of drill, Bosk felt he had them. To be certain, he wrote them on a scrap of vellum, following Laccodel's model syllabary, and tucked it into his pocket.

"I'll go first," said Rianna, and in a matter of heartbeats, she had shrunk to the size of the Twk-man.

Bosk gasped. Knowing it would be effective and seeing it happen were very different things.

Rianna's voice was tiny, piping, though he knew she must be shouting. "Come along!"

He took a deep breath and uttered the spell. He began to feel dizzy. As the walls of the tower chamber seemed to rush upward all around him, he fell to his knees, fighting to control his churning stomach. In a moment, though, the room steadied, the dizziness faded, and Rianna was beside him, helping him stagger to his feet. Nearby, the miniature castle was huge, and the ceiling of the chamber was as far away as the sky. Bosk took a few wobbling steps and laughed with the sheer joy of accomplishment. His stride was as firm as ever by the time he and Rianna entered the doll house version of Miir.

Bosk found their exploration beguiling. Everything was familiar yet simultaneously strange and wonderful. He would have lost himself in the place and stayed until dark to see the lights bloom, but Rianna was concerned that one of her parents might appear to fetch them to supper, and she fairly dragged him out. He was glad, then, that he had the scrap of vellum, for he had forgotten some of the reversal spell. Rianna cautioned him to stand well away from the gate for the process, and she herself trotted even farther off. While she sprouted upward like some impossible plant, he went over the sounds silently half a dozen times, listening to them in his mind.

"Bosk, we have to go to supper," said Rianna, and her voice was so loud he had to press his hands over his ears to bear it.

He needed three tries to get the spell right, but he finally saw the duplicate of Castle Miir shrink away from him and the ceiling of the tower chamber slam downward. He lost his balance again, and Rianna pulled at him with both hands to keep him from tumbling into her creation.

"The dizziness will be less with practice," she said. "Now tell me, apprentice Bosk, what do you truly think of my doll house?"

"Rianna," he said, "you and your doll house are astonishing."

She seemed pleased with that answer, and he guessed that he had finally been forgiven for his affront. He went to supper smiling, and when Turjan asked why he was so cheerful, he said only that he thought his studies were going well.

He liked Mazirian's Diminution, his first major spell, and over the next few weeks, he practiced to perfect both Evolutions, at first only when Rianna was present, but eventually alone in his bedchamber. There, too, he worked on the Spell of the Insinuating Eye. Turjan knew about the latter and let him continue, as long as he also spent time with the appropriate preceding books. The Insinuating Eye had little potential for damaging the practitioner; it simply allowed him to see things that were far away.

At the creator's end, the Eye occupied an onyx ring the size of the circle made by the tips of his thumb and forefinger set together, and at the far end it manifested as a fuzzy loop floating in air. His initial attempts to control it resulted in wild oscillations of the view from the forest to the river to the sky. Soon, though, he learned to hold it steady no matter how quickly he moved it, and to adjust distance and direction with delicate precision. In most places, the smoky loop appeared to go unnoticed. Certainly, when he practiced spying on Boreal Verge, neither his father nor Fluvio paid it any attention.

Bosk led Turjan to believe that homesickness was his motive for generating the Eye, but his true goal was the hall of Chun the Unavoidable. He had little trouble locating the ruins north of Kaiin, and the hall, the only undamaged structure there, was easy enough to identify. He circumnavigated the exterior, watching for Chun to emerge, and when twice he glimpsed the creature from afar, he immediately terminated the spell, each time allowing some days to pass before taking up his vigil again. When the singularly grotesque Chun, wearing a cape studded with golden-irised eyeballs, came forth a third time, Bosk observed him recede beyond the city before attempting to slide the Eye inside.

The hall was a surprisingly spare dwelling, with a few pillars supporting the roof and walls as pale and blank as alabaster. There was no couch, no hearth, no curio cabinet; its sole furnishing was a small, round table set in an alcove opposite the entrance. Upon the table rested a graceful tourmaline vase, green below and magenta above. But there was no golden thread wrapped about its slender neck.

Sharply disappointed, Bosk searched the hall again, to no avail.

At supper that night, Turjan looked so long and so silently at Bosk that the boy squirmed in his chair. "Have I done something wrong, sir?"

"I received a visitor this afternoon," said Turjan.

Bosk waited, both curious and apprehensive.

"I believe you know something of him. Chun the Unavoidable."

Bosk stopped breathing.

"He asked that you leave off spying on him. He said it in stronger terms, but that is the gist. We spoke of Chun when you first arrived, and now I realize that I did not sufficiently warn you against him. Fortunately, you are safe within these walls. However, he did require payment for his discomfiture. Breathe, boy, else you'll fall over in a faint."

Bosk gulped air. "Sir...do you intend to dismiss me?"

"We all do foolish things occasionally. We can hope none of them cost us more than a vat-grown golden eye." One side of his mouth quirked. "It seemed an appropriate exchange for your use of that other Eye."

"Then...you don't intend to dismiss me?"

Turjan leaned back in his chair. "On the contrary, I am pleased you were able to use the Eye so well. Therefore, this is not such a negative as you might think. Now, what were you seeking at Chun's hall"

"Nothing," said Bosk. "It was simply experimentation."

Turjan sighed. "It is early in your apprenticeship to lie to your master. Subterfuge, I expect." He glanced at his daughter, who immediately looked down at her plate. "But outright lying is a poor basis for a master-student alliance."

Bosk straightened his back. "Sir, I was seeking a golden thread ripped from a tapestry."

"Ah. Lith."

Bosk nodded. "But he did not seem to have it."

"I believe I suggested that Lith was a lady to be avoided."

"I owe her my life, sir. I would prefer not to remain in her debt."

"Or perhaps she saved you in order to establish that debt?"

Bosk turned that over in his mind, and he did not find it an outrageous suggestion. Even so, he could not forget the sadness in Lith's eyes as she

spoke of Ariventa. "At any rate," he murmured," I don't know what else I can do for her. Unless Chun can be persuaded to reveal its location, the thread is gone." He gazed at Turjan hopefully. "Perhaps another golden eye?"

"I would prefer not to deal with Chun again, young Bosk."

"The Twk will know where the thread is," said Rianna.

Bosk turned to her.

"You'll have to pay them, of course."

The boy looked back at Turjan. "You know the things they covet. I will repay you, I swear it."

"This is your endeavor, young Bosk," said Turjan. "Continue your studies. Perhaps someday you will find a way to achieve your desire."

"Perhaps," said Bosk, but he felt helpless.

He thought of Lith that night, as he had on many a night. But recalling the fear he had felt at the possibility of dismissal, he also thought of his own home. Would they have welcomed him back, as Turjan once assured him, or was his father as glad as Fluvio to be rid of him? As the ageing sun was just beginning to illuminate his bedchamber, he decided to send the Insinuating Eye to Boreal Verge, perhaps to find some evidence one way or the other. Morning twilight showed his old room just as he had left it; not even dust had accumulated, as if the place were being held in readiness for his return. For a moment, that made him feel better; then he realized that the servants would never allow any part of the manse to become dusty.

He did feel the touch of homesickness then. The memories of his childhood were in that room—a handful of green serpentine pebbles, collected on his first journey to the mines, a few fragile bird skulls, found under a shrub on the estate, a cup he had molded from clay and fired in a makeshift kiln. The cup was blackened and cracked, remnant of the flames that had spread from the kiln and destroyed the outbuilding he had been using as his workshop. His father had not been happy about that.

He shifted the Eye close to the pebbles. He wished now he had taken one with him. Such a small thing, it would have fit easily in his pocket. Through the Eye, it seemed close enough to touch. With the tip of one finger, he tapped at the space within the onyx ring, expecting some sort of resistance, but there was none. He pressed his finger into it, and when he withdrew, the finger seemed unharmed, and so he pushed more boldly, trying to touch the pebbles, but they were farther away than they seemed. He pulled out his knife and slipped it through the ring, but the point fell short. He ran downstairs to the kitchen, where a sleepy cook was just beginning to prepare rolls for the morning meal and had no objection to lending him a pair of kitchen tongs and a skewer the length of a sword. Both fit through the ring, but only the skewer could reach the pebbles, and it was so difficult to control that it knocked several to the floor. He pulled it back, wondering if he could fasten a pouch to its tip or daub it with some sort of glue. Neither notion seemed likely to work. He could think of only one other possibility.

He propped the onyx ring against his pillow and slid his copy of the Second Evolution of Mazirian's Diminution into his pocket. Then he shrank himself to doll size and stepped through the ring. He only had to dip his head slightly to fit.

That single step revealed a tunnel, cool and dark, with walls slick as polished metal. The far end was no longer the clear view of his old room that had been visible to full-size Bosk; rather, it was merely a speck of light in the far distance. He moved toward it, hands braced against the walls, the curved floor making for uncertain footing in the darkness. The speck expanded slowly, and after a time he could discern a blur of green within it, which he guessed must be the pebbles. He walked faster and finally began to run. The light loomed, and he emerged from the tunnel and fell headlong over one of the pebbles, boulder-size to his shrunken self. He clutched at it, the breath knocked out of him. The pebble had not moved at the impact, and he realized that he did not have the strength to transport any of the stones back to Miir. But he did not care. He felt triumphant at merely making the journey. He was a true sorcerer now. He pulled himself up to sit on the pebble and contemplate his old room grown huge.

A soft noise startled him. It might have been the door opening, perhaps a servant coming in to clean. He did not wait to find out. He turned to the faint gray ring of the Eye, dived into it, and ran. He stumbled a few times on the curve of the tunnel floor, and once his head grazed the ceiling, but he managed to reach Miir. Leaning against the pillow, he reached into his pocket for the Second Evolution.

It was gone.

He thought it must have fallen in the tunnel or among the pebbles at Boreal Verge, a speck of paper that no one would ever notice. He was not greatly concerned, though, for the spell was clear in his memory. He spoke it.

Nothing happened.

He tried several more times before admitting to himself that he truly needed the written version. With a sigh, he pushed the onyx ring under the pillow and settled himself over it, hoping that Rianna would be the one to find him. He was disappointed in that. Turjan himself read the Fourth Evolution from the book of spells and restored him to his normal size.

"These are difficult spells," Turjan said, closing the book. "Even the greatest of us have some difficulty maintaining more than three or four of them in our memories at any one time. You are fresh at the lore to recall even two."

"Which is why I wrote down the Second Evolution."

"Perhaps you should have inked it on your arm instead of on paper."

Bosk brightened. "I'll do that next time."

Turjan laughed. "As you wish, young Bosk. Then you'll have no trouble restoring yourself at either end of the Eye." At Bosk's wary expression, he added, "Oh come now—don't you think I know every instance of sorcery within these walls? Now, if you intend to range so far at the size of a caterpillar, you should know another spell to keep you safe. I would not wish to tell your father that a house cat ate his son."

Bosk swallowed hard.

For the rest of the day, he and Turjan were cloistered in the anteroom to Turjan's own quarters while Bosk learned the spell of the Omnipotent Sphere. When he was certain he had it, Turjan tested him again and again. In the end, Bosk did write it on his arm in indelible ink.

"Write it and rewrite it," said Turjan. "Until you have it so committed to memory that you will never forget it."

Bosk nodded.

"We will repeat the test from time to time."

Bosk nodded again.

"Now go ask the Twk where your golden thread can be found."

"But sir, I have nothing with which to pay them."

Turjan smiled at him. "Are you so sure of that?"

Bosk raised his hands in perplexity.

"Well, young Bosk, perhaps it will help you to know that the Twk are very fond of mushrooms."

"But I have none," said Bosk.

"Indeed? What a shame."

And then it was time for dinner, which included no mushrooms at all.

In his bedchamber that night, Bosk searched through his panniers, but as he had thought, his mushrooms had all been used up in the journey to Ascolais. He climbed into bed, and when he slid his hand beneath the pillow to tuck it against his cheek, there was the onyx ring of the Insinuating Eye.

And he realized that mushrooms, even fresh ones, weighed far less than pebbles.

With the dawn, he was in the cold pantry of Boreal Verge, where the family's private stock of fresh mushrooms was kept. He could only carry one at a time, and so he made half a dozen trips from there to his bedchamber at Miir.

At the morning meal, he asked how one of the Twk could be summoned.

"They visit when it suits them," T'sain said. "They answer no one's call."

"Then I must go to them," said Bosk. "Can someone give me directions for the journey?" He looked to Turjan.

Turjan glanced at Rianna.

"I've been to Twk town," she admitted.

In the library, she drew a map. The Twk lived in the forest, with no signposts showing the way, but there was an unmistakable pattern of boulders and trees leading to them, with the largest tree of all the destination. "If you stand below and call for Dandanflores, he will come," she said. "Tell him you're there at Rianna's request."

That afternoon, in his bedchamber, he guided the Eye to the Twk town, a cluster of perhaps a hundred hollowed-out gourds set high in the branches of that enormous tree. For a time, he watched the Twk and their dragonfly mounts ferrying goods to homes that were as large to them as his room was to him. He peeked inside a few gourds and found Twk families gathered at tiny tables and chairs, searching in tiny chests and cabinets, or napping in silky hammocks, each no larger than the finger of a glove. Seeing them so, he could well understand Rianna's wish for Twk to live in her doll house.

He set the far end of the Eye near the round entrance of one of the larger gourds, shrank himself to Twk size, and perched at the terminus of the tunnel, legs dangling over the edge of the smoky ring. Presently, a dragonfly emerged from the gourd and hovered beside him, and the draft from its wings was strong enough to make him hold tight to his seat. At his size, the rider's voice seemed deep as any human's.

"Who are you," said the Twk-man.

"Rianna sent me. I am Bosk, and I seek Dandanflores."

The dragonfly darted away. Shortly, another rider arrived. "I remember you," he said. "You were formerly larger."

"It's Rianna's spell," said Bosk.

"Oh, has she put you in her doll house?"

"I have visited it."

"A vile place," said the Twk chieftain. "No Twk would consent to inhabit it."

"So I understand. But I have not come to ask it of you. Rather, I seek information."

"Many do. And what do you have to offer in exchange?"

"I am Bosk Septentrion. Perhaps you have heard of my family."

"I have," said the Twk-man.

Bosk leaned back into the tunnel and brought forth a mushroom larger than his head. "This is an excellent example of our wares," he said, "and fresh, not dried, with all the nuances of its flavor intact. Steamed, sautéed, or even raw dipped in mustard sauce, it makes a royal dish. It is my gift to the chieftain of the Twk." He held it out. "I have others to offer if you and I can strike a bargain."

Dandanflores curved an arm around the mushroom, pinched off a fragment, and popped it into his mouth. He chewed it with a thoughtful expression. After a moment, he said, "Now what could a creature who emerges from nothingness and sits on its edge want from me?"

"The location of a certain golden thread," said Bosk, "formerly in the possession of Chun the Unavoidable but the property of one Lith, a witch with golden hair and eyes."

"Oh, that," said Dandanflores.

Bosk nodded. "I seek to return it to the lady."

The Twk-man shifted the mushroom to a net behind his left hip. "The thread changed hands in most equitable fashion."

"Yet it was stolen property."

"The new owner did not steal it. That fault was Chun's."

"If the new owner will not surrender it for the sake of conscience, then I will buy it. To whom shall I make the offer?"

The Twk chieftain cocked his head to one side. "Let us discuss the situation in more detail. My home is nearby, and my steed is strong enough to carry two."

The chieftain's home was one of the larger gourds. Within, it was like the other Twk dwellings, the space illuminated by windows cut in the walls and partitioned by shelf-like platforms that held the furniture. A Twk-woman and several children were there. Dandanflores and Bosk dismounted from the dragonfly at the lowest platform and climbed several ladders to the uppermost. From there, the family's sleeping quarters were within easy reach, a hammock for each suspended from the rounded ceiling, loosely woven of thick fibers and padded with dandelion fluff. The largest hammock was trimmed with spiral-wound golden rope.

"It's handsome, is it not?" said the Twk chieftain

Bosk made no reply. He knew what he was looking at.

"Part of my bargain with Chun was that I would never return the thread to Lith. So you can see my dilemma."

"I am not Lith," said Bosk. "In fact, the thread has so struck my fancy that I would prefer to keep it for myself. It would make a handsome ornament for my hat."

"You wear no hat," observed the Twk-man.

"That can be remedied. What will you exchange for the thread?"

Dandanflores contemplated the hammock. "I am reluctant to part with it."

"I can offer a large quantity of fresh mushrooms of many varieties."

"Yet how many mushrooms could my family consume before they spoiled?"

"There could be an ongoing supply over a period of weeks or months."

"Even so. After a time they would surely pall."

Bosk had to admit that he understood the complaint. In his memory, he could see his father at the dining table, happily eating his own mushrooms and urging his sons to eat theirs. He wondered if his father had been told of the missing mushrooms. Probably no one had noticed, they were so few. An ongoing supply, though, would have been more obvious, and some servant at Boreal Verge would have been blamed for the theft. Bosk felt suddenly guilty for having no way to pay for the mushrooms he had so blithely offered. Sorcerer or no, he was still a merchant's son and he had not been raised to cheat the family.

And then, the merchant's son truly awoke in him. The Twk, small enough to live in Rianna's doll house, were small enough to pass through the Insinuating Eye.

"I have a proposition for you," he said, and he outlined a partnership between the house of Septentrion and the Twk-folk. With the Eye as their highway, the Twk would convey fresh mushrooms from the north to the city of Kaiin, where Bosk would purvey them to the jaded appetites of the rich. The Twk would receive a commission for their labors, Bosk would take one for his enterprise, and the Septentrion family would profit from a previously nonexistent commerce.

Dandanflores looked dubious.

"Dried mushroom are excellent," said Bosk, "but as you yourself so recently observed, the fresh are superior. They will command a premium, but are unlikely to diminish sales of the dried significantly, if they are only available in a limited supply, let us say, once a month."

"I was thinking more of your magical tunnel," said Dandanflores. "Magic has its dangers and is generally best avoided."

"I have come to no harm," said Bosk.

"You are a sorcerer."

Bosk thought of the spells written on his arms, covered by his loose sleeves. "I am a mere apprentice. If there were danger, it would have found me." When Dandanflores made no reply, Bosk pushed harder. "I thought the chieftain of the Twk would be wise and brave in the service of his people. Would you deny them such profit as would enhance their lives?"

Dandanflores crossed his arms and looked past Bosk. The children had climbed to the platform below and were listening to the conversation. One of them shouted, "Take me along, Da!"

His father glared at him. "Boys," he muttered, and shifted the glare to Bosk. "You are all alike."

Bosk shrugged. "Someone has to dare."

"Very well," said the Twk chieftain. "Show me this Eye, and I'll judge for myself."

They mounted the dragonfly and returned to the smoky ring floating among the branches. Bosk dismounted first, stepping into the tunnel. He braced his back against one side and held a hand out to the Twk-man. Dandanflores did not take it but rather ran his own hands around the ring until he seemed satisfied with its solidity. Only then did he test it with one foot. Bosk eased back to allow him into the tunnel.

"Once inside the ring, you became a wraith of thinnest smoke," said the Twk chieftain. "I suppose the same has happened to me."

"It only appears so from the outside," said Bosk.

"Obviously," said Dandanflores. "Let us continue this adventure."

They reached the opposite end of the Eye and emerged into Bosk's bedchamber.

"The tunnel can be shifted until its two ends are anywhere I choose," said Bosk.

The Twk-man flexed his hands and looked down at his body. "I am unharmed," he said, "and therefore we have a bargain. When does our commerce begin?"

"As soon as I make the arrangements with my father. And may I suggest that your payment will be due after the first consignment of mushrooms is sold in Kaiin."

"That seems satisfactory."

Bosk conducted him back to the Twk town.

Bosk's father and Fluvio were at supper when Bosk descended the main stairway at Boreal Verge. Fluvio occupied the chair that once had been Bosk's, and he had been listening to some fatherly declamation before his father stopped speaking in mid-sentence. They both stared as Bosk approached the table.

"Good evening, Father, Fluvio." He pulled out a chair for himself. "I hope I find you well. Ah, I see the evening meal is based upon mushrooms again."

His father found voice first. "Shall I order some for you?"

"No need, Father. I'll sup at Miir." He nodded. "Yes, I travel in magical fashion these days. I have spent a most productive time at Miir and expect to learn more in years to come."

His father cleared his throat. "Master Turjan sent us word. He has been pleased with your progress. I still disapprove, but you do seem to have an aptitude for it."

"True as that may be," said Bosk, and he laced his fingers together upon the table, "I have not forgotten what I learned at your side." He outlined his plan to employ the Twk, citing unspecified sorcery as the means rather than giving any details of the Eye. "The family will profit from this. All we need to begin the operation is a small amount of silver for rental of a modest shop in the heart of the city and a sufficient supply of the commodity for our first consignment, which will be limited but choice. Once the wealthy of Kaiin sample our wares, they will not hesitate to purchase. Possibly we will gift the Prince with a selection, given his penchant for setting the fashion. Does this appeal to you, Father?"

"The price must be high," said his father. "Commensurate with the complexity of the transport."

"Exactly my thinking."

His father regarded him with narrowed eyes. "I did not expect you to use sorcery to profit the family."

Bosk met his gaze. "I am a Septentrion."

His father nodded. "This is a good plan. We will implement it." He turned to Fluvio. "You will help your brother as necessary. I will fetch the silver."

Fluvio watched their father leave. "We should talk," he said. "Shall we walk out on the grounds where we cannot be overheard?"

"As you wish," said Bosk.

Outside, Fluvio spoke in a low voice. "We have two new servants. What you have said already will fly back to the mines, and the miners will want higher pay for their goods. Father should have thought of that. Perhaps his age is beginning to tell on him."

"Father is hardly old. And there is no reason why the miners should not share in this new source of income."

Fluvio shook his head. "For doing nothing more than they have always done? I think not."

Bosk shrugged. "Father will decide."

"We should unite in our opinion. Then he will listen."

"Perhaps," Bosk said, though he doubted it.

"We are the new generation of Septentrions," said Fluvio. "The family commerce will be ours."

Bosk laughed softly. "Yours," he said. "I have made another choice."

"Then why have you come back? Why have you brought this proposal?"

"I have my reasons."

They walked in silence for a time, Fluvio looking down at the grass, Bosk waiting for him to speak again, for he was sure there would be more speaking.

Instead, Fluvio turned and struck him, and the blow was so hard that Bosk did not even feel himself fall. When he came to his senses, head spinning and sour bile filling his nose and throat, he found himself slung over something that moved, and for a moment he thought the Deodand had him once more. He coughed the bitterness away and clutched at his captor's back. It seemed to be covered with cloth, and he was certain that was wrong; the Deodand's back should be naked. Then reality returned, and he knew Fluvio was carrying him.

He had written the Spell of the Omnipotent Sphere on his arm in indelible ink, but he was too dizzy to read it. Dozens of repetitions, however, had engraved themselves on his memory. He began to murmur the spell, and by the time Fluvio did as he expected, the Sphere was springing into being around him, and instead of falling, he floated into the gorge of the Derna light as dandelion fluff, rebounding gently from the near wall as the Sphere repelled anything that might harm him. For the first few seconds, he could see Fluvio standing at the verge, staring, and then all he could see was rock and sky.

The dizziness had passed by the time he settled beside the river. By then his jaw had begun to ache fiercely, and he had been forced to press his sleeve into his mouth to stop the bleeding of his bitten tongue. He opened the Sphere and knelt to scoop up some water to rinse his mouth. There was no easy returning to Boreal Verge from this location. Upriver, though, at the mines, at least one of the green serpentine trails extended all the way to the bottom. It would take him two days of walking to reach it.

He was tired and hungry when he arrived at the mines, so hungry that he was glad to eat mushrooms. A few days later, three miners escorted him back to Boreal Verge, where he told his father only that he had decided to visit them before returning to Miir. He made no reference to the unpleasantness with Fluvio, nor to the bruise so evident on his jaw. For his part, Fluvio stayed well away from his brother and spoke little, though Bosk fancied he saw fear in Fluvio's eyes every time their gazes met. That seemed like a very good thing to Bosk.

His father had the silver ready, as well as a suggestion for a good location in Kaiin. As expected, Mazirian's spells worked as well on the coins as they had on Bosk, and he returned to Miir wealthier than he had left. No one asked where he had been, though Rianna did look long at the bruise, nor did they question his new enterprise.

"I thought you might find some simpler bargain," said Turjan, "but you are, after all, a Septentrion. Does this mean your apprenticeship has ended?"

"That is not my intention," said Bosk.

"So we speak of compromise. You will serve both your father and me."

"As I hope."

Turjan shook his head. "She does not deserve all of this."

"I am doing it for myself and my family, not for her."

Turjan's expression was enough to show his doubt.

Once the shop was secured, a dozen Twk-men became mushroom haulers. Bosk had already dispatched a gaudily wrapped packet of fresh mushrooms to the Prince, and now he posted a notice on the shop door that the goods would be available on a certain date. That morning, when he restored himself to his proper size on the premises, a crowd of satisfying proportions was already waiting outside the door. Many coins changed hands before the stock was exhausted, and Bosk noted all in a small account book. He closed the empty shop at noon, and after locking the door, he went back to Miir and shared the midday meal with Turjan, Rianna, and T'sain.

The next morning, the mushrooms haulers carried one silver coin each through the Eye, and Bosk helped Dandanflores unwind the golden thread from his hammock.

"I understand you have no intention of visiting her," said the Twik chieftain, "but you might find it interesting that Lith has established herself in Thamber Meadow." Casually, he suggested a route to the place.

"It is unlikely that she and I will ever meet again," Bosk agreed. He coiled the golden thread and slung it over his shoulder. It was quite heavy. He considered using Mazirian's spell to shrink it, but decided that he would not chance the effect on its intrinsic magic.

Back at Miir, he regained his true size, and the rope became a glittering thread. He looped it about his neck and tucked it under his shirt.

His horse was saddled and waiting at the gate. A brief sortie, he had told his master's family, though he had known from their faces that he was not deceiving them. He had left a sealed envelope on his pillow, with instructions for his father, for Fluvio, for Turjan, to continue the commerce with the Twk in his absence. As he rode away, he looked back more than once and saw Rianna watching from the tower garden. The last time, distance made her seem small enough to visit her own doll house, and he almost went back to thank her because everything he had accomplished would have been impossible without her. But he did not.

He found Thamber Meadow casily enough, on the second day of travel, near dusk. The house was small, with a thatched roof and ivy-covered walls, and it stood close beside a brook. Lith was in the water, her gown gathered up around her knees, and as he approached, she scooped up a fish, which struggled vigorously until she gave it a quietus with her fist.

She looked up as he dismounted, and her beauty was all that he remembered and more. "The boy from the north," she observed.

"I brought you gifts." He drew a sack of mushrooms from one of his panniers. "The finest the north has to offer. And bread fresh from the kitchens of Castle Miir." Another sack.

"You are kind. With such additions, I would be inhospitable if I did not share my supper with you. Bosk, was it not?"

He nodded, and his heart quickened at the sound of his name in her mouth.

As he helped her prepare the fish and the mushrooms, they exchanged scant information—he had begun his apprenticeship, and she had traveled a trifle, but nowhere that mattered. When their meal was finished, he did not wait for the dishes to be cleared away to show his other gift.

At the sight of the thread, her hand went to her mouth, and her cheeks paled. Her fingers trembled as she accepted it. "How?" she whispered.

"Too long a tale," he said. "Let it be enough that you have it back."

She bowed her head then, and her shoulders shook with weeping.

He reached across the table and touched her arm gently. "This should be a happy time for you."

She covered her face with her hands. "You don't understand. Leave me, please. Please."

Uncertainly, he stood, not knowing what to say. She did not look up at him. Finally, he went outside, led his horse some distance from the house, and tied it where the grass was plentiful. With the saddle for a pillow, he curled up in his blanket and watched the stars until he fell asleep.

In the morning, the hut still stood in Thamber Meadow, but when he called her name, she did not answer. He tried the door. It was not locked, and so he went in. The supper dishes were still on the table, and he took them to the brook to wash, dried them with a cloth from the cupboard, and put them away. He saw that the golden tapestry was complete, and he leaned close to peer at the village, the mountains, the river. From one angle, the golden sunlight seemed to glint on the water as if the current were actually moving within the weave.

At the couch, he stacked all the cushions atop one another, pushing them hard against the tapestry, and they reached as high as a tiny path just visible in the gold. He knelt on them and spoke the First Evolution of Mazirian's Diminution, but doll-size he was still too large and had to use the spell a second time. This time, the cushion was a vast plain stretching

behind him, and he could leap from its edge to the path, through a membrane thin as a soap bubble.

Ariventa surrounded him, bathing him in golden light. The village was farther off than he expected, but he reached it at last and marveled at its dwellings, every one as small as Lith's own but made of precious metal, reflecting the golden light with dazzling intensity.

Among the closed doors and shuttered windows was not a single sign of life.

He found Lith in the village square, sitting on a golden bench, her hands folded on her knee. He sat down beside her.

"They are all gone," she said. "Everyone I knew, everyone who called me family. Everyone who lived here. Gone." She was staring down at her hands.

"Perhaps they are farther down the river. Or in the mountains."

She shook her head.

"How can you be certain?"

"This is my land. I am very certain."

"Then Lady Lith…come back to my world."

Slowly, she turned her head and looked at him with her great golden eyes. She seemed older suddenly, fine lines showing at the corners of those eyes and dark smudges beneath. Or perhaps, he thought, that was only because she had been awake all night. "Ariventa is mine," she said. "I will not abandon it."

"But if no one is here—"

"I will not abandon it!" she shouted, and she slapped him full across the face, her nails raking his cheek like so many talons. "Go away! Ariventa is mine!"

He leaped up, one hand pressed against the starting blood. "I only meant to help you."

"Go away, boy!"

Without another word, he began to back down the golden path, and at the edge of the village, he turned and ran. By the time he burst through the tapestry, his lungs were afire, and he fell to his knees, gasping, on the plain that was the cushion. Two repetitions of the Second Evolution restored his full height, and he rolled to the floor. When he looked up at the tapestry, it had already dwindled to the size of his thumb, and a moment later, it disappeared entirely. Around him, the house began to shake as in a high wind, and he was barely able to stumble out the door before the entire place collapsed into a pile of rubble.

Two nights later, he was at Miir, and this time Rianna was waiting for him at the gate.

"Is it over?" she asked as he handed his reins to the groom.

"Yes," he murmured.

"Truly over?"

He nodded.

"Good. Now you can begin to wait for me."

"To wait for you?"

She tucked her hand into the bend of his elbow. "To grow up, of course." She smiled with just a corner of her mouth. "Come along now. We've saved some supper for you. With no mushrooms at all."

He took a deep breath and answered her smile with his own. Together, they walked into Castle Miir.

AFTERWORD:

I FIRST read Jack Vance's fiction when I was around ten years old. I was working my way through my older brother's science fiction collection, picking up whatever looked interesting, when I reached his cache of pulp magazines: a handful of coverless copies of *Planet*, *Space*, and *Startling*. The stories sucked me right in, especially three of them: a Brackett, a Williamson . . . and Vance's "Planet of the Damned," a kind of mean-streets space opera featuring one of his trademark enigmatic imperious women. I realized I wanted to read a lot more stories like this one. However, back then Vance books seemed hard to come by. By the time I was a junior in high school, I'd read only a couple more of his novels and a scattering of his shorter fiction. And then I found *The Dying Earth*.

In spite of the fact that it was a legendary book, known to every dyed-in-the-wool fantasy fan, I had never heard of it. But the byline alone was enough to make me dig up 75 cents for that Lancer paperback with the odd leathery cover. Only many years later did I learn that this was its first printing since the scarce 1950 Hillman edition. I can't say I read it; rather, I inhaled it. It was fantasy, it was science fiction; it was a wonderful amalgam of the two. I was sixteen, already collecting rejection slips from

the magazines, and I realized I'd found the target I should aim at. I couldn't duplicate Vance, of course. But when I finally wrote my first Alaric story half a dozen years later, my mantra was "Think Jack Vance," and so it has remained throughout that series. Echoes of *The Dying Earth* also crop up elsewhere in my fiction. Sometimes I'm surprised to recognize them, years later, and I'm reminded once more of how much Vance has influenced my writing.

So, when I was invited to join this voyage back to the Dying Earth, it wasn't possible for me to say no. And not because I thought it would be easy: you don't assume the cape of The Master without trepidation. It's been a special challenge to revisit the esoteric sunset world that Jack Vance minted half a century ago, but in the end, an exceedingly rewarding one. For this is a world—of danger, wonder, and delight—that has been impressed on our imaginations as few others have.

—Phyllis Eisenstein

ELIZABETH MOON

An Incident in Uskvosk

ELIZABETH MOON has degrees in history and biology and served in the US Marine Corps. Her novels include *The Sheepfarmer's Daughter*, *Divided Allegiance*, *Oath of Gold*, *Sassinak* and *Generation Warriors* (written with Anne McCaffrey), *Surrender None*, *Liar's Oath*, *The Planet Pirates* (with Jody Lynn Nye and Anne McCaffery), *Hunting Party*, *Sporting Chance*, *Winning Colors*, *Once a Hero*, *Rules of Engagement*, *Change of Command*, *Against the Odds*, *Trading in Danger*, *Remnant Population*, *Marque and Reprisal*, and *Engaging the Enemy*. Her short fiction has been collected in *Lunar Activity, Phases*, and *Moon Flights*, and she has edited the anthologies *Military SF 1* and *Military SF 2*. Her novel *The Speed of Dark* won a Nebula Award in 2004. Her most recent book is a new novel, *Victory Conditions*.

Here she gives us ringside seats for an exciting day at the races—Dying Earth style.

An Incident in Uskvosk

ELIZABETH MOON

O*nce a mighty* city rose beside the head of a deep gulf in the Sea of Sighs, and its ships plied their trade, and the magnificence of its buildings proved its wealth…but in these latter days, only a dusty town remained, buildings shabby, patched with stones from its earlier grandeur. Unimportant to most, a minor port, a stop on the caravan route across the land, Uskvosk had shrunk and faded in the bleak millennia of the sun's decay, and its population held many idiosyncratic beliefs with ferocious tenacity.

Midafternoon in the dry season, with the bloated sun hanging sullenly over the town, and most folk with nothing better to do than slump by a window and watch passersby, was not the best time for an assignation. It was, however, the only time that Petry, general dogsbody at the Bilge & Belly, the locals' name for *Herimar's First-class Drinking & Dining, Superior Rooms Available, Sea Views Extra*, could be sure his chosen outbuilding was empty.

In caravan season, the stable would have been full and busy, but caravan season was a quarter year away. Now the partitions intended to keep beasts separate made private nooks, suitable, Petry thought, for an afternoon's exploration of the town lady of pleasure he most favored. He had saved enough for her reputed fee, in battered copper slugs stolen, one by careful one, from under the beds of drunken merchants, while removing their stinking chamber-pots. She would not be busy at this hour. And surely she would rather lie with him, a sweet innocent lad as he appeared, than with the kind of men who came to the Bilge & Belly before attending Aunt Meridel's Treasure-house, the high-walled establishment in which the fairest of the town's professional ladies spent their evenings.

Now Emeraldine stood in the doorway, all ripe lips and riper body, golden curls tumbling to her plump shoulders, but scowling instead of smiling—eyes narrowed to slits, chin jutting, arms folded stiffly. "What's this? The stable? Where's my surprise?"

"In here," Petry said, doffing his boy's cap and making a broad gesture, such as storytellers made. "Ten coppers' worth, I'm telling you truly." He opened his hand so she could see the coppers.

Her face relaxed a little, but she did not step forward, despite his bow and second flourish of the cap. "Petry—you're a sweet boy, but I fear you have mistook me. Pillow companion I am, and will be till the day I die, but I do not lie with children. You are but half-grown, lad. Talk to me again in a year or two, when you've some *growth* and we can both take pleasure in it."

"But—but I am old enough—" Petry struggled to keep his voice high enough for a boy's.

Her eyes narrowed again. "If you were able, Petry, it would mean you were a dwarf, and while I do not lie with children out of care for them, I would not lie with a dwarf for care of my pride. As you surely know, such are unlucky and deserve the stoning our custom demands. Are you then a dwarf pretending to be a boy? I'm sure Master Herimar, who gave you work out of pity for an orphan, would be glad to know—"

Petry cringed. Discovery would be disastrous. Besides, he wasn't a dwarf, he was simply a very small man. "I'm not! I'm not a dwarf! I just thought—there's a boy on the docks, said he'd had a woman and he's just a half-year older than me—" Older than his apparent age; he had topped thirty in the previous dry season.

She snorted. "If you mean Katelburt, he's a very young looking fifteen; he lies about his age all the time. But you, young Petry—" She came a step nearer, put out a hand to his face, stroked his cheek, kept boy-smooth by use of a depilatory. "You, lad, are too young. I understand your curiosity, and honor your effort to save up my fee. I'll tell you what. You can look all you want at what awaits you when you're old enough, so that the first sight of a woman's body won't affright you." She undulated into the stable; Petry scampered past her, not daring even a pat on her hip, to the stall he had prepared with stolen straw and borrowed bed linens. Smaller than the great roach stalls, it would have made a cozy nest for lovers.

"You sit there," she said, pointing to the far corner of the stall. "Be a good lad now, and do not think of trying to touch. This is education, not entertainment."

Petry sat where she indicated, cursing the superstition that forced him to maintain the illusion of boyhood. With no more delay, she lifted her striped skirts to reveal dimpled knees, then plump white thighs, then—he gaped at the view as she held her skirts aside with one hand and fumbled down her bodice for a key to unlock the cage of her secrets.

"PETRY! Lazy mudspawn! These pots are still filthy!"

At Herimar's bellow, Emeraldine grimaced, shrugged, and dropped her skirts as Petry scrambled up.

"Better go, boy, or you'll lose your—"

"PETRY, damn you! If I find you loafing in the shade I'll kick your skinny ass halfway to the docks—"

Petry seethed with frustrated lust, and darted forward; Emeraldine grabbed him by the arm, forced his hand open, and peeled the coppers out of it like peeling seeds from a melon. "You surely didn't intend to rob me of my fee," she said too sweetly, as she dropped the coins into the pocket of her wide sleeve. Petry jerked away; her chuckle followed him out into the hot afternoon, where Herimar, vast and purple with rage, grabbed him by the ear, belabored his backside with a billet, and flung him in the general direction of the cook, who thumped his head with a spoon and soon had him head-down in the dirtiest cauldron, scrubbing until his fingers were raw. It was no benefit to his feelings when he heard Emeraldine and Herimar talking. Would she tell Herimar about the straw and the sheets? If so, he was as good as dead.

The sun went down, a soft ooze of deep crimson, but Petry's work did not end until late night, when he finished the last of the dinner cookpots to Cook's satisfaction. Herimar shoved him out the door. "You lazed all afternoon," Herimar said. "You don't get a place to sleep for that. Be here at first light, or else."

Petry found a snug spot under a pile of trash two alleys down, but the day's misfortune hunted him down even there, for in the middle of the night a cutpurse ran down the alley, pursued at a distance by one of the

town's heavy-footed nightwatchmen. Petry woke when the thief stepped on him, tripped, and fell; Petry yelped aloud; the thief, cursing, leapt up and ran on. Petry struggled up, hearing more footsteps coming, and one hand came down on a soft, lumpy object. Muddled with sleep as he was, he did not recognize it in time to toss it away, but picked it up just as the watchman rounded the corner.

Very shortly, he stood before the serjeant of the watch, hands bound and the evidence of his thievery laid out on the serjeant's desk. A rich velvet purse, a lady's purse, heavily embroidered with flowers and stinking of perfume, now empty: when the serjeant had tipped out its contents, gold terces and silvers of local coinage glinted as they fell, chiming a dangerous melody on the desk.

"Well, boy," the serjeant said. He was both tall and wide, straining the buttons of his bright yellow uniform. Two men stood leaning on the wall behind the serjeant, one caressing the handle of a cat-o'nine-tails. "Proper little thief you are, ain't you? Been seein' you at the Bilge & Belly, been hearing of missing coppers here and there—your work, I don't doubt."

"I—I didn't—this isn't—"

"You expect me to believe someone just came by and dropped a fancy lady's purse with gold and silver coins on your head while you were innocently—what were you doing in that alley, anyway?"

"Sleeping," Petry said.

"Sleeping," the serjeant said, in a tone that conveyed how little he believed that. "In a trash pile. Of course. When everyone knows you should be asleep in the Bilge and Belly stable…unless Herimar found you thieving and threw you out—"

"No!" Petry tried to think of am explanation that would get him out of trouble but hold up if they talked to Herimar. "He didn't throw me out. He just said I couldn't sleep there tonight but to be back in the morning…"

"Why couldn't you sleep there tonight? He have a full house?"

"I dunno," Petry said. "I mean, I dunno if he had a full house. He just said…"

"And here you are with a purse full of gold and silver. If you didn't have a steady job with Herimar, boy, it'd be thumbs and toes for you right now. As it is…a public stripping and a day in the stocks…"

Petry tried to look pitiful and young. Public stripping would reveal the truth—that he wasn't a young boy at all, but a very small man—what some would call a dwarf, a freak, a mutant, and send to the stake for stoning.

A night and day without the depilatory he'd obtained with so much effort and cunning from the witches of the waste and his beard would show. Then the stones would come…and he'd die, painfully and thoroughly. So it wasn't hard to look pitiful and scared. It wasn't working, either…no sympathy at all in the faces of the big men around him.

Then the serjeant pursed lips and sighed. "On the other hand…"

"The other hand?" Petry squeaked.

"It's the races, you see."

Petry didn't see, but anything that might save him from exposure he wanted to hear.

"The roach races, boy. Just a few days away, the south-coast yearly race meeting. We thought we had a sure thing, this year. Old Maggotory, used to be head of the local constabulary—that's us—went to breeding racing roaches when he retired. He's got a good one now, real good. Won some races out of town, healthy, training well. Sure thing to win the Cup this meet…or so we thought, when we wagered the entire pension fund on it, against those fool wormigers who think because their ships move fast across the sea, they can judge the speed of a roach."

Petry could see where this was going. "But?"

"But now the word is that the Duke of Malakendra, who's never bothered to send any of his prize beasts here before, has noticed the size of the purse and is sending his champion, undefeated winner of a hundred races. And it is this roach, whom the wormigers saw run in another place, they bet upon."

"Why do you tell me this?"

"Because every roach has its cuttlemites, as you surely know—you work in the stables, betimes; you have seen them, no doubt, scribble-scrabbling in the interstices of the roaches' cuticles, nibbling away those itchy accumulations. And you'll have noticed, maybe, that if one drops off, sated with its meal, it always returns to the same beast, does it not?"

"Aye…it does."

"We consulted the mage Kersandar, who by diverse arts and for a sum I will not reveal told us that the Duke's roach owes its celerity to a special breed of cuttlemites, not known to this region. The Duke obtained their eggs and established them in his stables, where they reproduced and attached to each of his own roaches…and to this champion sent to ruin us."

Petry examined the nails of one hand as if fascinated by the sediment thus revealed. "I pray you, explain—"

"Do you not see? A racing roach must have its cuttlemites, to keep its cuticle clean and its crevices free of those exudations which by nature the creatures produce, and which, accumulated, irritate and annoy, so the roach moves erratically at best, and always slowly. If we but remove the cuttlemites from Duke Malakendra's roach, and transfer them to Maggotory's beast, the Duke's will not run so well, ours will run better, and our funds are safe. If not—we lose all. None of us has any excuse to be working around the Duke's roach, nor is small enough, light enough, to infiltrate the stable without being noticed, but you, my lad, are the one who might save us."

"How?"

"It is certain that the Duke's roach will be stabled at Herimar's from tomorrow or the next day. You will surely have access to it; Herimar has no one else to clean the stable. If you perform this task, it might be possible to overlook your thieving, since you are so young and can be retrained…"

Petry bethought himself of the certainty of death if he failed, and quickly agreed to do his best. The serjeant kept him close in the watch-house until it was time for him to return to Herimar. "Abase yourself," the serjeant said. "Whatever is necessary to regain your place—for I am sure you did not tell us the whole truth. It matters not, if you are able to perform your task."

Before dawn, Petry crouched outside the main door of the Bilge and Belly, face washed, hair combed, cap tipped rakishly to one side. When Herimar threw open the door at last, Petry leapt up and bowed, bowed once, twice, thrice, sweeping his cap to the dust each time.

"Well, you rascal," Herimar said. "Are you ready to work, then?"

"With all my heart," Petry said.

"It's your hands I want," Herimar said. "At work. You can start by cleaning the stable; we have a valuable beast coming in." He led Petry through the inn's main downstairs room without even time to snatch a crumb from the bar. Still talking, he led the way to the stable. "The Duke of Malakendra's famous racing roach, here—and a premium paid for the exclusive use of the entire stable. Every stall to be cleaned, swept, and raked. No dung, no webs, no loose dirt. In this one, spread straw, make it level. I shall inspect your work later. It's essential the creature win—for to obtain the custom, I had to lay a wager risking all my possessions, including this inn. You may earn yourself bread and cheese, if you do well."

When Herimar was well out of the way, Petry slunk down to the end of the row and dug up his small pot of depilatory, smearing it on his face and body. The bristly hairs already rising from his skin fell off at once. Then he set to work, his belly clinging to his backbone with hunger, but he had no choice. He thought of many potent curses to lay on Herimar, but if the man sickened or died before the Duke's roach arrived, the constabulary would blame him.

When Herimar came back, Petry had cleaned all the stalls to the walls and bedded the one Herimar specified with straw to the depth of his elbow. Petry bowed, doffing his cap and waving it about. "You see, gracious Master, I have performed all you asked, to the last detail. Please, sir, a morsel to break my fast."

Herimar dug his hand into the straw. "Deeper," he said. "Twice as deep. I didn't mean a boy's elbow deep, but a man's. Are you stupid as well as lazy? Do that, and you can come to the kitchen door. You are at least working."

Grumbling to himself, but no louder than his empty belly, Petry added straw until it reached his own armpit, then went to the kitchen where the cook, without looking at him, handed out a half-loaf of stale bread and a lump of hard cheese rimed with mold.

He was halfway through his lunch when the Duke's roach arrived, surrounded by liveried roachifers, each holding one of the sandspider-fiber ropes that kept the creature in check, their black-and-white tunics and red leggings setting off the roach's gleaming dark crimson elytra with inlaid silver scrollwork. The Duke's own Roachkeeper Extraordinary led the way, wearing a wide hat layered in black and white plumes, a white cape edged in black and white sand-spider fur, a crimson shirt with full sleeves and baggy black trousers tucked into crimson boots. He led a pack animal carrying sacks of roach-bait that kept the creature moving forward.

Herimar, bowing and scraping for all he was worth, led the way into the stables; the Roachkeeper signaled his assistants to follow, and the great roach, leg by leg, squeezed through the gateway and into the stall prepared for it.

"We require a dungpicker," the Roachkeeper said, in a tone that suggested he expected Herimar to offer a selection of them for his inspection.

Herimar grabbed Petry by the shoulder and shoved him forward. "Here you are, good sir. Name's Petry—smart lad, does exactly what you tell him."

The Roachkeeper stared at Petry as if at dung on his shoe. "Well...if that's the best you can do...you, boy, you do exactly what you're told and nothing else, hear? And no gossiping about Magnificence out in town!"

"No, sir," Petry said.

"And no eavesdropping!"

Petry attempted a shocked expression that seemed to satisfy the Roachkeeper, who turned to Herimar. "I will require your best room for myself. My roachifers will stay with the champion and will require bedding in the stable, and their meals served to them there."

"Of course," Herimar said. "Come this way, good sir."

The rest of that day, the roachifers ordered Petry about as if he were their exclusive servant. He had to bed a stall to either side of the roach with straw, and fetch sheets to lay over it; he had to bring buckets of water; they demanded dishes not on the menu and complained about the quality of the crockery. During that time he had no need to eavesdrop, as they talked freely as if Petry had no ears. He heard the gossip of the Duke's court—which girls they'd bedded, which they fancied, when the Duchess might birth the next, which servants were cheating the steward. The only matter of interest to him was the recent illness and death of the Duke's dwarf jester.

"Such an easy life," said one. "Fed from the Duke's own table and all the ale he could drink, all for acting the fool and letting people laugh at him."

"I wouldn't like that," said another.

"For meat every day and a skinful of ale? They could laugh all they wanted, and I would be laughing too."

Petry felt the same way, but saw no way to get the Duke to hire him. Here, he was known as a beardless boy of no particular talent, fit to carry straw and dung and scrub pots. How could he prove himself without getting killed for it?

The next afternoon, when the roachifers had taken the roach out of town for a workout and Petry was hoping for a quick nap, one of the watchmen came to the inn and demanded to have a cask of ale delivered to the watch-house. Herimar beckoned to Petry. "Take the handcart, and be very sure you do not crack the hogshead or damage the cart or it will be the worse for you." Accompanied by the watchman, Petry pushed the cart down to the watch-house.

"Tell me all," the serjeant said, once the cask had been set up and broached. He sucked the ale off his whiskers; no one had offered Petry any.

Petry recounted the little he knew—the creature's size, its name, and the care being taken of it.

"Well, then. First we'll need a pellet of its dung, to season the bait. Then we'll give you the cuttlemite bait, and a jug to put them in. Drag the cuttlemite bait from its side to the jar; they'll follow the scent."

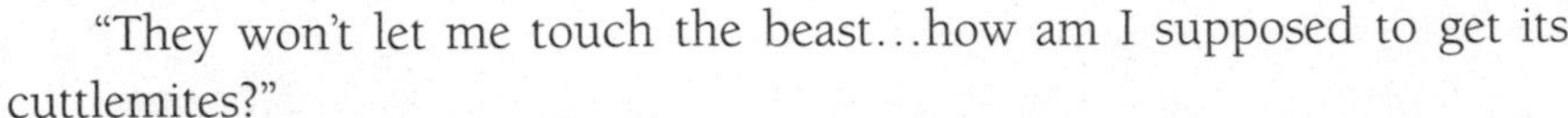

"They won't let me touch the beast…how am I supposed to get its cuttlemites?"

"You collect its dung…surely you have to be close to it to do that."

"No—they take it out to exercise; I'm only allowed in the stall then. And the roachifers sleep in the stable with it—they never leave it unguarded."

The serjeant exchanged glances with his men. "That still might work. We get the dung and make the bait, then—you take their meals to them, don't you?" Petry nodded. "Then you'll have to drug them." The serjeant pulled out a box from below the desk and rummaged in it, coming up with a flat-sided bottle, glass-stoppered. It had no label. "See that you drop a thimbleful in the food or drink of each roachifer this evening. Daggart will obtain a sample from the dungheap on his afternoon rounds. When your work's done and the inn's locked up, one of us'll be out behind the stable, on guard as it were, with the cuttlemite bait."

"What if the roachifers taste something?"

"They won't. The wizard Kalendar created for us this most potent soporific, undetectable but by another wizard. Very useful for those times when—" The serjeant stopped abruptly, flushing. "Never mind. Use it tonight; the race is day after tomorrow, time for the roach to miss its cuttlemites, but not time enough to fetch any from the Duke's stronghold."

Petry put the potion in the pocket of his vest and raced back to the inn, turning in the handcart to a scowling Herimar.

"Get yourself out there and make sure the stall is clean," Herimar said. "They'll be back from its training run soon."

Petris found only two more dung pellets in the stall and carried them out just as the roachifers led their charge in the gate. "Just a moment, goodsirs," Petry said, bowing. "And I will bring your supper."

"I don't think so," one of them said. "Not with the filth you've got on you. We'll have a nice fresh serving wench, and you can tell the Cook that—without touching our trays, understand?"

The Roachkeeper Extraordinary had already gone inside by that time; the roachifers led Magnificence into the stall. Petry wished blisters on their feet and hands and boils everywhere else as he carried the dung across the yard to the dungheap and jogged over to the kitchen door. Daggart came out of the inn, hitching up his belt and twirling a billet, just as one of the watchmen did every day. Petry ignored him. Cook was piling the trays with pannikins of sliced meat and gravy, bowls of deep-fried insects, boiled vegetables, and a whole loaf each of fresh bread, still steaming.

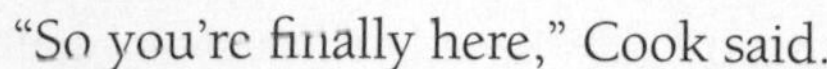

"So you're finally here," Cook said.

"Please, Cook, the roachifers want a serving wench instead of me..."

"I don't wonder. Boys are always dirty," Cook said. "Put anyone off their feed, the way you look and smell." He sighed heavily. "I'll have to fetch one of the girls..." He turned away, bellowing.

Petry pulled out the potion bottle and put two drops in each serving of meat, each serving of vegetables, and then, with great care, spat in them as well, and stirred them with a grubby finger. If they all sickened...it would not be counted his fault. The rest of the potion he poured into the jug of ale. He was across the yard, lifting a bundle of thorny sticks for Cook's oven, when one of the girls came out, whining that she couldn't possibly carry that many trays at once. Cook yelled, she yelled, and eventually another girl came out. They both carried trays to the stable.

It was well into the second watch when Petry finished the last of the supper pots, got his meager supper—no meat or gravy for him—and heard the kitchen latch snick to behind him. He sauntered across the yard to the wash house, biting hunks off his stale bread, and adding another curse to the pile of them he planned to topple on Cook's head when he had enough money for a magician's fee. From the stable, he heard snoring—at least two of the roachifers were sleeping soundly and perhaps the rest did not snore.

At the back of the wash house, he wiggled out the supposedly thief-proof window, having loosened the bars in advance, and moved silently along the alley wall to the end wall of the stable, then around to the back, where he found the serjeant and several watchmen waiting with an earthenware jug: the cuttlemite baited rag, the cord to lower it by, and a rope through the handle to lift the jug. Petry tied the rope around his waist.

Two men lifted him high enough to reach the edge of the roof. Petry shinnied over the edge and pulled himself onto the mismatched collection of warped boards, tiles, shingles, branches, and thornbush thatch that served now in place of the original roof. Herimar, always unwilling to spend a copper without need, insisted that his stable roof offered superior ventilation and was healthier for any beasts housed therein. Petry untied the rope from his waist and looped it around the board he'd pushed through the roof and tied in place for just this purpose.

Slowly, carefully, Petry crept forward, testing each separate unstable surface, wary of the slightest noise, which the roachifers below would surely hear if not adequately under the influence of the drug. Fortunately, the multiple glowspheres the guards had deployed against thieves gave sufficient light to outline the roof sections, and made it easier for him to keep from falling through.

Something rustled below. Petry put his eye to one of the many vacancies and looked down on the great roach, stirring restlessly in its stall. The silver scrollwork inlaid on its elegant elytra left bare the area where its rider would sit. The roach lifted its elytra, releasing the gauzy underwings, fluttering them, and a strange eldrich fragrance, heady and alluring, rose to Petry's nostrils. And there, for the first time, Petry saw the glitter of something moving, something that must be the cuttlemites, gently grooming the great beast. He peered as far headward of the beast as he could. The long, sensitive antennae waved about, one almost reaching the roof.

Petry shifted the shingle nearest him—now he could see the liveried roachifers, sound asleep in the stalls on either side of the great roach. So the potion had worked, or apparently so. He slithered ungracefully down the slant of the roof, unlooped the rope from which hung the jar of cuttlemite bait, and pulled it up. After a dicey crawl back up the roof, he unplugged the jar, pulled out the bait-soaked rag already knotted to a cord, and sniffed it. He could detect nothing but a faint smell of roach, but the serjeant had sworn it would attract cuttlemites better than a roach itself.

He lowered it through the gap he'd made between two boards until it touched Magnificence of Malakendra's back, right where the jockey would sit. The pronotum, the serjeant had said that was. Nerves had been cut, so the roach would not reflexively open its wings at the sensation of the jockey's weight.

The roach's antennae wiggled, but it did not react otherwise. Petry wondered if the roach could smell the bait, as well as its cuttlemites. He began counting, as instructed. At first he saw nothing, then a faint ripple, moving forward from the roach's rear, and backward from its head, that must, he thought, be the cuttlemites. The cord began to cut into his hand as the cuttlemites crawled onto the rag. The lower end, above the rag, appeared frayed as cuttlemites climbed up it, as well, to get their palps on the bait. At last, and some unimportant number less than he'd been told to count, he had enough, and pulled the cord up, smoothly, not too fast.

The hardest part was getting the rag and its cuttlemites through the gap in the roof without letting them bump against it. Once they were out, he poked the rag back into the jar with a stick, coiled the cord on top of it, plugged the jar, and crawled back down the roof to the back stable wall, where he lowered the jar to the serjeant. When he landed in the alleyway,

the serjeant and his men were already out in the street beyond; he made it back to the wash house with no alarms, and set the bars back in place before stretching out on the floor.

Next morning, he woke to shouts that mingled worry and anger, just as someone kicked open the wash-house door.

"No, he's here!" That was one of the roachifers. "Sound asleep, too. Get up, roach-dung! Get out. We're searching for evidence."

"Evidence?" Something tickled in Petry's hair and he was instantly sure it was a cuttlemite that would prove him guilty. He struggled not to scratch.

"Did you drug that swill you fed us last night?" the roachifer said, shaking his shoulder. "Couldn't have tasted anything in that disgusting liquid they call ale around here—"

"Hold on there," Herimar said. He was turning purple again, Petry noticed. "That's an insult, sir. There's nothing wrong with my ale. Brew it ourselves we do, best quality…"

"Out of dirty socks and chamberpots, by the way it tastes," the roachifer said, still holding Petry. "If it wasn't drugged, it was poison to start with. We'd none of us sleep on watch without—" The roachifer was eyeing the Duke's Roachkeeper Extraordinary, who had slept in the inn's best room, due his position.

"Let us consider all possibilities," the Roachkeeper Extraordinary said. "Our host has not had the benefit of comparing his ale to that brewed by the Duke's brewmaster, but though it is of course inferior to that served the Duke at his own table, I found it not undrinkable at all—intriguing, really, the hint of delunkin berries and just a touch of saltgrass."

Herimar's face went through several expressions and finally settled into a nervous grin that Petry judged related to the bulk of the Roachkeeper Extraordinary and his weaponry…and the fat wallet at his belt.

"This boy, now," the Roachkeeper said. "Boy, did you bring the men their food last night, as always?"

"N-no," Petry said. "They—the roachifers—asked to have a girl bring it—"

"Oh, did they!" The Roachkeeper Extraordinary shot his men a look of disdain. "A pretty one, did they specify that?"

"No, no," one roachifer said. "This boy was hauling dung, is all, and we didn't want his dirty fingers in our food. The lasses inside, they're cleanly. And we were hungry and didn't want to wait."

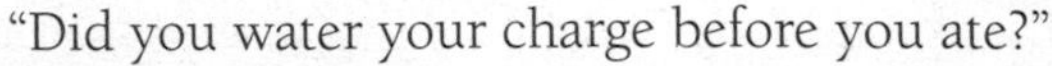

"Did you water your charge before you ate?"

"Yes, Roachkeeper—" "Of course, Roachkeeper—"

"And where was the boy, when the serving girl brought you your supper?"

The roachifers didn't know, but when all the servants were questioned, Cook's evidence was conclusive: Petry had come to tell him the men wanted a serving girl that night; Cook had agreed the boy stank of roach dung, and sent him to get firewood for the morning's baking. Cook had fetched Pecantia, who argued the job was too hard, and then Scyllinta to help her, and the two girls had come back after awhile, flushed and giggling...he had seen Petry carrying bundles of wood to the side of the oven.

"Did they..." The Roachkeeper Extraordinary eyed his men again, and they shuffled their feet. "Well, let the boy go, Jost. If anyone drugged your food, if you didn't drop off on your own from drinking too much of Master Herimar's unique ale and pillow-dancing with those girls, it certainly wasn't this little fellow."

The roachifer let go Petry's shoulder and shoved him away; Herimar pointed at him. "Now you're up, you'll start sweeping—unless, gentlesirs, you wish the roach's stall cleaned immediately—"

"No!" all the roachifers said at once. The Roachkeeper Extraordinary expanded on that. "The beast is not himself this morning, some trifling irritation perhaps, and it is best not to introduce strangers to it at such times."

"Sick?" Herimar asked. "The race—" His face paled; Petry knew he was thinking of the wager he had made.

"It will be fine by race time," the Roachkeeper Extraordinary said. "Roaches in training do often develop minor problems—sabotage is the only thing we have to fear, really, and I suspect my roachifers simply drank so much last night the fumes affected the creature's breathing orifices. Today—" He glared at his men. "Today, serve them nothing but plain water and bread. It will clear their heads."

For the rest of that morning, Petry swept and carried, fetched out full chamber pots and scrubbed them, all the while listening, listening. The two girls burst into tears when accused and denied all, even the obvious—for both had the signs of illicit encounters on their persons, the telltale little bruises and rednesses which could be expected, and a silver each in their sleeve pockets that Herimar had certainly not paid them.

Herimar was furious, Petry gathered, not because the girls had been playing bounce-the-bunnies in his inn, but because they had not paid him his share of their fee. He took both silvers to teach them a lesson; they glared at him behind his back, and fell to whispering. He called for the pot the ale had been in, but Petry had already washed it—"Cook said clean up all the dishes," he said.

Herimar glared at him. "Don't act so virtuous, scum-boy. You are up to something, don't think I don't know it! Stealing a finger of sugar from the kitchen, or grabbing a girl behind my back...you watch yourself, see?"

Petry thought it wise to withdraw, and finished cleaning the upstairs rooms without moving a single copper slug from its owner's possessions.

All the rest of that day, he saw roachifers going in and out of the stable. He came at their call to the stable doors, fetching water and carrying away wet towels to dry in the sun.

"Is your beast fevered?" Herimar asked on one of his own frequent trips to the stable doors. "Would he not be better in the open air of the yard?"

"No," the Roachkeeper said. "He is merely a little uncomfortable and we are massaging him...there's a spot where the saddle may have galled." Petry could hear rustling from within, as if the roach were scrabbling in the straw, not just shifting in its stance.

A spot where the saddle might have galled? Where the rag soaked with cuttlemite bait had rested through that long, long count? Was it the bait, or was it the many cuttlemites that had gathered there to feed on the bait?

Later in the afternoon, Petry went once more with a large jug of ale to the watch-house—again, a watchman had stopped by the Bilge & Belly to ask for a delivery—and he reported to the serjeant all he had seen and heard.

"You give a good report, boy," the serjeant said. "Ever think of becoming a watchman when you grow up?"

"Er...I hadn't, sir..."

"That's good, because you're far too young and there's still the little matter of your thievery. But there might be work for you, now and then, since you've proved yourself so far. If the Duke's roach loses, and Herimar's bankrupt, you'll need another way to live, and I'd hate to see a lad with your talents taken up as a pickpocket."

In other words, Petry realized, he would not be free of his obligation to the serjeant even after this.

Race Day at last—the townsfolk crowded the lanes on the way out to the ancient track, once used for racing chariots but now modified for giant roach racing. Herimar left early to get a seat in the Merchant's Box. Petry tried to sneak out the window of the wash-house again with a couple of wooden house-tokens he'd pilfered and hoped to trade for drinks at the track, but a grinning watchman waited outside and delivered him to the serjeant, who kept a firm fist knotted in Petry's collar all the way to the racetrack.

Roaches, unlike the other species humans had raced over the millenia, had neither the innate desire to run, nor the desire to chase down prey. Instead, roaches ran because they were chased, chased by something that ate roaches. At minor race-meets, the more common and less expensive gritches were used as chasers, so that even the slower race-roaches came home alive, but for important races such as this, owners hired a giant shrew, and had to commit a certain percentage of the roaches themselves to the fee. This was non-negotiable, since otherwise the shrews would attack the humans. Only when sated with roach-flesh could they once more be muzzled and sedated.

The roaches ran the prescribed course only because, with their wings disabled, they could not fly, and the incurved track boundaries gave their jockeys a leverage advantage if they tried to run up and over them. A series of winches mounted to the high pommel of the saddles gave the jockeys control of the roaches' front legs.

In the post parade, teams of roachifers led the race-roaches past the shrew's wheeled cage, to get its scent and understand their peril. Maggatory's entry, a gleaming golden-copper named "Arresting," high-stepped past the chittering shrew, flicking its antennae. It was ranked second in the betting. Petry had not seen it before; it was a little longer and slimmer than Magnificence of Malakendra, but moved smoothly despite its agitation. After it came a dark brown roach belonging to the Harbormaster, its elytra inlaid with a turquoise wave design.

"No threat," the serjeant said. "Now if this was a sprint, maybe, but it won't make the distance. There's money on it to place, though."

Another, a lustreless tan, followed. Its jockey looked nervously at the shrew.

"He'll have to be quick, when it's caught," the serjeant said, chuckling. "He knows he's on the slowest roach in the race. Bet he tried to get out of his contract."

The Duke's Roachmaster Extraordinary appeared now, leading Magnificence, the stunning dark crimson elytra with their silver inlays

gleaming in the sun and the roachifers in their formal livery. It stopped, had to be prodded on, lifted one leg and twitched it. Its elytra lifted as far as possible, and the gauzy wings fluttered; its head jerked from side to side. The jockey, also in the Duke's livery, played with the lines.

"They're makin' it do that, to scare bettors off and get good odds," someone said from behind Petry.

"I dunno..." said someone else. "Looks poorly to me, it does."

The serjeant's fist tightened on Petry's collar; he said nothing.

The fifth roach, a light brown with green stripes merely painted on, not incised, skittered past the shrew's cage, half-dragging its roachifers.

Now, in the starting chutes, the roaches waved their antennae frantically and tried to lunge ahead, but each had a stout roachifer hauling on each leg. When the starter dropped his flag, the roachifers released their grips, and two hundred paces back, the shrew's keepers released the shrew.

The crowd roared. The Harbormaster's roach shot into the lead, closely followed by Arresting. Magnificence, though equal with Arresting at first, quickly veered to the outside, rubbing against the rail like a hog scratching an itch, despite its jockey's frantic work on the winches. It was running fast, but a longer distance than the others. By the time the jockey was able to steer it back to the middle of the track, it was last, and the shrew was chittering a bare length behind. Thoroughly frightened, it raced ahead, catching up with the last roach, the dull tan one, and then passing the next before the next turn. Down the backstretch, the Harbormaster's roach faded, leaving Arresting in the lead. Magnificence continued to gain, passing the Harbormaster's roach, but even at a distance Petry could see that Arresting had the smoother stride, wasting no energy on popping its elytra. It was also clear that Arresting had more speed in hand, for it flattened out as Magnificence came alongside, opening a lead again. Magnificence challenged again, as they neared the far turn.

Neck and neck the two roaches ran, legs scuttling so fast they were nearly invisible. First the red and then the gold would get a lead. Far behind, the other three roaches were clearly outmatched, and the shrew snatched a leg off the last as it chased the next. The jockey leapt clear and ran for the protection of the inside rail—and made it, somewhat to the disappointment of the infield crowd.

Petry watched all this with interest, as the serjeant's grip never loosened and he was keenly aware what fate awaited him if Arresting should lose. He had done all that the serjeant had asked of him but that would not be enough to save him. And yet, there in the merchants' box was his present employer, who would be equally wroth if Magnificence lost. Never mind that Herimar had no idea it was Petry's doing; he would be angry enough to make Petry's life hell anyway.

"Get him away," the serjeant muttered, over Petry's head. "Get him away from that beast—"

"The shrew, sir?" Petry said. "He's well ahead—"

"No, you fool! Away from Magnificence! It's not good to be too close—"

Down the stretch they came now, with Arresting, on the rail, pulling slowly ahead...a handspan, an armspan. Magnificence's jockey leaned forward, urging him on...when suddenly a glittering cloud lifted from Arresting and settled on Magnificence. The jockey on Magnificence waved his arms like a man threatened by a swarm of bees and nearly fell off.

"May all the devils in all the hells take him!" the serjeant said. "We warned him!"

"Warned who?" Petry said. "What happened?" But before the serjeant could speak, he knew. The cuttlemites, transferred to Arresting, had smelled their born-host nearby, his smell stronger for the race he'd been running and the accumulation of secretions, and transferred back. In an instant, they seemed to disappear, diving into the great beast's crevices to groom him. Magnificence slowed and stopped as Arresting raced on and crossed the finish line; despite all his jockey could do, he crouched low to the track, antennae outspread. Petry imagined the relief the roach was feeling...all those itches scratched, expertly at once, as blissful comfort overrode fear. But now the Harbormaster's roach, only slightly ahead of the shrew but far ahead of the two roaches the shrew had crippled, scuttled past Magnificence. Too late, the champion sensed the danger; too late it gathered its slender legs and tried to run...too late and too slow.

The crowd's cheers for the winner died away as they watched the unthinkable...the Duke's renowned racing roach losing leg after leg to the shrew; the jockey's brave attempt to fight it off, until the shrew, annoyed, snapped at the man and bit off his leg. Though a dozen men with weapons ran out to save the jockey, he died before a healer could be found, and the great roach was eaten entire. The Duke's Roachkeeper Extraordinary had flung his feathered hat on the ground and was jumping up and down on it, screaming; the roachifers huddled together, wailing.

"Well," the serjeant said, loosening his grip at last. "As I said, boy, it's time to cut your losses with Herimar and consider other opportunities. If you came to us, the work's no harder and you might have that chance to become a watchman, when you've got some growth on you."

And when he did not grow, they would begin to wonder why, and when they found out…

Petry fixed a bright smile on his face. "Could I really? But I need to pick up my things at Master Herimar's, before—"

"Before he comes to himself and takes a billet to everyone," the serjeant said. "Sure, then. Go on. I'm stuck here—no odds taken that Roachkeeper's going to enter a formal protest, for all the good it'll do him. He can't prove anything. Come by the watch-house after sundown…and here's a few coppers for you in earnest of the offer. No stealing purses, now…" He counted out five copper slugs.

"No, sir! I wouldn't think of it." Petry took the coppers then turned and elbowed his way through the crowd. Not enough for a stake, not enough for a pillow dance or even a good meal, but more than he'd had since Emeraldine ran off with his entire stash. And…neither Herimar nor the serjeant were in their usual places.

He might be able to diddle them both. It was time for him to leave the place anyway—one year without growing could happen to any young boy, but two was pushing it, and anyway he'd like to be someplace he didn't depend on a magic depilatory to maintain his appearance.

Sure enough, all the watch were out on the streets, leaving the watch-house locked but unguarded. Locked, but not impregnable to a boy-sized man with the right experience. There in a drawer of the serjeant's desk was the velvet purse and its jingling contents. Petry tucked that away in his vest pocket, scratched Herimar's initials on one of the wooden house-tokens and dropped it on the floor, nudging it under the serjeant's desk next to the lock-box. He scratched around the lock, as if trying to pick it, but left it locked. Then he relocked the watch house, and made his way to the Bilge & Belly.

The main room bustled with those returning from the race, downing jugs of ale as they told each other what they'd seen at the top of their lungs. Serving wenches rushed back and forth and half the professional ladies of pleasure from Aunt Meridel's Treasure House were there, too, including Emeraldine, the cause of all his recent troubles.

Herimar, however, was missing. Arguing with the bookmakers about the extent of his losses, no doubt, for all the good it would do him. With any luck, he would quarrel with the Roachkeeper Extraordinary and be gone for hours.

Petry slipped into Herimar's private apartment and left the purse, minus two of the gold coins, under his mattress. Then upstairs, to the Roachkeeper's room, where he found, as expected, that the man had hidden a stash of coins in his chamber-pot. And he'd marked them in the usual amateurish way, scratching his initials into the space between the Prince's head and the motto. Easy enough to rub out, but Petry had a better idea. He took them all but one, tying half of them into a rag so they wouldn't jingle, and put them down the back of his vest, under his shirt, with a string. That one, a silver, he held in his hand. The other half joined his earlier stash, inside his vest.

Downstairs again, with a chamberpot in each hand as if he were working, he looked to see if Herimar had returned. Not yet...very good. The rag with the Roachkeeper's coins in it went under Herimar's pillow; Petry came out of Herimar's rooms with three chamberpots, just in case anyone noticed where he'd been, and out the back door to empty them in the pit. While appearing to scrub out the chamberpots, he scoured off the Roachkeeper's initials from the coins he'd kept and then dirtied them in the quickest way, so they weren't too shiny.

Still the Roachkeeper did not return; he imagined the man and his roachifers arguing with the serjeant, and smiled. Nor had Herimar returned. Petry's smile widened. He didn't need much more time...back inside, he slipped the Roachkeeper's marked silver into Emeraldine's sleeve-pocket while she had her tongue down some wormiger's throat, then made his way to the stable and retrieved his pot of depilatory.

Now to the Duke's, to apply for the job of fool. He sauntered through the town's market square, stopping to buy himself a fruit pasty for the journey, trade the jar of depilatory for one guaranteed to speed hair growth, and fill the empty potion bottle from a dyer's pot, then strolled out the unguarded west gate. When the thefts were discovered and he wasn't around, someone might try to blame him—but the house-token should result in a search of Herimar's—where the evidence he'd planted should point to Herimar—his greed and his need both being public knowledge. If not, Petry the boy would soon cease to exist anyway.

By the time the Roachkeeper Extraordinary and his roachifers dared return to the Duke's court, only to be summarily dismissed, a very hairy dwarf known to that noble lord as Otokar Petrosky might be seen capering about the Duke's hall each night in motley and a belled cap. With his hair dyed blue and done up in ribboned plaits, and his long braided beard dyed red with a bell on the end for the Duke to pull, he resembled in no way the beardless skinny orphan boy from the Bilge & Belly, and his short stature was in no wise a hindrance to his other ambitions...since not all of him was short.

AFTERWORD:

I DISCOVERED Jack Vance while in high school, a few years into my attempt to read every scrap of science fiction I could find. Compared to my previous reading, Vance, like Sturgeon, was exotic—his imagined worlds as different from a small city in south Texas as a dreamer could wish. Later, other writers lured me away from Vance, but he was a bright-colored thread in the tapestry of writers whose work I read. I suspect, though, that he's the reason I spent one whole summer writing (very bad) stories with purple ink.

—Elizabeth Moon

LUCIUS SHEPARD

Sylgarmo's Proclamation

REVENGE IS one of the oldest and most primal of human motives, and in the fast-paced tale that follows, it drives a battle-scared warrior to the ends of the Dying Earth—and perhaps to the end of the Dying Earth itself!

Lucius Shepard was one of the most popular, influential, and prolific of the new writers of the '80s, and that decade and much of the decade that followed would see a steady stream of bizarre and powerfully compelling stories by Shepard, stories such as the landmark novella "R&R," which won him a Nebula Award in 1987, "The Jaguar Hunter," "Black Coral," "A Spanish Lesson," "The Man Who Painted the Dragon Griaule," "Shades," "A Traveller's Tale," "Human History," "How the Wind Spoke at Madaket," "Beast of the Heartland," "The Scalehunter's Beautiful Daughter," and "Barnacle Bill the Spacer," which won him a Hugo Award in 1993. In 1988, he picked up a World Fantasy Award for his monumental short-story collection *The Jaguar Hunter*, following it in 1992 with a second World Fantasy Award for his second collection, *The Ends of the Earth*.

In the mid to late '90s, Shepard's production slowed dramatically, but in the new century he has returned to something like his startling prolificacy of old; by my count, Shepard published at least ten or eleven stories in 2003 alone, many of them novellas, including three almost-novel-length chapbooks, *Louisiana Breakdown*, *Floater*, and *Colonel Rutherford's Colt*. Nor has the quality of his work slipped—stories like "Radiant Green Star," "Only Partially There," and "Liar's House" deserve to be ranked among his best work ever, and his "Over Yonder" won him the Theodore Sturgeon Memorial Award. And it may be that he's only beginning to hit his stride. Shepard's other books include the novels *Green Eyes*, *Kalimantan*, *The Golden*, and the collection *Barnacle Bill the Spacer*, *Trujillo*, and *Two Trains Running*. He has also written books of non-fiction essays and criticism such as *Sports and Music*, *Weapons of Mass Seduction*, and *With Christmas in Honduras: Men, Myths, and Miscreants in Modern Central America*. His most recent books are two new collections, *Dagger Key and Other Stories*, and a massive retrospective collection, *The Best of Lucius Shepard*. Born in Lynchberg, Virginia, he now lives in Vancouver, Washington.

Sylgarmo's Proclamation

LUCIUS SHEPARD

From a second-story window of the Kampaw Inn, near the center of Kaspara Viatatus, Thiago Alves watched the rising of the sun, a habit to which many had become obsessively devoted in these, the last of the last days. A faltering pink ray initiated the event, probing the plum-colored sky above the Mountains of Magnatz; then a slice of crimson light, resembling the bloody fingernail of someone attempting to climb forth from a deep pit, found purchase in a rocky cleft. Finally the solar orb heaved aloft, appearing to settle between two peaks, shuddering and bulging and listing like a balloon half-filled with water, its hue dimming to a wan magenta.

Thiago grimaced to see such a pitiful display and turned his back on the window. He was a powerfully constructed man, his arms and chest and thighs strapped with muscle, yet he went with a light step and could move with startling agility. Though he presented a formidable (even a threatening) image, he had a kindly, forthright air that the less perceptive sometimes mistook for simple-mindedness. Salted with gray, his black hair came down in a peak over his forehead, receding sharply above the eyes—a family trait. Vanity had persuaded him to repair his cauliflower ears, but he had left the remainder of his features battered and lumped by long years in the fighting cage. Heavy scar tissue thickened his orbital ridges, and his nose, broken several times during his career, had acquired the look of a peculiar root vegetable; children were prone to pull on it and giggle.

He dressed in leather trousers and a forest green singlet, and went downstairs and out onto the Avenue of Dynasties, passing beneath several of the vast monuments that spanned it; a side street led him through a gate in the city wall. Swifts made curving flights over the River Chaing and a tall two-master ran with the tide, heading for the estuary. He walked briskly along the riverbank, stopping now and again to do stretching exercises; once his aches and pains had been mastered by the glow of physical exertion, he turned back toward the gate. The city's eccentric spires—some capped by cupolas of gold and onyx, with decorative finials atop them; others by turrets of tinted glass patterned in swirls and stripes; and others yet by flames, mists, and blurred dimensional disturbances, each signaling the primary attribute of the magician who dwelled beneath—reduced the backdrop of lilac-colored clouds to insignificance.

In the Green Star common room of the Kampaw, a lamplit, dust-hung space all but empty at that early hour, with carved wainscoting, benches and boards, and painted-over windows depicting scenes of golden days and merrymaking through which the weak sun barely penetrated, Thiago breakfasted on griddlecakes and stridleberry conserve, and was contemplating an order of fried glace[2] to fill in the crevices, when the door swung open and four men in robes and intricately tiered caps crowded inside and hobbled toward his table. Magicians, he assumed, judging by the distinctive ornaments affixed to their headgear. Apart from their clothing, they were alike as beans, short and stringy, with pale, round faces, somber expressions and close-cropped black hair, varying in height no more than an inch or two. After an interval a fifth man entered, closed the door and leaned against it, a maneuver that struck Thiago as tactical and put him on the alert. This man differed from his fellows in that he walked without a limp, moving with the supple vigor of youth, and wore loose-fitting black trousers and a high-collared jacket; a rakish, wide-brimmed hat, also black, shadowed his features.

2 A variety of mollusc valued for their succulent flesh. It was once proposed that glace possessed a form of intelligence, this based on the fact that many who consumed them raw reported experiencing poignant emotional states and hearing what seemed to be pleas in an unknown tongue. For this reason, they are now served either fried or broiled. As to the question of their sentience, their severely depleted population prevents a comprehensive study.

"Have I the pleasure of addressing Thiago Alves?" asked one of the magicians, a man whose eyes darted about with such an inconstancy of focus, they appeared on the verge of leaping out of his head.

"I am he," Thiago said. "As to whether it will be a pleasure, much depends on the intent of your youthful associate. Does he mean to block my means of egress?"

"Certainly not!"

The magican made a shooing gesture and the youth stepped away from the door. Thiago caught sight of several knives belted to his hip and remained wary.

"I am Vasker," the magician said. "And this worthy on my left is Disserl." He indicated a gentleman whose hands roamed restlessly over his body, as if searching for his wallet. "Here is Archimbaust." Archimbaust nodded, then busied himself with a furious scratching at his thigh. "And here Pelasias." Pelasias emitted a humming noise that grew louder and louder until, by dint of considerable head-shaking and dry-swallowing, he managed to suppress it.

"If we may sit," Vasker went on, "I believe we have a proposal that will profit you."

"Sit if you like," said Thiago. "I was preparing to order glace and perhaps a pot of mint tea. You have my ear for as long as it will take to consume them. But I am embarked upon a mission of some urgency and cannot listen to distractions, no matter how profitable."

"And would it distract you to learn…" Archimbaust paused in his delivery to scratch at his elbow. "…that our proposal involves your cousin. The very one for whom you are searching?"

"Cugel?" Thiago wiped his mouth. "What of him?"

"You seek him, do you not?" asked Disserl. "As do we."

"Yet we have an advantage," said Vasker. "We have divined his whereabouts." Thiago wiped his mouth with a napkin and glared at him. "Where is he?"

"Deep within the Great Erm. A village called Joko Anwar. We would travel there ourselves and secure him, but as you see we lack the physical resources for such a task. It requires a robust individual like yourself."

The young man made a sound—of disgust, thought Thiago—and looked away.

"It is possible to dispatch you to the vicinity of Joko Anwar within minutes," said Archimbaust. "Why risk a crossing of the Wild Waste

and endure the discomfort and danger of a voyage across the Xardoon Sea?"

"Should you travel by conventional means, you may not achieve your goal," Disserl said. "If Sylgarmo's recent projections are correct, we might have as little as a handful of days before the sun quits the sky."

The wizards began debating the merits of Sylgarmo's Proclamation. Vasker adhered to the optimistic estimate of two and a half centuries, saying the implications of Sylgarmo's equations were that there would soon be a solar event of some significance, yet not necessarily a terminal one. Archimbaust challenged Sylgarmo's methods of divination, Disserl held to the pessimistic view, and Pelasias offered a vocabulary of dolorous hums and moans.

To silence them, Thiago banged on the table—this also had the effect of summoning the serving girl and, once he had given her his order, he asked the magicians why they sought Cugel.

"It is a complex issue and not easily distilled," said Vasker. "In brief, Iucounu the Laughing Magician stole certain of our limbs and organs. We sent Cugel to retrieve them, armed with knowledge that would put an end to Iucounu for all time. Our limbs and organs were restored, but they were returned to us in less than perfect condition. Thus we limp and scratch and shake, and poor Pelasias is forced to communicate his dismay as might a sick hound."

It seemed to Thiago that Vasker had summarized the matter quite neatly. "And you blame Cugel ? Why not Iucounu or one of his servants? Perhaps the manner in which the limbs and organs were stored is at fault. It may be that an impure concentrate was used. Your explanation does not ring true."

"You fail to comprehend the full scope of Cugel's iniquity. I can…"

"I know him as well as any man," said Thiago. "He is spiteful, greedy, and uses people without conscience or concern. Yet never has he acted without reason. You must have done him a grievous injury to warrant such vindictiveness."

Led by Pelasias' groaning commentary, the magicians vehemently protested this judgment. Archimbaust was eloquent in their defence. "Our last night together we toasted one another with Iucounu's wine and feasted on roast fowl from his pantry," he said. "We sang ribald tunes and exchanged amusing anecdotes. Indeed, Pelasias performed the Five Amiable Assertions, thus consecrating the moment and binding us to friendship."

"If that is the case, I would counsel you to think well before you dissemble further." The serving girl set down his tea and Thiago inhaled the pungent steam rising from the pot. "I have little tolerance for ordinary liars and none whatsoever for duplicitous magicians."

The four men withdrew to the doorway and talked agitatedly among themselves (Pelasias giving forth with plaintive whimpers). After listening for a minute or so, the young man hissed in apparent dissatisfaction. He doffed his hat, releasing a cloud of dark hair, and revealed himself to be a young woman with comely features: a pointy chin and lustrous dark eyes and cunning little mouth arranged in a sullen pout. She would have been beautiful, but her face was so etched with scars, she resembled a patchwork thing. The largest scar ran from the hinge of her jaw down her neck and was wider than the rest, looking as though the intent had been not to disfigure, but to kill. She came toward Thiago and spoke in an effortful hoarse whisper that he assumed to be a byproduct of that wound.

"They claim that while taking inventory of Iucounu's manse, Cugel happened upon a map made by the magician Pandelume, who dwells on a planet orbiting a distant star," she said. "The map marks the location of a tower. Within the tower are spells that will permit all who can master them to survive the sun's death."

"Cugel's behavior becomes comprehensible," said Thiago. "He wished to disable his pursuit."

The magicians hobbled over from the door. Vasker cast a sour glance at the young woman. "This, then, is our offer," he said to Thiago. "We will convey you and Derwe to a spot near Joko Anwar, the site of Pandelume's tower. There you will…"

"Who is this Derwe?"

"Derwe Coreme of the House of Domber," the woman said. "I ruled in Cil until I ran afoul of your *cousin*." She gave the word a loathing emphasis.

"Was it Cugel who marked you so?"

"He did not wield the knives. That was the fancy of the Busacios, a race vile both in form and disposition who inhabit the Great Erm. Yet Cugel is responsible for my scars and more besides. In exchange for information, he handed me over to the Busacios as if I were a bag of tiffle."

"To continue," said Vasker in a peremptory tone. "Once there you will enter the tower and immobilize Cugel. He must be kept alive until we have questioned him. Do this and you will share in all we learn."

The serving girl brought the glace—Thiago inspected his plate with satisfaction.

"When we have done with him," Vasker went on, "you may extract whatever pleasure you can derive from his torment." He paused. "Can we consider the bargain sealed?"

"Sealed?" Thiago hitched his shoulders, generating a series of gratifying pops. "Our negotiation has just begun. Is that a spell sniffer I observe about Archimbaust's neck? And that amulet dangling from Disserl's hat, it is one that induces a sudden sleep, is it not? Such trinkets would prove invaluable on a journey such as you propose. Then there is the question of my fee. Sit, gentlemen. You may pick at my glace if you wish. Let us hope by the time the meal is done, you will have succeeded in satisfying my requirements."

THE FOREST known as the Great Erm had the feeling and aspect of an immense cathedral in ruins. Enormous trees swept up into the darkness of the canopy like flying buttresses and from that ceiling depended masses of foliage that might have been shattered roof beams shrouded in tapestries ripped from the walls, the result of an ancient catyclysm. Occasionally Derwe Coreme and Thiago heard faint obsessive tappings and cries that could have issued from no human throat; once they saw an ungainly white shape drop from the canopy and flap off into the gloom, dwindling and dwindling, becoming a point of whiteness, seeming to vanish ultimately into a distance impossible to achieve in so dense a wood, as if it had burrowed into the substance of the real and was making its way toward a destination that lay beyond the borders of the world. The hummocky ground they trod broke into steep defiles and hollows, and every surface was sheathed in moss and lichen, transforming a tallish stump into an ogre's castle of orange and black, and a fallen trunk into a fairy bridge that spanned between a phosphorescent green boulder and a ferny embankment beneath which long-legged spiders with doorknob-sized bodies wove almost invisible webs wherein they trapped the irlyx, gray man-shaped creatures no bigger than a clothespin that struggled madly against the strands of silk and squeaked and thrust with tiny spears as the hairy abdomens of their captors, stingers extruded, lowered to strike.

It was Derwe who first sighted Pandelume's tower, a slender needle of yellowish stone showing the middle third of its height through a gap in the foliage. From atop a rise, they saw that beyond the tower, the land declined into a serpentine valley, barely a notch between hills, where several dozen huts with red conical roofs were situated on a bend in a river; beyond the valley, the Great Erm resumed. They hastened toward the tower, but their path was impeded by a deep gorge that had been hidden from their eyes by vegetation. They walked beside it for half an hour but found no spot sufficiently narrow to risk jumping across. The walls of the gorge were virtually concave and the bottom was lost in darkness, thus they had no hope of climbing down and then up the opposite side.

"Those fools have sent us here for nothing!" Derwe Coreme rasped.

"Patience finds a way," Thiago said. "Soon it will be dark. I suggest we camp by the stream we crossed some minutes ago and wait out the night."

"Are you aware what night brings in the Great Erm? Bargebeetles. Gids and thyremes. Monstrosities of every stamp. A Deodand has been trailing us for the past hour. Do you wish to share your blanket with him?"

"Where is he? Point him out!"

She gazed at him quizzically. "He stands there, in back of the oak with the barren lower limb."

Thiago strode directly toward the oak.

Not having anticipated so bold an approach, the Deodand, upon seeing Thiago, took a backward step, his silver eyes widening with surprise. His handsome black devil's face gaped, exposing an inch more of the fangs that protruded from the corners of his mouth. Thiago gave him a two-handed push, adding to his momentum, and sent him sprawling. He caught one of his legs, stepped over it, dropped to his back and, holding the foot to his belly, he braced against the creature's body and rolled, wrenching the knee from its socket and—though the flesh felt like petrified wood—fracturing the ankle. The Deodand emitted a throaty scream and screamed again as Thiago stood and drove a heel into his other knee. He repeated the action and heard a crack. Unable to stand, the Deodand crawled after him, his breath hissing. Thiago nimbly eluded his grasp and snapped the elbow joints with deft heel-stomps. He kicked him in the head, to no visible affect. However, he kept on kicking and at last a silver eye burst, cracks spreading across it as they might in a sheet of ice, and fluid spilled forth.

The Deodand thrashed about, keening in frustration.

"How can this be? That you, a human, could have bested me?"

He spoke no more, for Derwe Coreme kneeled at his side and pricked his throat with a thin-bladed knife, causing him to gag, whereupon she

sliced off his carmine tongue and stuffed it into his mouth. Within seconds, he had drowned, choking on the blood pouring into his throat.

"I could have dealt with the Deodand," Derwe Coreme said as they retraced their steps toward the stream. "And with far greater efficiency."

Thiago made an impertinent sound with his tongue. "Yet you gave no sign of doing so."

"An auspicious moment had not offered itself."

"Nor would it have until the Deodand pounced."

She stopped walking and her hand went to the hilt of a hunting knife. "You fight well, but your style is not one that will allow you to survive long in the Great Erm. I, on the other hand, survived here for three years."

"Under the protection of the Busacios."

Her hand tightened on the hilt. "Not so. I escaped after eight months. The remainder of those years I spent hunting Busacios." She shifted her stance the slightest bit, easing back her left foot and resting her full weight upon it. "Do you know why Vasker hired you? They expect you to control me. They are afraid I will be so inflamed by the sight of Cugel, I may not be able to restrain myself from killing him and all the knowledge that can save them will go glimmering."

"Are they correct in that assumption?"

"Only in that I will not be controlled." With her left hand, she brushed a stray hair from her eyes, carefully laying it in place behind her ear. "It is impossible to discern the depths of one's own heart. My reaction to meeting Cugel again is thus unknowable. If you intend to thwart me, however, perhaps now would be the time."

Thiago felt the push of her anger; her pulse seemed to fill the air. "I will await a more auspicious moment."

He began walking again and after a second or two she ran to catch up.

"What are your intentions toward Cugel?" she asked. "I must be the one to kill him."

"A seer of peerless reputation in Kaiin has assured me that Cugel will not die by my hand, but by his own."

"He said that? Then he is a fool. Cugel would never take his own life! He defends it as a pig his last truffle."

Thiago shrugged. "The seer is not often wrong."

A frown notched Derwe Coreme's brow. "Of course, if I were to force suicide upon him, if I were to torture him and then offer a choice of more pain, unbearable pain, or the use of one of my knives to end his suffering…

That would be delicious, would it not? To watch him slice into his body, seeking the source of his life's blood, his hands trembling, almost too weak to make the final cut?"

"It would serve a purpose," said Thiago.

She went with her head down for a few paces and then said, "Yes, the longer I think about it, the more certain I become of your seer's acumen."

AT TWILIGHT Thiago built a fire that illumined a ragged clearing some fifteen yards in diameter. The stream cut through the edge of the lighted area and, after staring at it yearningly for several minutes, Derwe Coreme stood and removed her jacket.

"I intend to bathe while the warmth of day still lingers," she said. "There are scars on my body as well as my face, but if the urge to see me at my bath persists, I cannot prevent you from watching. I would caution you, however, against acting upon whatever attendant urges may spring to mind. My knives are never far from hand."

Thiago, who was eating parched corn and dried apples, grunted to signal his indifference. Yet though he determined not to watch, he could not resist. At that distance the scars resembled tattoos. Kneeling in the stream, the water running about her waist, she was lovely and clean-limbed, an image from legend, the nymph unmindful of a spying ogre, and he wondered at the alchemy that had transformed her into such a hate-filled creature…though he had witnessed such a human result on many previous occasions. Cupping her hand, she sluiced water across her shoulders. He imagined that a woman's back must be the purest shape in all the world.

Darkness fell. She stepped from the stream, dried herself, probing him with glances as though to know his mind, and then, wrapping herself in a blanket, came to sit by the fire. He maintained a stoic reserve and thought to detect irritation in her manner, as if she were annoyed by his lack of reaction to her nudity. Her scars were livid from the cold water, but now he saw them as designs and irrelevant to her beauty. The fire spoke in a language of snaps and crackles, and a night thing quarreled with itself, its ornate chortling echoing above a backdrop of lesser hoots and trills. She asked why he had chosen fighting as a profession.

"I liked to fight," he said. "I like it still. In Kaiin there is always a call for fighters to fill Shins Stadium. I did not enjoy hurting my opponents as

much as some of the others. Not in the beginning, anyway. Later...perhaps I did. I became First Champion of Kaiin for six years."

"Did something happen?" she asked. "To make you better or more fierce."

"Cugel."

She waited for him to go on.

"It's an old story." He spat into the fire. "A woman was at issue."

When he did not elaborate, she asked why he had waited so long to even the score.

"I lost sight of the matter," he said. "There were other women. I had money and a large house and friends with which to fill it. Then Sylgarmo's Proclamation alerted me to the fact that time was growing short. I began to miss the woman again and I recalled the debt I owed my cousin."

They were silent a while, each absorbed in their own thoughts. Something stirred in the bushes; then a feral outcry, the leaves and branches shook violently; then all was quiet. Derwe Coreme shifted closer to Thiago, reached out tentatively and touched the tip of her finger to a scar that transected his eyebrow, turning a portion of it gray.

"Mine are deeper, but you have more scars than I," she said wonderingly.

She seemed animated by something other than her usual sullen fury. Her hand lingered near his cheek and in the unsteady light of the fire her expression was open and expectant; but she snatched back her hand and, like an old sun restored for an instant to youthful radiance, its burst of energy spent, she lapsed once again into a funereal glow.

THIAGO'S IMAGINATION peopled the avenues among the trees with sinister ebony figures whose eyes were the color of fire. Dark spotches the size of a water-shadow filtered down through the canopy. He blinked them away and fought off fatigue. Some time later Derwe Coreme shook him awake. He was dazed, mortified, sputtering apologies for having fallen asleep.

"Keep quiet!" she said.

He continued to apologize and she flicked her hand at his cheek, not quite a slap, and said, "Listen!"

A sound came from the direction of the gorge. He thought initially it was that of a large beast munching greenery, smacking its lips and making pleased rumbles between bites; but as it grew louder and more distinct, he decided this impression had been counterfeited by many voices speaking at once. It grew more distinct yet and he became less certain of its nature.

The gorge brimmed with a night mist. Three pale lights, halated by the mist, rode atop an immense shape that moved ponderously, sluggishly, surging forward one plodding step after another, as though mired in mud. Peering into the murk, Thiago heard laughter and chatter, such as might be uttered by a great assemblage; then a piercing whistle came to his ears. The beast rumbled in apparent distress and flung up its head so that it surfaced from the mist. The sight of its coppery sphinx-like face, bland and empty of all human emotion, struck terror into his heart. A gid![3] Beside him, Derwe Coreme let out a shriek. The gid halted its progress, its cavernous bleak eyes fixed on the thicket where they were hiding. Its nose, the merest bump perforated by two gaping nostrils, lent it a vaguely amphibian aspect, and the lights (globes affixed to its temples and forehead) added a touch of the surreal. Mist obscured its wings and sloping, muscular body.

"Show yourselves!" a booming voice sang out. "It is I, Melorious, who speaks! I offer safe passage through the Great Erm."

This pronouncement stilled the babble of voices, but soon they returned, directing merry insults and impudent remarks toward Melorious. The gid surged forward and again lifted its head, trying to wedge it through the break in the earth, but failed in the attempt—it was too wide by half. Thiago was now situated directly above the gid's back and through the mist he saw what looked to be steel panniers strapped to its side. The panniers were each divided into four segments and each segment served as a cage in which forty or fifty men and women were kept. Thiago estimated there were several hundred people so encaged, yet none exhibited the attitude of captives, but rather acted like the passengers on a pleasure barge. Amorous couples lay intertwined on the floor. In another of the panniers, a band consisting of lutes, quintajells and nose-trumpets began tuning their instruments.

3 The gid is a hybrid of man, gargoyle, whorl, and leaping insect. In their "newt" stage they are relatively harmless, yet they inspire an atavistic fear. Once they have tasted human blood a metamorphosis occurs within minutes and they acquire mental powers that permit them to dominate lesser minds with ease. The physical changes are, reputedly, also extreme, but this is unproven, since a mere handful of men and women have survived the sight of an adult gid and none have been capable of reporting coherently on the particulars. The "newt" gid is copper in color, with black facial markings. As to the adult's coloration, we have only the word of Cotuim Justo, blind since birth, who claimed that the beast's colors "burned my eyes."

"You need not fear the gid," boomed Melorious. "I have bound it with a potent spell that renders it as docile as a pet thrail. Travel the Great Erm in complete security! Enjoy the companonship of beautiful women lacking all moral rectitude! Come away to Cil and Saskervoy…with first a stop at my subterranean palace for a feast to end all feasts."

The gid rumbled again, attempting to push the top of its head up through the gorge; a piercing whistle caused it to cease. Thiago perceived an opportunity. He sketched out his scheme with whispers and hand signals. Derwe Coreme looked at him aghast, shook her head vigorously, and shaped the word, no, with her mouth.

"Conscience will not permit me to leave you to the perils of the forest." A bald, honey-colored man clad in a jacket and trousers of dark blue silk worked with gilt designs, ostensibly Melorious, appeared on the gid's neck, tethered by a line; he spoke into a small hand-held device. Several other figures, untethered, cowered at his side, clinging to folds of the skin. "Make yourself known at once or I will have to send my minions after you. Wood gaunts and Deodands, beware! The flesh of my men bears a fatal taint that causes demon mites to breed in the belly of whatever consumes it."

Thiago burst from the thicket, half-dragging Derwe Coreme. She resisted, but upon realizing there was no going back, she outsped him to the edge and leaped, landing atop the gid's head, now a few feet beneath the lip of the gorge, and sprinted across his brow for the opposite side. Thiago also leaped, but did not land where he had intended. The gid, alarmed by Derwe's impact, trying to learn what had struck it, tipped its face to the sky, and Thiago came down feet-first near the center of its left eye. He expected to penetrate the membrane, to drown in the humor, but instead he slid along the clammy surface of the eye, fighting for purchase. The gid roared in anguish and tossed its head violently, sending Thiago hurtling through the air and crashing into a ragthorn bush. Screams from the men and women in the panniers stabbed at the air, but he could scarcely distinguish them from the ringing in his ears. Stunned, not knowing where he was, he peeked out and discovered that the ragthorn bush overhung the gorge. A little honey-colored bug in dark blue silks, Melorious dangled from his tether, hanging in front of the gid's vast, empty face. As Thiago looked on, he managed to set himself aswing by kicking at the gid's monstrous cheek, but every swing carried him back to the creature, nearer its unsmiling mouth. He had lost the hand-held device and thus his voice (and his whistles) went unheard. It seemed to Thiago that the gid stared at Melorious with a certain melancholy, as though it realized its youth was about to end and was made reluctant by the idea, by the grisly requirements demanded by this rite of passage. Melorious bumped against the creature's nose and, as he swung out wide again, the gid extended its neck and lazily snapped him up.

Ignoring his hurts, Thiago scrambled to his feet and ran, beating aside branches, tripping over roots, half-falling, intent on putting distance between himself and the gid. Behind him, the creature roared and, though no less loud, it seemed a narrower throat had shaped it—a snarly, grating sound with an odd buzzing quality. There was no sign of Derwe Coreme. He tried to recall if he had seen her clamber up onto the far side (this side) of the gorge, but without success. His lungs began to labor and, after a passage of seconds, he threw himself down under the snakelike roots of a mandouar and burrowed furiously until he was covered with black dirt. A minute or so later he felt a discharge of heat as if something on fire had passed close overhead. He put his head down and lay still for quite some time. When at length he sat up, he kept watch on the sky, picking thorns from his flesh, ill at ease and alert for the slightest sound.

A torrential shower dowsed the first of daylight, a pulsating redness in the east, and thereafter the overcast held. Wind herded black and silver clouds across the sky, accompanied by fitful thunder. Thiago felt around for his pack. It was gone, along with their supply of food and the various runes and devices he had coerced Vasker into giving him. The tower's summit was visible above a high hill and as he went toward it the rain started up again, blowing sideways into his face, drenching him to the bone. Just below the crest of the hill stood the ruins of a shrine. Its stone porch was more or less intact and beneath it a figure dressed in black sat cross-legged beside a crackling fire. Derwe Coreme. The carcass of a small animal, its bones picked clean, lay beside her. She looked at him incuriously and licked grease from her fingers.

He sat facing her, miserable as mud. A thorn he had been unable to dig out of his back gave him a fresh jab. "Do you have anything to eat?" he asked.

"Where is your pack? Is our food then at the bottom of the gorge?" She gave a rueful sigh, dug into a pocket and handed him a cloth in which a few edible roots and nuts were wrapped.

The roots yielded a bitter juice and, as he gnawed on one, he experienced a sharp pain in his jaw.

She watched him probe the inside of his gum with a forefinger and said, "When we met in Kaspara Viatatus, I worried that you were much like Cugel. The manner in which you dealt with Vasker and the rest reminded me of him. After you crippled the Deodand, I understood you were nothing like Cugel. He does not have your courage and, though your fighting style is not optimal, it reflects a directness of personality. A type of honesty, I thought. Now, having seen you destroy hundreds of lives by means of a foolhardy act, I wonder if what I assumed to be honesty was simply brute stupidity. And I ask myself, is moral incompetence any different from outright iniquity? The result is the same. Innocents die."

"Are you so naïve that you believe Melorious had a festive weekend planned for those in his cages? His spells had bedizened them—they were dead already. Or perhaps it is for Melorious you grieve?"

She seemed about to speak, but bit back the words. Finally she said, "You forced me to jump into the gorge and race across the forehead of a gid. Does this not, in retrospect, seem ill-considered?"

"Risky, yes. But we have reached our objective, so it can hardly be countenanced ill-considered."

"'Patience finds a way', you said. I suppose this is exemplary of the quality of your patience?"

"One must recognize when the time for patience has passed. I made a decision."

She brushed dirt from her trousers. "Kindly consult me in detail as to all your future decisions."

THE SKY cleared by mid-morning and the sun struck shifting black crescents of shadow from the field of boulders that lay beneath the tower; but the tower itself cast no shadow, a fact that gave Thiago pause, as did the presence of a pelgrane that flapped up from the summit and briefly circled above them before returning to her perch. A female and, judging by her clumsy and erratic flight, gravid—a condition that would render her especially vicious and unpredictable. None of this had a discernable effect upon Derwe Coreme, whose eagerness increased with every step. As they drew near, she could no longer contain her enthusiasm and broke into a trot. By the time Thiago reached the base of the tower, however, she was the picture of

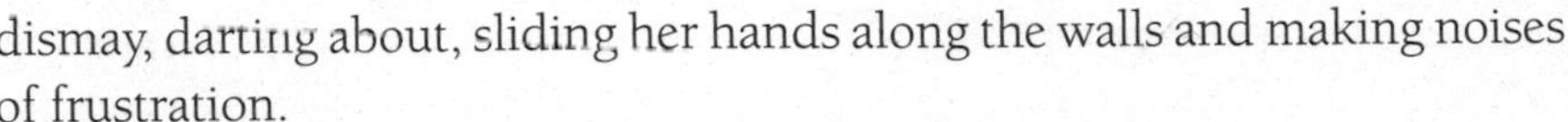

dismay, darting about, sliding her hands along the walls and making noises of frustration.

"There's no door!" she said. "Nothing. There's nothing!"

The tower was a seamless flow of stone, a single unbroken piece more than a hundred feet high, evolving at its top into a bulbous shape—this had been cut into an intricate filigree pattern of windows that would allow someone inside to scan the area below without revealing themselves. Leaving Derwe Coreme to vent her anger, Thiago began a circumnavigation of the base, testing each slight declivity and projection in hopes that pressing upon one of them would cause a hidden door to open. After an hour or thereabouts, his circuit less than a third complete, he heard bellicose voices coming from the opposite side of the tower, Derwe Coreme's hoarse outcries loudest of all. She had struck a defensive pose, knives in both her hands, and was fending off five men who encircled her. A sixth lay upon the ground, bleeding from slashes on his arm and chest. On seeing Thiago, the men fell back and their menacing talk subsided. They were a motley group, ranging in age from a mere lad to an elderly, weather-beaten individual with a conical red hat, identical to the roofs of the village below, jammed low onto his brow so that wisps of gray hair stuck out beneath it like bent wires. They were armed with rakes and clad in coarse white garments that were belted about their waists with green sashes. Lead amulets bearing the image of a crude anthropomorphic figure hung from their necks.

"Ho! What's this?" Thiago gestured with his fist and this served to drive the men farther from Derwe Coreme. "Explain yourselves at once."

The elderly man was pushed to the fore. "I am Ido, the spiritual charge-man of Joko Anwar. We sought only to inquire of the woman in the name of Yando and she rasped at us in a demon's voice and attacked. Poor Stellig has suffered a dreadful wound."

"Lies! They laid hands on me!" Derwe Coreme surged toward the men and Thiago side-stepped to block her way.

"Enlighten me as to the nature of this Yando," he said.

"He is the god of Joko Anwar," Ido said. "Indeed, it is said he is the god of all forlorn places."

"By whom is this said?"

"Why, by Yando himself."

A portly man with a patchy beard whispered in his ear and Ido said, "To clarify. Yando often appears as a man of burning silver and in this

guise he does not speak. But of late he sends his avatar, who confides in us Yando's truth."

Derwe Coreme, who had relaxed from her defensive posture, laughed derisively and started to speak, but Thiago intervened.

"Lately, you say? Did the appearance of the avatar predate Sylgarmo's Proclamation?"

"On the contrary," said Ido. "It was not long after the Proclamation that Yando sent him to instruct us so we might be saved by the instrumentality of his disciple, Pandelume."

Thiago gave the matter a turn or two. "This avatar…does he bear some resemblance to me? Does, for instance, his hair come down in a peak over his forehead? Like so?"

Ido examined Thiago's hair. "There is a passing similarity, but the avatar's hair is black and of a supreme gloss."

Derwe Coreme hissed a curse. Thiago laid a hand on her arm. "What form did the avatar's instruction take?"

All the men whispered together and after they had done, Ido said, "Am I to understand that you wish to undergo purification?"

Thiago hesitated, and Derwe Coreme sprang forward, putting her knife to Ido's throat.

"We wish access to the tower," she said.

"Sacrilege!" cried the portly man. "The Red Hat is assaulted! Alert the village!"

Two men ran back toward the village, giving shouts of alarm. Derwe Coreme pressed on the blade and blood trickled from its edge.

"Grant us immediate access," she said. "Or die."

Ido closed his eyes. "Only through purification can one gain entrance to the tower and the salvation that lies beyond."

Derwe Coreme might have sliced him open then and there, but Thiago caught her wrist and squeezed, forcing her to relinquish the knife. Ido stumbled away, rubbing his neck.

Thiago sought to pacify Ido and the portly man, but they refused to listen to his entreaties—they huddled together, lips moving silently, offering ornate gestures of unknown significance to the heavens. At length, giving up on reason, he asked Derwe Coreme, "Can you persuade them to instruct us in the rite of purification?" She had retrieved her knife and was testing the edge with her thumb, contemplating him with a brooding stare.

"Well," he said. "Can you do so? Preferably without a fatality? I would consider it a personal favor if we could avoid a pitched battle with the villagers."

She walked over to Ido and held up the blade stained with his blood to his eyes. He loosed a pitiable wail and clutched the portly man more tightly.

"Without interference, I can work wonders," she said.

AT DARKEST dusk, Derwe Coreme and Thiago stood alone and shivering in the boulder-strewn field beneath the tower. They wore a twin harness of wood and withe that culminated in a great loop above their heads—this, Ido explained, would allow Yando's winged servant to lift them on high and bring them to salvation. Except for a kind of diaper, designed so as to prevent the harness from cutting into their skin, they were naked and their bodies were festooned with painted symbols, the purpose of which had also been explained in excruciating detail.

Though no more risible than the tenets of other religions, the rites and doctrines of Yando as dictated by the avatar revealed the workings of a dry, sardonic wit. Thiago had no doubt they were his cousin's creation.

"Consider the green blotch currently being applied," Ido had said. "By no means is its placement arbitrary. When Yando was summoned from the Uncreate to protect us, he woke to discover that he had inadvertently crushed a litter of copiropith whelps beneath his left thigh. The blotch replicates the stain left by those gentle creatures[4]."

A last blush of purple faded from the sky. Thiago could barely make out Derwe Coreme beside him, hugging herself against the chill. He cleared his throat and launched into a hymn of praise to Yando, stopping when he noticed that Derwe Coreme remained silent.

"Come," he said. "We must sing."

4 It is something of a euphemism to describe the behavior of the copiropith whelp or imp (the term more commonly used) as "gentle." After devouring their mother and a majority of their siblings, the litter typically invade the nasal cavities of humans and attach themselves to certain nodes of the nervous system, provoking the victim to grin broadly and to hop and caper about in dervish fashion, all while experiencing terrible pain that results, after some weeks, in death. As adults, however, the whelps acquire an affectionate personality, soft, bluish gray fur, and a pleasing, cuddlesome look. In this form they are greatly prized as pets and believed by some (particularly residents of the Cloudy Isles) to house the souls of the men and women they have killed, and thus are treated as family members.

"No, I will not," she said sullenly.

"The winged servant may not appear."

"If by 'winged servant' you refer to the pelgrane, hunger will bring her to us. I refuse to play the fool for Cugel."

"In the first place, that the pelgrane and the winged servant are one is merely my hypothesis. Granted, it seems the most likely possibility, but the winged servant may prove to be another agency, one with a discriminating ear. Secondly, if the pelgrane is the winged servant and notices that we are less than enthusiastic in our obedience to ritual, this may arouse its suspicions and cause it to deviate from its routine. I feel such a deviation would not be in our best interests."

Derwe Coreme was silent.

"Do you agree?" Thiago asked.

"I agree," she said grudgingly.

"Very well. On the count of three, may I suggest you join me in rendering with brio, 'At Yando's Whim, So We Ascend In Gladness'."

They had just begun the second chorus when the oily reek of a pelgrane filled Thiago's nostrils. Great wings buffeted the air and they were dragged aloft. The harness swayed like a drunken bell, making it difficult to sustain the vocal, yet they persevered even when the pelgrane spoke.

"Ah, my lunchkins!" it said merrily. "Soon one of you will rest in my belly. But who, who, who shall it be?"

Thiago sang with greater fervor. The pelgrane's egg sac, a vague white shape, depended from its globular abdomen. He pointed this out to Derwe Coreme and she reached into her diaper. He shook his head violently and added urgency to his delivery of the words "not yet" in the line, "...though not yet do we glimpse the heights..." Scowling, she withdrew her hand.

A pale nimbus of light bulged from the sloping summit of the tower. As they were about to land, Derwe Coreme unhitched herself from the harness. She clung to the loop by one hand, slashed open the sac with the knife that had been hidden in herd diaper, and spilled the eggs into the dark below, drawing an agonized shriek from the pelgrane. Thiago also unhitched. The moment his feet touched stone, he made a leap, grabbed a wing strut and sawed at it with one of Derwe Coreme's knives. With a wing nearly severed from its body, the pelgrane lost its balance, toppled onto its side and slid toward the abyss, gnashing its tusks and tossing its great stag-beetle head in pain. It hung at the edge, frantically beating its good wing and clawing at the stone.

Breathing heavily, Thiago sat down amongst the bones that littered the summit and watched it struggle. "Why only one of us?" he asked.

The pelgrane continued to struggle.

"You are doomed," Thiago said. "Your arms will not long support your weight and you will fall. Why not answer my question? You said that soon one of us would be in your belly. Why just one?"

The pelgrane achieved an uneasy equilibrium, a claw hooked on an imperfection in the stone. "He only wanted the women. The men provided me with sustenance."

"By 'he', do you mean Cugel?"

Drool fettered the pelgrane's tusks. "My time was near and it was onerous for me to hunt. I struck a bargain with the devil!"

"Was it Cugel? Tell me!"

The pelgrane glared at him, loosed its hold on the edge and slipped away into the darkness without a sound.

At the apex of the summit, pale light that emanated from no apparent source spilled from a shaft enclosing a spiral staircase. With her prey close at hand, Derwe Coreme lost all regard for modesty. She ripped off the diaper and, a knife in each hand, began her descent. Thiago's diaper caught on the railing and he, too, rid himself of the garment.

The shaft opened onto a circular room into whose walls the windows Thiago had seen from the ground were cut. It was absent all furnishings and lit by the same pale sourceless light. A second stairway led down to an even larger room, pentagonal in shape, its gray marble walls resplendent with intricate volutes and a fantastic bestiary carved in bas relief. The air retained a faint sourness, as of dried sweat. Cut into the floor, also of gray marble, was a complicated abstract design. Five curving corridors angled off from the room, receding to a depth Thiago would have believed impossible, given the dimensions of the tower; but this, he reminded himself, was a magician's tower that cast no shadow and likely was governed by laws other than those to which he was accustomed.

They went cautiously along the first of the corridors, passing a number of doors, all locked, and came at last to a door at the corridor's end that stood open and admitted to a room, a laboratory of sorts. Derwe Coreme made to enter, but Thiago barred her way with his arm.

"Look first," he said.

She frowned, yet raised no objection.

Many-colored light penetrated the room from panels in a domed ceiling, shifting from dull orange to peach to lavender. Volumes of obvious antiquity lined the walls. Upon a long table, vials bubbled over low flames and the components of a mysterious device, a puzzle of glittering steel and crystal, lay scattered about. An immense bell jar contained dark objects suspended in what looked to be a red fluid. Several more such jars held items that Thiago could not identify, a few of which appeared to be moving. Then the scene changed. Their view was still of the same room, yet they were considerably closer to the table. The objects submerged in red fluid were fragments of a sunken ship. Gray creatures with sucker mouths, elongated hands and paddle feet crawled over the wreck, as if searching for something. Another jar enclosed a miniature city with a strange geometric uniformity to its architecture whose two tallest towers were aflame. Beneath the largest glass bell, a herd of four-legged beasts with flowing blond hair and womanly breasts fled across a mossy plain, pursued by an army of trees (or a single multi-trunked tree) that extended root-like tentacles to haul itself along.

Unsettled, Thiago and Derwe Coreme returned to the room of gray marble and entered a second corridor, passing along it until they reached a door at its nether end. Through it they saw a valley of golden grasses lorded over by hills with promontories of corroded-looking black rock that might have been the ruins of colossal statuary rendered unrecognizable by time. They could discern no signs of life, no movement whatsoever. The absence of all kinetic value bred a sense of foreboding in Thiago. At the end of a third corridor they stood overlooking a vista that could have been part of the Sousanese Coast south of Val Ombrio: a high reddish sun, barren hills, a stretch of forest, and then a lowland declining to water that glowed a rich pthalocyanine blue. All seemed normal until a flight of winged serpents the size of barges soared low along the coast and in the eye of one that flew straight at the door, veering aside at the last second, Thiago glimpsed their terrified reflection.

They had quit trying the doors, but as they retreated toward the marble room, Thiago idly turned a doorknob and thought to hear a gasp issue from the other side.

"Who's there?" Thiago gave the door a shake.

He received no answer. Again he rattled the door and said, "We have come to free you. Let me in!"

After an interval, a woman's voice cried out, "Please help us! We have no key."

Derwe Coreme pressed on; when Thiago called to her, she said, "Whoever she is, she can wait. I have two more corridors to inspect."

Before he could speak further, she passed beyond the bend in the corridor. He felt diminished by her absence and this both surprised and iritated him.

He examined the hinges of the door. The bolts were flush to the metal and he did not think he could loosen them with a knife. He set his shoulder to the planking and gave it a test blow. Solid. The corridor, however, was narrow enough that he could brace his back against the opposite wall and put all his strength into a kick. He did so and felt the lock give way the slightest bit. The sound of the kick was startlingly loud, but he drove his foot into the lock again and again until the wood splintered. A few more blows and the door swung open. Two beautiful dark-haired women attired in gauzy costumes that left little to the imagination stood gaping at him in the center of a room furnished with a bed, an armoire, and a mirror. In reflex, Thiago covered himself as best he could.

The younger of the women, scarcely more than a girl, prostrated herself. The older woman regarded him with a mix of hauteur and suspicion; then she stepped forward, standing almost eye-to-eye. She had the well-tended look and fine bone structure of the patrician women with whom he had consorted in Kaiin. Her hair was bound with an ivory and emerald clip. He could not picture her ladling dumplings onto a farmer's plate in Joko Anwar.

"Who are you?" she asked in a firm voice.

"Thiago Alves of Kaiin."

"My name is Diletta Orday. I was traveling in…"

"We have no time to exchange personal histories. Is there somewhere you can hide? I cannot fight and watch over you both."

Diletta's eyes darted to the side. "There is no hiding place for us so long as the avatar lives."

The girl on the floor moaned and Diletta said in a challenging tone, "Ruskana believes you will rape us."

"That is not my intent." He cast about in the corners of the room. "There were more of you, were there not?"

"We were nineteen in all. The avatar led seventeen along the corridors. None returned. He claims they are with Yando."

Cugel, Thiago told himself, must have been testing the open doorways, sending the women through and observing what happened. Chances were, he had not liked the results.

"He is no avatar," Thiago said.

"I am not a fool. I know what he is." She pointed to the armoire and said archly, "If your intent is to fight, you may need your hands. His clothes are there. Perhaps something will fit."

Within the armoire was an assortment of men's clothing. The shirts fit too snugly, hampering his freedom of movement; but he found a pair of trousers that he could squeeze into.

"Can you tell me where he is?" he asked.

"Oh, you will see him shortly."

As he turned, made curious by the lilt in her voice, he felt a sharp sting in his neck and saw Diletta pulling back from him, wearing a look of triumph. He staggered and, suddenly dizzy, went to one knee. Something struck him in the back and he toppled on his side. A second strike rolled him onto his back. The girl, Ruskana, was engaged in kicking him, grinning like a madwoman. He tried to focus on Diletta, but his vision clouded. Her voice echoed and faded, losing all hint of meaning and tone, becoming an ambient effect, and the kicks, too, became a kind of effect, no longer causing pain, each one seeming to drive him farther from the world.

Voices, too, ushered Thiago back to consciousness. A woman's voice complaining…Ruskana? Another woman, lower-pitched, asking what she should do. Diletta. Then a familiar man's voice that brought Thiago fully awake. He lay on his back, his hands bound beneath him, and began to work at loosening his bonds even before he opened his eyes.

"There must have been a woman with him," said Cugel from a distance. "The pelgrane would not have flown him to the summit, otherwise."

"Hunger may have overwhelmed its sense of duty," said Ruskana.

"I attribute no sense of duty to the pelgrane," said Cugel peevishly. "I suggest that if Thiago had come alone to the field, it would have gained nothing by flying to the summit. It would have eaten him where he stood."

"We have searched most of the night," Diletta said. "If a woman *was* here, she is not here now. Perhaps she took refuge at the end of one of the corridors. If that is the case, we have no need to worry."

Thiago could not make out Cugel's response. He slitted his eyes and saw he was lying in a small featureless room with gray marble walls close beside a bluish metal egg some fifteen feet high and ten feet wide, supported by six struts. Beyond lay a stair on the bottom step of which Ruskana stood. It led upward to a ceiling of gray marble. Thiago assumed there was a concealed exit and this would open onto the room

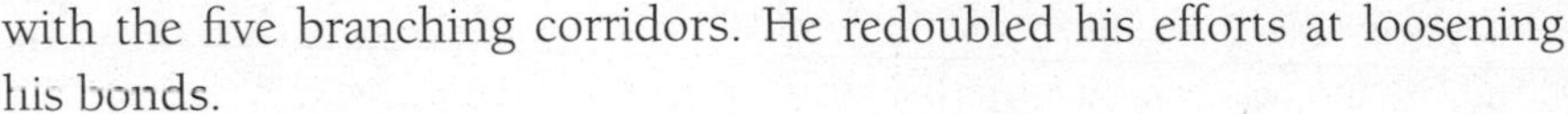

with the five branching corridors. He redoubled his efforts at loosening his bonds.

"Is it ready?" Diletta asked, moving into view.

"I must refer to Iucounu's notes. Minor adjustments may be required."

Cugel came out from behind the egg. He wore a high-collared black cape, gray trousers, and a velvet tunic of striped mauve and black. On his right thumb was a ring of black stone. His sharp features seemed a perversion of Thiago's own. What had once manifested as a roguish quality, the product of a quick wit and a penchant for irreverence, seemed to have been eroded by the years, resolving into an imprint of cruelty and capriciousness. The sight of him captivated Thiago. It was as if his view of the world had lacked only this lean figure to complete it. Now, seeing him in the flesh, his loathing for Cugel was given such weight and substance that he understood what he had felt before was a shadow of his true hatred of the man. He was so overwhelmed with revulsion that he could not even make a pretense of being unconscious; he stared at his cousin like a hawk watching supper emerge from a hole until Cugel directed a cursory glance his way.

"Cousin!" A smile sliced Cugel's features, but did not touch his eyes. "I would not have recognized you if you hadn't declared yourself to Diletta. You've grown so formidable. You have been exercising, have you not? All those scars, so much gray in your hair! I trust life has not treated you unkindly."

Thiago was unable to muster speech.

"What has led you to seek me out after all these years?" Cugel asked. "A desire to rekindle our childhood bond? Judging by your expression, I think not. An old enmity, perhaps. But what? I cannot recall ever having done you injury. Certainly none to warrant so desperate a journey as you must have made."

Thiago managed to croak a single word: "Ciel."

Cugel squatted beside him, tipped his head to one side. "Ciel? It has a ring, I admit, but…" He smacked his forehead. "Not that blond poppet you were smitten with during our formative years? A sweet bite of the apple, that one. By now, she must be a grandmother. Is she well?"

"You know she is not." Thiago worked at his bonds.

"Ah, yes. I remember. A pity you weren't there to save her, but you had your priorities in those days, always busy at your brutish sport and your revels. Blaming me for Ciel's death…you would do as well to blame a bee for sipping from a flower."

Thiago tried to sweep his legs out from beneath him with a kick, but Cugel, agile as ever, avoided it and caught his ankle. He dragged him forward and left him in front of the machine.

"I have better to do than listen to you whine about a girl dead a quarter of a century." Cugel flung open a transparent door in the face of the machine and indicated the ovoid chamber within—it contained two padded seats. "In moments, we will be away to a pleasant world far from this moribund planet and its dead sun."

"Sylgarmo's Proclamation has yet to be proven," Thiago said.

"Has it now?"

Smirking, Cugel went to the wall and pressed an indentation. With a grating noise, a portion of the wall retracted, creating as it did a large circular window.

"Welcome to the last morning of the world," said Cugel.

The sky as revealed by the window was black. Not pitch black, but black pervaded by a sickly glow, the source of which hung nearly dead-center of the window: the sun. Though it was at ten o'clock high, he could look directly at it and for a long moment he could do nothing else. Pale orange plasma filmed across the surface of a sphere that resembled an ember left over from a blaze, a great round ball of crusted carbon cracked and seamed with fire. From points on opposite sides of the sphere there arose enormous crimson effulgences, plumes of solar flame with the aspect of two mismatched horns, flares flung out into space that seemed as though they would eventually form into pinchers that would pluck the earth from its orbit. It was a ghastly, soul-shriveling thing to see. A dread weakness invaded Thiago's limbs. Ruskana clapped a hand to her mouth and Diletta put a hand on the wall for support. For his part, Cugel appeared enlivened by the sight.

"Ruskana! Take a last look around," he said, rubbing his hands together. "We want no interruptions. Quickly, girl! Diletta! See to the provisions."

The sound of Cugel's voice enlisted Thiago's hatred once again. He had made progress with his bonds, but needed more time.

"Ruskana!" he shouted as the girl mounted the stair. "There are only two seats inside the machine. Do you believe he will be here when you return? Every woman he has ever known, he has played her false."

"Ruskana is to ride astride my lap," said Cugel. "This has been discussed. Now go!" He waved her on.

"There have been a thousand Ruskanas before you," Thiago said. "Beginning with my Ciel. We quarreled, she and I. Cugel lured her to a solitary place on the outskirts of Kaiin, under the guise of offering advice on how she might repair the relationship. There he drugged her and she died...whereupon he fled. Do not expect better of him, I caution you."

Ruskana hovered near the top of the stair, the picture of uncertainty.

"Did you expect me stand my ground while you raised a mob?" Cugel made a derisive noise. "That was ever your way. To choose someone you believed was weak for a scapegoat and excite the public temper. But there is no mob here, only these two devoted women. I have come too far and endured too much to be thwarted by the likes of you." He held his fisted right hand to Thiago's face, showing him the ring of black stone. "This is Iucounu's ring. I bested him with his own magic. I have bested demons, giants, creatures that would leave you trembling. What did you hope to achieve against me?"

Cugel stood over Thiago, his face a neutral mask. He reached into the folds of his cape, produced a parchment scroll and tossed it onto Thiago's chest.

"A gift, cousin," he said. "The Spell of Forlorn Encystment. It is an option you may wish to exercise. Ask yourself if life is worth living imprisoned within the earth when there is no other choice, and act according to your answer." He turned to the stair. "Quickly now, Ruskana!"

The girl darted up the last few steps and pressed a stud in the ceiling; a section of the ceiling began to lift.

"She was done with you, Thiago," Cugel said. "She complied with my every desire."

Ruskana shrilled a warning. Derwe Coreme had slipped through the opening and stood at the top of the stair, wearing a man's shirt and trousers. The two women grappled briefly and Ruskana fell, cracking her head on the marble floor. Derwe Coreme spied Cugel and came toward him, knife in hand, face twisted with rage. Cugel darted for the egg and she screamed—it seemed ripped from her chest, furious like a raptor's scream. She hurled the knife, but Diletta pushed Cugel aside. The knife took her in the throat, penetrating both sides of her neck, and she collapsed. Derwe Coreme hurled a second knife, but it clanged off the door of the egg, with Cugel safe inside. Spatters of Diletta's blood dappled his cheek, lending him a clownish aspect.

Derwe Coreme sprinted down the steps and pounded on the door, screaming all the while. Cugel's expression was one of bewilderment. It was as though he were asking, Who is this scarred termagant? He busied himself with final preparations, ignoring her screams…if, indeed, he heard them.

Thiago burst the cords that constrained him.

A humming proceeded from the egg as Cugel, eyes closed in concentration, spoke the activating spell. Thiago got to his feet, and, standing beside Derwe Coreme, confronted him through the door. His spell complete, Cugel opened his eyes and smiled at them with the sweet tranquility of a man gone beyond judgment. The humming rose in pitch.

Thiago gave the egg a tentative push. He cleared Derwe Coreme away from the door, backed off several paces, and ran at it, striking it with his shoulder.

Cugel's smile faltered. Thiago had another run at the egg, and this time moved it slightly. His shoulder ached, but he made a third run. Concern was written on Cugel's face, but then the humming evolved into a keening and the egg appeared to be covered in sparkling silt, a film that vibrated over the metal surfaces. Cugel's smile returned. Thiago charged again, but was repulsed violently and thrown onto his back. The egg rippled, winking bright to dark. Soon it grew insubstantial and vanished, leaving a translucent afterimage in the air.

Thiago studied the afterimage as it faded. Was there a trace of desperation in Cugel's smile? The beginnings of fear? Was it a true smile or a rictus leer, a sign that his cousin was at the end *in extremis*? Perhaps Thiago's bullrushes had taken a toll, or perhaps Pandelume's egg had borne Cugel to a less pleasant world than he had imagined and his expression was the initial register of that place. It was useless to speculate. One could but hope. He sank to the floor beside Derwe Coreme, who sat with head in hands.

"He did not know me," she said mournfully.

Thiago thought to reassure her, but had not the energy to do so. After a bit, he put a hand on her shoulder. She stiffened, but permitted the contact.

"What happened to you?" he asked. "You were gone the entire night."

"It was strange," she said. "They searched for me carrying tubes of blue concentrate. I might have killed one, but not both, so I hid in the room at the end of the corridor we first explored."

"The study…the laboratory?"

"Yes. I met someone there. I…It was an old man, I think. He gave me these clothes and spoke to me of many things. Yet I cannot picture him, nor do I recall a word he said."

"Pandelume," said Thiago.

"If it was he, I cannot remember."

A curious white flickering, a discharge of some type, passed across the face of the sun. They stared hopefully, but it remained a molten horror, like an emblem on an evil flag. Some of the cracks in the black crust were sealing over and the coating of orange plasma looked to have thinned; but it was otherwise unchanged.

"We have to go!" Derwe Coreme sprang to her feet.

"It is a fine notion, but how?"

She went to the wall, pressed an indentation next to the one Cugel had pressed. A wide section of the floor retracted with an accompanying grinding noise. Light streamed upward from a hole. Another staircase spiraled downward. Thiago asked how she had known about the stair. She shook her head and set about retrieving her knives. To remove the blade from Diletta's neck, she was forced to wrench and tug, her foot pinning the corpse's shoulder in place, until it came free with a sucking noise. She wiped it clean on her trousers and started down the stairs. Thiago could find no reason to stir himself. One death was like another.

A whisper, one that seemed shaped by the tower itself, as if it were a vast throat enclosing them, said, "Go. Goooo…" The walls of the room wavered like smoke and Thiago had an apprehension that Pandelume was all around them, that the voice was his, and that his substance *was* the stuff of the walls, the floors, that this was not merely his place…it was *him*. Deciding that the prospect of a bottomless stair was less fearful than what he might face were he to remain, Thiago came wearily to his feet and began his descent.

It was a long way to the bottom of the stair, longer than would accord with the tower's height, and they stopped to rest on several occasions. During one such rest period, Derwe Coreme said, "How could those women stay with him?"

"You were with him once."

"Yes, but I would have left at the earliest opportunity. Our association was based solely on necessity."

"The women may have been no different from you at the outset. Cugel has a knack for bending people to his will, even when they do not care for him."

"Do you think he is alive?"

Thiago shrugged. "Who can say?"

At the bottom of the tower was a partly open door. They passed through it and into the field of boulders. The sun was at meridian, shining down a reddish light that, though a shade dimmer than usual, was well within its normal range of brightness. They gazed at it, silent and uncomprehending, shielding their eyes against the glare.

"I am afraid," said Derwe Coreme as they walked toward the edge of the Great Erm. "Did the sun rekindle as we descended? Have we crossed over to another plane of existence? Did Pandelume intercede for us? Life offered few certainties, but now there are even fewer."

The high sun burnished the massy dark green crowns of the trees, causing them to seem drenched with blood. Derwe Coreme passed beneath the first of them and along an avenue that ran between two mandouars. Thiago glanced back and saw the tower dissolve into a swirling mist; from the mist another image materialized, that of a gigantic figure who looked to be no more than emptiness dressed in a hooded robe, the features invisible, the body apparent yet unreal. For an instant, something sparkled against the caliginous blackness within the cowl, a blue oval no bigger than a firefly. The same blue, Thiago noted, as the egg in which Cugel had escaped, pulsing with the same vital energy, twinkling like a distant star. It winked dark to bright to dark and then vanished, swallowed by the void.

Intially, Thiago was distressed to think that Cugel might be alive, but when he considered the possibilities, that Cugel might travel on forever in that void, or that he might be bound for some hell of Pandelume's device, or for one of the worlds they had glimpsed at the ends of the corridors, for the table in the workshop, say, where he would be imprisoned beneath a glass bell and subject to exotic predation...though a clear judgment on the matter was impossible, these notions dispelled his gloom.

Pandelume's figure dispersed, fading and fading until only the feeble red sun and some puffs of cloud were left in the sky. Thiago broke into a jog in order to catch up with Derwe Coreme. Following her trim figure into the shadows, he recognized that though nothing had changed, everything had changed. The sun or something like it lived on, and the world below was still ruled by magicians and magic, and they themselves were ruled by the magic of doubt and uncertainty; yet knowing this no longer felt oppressive, rather it envigorated him. He was free for the moment of gloom, lighter at heart by one hatred, and the next time Derwe Coreme asked one of her imponderable questions, some matter concerning fate or destiny or the like, he thought he might be inclined, if he deemed the occasion auspicious, to provide her with a definitive answer.

AFTERWORD:

I FIRST encountered Jack Vance's work in junior high, when I read a paperback edition of *The Dying Earth* sheathed in one or another textbook (I hated mathematics, so most often I read it during math class). I was immediately hooked. I searched the newsstands for Mr. Vance's books—I recall being exhilarated when I stumbled across *The Languages of Pao*, and later, in college, when I discovered the first three novels of his Demon Princes series, which I also read hidden in textbooks. I think I began to associate the reading of Vance with a certain criminality and, in this particular instance, with an aversion to a certain history professor who spoke with a Southern drawl and pronounced "feudalism" as *fee-yood-a-lism*.

Of the many books I have read by Jack Vance, and I think I've read them all, I suppose it was *The Dying Earth* that was the biggest influence on my writing simply because it was the first to introduce me to the Vance-ian syntax and formality of language. I was already on a path that would lead to a complicated syntax and formal style, thanks to my father's pushing me that way, but Vance was *my* discovery and I accepted the lessons more willingly and more naturally from him than from an authority figure. Aside from the odd movie, Vance was my first exposure to science fiction—my father had forbidden all such reading material—and as such he was a revelation. That one could write stories about a dying sun and the peculiar folk who lived beneath it came as a shock, one from which I never recovered. Most of my stories are set in contemporary times, but were it not for Vance I think I might have been one of those writers who examine the psychological nuances of their failed marriages. Not that there's anything wrong with that, but this way it's been so much more fun…

Thanks, JV.

—Lucius Shepard

The Lamentably Comical Tragedy (or The Laughably Tragic Comedy) of Lixal Laqavee

TAD WILLIAMS

"*I am not a* magician," Lixal Laqavee announced to the shopkeeper who had come forward at the ringing of the bell upon the counter, "but I play one in a traveling show."

"Then you have come to precisely the right place, sir," the man said, smiling and nodding. "Twitterel's Emporium is known throughout the length of Almery for its unrivaled selection of effects, marvels, and confidence enhancers."

"And are you Twitterel?" Lixal inquired. "The one whose name is above the door of this establishment?"

"I have that honor," said the small, bewhiskered man and brushed a fleck of dust from his velvet robe. "But let us not waste time on such trivia as my name. How may I serve you, sir? Flash-dust, perhaps? It gives the impression of a great outrush of thaumaturgical energies while posing no great danger to its employer." Twitterel reached into a ceramic jar on the scarred counterop and produced a handful of silvery dust, which he threw to the floor with a flick of his wrist. It burst with a percussive crack and produced a voluminous puff of white smoke. The shopkeeper then fanned vigorously with his hand until he and Lixal were face to face again. "As you see, it also provides ample distraction for a well-conceived disappearance or sleight-of-hand effect."

Lixal nodded thoughtfully. "Yes, I think a portion or two of flash-dust might serve admirably, although by no means will it fulfill all my needs."

"Ah!" Twitterel smiled, showing fewer teeth than one might expect even in a man his age. "A gentleman who wishes his impostures to be both believable and exciting. May I say, sir, that your audience will thank you for your care. Perhaps this length of rope, which when properly exhibited seems to have the living qualities of a serpent? Or this Benaraxian Cabinet, whose interior can comfortably contain a shapely female assistant—the type whose curvaceous form, and your menacing of same with these cleverly constructed sabers, will particularly stimulate your audience…"

"No, no," said Lixal, waving his hand. "You have incorrectly conceived my needs. I do not wish to employ mere trickery, especially of the expensive variety embodied in this monstrous, mirrored sarcophagus." He flicked a finger at the lacquered surface of the Benaraxian Cabinet. "The performing troop with which I ply my trade is a small one, accustomed to the back roads of Almery, and we have but one wagon to carry all our goods. Also, and far more importantly, in the vicinities we frequent the distinction between performing the *role* of magician and *being* a magician is often a blurry one."

The shopkeeper Twitterel paused. He reached up and plucked out a bit of his breakfast that had lodged in his beard (or at least Lixal hoped it was from a meal no less recent.) The old man seemed oddly disturbed by his customer's words. "I am not sure I grasp the sum of your meaning, sir," Twitterel said. "Elucidate, please, so that I may better serve your needs."

Lixal frowned. "You force me to greater crudity than I would prefer. However, I will do my best to make plain my desire." He cleared his throat. "I travel with a troop of performers, providing entertainment and instruction, and sometimes even hope to those who previously found that quality in short supply. Not all perceive us in this wise—in fact, some ungenerous souls have suggested that I and my associates are little better than venal tricksters, a claim I reject vigorously.

"In the course of our educational performances, we offer to our auditors certain medicines and tonics of a curative nature. Despite the slurs of the uncomprehending, our record of cure is bettered by no other similar organization, and even compares favorably with the more common medicinal advice offered by the sort of physic to which our rustic audiences generally have access. Do you grasp my meaning?"

"You sell dubious cures to the peasantry."

"In a nutshell, good shopkeeper, in a nutshell, although I might take exception to the word 'dubious'. By certain measures, life itself is dubious. However, generally speaking, your perception is admirable. Now, because my part in this organization is a portrayal of magicianship, at times I am approached by members of the buying public separately from the rest of the cast, customers who believe the illusions they have seen are real. Many of them wish only to know whether the silver coin I produced had truly been lodged in their ear in the first place, and if so, should it not then belong to them." Lixal shook his head ruefully. "Others, though, have requests for magical assistance of a more precise nature, usually concering some petty problem in their lives—a failure of certain human apparatus of a privy nature being the most common. Then there are those who would like to see a family member hastened to peace so that the division of his or her possessions might be practiced sooner rather than later." Lixal held up his finger. "These commissions I would not take, I hasten to assure you, even had I the means, and not only because of my naturally ethical composition. Our rural folk tend to carry both grudges and sharp hand tools, so I have no urge to excite malice." He cleared his throat. "Other supplicants have desired lost objects found, unpleasant creatures or relatives confined, and so on—in short, a galaxy of requests, most of which I am unable to fulfill, and so a healthy sum remains dispersed in the pockets of the rustic population instead of concentrated in my own, where it might form the foundation of a burgeoning fortune." Lixal shook his head sadly. "I have come to tire of this woefully imbalanced state of affairs. So I come to you, good shopkeeper."

Twitterel looked back at Lixal with more consternation than the casual observer might have expected. "I still do not grasp with certainty your desires, sir," the old man said nervously. "Perhaps you would be better off visiting the shop of my good friend and colleague Dekionas Kroon, a scant four leagues away in the pleasant hamlet of Blixingby Crown Gate—he also specializes in fine acoutrements for the performing of magic to discerning audiences…"

"You tease me, sir," said Lixar sternly. "You must have grasped by now that I am not interested in the *acoutrements* of the magical arts, not

in elaborate stage artifices, or even the potware and piping of alchemy or other scholarly but unsatisfying pursuits. I wish to buy actual *spells*. There—I can make it no clearer. Just a few, selected for one like myself who has no magical training—although, it must be said, I do have a wonderful, firm voice that any magician might envy, and a certain physical presence concomitant with a true thaumaturge, as you must have noticed yourself." Lixal Laqavee stroked his full brown beard slowly, as if comparing its lushness to the sparse clump of yellowed whiskers which decorated the shopkeeper's receding chin.

"Why would I, a mere merchant, have such things?" Twitterel questioned in what was almost a squeak. "And why, even if I did possess such objects of powerful wisdom, would I share them with someone whose only claim to wizardly dessert is a velvet robe and an admittedly handsome beard? Sooner would I put a flaming brand into the hands of a child residing in a house made of twigs and dry leaves!"

"You misunderstand me again, good Twitterel," Lixal replied. "You protest that you are a mere merchant, and yet unless I much mistake things, the name etched above your door does not conform to your true identity. In other words, I believe you are in fact not 'Twitterel' at all, but rather Eliastre of Octorus, who was once reknowned in the most powerful circles as 'The Scarlet Sorceror'—a pleasantly dramatic name, by the way, that I would quickly adopt for my own performances were it not that I make a better appearance in dark colors such as blacks and moody, late-evening blues." Lixal smiled. "You see, it happens that by mere chance I studied your career while honing my impersonation of someone in your line of endeavor. That is also how I recognized you when I saw you drinking in the tavern up the road yesterday and began to conceive of my current plan. What a piece of luck!"

"I...I do not understand." Twitterel, or Eliastre, if that was indeed his name, retreated a little farther from the countertop behind which he stood. "Why would such an unlikely set of affairs mean luck for you?"

"Step back in this direction, please. Do not think to escape me," Lixal said. "And neither should you attempt to bluff me with the powers you once so famously owned. I know full well that after you failed in an attempt to seize leadership among your fellow magicians and wizards, the Council of Thaumaturgic Practitioners removed said powers and placed you under a ban of trying to regain them or *in any other way dabbling in the profession of wizardry*, under pain of humiliating, excruciating, and lingering death.

Please understand that I will happily inform the Council of your whereabouts and your current occupation if you resist me. I am inclined to believe your current profession, peddling alembics and flash-dust, might well fall within the scope of their ban."

Twitterel seemed to have aged twenty years—decades he could ill-afford to add to his tally—in a matter of moments. "I could find no other way to make a living," he admitted sadly. "It is the only craft I know. The Council did not take that into account. Better they should have executed me outright than condemn me to starve. In any case, I wished only to reform certain insufficiencies of the transubstantive oversight process—what was once a mere prophylactic has become a hideous, grinding bureaucracy…"

Lixal held up his hand. "Spare me. I care not for the details of your rebellion, but only for what you will do next—namely, provide me with several easily-learned spells that will allow me to supplement my performing income by rendering assistance to those pastorals who seek my aid. I am not a greedy man—I do not wish to raise the dead or render gold from dry leaves and river mud. Rather, I ask only a few simple nostrums that will put me in good odor with the country-folk—perhaps a charm for the locating of lost livestock…" He considered. "And surely there is some minor malediction which would allow the sending of a plague of boils to unpleasant neighbors. Such a thing has been requested of me many times, but heretofore I had no means of answering the call."

Eliastre, or Twitterel as was, rubbed his hands together in what looked like genuine unease. "But even such minor spells can be dangerous when improperly used—not to mention expensive!"

"Never fear," said Lixal, with a certain air of *noblesse oblige*. "When I have begun to earn the money I so richly deserve by employing these spells, I will most certainly return and pay you their full worth."

"So," the shopkeeper said bitterly. "You would extort me *and* rob me."

"Not at all." Lixal shook his head. "But lest such an ill-considered notion set you scheming to punish me somehow for merely trying to better my situation in this uncertain life, let show you the warding bracelet on my wrist, an object of true power." He flourished the twist of copper he wore around his arm, which indeed seemed to have a glow greater than the ordinary reflection of metal. It had been given to Lixal by a young lady of the troop during a time of pleasurable intimacy—a charm that she swore would protect him from premature death, inherited by her from

her aunt at the time of that elderly lady's quite timely demise. "Oh, by the by," Lixal continued, made uneasy by the speculative way Eliastre was examining his wrist jewelry, "if in your misdirected bitterness you decide that some knowledge or stratagem of yours could overcome the efficacy of this ornament, I would like you to be aware that the bracelet is not my only protection. Should anything untoward happen to me, an associate of mine unknown to you will immediately dispatch to the Council of Thaumatrugic Practitioners a letter I have prepared, detailing both your recent crimes and your exact location. Remember that as I choose my spells and you guide me in their recommended usages."

The old man stared at him for a long time with an expression on his face that it would have been difficult to call either friendly or forgiving. "Ah, well," Eliastre said at last. "My hands appear tied, as it were, and the longer I resist the more the binding rope shall chafe me. Let us proceed."

WHEN HE had completed the transaction with the ex-wizard to his satisfaction, Lixal took the manuscript pages of the new spells and bade Eliastre goodbye.

"By the by, I frown on the word 'extortion'," Lixal called back to the old man, who was still glaring at him from the doorway of the shop. "Especially when I have given you my word of honor that I will come back at a time when my pockets are full and repay you at market rate. The expression on your face suggests that you doubt this promise, or else that you are otherwise unsatisfied with our exchange, which to me seems to have been more than fair. In either case, I am displeased. Until that cheerful day when we meet again, I suggest you cultivate an attitude of greater humility."

Lixal made his way back out of the city of Catechumia toward the forested outskirts where his traveling theatrical company had made its camp. He wished he had been able to force the old man to recite the spells himself, as proof that none of them had been primed like a springe trap to rebound painfully or even fatally on its user, but since Eliastre had been forcibly curtailed from using magic by the Council of Thaumaturgic Practitioners, Lixal knew there would have been little point: no flaws would have been exposed, because the spells themselves would not have worked. He would have to trust to the curbing effect of his threat to have a colleague notify the Council if anything hurtful should happen to Lixal.

The fact that this colleague was an invention, created on the spur of the moment—Lixal had long practice in improvisation—would be unknown to Eliastre, and therefore no less effective an intimidation than an actual confederate would have been.

Most of the rest of his fellow players were still in town, but Ferlash, a squat, ill-favored man wearing the cassock of a priest of the Church of the Approaching Horizon, was toasting a heel of bread at the campfire. He looked up at Lixal's approach.

"Ho!" he called sourly. "You look cheerful. Did you bring something to eat? Something which, by sharing it with a deserving priest, you could store up goodwill in the afterlife? I do not doubt your soul's post-horizontal standing has need of a little improvement"

Lixal shook his head in irritation. "As everyone in our company knows, Ferlash, you have not been a celebrant in good standing of your order since they expelled you years ago for egregious impregnation of congregants. Thus, I suggest you leave off discussion of my own particular afterlife. I would no more listen to your speculations about the health of my soul than I would accept similar advice from the piece of bread you are toasting."

"You are a testy young man," Ferlash said, "and too pleased with yourself by half. In fact, I must say that you seem even more self-satisfied than usual today."

"If I am, it is a condition well-earned. I have made no small contribution today to my own well-being, and, indirectly, yours as well, since the spread of my fame as a thaumaturge will bolster the reputation of our entire troop."

Ferlash scowled. Along with Lixal and another man who called himself Kwerion the Apothecary, the once-priest acted the part of authority figure for the troop, explaining matters of religion and its accommodations with commerce to the rural audiences. "Your thaumaturgic credentials are even more tenuous than mine as a priest," he now told Lixal, "since I at least once legitimately wore the sacred mantle. What claim to genuine wizardship have you?"

"All the claim in the world, as of today." And, because he was indeed pleased with himself, he went on to tell Ferlash what he had done. "So here you see the fruits of my intellect and ambition," he finished, waving the sheaf of spells. "Once I have conned these, I shall be a form of magician in truth, and thereafter I will rapidly better myself."

Ferlash nodded his head slowly. "I see that you have indeed done well today, Lixal Laqavee, and I apologize for lumping you in with the rest of us poor posers and counterfeits. Since you are soon to become such an accomplished wonder-worker, I suppose you will no longer have any use for that bracelet you wear, the one that is such a fine talisman against premature death? There are times during our travels when the agnosticism of our audiences slips from doubt of my sincerity into actual bad temper—especially among those for whom the prayers and holy artifacts I sold to them did not work as effectively as they had hoped. I would value such a protection around my own wrist against those more strenuous gainsayers of my methods."

Lixal drew back in irritation. "Nothing like that shall happen, Ferlash. The bracelet is mine and mine alone, given to me by a woman who loved me dearly, even though she chose security over romance and married that toadlike proprietor of a livery stable last year. The idea that you would be rewarded for nothing but beggary with such a puissant token is laughable." He sniffed. "I go now to learn my spells. When next you see me, I shall be even less a person with whom you might wish to trifle."

The thaumaturge-to-be left Ferlash sitting by the fire, staring after him with envy and dissatisfaction.

LIXAL LAQAVEE had chosen the incantations carefully, because without the decades of conscientious practice which most wizards devoted to their craft—a routine far too much like hard work to attract Lixal, who knew there were many more amusing uses for his spare time—it was entirely possible to misspeak an incantation or muddle a gesture and find oneself in an extremely perilous situation, taslismanic bracelet or no. Also, due to his lack of experience, it was doubtful that Lixal Laqavee would be able to employ more than one spell at a time, and, of course, after each employment he would need to learn the spell anew before its next usage. Thus, Lixal had demanded only four spells of Twitterel-who-was-in-truth-Eliastre, a selection that he believed would prove both versatile and easy to manage.

The first was the Rhinocratic Oath, which allowed its perpetrator to create amusing or horrifying changes to the nose of anyone he designated, and then to undo those changes again if he so desired. The second, the

Cantrip of Notional Belittlement, allowed its wielder to make any idea or sight seem smaller or less important to one or more people, the length of the effect varying with the amount of people ensorceled. The third was a charm of romance named Dormousion's Pseudo-Philtre, which tended to create lust even when lust would normally not have existed or exacerbate it in even its most tenuous manifestations until the designated recipient of the pseudo-philtre would take ridiculous risks to scratch the amatory itch.

Last, most difficult to memorize, but also undoubtedly the most powerful of all the spells he had chosen, was the Thunderous Exhalation of Banishment, a weapon which would instantly move an unwanted personage or creature to the farthest end of the earth from the point at which the spell was employed, and then keep that individual there perpetually. An enraged husband or hungry leucomorph so banished anywhere in Almery would instantaneously be flung to the farthest ends of the unknown regions of ice on the far side of the world, and be held in that vicinity in perpetuity as long as he lived.

This spell drew such great reserves of strength from its user that it was practical only for select occasions, but since those occasions would likely be of the life-or-death variety, Lixal did not doubt it had been a wise and valuable choice. In fact, his selection of the Thunderous Exhalation had particularly seemed to nettle old Elisatre, so that the shopkeeper muttered the entire time he transcribed it, which only convinced Lixar he had done well in his selection.

And indeed, over the following months, Lixal and his newfound thaumaturgical skills did prosper. He enlivened countless local feuds with the sudden provision and subsequent recusal of nasal grotesqueries, and created a giant efflorescence so like a starfish on the end of one old woman's nose that she completely rewrote her will in favor of a nephew she had not previously favored, who happily passed on a percentage to Lixal, who then rewarded the old woman's good sense by returning her proboscis to its natural (if only slightly less unlovely) state. On separate occasions, he used the Exhalation to banish three mad dogs, one dauntingly large and aggressive tree-weasel, and two husbands and a father who had all taken violent issue with Lixal's use of the Pseudo-Philtre on their wives and daughters, respectively. (Two wives and two daughters, because one of the cuckolded husbands also had a comely daughter slightly past the age of consent. Lixal had made sure of this last—he was scrupulous that his amatory coercions should be used only on adults, another of his many traits that he felt was deserving of greater admiration than it received.) And the belittling cantrip had also been employed in several cases where his other methods could not prevail, enabling Lixal to find escape and even reward when he might otherwise fail in one or both areas. He began to develop no small reputation in the environs through which his troop traveled.

Thus, one evening, in a town called Saepia, a committee of local grandees led by Saepia's aldermayor approached Lixal at the conclusion of the troop's nightly show with a request for his assistance. He invited them to drink a glass of stock wine with him and discuss their needs. After a string of successes in surrounding towns, Lixal felt secure in what he had to offer, and thus in what he was empowered to charge.

"We could not help admiring your demonstrations tonight," the aldermayor opened, clutching his many-pointed ceremonial wool hat in his hands in the submissive manner of a tardy schoolboy. "Nor could we help to be impressed by the arguments of your colleagues, Kwerion and Reverend Ferlash, as to the value to a town like ours of being forward-thinking in regard to the benefits of your advanced knowledge."

"By the way, speaking of such aids to fortune, is it true that those apothecarical potions will allow me to satisfy my wife?" asked one of the grandees shyly. "If so, I would like to buy some from your colleague Kwerion. My lady has a powerful appetite, if you know what I mean, and I often despair of being able to keep her from looking elsewhere for sustenance."

"Oh, Kwerion's potions could no doubt help," Lixal assured him. "But if you will send your wife to me to be examined, as a personal favor I will give her something to curb those hungers—and I will not charge you a single terce! Is that all you good folk wished, then?" he asked as the local grandee stammered his thanks.

"In fact, there is another matter," said the aldermayor. "Small and insignificant to the great and powerful Lixal Laqavee, but large and ruinous to such as ourselves, and to the resources of our small backwater. A Deodand has taken up residence in the local cuttlestone quarry, and we can no longer work the crystal beds there, which had long been source of the greatest part of our revenue. To add to the indignity, not only does his presence inhibit the quarry's workings, but also he sallies forth at intervals to steal our town's babies from their cribs or seize unwary citizens walking home by night. He then takes these unfortunates back to his cavern and devours them. We have sent several doughty hunters after him, and he has defeated and digested them all. It has cast a pall over even the smallest activities in Saepia's usually vibrant civic life."

"And you would like me to rid you of this vile creature?" said Lixal, thinking cheerfully of the Thunderous Exhalation of Banishment. "Easily done, but owing to the danger of the work, even to a trained and experienced practitioner of the mystical arts such as myself, the price will not be insignificant." And he quoted them an amount in gold that made the grandees blanch and the aldermayor fretfully detach one of the wool horns from his ceremonial hat.

After a great deal of bargaining, they settled on a slightly lower amount, although it was still as much as Lixal would have expected to make over the next half-year in the ordinary course of things. He pleaded weariness that evening, wanting a chance to study and memorize the banishing spell, then bade them goodnight with a promise to meet them in the morning and solve their problem.

The next day, after a leisurely breakfast with the grandee's wife, whose curative visit had run long, Lixal made his way from his wagon in the troop's camp—he now had one all to himself—to the aldemayor's house, a humble but well-constructed building in the domelike local style. That gentleman stood waiting in the road with an even larger swarm of townsfolk than had accompanied him the previous night. Lixal greeted them with casual nonchalance and allowed himself to be led up the hill toward the cuttlestone quarry behind the town.

He was left at the edge of it, without guides, but with directions toward the Deodand's cave. Lixal made his way across the floor of the silent quarry, noting with interest the tools dropped as though their users had simply run away and never returned, which had likely been the case. Dispersed among these discarded tools were the bones of both animals and people, most of which had been snapped in half so that their marrow could be accessed. The quarry itself was hung with early morning mist that mostly blocked the sun and made it hard for Lixal to see what was around him, which might have made a less confident man nervous, but he knew it took only a heartbeat to shout the single, percussive syllable which enacted the Thunderous Oath. After all, had he not been surprised by that cuckold back in Taudis, so that he had only begun to speak the word as the ax was already swinging at his head? And yet was not he, Lixal, still here, while the ax-wielder was doubtless shivering miserably in the snows of uttermost Ultramondia, wishing he had thought twice before assaulting the Dire Mage Laqavee?

"Hello!" he called now, tiring of the walk. "Is anyone here? For I am a lost traveler, plump and out of shape, wandering helplessly in your abandoned quarry."

As he expected, a dark form came toward him out of the mists, in no great hurry, lured by the promise of such an easy meal. The Deodand, in the manner of its kind, looked much like a man except for the flat, sooty black of its skin and the bright gleam of its claws and fangs. It stopped now to inspect him through slitted, bile-yellow eyes.

"You exaggerate your own plumpness, traveler," it said disapprovingly. "Except for that moderate roll of fat around your middle I would not call you plump at all."

"Your eyes are as faulty as they are inhumanly strange," cried Lixal. "There is no such roll of fat. I described myself thusly merely to lure you out so that I might dispose of you without wasting my entire morning in search."

The Deodand looked at him curiously. "Are you a warrior, then? I confess you do not resemble it. In fact, you have the slack, well-fed look of a merchant. Do you plan to end my reign of terror here in Saepia by offering me better employment elsewhere? I confess that I feel an urge to explore other places and to eat newer, more exotic people."

Lixal laughed in scorn. "Do not be impertinent. I am no simple merchant, but Lixal Laqavee, the Dire Mage in Late-Evening Blue. If you do not know my name already, you will have ample time to reflect on it with rue in the cold place to which I will send you."

The Deodand moved closer, stopping only when Lixal raised a hand in warning. "Strange. I have never heard of such a magician as yourself, and other than that small talisman on your wrist, I see no evidence of power about you. If I wrong you, please forgive me, but you do not strike me as much of a wizard at all. Could you be mistaken?"

"Mistaken? Can you mistake *this*?" His irritation now become something closer to blind rage, Lixal waved his hand and uttered the Thunderous Exhalation of Banishment in his loudest and most impressive voice. The sky rumbled as if in terror at the great forces employed and a flash of light surrounded the Deodand as though lightning had sprung out of the creature's carbon-colored pores. But the next instant, instead of shrinking into utter vanishment like a man falling down an endless well, as all the previous men and beasts struck with the Exhalation had done, the Deodand suddenly came sliding toward Lixal as rapidly as if the foul creature were a canal boat dragged by a magically superanimated donkey. Lixal had time only to throw his hands in front of his face and give out a brief squeak of terror, then the Deodand smacked to a sudden halt a scant two paces away from him as though the creature had run into a soft but inflexible and unseen wall.

Lixal looked between his fingers at the Deodand, whose hideous aspect was not improved a whit by close proximity. The Deodand looked back at him, an expression of bemusement on its cruel, inhuman features.

"A strange kind of banishment," it said, taking a step back. A moment later it leaped at Lixal, fangs bared. Whatever had prevented it from reaching him before stopped it this time as well: the Deodand bounced harmlessly back from him. "Hmmm," the creature said. "Your spell seems to have worked in reverse of the way you intended it, drawing me toward you instead of exiling me." The Deodand turned and tried to walk away but could not get more than a step before it was again brought up short. "I am held like a leashed moon circling a planet, unable to move away from you," it said in frustration. "But that talisman on your wrist seems to prevent me reaching you and completing my earlier intention, namely, to destroy you and eat you." It frowned, hiding its terrifying pointed teeth behind a pouting lower lip. "I am not happy with this state of affairs, magician. Release me and I will go my way without molesting you further. You have my word."

Lixal stared at the creature, who was so close he could smell its sour, feral scent, the odor of bones and rotting flesh that hovered in its proximity like the morning fogs that hung over the quarry. "I…I cannot," he said at last. "I have not the capability to undo the spell."

The Deodand made a noise of disgust. "As a both a wizard and Deodand-slayer, then, you are close to an utter failure. What are we to do now?" A look of calculation entered its yellow eyes. "If you cannot release me in the conventional way, you must consider removing your bracelet and letting me kill you. That way, at least one of us will live his life out the way the spirits of the void intended."

"On the contrary!" said Lixal, piqued. "Why would I permit you to kill me? You may just as easily kill yourself—I imagine those sharp claws will work as efficaciously on your own jugular as mine. Then I can go on with my own life, which has much more to recommend it than your skulking, marrow-guzzling, baby-stealing existence."

"Clearly we will not easily find agreement on this," said the Deodand. "A thought occurs to me. Have you offended another wizard lately?"

Lixal thought immediately of Eliastre and the impression of dissatisfaction he had displayed at their parting, but was unwilling to broach the subject to the Deodand after such a short acquaintance. "Anything is possible in the rarefied yet contentious circles in which I travel. Why do you ask?"

"Because if so, it is likely that even death will not release us. If this misfiring of your incantation is the result of thaumaturgical malice, it may well be designed so that even if one of us dies, the other's fortunes will not improve. For instance, I am compelled to be in your vicinity. If you die and become motionless bones, it is quite logical that I will be compelled to remain in the spot where you fell. Similarly, should you achieve the unlikely result of killing *me*, the corpse would probably still adhere to your person no matter where you traveled. The material shells of my tribe decay loathsomely but extremely slowly. In short, you would spend the rest of your life dragging my rotting corpse behind you."

Lixal closed his eyes in disgust and dismay. "Eliastre!" he said, and it was a bitter curse upon his tongue. "I know this is his hand at work. He has treated me shamefully with this trick and I will have revenge on him, somehow!"

The Deodand stared at him. "What name is this?"

"It is the name of one we apparently must visit," Lixal said. "That is our only hope to escape our unpleasantly twinned fate. Come with me." He grimaced sadly. "I think we must steer clear of Saepia as we leave these environs. The townspeople now will have several reasons not to love me, and I will tell you honestly that they never cared much for you."

LIKE TWO climbers bound by a rope, Lixal and the Deodand made their way through the forest and back to the camp outside town where the traveling troop was still ensconced. The players would have been at worst indifferent to the arrival of Lixal in other circumstances, but his companion filled the whole camp with unhappiness.

"Do not move," shouted the apothecary Kwerion. "A terrible beast pursues you! Throw yourself down on the ground and we will do our best to slay it!"

"Please offer the creature no harm," said Lixal. "Otherwise, and in the doubtful circumstance that you destroy it, I will be condemned to drag its stinking, putrefying corpse around with me for the rest of my natural days beneath our dying sun."

When Lixal had explained what had befallen, the rest of the troop was much amazed. "You must find a sorceror of great power to help you," said Kwerion.

"Or a sympathetic god," suggested Ferlash, who was having trouble keeping amusement off his face.

"Surely someone as clever as yourself will find a solution," said a girl named Minka, who had replaced the young woman who had given Lixal the bracelet in the role of the troop's primary educational dancer. Minka had of late expressed a certain warmness toward Lixal, and though she was clearly disappointed by this latest turn of events, she seemed determined at least to keep her options open. "Then you will find your way back to us."

"In any case," Kwerion said authoritatively, "you must embark on your quest for salvation immediately!"

"But I think I should prefer to remain with you—the troop is headed back toward Catechumia soon," Lixal said. "I would appreciate the security of company. I will find some way to incorporate the Deodand into our presentation. It will be a sensation! What other troop has ever boasted such a thing?"

"No troop has ever performed while infected with the Yellow Pestilence, either," said Ferlash. "Novelty alone is not enough to promote attendance, especially when it is the novelty of horrid mortal danger, and is accompanied by such a dreadfully noisome and pervasive odor of decomposing flesh."

The rest, even Minka, seemed to agree with the false priest's objections, and despite Lixal's arguments and pleading he and the Deodand were at last forced to set off on their own toward distant Catechumia with nothing more in the way of possessions than what they could carry, since the troop also saw fit to withdraw their gift to Lixal of his private wagon, as being inappropriate for one no longer appearing in their nightly dissemination of knowledge to the deserving public.

Lixal Laqavee's first night in the wilderness was an uncomfortable one, and the idea that he was sleeping next to an inhuman creature who would happily murder him if it could did not make Lixal's slumbers any easier. At last, in the cold hours before dawn, he sat up.

The Deodand, which did not seem to have even tried to sleep, was visible only as a pair of gleaming eyes in the darkness. "You awaken early.

Have you reconsidered letting me take your life and now find yourself eager to begin your adventurous journey into That Which Lies Beyond?"

"Unequivocally, no." Lixal built the fire back up, blowing until it filled the forest dell with reddish light, although the Deodand itself was still scarcely more than a shadow. He had no particular urge to converse with the ghastly thing, but neither did he want to sit beside it in silence until sunrise. At last, Lixal reached into the rucksack that contained most of his remaining possessions and pulled out a box which unfolded into a gaming board of polished wood covered with small holes. He then shook a handful of nail-shaped ivory spikes from a bag that had been inside the box and began to place them in holes along the outer edge of the board.

"What is that?" asked the Deodand. "An altar to your god? Some kind of religious ritual?"

"No, far more important than that," Lixal said. "Have you ever played King's Compass?"

The glowing eyes blinked slowly—once, twice, three times. "Played King's Compass? What do these words mean?"

"It is a contest—a game. In my childhood home in the Misty Isles, we play it for amusement, or sometimes as a test of skill. At the latter times, money is wagered. Would you like to learn the game?"

"I have no money. I have no need of money."

"Then we will play for the sheer pleasure of the thing." Lixal extended his arms and set the game down an equal distance between the two of them. "As for the distance that perforce must always separate us, when you wish to reach out and move your pieces I shall lean back a compensatory amount, allowing you to manipulate the *spinari*."

The Deodand stared at him, eyes narrowed in suspicion. "What is a spinari?"

"Not 'a spinari'—it is plural. One is called a '*spinar*'. The collective refers to these pale spikes. For every one you move to your right, you must move another to your left. Or you may choose to move two in the same direction. Do you see?"

The Deodand was silent for long moments. "Move one to my right...? What is the point of it?"

Lixal smiled. "I will show you. You will learn it in no time—in the Isles even the youngest children play!"

BY THE time they reached Catechumia they had traveled together nearly a month and played several hundred games of King's Compass, each of which Lixal had won handily. The Deodand was somewhat literal in its employment of strategy and had trouble understanding Lixal's more spontaneous decisions. Also, the concept of bluffing and feinting had not yet impinged on the creature's consciousness in the least. Still, the Deodand had improved to the point where the games were now genuine, if one-sided, and for that at least Lixal was grateful. The life of a man tethered to a living Deodand was bound to be a lonely one, and so his had proved in these last weeks. Solitary travelers fled them without even stopping to converse on the novelty of Lixal's situation. Larger groups often tried to kill the Deodand, the reputation of whose kind was deservedly dark, and such groups bore scarcely more good will toward Lixal, who they deemed a traitor to his species: more than once he was forced to flee with the creature beneath a hail of fist-sized stones. Twice the barns in which they had taken refuge for the night were set on fire with them inside, and both times escape had been no certain thing.

"I confess I had not fully understood the unhappiness of your existence," Lixal told the Deodand. "You are hunted by one and all, with no succor to be found anywhere."

The creature gave him a look that mingled amusement with scorn. "On the contrary, in the general run of things, one and all are hunted by *me*. In any average meeting, even with three or four of your fellows, the advantage is mine, owing to my superior speed and strength. Our current plight is unusual—no sensible Deodand would go into the midst of so many of his enemies in broad daylight when his inherent duskiness provides no shield against discovery. It is only being tethered to you by this confluence of spells that puts me in such a vulnerable position. Not to mention how it hampers my diet."

This last remark, the most recent of several, pertained to Lixal's insistence that the creature with whom he was bound up not consume the flesh of human beings while they were in each other's company—which meant, perforce, all the time. This the Deodand had acceded to with bad grace, and only after Lixal pointed out that he could easily warn away all but the most deaf and blind of potential victims. When he accompanied this injunction by employing the Rhinocratic Oath, showing the Deodand how Lixal could cause the creature's nose to grow so large as to block its sight entirely, the Deodand at last submitted.

They both needed to eat, however, so Lixal had a first hand view of the sharpness and utility of the Deodand's claws and teeth when they were employed catching birds or animals. Because the distance between them had to remain more or less identical at all times, it meant that Lixal himself also needed to learn something of the Deodand's arts of silent hunting and swift attack. However, this level of cooperation between the two distinct species, although interesting and unusual, only made Lixal Laqavee more aware of how desperately he wanted to be out of the creature's presence.

Since the Exhalation of Thunderous Banishment had proved worse than useless when employed on Deodands—and that, Lixal suspected, had been the exact nature of Eliastre's deadly ruse—it was only the talismanic bracelet around his wrist which kept the Deodand at a distance. He no longer had any illusions that he could resist the creature's fatal strike in any other way: the Rhinocratic Oath would not deter it for more than a moment, the Pseudo-Philtre was laughably inappropriate, and even the Cantrip of Notional Belittlement, which Lixal had employed early on in their forced companionship, had only slightly reduced the creature's obsession with the day when it would be free of him (and, the implication was clear, equally free to destroy him.) He might have used the cantrip on himself to reduce his own level of unease but feared becoming oblivious to looming danger.

One interesting concomitant of the situation was that the cantrip-calmed Deodand became more conversational as the weeks rolled on. There were evenings, as they leaned back and forth like rowers to access the King's Compass gaming board, that the creature became almost chatty, telling of his upbringing as an anonymous youngster in a teeming nest, surviving against his fellows only by employing those impressive fangs and talons until he was old enough to escape the nest and begin killing things other than his own siblings.

"We do not build towns as your kind does," the Deodand explained. "We share territories, but only at a distance except for those times when we are drawn together to mate and settle grievances, the latter of which we effect by contests of strength which inevitably end in exoneration for one party, death for the other. I myself have survived a dozen such disputes. Here, see the deep scar of one such honorably concluded disagreement." The creature raised its arm to show Lixal, but in the firelight he could make out nothing against the flat darkness of its skin. "It has never been in our nature to cluster together as your kind does or to build as your kind builds. We have always been content to take shelter where it is found. However, as I play this game of yours, I begin to see advantages in the way your kind thinks. We Deodands seldom plan ahead beyond the successful conclusion of a given hunt, but I see now that one of the advantages your people has over mine is this very quality of forward thinking. Also, I begin to comprehend how misdirection and even outright untruth can be useful for more than simply catching a wary traveler off-guard." The Deodand abruptly moved two spinari in the same direction, revealing a sortie he had prepared, but which had been previously hidden behind them. "As you see," he pointed out with a baring of fangs which was the Deodand equivalent of a self-satisfied smile.

Despite the creature's unusual strategem, Lixal won again that night. He had been put on notice, however: the Deodand was learning, and he would have to increase the effort he put into the games if he wished to maintain his supremacy and his unbroken record. He found himself regretting, as he had many times before, that hundreds of consecutive victories in a game of skill should net him exactly nothing in the way of monetary reward. It was a suffering more poignant than anything Eliastre could have devised for him.

AT LAST, they reached the small metropolis of Catechumia, home of Twitterel's Emporium. Lixal and the Deodand paused and waited for nightfall in a glade on the outskirts of town, not far from the place where Lixal's troop had once camped.

"Do not trouble yourself with speech when we meet Eliastre," he warned the Deodand. "It will be a tense negotiation and best served by devices I alone can bring to bear. In fact," he said after a moment's thought, "It may be best if you remain outside the door while I step just inside it, so that the treacherous onetime mage knows nothing of your presence and can prepare no defense against you, should I find it necessary to call upon you."

"You have tried once already to trap me on the other side of a door, Laqavee," the Deodand said sourly. "Not only that, but it was a church door, which you thought might increase the efficacy of the strategem. And what happened?"

"You wrong me! That was weeks ago and I intend no such trickery here...!"

"You discovered you could not go forward while I remained on the other side of the door," the creature reminded him. "Like the golden links of a magister's cuff, we are bound together, willy-nilly—one cannot proceed without the other."

"As far as our current plan, I desired only to keep your presence a secret at the outset," Lixal said in a sulky voice. "But you will do as you feel you must."

"Yes, I will," said the Deodand. "And you would be wise to remember that."

When midnight came, they crossed town swiftly and mostly silently, although Lixal was forced to remonstrate severely with the Deodand, who would have eaten a drunkard he found sleeping in an alcove outside a shuttered tavern.

"He is of no interest to anyone except me," the creature argued. "How can you prevent me when you have starved me of proper man-flesh for so long?"

"Because if we are discovered, things will go badly for both of us. If the gnawed bones of even the lowliest of townsfolk come to public attention, will not the presence of such as yourself in Catechumia instantly be inferred?"

"They might suppose a wolf had snuck into town," suggested the Deodand. "Why do you continually thwart me? You will not even let me eat the flesh of the dead of your species, which your people scorn so much they bury it in the ground, far from their habitations!"

"I do not let you eat the flesh of corpses because it sickens me," replied Lixal coldly. "It is proof that, no matter how you aspire to be otherwise, you and your ilk are no better than beasts."

"Like those you call beasts, we do not waste perfectly edible tissues. Our own kind, at the end of their days, are perfectly happy to be returned to the communal stomach."

Lixal shuddered. "Enough. This is the street."

But to his great unhappiness, when Lixal approached the doorway of what had once been Twitterel's Emporium it gave every sign of being long deserted. "Here," Lixal cried, "this is wretched in the extreme! The coward has decamped. Let us enter and see if there is any clue to his present whereabouts."

The Deodand easily, if somewhat noisily, broke the bolt on the door, and they went into the large, dark room that had once been densely packed with Twitterel-who-was-Eliastre's stock in trade. Now nothing lined the shelves but cobwebs, and even these looked long-abandoned. A rat, perhaps disturbed by the Deodand's unusual scent, scurried into a corner hole and disappeared.

"He seems to have left you a note, Laqavee," said the Deodand, pointing. "It has your name on it."

Lixal, who did not have the creature's sharp vision, had to locate the folded parchment nailed to the wall by touch, then take it outside into the flickering glow of the street-lantern to read it.

To Lixal Laqavee, extortionist and counterfeit thaumaturge,

the missive began,

If you are reading this, one of two things has occurred. If you have come to pay what you owe me, I stand surprised and pleased. In this case, you may give thirteen thousand terces to the landlord of this establishment (he lives next door) and I will receive it from him at a time in the future and in a manner known only to myself. In a spirit of forgiveness, I will also warn you that at no time should you attempt the Exhalation of Thunderous Banishment on a Deodand.

If you have not returned to erase your debt, as I think more likely, it is because you have used the Exhalation on one of the dusky creatures, but for some reason my intention of teaching you a lesson has been thwarted and you mean to remonstrate with me. (It is possible that my transposition of two key words, because hurried, was not as damaging to the effect as I hoped. It is even remotely possible that the protective charm you wore on your wrist was more useful than it appeared, in which case I must blame my own overconfidence.) If any combination of these is the case for your return, my various curses upon you remain in force and I inform you also that I have moved my business to another town and chosen another name, so that any attempt by you to stir up trouble for me with the Council of Thaumaturgic Practitioners will be doomed to failure.

You, sir, may rot in hell with my congenial approval.

signed, He Who Was Twitterel

LIXAL CRUMPLED the parchment in his fist. "Repay him?" he growled. "His purse will groan indeed with the weight of my repayment. His account shall be paid to bursting!"

"Your metaphors are inexact," the Deodand said. "I take it we shall not be parting company as quickly as we both had hoped."

LIKE TWO prisoners condemned to share a cell, Lixal and the Deodand grew weary of each other's company in the weeks and months after they left Catechumia. Lixal searched half-heartedly for news of the ex-wizard Eliastre, but he was inhibited by the constant presence of the Deodand, who proved a dampening influence on conversation with most of humankind, and so he all but gave up hope of ever locating the author of his predicament, who could have set up shop anew in any one of hundreds of towns and cities across Almery or even farther countries still.

While they were everywhere shunned by men, they came occasionally into contact with other Deodands, who looked on Lixal not with fear or curiosity, but rather as a potential source of nutrients. When his bracelet proved more than these new Deodands could overcome, they settled instead for desultory gossip with their trapped comrade. Lixal was forced to listen to long discussions criticizing what all parties but himself saw as his ridiculous opposition to the eating of human flesh, living or dead. The Deodand bound to him by the Exhalation was inevitably buoyed after these discussions with like-minded peers, and would often bring an even greater energy to bear on their nightly games of King's Compass: at times Lixal was hard-pressed to keep up his unbroken record of victories, but keep it he did, and, stinging from the Deodandic imputation of his prudishness, did not hesitate to remind his opponent as often as possible of that creature's campaign of futility.

"Yes, it is easy to criticize," Lixal often said as the board was packed away. "But one has only to review our sporting history to see who has the superior approach to life." He was even beginning to grow used to this mode of existence, despite the inadequate nature of the Deodand as both a conversationalist and competitor.

Then, almost a year after their initial joining, came the day when the talismanic bracelet, the admirer's gift that had so long protected Lixal Laqavee's life, suddenly ceased to function.

LIXAL DISCOVERED that the spell was no longer efficacious in a sudden and extremely unpleasant manner: one moment he slept, dreaming of a charmed scenario in which he was causing Eliastre's bony nose to sprout carbuncles that were actually bigger than the ex-wizard himself, and laughing as the old man screeched and pleaded for mercy. Then he awoke to discover the Deodand's stinking breath on his face and the demonic yellow eyes only an inch or two from his own.

Lixal had time only for a choked squeal, then the taloned hand closed on his neck.

"Oh, but you are soft, you humans," the thing whispered, not from stealth it seemed but from pure pleasure in the moment, as if to speak loudly would be to induce a jarring note into an otherwise sublime melody. "My claws would pass through your throat like butter. I will certainly have to choose a slower and more satisfying method of dispatching you."

"M-my b-b-bracelet," stuttered Lixal. "What have you done to it?"

"I?" The Deodand chortled. "I have done nothing. But as I recall, it was meant to protect you from untimely death. Apparently, in whatever way these things are calculated, your time of dying has arrived. Perhaps in a different state of affairs, a paralleled existence of some sort, this is the moment when you would have been struck lifeless by a falling slate from a roof or mowed down by an overladen horse cart whose driver had lost his grip on the reins. But fear not! In *this* plane of reality, you shall not have to go searching for your death, Laqavee, since, by convenience, I am here to make certain that things proceed for you as just the Fates desire they should!"

"But why? Have I mistreated you so badly? We have traveled together for a full round of seasons." Lixal raised a trembling hand with the intention of giving the Deodand an encouraging, brotherly pat, but at the sight of the creature's bared fangs he swiftly withdrew it again. "We are as close as any of our two kinds have ever been—we understand each other as well as our two species have ever managed. Surely it would be a shame to throw all that away!"

The Deodand made a noise of sarcastic amusement. "What does that mean? Had you spent a year chained against your will to a standing rib roast, do you suggest that when the fetters were removed you would suddenly wish to preserve your friendship with it? You are my prey, Laqavee. Circumstances have pressed us together. Now circumstances have released me to destroy you!"

The grip on his neck was tightening now. "Hold, hold!" Lixal cried. "Do you not remember what you yourself suggested? That if I were to die, you would be held to the spot where my bones fell?"

"I have considered just that during this long night, since I first realized your magical bracelet no longer dissuaded me. My solution is elegant: I shall devour you bones and all. Thus I will be confined only to the vicinity of my own stomach, something that is already the case." The Deodand laughed in pleasure. "After all, you spoke glowingly yourself of the closeness of our acquaintanceship, Laqavee—surely you could wish no greater proximity than within my gut!"

The foul stench of the thing's breath was almost enough to snatch away what little remained of Lixal's dizzied consciousness. He closed his eyes so that he would not have to see the Deodand's terrible gaze when it murdered him. "Very well, then," he said with as much aplomb as he could muster, although every limb in his body trembled as though he had an ague. "At least I die with the satisfaction of knowing that a Deodand has never beaten a human at King's Compass, and now never shall."

He waited.

He continued to wait.

Lixal could not help remembering that the Deodand had earlier spoken of a death both slower and more satisfying than simply having his throat torn out—satisfying to the murderous creature, Lixal had no doubt, rather than to himself. Was that why the thing hesitated?

At last he opened his eyes again. The fiery yellow orbs were asquint in anger and some other emotion, harder to discern.

"You have put your finger on a problem," the Deodand admitted. "By my account, you have beaten me thrice-three-hundred and forty-four times out of an equal number of contests. And yet, I have felt for some time now that I was on the verge of mastering the game and defeating you. You yourself must admit that our matches have become more competitive."

"In all fairness, I must agree with your assertion," said Lixal. "You have improved both your hoarding and your double sentry maneuver."

The Deodand stood, keeping its claw wrapped around Lixal Laqavee's neck, and thus forcing him to stand as well. "Here is my solution," the creature told him. "We will continue to play. As long as you can defeat me, I will let you live, because I must know that when I win, as ultimately I feel sure I must, it will be by the sole fact of my own improving skill."

Lixal felt a little relieved—his death was to be at least momentarily postponed—but the knowledge did not bring the quickening of hope that might have accompanied such a reprieve in other circumstances. The Deodand did not sleep, while Lixal felt the need to do so for many hours of every day. The Deodand was swift and powerful while he, Lixal, was a great deal less so. And no human with any wit at all would try to help him.

Still, perhaps something unforeseen might happen that would allow him to conquer the beast or escape. The events of Lixal's life had taught him that circumstances were bound to change, and occasionally even for the better.

"You must also keep me well-fed and healthy," he told the Deodand. "If I am weakened by hunger or illness, any victory of yours would be hollow."

"Fair enough." The creature transferred its iron grip to his arm, then, without further conversation began to walk. It made a good speed through the patchy forest, forcing Lixal to hurry to keep up or risk having his limb pulled from its socket.

"Where are we going?" Lixal called breathlessly. "What was wrong with that particular camping spot? We had a fire, and could have started a game at our leisure once you had provided us with some dinner."

"I am doing just that, but dinner of the kind I seek is not so easily obtained near our previous camping site."

Sometime after this unsettling declaration, just as the morning sun began to bring light to the forest, the Deodand dragged Lixel out of the thickest part of the trees and into an open grassy space dotted with lumps of worked stone, some standing upright but many others tumbled and broken, all of them much patched with moss.

"Why have we come here?" Lixal asked. "This is some ancient graveyard."

"Just so," said the Deodand. "But not truly ancient—burials have taken place here within relatively recent years. You have long forbidden me the chance to dine as I please, on the meat that I most like. Now I shall no longer be bound by your absurd and cruel strictures. And yet I do not want the vigilante impulses of your kind to interfere with our contest, so instead of sallying forth for live human flesh, we will encamp ourselves here, where suitably aged and cured specimens wait beneath only a shallow span of topsoil." The creature grinned hugely. "I confess I have dreamed of such toothsome delicacies for the entire span of our annoying and undesired companionship."

"But what about me?" said Lixal. "What shall I eat? Will you hunt game for me?"

"You seem to think you still hold the upper hand, Laqavee." The Deodand spoke as sternly as a disappointed father. "You are far away from the assistance of any of your fellows, and in the passing of a single heartbeat, I can tear your throat with my talons. Hunt game for you? Nonsense." The Deodand shook its head and shoved him down onto his knees. "You will eat what I do. You will learn thrift as the Deodands practice it! Now set up the gaming board and prepare to defend the honor of your species, Lixal Laqavee! In the meantime, I will begin digging for breakfast."

AFTERWORD:

TO BE honest, I couldn't say exactly when I discovered the Dying Earth. Since it happened during my first great flowering of love for science fiction, the time I was about eleven to fourteen, I suspect my primary encounter must have been *Eyes of the Overworld*, the opening tales of Cugel the Clever. What I do remember was the delight with which I encountered both Jack Vance's fabulous imagination and the chortling joy with which I followed the elaborate, circumlocuitous conversations between his wonderfully amoral characters in a thousand different strange situations. Dickens and Wodehouse had prepared me for this sort of word- drunkenness, but I had never encountered anything quite like it in science fiction (nor have I found anything quite so piquant in the many years since.)

I was definitely in love, and I have remained so ever since—not just with the Dying Earth, but with all the products of Vance's imagination. I only hope that seeing how he has influenced some of the best writers of today (and me, too!) will bring new readers to Vance's work. Not just because his work deserves it—although it does, it does, it does—but because readers who love wit and imagination have not fully lived until they have spent a while sitting at the master's feet, laughing and marveling.

You lucky readers, who still have that discovery ahead of you!

—Tad Williams

JOHN C. WRIGHT

Guyal the Curator

JOHN C. Wright attracted some attention in the late 90s with his early stories in *Asimov's Science Fiction* (with one of them, "Guest Law," being picked up for David Hartwell's *Year's Best SF*), but it wasn't until he published his "Golden Age" trilogy (consisting of *The Golden Age*, *The Golden Transcendence*, and *The Phoenix Exultant)* in the first few years of the new century, novels which earned critical raves across the board, that he was recognized as a major new talent in SF. Subsequent novels include the "Everness" fantasy series, including *The Last Guardians of Everness* and *Mists of Everness*, and the fantasy "Chaos" series, which includes *Fugitives of Chaos*, *Orphans of Chaos*, and *Titans of Chaos*. His most recent novel, a continuation of the famous "Null-A" series by A.E. van Vogt, is *Null-A Continuum*. Wright lives with his family in Centreville, Virginia.

Here he regales us with the story of the last Remonstrator of Old Romarth, who keeps civic order in the streets of the city with the mystic weapon called the Implacable Dark Iron Wand of Quordaal, but who soon will find himself facing threats of unprecedented severity from demons, evil magicians, and immense, sky-towering giants. Fortunately, he—and the Wand—will get some help from an unexpected source…

Guyal the Curator

JOHN C. WRIGHT

In Old Romarth

Manxolio Quinc was a Grandee of Old Romarth, who dwelt in the Antiquarian's Quarter, and enjoyed a life of leisurely routine.

Due to the peculiar nature of the Antiquarian delving, a wall of dark red stone, one fathom thick and five ells high, had been raised around the whole quarter. At equal intervals along it had been erected towers mitered with immense lanterns of Lucifer-glass and cunning amplifying lenses brought at great expense from glassblowers in Kaiin, so that beams of particular penetration could transfix any effluvia, grues, dire-sloths, revenants, melancholics, or apparitions that might appear, or illume fugatives. The well-lit avenues allowed citizens to walk abroad at night without fear of pelgranes or press gangs. Murders, thefts, and morbid eventualities were rare.

These lights did not reach into the Cleft, a huge well piercing the Magistrate' s square in the center of the Quarter, which gaped beneath the shadow of a skeletal derrick. The cries and moans that issued from the Cleft reminded passers-by of the stringency of the law in the Antiquarian Quarter.

The other quarters of the city were not so orderly. Scofflaws and smugglers haunted the wharfs of the Mariner's Quarter, and the ruffian gangs there were said to be organized by a voice that spoke out of the waters of the bay on moonless nights. A nest of Deodands occupied the empty mansions of the Old Quarter and had ferociously repulsed recent attempts to unseat them. Nomads from the Land of the Falling Wall moved into the deserted buildings and shops of the Carcass-Delver's Quarter, housing their animals in the empty Odeon, penning their oasts in deserted arcades, pulling down mansions for firewood, and driving away Invigilators with glass-tipped arrows from their tiny, recurved bows. Each time they slew a patrol, the tribesmen could be seen in their painted contumely-masks dancing naked jigs on the rooftops.

The Invigilators manned the gates leading to the Antiquarian Quarter as if against besiegers. Only Manxolio Quinc made it his habit to travel into the ulterior parts of the city, where the laws held no control. He walked the route his fathers and grandfathers had walked during their tenures of office as Civic Remonstrators. The lictors whose duty it was to accompany the Remonstrator on patrol, carrying lancegays aflame with luminous venom, allowed their obligations to lapse, under the excuse that he needed no protection.

The fame of Manxolio Quinc rested on a mystic weapon thickly fraught with ancient reputation, called the Implacable Dark Iron Wand of Quordaal, which he was seen to carry with him, and from which a ominous susurration oft could be overheard.

Not even the Deodands in their fury dared molest him, as he strode each day at dawn to the highest point of the ruined citadel in the Old Quarter.

From here, the crumbling streets and ruins of the outer city lay outspread in the musty, wine-colored light like the intricate diorama a sorcerer's table might hold.

The prospect included both the mountains to the north, their peaks stained cerise by the intervening air, and the sweep of the sluggish Szonglei River to the south, where feluccas with slanted sails and many-oared galliards brought silks and spices from Almery and Nefthling Reach and Lesser Far Zhjzo. These same galliards bore away the unearthed findings of Antiquarian Quarter: books and folios leathered in the skins of extinct animals, set with clasps of amethyst, citrine, or ametrine. Each outbound ship was a melancholy sight, for she carried away a treasure never to be replaced.

To the east, on the barren slope of Sunderbreak Fell, sometimes were glimpsed the strange lights that hovered unwinkingly over the onyx tower of the Sorcerer Iszmagn. To the west lengthened the dun shadows of the Ineluctable Forest, slowly overrunning roofless crofts and weedy plantations. The forest garmented the abandoned hill-land beyond, which was said to now be the haunt of the titan Magnatz, recently come from destroying the great metropolis of nacre-walled Undolumei, where the Three Ivory Princesses once dwelt in opiate bliss. From this direction, as if to lend gravity to the rumor, oft could be heard the echo of enormous convulsions, for whose origin no antiquarian of Old Romarth could offer an undisquieting theorem.

The sorcerer Iszmagn was known to have sent a split-tongued crow to the Chief Invigilator of the city, with this offer: to bend his unearthly art to the task of turning aside Magnatz. The price for this theurgy was exorbitant: six hundred fair gem-studded illuminated folios unearthed from beneath Romarth, and twelve of the fairest virgins in the city, blonde of hair and younger than sixteen winters, and two thousand talents of gold-weight, and the sacred white monkey from the pagoda of the beast-god Auugh. The Chief Invigilator pondered the decision, consulting with augers who watched the birds and astrologers who watched the stars.

From that high place, seeing all the world underfoot, all things in order, and with the great city and its red-tiled roofs and green glass towers silent below, chimneys threaded with blue smoke, Manxolio Quinc would be aware of a profound satisfaction. Certainly there were sorcerers, dark forests, titans, smugglers, nomads, and Deodands. But, what of them? What harm could they do, in the little time that remained to the world? History had entered its repose. No further great wars, experiments, or deeds were left to be done. It was an era for no effort more excessive than quaffing a hot rum toddy, before life on earth closed its eyes and sank into rest.

An Importunity

THIS ROUTINE was interrupted one morning as he descended the municipal stairs from the Citadel down toward the human-occupied Antiquarian Quarter. The third landing, called Leaper's Landing, was hemmed in on two sides by statues of famous suicides in postures of defenestration. The

dawn was wan that day, and the sun had a number of pustules on its surface: in the uncertain illumination, there seemed to be an extra figure among the statues.

Manxolio thought that the figure was contemplating a suicide in the gulf of air underfoot, as the hunched shoulders of this silhouette seemed poised as if to leap. It being no concern of his, he made as of to stroll past. Only then did Manxolio realize that the silhouette was facing him, and its posture suddenly seemed one of menace.

A man's voice issued from the hood. "You are Manxolio Quinc? I seek you."

"I bear that name." Manxolio casually lifted the Implacable Dark Iron Wand and extended it to its full length. "Observe this instrument! It dates from the Nineteenth Eon, the time of the Knowledgeable Pharials. It is said to govern eight different actuators of energy, three aspects of visible refulgence, four more no longer visible, and an astute principle of anti-vitalistic projection."

The man came closer. Manxolio tapped the heel of the rod on the flagstones of the landing, eliciting an almost-inaudible throb from the shaft. A dark nimbus shivered through the surface of the dull metal.

"With this," continued Manxolio, "Quordaal the Rarely Compassionate slew the leviathan Amfadrang at a single impulse, annihilating the beast! See! The otherworldly vigor already begins to tremble through the weapon's unquiet heart!"

The figure said, "No."

Manxolio waited to hear more, but the cloaked man was now apparently caught in a reverie. "No? To what purport do you utter that monosyllabic negative?"

The figure sighed, and then spoke. "I mean, no, your estimation is understated. The wand is from an earlier time, the middle Eighteenth Eon: the design follows the precepts of Thorsingolian engineers. The energetic forces it commands are correctly numbered at twenty-one. Stroking the Implacable Dark Iron Wand to the ground merely activates its repair-cycle, which, if the cells had not been drained by effusion, would make no noise. Only an empty jar rattles so. The connection with the central potentium has been abrogated, leaving only secondary functions viable. Also, the Leviathan was not evaporated, as you said. The incorrupt serpent-corpse clogged the Szonglei River and blocked the harbor of Romarth for three centuries and a half, and thence was mined for bone and scale and cartilage, and other valuable by-products, for several luxurious decades."

Hiding a sensation of dread, Manxolio tapped the wand again, silencing it, wondering what would next eventuate. But the hooded stranger stood motionless.

Manxolio spoke in a voice of studied casualness: "This wand is the brother of the baton of the Curator of Man, and the Antiquarians of this city once, ages ago, communed with his archives. In my grandfather's time, the weapon blew a vent through the north slope of Mount Scagg and out the other side. The tunnel exists to this day. My father, the last of the Remonstrators, could unsaddle a cataphract with a jolt. When I was younger, enough virtue remained in the marrow to deliver a vehement twinge that could unnerve even a full-grown forest-gleft. In any case, it is a stout truncheon, and I know how to break bones with it, and a hook unfolds from the end to allow me to use it like a peavey or picaroon, or, if my work require it, to impale a skull." He opened this spike, which stood out from the shaft like a gnomon, giving the wand the aspect of a long-handled pickaxe.

The hooded man said, "Your work! What is its nature?"

"A strange question! You know the secrets of the greatest heirloom of the Quinc bloodline, and my name, and seek me, and do not know what I am in this town, splendid Old Romarth?"

"Your name was suggested to me by a pot-boy in the tavern, for I pestered him with questions while the landlord beat me."

"Why did the landlord beat you?"

"Inadvertently, I cheated him of his due: your coinage is unfamiliar. Your people use scales pried from the belly of a aquatic megafauna for your bezants."

Manxolio was taken aback at this comment. Could it be so? Putting his hand into his poke, he drew out two large blue bezants and a smaller pink. These were hemi-circular flakes of steel-hard substance. Enamel? Armor? In the dim rose light, Manxolio squinted at the coins in new wonder. The scales of Amfadrang, perhaps? The notion was unnerving.

Manxolio dismissively put away his coins. "I am an Effectuator—the last of that profession on all of Old Earth. The nature of my work is, in return for suitable remuneration, to expedite legal awkwardnesses, gather information of value, discourage effrontery, observe nuances, and to apply, when needed, deterrents to malefactors."

"A resolver of mysteries?"

"Ahh…! You seek an Effectuation? No doubt your paramour sweats and swoons in the arms of another! Your outrage is understandable. With a clew-hook and fine thread, I can hoist myself to the most difficult vantages by rooftop or wall, and peer in through casements or chimneypot, using a technique I call the Surreptitious Dangle-Glass."

"Suspicion of infidelity is not my impetus."

"You display a charming innocence! Best to be sure. With no more noise than a shadow glancing along the snow, I can trail even an alert woman to discover the meaning of her unexplained absences, or rare lapses of memory."

"While your clandestine skills are doubtless unparalleled, my needs are otherwise. Can you find missing men? Lost goods?"

"Such is a specialty of mine, if I may speak without boasting. What have you lost? What is your name and family? What man do you want me to find?"

"I wish to engage your services," declared the young man. "I have lost my essential being. I cannot answer you my name: it is gone. The missing man…is me."

The man threw back his hood. He was bruised along his cheek, and the quirk of his mouth suggested pain in his tooth or jaw. He was a slight but well-knit youth with clear eyes, who carried himself with an unconscious dignity so natural that Manxolio did not at first realize that, beneath the heavy cloak, the youth wore slops apparently from a ragpickers wagon.

A Question of Memory

THE STRANGER was exasperating to the patience of even so equitable a temper as Manxolio's. His conversation consisted of a never-ending series of inquiries, over matters both small and great, philosophical and childlike, to the point of bewilderment. The stranger was also prone to eccentric behavior, stooping to examine objects in the street, craning his neck to see details of the rooftops.

They soon came to the domicile of Manxolio Quinc. Within, the parlor was walled with green and gold, and the posts had been carved into an intricate pattern of birds and lianas.

A fire crackled warmly on the grate to one side, and Bittern, the only servant in the house, set out warm drinks in porcelain cups. Garments of Manxolio's father found in an old chest, able to fit the frame of the young man, had been exchanged for the rags, which Manxolio had decreed insufficient for a patron of the art of effectuation.

Only with difficulty could Manxolio restrain the young man from crawling the carpet to inspect the wainscoting joists, or fingering the carven roof-posts, asking questions about the artist, his school of craft, and the tools used in the woodwork. Finally, he was settled in a wing-backed chair near the fire.

Manxolio spoke meditatively, "Before I speak, let me impart my wisdom, an old man to a young."

"Speak on. I have a deep thirst for wisdom."

"Just this: ponder the advantage of ceasing to inquire further into your lost self-being."

The youth raised his eyebrows. "What advantage?"

"The red sun shivers and is soon to die, whereupon all life on Old Earth will grope in the gloom and freeze. In the face of such an impending actuality, you must weigh the chance that your lost essential self once enjoyed a happy life, and that the restoration of your essence would return you to that happiness: over against this, weigh the carefree solitude you currently enjoy, a man with neither known debts nor parental obligations. Consider! What if you recovered your selfhood, and learned that a long voyage was required to return you to your proper place? The sun could fail before the voyage was done. Reaching home, perhaps an unadvantageous marriage, or durance in military service, or the completion of an onerous religious vow awaits you, involving acts of unusual and disquieting self-abnegation, chastity, or temperance. No, the statistics do not favor the resumption of an interrupted life. The wise course is to accept your condition with the equilibrium of a philosopher."

The youth shook his head briefly. "The hunger for knowledge aches in my soul like an intrusive void."

Manxolio nodded. "You speak like one who is well-read (indeed, one whose knowledge is beyond credible belief) but nothing of the strangeness of wizardry hangs about you: too hale a look gleams in your eye for you to be one who has memorized the polydimensional runes of continuum-jarring magic, nor have your finger-nails been yellowed and stained by trifling with alchemic reagents. Not a wizard, then. But who else studies?

You are not an Antiquarian. And yet your color and accent are local. You are from this land."

"Then who am I? What befell me?"

"A dereliction of the mnemonic centers of the cortex can sometimes be caused by a shock to the skull that disarranges the fibers and nodules of the brain. You have no head wound sufficient for this. A second alternative is psychic distress, or a convulsion of purely spiritual influences caused by phrensy. Again, you are too oriented, too knowing, to be a sufferer of this type of malady. The final alternative is magic."

"Are there theurgist's draughts to enchant the memory?"

"Perhaps, but you exhibit none of the signs. No. I deduce a power more primal than mere pharmacopoeia at work. The IOUN stones, geodes of solidified primal ylem, collapsed by gravity in the heart of dead stars, and extracted by means too exotic for description, represent an ulterior order of being: they are said to be able to soak up the vibrations of thaumaturgy like a tippler drinking wine, and to drain soul and vital quintessence. I know of but one agency able to drain the very memories from the intellect: the IOUN stones!"

"Who controls this astonishing efficacy?"

"To my knowledge, none. The wizards of the various lands fritter away their lore in exchanges of morbid glamour and poisonous dreamweft, belittling each other with tricks, or devising homunculi. Any wizard administering such matchless strength as the IOUN stones bestow would have made himself supreme over his peers forthwith."

The youth nodded. "This implies I was bereft by a wizard only recently come into the possession of such stones, who has not yet had time—or lacks utterly the inclination—to impose his will on the world."

Manxolio sipped his tea meditatively. "You seem capable of clear deductions, which is at odds with your mental defect. How do you know of such mysteries, as, to pick a merely random example, the exact specifics of the Dark Iron Wand?"

"An afflatus, a ghost, an echo, seems to tremble in my brain. Now it is gone." A haunted look shivered through the young man's countenance. "I seem to see the tapestry of knowledge as a vast and varied landscape, picked out with fulvous hues of gold, tawny, or silver-white, emerald and aquamarine, seething with the shapes of man and beast, dates and places, an intricate structure of mathematics, more colossal than a tower. Then the mind-cloud returns, and all is snatched away."

Manxolio, who knew friends of his own age that suffered from senility or depredations of time, was disquieted. "In any case, there is a second and obvious clue as to your origin. The question arises: how long across the surface of the senile Earth could a man bereft of memory, penniless and weaponless, wander? Your face betrays no signs of long fasting; your flesh is not cracked with thirst, nor do you bear scars such as might be found upon someone who has escaped the alarming claws of forest Deodands, dire-wolves, flesh-eager anthropophages, or one-eyed Arimaspians. You have hardly even a growth of beard. What is your earliest memory?"

"I saw a star. I was standing near a great rock covered with ochre moss, and I wept."

"From what direction did you approach this city?"

"I am not sure. The stars look wrong to me, as if they are shifted from their accustomed positions."

"Curious. I can put no meaning to that comment."

"I remember walking along a dry stream-bed."

Manxolio spread his hands, breaking into a smile. "That is the river Scaum, drunk dry by the titan Magnatz, who is rumored to be lumbering through the lands west of here, toppling mountains and trampling towers. If you came afoot, it will be a simple matter, less than an afternoon's ride, to follow your trail on mounted steeds, perhaps with an ahulph to track the scent, and discover where your essence was lost."

The young man came to his feet. "Your thought process has struck upon an elegant solution! When can we begin?"

"Ah! I do not wish to trifle with a magician who controls the efficacy of IOUN Stones. Even to have spoken to you involves me in discomforting jeopardy. Who knows what clairvoyance this mage might command? His sandestins could be anywhere. A whorl of mystic excrescence could even now be being parsed from the hide of some chained demon-being, to be flung across intervening miles from some warlock's laboratory, to shatter the panels of my doors, intrude into the chamber, and reduce me instantly to soot. No! The question of proper remuneration asserts itself."

And, with a delicate motion, he drew the Implacable Dark Iron Wand from its holster, and laid it in the young stranger's lap.

A Question of Proper Remuneration

MANXOLIO QUINC said meditatively, "While I might, hypothetically, be delighted to exert my proficiency on your behalf merely for the intellectual pleasure that comes of the exercise of one's faculties, in practice, the Law of Equipoise must intercede. Savants have studied the cosmos and determined that for each action there must be a corresponding counter-action; for each debt, payment; for each effort, recompense; for each injustice, revenge! When all the balancing forces have countered each other, all stresses released, neutrality will dominate, and the universe sink into peaceful, if exhausted, oblivion."

"A dismal theory. Suppose it so: then what did those who concocted it receive in return for its invention? If they acted from selfless love of truth, their theory is invalidated."

Manxolio scowled in confusion. "Tell me, first, can the force ever be restored to this wand?"

The youth gazed at him with narrow eyes. "You could make yourself a power greater than ever was the Grand Motholam. Is that the payment you wish?"

Manxolio shook his head. "My ambitions are far less exquisite. I crave that the Implacable Dark Iron Wand be restored to its legendary magnificence that I might protect myself."

"From your enemies?"

"Mine are not so fearsome. From *yours*."

The youth, without a further word, unfolded the wand, touched a section with a quick flick of his fingers. To Manxolio's astonishment, the outer surface of the Implacable Dark Iron Wand opened with a ringing like the clatter of coins.

The innards thus exposed consisted of a tightly-wound spine of multicolored strands and curving threads of glass and metal and fire, to which were affixed black metallic disks, slivers of pale crystal, hissing orbs of eye-defeating nothingness, and points of light smaller and bluer than the tails of fireflies.

"How did you open it?" asked Manxolio in a strangled voice.

"Manually. The thought-sensitive nodes that would normally render the wand dehiscent upon unspoken command are inoperative. Depressing these two carbuncles works the molecular latch."

"Those two… How abnormal!" Manxolio found himself leaning foreword. Recovering his dignity, and not wishing to seem at a loss, now he sank back in his chair cushions, saying nonchalantly, "Neither my father nor my grandfather imparted to me that such a latch existed. Obviously, there was no need."

The young man gave him a penetrating look. "You have owned this instrument for how many years, and you never made a systematic inspection of it?"

Manxolio groped for an answer, but the youth had already returned to his task. "What are you doing now?"

"I am tuning the internal register to my life-patterns, so that I may have the diagnostic index inspired into my conceptual lobe. There is a sufficient residual charge of nervous flux remaining, I hope: otherwise, I will not be able to read the instrument."

At once, the little blue dots of light shining from the inner works flickered and went dim.

The young man seemed distraught. "A piece of ill luck! Even a partial investment of the thought-energy extender has drained the primary operative!" He closed the hemicylindrical housing, and telescoped the Wand back to a short baton. No whisper came from the black metal

"It is inert! You've killed it!" cried Manxolio, leaping to his feet. "I have known that artifact since childhood! You are a murderer!"

"Do not indulge in anthropomorphism. I am still effecting a repair." The young man rose unhurriedly to his feet, unfolded the wand once again, and tapped the heel sharply against the carpet. To the infinite relief of Manxolio, the familiar low moan, a throb of power, issued softly from the wand.

The youth now performed a strange act. Facing one direction, then another, he moved the wand back and forth in a slow arc. The susurration rose and fell in pitch.

"What do these antics mean?" said Manxolio, his eyes wide.

Again, the youth gave Manxolio an odd look. "You have never noticed that the sound given off by the repair cycle alters in pitch and consistence?"

Manxolio nodded brusquely. "Of a certainty! Am not I the Earth's last Effectuator, a man of perspicacity, an acute observer of details? I have often waved the wand to make the pitch oscillate. It frightens suspects into odd confessions."

The young stranger said, "But the cause of the change did not provoke your curiosity? You never mapped the waveforms against a graph? You never followed the variation in sound to its source?"

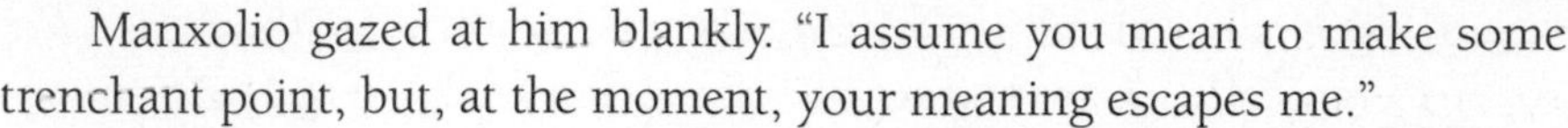

Manxolio gazed at him blankly. "I assume you mean to make some trenchant point, but, at the moment, your meaning escapes me."

The youth favored him with an easy smile. "Grasp the Wand lightly. The sound will climb in pitch as we grow closer to the source of the signal, which implies an energy supply. There may be a potentium nearby, at which we can restore the instrument to power."

A Question of Descent

IN THE middle of a wide square paved in alternating brown and black tile, the two men walked beneath the shadow of a black derrick. A ring of knee-high white stones surrounded a chasm. They stepped over and stood at the lip, looking down into the Cleft.

The lip itself was ragged, and broken tiles canted dangerously over the dark hole. The sun, like a bubble of rosy wine, had risen toward noon, and the rust-colored light slanted wanly into the pit. A vast space was revealed, with what seemed colonnades and corridors opening up upon a central well.

The tiles of the street were nothing more than the rooftiles of a building immense beyond description: soil and stone had accumulated atop this roof. The city later erected atop it was no more significant than the nests of rooks found in the eaves of barns.

The architecture underneath was old, with that exactitude of beauty and detail evidenced nowhere in the above-ground buildings; but rubbish and broken rock, slick with mushrooms and spores, lay everywhere. There was a noise of dripping water echoing from the gloomy depths.

A squadron of soldiers, led by two officers in square-topped plumed helmets, and wearing scaly jackets made of hard, brightly-colored flakes, approached at a quickstep from the wrought-iron wickets fronting the Magistracy building. In their hands were lances with tips of sharpened glass, and large round shields of transparent substance.

Manxolio said in a low voice: "We are discovered. These are the Uhlan Elite, the privy guard of the Invigilator's Order. Such is the price of overzealous curiosity. I might be able to deter them from trifling with us, if they respect my rank. Do not aggravate them with questions!"

The young man lifted his eyes and saw them. "Note the vermeil, purple, rose, and lavender hue of the scales they wear. Their armor is worked from a leviathan's hide. The bucklers are made from shed eye-cusps." He seemed not overly concerned with their approach. "The Dark Iron Wand points downward, and south-southwest. That third level: see the dark residue of the radium lamps? Behind those cracked valves beneath that fallen architrave is an energetic source."

Now the men-at-arms were at hand. The men saluted Manxolio with a flourish of their glassy spears and a click of their boots, and the two officers greeted him with polite words.

Manxolio said genteelly, "Permit me to introduce two of the Invigilators, upon whose valor the peace of Old Romarth with tranquil confidence depends: here is Ullfard of House Urilim, son of Oothbard; and this is Right-Lieutenant Mmamneron of House Mm, son of Mmaeal, a didact and antiquarian. Much of his family's riches come from the Cleft, and so his fathers have made an avocation of its study." Then, turning to them: "This is…ah…call him Anomus. He is assisting me in effectuating a case. The details of the matter are delicate, and a nicety of discretion is called for. I trust I need say no more?" He favored them with an engaging smile.

In a soft voice, Ullfard said, "Noble sirs, I cannot help but trouble you to notice that you have overstepped the bounds of demarcation, quite clearly inscribed in this circle of white stones circumvallating the aperture of the Cleft. This is a dereliction of the First Order against the civic mandates. I enjoin you, out of the graciousness of your high station, sirs, to remove yourselves with no delay."

Even as he spoke, there came a voice from the pit, a hushed whisper, and then a murmur as of many voices. In the dim light, figures could be seen, thin, bone-white and wild-eyed, dressed in rags. These men were peering from the tumbled rocks that clustered near the corridor-ends. The Cleft itself was infundibular, so that the Cleft offered a diminishing view of each successive level. The ragged men among the columns and broken walls of the first level seemed fully human; lower down, where there was less light, could be glimpsed larger, thinner shapes, perhaps of Ska or Visitants or beast-human hybrids.

Anomus (or so he was called now) spoke up. "Sirs! I see children's faces down there, thin and scarred with disease. If this is where you emplace your criminals, how came these to be there?"

Manxolio winced.

Ullfard politely answered, "In the ordinary course of nature, once female felons, murderesses, mulct-evaders, scolds, harridans, or strumpets,

run afoul of the edicts, they are lowered into the Cleft. The convicted women wed, or are taken without wedlock, there in the dark, and produce whelps, who are the small faces you see."

Anomus said, "But why is not the platform of your derrick lowered for the children to ascend? They have committed no offense."

Ullfard smiled. "In principle, I suppose you are correct, but modern legal theory holds that no child is truly human unless raised into the sunlight, since our race is self-evidently a diurnal one. These creatures are nocturnal. While they might biologically be children, in the legal sense they occupy a less dignified category. Besides, who knows what crimes these dark beings commit against each other in the wet and stinking pits of under-earth? They are surely guilty of something! In any case, I fear, gentle sirs, that I must insist with unseemly persistence that you remove yourself from this area. None may approach the Cleft."

Now a voice spoke from underfoot. "Ullfard, Ullfard, of Urilim! We ache with hunger! Lower the platform, let the viands and good brown beer be bestowed! We thirst! We sicken of eating mushrooms! It is I, Chomd, the chieftain of the Northwest Buried Corridor, who speaks!"

Ullfard clashed his spear against his transparent shield, producing a ringing clatter, surprisingly loud. "Silence, worms of the underworld! I speak with men of stature and distinction! Draw back from the open air! Now is not the hour when you are allowed to see the sunlight! Draw back, I say, or I will call the archers. They have plucked fresh needles of potent import from the gnarled limbs of cacti, which you will mourn to find embedded in your flesh! Draw back!"

The voice spoke again: "Noble and kindly Ullfard of Urilim! Important news! A swimmer in the mud discovered an inundated hatch in the second level, leading into the treasure houses of the third level, where, dry and untouched, corridor upon corridor of mummified remains, still seated in the postures they assumed in life, rear among the broken splendor of their libraries and relict-halls! Rare crystals taken from a mausoleum we have found, the brain-stone of a grue, the vestments of the matriarchs of the Nineteenth Aeon, as well as codices and tomes. All rarities, worth stoops of wine and fat hens! The books are illuminated in precise hand, crafted with capitals in red ink, and set with tiny nodules of malachite. Lower the platform, the beloved platform, forty-nine feet. Send us the hens, for we hunger, or we will burn the books, and no advantage will there be to your fairs and merchant houses!"

A second voice, this one dimmer, as if farther off, cried out then: "Heed him not, Ullfard! Gward the Huge, hetman of the Third Dungeon importunes! We have legal title to those books; they were found on our level. Lower the platform ninety-one feet, and we will pour out with abundant hand the folios and geodes from the ancient glory of Romarth! Send us lamps, lamps with oil, and more treasures will be yours! Send us weapons, dirks and derringers, petards and partisans, ranceurs and guisarmes with iron beaks, that we may drive back the impertinent trespassers of the second level! We are harder-working, and will heap up in vertiginous piles the ancestral heirlooms for you to sell!"

Ullfard clashed his spear against his shield. "Silence! Draw back! Or shall I order the sluices opened?"

Mmamneron of Mm said nervously to Anomus, "The talk of the Inhumed is often wild, and full of rare allusions, difficult to interpret! When they speak of selling the priceless archeological treasures of Old Romarth, of course, this is a short expression, a synecdoche, really, for reposing these rarities in the museums of the Antiquarians, where they are preserved for scholarly study."

Anomus said to the Invigilators, "We mean to enter the Cleft, explore certain corridors and shafts of the buried city, and return. We will lose the signal if we delay. What is the procedure?"

Ullfard said unctuously, "There is no procedure. Without the Magistrate's order, none can be lowered into the Cleft, and even that only after a disquisition and official hearing, and a consultation of the auguries. As for now, by approaching the Cleft, you trespass, and you must withdraw. Such is the unrelenting law."

Anomus said, "What is the penalty for defying this law?"

Ullfard blew out his cheeks. "Why, in a severe case, or if the workforce needs replenishment, the punishment for trespass would be introduction into the Cleft."

"So, the punishment for attempting to enter the Cleft, is that one is allowed to enter the Cleft?"

Manxolio Quinc spoke hesitatingly. "Anomus, it is no use. We cannot offend the ancient ceremonies. If the Magistrate were here…but even so, there is no provision for introducing innocent men into the Beneathworld. The concept is novel, perhaps even obscene…perhaps we can retire to yonder legal library. A narrow examination of the Edicts might elucidate an overlooked exception."

Anomus, without a word, plucked the Dark Iron Wand from Manxolio's surprised fingers and tossed it lightly into the air. It fell into the Cleft, ringing against the broken columns and canted floors as it toppled, glinting in the rosy light. Eventually the chiming clatter ceased. Faintly came also the sinister whispering moan of the Wand.

The pale faces peering between the columns underfoot, startled by the noise, ran away.

Anomus said, "Behold. I confess to both tortuous battery, impertinence, and theft of a priceless heirloom. Rather than trouble your magistrate, I hereby condemn myself. Will you lower me on the chain of the derrick? Otherwise the legacy of House Quinc is forever lost."

The Invigilators said nothing, but stood blinking.

Up the Scaum

THE AFTERNOON sky was dark with cloud. Manxolio Quinc rode an oast, a disturbingly humanoid biped, which he controlled by thongs through its nose. Anomus was mounted on a more traditional blue-feathered horse.

The men rode along the dry streambed of the dead river Scaum. To either hand rose the barren earth walls of an old streambed. A line of crooked trees, ginkgo and gumwood, grew along what had once been the riverside. The landscape around was rolling slopes of waist-high grass, dry and gray, interrupted by lumps of granite and flint.

A remnant of the river, a mere stream a boy could have waded, slid noiselessly through a trough of mud and rocks, amid the bones of many fishes. Lily pads and lotus plants grew there, half masking the yellow water in green.

Manxolio toyed with the Implacable Dark Iron Wand as they rode. The metal of the shaft was blacker than heretofore, rich and shining with dark luster. A spark of greenish-white acetylene light appeared at the blunt tip of the wand whenever Manxolio, astonishment in his eyes, squinted at it. He would laugh; the spark would vanish, and then, a moment later, with innocent glee, he would squint again, and make the burning spark reappear.

Anomus said, "Do not exhaust the charge. As I warned, I was only able to stir to action two of the secondary functions: first, the Zone of Intrusive Nigrescence, which darkens the luminary spectrum in all its phases; and second, the Many-valued Magnific Exultation. This is a complex vibration of sympathetic pulses, which will enable partial amplification of any third-order force or lower, and follow its vector and configuration, and augment it. Of the primary functions, I performed a bypass by means of a shunt, but it is frail. The phlogiston chambers have sufficient vehemence to produce a single lance of fire in the pyroconductive mode. I could not restore variant control, as the aperture valve is lost; the cell will discharge all its power at once."

Manxolio contented himself with silently commanding the picaroon hook to open or shut with a satisfying snap. He could feel the power of the wand in his brain, present, but unobtrusive, like a whisper from a dark closet into a sunlit room. "How did you survive the Cleft? What happened beneath the Earth?"

"I discovered the node buried beneath the rubble of a flooded museum-chamber, but it still glistened with sufficient power that I was able to recharge auxiliary manifestation. Three times I held my breath and dived beneath the still, dark, freezing waters of the mausoleum floor. The only tools I had to work with were those the Wand itself temporarily solidified out of hardened air. I could not repair the main cells. However, when in contact with the potentium node, the wand was able to detect a second, but very faint, whisper of power. It lies in this direction. That is what you are supposed to be seeking with the Wand, and why it is, in theory at least, in your hand now."

"Of course! I was just, ah… In any event, how was it that the Inhumed did not rip your body to bits, and consume the flesh of your limbs and frame?"

"Once I restored power to the lighting elements, they were grateful, and were willing to stay out of sight while I negotiated with you to lower a sturdy chain. I promised I would secure their release."

"And your threat to unleash a cataclysm of fire, I assume, was a similar falsehood? The wand, if it is still as weak as you say, could not cut through bedrock and flagstones to envelope the Magistracy building in a holocaust!"

Anomus gave him a quizzical look. "My comment, if anything, was an understatement. As I said, I could not replace the aperture valve on the main beam emitter."

Manxolio sniffed. "You are merely fortunate that I recalled that one of the ancient prerogatives of the Civic Remonstrator was to commute

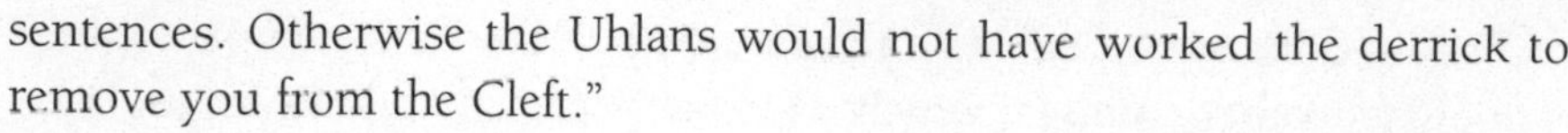

sentences. Otherwise the Uhlans would not have worked the derrick to remove you from the Cleft."

Anomus said blandly, "Yet I was not sentenced by any lawful process."

"A mere technicality. Your act was an eccentric affront to conformity. But no matter, for, look there!" He pointed up to where the brush and grasses by the river bank had been disturbed. "Our investigation nears a definite result. Your trail here entered the stream-bed."

The Dead Town of Sfere

PLAINLY VISIBLE were naked footprints in the clay of the slope. "There is your foot, preserved in a muddy petrosomatoglyph. Observe the disturbance in the eucalyptus leaves, elsewhere fallen evenly, and the snapped twigs. There was rain two days ago, and water would have smoothed the edges of these prints, or sponged them away in a wash of mud. This gives us an upper limit for the time. Do you recall pushing through the brush here?"

Anomus squinted and shook his head. "I recall tumbling. Perhaps it was this slope."

"What else do you recall?"

"It was night. As I said, the stars seemed out of place. I fell down the slope because I came upon it unawares."

"Why did you not await the dawn-light?"

"I did not know how long the nights lasted on this world."

Manxolio's face grew long with surprise. "A singular comment, even eccentric. This leads to a strange supposition."

With some difficulty, the two men drove or lead the biped and the blue-feathered horse up the muddy slope. They pressed past the brush and gumwood trees. Unlimbering a lantern made from the carbuncles of luminous fish, Manxolio narrowly inspected the ground. For an hour, they followed the meager traces: a broken leaf, a displaced pebble sitting pale-side up.

They debated for a time what to do, whether to return to Old Romarth and secure a hunting pack of ahulphs, or set out sugar to attract a Twk-man, when the upper winds, breaking apart the cloud cover, allowed cerise, rose, and orange beams of light to touch upon the landscape. The ruddy light caught a tumble of bright stones in the distance.

Below them was a wide valley, bisected by the riverbed. The lower parts of the valley were inundated, for the Scaum was blocked. A great topple of stone formed a crude dam, and, behind it, a lake had spread. From the waters rose broken columns, and mossy, topless towers, broken arches, and vacant windows. From their shape, it was clear that the stones forming the dam were nothing other than the houses and towers, fortresses and defensive walls, of what had once been a small city, pulled up by some unimaginable force and heaped into a dike.

Not far from where they stood and observed these melancholy ruins, rose a single standing stone, incised with moss-obscured designs. Here and there, poking through the clumped grass and bushes, rose statues of graceful maidens, now armless, their piquant features blurred with rain. Between these statues ran a roadway of white stone, now green and cracked with overgrowth. Sections of the city walls were still standing, triangular as broken teeth, and not all the houses and mansions of the suburbia were inundated, though all were unroofed, doorless, weed-choked.

Anomus pointed: "That is the stone I recall in my first memories."

Manxolio approached, leaned precariously from the saddle on the shoulders of his oast, and scraped some of the moss free with a broad-bladed dagger. "This is the City of Sfere, founded in the third year of his reign by the Hero-King Sferendur, and is under the protection of the nine goddesses of Good Fortune, Long Life, and Tranquility. The words of a curse against trespassers who would disturb them is inscribed on the reverse: if I might venture an opinion…" (he gazed in bitter awe at the sheer volume of destruction involved in upending an entire city) "…the curse proved nonoperative." He twisted in the saddle and looked toward Anomus. "If this is your home, you escaped a decisive disaster."

Anomus was looking with great curiosity at the ruins. White stones shined in the sunlight. The square foundations of vanished buildings were arranged in rows like a graveyard. Sheep grazed among the broken columns. Down the slope, beneath the lake, could be glimpsed houses and towers, and the concentric stone benches of a great amphitheatre or coliseum, half-buried in mud and waterweed.

"Within myself, I observe merely a blank." Anomus said, "If this was my home, even the grief I should feel has been taken from me."

"Your trail ends here," said Manxolio. "There is nothing more to discover." Anomus seemed not to hear, and his face was set without expression.

Manxolio felt an unexpected compassion rising in him, like a bubble in the mud, and bursting forth. "Come! Return with me to Old Romarth, and I will, despite my age, make you my apprentice. You will learn the slights and craftsmanship of investigation, and become as watchful as a cat, loyal as a dog, dangerous as an erb! A man to be respected! We can start by learning the strangle-grips to use on a prisoner, which elicit pain, but leave no marks, or only such bruises as admit of ambiguous explanation."

Anomus said, "I do not quit yet. Whatever stole my essential self did not commit the deed when this disaster befell. When did the river Scaum run dry?"

"Seven years past, no longer."

Anomus said, "If your arts as an Effectuator can tell us nothing more, then mine as a scholar can do otherwise. Hold forth the Implacable Wand once more: the single question remains to us—to find the source of the invisible pulse the wand detected. Now that we are closer, a clearer sign may eventuate."

Manxolio and Anomus dismounted, and trod the wintery grass. They came upon a wide square of colored tiles, cracked and faded, in the midst of the grass like an island, covered with an inch or two of stinking, standing water. In the midst was the rubble of a well mouth, clogged with a litter of branches and floating rubbish, and with weathered statues of river-goddesses still tilting dry pitchers above it.

The rains from two days ago apparently had overflowed the well, for now several trickles of water spilled over the cracked lip. Transparent insects with exaggerated legs danced across the stagnant surface, leaving tiny ripples. The image was one of desolation.

"The source is near," Manxolio reported.

Anomus splashed across the stagnant water, sending irked insects to the air, and plunged his arm into the litter occupying the well mouth. Manxolio saw a glint of metal. In a moment, Anomus returned with an object, no larger than a tambourine.

"Here is a Transmultiangular Peripatetic Analept, flung into a well and abandoned as junk. By mere chance, it fell onto a mat of branches, and was carried to the surface again when the water rose. Who would dispose of such a remarkable artifact in so casual a fashion?"

The object in the hands of the young man was a twisted shape of brass and mirrored crystal, but an eye-defeating visual effect made Manxolio unable to register the shape in his mind. It seemed, from one viewpoint, to be a Penrose triangle, with some sort of strange depth held in the center; but when Anomus twisted it, it folded into a shape like a Moebius strip, a flat circle with a half-twist in it.

Anomus said thoughtfully, "It seems of new fabrication. None of the elements have suffered elution. There is no yellowing of the crystals, no Doppler effect due to expansion of microcosmic venules."

Manxolio laughed without mirth. "It is yours."

"In what sense? I would not throw such a thing down a well."

Manxolio said heavily, "Nonetheless, it is yours. This is an instrument to induce a portcullis into some demon-world beyond the warp and woof of space, or a portage to the transplutonian worlds which whirl through the upper abyss."

Anomus replied, "It is the end point of the Indigo Path of Instantaneous Motion, which allows for superluminal passage of energy and matter across any distances. The Path, to operate, must be maintained at both ends: there is no fixed anchor established at this end. But how do you know of it?"

"By deduction. And yet you seem, outwardly, to be human; indeed, you have the same color and accent as a man of Old Romarth: but this carried you here from elsewhere. You…" But he stopped, for the Dark Iron Wand was vibrating in his hand.

"What does this mean?" Manxolio asked.

But Manxolio was answered by the Wand itself, which reacted to his words, and imposed knowledge directly into his consciousness: the tension in time-space had reached a cusp, beyond which natural law is inoperative.

The sun passed behind a thin cloud, and, in the dim light, the full moon could be seen faintly in the east, surrounded by stars. The insects, which normally sang when the sun was dim, and the birds, which sang when it was shining, both were silent. The wind itself was still.

Manxolio said, "A supernatural event is occurring!"

The Dead Lord of Sfere

HE SPOKE truly: bells and gongs could be heard tolling from beneath the waters. Beneath the lake, the lifeless buildings now seemed whole, their roofbeams gilded and painted, and lights shined through their stained glass windows, painting the underwater with delicate colors.

While the two men stood in awe, the oast and the blue-feathered horse bellowed and whinnied, and fled away.

Arms of white mist, spangled as if with fireflies, had collected over the lake, then thickened and formed into a transparent figure, robed in shimmering iridium, and bearing a coronet of thirteen moonstones.

It spoke, and even though its voice made no noise, both men understood the meaning without hearing any words. *Behold me, the shade and echo and remnant of Sferendur, whose sacrifice founded this fair town.*

Anomus knelt, and addressed the disembodied shadow. "Illustrious specter, who am I and whence did I come? By what means might I recall my lost being?"

Again, the strangely wordless meaning was imparted into their understanding.

You are Guyal of Sfere, son of Ghyll, last of my bloodline, last indeed of all my people, foully slain seven years agone. But I name you anew: Guyal of Sferendelume. You are the Curator of the Museum of Man, which by your arts you lifted, huge and weightlesss as a thundercloud, above the regions of the sky and into the ulterior void.

Anomus, or Guyal, listened with intent curiosity, but it was Manxolio who gaped in astonishment. "The Curator!" he whispered in awe.

Longing to soar the starry path of heaven, and with all the gathered knowledge of countless aeons, you followed the wake of the Pharials and the ambitious Clambs who departed Earth; as did the lordly Merioneth ages before them, whose children were remade into pitiless star-gods beyond Antares; and the Gray Sorcerers still earlier, who departed Earth in secret. In the Pleiades, of filial courtesy, you named a virginal and shining world of my name, calling her Sferendelume.

Whereas the Earth has rolled in her orbit so long that the threads of timespace have frayed, allowing dark visitants from the nooks of nether-space to intrude, and the weight of time has overlaid the substance of the world with a patina collected from untold millenniums of fear and human pain—in stark contrast, azure Sferendelume is fresh and unstained, the giant sun Alcyone is dazzling bluish-white and vehement, her littler companion suns bathe the globe with radiance of vermilion, blue, and fulvous gold: and no ear there has heard rumor of the demon realm of La-Er, or the imperturbable hungers of Blikdak of the under-gloom.

The knowledge of the Museum of Man you unhoarded, and built tools and servant-beings to wield them, and the lost star lords from the Cluster of Hyades to the Clouds of Magellan you called to you: the Sacerdotes of forgotten Aerlith, and the Pnumekin, who toiled in the service of the buried kingdoms of a war-torn orb in Argo Navis, you freed and restored their humanity.

When all was prepared for the lost peoples of Earth, and golden mansions readied to receive them, you descended to this globe.

The apparition raised its head, and the nothingness of its eyes blazed with emotion: *To your first home of Sfere out of compassion for your father, nine brothers and twelve uncles, you came, to call them to the hither shore of the seas of night. His death you must avenge: that* gaes *lay I upon you.*

To find his slayer, and your lost remembrance, await the monster that approaches, for my appearance has enraged him. Now he comes. And throwing his mantle over his head, the vision evaporated, leaving the lake water roiling and disturbed.

A moment later, and the ringing gongs fell silent; the walls of the drowned city were dark, blind and broken as before.

The Titan

Manxolio said, "There is a tale of Guyal of Sfere, a boy born bereft of wits. In punishment for his endless curiosity, he was sent forth to seek the mythical Museum of Man beyond the lands of the Saponids. What he found there, none know."

The youth, now called Guyal of Sferendelume, Curator of the Museum of Man, addressed Manxolio Quinc: "Evidently Guyal of Sfere—if I am he—found the Curator and assumed his post."

"Nothing else could explain the bizarre expanse of your knowledge. Your ancestral specter spoke words of ominous import. It is the titan Magnatz—a name of terror—who destroyed your ancestral home here, and who approaches now."

"By what do you deduce this?"

"First, many of the craters here look suspiciously like footprints of vast dimensions; second, rumors spread in my city to the effect that the Sorcerer Iszmagn seeks to extort vast wealth from Romarth, feeding on our fear of Magnatz as a vulture feeds on rancid meat; third, I see between the crest of yonder two hills the motion as of a third hill, but this one covered with hair, not trees, and two lakes suspiciously like eyes. Magnatz is upon us!"

"Since we cannot outrun the event, our choices are limited to seclusion, negotiation, and deterrence."

The noise of the footfalls was like repeated thunder. Like a rising harvest moon, the head of Magnatz hove into view between the hilltops, huge and pale.

Manxolio draw himself to his full height. "What need have we to talk or run? Does this monstrosity not also threaten Romarth? Then he is my foe as well! Have you not restored this dread weapon, the very Implacable Dark Iron Wand itself? One bolt remains, you said! Hah-La! I have no need of two!"

Unlimbering the Wand to its full length, Manxolio flourished it the direction of the monster, whose shoulders and torso were now visible over the hilltops. A secondary aiming-beam lashed out with a finger of red fire, scorching Magnatz slightly along one cheek. Instead of a beam of furious destruction, a whining note issued from the rod, which plaintively dropped in pitch and trailed off.

"Ah," exclaimed Guyal, "That was unexpected."

Magnatz roared in fury, and pulled up the crest of a hill to hurl at them. While the titan was still hefting the broken peak aloft, Manxolio called on the Wand and established a zone of lightlessness like a smothering cloud. Both men sprinted with agility: they heard a noise like the end of the world as numberless tons of rock and dirt, trees and topsoil, fell short and missed them. Only gravel like stinging hail smote them.

Manxolio adjusted the Zone of Primary Nigrescence to position it overhead. To them, it was a roof; to the titan, a lake to wade in.

He displayed the Wand to Guyal. "Examine this. What is the error?"

Guyal communed with the instrument. "No error. It is a safety feature. The aiming register senses that the titan has a charmed life, rendering him immune to fire, fear, iron, pain, or directed energy. Magnatz can neither starve, choke, nor drown, because he is surrounded by a system of runic pulses that ward his vitality in nine directions. The rod will not discharge, as the bolt would have merely returned on its flow path, and slain you."

"Perhaps we could lure him into a pit of eighty fathoms."

"The plan is commendable in theory, but otherwise not actionable."

Manxolio said, "Your Analept! I can see that it seethes with eldritch ultra-dimensional energies. Can it blast Magnatz with a spurt of extraordinary fire, or, failing that, open a port to a far world wherein we might end our days, perhaps as unhappy exiles solacing ourselves with exotic native girls and strange unearthly wines, but end our days, lo, long years rather than short minutes hence?"

Guyal twisted the shining object from a square to a cruciform to a triangle, and between the brass bars of the armature there seemed to hang distant stars in a void. "I fear not. The effluvium of nullity is not anchored on this end, and there is no potentium closer than Romarth wherewith to affix it. If I put tension on the strand through overspace, the mass would merely be drawn to the nearest gravitating body. Portage to Sferendelume this cannot presently supply."

"Useless geegaw! Then what *can* it do?"

"By itself, it has sufficient lifting force to hale a man, nothing more massive, into the upward spaces."

But there was no more time for speaking. Large as the funnels of two strangely parallel tornados, the legs of the titan were visible beneath the cloudy zone of darkness, wading toward them, a stormcloud of dust and brush and broken stones at his heels.

Then came a sound like the wind being torn in two, and a mighty truncheon, some huge fasci made of bundled pine trunks, came through the nigrescent zone and smote the ground. But the blow went astray: a hundred feet to the east of the two men, there was a cataclysm; the earth puked up a fountain where the bludgeon struck, and now there was a little, barren valley, half a dozen paces across, filled with steam.

Manxolio looked at the Dark Iron Wand. "Well, perhaps negotiation should have been our first attempt. Was there not a second efficacy you restored to this instrument?"

Guyal did not answer him, for the two men heard the noise of the descending bludgeon and took to their heels. The cloak of darkness under which they cowered permitted the two adventurers, for frantic minutes while they hopped and dodged in wild, eccentric leaps, to evade the thunderous blows of the truncheon of Magnatz.

Guyal hissed over the noise of tumbling stones, "Address him! Mask my motions!" and he ran swiftly toward the huge, creaking feet of the giant.

Manxolio, white-faced with terror, for a moment could not bring himself to speak. Then he saw his fastidiously lacquered and brushed hat, which had fallen from his head in his gyrations, laying in tatters in a smoking crater-mouth. That image resolved his courage.

He called out, "Magnatz! Heed me! Destroy me not, for I have news that concerns you!"

The truncheon went above the dark cloud, as if readying for another blow, but instead came words, huge and deep, as if a volcano spoke: "What news of little men could concern me? My life is charmed, and nothing can destroy it. Each year I grow in size. I push up mountains with my stride, fill wide valleys with my spew. I am as vast and as terrible as the sea."

Manxolio drew a shivering breath, clenching his teeth to prevent them from chattering. "All too true, great Magnatz! And yet I have dire news. The Sorcerer Iszmagn cheats you!"

"My brother? Cheats me how?"

"Iszmagn foretells your coming to quaking towns, and extorts from them rich treasures, women of allure, gold and bezants plentiful beyond count. Does he share these assets with you? He bathes in a tub of porphyry filled with steaming milk, while round-hipped virgins feed him delectable grapes and coo amorous ditties to trifle away the nights! What does he do for you? Where is the gold of Magnatz?"

A laugh answered him, like the gust of a hurricane. "Nay, it is I who cheat him! For all his dreadful lore, he flitters away his time chasing dream-bubbles, which he captures in living lenses. At my order, he exacts from men, terrified by the rumor of my coming, all the taxation any emperor might require. The gold and women I take to myself, to use or consume in sport. To him, I leave nothing by baubles and trash! Why, just yesterday, following certain dream-signs, we came upon a star-wanderer and robbed him—but Iszmagn took nothing but worthless stones to float round his head. Worthless! For they could protect no one from the strength of my hands. The wanderer we spared, merely so the curiosity of Iszmagn could be sated, to see how long his amnesia would obtain. Our hope was that the press-gangs of Romarth would throw him in the Cleft for vagrancy."

At that moment, Guyal seemed to fall beneath the feet of Magnatz; or, at least, Manxolio lost sight of him. Then Guyal called out: "The second restored efficacy is the magnific adumbration! Use it now on the Analept!"

Manxolio squinted. The iron pulsed in his grip. The dark zone dispersed. For one terrifying heartbeat of time, the titan reared above them, visible, a vast bulk. At that same moment, from beneath the giant's toe, issued a strange, piercing, three-toned note. There was a wash of motion, a curtain of upward-rushing dust and wind. Manxolio blinked, caught a last sight of Magnatz the titan dwindling to a mote in the dark blue spaces of the upper sky.

Perhaps a minute later, the pale disk of the full moon formed a new crater, large as Tycho, and rays of moondust scattered far across the airless surface, forming an asterism. The crater was white-hot with the impact of some vast body, but the glow soon diminished through yellow to pink to a sullen red.

The Call to the Violent Cloud

GUYAL ROSE from the footprint-shaped crater of broken rock where he lay, and made his way wearily to the side of Manxolio.

Manxolio spoke: "How did you survive the pressure of the giant's foot?"

Guyal said, "The Analept was able to produce a repulsive force, under which I hid, like a turtle in a shell. It was not until you employed the many-valued magnific adumbration that the Analeptic lifting energies were augmented to hurl the monster aloft. Unfortunately, I lost my grip on the Analept, and the strand of star-stuff that connected it to Sferendelume in the Pleiades yanked it to an unknown location. Magnatz will not perish, being charmed against suffocation, and neither will he die of old age, so he will remain in the discomfort of decompression, bleeding from his eyes, nose, ears, and mouth, until entropy halts the universe. How did you know Iszmagn and Magnatz were in league?"

"The honed intuition of an Effectuator. The similarity of names. I told myself that a charmed life implies someone to cast the charm; and the magic which swelled his bulk implied a magician. I asked myself why Iszmagn benefits from the depredations of Magnatz; where there is benefit, might there not be alliance?"

"A correct guess. I am relieved to satisfy, and within moments, the gaes placed by my ancestor, but I am no closer to achieving the resumption of my inner self."

Manxolio stared incredulously. "Did you not hear? The titan himself described the theft, and identified its perpetrator."

"I was preoccupied by being trod upon, and so some nuances of the conversation regrettably escaped me," admitted Guyal.

"The Sorcerer Iszmagn overcame you and took your IOUN stones and your recollections, leaving you alive to study the effects of his experiment in mind-theft. Your dream of revenge is nuncupatory, since so powerful an adversary cannot be overcome."

"Was it not you who, earlier this day, spoke of the Law of Equipoise, which demands retaliation for each affront?"

"And you denied its self-evident verity."

Guyal looked up at the sky and uttered a deep sigh.

Manxolio said, "You are resigned, then, to omit this quest? Return with me to Romarth; we will live lives of ease."

"No, I sigh because we go to our fates with no time to prepare: for the sorcerer manifests the Call of the Violent Cloud to ensnare us."

There was an noise in the air as of many voices roaring. At once, a column of boiling black smoke hurled down from the sky. Manxolio again commanded the baton to issue the Zone of Primary Nigrescence, which instantly blotted out all sight, but did nothing to impede the Violent Cloud. The two were snatched up, whirled abominably, yanked and jerked in four directions, and then hurled contemptuously to the ground in a spasm of motion.

It was still dark as pitch. Guyal was surprised not to find himself in the crater of a volcano or the midst of a sea of ice, which would have been the most efficient way to extinguish their lives. Instead, he groaned on pavement, aware of his bruises. As he rose to his feet, he heard a peculiar hissing sound, as if white-hot wires were plunged into sizzling wine. The odor of burning, the smell of hot rock and molten metal came from every side.

"Do not yet lift the Zone, Manxolio!" warned Guyal, hoping Manxolio was alert. "Someone employs the Excellent Prismatic Spray against us—while the visual phase of reality remains inoperative, the photonic eruption cannot scald us."

In a moment, the commotion fell silent. Manxolio lifted the Nigrescent Zone, and visible light returned to the area.

The Dreaming Sorcerer

THEY STOOD in the courtyard of a tower of onyx and dark basalt, fantastically carved in rococo designs, and upheld by wide flying buttresses. The courtyard held smoldering urns filled with burning floral displays, a dozen cracked statues of glyptodonts from the First Aeon, and a silver-basined fountain, now a mass of boiling steam. The flagstones in each direction were pitted with tiny dark asterisks, evidence of a recent rain of incandescent darts.

A hundred smoldering little streamers led from the courtyard to a high balcony, where the sorcerer Iszmagn stood, hand still raised and fingertips still glowing, a look of dark satisfaction beginning to elongate into an expression of surprise.

He wore a knee-length jacket of green cusps, and in the center of each there flashed and floated colors never seen in waking life. The cusps also blinked and stared in alarm, and showed other evidence that they were animate objects, stirred at least to a mockery of life. In the middle of his forehead was the eye of an Archveult of Sirius grafted to his brow, a tendril root no doubt sunk deeply into his brain-pan.

In a galaxy around his head swarmed and danced the colored polygons of IOUN stones: spheres, ellipsoids, spindles, each the size of a small plum, and vibrant with inner auroras.

With the merest of hesitations, the sorcerer raised his fingers and the syllables of the Instantaneous Electric Effort gushed forth from his mouth. Tridents and biforks of lighting fell from the balcony, but Manxolio manifested a thick disk of the Nigrescent Zone in midair between them, and the fulgurations were absorbed without effect.

While the dark zone hung overhead, obscuring their motions, Guyal pointed to the iron-bound oaken doors leading into the tower. Manxolio placed the heel of the Wand on the stones, and jammed the head beneath an ornamental boss. He unfolded the Wand, and augmented the motive force with the Magnific Adumbration. The locks shattered and the door sagged open.

The Onyx Tower

MANXOLIO AND Guyal crept into the entrance hall. The wonders of the sorcerer's walls and ceilings were hidden by Manxolio's cloud of darkness, but the floor was visible: blocks of hollow glass, each one of which held a different brightly-colored fish. To one side, the first few steps of an insubstantial, spidery, curving stairway were visible.

There was a snap of energy, and the zone vanished.

Guyal said, "Unexpected! Iszmagn has discovered how to abjure the primary nigrescence."

Manxolio said in a low voice: "I suspect the IOUN stones. Let us retreat, and calculate a more complete stratagem in a leisurely fashion, perhaps over a beaker of Old Golden in the taproom of the Scatterlamp Hotel."

Guyal said, "Retreat is unlikely, as the tower is now surrounded with blue extract." Nearby was an arched window carved with grimacing gnomes. The ground below was infected with aquamarine pulsations of singularly uninviting aspect.

Up the stairs, they passed through an alchemical lab, seething with alembics and bubbling retorts, and then a chamber composed of looking glasses, each face of which showed a different landscape, none of which were of Earth.

They came upon Iszmagn in the astrological copula, laying at ease upon a pink couch, a plate of candied figs at his elbow, a hookah in his hand. Huge crystalline windows loomed behind the couch of Iszmagn, showing the sky, the red sun, and the faint full moon with its new crater. The IOUN stones swarmed the glass-domed chamber like bees.

"Leave me in peace, you clumsy creatures of the waking world!" called Iszmagn. "I have no ambitions, save to live out the remainder of human life on earth in comfort, collecting my dream-lenses. They are my companions, they whisper love-songs to me as I sleep!"

Guyal spoke in a voice of doom: "Iszmagn the Sorcerer, for the death of the peoples of Sfere and Vull and gay Undolumei and countless others, and in recompense for the murder of my father and brothers, I call on you to surrender, that your life might be spared. Here stands the Remonstrator of Old Romarth: he will take you into custody, and you will receive the justice of their Magistrates."

"What? And toil in the Cleft for my daily ort of bread, and firken of unclean water?" called out Iszmagn in a strange, strangled, high-pitched voice. He gave a shrieking giggle of laughter. His two eyes seemed dull and listless; only the third eye, taken from a nonhuman being from Sirius, glittered with intention.

Said Guyal. "Will you capitulate? Human life is rare: in all eternity, each man has but one. Better to toil than to perish."

"So, I killed your father and all your kin! What of it? I have arranged that you have no memory, so it causes you no real grief: your complaint against me is highly theoretical, if not absurd."

Manxolio, made courageous, perhaps, by desperation, spoke up: "Behold, I hold in hand the Implacable Dark Iron Wand of Quordaal."

The lenses in Iszmagn's coat flickered with emotion: the dream images surged and darkened. The sorcerer rose to his feet, saying, "I have attempted reason, but you are stubborn! Enough!" and then he uttered Lispurge's Vexatious Thrust.

A gust of the distilled motion darted out toward Manxolio. Guyal leaped in the way: the line of force passed through his chest; Guyal was flung like a rag doll up against a rack of plates of gold, silver, and green iridium; all clattered to the gemmed floorstones.

Manxolio flourished the Wand: a lance of thousand-lightninged brilliance roared out. Manxolio could not diminish the rush of white fire.

When at last silence fell, Manxolio blinked purplish dots from his eyes. The Wand was dull and exhausted.

Iszmagn was unhurt, his chamber undamaged, and the tumbling shapes circling his head were brighter. He emitted a cackle, and the lenses in his coat looked merry. "My IOUN stones drink magical vibrations! I am proof from all attack! Your zone of darkness, I have already deduced how to negate. Your Implacable Iron Wand has no further powers against me!"

Guyal rose to his feet. There was a hole in his coat, but the flesh beneath was untouched. "You do not know my powers," he intoned.

At that moment, there came a momentary lull in the radiation of the sun—it flared like lightning, and then the world was plunged into a jet-black gloom, with the iron-red face of the moon flickering into darkness a half-second later.

The mage clutched his three eyes and screamed in terror. "The Sun! The death of all life is come!"

From the window came a noise: beneath the black sky, a lamentation passed across all the lands and seas, as every living man, and other creatures, talking beasts and semihumans, all who knew the meaning of this gloom, let out a cry. The noise was very faint indeed, for the tower was far from any dwelling of man, but it came from all quarters.

And yet, as good fortune would have it, this was merely a solar spasm of unusual opaqueness: the sun trembled with new effort. Ember-red light seeped forth from scabs on the sun's surface, and flares clawed their way into visibility like volcanic eruptions. In a few moment, more than half the sun was re-ignited from its buried fires, the world was as well-lit as before, or very nearly.

When vision returned to the cupola of the tower, the spike of the Implacable Iron Rod could now be seen, having penetrated the skull of the Sorcerer Iszmagn. A river-delta of blood and brain matter, as well as other

fluids the sorcerer had introduced into his nervous system, dripped along his neck and down his coat. The lenses were dark, their vitality exhausted: all the carefully collected dreams of the sorcerer were dead.

The Restoration of Guyal of Sfere

MANXOLIO, WHO held the haft in both hands, and stared in awe at the corpse, only slowly straightened and regained his composure. When he clicked shut the spike, the body slid heavily from the end, and splashed to the floor, already beginning to dissolve. It was clear that the IOUN stones did not protect physical flesh from merely physical assault.

He turned to Guyal, who seemed whole and unblooded. Manxolio said, "Difficult as this is for an Effectuator to admit, I confess I cannot fathom how you survived a cantrip that normally pierces quenched steel."

Guyal smiled and held up his fist. Light shined between the cracks of his fingers. Opening his hand, he let loose a small IOUN stone, which darted like a fish, and took up orbit around the young man's head. "These stones are mine, or so we deduced. I snatched one from the air as I jumped to take the blow."

One by one, the other stones departed from their position near the corpse, and, following the first, took up positions in concentric circles around Guyal. The IOUN stones changed hue and grew duller, as first the oblongs, and then the spindles and spheres, gave up their essence. Guyal of Sferendelume stood taller, and majesty seemed to shine from his face.

His voice was now stronger, as if vibrant with unearthly wisdom. "I now recall my destiny and fate. Iszmagn was more foolish than I guessed, for the potentium of the Museum of Man upon Sferendelume in Pleiades, a trifling 440 lightyears from Earth, reaches me here still, and, like your Wand, it is directed by thought-pressure alone. Had I known, merely my wish could have set free powers of the first magnitude. Observe!"

Guyal made no gesture and spoke no spell, but Manxolio felt the floor cant like the deck of a ship. There was a sensation of rushing motion. When it ceased, outside the many windows of the cupola, Manxolio saw that the onyx tower now rested in the midst of the ruins of Sfere.

An invisible force was lifting the stones of the dam, one by one, and threads of silver water were beginning to return to the dry streambed of the lower Scaum.

"With the IOUN stones once more in my command, I can seek in the limitless void, discover and recall the Analept to Earth, and anchor it. It is done! Let there be the first anchor point here, in Sfere.

"The river Scaum shall live again, and bear the traffic of boats and rafts of pilgrims. The Indigo Path of Instantaneous Motion will loft all those who seek to depart the Dying Earth away, beyond the sky, to fair Sferendelume!"

Manxolio felt the Implacable Wand begin to vibrate in his hand, and it grew heavy as lead.

"As promised, the wand is restored." The ringing voice of Guyal of Sferendelume continued, "Manxolio, I charge you to return to Old Romarth and tell them of this hope I bring. The end of Earth need not be the end of Man.

"As men from all the lands and continents of Earth gather, your decaying city shall be rich once more with the trade of passers-by, both of pilgrims fleeing this dying world, and scholars descending from the stars to gather up the mementos and mysteries of Earth, and buried cities hale aloft from the bottom of the sea. Surely, the lore of the Antiquarians of Romarth will be a signal study, and the treasures of your past no longer need be sold as curios, but shall be properly collected, indexed, and examined by experts.

"I must now depart, before the IOUN stones grow exhausted, and go to my new world, not with my father, as I'd hoped, but alone.

"Tell all men that life on Earth is precarious, and commend to them to seek out the bright fields of the ulterior world: but warn them that, if this world holds no souls curious, like me, to seek the stars, I shall not return, and the path be closed forever. With my people slain, what is there for me? I have other duties and other loves beyond the Pleiades, and I hear the silver song of Sheirl calling me to the stars. Ah! Sheirl! I return to you!"

The Remonstrator of Old Romarth

MANXOLIO LISTENED to this with growing disquiet, but said nothing. Guyal flung open the dome of the tower's cupola, ascended into the sky, and vanished in a flare of indigo light.

When Guyal the Curator vanished, there came at that moment the strange three-tone chime of the Analept, even though that instrument was nowhere to be seen.

Now alone, Manxolio spent the afternoon investigating the various periapts and amulets horded in the store of Iszmagn. He discovered a curious property of the lenses of the sorcerer's emerald coat: seemingly dead, nonetheless a simple pulse of meaning from the Implacable Wand could elicit an image from them, nightmarish, something from the dark undermind of humankind, along with a disquieting aura.

Manxolio selected the most hideous of these lenses, and buried them, one after another, in a rough circle all about the valley of Sfere. He took care to place more of them near the river, or in any direction that promised an easy approach. He invoked them with his Wand, and at once a legion of specters, half-seen, terrifying, crowded the edges of vision.

He spent an hour cutting warning signs, in as many languages and scripts as he knew, into various rocks and standing walls, or along the bare side of a hill he cleaved in two with the Dark Iron Wand. Blood-curling threats and fanciful implications were abundant. All were warned to stay away, and sinister references were made to the Indigo Path of Death.

Another application of the power of the Implacable Wand, returned him in a whirl of motion to Old Romarth, indeed, to the very stoop of the Admonastic gate.

He strolled with stately stride up the narrow streets of the Antiquarian's Quarter toward his abode, reflecting with infinite satisfaction on the consequence of events.

"The ancient power is restored to the Implacable Dark Iron Wand of my ancestors. I hold, a single man, the power of a brigade nay, a legion. I have slain a warlock, and a titan, without wound or scar. And, best of all, I now return to the comfortable and expected routine of retiring leisure! The clamor of ten thousand pilgrims, with all their crimes and diseases and strange food flooding into my fair city, has been averted. The learning and wisdom from beyond the stars, which is immense to the point of terror, will not be known on Earth, and the reputation of the Antiquarians will linger undisturbed, and unchallenged.

"And why should any one wish to flee the earth? A few are born here to high position: rulership is our duty and burden. The rest are born to ache and sweat with endless labor. It would be disloyal, nay, treason, for a man to depart the Earth merely because she is dying! Why, what kind of cad would abandon an ailing mother? The case is parallel, the moral maxim is the same!"

As he strolled near the Cleft in the central square of the quarter, he paused, for a strange light was shining up from underground. He heard the noise of the buried world on which the foundations of his house were planted: instead of the weeping and begging of the inhumed, the whines of their children for bread, he heard a solemn song. He could not distinguish words, but the tones were rich with joy.

Next he heard, not in the air, but inside the inner works of his ear, of an unearthly three-toned chime, and he realized that Guyal had established more than one anchor for the Analept.

The first of a countless number of soaring men, women, and children rose weightlessly from the cleft, poised in swan-dive against the infinity of the sky, were wrapped in the shining indigo light, and were gone.

AFTERWORD:

IN MY long vanished youth, time was abundant and book money was dear, and so each book I owed was read and reread until its contents were nearly memorized.

Paperbacks, which cost (at that time) less than two dollars, were treats bestowed by the indulgence of a parent as rare as an oasis in a wasteland, a green garden-spot to which the imagination could escape the burning sun of reality for refreshment.

I remember the order of my first three fantasy purchases: the first book I ever bought was H.P. Lovecraft's *Dream-Quest of Unknown Kadath*, edited by Lin Carter; the second was *The Last Unicorn*, by Peter S. Beagle; and the third was an eerie slim volume of tales from a world with a dying sun, where eldritch magicians, and eccentric rogues awaited the final darkness of the world with nonchalant elegance: Jack Vance's *The Dying Earth*.

I am old enough to remember the days before *Dungeons and Dragons*, when the fantasy books were so rare and strange that no two were alike. *Gormenghast* sat on the shelf next to *The Worm Ororboros* next to *Well At the World's End* next to *Xiccarph*. The sword of Shanarra had not yet been drawn; the dragonlance was decades away.

Most unalike of all was the fantasy of Vance, where the magic and the superscience were strangely blended. Human nature was on pitiless

display, warts and all, but mingled with the finely-mannered and drily ironic affectations of over-elegant speech. It was an unforgettable mix.

Back in those days, fantasy avoided the journalistic prose of Hemingway, the simple straightforward taletelling of Heinlein, Clarke, and Asimov. Clarke Ashton Smith had a voice and vocabulary distinct from that of William Morris, from E.R. Eddison, from Mervyn Peake. These men penned symphonies, arpeggios, arias and arabesques of English language. Most distinctive of all was Jack Vance.

There were many a strange and brilliant idea to be found in these older fantasies. The central problem confronting any author of magical tales was how to write a convincing drama where the magic does not solve too easily any and all dramatic conflicts, and for this Vance had a unique and frankly brilliant solution: wizards can memorize only a certain number of the half-living reality-warping syllables of magical spells per day, and, once expelled from the mouth, the spell vanished eerily from the memory. Of course, this seems as a commonplace today, thanks to Gary Gygax borrowing the idea (and indeed the names of several spells) from Vance, but it is not a commonplace idea. It is still as strange and as brilliant as everything Vance does.

Even now, when fantasy is so common that it outsells science fiction, and every book seems oddly bland and similar, the work of Vance from half a century ago still stands out, an oasis for the imagination, an airy garden in the midst of an overfed swamp.

As I aged, my taste changed in many predictable ways. Few of the books I so adored in youth can I read again with undiminished pleasure. Jack Vance is the great exception.

And now, when book-buying money is abundant, but time is dear, and I have no idle hours to beguile with fantasies, Jack Vance is the author for whom I will always make time, to read and read again.

The Dying Earth will always for me live in the shining treasure house of imagination: that oasis will always for me stay green.

—John C. Wright

Glen Cook

The Good Magician

HERE A fleeting vision glimpsed high above the River Scaum sends Alfaro, the Long Shark of the Dawn, and a motley, ill-assorted collection of squabbling wizards, on a perilous quest to find a fabulous lost city—one which, it turns out, might have been better *left* lost...

Glen Cook is the best-selling author of more than forty books. He's perhaps best-known for the *Black Company* books, which include *The Black Company*, *Shadows Linger*, *The White Rose*, *The Silver Spike*, *Shadow Games*, *Dreams of Steel*, *The Silver Spike*, *Bleak Seasons*, *She is the Darkness*, *Water Sleeps*, and *Soldiers Live*, detailing the adventures of a band of hard-bitten mercenaries in a gritty fantasy world, but he is also the author of the long running *Garrett P.I.* series, including *Sweet Silver Bells*, *Bitter Gold Hearts*, *Cold Copper Tears*, and nine others, a mixed fantasy/mystery series relating the strange cases of a Private Investigator who works Mean Streets on both sides of the divide between our world and the supernatural world. The prolific Cook is also the author of the science fiction *Starfishers* series, as well as the eight-volume *Dread Empire* series, the three-volume *Darkwar* series, and the recent *Instrumentalities of the Night* series (two volumes to date), as well as nine standalone novels such as *The Heirs of Babylon* and *The Dragon Never Sleeps*. His most recent books are *Passage At Arms*, a new *Starfisher* novel; *A Fortress in Shadow*, a new *Dread Empire* novel; and *Cruel Zinc Melodies*, a new *Garrett, P.I.* novel. Cook lives in St. Louis, Missouri.

The Good Magician

GLEN COOK

1

Alfaro Morag, who, in his own mind, styled himself The Long Shark of Dawn, rode his whirlaway high above a forest. Ahead lay the bloody glimmer of the Scaum and his destination, Boumergarth, where he meant to assume protection of a rare tome currently in the collection of Ildefonse the Preceptor. As a precaution against the likelihood that Ildefonse was not prepared to cooperate in the transfer, Alfaro had surrounded himself with Phandaal's Mantle of Stealth.

His desire was *The Book of Changes*, subtitled *Even the Beautiful Must Die*. All secrets of protracted vitality and unending youth were contained therein. The Preceptor's volume was the last known copy.

Ildefonse was unreasonably narrow about sharing. He would not allow *The Book of Changes* to be borrowed or copied, definitely an unenlightened attitude. Certainly Alfaro Morag had a right to review the spells therein. Surely he should have access to the formulae for puissant potions.

Such were Morag's thoughts as he peddled across the sky, ever more displeased with the Preceptor and his hidebound coterie, some of whom

had been around since the sun was yellow, half its current size, and not nearly so far away. Those antiquities considered Alfaro Morag a pup, a whippersnapper, a come-lately interloper enslaved by impatience and lack of subtlety in acquiring properties he desired.

Bah! They just felt threatened by the refugee from somewhere so far south no local map revealed it.

Alfaro drifted right, left, up, down. How best to proceed? He spied a silhouette masking the sun, there so briefly he suspected it must be a time mirage. Yet he felt it was familiar.

He swung back, dancing on the breeze. He found the silhouette again, for seconds only. He had to climb to gain the right angle, up where pelgrane would soon cruise, watching the roads for unwary travelers as the last bloody light faded. Or for other things that flew: gruehawks and spentowls. And whirlaways too small and primitive to be protected by more than a single spell.

Alfaro's machine could not be seen but made noise thrashing through the air. Morag himself shed odors proclaiming the presence of a delicious bounty.

Alfaro veered off Boumergarth. Shedding altitude, he hastened to his keep in the upper valley of a tributary of the Scaum, the Javellana Cascade. He touched down yards from the turbulent stream, pausing only long enough to assure that his whirlaway was anchored against mischievous breezes, then headed for the ladder to his front door. "Tihomir! I come! Bring my vovoyeur to the salon. Then prepare a suitable repast."

Tihomir appeared at the head of the ladder, a wisp of a man featuring sores and seborrheas wherever his skin could be seen, topped by a few strands of fine white hair. His skull had a dent in back and was flat on the right side. He resembled a sickly doppelganger of Alfaro and was, in fact, his unfortunate twin.

Tihomir assisted Alfaro as he stepped off the ladder. "Shall I pull the ladder up?"

"That might be best. It has the feel of an active night. Then get the vovoyeur."

Tihomir inclined his head. Alfaro often wondered what went on inside. Nothing complex, certainly.

Alfaro's tower was nowhere so grand as the palaces of the elder magicians of Ascolais. But it was inexpensive. It had been abandoned when he found it. He hoped to complete renovations within the year.

His salon on the third level doubled as his library. A library bereft of even one copy of Lutung Kasarung's masterwork, *The Book of Changes*. He took down several volumes uniformly bound in port wine leather, each fourteen inches tall and twenty-two wide, with gold embossing on faces and spines.

Cheap reproductions.

All Alfaro's books, saving a few acquired under questionable circumstance, were reproductions created in sandestin sweat shops far to the east. Those he chose tonight were collections of artwork, volumes I through IV and VI, of the fourteen volume set, *Famous Illustrations of Modern Aeons*. Six volumes were all Alfaro could afford, so far. Volume V never arrived.

He finished a quick search of volumes I and IV before Tihomir brought the vovoyeur. "Are the experiments proceeding correctly?"

"All is perfection. Though the miniscules are asking for more salt."

"They're robbers." Literally, actually. There had been a noticeable decline in the number of wayfarers and highwaymen since Alfaro's advent in Ascolais. He did not boast about it. He doubted that anyone had noticed. "Give them another dram. In the morning."

"They're also asking for brandy."

"As am I. Do we have any? If so, bring a bottle with the meal."

Tihomir went. Morag lost himself in illustrations.

The one that fickle recollection insisted existed was in the last place he looked, the final illustration in Volume III.

"I thought so. It would be identical if the sun were behind me. And aeons younger."

He warmed the vovoyeur.

Strokes with a wooden spoon did not spark a response. More vigorous application of an iron ladle enjoyed no more success. Alfaro found himself tempted to suspect that he was being ignored.

Perhaps the Preceptor was too engrossed in his pleasures to respond.

Irked, Alfaro selected a silver tuning fork. He struck the face of the farseeing device a half dozen times while declaiming, "The Lady of the Gently Floating Shadows makes way for the Great Lady of the Night."

The surface of the vovoyeur brightened. A shape appeared. It might have been the face of a normally cheerful but time-worn man. Alfaro could not improve the clarity of his fourth-hand device. "Speak, Morag." Uncharacteristically brusque.

"See this illustration." Morag held the plate from Famous Illustrations to the vovoyeur. "Do you know this place?"

"I know it. To the point, Morag."

"I saw it this evening while enjoying an aerial jaunt above the Scaum."

"Not possible. That place was destroyed aeons ago."

"Even so, I spied it in a place where nothing stands. Where no one goes because of the haunts."

Silence stretched. Then the vovoyeur whispered, "It might be best to discuss this face to face. Tomorrow. I will instruct my staff to permit the approach of your whirlaway, so long as it remains visible."

"I shall follow your instructions precisely, Preceptor." Stated while reflecting that his vision had been a stroke of good fortune.

There were reasons the Ildefonses of these fading times persisted.

He examined the plate he had shown the Preceptor. There was no accompanying text, just a word: Moadel.

Alfaro searched his meager library for references to Moadel. He found none.

2

ALFARO DISMOUNTED from his whirlaway, bowed to Ildefonse while noting that his conveyance was neither the first nor even the tenth to grace the broad lawn at Boumergarth. He was surprised to be greeted by the Preceptor himself, but more surprised to find that he had been preceded by so many beings of peculiar aspect, magicians of Almery and Ascolais, all. Panderleou, evidently having arrived only moments ago, was haranguing Barbanikos and Ao of the Opals about his latest acquisition, a tattered copy of *The Day of the Cauldrons*. "Hear this from the second chapter. 'So they killed a thief and gave the best parts to Valmur, to hasten him on his way.'"

Others present included Herark the Harbinger, Vermoulian the Dream-walker, Darvilk the Miianther, wearing the inevitable black domino, Gilgad, as always in red, Perdustin, Byzant the Necrope, and Haze of Wheary Water with a new green pelt and fresh willow leaves where others boasted hair. There were others, the quieter ones, and Mune the Mage made his entrance while Alfaro still silently called the roll. Mune the Mage preceded the foppish Rhialto the Marvellous by moments, and Zahoulik-Khuntze was scarcely a step behind the odious Rhialto.

These constituted the bulk of the magicians of Almery and Ascolais. Alfaro felt the oppressive weight of many gazes. He had not tried hard to win friends. Nor had felt any need. Till now, perhaps.

What was this? What had he stumbled across? As a group, these men—applying the collective in its broadest definition—consisted of the most unsociable, cranky, and iconoclastic denizens of the region. Some had not spoken for decades.

The magicians watched one another with a casual wariness equaling what they lavished on the interloper.

Ildenfonse stepped up to a podium, raised his hands. The approximation of silence gathered shyly. "I do not believe the others will join us. Let us repair to the solarium. I've had a light buffet set out, with breakfast vintages and a selection of ales and lagers. We shall then consider young Alfaro's news."

The magicians brightened. Elbows flew as they jostled for precedence at the buffet. Ildefonse's pride did not let him stint.

Alfaro reddened. The loathsomely handsome Rhialto was heads together with the Preceptor. They kept glancing his way.

Alfaro headed for the buffet, only to find it reduced to bones, rinds, pits, and feathers. Some of the 21st Aeon's finest costumery now featured stains of juice, gravy, grease, and wine.

Clever Ildefonse. Magicians with full bellies and wine in hand soon relaxed. His servants moved among them, keeping their favorite libations topped up.

Ildefonse called for attention. "Young Alfaro, taking the upper airs yester eve, chanced to see something that none of this aeon ought, unless as a time mirage. Amuldar."

Susurrus, not a syllable of which Alfaro caught.

"He did not recognize what he saw. He did know that it did not belong. A clever lad, he has built himself a library of inexpensive reproductions of masterworks. In one of those, he found an illustration of what he had seen. Suspecting this to be of importance, he contacted me by vovoyeur." The Preceptor gestured, left-handed, across, up, fingers folded, then open. The Moadel illustration appeared at the western end of the solarium.

A glance at the collective showed the majority to be unimpressed. "Before my time," grumbled the usually reticent Byzant the Necrope. "And, considering the history, definitely a time mirage."

Haze of Wheary Water, leaves up like an angry cat's fur, demanded, "And if it were purest truth, what would it be to us?"

Questions arose.

Likewise names.

Historical events were enumerated.

Accusations flew.

The image did mean something to several magicians.

Arguments commenced, only to be shut down by the host when the spells supporting them threatened damage to his solarium. The magicians were accustomed to making their points briskly, with enthusiasm.

Rhialto approached Alfaro. In Morag's opinion, he did not deserve his sobriquet. Nor was Rhialto half the supercilious fop of repute. "Alfaro, what moved you to stir all this ferment?"

"I intended nothing of the sort. By chance, I spied an ominous structure where none ought to stand. Amazed, I hurried home, did some research, chanced on the illustration floating yonder. I reported the evil portent to the Preceptor." Alfaro meant to pursue exact clarity in all aspects, unless interrogated as to why he happened to be where he had been when he had spied this Moadel.

Alfaro posed a question of his own. "Why all the excitement? I didn't expect to find the entire brotherhood assembled."

"Assuming you actually saw…that…many magicians' lives might be impacted." Rhialto stalked off, having forgotten his usual exaggerated manners. He intervened in a dispute between Byzant the Necrope and Nahouerezzin, both of whom had honored Ildefonse's vintages with excessive zeal. Nahouerezzin further suffered from senile dementia and thought he was engaged in some quarrel of his youth.

The mood of the gathering changed as the magicians made inroads into Ildefonse's cellar. The oldest became particularly dour and testy.

Rhialto having demonstrated no interest in further converse, Alfaro slipped off into anonymity. The others preferred to ignore him? He would not fail to enjoy the advantages. He made an especial acquaintance with the buffet once the Preceptor's staff refurbished the board. The long gray coat he affected boasted numerous capacious pockets, inside and out, as a magician's coat should. When those pockets threatened to overflow, he strolled down to the lawn. His whirlaway sagged on its springs as weight accumulated in its cubbies and panniers.

During Alfaro's third taking of the air, he realized that chance had granted him an opportunity he had come near failing to recognize.

He was inside Boumergarth, with a rowdy mob, all of whom would be equally suspect if *The Book of Changes* went missing.

3

AMONG ALFARO Morag's gifts was a near eidetic memory. First time through Ildefonse's library, he touched nothing. He examined spines, read titles where those were in languages he recognized, and, so, had nothing in hand when Ildefonse caught him staring at a set of slim volumes purportedly written by Phandaal of Grand Motholam.

"Morag?"

"Preceptor? I overstepped, surely, but I can't help being awed. I might suspect that there is no other library as extensive as yours. Already I've noted three books my teachers assured me were lost forever."

"You suspect wrong, Morag. As you often do, to no great disadvantage to yourself yet. There are much grander collections, all even more direly protected." Ildefonse was in a bleak mood. "Return to the solarium. Do not roam unescorted. Even I don't remember all the traps set to take an interloper."

Alfaro did not doubt that. Neither did he doubt Alfaro Morag's ability to cope with petty snares.

He followed Ildefonse to the salon, where the older magicians formed ever-changing groups of three or four. Knowing smirks came his way, from faces capable of smirking.

A servant in livery boasting several shades of orange on dark violet blue entered. "Should Your Lordships be interested, an historic solar event appears to be developing. It can be best viewed from the upper veranda."

The magicians topped up their drinks and climbed to the veranda, impelled by the servant's intensity.

The fat old sun had completed a third of its descent toward the western horizon. It revealed a portentous case of acne, a dozen blotches that swirled and scurried around its broad face. Some collided and formed larger blemishes, while new blackheads developed elsewhere. Soon a quarter of the red face was hidden behind a shape-shifting dark mask.

"Is this it?" someone asked. "Has the end finally come?"

The sun flickered, grew by perhaps a tenth, then shuddered and shook it all off. It returned to its usual size. The blotches dispersed. The smallest sank into the dark red fire.

Hours fled while the magicians remained transfixed by the drama.

Ildefonse began to issue orders. His staff unfroze. He announced, "The lower limb of the sun will reach the horizon within the hour. I have ordered my largest whirlaway readied. Let us go. Young Morag will guide us to the point where he spotted his untimely marvel."

Apparently at random, Gilgad remarked, "The sun has developed a green topknot. And tail." An eventuation apparent only to his unique eye. He dropped the matter quickly.

4

ILDEFONSE'S LARGEST whirlaway was a palace in itself. Alfaro was hard pressed to conceal his envy.

As yet, he had no clear idea why the magicians were interested in Moadel. They ignored his questions. They were not pleased, that was plain. They were nervous. Some might even be frightened. More than a few sent dark looks Alfaro's way, sure that he was a taunting liar working a confidence scheme.

Only Ildefonse spoke to him, and that with obvious distaste. "The sun will be behind Amuldar shortly. Where do I situate us?"

"Amuldar? I thought it was Moadel."

"Amuldar is the place. Moadel was the artist."

"Oh." Alfaro had spent some energy seeking an alternative to admitting that he had been near Boumergarth. He had come up with nothing. Nor was it likely that any disclaimer would be accepted. Ildefonse had dropped hints enough.

Morag delivered the true ranges and bearings.

He would build an image of honest cooperation. That might prove useful should flexibility be called for later. "It's difficult to judge from so grand a standpoint but I would move a hundred yards back from the Scaum and rise half a dozen."

The palatial conveyance adjusted its position, possibly in response to the Preceptor's thoughts.

"Here. This is almost exactly…"

"Excellent." With an undertone suggesting that Alfaro Morag had won a stay.

Alfaro had spent little time with the elder magicians since his advent in Ascolais. Now he suspected that they were deeper than they pretended. And were very clever at making outsiders feel small.

5

THE TIPS of the spires and bulbous towers of Amuldar rose stark black against the sun, seeming to climb it. Beforehand, the magicians had been indifferent. Now they were interested. Some dramatically so.

Ildefonse and Rhialto lined the rail of the promenade. Alfaro leaned against that rail between them. Rhialto mused, "We may have misjudged our new associate."

"Possibly." Ildefonse seemed to doubt that.

"I, for one, am pleased. This could be a splendid opportunity. Alfaro, tell us more."

"There's nothing to tell that hasn't been told."

"Indeed? So. Why go home and contact Ildefonse rather than investigate?"

"I am neither a fast thinker nor particularly courageous in the face of something that should not be."

Ildefonse said, "Any of these starry old bull erbs would have swarmed straight in, hoping to strike it rich."

Alfaro noted that Zahoulik-Khuntze and Herark the Harbinger, both, had developed a furtive manner. Nor were his immediate companions demonstrating their customary flash and bravura.

Panderleou presented himself. "Ildefonse, I have recalled a critical experiment I left active in my laboratory. Return to Boumergarth. I must get home quickly."

"And thence, whither?" Rhialto inquired.

"This is no time for your superior airs and snide mockeries, Rhialto. Preceptor! I insist."

"Dearest Panderleou, companion of my youth, you are entirely free to come and go as you will."

"A concept exceedingly appealing but one you have rendered impracticable."

The sun declined behind Hazur. The after light revealed no sign of Amuldar. Nothing could be seen but a brace of pelgrane circling.

With little expectation of a useful answer, Alfaro asked, "Will someone tell me something, now? Anything?"

Ildefonse said, "We will honor Panderleou's request. I set course for Boumergarth. After a suitable evening repast, we will repair to the library, research, and consider what actions we should take or should not take tomorrow."

The grand whirlaway soared, leaned, swept away across the dying light. The hundred colorful banners dressing its extremities cracked in the passing air.

6

A SCRAMBLE commenced as the whirlaway docked. Most of the magicians rushed the buffet, determined to further deplete the Preceptor's larder. A few fled to the lawn and their conveyances. Those returned in a squawking gaggle, righteously outraged.

Ildefonse said, "After protracted soul-searching, I suffered a change of heart. Prudence demands that we remain together and face the future with a uniform plan and resolute purpose."

Mune the Mage, mouth filled with lark's liver croquets, observed, "The most salubrious course would be to continue the exact policy pursued since the incident of Fritjof's Drive. Ignore Amuldar."

A strong minority were swift to agree.

Herark the Harbinger declared, "I put that into the form of a motion. Though it would seem that Amuldar inexplicably survives, it has offered no provocation since the age of Grand Motholam. Let sleeping erbs lie." The Harbinger had not yet recovered his color. Alfaro feared the man might have caught some dread scent drifting in from the future.

Rhialto said, "An admirable strategy, tainted by a single flaw. When Alfaro became aware of Amuldar, Amuldar became aware of Alfaro."

Morag enjoyed a barrage of dark looks. These magicians seldom let reason sweep them away.

"When we went out to learn the truth of Alfaro's sighting, Amuldar sensed us looking. Te Ratje knows we know."

"Unacceptable," Panderleou declared.

And Herark, "I call for a vote of censure against Alfaro Morag, the penalty to include confiscation of all his possessions."

Ildefonse stepped in. "Control yourselves. Alfaro is but the messenger. In any event, did he possess anything of merit someone would have taken it for safekeeping already."

Alfaro suffered a chill. This might be an ideal time to refill his pockets and hurry home, then move on, perhaps into the wastes beyond the Land of the Falling Wall.

Herark grumbled, "Will no one second either of my motions?"

No. But Haze of Wheary Water, leaves again in a ruff, offered, "I make a motion that Ildefonse, Rhialto, and others with the apposite knowledge, render the rest of us fully cognizant of the truths concerning Amuldar, being candid in all respects and reserving no salient point."

"Hear! Hear!" from a dozen throats. The young insisting on knowing what the old had gotten them into.

Alfaro, having heard no actual second, declared, "I second the motion offered by the esteemed Haze."

The "Hear! Hear!" chorus gave way to protests of Alfaro's audacious conceit. He had no standing.

"Quiet," Ildefonse said. "I have another second from Byzant."

Startled, the Necrope turned his back to the buffet and glared at the Preceptor.

"Panderleou, you were in the front rank at Fritjof's Drive. You have an agile tongue. Tell the tale. Cleave close to the truth. Neither fanciful embellishment nor self-effacing modesty are appropriate."

Sourly, Panderleou suggested, "Let Rhialto tell it. He was nearer the action than I."

Ildefonse demurred. "Rhialto was too near. And, as we well know, Rhialto holds himself too dear to relate any story involving Rhialto with precise accuracy."

Morag smiled. Even Rhialto's closest crony had reservations about his character.

Sullen, Panderleou growled, "All right. Gather round. I'll tell this once, touching only the critical moments."

The magicians gathered. Those with only two hands had difficulty managing their food and wine. And Ildefonse was of that inhospitable breed who did not allow guests to use magic inside his house. Which could explain his continued robust health.

Panderleou said, "At some undetermined point in the 16th Aeon, the first Great Magician rose, Te Ratje of Agagino, who may have been greater than Phandaal himself. Long gone, he is recalled only in footnotes in the most ancient tomes, where his name is inevitably misspelled Shinarump, Vrishakis, or Terawachy."

Panderleou headed for the buffet.

Ildefonse cleared his throat. "Panderleou, that was far too spare for those unacquainted with the name or situation."

Panderleou grumbled, "I blame modern education. Very well. In his day, Te Ratje was known as the Good Magician. All magic, he claimed, was a gift that should be used to benefit mankind as a whole. In his self-righteousness, he was more objectionable than is Rhialto in his egotism. He was smug, he was absolute, he was too much to endure. His fellow magicians concluded that an intervention was necessary. Te Ratje's eyes had to be opened. In consequence, much of the earth was burned clean of life. A wave of emigration took most of the survivors to the stars. Their descendants return occasionally, so changed we fail to see them as human."

Alfaro scanned faces. None of the magicians resented that remark.

"This was in the time of Grand Motholam. Many magicians since have wondered how Valdaran the Just, a mere politician, could have decimated the mages of Grand Motholam. The answer is, Te Ratje, the Good Magician. In the end, though, Te Ratje and his perambulating city were extinguished. Or driven into the demon dimensions. Valdaran succumbed to time's bite. The Earth went back to being what it always was, absent a few hundred million people."

"Until today," Ildefonse observed. He gestured. Amuldar reappeared. "Moadel painted this after Te Ratje disappeared. From a dream, he said. From a time mirage haunting the dreamlands, Vermoulian said at the time."

Vermoulian the Dream-walker pulled a thrush's drumstick out of his mouth. "I did advise you that I had found no trace of any such dream when Moadel made his claim."

"Yes, you did. I was complaisant. Te Ratje was no longer under foot. Evidence sufficient to consider the problem solved."

Alfaro tried to think himself beneath notice. He was at risk of being swept up in a quarrel that harkened to an ancient confrontation between vigorous rectitude and a relaxed attitude toward corruption.

The past might have come back.

Alfaro worried that it might bite him, too.

7

ONCE BOUMERGARTH was a palace of vast extent. The countless towers and rooms—some in realities not of Earth—were fading with their master. Ildefonse was nearing his dotage, despite the mysteries spun by Lutung

Kasarung. Or had lost his taste for the grand show. When guests were not present, he and his staff lived no better than common tradesmen, in a fraction of Boumergarth. Heroic expenditures of effort had been needed to provide for the current infestation.

It was, indeed, tempting misfortune to roam Boumergarth without Ildefonse. Who, occasionally, fell prey to his own forgotten snares.

So Alfaro learned in discourse with Ildefonse's staff, during a night when sleep proved hard to secure. During a night when discontent plagued the full company.

Ildefonse was determined to deal with Amuldar as soon as daylight drove more mundane dangers into forests and caves.

The breakfast buffet was basic. Fuel for a hard day's work.

Why go gourmet for the condemned?

By way of elevating spirits, the Preceptor announced, "I deployed my sandestins during the night. Expect a dead city, if we find anything more than a time mirage. Te Ratje detected would have acted by now. His recollections of us would be less affectionate than ours of him. So. One last sup of wine, and away!"

The magicians arrived on the lawn in a grumbling scrum, only to be disappointed again. Ildefonse did grant leave for individuals to provide their own transport. Woefully, that transport would proceed exclusively to the destination the Preceptor chose.

Most whirlaways used a minor demon called a sandestin to move them about. The Preceptor had suborned those with threats and loose talk of a release of indenture points, which were within his power to award.

He told Rhialto, "Lead the way, with young Alfaro. I will come last, sweeping up stragglers."

Alfaro thought Rhialto approached this morning with no more enthusiasm than did Panderleou or Zahoulik-Khuntze. Both continued to plead a pressing need to attend to business at home.

Ildefonse, from behind, shouted, "Each of you came to Boumergarth armed with several spells. I hope that, collectively, we're armed with a broad variety."

"Spells?" Alfaro gobbled. "I didn't... Why would..."

Rhialto looked at him with what might have been pity. If not disdain. Assuming that was not just the wind in his eyes.

8

THE MAGICIANS neared Hazur. Ildefonse relaxed control. They buzzed round the headland like giant gnats. Alfaro remained near Rhialto, keeping that magician between himself and the haunted country the best he could.

Magicians sparking about attracted attention, first from the road hugging the far bank of the Scaum, then from above. Yonder, travelers stopped to gawk. Above, the activity attracted pelgrane, monsters remotely descended of men. Their slow brains understood that all that sweet meat bobbing around Hazur could be deadly. Ao of the Opals underscored the point with his Excellent Prismatic Spray.

The gallery beyond the river roared approval when a hundred scintillant light spears pierced a too daring pelgrane. Sizzling, the monster plunged toward the Scaum.

The magicians closed with the headland, which consisted of rocky ground strewn with deadwood and clusters of stunted brush.

Ildefonse called to Rhialto, "Do you apprehend any cause to avoid the Forthright Option of Absolute Clarity?"

"It costs but a spell to try. Though it is absolute. And unlikely to have a broad impact on a target as grand as Amuldar."

The Preceptor made sure none of the magicians were slinking away. He whispered. His whirlaway plunged toward the forest choking the approaches to Hazur. He curved round above the treetops and hurled his spell.

The Forthright Option was new to Alfaro. Few magicians used it because it banished all illusion, not just what the spell caster wanted brushed aside.

The air coruscated. A patch an acre in extent became the flank of a transparent dome rising from barren rock. A city lay behind that patch.

The orbiting magicians swooped in to look.

The Preceptor preened.

Rhialto told Alfaro, "That took the aeons off. He's a boy again."

Morag was more interested in the city. The not-mirage.

Nothing moved there. There was no obvious decay, but the place had the look of having been abandoned to vermin and dust for ages.

For aeons, Alfaro reminded himself. Meaning there were potent sustaining spells at work.

The older magicians, so recently determined to attend interests elsewhere, now chattered brightly of what might be unearthed here.

Terror had been forgotten. Greed reigned. There was much snickering at the certain disappointment soon to grip those who had failed to respond to Ildefonse's summons.

The Preceptor observed, "Once again avarice trumps caution."

Alfaro saw something. "There! Did you see?"

"What?"

"A blue moth. It was huge."

Ildefonse said, "Blue was not Te Ratje's favorite color."

"An understatement," said Rhialto. "Te Ratje appears to be out of patience. He is ready for the test direct."

The Preceptor's whirlaway rose and darted away. Alfaro followed, as did Rhialto. Below, Barbanikos launched a spell with dramatic results.

The spell struck the dome, flashed brilliantly, rebounded, caught Barbanikos before he could dodge. His great dandelion puff of white hair exploded. Down he went, smoldering, whirlaway shedding pieces, its animating sandestin shrieking. Wreckage scattered down the flank of Hazur. Small fires burned out before they could spread.

Rhialto observed, "Barbanikos succeeded."

A black O ring a dozen feet across pulsed in the surface of the dome. Haze of Wheary Water darted through. No instant doom struck him down. Mune the Mage followed. The other magicians wasted no time.

Rhialto remarked, "Our reputations are unlikely to recover if we fail to follow."

Alfaro had a thought about opportunity knocking. Should that slowly shrinking O ring close a dozen estates would become masterless.

Ildefonse caught his eye. "Learn to think things through."

Alfaro opened his mouth to protest.

"Had you developed that skill early you would have had no need to migrate in haste."

Rhialto observed, "You are a slow learner. Nevertheless, you show promise. And you have youth's sharp eye."

Youth's sharp eye, unable to meet Ildefonse's fierce gaze, wandered to the pelgrane contemplating prospects on the river road, then to the feeble sun. "Gilgad was right. The sun has a green topknot. And maybe a beard or tail." Both discernable when considered from a dozen degrees off direct.

Rhialto and Ildefonse discovered it, too. And Rhialto saw something more. "There is a line, fine as a thread of silk, connecting the earth to the sun."

Ildefonse said, "Would that we had Moadel here to sketch it."

Alfaro suggested, "I could get my brother. He has a talent for drawing." Tihomir was immensely blessed in that one way.

"Unnecessary. The sun will persist for a few more days. Our task is more immediate. Rhialto. Lead the way. I will sweep up the rear."

Rhialto tilted his jeweled whirlaway toward the shrinking O ring. Disgruntled, Alfaro followed.

9

"THERE'S NO color," Alfaro exclaimed.

"But there is," Rhialto countered. "Te Ratje's gray, in all its thousand shades. Gray is the color of absolute rectitude."

"Unsettling news," Ildefonse said. "Barbanikos's aperture has closed."

The hole had become a black circle floating in the air. The acre unveiled by the Forthright Option of Absolute Clarity had dwindled to a patch a dozen yards in its extreme dimension, too.

Rhialto said, "I have not been here before."

Ildefonse confessed, "My visit has become so remote that I might need weeks to exhume the memories. Alfaro was correct. There is a blue moth. I need recover no memories, though, to understand that the street below leads to the heart of Amuldar."

The others had gone that way. Dust hung in the air, stirred by their passage. There was nothing here to seize their attention. This was the most bland of cities. No structure stood taller than three stories, nor wore any shape but that of a gray block, absolutely utilitarian.

"Where are the towers? The minarets? The onion-domed spires?"

Ildefonse said, "The silhouette was what the Good Magician believed he was creating. Now we are inside what actually came of his vision."

"Valdaran the Just destroyed the magicians of Grand Motholam for this?"

Rhialto chuckled. Ildefonse did not respond.

Alfaro squeaked, startled by a big blue moth that just missed his face.

The elder magicians slowed. "Time for caution," Rhialto said, indicating a strew of polished wood and wickerwork that had been a whirlaway not long ago.

"Mune the Mage," Ildefonse decided. "I don't see a corpse, so he walked away."

Several large moths, or maybe butterflies, flitted randomly nearby. They ranged in color from dark turquoise to pale royal blue. Alfaro said, "Looks like writing on their wings."

"Those are spells in Te Ratje's own script." The Preceptor evaded a moth as big as his spread hand. "One of his contributions to magic. Even he could encompass no more than four spells at a time. So he made these creatures. He could read a spell if he so chose, or he could arm them so the insects could deliver disaster by fortuitous impact. This would be an instance of the latter."

Rhialto prized a small purple stone from its mount on the tiller bar of his whirlaway, whispered to it, pegged it at an especially hefty moth. The moth turned onto its back and wobbled downward.

Ildefonse observed, "That one carried the Dismal Itch."

"They're all nuisance spells." Rhialto's right hand danced. His purple stone zipped from butterfly to moth, trailing ichors and broken wings.

They fell where others had fallen already. Then there was Mune the Mage, clumping onward with inspired determination, his iridescent cape an aurora against the gray. Ghostly, shimmering footprints shone where he trod but faded quickly. Ildefonse observed, "I believe his temper is up. Forward, Mune! Forward, with alacrity!"

Mune the Mage made a rude gesture. Even so, Rhialto swooped down for a few words. He returned to report, "Only his dignity is injured. As you might expect, though, he's already grumbling about restitution."

Alfaro said, "I see something."

All three slowed.

There was a hint of color at the heart of Amuldar, about as lively as that of a plant found lying beneath a rock. It filled the spectrum but every shade was washed out, a ghost of what it might have been.

Thither, too, stood a scatter of structures resembling those seen against the sun. None were the size the silhouette had suggested.

An expansive plaza lay surrounded by those. A squadron of unmanned whirlways sat there. The Preceptor said, "They're all here but Barbanikos and Mune the Mage."

The three settled to the gray stone surface, which trembled with ribbons of color for an instant after each dismounted.

Alfaro understood. The color here, weak as it might be, existed only because outsiders had tracked it in.

10

FALLEN LEPIDOPTERA marked the path into thc squarest and grayest square gray structure, where no light lived. Alfaro drew his short sword from beneath his coat. A moonstone in the pommel, properly seduced, shed a brisk light, which illuminated a circle twenty feet in radius. Rhialto and Ildefonse were impressed. "An heirloom," Alafaro explained. The acquisition of which had precipitated the cascade of events that had brought the Morag brothers to Ascolais.

"Amazing," Ildefonse said. "But we need something more."

The hall seemed to have no boundary but the wall through which they had entered. The other magicians were around somewhere, though, as evidenced by remote echoes and flashes.

"What is this place?" Alfaro asked.

The Preceptor said, "Your guess will be as good as any."

There was a deep mechanical clunk. The floor shuddered. Light began to develop, accompanied by a rising hum. The distant voices sounded distraught.

Alfaro damped his moonstone, turned slowly.

The wall behind boasted countless shelves of books, up into darkness and off into the distance to either hand. "Preceptor..."

"I did tell you there were libraries superior to my own. Forward!"

Ildefonse stepped out. Alfaro followed. He did not want to be alone, now. There was danger in the air. Rhialto felt it, too. He appeared uncharacteristically nervous. Ildefonse followed tracks in dust disturbed by those who had run the gantlet in the dark.

"Ghosts," Alfaro said as they moved through acres of tables and chairs, all dusty.

Creatures high in the air floated their way. Both were near-naked girls who appeared to have substance. Rhialto murmured approval. He had a reputation concerning which no one had yet produced hard evidence.

"Take care," Ildefonse warned. "They'll be more than they seem."

Rhialto added, "I suspect a sophisticated twist on the theme of the moths. The one to the left seems vaguely familiar."

The Preceptor said, "She is showing you what the secret Rhialto wants to see. This trap consists of choice. You have to chose to touch. But if you do, you'll have no time for regrets."

"Te Ratje's way. Destroy you by pandering to your weaknesses."

Similar ghosts floated ahead. They formed an aerial guide to other magicians. Not all those ghosts were female or young.

A scream, yonder. A brilliant flash. Then a half minute of utter silence during which the ghosts hung motionless. Then a grinding began, as of hundred ton granite blocks sliding across one another.

Ildefonse stepped out vigorously. Alfaro, perforce, kept up. Rhialto remained close behind, muttering as he wrestled temptation.

11

PERDUSTIN HAD screamed. Gilgad reported, "He touched a girl. Haze saw it coming. He interceded."

Perdustin was down and singed but alive at the center of an acre of clear floor under the appearance of an open sky.

"And the girl?" Ildefonse asked.

"Shattered." A red-gloved hand indicated a scatter that appeared to be bits of torn paper. "Sadly, none of the young ladies are any more real."

"It's all illusion," Haze said, before retailing his version of events.

Ranks of gargantuan, dusty machines surrounded the acre. "Where did that come from?" Alfaro asked. "We saw none of it till we got here."

Gilgad shrugged. "Things work differently inside Amuldar." He was frightened. And, in that, he was not unique.

"What is that?" Morag indicated the sky, where alien constellations roamed. Where fine lines, plainly visible despite being black, waved like the tentacles of a kraken eager to feast on stars.

Someone said, "Ask Te Ratje when he turns up."

A dozen pairs of eyes contemplated the wispy curve of pale green trailed by a sun that had set.

Ildefonse knelt beside Perdustin. Rhialto hovered. The other magicians grumbled because not one worthy souvenir had surfaced.

Alfaro glanced back. What about those books? Then he resumed studying the sky.

Saffron words, written on air, floated over his shoulder. YOU WITNESS THE EVOLUTION OF THE STARS. A MILLION GALACTIC YEARS PASS FOR EACH THREE MINUTES YOU WATCH.

Stricken, Alfaro watched black tentacles for a moment before he turned to face the oldest little old man he had ever seen. Liver spotted,

nearly hairless, with a left eyelid that drooped precipitously. The left end of his mouth sagged, too. His wrinkles had wrinkles. He had an arresting nymphet under either arm. His toes dragged when they moved. They were no ghosts. Alfaro felt the heat coming off them. They would bleed, not scatter like bits of torn paper.

Alfaro watched the improbable: self-proclaimed fearless magicians of Almery and Ascolais began to mewl, to wet themselves, and, in the case of Nahourezzin, to faint. Though, to be exactly reasonable, his faint had exhaustion and prolonged stress behind it. Morag noted, too, some who were not obviously intimidated, the Preceptor and Rhialto the Marvellous among them.

12

"TE RATJE?" Rhialto asked.

The old man inclined his head. After a pause. He did not seem quite sure. More girls gathered to support him. Their touch did not inconvenience him.

"Their concern is intriguing," Ildefonse murmured. "They exist at his will. And he isn't healthy."

Rhialto opined, "Even my formidable resources would be taxed were I tasked to entertain so many gems."

Alfaro asked, "Who are they? They're exquisite. Does he create them himself?" His own such efforts always turned ugly.

"No. Long ago he traversed time, harvesting the essences of the finest beauties and most accomplished courtesans, each at her perfect moment of ripeness: firm, unblemished, and a trifle green. He decants their simulacra at will."

Ildefonse added, "Youth's fancy."

Rhialto said, "The girls are not precisely aware of their status, but do understand that they have been fished from time's deep and are dependent on his affection for their immortality."

Alfaro wondered, "Why is he so old?" By which he meant: Why had Te Ratje let himself suffer time's indignities?

According to Rhialto, "His mind never worked like any other. Belike, though, this is just a seeming, like Ildefonse, or Haze, or Zahoulik-Khuntze with his illustrated iron fingernails."

Alfaro examined the Preceptor. As ever, Ildefonse seemed a warm, plump, golden whiskered grandfather type. Had he a truer aspect?

The Good Magician became someone dramatically less feeble. He stood tall, strong, hard, saturnine, and entirely without humor. But his eyes did not change. They remained ancient and half blind. Nor did he speak.

Te Ratje stabbed the air with his left forefinger. His fingernail glowed. He wrote: WELCOME, ALL. ALFARO MORAG. SCION OF DESTINY. YOU HAVE BEEN A LONG TIME COMING. His lines were thirty characters long, floated upward to fade in tendrils and puffs of yellow-lime vapor.

"Always a showoff!" Herark the Harbinger sneered.

TIME HAS BETRAYED ME. MUST YOU SABOTAGE MY GREAT WORK AGAIN?

Rhialto was skeptical. "I see no sign of work, great, trivial, wicked, or otherwise. I see the dust of abiding neglect."

I HAVE ABANDONED ALL EFFORTS TO IMPROVE MANKIND. THE BEAST IS A SHALLOW, SELFISH, INNATELY WICKED INGRATE. I LEAVE HIM TO HIS SELF-DESTRUCTIVE AMUSEMENTS. I FOCUS SOLEY UPON THE PRESERVATION OF KNOWLEDGE AND MINISTRATION TO THE SUN.

The Good Magician gestured. The air between himself and the magicians resolved into a diorama six feet to a side and three deep. An exact replica of the space they occupied revealed itself, with miniscules of magicians and girls at its center.

Te Ratje's illuminated forefinger extended to become a slim four foot yellow-green pointer. LIBRARY. INCLUDING EVERY BOOK WRITTEN SINCE THE 13TH AEON.

Ildefonse actually winked at Alfaro.

THESE ENGINES DETECT CREATIVE WORK IN PROCESS. WHEN A WORK IS COMPLETED, A SUITE OF SPELLS INTERRUPTS TIME, AN ASSOCIATE TRAVELS TO THE CREATION POINT AND RENDERS AN EXACT DUPLICATE. NO POEM, NO SONG, NO ROMANCE, NO MASTERWORK OF MAGIC OR HISTORY IS EVER LOST, THUS.

Alfaro detected a taint of madness.

The magicians had ignored the books in their haste to find more worldly treasures. But, now, every book written for eight aeons? Including the lost grimoires of Phandaal, the Amberlins, the Vaspurials, and Zinqzin? Three quarters of all magical knowledge had been lost since Grand Motholam.

A blind man could smell the greed beginning to simmer.

Deliberately provoked? Alfaro wondered.

Inside the diorama several engines turned a pale lilac rose. THERE BEATS THE HEART OF AMULDAR. THOSE DO THE GREAT WORK OF TIME. THOSE REACH OUT TO THE STARS AND DRAW THE SUSTENANCE FOR WHICH OUR SUN HUNGERS.

Gesture. A sphere of denominated space appeared overhead, the sun a bloody pea at its center. A scatter of latter age stars blazed at the boundary, true scale of distance ignored. Threads of black touched those and lashed the empty regions between. Every thread pulled something unseen into one of the two green tails spiraling out from the sun's poles.

AS I GIFT MY ANGELS LIFE, SO DO I GIFT LIFE TO ALL THAT GOES UPON THE EARTH. COME.

Alfaro blurted, "Me?"

YOU. YOU ARE THE ONLY INNOCENT HERE.

Morag gulped air. He felt like a small boy caught with his hand in a purse that was not his own. A situation in which he had found himself more than once. A glance round showed him none of the magicians moving, or even aware. "A stasis? One that exempts me, though I'm at a distance and did not initiate it?"

YES. Wicked smile. The Good Magician continued to grow stronger and younger. THERE IS LITTLE TO DO HERE BUT TEND THE ENGINES, STUDY, AND INDULGE IN RESEARCH. He smiled more wickedly as two of his pets slipped under his arms. Another, a sleek black-haired beauty wearing a pageboy cut like a visorless bascinet, who roiled Morag's thoughts from the moment he spied her, sidled up beside Alfaro. Her wicked eyes told him she knew perfectly well that she could make him her slave in an instant.

Te Ratje said, WITH ALL THE GREAT MAGICAL TEXTS AT HAND, AND TIME IN NO SHORT SUPPLY, EVEN A DILITANTE CAN FIND CLEVER NEW WAYS TO USE MAGIC.

Distracted by the nymph and natural flaws in his character, Alfaro followed Te Ratje's speech only in its broadest concept.

The story Te Ratje told was dubious even to a naïve youth just beginning to grasp how far out of his depth he was with the magicians of Almery and Ascolais. Who had begun to understand that he needed, desperately, to rein in his natural inclinations, lest he suffer a fate not unlike that enjoyed by his miniscules.

From glances caught, hc knew that Byzant the Necrope had something in mind.

13

THE NYMPH rubbed against Alfaro like an affectionate cat. He asked, "Is this distraction necessary?"

I CANNOT CONTROL THEIR AFFECTIONS.

Alfaro remained unsure of how he had moved from the plaza of the engines to a cozy little library rich with comfort and polished wood. It could not possibly hold all the books created across eight aeons. It was crowded by two magicians and three girls.

WHAT BOOK WOULD YOU LIKE TO SEE?

Because a lust for its possession had brought him to this pass, Alfaro said, "Lutung Kasarung's *The Book of Changes*."

Te Ratje extended an arm impossibly far, retrieved a volume. He presented it to Alfaro. It was a pristine copy, never opened. Alfaro placed it gently on a small teak table featuring a finish so deep the book seemed to sink. Shaking, he asked, "What are you doing to me?"

I WANT YOU TO BECOME MY APPRENTICE.

"Why?" Morag blurted.

YOU ARE THE FIRST TO FIND AMULDAR IN AEONS. YOU COME BURDENED BY NEITHER PREJUDICE NOR GREEDS FROM THE PAST, ONLY BY PICAYUNE WEAKNESSES EXAGGERATED BY YOUR TALENT.

"Why would Te Ratje want an apprentice?"

EVEN THE BEAUTIFUL MUST DIE.

Alfaro was baffled. He was confused. In moments of honesty, he could admit that he was not a good man, just a man who excelled at self-justification. He was not a man made in the style of the Good Magician.

There was a trap here, somewhere.

COMES THE DAY, COMES THE MAN. THE CHALLENGE CREATES THE MAN. I HAVE STRIVEN, ACROSS AGES, TO PRESERVE KNOWLEDGE AND PROLONG THE HOURS OF THE SUN. THE STRUGGLES OF THE 18TH AEON COST ME MY POWER AND AFFLICTED WOUNDS THAT GNAW ME TODAY.

Could the snare be emotional?

EVEN HIDDEN, UNKNOWN, WITH ALL THE KNOWLEDGE OF THE AGES, I COULD NOT RECLAIM WHAT HAD BEEN RIPPED AWAY. BUT NOW CHANCE OFFERS AN OPPORTUNITY. I CAN PREPARE A REPLACEMENT.

Alfaro concealed all cynicism. He did not believe. He could envision reality only through his own character. Te Ratje must be another Alfaro Morag, ages subtler and craftier.

Even so, Alfaro sustained his resolution to honesty. "I'm not the man you need. The best I can be called is rogue or scoundrel." And he did have obligations elsewhere.

YOUR BROTHER. OF COURSE. YET I HAVE ALL THESE DELICACIES. TEN THOUSAND OF THE SWEETLINGS, WHO LIVE BUT A DAY OF EACH HUNDRED YEARS. I HAVE THE WORLD, WHERE THE SUN'S TIRED OLD LIGHT WOULD BE EXTINGUISHED BUT FOR TE RATJE'S MIRACLE ENGINES.

"You read minds?"

SOME, I DO. YOURS IS OPEN. THOSE OF MY ANCIENT ANTAGONISTS, THOSE PRINCELINGS OF CHAOS AND SELFISHNESS IN THE SQUARE, NO. BUT I KNOW THEM. AND THE ENGINES UNDERSTAND THEM.

IT IS DETERMINED. AFARO MORAG WILL BEGIN TRAINING TO BECOME THE GOOD MAGICIAN.

Alfaro's companion snuggled close and purred.

14

ILDEFONSE STEPPED into the library. The girls squeaked in surprise. The Good Magician shimmered.

The Preceptor asked, "Morag, what is this?"

Alfaro blurted, "What happened? How did?..."

"Mune the Mage arrived. He broke the stasis. Only, I'm sure, after making sure there were no loose treasures in need of pocketing. Answers, please."

"Te Ratje would like me to become his assistant."

The Preceptor chuckled wickedly, his mirth echoed by the other magicians, outside. Ildefonse turned to the doorway. "I spent my Forthright Option of Absolute Clarity. Does anyone have a spell meant to disperse illusion?"

Vermoulian the Dream-walker pushed forward. "I have a charm, not a true spell, which will distinguish illusion from waking dream."

"Try it. Young Alfaro needs to see how far in he has been drawn."

"That seems profligate."

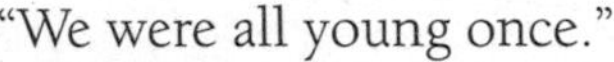

"We were all young once."

"Very well. The charm is renewable." The Dream-walker gestured, said a few words.

Ildefonse asked, "Is it time release? Nothing happened."

"The effect is instantaneous."

"Nothing has changed."

Not strictly true. Nothing he wanted to be illusion had changed. Ildefonse himself reverted to his natural form. The change lacked drama. He developed a paunch and lost some looks, hair, and his avuncular warmth.

A brief disturbance arose outside the library, where the magicians saw one another clearly for the first time.

The library remained precisely unchanged. Likewise, the three beautiful girls. But an odor pervaded the scene.

"Ach!" Alfaro gasped. "Te Ratje!"

The Good Magician's response to the charm was to grow old again, to become the wizened gnome, then to stop moving.

Nearest, Alfaro pronounced, "Dead! A long time dead. A mummy. Have we been dealing with a ghost?"

A shimmer formed about the husk. A voice inside Alfaro's head said, *I am a memory in the same engines that recall the delicate legion. Even the beautiful must die. But an idea, a dream, lives forever in Amuldar. The engines will labor on after the last star gutters.*

"Not a dream," Vermoulian opined. "A nightmare, brought to life."

Ildfonse nodded. Alfaro failed to comprehend. His kitten slithered up him and nipped at his left earlobe. "I lack key information. Te Ratje did not discuss his old feud. He dismissed it as of consequence only insofar as it might interfere here."

"Te Ratje was a zealot, of the narrowest focus, prepared to wreck civilizations to enforce his concept of right. The city outside, the gray, is the gift the Good Magician planned for us all." Ildefonse spoke passionately.

"And yet, after the excesses of Grand Motholam, he ceased intercourse with mankind. He focused on sustaining the sun."

"For which we must express gratitude, of course. But..."

The nymph had a hand inside Alfaro's coat and shirt. He had trouble concentrating.

The Good Magician—or the machine inside which his ghost still conspired—read his mind.

The truth is the truth, whatever hat it wears.

Alfaro disagreed. "The truth is different for each observer. Even the laws of nature are protean in some circumstances." He eased the hand from beneath his shirt, pushed the girl far enough away that her warmth no longer heightened his blood. "Forces try to enlist me, by seduction or implied threat. Why?"

Ildefonse betrayed a momentary surprise.

"The seducer is easily understood. My wants and fantasies will be fulfilled. The Preceptor, on the other hand…"

Ildefonse visibly controlled his tongue.

Truth is truth. The spell has been spun. Henceforth none can lie, save by silence. But truth will fill their thoughts. The Preceptor wishes to plunder Amuldar, then complete its destruction. So much does he loathe the vision of the Good Magician.

"Even to the cost of the sun?"

Even the beautiful must die. There are other suns. The magicians of Ascolais can travel in the palace of Vermoulian the Dream-walker.

Why did the magicians so hate the Good Magician's vision?

The engines showed him the world Te Ratje would have made, first according to his truth, then according to neutral machines capable of calculating the sum vector of all the stresses presented by the ambitions of the beings within that world. There was little resemblance.

Morag rode the engines' memories, observing incident and fact, absorbing the truths lurking between the biases.

15

TIME HAD fled. Ildefonse had gone into a stasis again, his mouth open to protest. Likewise, the girls and the mummy.

Who had not been the Good Magician. Te Ratje had perished in the ancient conflict. He had been replaced by a follower with a lesser grasp of magic.

And had been replaced himself, in time.

"Relax the stasis."

Ildefonse resumed protesting. The yelp of his stasis alarm interrupted. "What happened?" he demanded.

"The engines shadowed me through history."

Ildefonse had no comment. Neither did the magicians outside.

"Preceptor, Te Ratje did fall at Fritjof's Drive. The Good Magician here was a follower who salvaged Amuldar and carried on in secret. He made sure the engines will not fail in the lifetime of this universe. Amuldar is no threat to you. It will tend to the sun. It will care for Te Ratje's beloved daughters. It will protect itself."

Ildefonse absent his normal semblance could not conceal his inner self. Nor could he hide from Amuldar, which did not withhold salient information from Alfaro.

Morag said, "You all need to understand that none of the things you're thinking will work. Content yourselves with the status quo."

"Which is?" Vermoulian demanded.

"We are guests of Amuldar. For so long as Amuldar wishes." Alfaro flung a thought at the engines. "A buffet is being set out. Follow the young women with the lights. Restrain your lusts. Vermoulian, go. Preceptor, stay. Rhialto, join us in here." At a thought from Alfaro, the husk of the Good Magician floated away. Morag did not look. He feared it might be watching him as it went.

The dimensions of the library shifted. There was room for three men in three comfortable chairs attended by three implausibly beautiful young women. Alfaro reviewed his own sour history. One vision plagued him: Tihomir's injury.

Several new girls appeared. They brought wines and delicacies.

Alfaro said, "I've been bitten by the serpent whose venom moved Te Ratje. I'll do as he asked. So, now, the question. What to do about you?"

"Release us," Rhialto said, distracted. He had a princess on either knee.

"The machine considers that dangerous. It knows your minds. You are who you are. Yet returning you to Ascolais would be my preference."

Alfaro was amazed. He was talking like the man in charge.

He asked, "Who among you can be trusted?"

Rhialto and the Preceptor instantly volunteered.

"I see. The engines disagree. I want to send for something. But whoever I send is likely to plunder those who stay behind. Excepting Nahourezzin, who would fail to remember his mission. Yes. An excellent strategy. There. And done."

"What is done?" Ildefonse asked, nervously.

"The sandestins from the whirlways have been enlisted for the task, in return for remission of their indentures."

"In just such manner did Te Ratje become unpopular, making free with the properties of others."

"A paucity of otherworldly servants should make actions against Amuldar less practical. Enjoy the wine. Enjoy the food. Enjoy the company." Alfaro leaned forward to whisper, "I'm doing my best to get you out of here alive."

16

TIHOMIR STARED at the gray city, childlike. The sandestins had deposited him, and the contents of the tower beside the Javellana Cascade, in the center of the acre square. Alfaro rushed to greet his brother. Several favorite nymphs followed. He anticipated meeting the others wholeheartedly. Ten thousand of those precious, wondrous gems!

There were no magicians or whirlways in the square.

After embracing his brother Alfaro commenced the slow process of making Tihomir understand their new situation. He worried overmuch. Tihomir would be comfortable so long as he remained near Alfaro. He had arrived frightened only because they had been separated for a time, then strange demons had come to carry him away.

Alfaro Morag. The bad magicians are escaping.

"How can that be?" Though he had noted the absence of the whirlaways, including his own.

The one called Barbanikos propped the way open when the demons returned. The demons themselves had no confidence in your promise to relax their indentures.

Golden-tongued Rhialto and Ildefonse would have leveraged any demonic doubt to adjust notoriously evanescent sandestin loyalties.

There was a reason they were indentured rather than hired.

Alfaro shrugged. He remained irked that his whirlaway had been appropriated—by Mune the Mage, surely—yet here was a problem solved without his having to offend Amuldar. A prodigy. He was free to be the Good Magician and free to make Tihomir whole.

A dozen more girls arrived to help Alfaro move his possessions into his wondrous new quarters, shaped by Amuldar's engines based on his deepest fantasies.

Not even Ildefonse's Boumergarth could match their opulence.

He had fallen into paradise.

PARADISE WAS a blade with vicious edges.

Across subsequent centuries, individual magicians, or, occasionally, a cabal, attempted to avail themselves of the riches of Amuldar. Every stratagem failed.

Only Vermoulian the Dream-walker penetrated Amuldar's shell—by stalking the nightlands. The Dream-walker traced the nightmare into which the Good Magician descended.

Alfaro Morag, as all the Good Magicians before him had, discovered that only a few millennia of this paradise left him unable to continue to endure the cost. As had they, he began to yearn for the escape of the beautiful.

The better grounded and rounded Tihomir Morag would gain fame as his brother's successor.

AFTERWORD:

I entered the Navy out of high school in 1962, severely afflicted by Ambition Deficit Disorder. Nevertheless, when the Navy offered to send me to college for an additional four years of my life I said "Yo-ho-ho!" and went off to the University of Missouri. As a gangly, uncoordinated freshman I lurched about in the wake of a senior keeper whose name I have forgotten but whose greatest good turn remains with me still.

On learning that I favored science fiction, too, he dragged me into the independent bookstore next door to the tavern where we spent our evenings practicing to become sailors on liberty. There he compelled me to fork over the outrageous sum of, I believe, 75 cents (plus tax!) for the Lancer Limited Edition paperback of Jack Vance's *The Dying Earth*. I was aghast. Paperbacks were 50 cents or, at most, 60 cents at the time. But I got my money's worth, yes I did. That book is gone, along with a couple of subsequent editions, because I have read and read and read, I cannot say how many times.

I was hooked from the first page. This was intellectual meth. I cannot shake the addiction, nor have I ever lost the tyro's longing to create something "just like—" What every author feels about favorites who blazed new roads throught the ravines and thickets of literature's Cumberland Gaps. One of the great thrills of my writing career was being invited to participate in this project. So, for the first time in two and a half decades, I wrote a piece of short fiction, to honor one of the greats who lured me into this field.

Events here chronicled occur at the extreme end of the 21st Aeon, in an otherwise dull epoch some centuries after happenings recorded in *Rhialto the Marvellous*.

—Glen Cook

ELIZABETH HAND

The Return of the Fire Witch

ELIZABETH HAND is the author of ten novels, including *Generation Loss*, *Waking the Moon*, *Mortal Love*, and *Winterlong*, and three collections of short fiction, the most recent of which is *Saffron & Brimstone: Strange Stories*. She is a longtime contributor of book reviews and essays to the Washington Post, Village Voice, Salon, and the Magazine of Fantasy and Science Fiction, among many others. In 2008 her psychological thriller *Generation Loss* received the inaugural Shirley Jackson Award, and her fiction has also received two Nebula Awards, three World Fantasy Awards, two International Horror Guild Awards, the James M. Tiptree Jr. Award and the Mythopeoic Society Award. She recently completed *Wonderwall*, a Young Adult novel about the French Symbolist poet Arthur Rimbaud. She lives on the coast of Maine with her family, and is currently at work on *Available Dark*, a sequel to *Generation Loss*.

The Return of the Fire Witch

ELIZABETH HAND

Insensibility, melancholia, hebetude; ordinary mental tumult and more elaborate physical vexations (boils, a variety of thrip that caused the skin of an unfaithful lover to erupt in a spectacular rash, the color of violet mallows)—Saloona Morn cultivated these in her *parterre* in the shadow of Cobalt Mountain. A lifetime of breathing the dusky, spore-rich air of her hillside had inoculated her against the most common human frailties and a thousand others. It was twelve years since she had felt the slightest stirring of ennui or regret, two decades since she had suffered from despondency or alarm. Timidity and childish insouciance she had never known. There were some, like her nearest neighbor, the fire witch Paytim Noringal, who claimed she had never been a child; but Paytim Noringal was wrong.

Likewise, Saloona had been inoculated against rashness, optimistic buoyancy, and those minor but troubling disinclinations that can mar one's sleep—fear of traveling beyond alpen climes, the unease that accompanied the hours-long twilight marking the months of autumn. Despair had been effaced from Saloona's heart, and its impish cousin, desire. If one gazed into her calm, ice-colored eyes, one might think she was happy. But happiness had not stitched a single line upon her smooth face.

Imperturbability was an easy emotion to design and grow, and was surprisingly popular with her clients. So it was, perhaps, that she had inhaled great quantities of the spores of imperturbability, because that was the sole quality that she could be seen to possess. Apart, of course, from her beauty, which was noted if not legendary.

This morning, she was attempting to coax an air of distinction from a row of Splendid Blewits, mushrooms that resembled so many ink-stained thumbs. The blewits were saphrophytes, their favored hosts carnivorous Deodands that Saloona enticed by bathing in the nearby river. She disabled the Deodands with a handful of dried spores from the Amethyst Deceiver, then dragged them up the hillside to her cottage. There she split each glistening, eel-black chest with an ax and sowed them with spores while their hearts still pumped. Over the course of seven or eight days, the sky-blue sacs would slowly deflate as the Splendid Blewits appeared, releasing their musty scent of woodlice and turmeric.

After a week, she could harvest the spores. These became part of an intricate though commonplace formula usually commissioned by men with aristocratic aspirations—in this instance, a dull optimate of middle years who sought to impress his much younger lover, a squireen who favored ocelex pantolons that did not flatter him.

It was no concern of hers if her clients were vain or foolish, or merely jaded by a terminal ennui that colored their judgment, much as the sun's sanguine rays stained the sky. Still, she needed to eat. And the optimate would pay well for his false magnificence. So: arrogance and feigned modesty; a dash of servility to offset the stench of self-love…a few grains from the Splendid Blewits, and the physic would be complete.

But something was wrong.

Yesterday evening, she had unrolled nets of raw linen fine as froghair, arranging the filmy cloth beneath those indigo thumbs to catch the spores they released at nightfall. Morning should have displayed delicate spore-paintings, the blewits' gills traced upon the nets in powdery lines, pollen-yellow, slate-blue.

Instead, the gauze bore but a single bruised smear of violet and citron. Saloona bent her head to inspect it, holding back her long marigold hair so that it wouldn't touch the cloth.

"You needn't bother."

She glanced aside to see a Twk-woman astride a luna moth, hovering near her head. "And why is that?" Saloona asked.

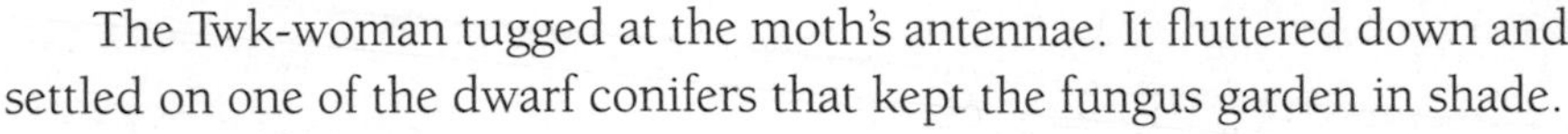

The Twk-woman tugged at the moth's antennae. It fluttered down and settled on one of the dwarf conifers that kept the fungus garden in shade.

"Give me salt," she said.

Saloona reached into her pharmocopia bag and handed the Twk-woman a salt pod, waiting as she lashed it to the moth's thorax. The Twk-woman straightened, adjusted her cap, then struck a pose like that of Paeolina II in his most well-known execution portrait.

"Paytim Noringal came here at moonfall and shook your spore-net. I watched unobserved. The resulting cloud gave me a coughing fit, but my leman swears I appear more distinguished than this time yestermorn."

Saloona cocked her head. "Why would Paytim do that?"

"More I cannot say."

The luna moth rose into the air and drifted off, its bright wings lost amid the ripple of jade and emerald trees crowding the hillside. Saloona rolled up the spore-net and set it with those to be laundered. She was neither perturbed nor angered by Paytim's action, nor curious.

Still, she had to eat.

She had promised the optimate his physic two days hence. If she captured another Deodand this evening, it would be a week before the spores were ripe. She secured the sporenets against rain or intruders, then walked to the paddock beside her cottage and beckoned her prism ship.

"I would see Paytim Noringal," she said.

A moment where only dappled sunlight fell through the softly waving fronds of cat-firs and spruce. Then the autumn air shimmered as with heat. There was a stinging scent of ozone and scorched metal, and the prism ship hovered before her, translucent petals unfolding so that she could spring inside.

"Paytim Noringal is a harlot and a thief," said the prism ship in a peevish tone.

"She now appears to have become a vandal as well." Saloona settled into the couch, mindful that her pharmacopoeia pouch was not crushed. "Perhaps she will have prepared lunch. It's not too early, is it?"

"Paytim Noringal will poison you in your sleep." The ship lifted into the air, until it floated above the hillside like a rainbow bubble. "If you're hungry, there are salmon near the second waterfall, and the quince-apples are ripe."

Saloona stared down at her little farmstead, a pied checkerboard of fungi, cerulean and mauve and creamy yellow, russet and lavender and

a dozen hues that Saloona had invented, for which there was no name. "Paytim is a very fine cook," she said absently. "I hope she will have blancmange. Or that locust jelly. Do you think she will?"

"I have no opinion on the subject."

The ship banked sharply. Saloona laid a hand upon its controls and made a soothing sound. "There, you don't need to worry. I have the Ubiquitous Antidote. It was a twenty-seven-year locust jelly. It was generous of her to send me some of it."

"She means you harm."

Saloona yawned, covering her mouth with a small freckled hand. "I will sleep, ship. Rouse me when we approach her enclosure."

The glorious spruce and granite-clad heights of Cobalt Mountain fell away, unseen by Saloona Morn and unremarked by the prism ship, which had little use for what humans call beauty.

THE FIRE witch's villa nestled in a small valley near the caves of Gonder. The structure had seen better days. It had been commissioned as a seraglio by the Crimson Court lutist Hayland Strife, whose unrestrained dalliances caused three of his aggrieved lovers (one of them Paytim Noringal) to first seduce then subject him to the torment known as Red Dip. When, after seventeen days, the lutist expired, the fire witch prepared a celebratory feast for her fellow torturers, using skewers of oleander for the satay. All died convulsing before daybreak. In the decades since then, the seraglio had been damaged by earthquakes, windstorms, and, once, an ill-conceived attack by Air General Sha's notorious Crystal Squadron.

And, of course, Paytim's own mantic enterprises had left the gray marble walls and sinuous columns blackened with soot, and the famous tapestries singed and smoke-damaged beyond repair. She paced now before the ruins of the arras known as The Pursuit of the Vinx, heedless of the geckos and yellow-snouted lemurs that clambered across the backdrop to one of her more notable love affairs.

Paytim disdained magic to enhance her charms, though she had for many decades employed the Nostrum of Prodigious Regeneration to retain the dew of youth. She remained a remarked beauty. Like her neighbor, she was flame-haired, though Paytim's was brazen tigerlily to Saloona's pale marigold, and Paytim's eyes were green. Her skin was the bluish-white of weak milk and bore numerous scars where she had been burned while conjuring, repairing the *bouche a feu*, or carelessly removing a pot from the oven. The scars were a mark of pride rather than shame; also a warning against over-confidence, in particular when dealing with souffles, or basilisks.

Today, her thoughts wandered along their customary paths: concocting a receipt for the season's bountiful quince-apple harvest; estimating when her young basilisk might be successfully mated; brooding upon various old wounds and offenses. She paused in her pacing, withdrew a shining vial like a ruby teardrop from the pocket of her trousers, and, with a frown, gazed into it.

A dark shape, so deep a red that it was almost black, coiled and uncoiled within the vial. At intervals, the shape cohered into the image of a gysart in scarlet and saffron motley, which would extend its arms—in joy or anguish, she could not say—then, in a voice pitched like a bat's, exhort her.

"*Paytim Noringal, Incendiary and Recusant! Your exile has been revoked, following the abrupt and unfortunate death of Her Majesty Paeolina the Twenty-Eighth. His Majesty Paeolina the Twenty-Ninth hereby requests your attendance at the after-ball following his coronation. Regrets only to be tendered by...*"

Here the harlequin doubled over in a spasm and began once more to writhe.

Paytim's frown smoothed into a small smile: for anyone who knew her, a far more alarming sight. She crossed the chamber to a low table, pressed a button that caused a cylindrical steel cage to rise from the floor. The young basilisk slept inside. Minute jets of flame flickered around its nostrils as it exhaled, also a faint sulfurous stink.

The vial bore a summons, not a request. Paytim's exile had been voluntary, although, in fact, she loathed all of the Paeolinas, going back to their progenitor, a court dancer who claimed to have invented the gavot.

His new Majesty, Paeolina XXIX, was indulging a customarily vulgar display of power. When Paytim had been at court, she had noted the lascivious glances he directed her way. The looks had been easy to ignore at the time—the present Paeolina had been little more than a spindle-necked boy. Now his attentions would be more difficult to deflect.

Despite this knowledge, she had already decided to attend the coronation's after-ball. She had not traveled beyond the mountains in some time. Also, she had recently made a discovery, an arcane and unusual spell

which she hoped to implement, although its success was dependent upon Paytim receiving some assistance.

Not, however, from the monad gysart. She lifted her hand and gazed impassively into the vial, then nudged the steel cage with her foot. The basilisk stirred. It made a soft croaking sound, opened its mouth in a yawn that displayed a fiery tongue and molten throat.

"Inform His Majesty that I will be delighted to attend," announced Paytim. "May I bring a guest?"

The mote ceased its wriggling to regard her with bright pinprick eyes. Flashes of silver phosphorescence overtook the whorls of crimson and jet. The gysart shuddered, then nodded.

"In that case," said Paytim, "Please inform His Majesty that I will be accompanied by Saloona Morn."

"*Your reply has been registered with the equerry of invitations. You are welcome to bring one guest. Further instructions will be—*"

Paytim's eyes narrowed. With one long finger, she flicked open a slot in the lid of the basilisk cage. Its inhabitant scrambled to its feet and stretched out its neck expectantly, as she held the ruby vial above the opening. A nearly inaudible shriek stirred the chamber, startling the geckos so that they skittered back behind the tapestry as the vial dropped into the basilisk's mouth, and, with a burst of acrid steam, disappeared.

FROM THE air, Paytim's villa resembled a toy that had been kicked to bits by a petulant child. Ivy and snowmoss covered heaps of hand-painted tiles fallen from the roof. The entire east wing had collapsed, burying solarium and manta pool. The collection of musical scrolls Hayland Strife had painstakingly assembled when not dandling some fawn-eyed courtesan was ash, destroyed when lightning struck the library tower. Its skeletal remains rose above the north wing like a blackened scaffold. Spiderwebs choked the famed boxwood maze, and the orchards of pomegranate trees and senna grew wild and blackly tangled. Saloona spied a thrasher's nest atop a quince-apple, the white bones of some unfortunate snagged in its branches like a broken kite.

Only the kitchen wing was intact. Smoke streamed from its five chimneys and the windows gleamed. Troilers wheeled through the herb and root-vegetable gardens, harvesting choi and sweet basil and yams. Sallona gazed down, her mouth filling with saliva.

"Poison," hissed the prism ship. "Ergot, chokecherry, baneberry, tansy!"

"Fah." Saloona waved a hand, signaling that they should descend. "Remain in the garden and do not antagonize her. I smell braised pumpkin."

Other, less attractive odors assailed her as she approached the dilapidated household, scents associated with the fire witch's metier: sulphur, burnt cloth, scorched hair, gunpowder; the odd sweetish reek of basilisks, reminiscent of barbecued peaches and fish. Paytim stood at the entrance to the kitchen wing, her wild hair barely restrained by a shimmering web of black garnets, her trousers flecked with pumpkin seeds and soot.

"Mother's sister's favored child." Paytim used the familiar, if archaic, salutation favored by the fourth caste of witches. "Will you join me for luncheon? Port-steeped pumpkin, larks-tongues in aspic, I just picked some fresh cheeps. And I saved some of the locust jelly. I remember how much you liked it."

Saloona dipped her head. "Just a bite. And only if we share it."

"Of course." Paytim smiled, revealing the carven placebit she'd made of the lutist's finger-bone and implanted in her right eye-tooth. "Please, come in."

Over lunch, they made polite conversation. Saloona inquired after the newest litter of basilisks and feigned dismay to learn that only one had survived. Paytim wondered innocently if the prism ship had been confiscated during the most recent wave of enforced vehicular inspections.

When the dishes were cleared and the last of the locust jelly spooned from a shared bowl, Paytim poured two jiggers of amber whiskey. She removed a pair of red-hot pokers from the kitchen athanor, plunged one into each jigger, then dropped the spent pokers into the sink. She handed a steaming whiskey to Saloona, and, without hesitation, downed her own.

Saloona stared at her unsteady reflection in the simmering liquid. When it cooled, she took a sip.

"What a remarkable cook you are," she said. "This is utterly delectable. And the aspic of larks'-tongue was sublime. Why did you shake my sporenets last moonfall?"

Paytim smiled unconvincingly. "I long for company. I wished to invite you for luncheon, and feared you would refuse an invitation."

Saloona thought on this. "Probably I would have," she conceded. "But your invitation has cost me a week's worth of spores I need for a client's physic. I can't afford to—"

"Your cantrap is a childish game," exclaimed Paytim. She could forestall her habitual impatience for an hour, no more. "I have discovered a charm of immense power, which Gesta Restille would have slain her own infant to possess! Eight sorcerers and twice that many witches died in their efforts to retrieve this spell. Do not think you can thwart me, Saloona Morn!"

"I have but this instant learned of your spell." Saloona set her unfinished tumbler of whiskey back upon the table. "I am unlikely to thwart you."

"Then you agree to assist me?"

Saloona raised a marigold-colored eyebrow. "I am a humble farmer of psychoactive fungus, not a fire witch. I can't be of any use to you."

"It's not an incendiary spell. It's far more lethal."

Saloona's lips pursed oh so slightly. "I have taken a vow not to cause death by intent."

"Any death would not appear intentional."

"I have taken a vow," repeated Saloona.

"I am without transport and require the use of your prism ship."

"No one but myself may use my ship."

"The aspic you just devoured was made with tingling spurge and an infusion of castorbean. I took a mithradatic dose two days ago."

Outside, the prism ship made a keening sound. Saloona began to unloosen the ribbons of her pharmacopoeia bag. "I have the Ubiquitous Antidote…"

"There is no antidote. Save this—"

Paytim opened her hand. In the palm quivered what appeared to be a drop of water.

"That could be rainwater," said Saloona. "I think you are lying."

"I am not. You will imbibe the last of your panacea and still die convulsively."

The ship's lament grew so loud that the dishes in the sink began to rattle. Saloona sighed.

"Oh, very well." She extended her tongue to Paytim's outstretched hand, felt a drop like freezing hail upon its tip, and then a pulse of heat. She grimaced. "What is the spell?"

Paytim bade her accompany her to the ruins of the library tower

"I found it here," the fire witch said, her voice hushed with excitement. "I have not removed it, lest someone arrive unexpectedly and sense my discovery. Clans have fought and died over this periapt. My

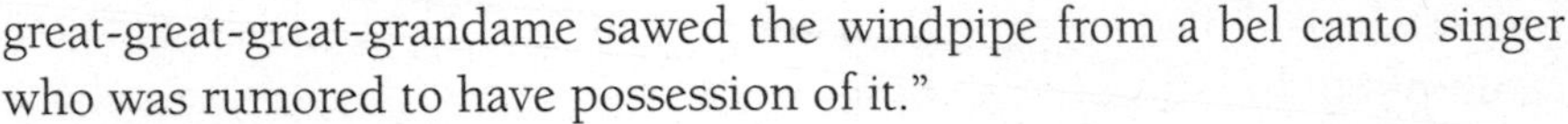

great-great-great-grandame sawed the windpipe from a bel canto singer who was rumored to have possession of it."

"In his throat?"

Paytim stood on tiptoe to avoid a puddle of green muck. "None knew where the spell might reside. Throats were slashed, golden thulcimers melted down, kettledrums covered with the skin of youths and maidens. Hayland Strife swore his father strangled his mother while she slept, then restrung his lute with her hair. All for naught—all for *this*."

She stopped at the foot of a crumbling stair that curved up and up into the skeletal remnants of the library tower. Swiftly, almost girlishly, she grasped Saloona's hand and led her up the rickety steps. Around them, the structure shuddered and swayed, its exposed struts of hornbeam and maskala tusk all that remained of the tower walls.

Cold wind tangled Saloona's hair. It carried the smells of fermenting quince-apple and moldering paper, scents overpowered by the stink of smoke and ozone as they approached the topmost level, which shook as though they stood atop a storm-tossed tree. They stepped out into a small platform, inefficiently protected by makeshift panels of oiled silk.

The fire witch dropped Saloona's hand, and, with care, crossed the unwieldy space. A single wall had miraculously survived that long-ago lightning strike, festooned now with cobwebs. Bowed and mildewed, it held row upon row of small round holes, so that it resembled an oversized martinhouse.

"Hayland kept his musical scrolls here," explained Paytim Noringal. "I use them to start the cookstove sometimes. It was purest chance, or mischance, that I found it."

She stepped lightly among the desiccated scrolls scattered across the uneven floor. Some had unspooled so that their singed notations could still be read. Others were little more than skeins of dust and vellum. More scrolls were wedged into the wall's pigeonholes, along with miniature assemblages of circuitry and glass, a theramin wand, coils of lutestrings and ivory lute-keys, stacks of crystal discs, a broken gamelan.

When Paytim reached the wall, she hesitated. A crimson flush spread across her cheeks; a bead of blood welled where she bit her lower lip. She drew a quick breath, then thrust her hand into one of the holes. Saloona was reminded of a time years before, when she had spent an idle afternoon with a lover, catching fileels in the shallows of the Gaspar Reef. The young man had reached into a crevice, intending to grasp a wriggling fileel.

Instead, he had inadvertently antagonized a luray. Or so she assumed, as a cloud of blood and pulverized bone bloomed around the crevice and she quickly swam back to their waiting caravel.

No luray appeared now, of course, though there was an instant where an inky blackness spread across Paytim's arm like a thrasher's bite. With a gasp, the fire witch snatched her hand back. The stain was gone, or perhaps had never been.

But her fingers were closed tightly around a shining silver rod, slender as a bastinado and half again as long as her hand. It was inscribed with a luminous equation, numerals unrecognizable to Saloona, and which even the fire witch seemed to regard with profound unease.

Saloona asked, "Is that the charm which Gesta Restille so desired?"

The fire witch nodded. "Yes. The Seventeenth Iteration of Blase's 'Azoic *Notturno*,' known by some as the Black Peal."

Her lips had barely uttered that final word when a frigid gale tore through the flimsy walls, shredding silken panels and making shrapnel of scrolls and shattered instruments. At the same moment, a strange sound clove the air, a sound which Saloona sensed in her bones as much as her ears: a deep and plangent *twang*, as though an immense theorbo, too tightly strung, had been plucked.

"Quickly!" gasped Paytim Noringal, and lunged for the spiral stairs.

Saloona ducked to avoid being decapitated by a brazen gong, then followed her. With each step, the stairs buckled and fell away behind them. What remained of the tower walls crumbled into ivory and sawdust. A steady hail of blasted scrolls and blackened silk fell upon their heads, until, at last, they reached the ground and dashed from the tower seconds before it collapsed.

Scarcely had they raced into the corridor before it, too, began to fall away. Marble columns and tiled floor disintegrated as though a vast invisible grinding wheel bore down upon the fortress. Saloona dashed through a narrow door that opened onto the kitchen garden. Paytim Noringal stumbled after her, still brandishing the glowing silver rod.

"Wisdom suggests you should divest yourself of that," Saloona shouted above the din of crashing stone and brick. She ran to where the prism ship hovered, a rainbow teardrop whose petals expanded at her approach.

"Calamity!" exclaimed the ship. Saloona touched it gently, settling into her seat; but the ship continued to express alarm, especially when Paytim Noringal hauled herself in beside Saloona.

"My poor basilisk." The fire witch gazed at the ruins of her home. A single tear glistened at the corner of her eye, before expiring in a minute puff of steam.

"Perhaps it escaped," said Saloona as the prism ship floated upward. In truth, her greatest regret was for the loss of Paytim's kitchen, in particular the last remaining globe of locust jelly. "It may well follow us."

She glanced at the silver rod Paytim grasped. The lustre of its glowing numerals had diminished, but now and then a bright ripple flashed across its surface. The sight made Saloona shiver. She seemed to hear an echo of that strange, plangent tone, and once she flinched, as though someone had struck a gong beside her ear. She wished that she had heeded the warnings of her prism ship, and remained at home among her mushrooms.

Now, no matter the imminent danger to herself, Saloona was bound by ancient laws of hospitality. It would be gauche to refuse an offer of refuge to the fire witch; also foolhardy, considering the power of the charm Paytim held. When the prism ship had traveled a safe distance from the fire witch's demesne, skimming above an endless canopy of blue-green spruce and fir, Saloona politely cleared her throat.

"I am curious as to what use a musical charm might be to one as learned in the incendiary arts as yourself."

Paytim stared at the rod in her lap. She frowned, then flicked her fingers as though they were wet. A thread of flame appeared in the air, darkened to smoke that, as it dispersed, left a fluttering fold of purple velvet that fell onto Paytim's knee. Quickly, she draped it around the silver rod. Both rod and cloth disappeared.

"There," she said, and Saloona noted the relief in her tone. "For a day and a night, we can mention it with impunity." She sighed, staring down at the foothills of Cobalt Mountain. "I have been summoned to the Paeolinas' court to attend the coronation after-ball."

"I was unaware the Queen was ill."

"The Queen was not aware of it either," replied Paytim. "Her brother poisoned her and seized control of the Crimson Messuage. He has impertinently invited me to attend his coronation as Paeolina the Twenty-Ninth."

"An occasion for celebration. The charm is then a gift for him?"

"Only insofar as death is that benefaction offered by envious gods to humankind. My intent is to destroy the entire lineage of Paeolina, so that I will never again be subjected to their abhorrent notions of festivity."

"It seems excessive," suggested Saloona.

"You have never eaten with them."

For several minutes, they sat without talking. The prism ship hummed high above the trees, arrowing homeward. A red-dimmed fog enveloped the sky as the dying sun edged toward the horizon, and the first mal-de-mutes began to keen far below.

Finally, Saloona turned to the fire witch, her gray eyes guileless. "And you feel that this—spell—will be more provident than your own fire charms?"

"I *feel* nothing. I *know* that this is a charm of great power that relies upon some subtle manipulation of harmonics, rather than pyrotechny. In the unlikely event that there are survivors besides ourselves, or an inquest, I will not be an obvious suspect."

"And *my* innocence?"

A flurry of sparks as Paytim made a dismissive gesture and pointedly looked away from Saloona. "You are a humble fungalist, awed by very mention of the Crimson Messuage and its repugnant dynasty. Your innocence is irrefutable."

The mal-de-mutes' wails rose to a fervid pitch as the prism ship began its long descent to Saloona's farmstead, and the humble fungalist gazed thoughtfully into the enveloping darkness.

PAYTIM WAS understandably disgruntled over the destruction of her home, and, to Saloona's chagrin, showed little interest in preparing breakfast the next morning, or even assisting her hostess as Saloona banged about the tiny kitchen, looking for clean or cleanish skillets and the bottle of vitrina oil she'd last used three years before.

"Your cooking skills seem to have atrophied," Paytim observed. She sat at the small twig table, surrounded by baskets of dried fungus and a shining array of alembics, pipettes, crucibles, and the like, along with discarded circuits and motherboards for the prism ship, and a mummified mouse. Luminous letters scrolled across a panel beside the table, details and deadlines related to various charms and receipts, several of which were due to be completed the next morning. "I miss my basilisk."

"My skills never approached your own. It seems a waste of time to improve them." Saloona located the bottle of vitrina oil, poured a small amount into a rusty saucepan, and adjusted the heating coil. When the oil spattered, she tossed in several large handfuls of dove-like tricholomas and some fresh ramps, then poked them with a spoon. "You have yet to advise me as to how I will address the customer whose charm you ruined."

Paytim scowled. The divining rod sat upon the table beside her, still wrapped in its Velvet Bolt of invisibility. She waved her hand above it tentatively, waited until the resulting flurry of silver sparks disappeared before replying. "That flaccid oaf? I have seen to him."

"How?"

"An ustulating spell directed at his paramour's bathing chamber. The squireen has been reduced to ash. The optimate's need to retain his affection has therefore diminished."

Saloona's nostrils flared. "That was cruel and unwarranted," she said, and tossed another bunch of ramps into the skillet.

"Pah. The optimate has already taken another lover. You are being uncharacteristically sentimental."

Saloona inhaled sharply, then turned back to the stove. Paytim was correct: this was more emotion than Saloona had displayed, or felt, in decades.

The realization unnerved her. And her dismay was not assuaged by the thought that this unaccustomed flicker of sensation had manifested itself after Paytim had uttered aloud the names of the harmonic spell that was, for the moment, contained by the Velvet Bolt.

Saloona shook the saucepan with more vigor than necessary. Since that moment in the tower, she continued to hear a low, tuneless humming in her ears, so soft she might have mistaken it for the song of bees, or the night wind stirring the firs outside her bedroom window.

But it was only late afternoon. There was no wind. There were no bees, which were unnecessary to propagate mushrooms and other fungi.

Yet the noise persisted. Saloona almost imagined that the humming grew more urgent, almost minatory.

"Do you hear that?" she asked Paytim. "A sound like hornets in the eaves?"

The fire witch cast her a look of such disdain that Saloona turned back to her stove.

Too late: the ramps were scorched. Hastily she dumped everything onto a single pewter dish and set it on the twig table.

"This—charm." Saloona pulled a stool alongside Paytim and began to eat. "Its potency seems great. I don't understand why you have need of my feeble powers to implement it at the Crimson Messuage."

Paytim regarded the mushrooms with distaste. "Your false modesty is unbecoming, Saloona. Also, I need your ship." She glanced out the window to where a maroon glow marked the onset of dawn. "The Crimson Messuage is gravely suspicious of me, as you well know, but that's never stopped them from wanting me to join their retinue as Court Incendiary. In addition, I have a torturous history with this particular Paeolina. He made disagreeable suggestions to me many years ago, and, when rebuffed, grew surly and resentful. I am certain that his invitation will lead me into a trap."

"Why didn't you refuse it, then?"

"It would merely have been tendered at another time. Or else he might have attempted to take me by force. I tire of their game, Saloona. I would like to end it now, and devote myself to more pleasurable activities. My basilisk." She dabbed at a sizzling tear. "And my cooking..."

A sideways glance at Saloona became a more meaningful look directed at the blackened saucepan. Saloona swallowed a mouthful of tricholomas.

"I still don't—"

Paytim banged her fist against the table. "*You* will be *my* Velvet Bolt! I need you to sow clouds of unknowing, of rapture, forgetfulness, desire, what-have-you—whatever you wish, whatever distractions you can conjure from *this*—"

She stormed across the cottage to the window, and pointed at the ranks of neatly-tended mushroom beds, flushed with the first rays of morning. "Disarm the Paeolinas and their subordinates, so that we enter the court unaccosted, and with the Black Peal intact. During the evening's entertainment, I will enact the spell: their corrupt dynasty will fall at last!"

Saloona looked doubtful. "What is to keep us from succumbing as well?"

"That too will be your doing." The fire witch cast a sly glance at the pharmacopoeia bag hanging at Saloona's waist. "You possess the Ubiquitous Antidote, do you not?"

Saloona ran her fingers across the leather pouch, and felt the familiar outline of the crystal vial inside it. "I do. But very little remains of last year's tincture, and I must wait another month before I can harvest the spores to infuse more."

Paytim sniffed.

Saloona finished the last of the mushrooms and pushed aside her platter. The faint pricklings of emotion had not subsided when her stomach was filled. If anything, she now felt even more distressed, and ever more reluctant to commit to this hapless venture. Paytim's must be a very powerful spell, to so quickly undo decades of restraint and self-containment. It would be dangerous if the fire witch were aware of Saloona's sudden lability.

"You require the use of my prism ship and my fungal electuaries. I remain uncertain of the benefits to myself."

"Ungrateful slut! I saved your life!"

"After you attempted to wrest it from me!"

Paytim tapped distractedly at the windowpane. The glass grew molten beneath her fingertips, then congealed again, so that the view outside blurred. "The robust holdings of the Crimson Messuage will be ours."

"I am content here."

"The Crimson Court has a legendary kitchen. Too long have you languished here among your toadstools and toxic chanterells, Saloona Morn! At great danger to myself, I have secured you an invitation so that you may sample the Paeolinas' nettlefish froth and their fine baked viands, also a cellar known throughout the Metarin Mountains for vintages as rare as they are temulent. Still you remain skeptical of my motivations."

Saloona rose and went to stand beside the fire witch. Small flaws now flecked the window, like tiny craters or starbursts. The scents of sauteed mushrooms and burnt ramps faded into those of ozone and hot sand. Her hair rose slightly, tingling as with electricity. If she were to refuse the fire witch, Paytim was likely to exact a disagreeable vindication.

"I will do what I can." Saloona pressed a palm against the glass. "I have heard that the Paeolinas' kitchen is extensive and the chef's repertoire noteworthy if idiosyncratic. But if I fail…"

"If you fail, you will die knowing that you have tasted nettlefish froth, a liqueur more captivating than locust jelly. And you will have heard the Seventeenth Iteration of Blase's "Azoic *Notturno*." Some have claimed that death is a small price to pay for such a serenade."

"I have never been a music lover."

"Nor I," said Paytim. She laid her hand upon Saloona's shoulder. "Come now. Time for a proper breakfast."

BY THE morning of the after-ball, Saloona had devised a half-dozen charms and nostrums of varying power. The fire witch wanted nothing to interfere with her deployment of the Black Peal: her plan, therefore, was to sow the air with sores and spells that would discourage or retard any effort to

restrain her once inside the court. The most severe was a spell of Impulsive Corrosion, caused by spores of panther caps, pink mycenas, and fragile elf cups infused with azalea honey and caladium. The rest made ample use of fungi that caused convulsions, temporary paralysis, hallucinations, reverse metamorphosis, spasms, twitches, and mental confusions.

Saloona refused to create any charm that might induce fatality. Still, for many years a favored entertainment had been researching the means by which her crop could depopulate large areas of the surrounding mountains. She grew poisonous mushrooms alongside their benign and sometimes all-but-indistinguishable relatives, and took pride in recognizing the subtle differences between, say, the devil's bolete and its honey-scented cousin, the summer bolete. Her longtime sangfroid had made this a macabre but innocent pleasure. It had never crossed her mind that she might someday harvest spores and stems and caps from this toxic wonderland.

She took no delight now in concocting her poisons. More alarmingly, she *did* feel guilt. This too she associated with the long echo of the Black Peal. It must be a most powerful charm, to overcome the emotional inoculation she had experienced from handling so many psychotropic substances for so long.

"It seems inappropriate to sow such tumult among innocent guests," she observed to the fire witch.

"I assure you, no one within the Crimson Messuage is innocent."

"*I* am innocent!"

Paytim held up a deadly gaelerina, a fatal mushroom which Saloona claimed tasted exquisite. "A dubious statement. Innocent? You use that word too often and inappropriately. "Naive" would be more accurate. Or "hypocritical."

"Hypocritical or not, we will be fully reliant upon the Ubiquitous Antidote," said Saloona, whose efforts to create a spell to cause temporary deafness had been ineffectual. "If this spell is as powerful as it seems…"

"So few spells are not reversed by your marvelous restorative," replied Paytim in silky tones. "You are certain there is sufficient to protect us both?"

Saloon removed the crystal vial from her pouch. A small amount of glaucous liquid remained, which the fire witch regarded dubiously. "There is enough to preserve us, if the Black Peal does not prove resistant. Its potency is such that a very small amount is effective. Yes, there is enough—but no more than that. We'll be cutting it fine, and not a drop can be wasted."

"If necessary, we can stop our ears with beeswax."

"If that succeeds, this is a far more feeble charm than previously suggested," said Saloona, and replaced the vial.

Paytim Noringal said nothing; only stood before a deeply recessed window and stared mournfully at the dark line of spruce and cat-fir that marked the horizon.

She was looking for her basilisk. Saloona considered a sharp retort about the unlikelihood of its return.

But pity stayed her tongue, and apprehension at the thought of annoying the fire witch, whose temper was formidable. Saloona had never seen her neighbor exhibit much fondness for other humans. Paytim's treatment of her former lover, the Court lutist, was not anomalous.

Yet she displayed great, even excessive, affection for the basilisks she bred. They were lovely creatures, otter-sized and liquid in their movements, with glossy, sharply defined scales in vibrant shades of coral, cinnabar, chocolate-brown, and orange; their tails whiplike and their claws sharp enough to slice quince-apple rinds. They had beautiful, faceted eyes, a clear topaz yellow. Unlike their mythological counterparts, their gaze was not lethal. Their breath, however, was fiery as an athanor, and could turn sand to glass at a distance of three paces.

They were almost impossible to tame. To Saloona's knowledge, only the fire witch had ever succeeded in doing so. Her affection was returned by her charges, who consumed whatever was offered to them, living creatures or inert matter, but showed a marked preference for well-seasoned hardwood. Saloona imagined that was why Paytim's gaze returned to the nearby forest, despite the inferior quality of the evergreens.

"Perhaps it will find its way here." Saloona wiped fungal detritus from her fingertips. "You have always claimed that they have a well-developed homing instinct."

"Perhaps." Paytim sighed. "But this is not its home. And in a few hours, we depart."

Saloona touched her hand. She hoped the gesture was reassuring—she was out of practice with such things. She very much needed the fire witch's assistance during this final stage of assembling each spell. Since breakfast, they had worked side by side in the small, steel-and-glass-clad laboratory that stood in the darkest corner of Saloona's farmstead, deep within a grove of towering black spruce.

There, beneath glowing tubes of luminar and neon, Saloona utilized an ancient ion atomizer that reduced spores and toxic residues to a nearly

invisible dust. The fire witch then used Saloona's telescoping syringes to inject the toxins into a series of jewel-toned vesicles. Paytim strung these gemlike beads onto a chain of finest platinum, which would adorn Saloona when she entered the after-ball. Saloona and Paytim had taken mithradatic doses of each poison.

When the last vesicle had been strung, they returned to Saloona's cottage. There she decanted half of what remained of the Ubiquitous Antidote into a vial and gave it to the fire witch. Paytim then organized lunch. Saloona continued to express reservations regarding the night to come.

"I received no personal invitation to this celebration. Surely they will not be expecting me."

Paytim stood beside the stove, preparing two perfect omelets laced with sauteed ramps and oryx bacon. "My response to the court was clear: you will be my guest."

"I haven't left this place for nine years."

"You are well overdue for a journey." Paytim slid an omelet onto a copper plate and set it in front of Saloona, alongside a thimble-sized lymon tartlet and a glass of fresh pepper jelly. "There. Eat it while it's hot."

"I have nothing to wear."

A wisp of white smoke emerged from the fire witch's left nostril. "It would be a grievous day indeed when a Cobalt Mountain witch could not conjure attire suitable for paying court to a ruler of such legendary incompetence as Paeolina the Twenty-Ninth."

"And if my incompetence outshines his?" Saloona stabbed irritably at her omelet. "What then?"

"It will be for such a brief moment, only you will be aware of it. Unless, of course, your spells of confusion fail, and the Ubiquitous Antidote is deficient against The Black Peal. In which case…"

Paytim's voice faded into an uncomfortable silence. The two witches looked at each other, contemplating this unsavory prospect. A spasm assailed Saloona, and she clapped her hands to her ears.

"Do you hear that?" she cried.

The fire witch paled. "I hear nothing," she said, then added, "but I suspect the Velvet Bolt has expired. We must not speak of the musical charm again. Or even think of it."

Saloona bit her lip. She prodded her omelet with her fork, and reflected unhappily on how little joy she had taken from Paytim's cooking in the last day and a half.

This too is due to that malign spell, she thought.

Before another fit of trembling could overtake her, she began to eat, with far less avidity than had been her wont.

SKY AND shadows mingled in an amaranth mist as twilight fell that evening. At the edge of the forest, the prism ship had for some hours kept up a high-pitched litany of admonition, interspersed with heartrending cries. Since Saloona now seemed to possess a heart, the ship's lament frayed her nerves to the snapping point, and drove the fire witch wild with anger. Twice Saloona had to physically restrain her from reducing the ship to smoking metal and charred wire.

"Then silence it yourself!" demanded Paytim.

"I cannot. The neural fibers that give it sentience also propel it and govern its navigation."

Paytim's eyes narrowed dangerously. "Then we will walk."

"And arrive tomorrow," said Saloona with impatience. "Perhaps this is an opportune moment to test your beeswax plugs."

The fire witch exhaled with such force that the hem of a nearby curtain curled into gray ash. Saloona ignored this and returned to her bedroom.

Clothes were strewn everywhere. Stained lab tunics; an ugly crinoline diapered with paper-thin sheets of tellurium that whistled a jaunty air as she tossed it aside; an ancient silk kimono, never worn, embroidered with useless sigils; rubber booties and garden frocks; a pelisse she had made herself from a Deodand's skin, which still gave off a whiff of spoiled meat and blewits.

Saloona stuffed these back into the armoire from which they'd emerged, then sat brooding for some minutes on the edge of her little carven bed. She had lived here alone, had taken no lover for many years now, and had virtually no interest in fashion. Still, a sartorial cantrap was well within her powers.

But if one lacked an affinity for fashion, or even a mild interest, what use was such a spell? Might not the attire it procured turn out be inelegant, even fatally offensive? Certainly it would be unsuitable for an affair of such magnificence as the after-ball.

Saloona was, in fact, naive. She shared the province's general disdain for the ruling dynasty, but she had never visited court, or entertained the

notion that she someday might. Her anxiety at the prospect was therefore extreme. She once more flung open the door of her armoire, inspected the garments she had just rejected, and continued to find them wanting.

After a fraught quarter-hour, she still wore her faded lab tunic.

"Are you ready?" Paytim's voice echoed shrilly down the hall.

"Another minute."

Saloona bit her lower lip. She undressed hastily, retaining only her linen chemise and crimson latex stockings—the color, she thought, might be viewed as a sign of admiration. She pulled on a pair of loose sateen trousers, a deep mauve, and then an airy silk blouson, white but filigreed with tiny eyes that opened to reveal scarlet irises whenever bright light shone upon the fabric.

"Saloona!" The fire witch sounded almost frantic. "*Now*."

Saloona gave a wordless cry, swept her marigold hair into an untidy chignon that she secured with a pair of golden mantids whose claws tugged painfully at her roots. A final glance into a mirror indicated that she looked even more louche than she'd feared. The subtly glowing necklace of toxic vesicles around her throat seemed particularly out of place, its false bijoux glowing like Viasyan adamant. The entire effect was not mitigated by her worn leather slippers, which had long curling toes that ended in orange tassels.

But she had no time to change her shoes. As Paytim's footsteps boomed down the corridor, Saloona grabbed the silk kimono and rushed from her room.

"I'm ready," she said breathlessly, wrapping herself in the kimono's folds.

The fire witch scarcely glanced at her; merely dug her fingers into Saloona's elbow and steered her out the front door and toward the paddock. "Your ship knows the way?"

An answering retort, midway between a turbine explosion and the shriek of a woman in childbirth, indicated that the prism ship was aware of the destination.

Saloona nodded, then glanced at her companion, her eyes widening.

The fire witch rewarded her with a compressed smile. "It's been such ages since I've worn this. I'm surprised it still fits."

From her white shoulders to her narrow ankles, Paytim was encased in a gown of pliant eeft-skin, in shades of beryl, sea-foam, moonlit jade. Where twilight touched the cleft between her breasts, opalescent sparks shimmered and spun. Wristlets of fiery gold wound her arms, wrought

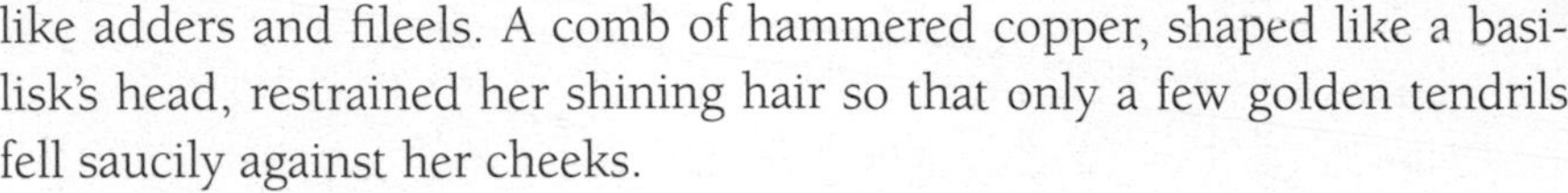

like adders and fileels. A comb of hammered copper, shaped like a basilisk's head, restrained her shining hair so that only a few golden tendrils fell saucily against her cheeks.

"Your attire becomes you," said Saloona.

"Yes."

The fire witch smiled mirthlessly, displaying the placebit carved from her lover's finger-bone; then raised her hand. The wand that had confounded even Resta Gestille glowed as though it were an ingot just hauled from the flames. It was so bright that Paytim blinked and looked aside.

More discomfiting to Saloona Morn were the sounds that emanated from the wand. A subtle, refined yet cunning cascade of notes, at once bell-like yet ominously profound, as though played upon an instrument whose tympanum was the earth's very skin, its sounding rods the nearby crags and stony spires. The notes rang inside Saloona's skull, and she gasped.

But before she drew her next breath, the sound faded. The ensuing silence, fraught with malign portent, Saloona found more disturbing than the uncanny music.

She had no time to ponder her unease. With a soft command, Paytim urged her toward the paddock. As they approached, the air grew increasingly turbulent. The evergreens' heavy branches thrashed. Dead fir needles and bracken rose and whirled in miniature wind-funnels. Fenceposts buckled, then exploded into splinters. A flock of mal-de-mutes rose from the topmost branches of the tallest spruce and fled screaming into the darkening sky.

"Can't you control it?" Paytim shouted.

Saloona shielded her eyes against a bolt of violet plasma. "I don't think it wants to go."

As she spoke, the air thickened until the ship's outlines grew visible, coruscant with lightning.

"BETRAYAL DEPRAVITY DISSOLUTION DESPAIR," the ship thundered. "INIQUITY CATASTROPHE DOOM DOOM DOOM."

"I'll speak to it." Saloona hurried past the fire witch, beckoning the ship open. Translucent petals emerged from the air and she slipped onboard.

"You must bear us to the Crimson Messuage without delay." Saloona pressed her palm against the navigational membrane. "We are, I am, a guest of his Majesty Paeolina the Twenty-Eighth."

"TWENTY NINTH," boomed the ship, but, as Saloona exerted more pressure upon the porous membrane, its violence abated and its voice dropped to a rasp. "A chaotic and incestuous heterarchy, their lineage is damned!"

"*I must go.*" Saloona glanced through the rippling plasma haze to where the fire witch stood, her mouth tight and her eyes fixed upon the blood-tinged western sky. "Paytim Noringal wields a terrifying spell. I fear to cross her."

"What is the spell?"

Saloona lowered her face until her lips brushed the ship's warm plasmatic membrane, and breathed her reply.

"Paytim Noringal claims it is the Black Peal; the Seventeenth Iteration of Blase's "Azoic *Notturno*," which Gesta Restille committed heinous crimes to employ. In vain," she added, and directed a cogent look toward the fire witch.

"A harmonic charm of indisputable force," the ship remarked after brief reflection. "Best I kill you now, painlessly."

"No!" Saloona snatched her hand from the navigational membrane. "It may be the spell can be averted. If not, I will certainly escape and you will bear me back home."

Her tone implied that she felt otherwise, but the ship's power field relaxed, from vivid purple to a more subdued shade of puce.

"Does it know the way?" Paytim Noringal demanded as the petals opened once more so that she could alight.

"Yes, of course," Saloona said. "Please, recline there upon the couch. I must offer my ship guidance for the first portion of the journey, then I will join you."

Without speaking further, they took their places in the cabin. Saloona closed her eyes and once again placed her hand upon the tensile membrane.

"Bear us to the Crimson Messuage," she commanded in a low voice.

The prism ship shuddered, but, after a momentary hesitation, rose smoothly into the air, and banked so that its prow pointed northeast. Lightning streamed from the thickening clouds as the ship sped above the mountains, its passage marked by violent bursts of blue-white flame and pulses of phosphorescence like St. Elmo's Fire. Those few persons who saw it from the ground took shelter, fearing one of the vicious tempests which shook the mountains from time to time.

Yet as they cowered in silos and subterranean closets, their skin prickled as a faint invidious music seeped into their consciousness, a sound at once aching and desperate. To those who heard it, sleep did not arrive that night, nor for some nights to come. When it did, the sleepers cried aloud, begging for release from the visions that overtook them. Even *en passant*, such was the power of the "Azoic *Notturno*."

THE CRIMSON Messuage first appeared as a twinkling of fallen stars, scarlet and gold and vermilion, scattered within a narrow cleft within the sharp-teethed Metarin Mountains. Once the prism ship began its descent, Saloona discerned the outlines of conch-shaped towers and minarets, outer gates with crenelated battlements built of crumbling soft cinnabar, and the extensive mazed gardens where great tusked maskelons prowled, and, it was said, fed upon bastard Paeolina infants.

"Is that it?" she wondered aloud.

"It is," said Paytim Noringal. She had been silent until now, her energies devoted to creating and maintaining a masking spell that would disguise the rod until they had gained entry to the after-ball. "Once, this was a great peak of friable red stone. An ambitious ancestor of the present King began its construction an eon ago. Twelve hundred slaves spent fifteen years clearing forest and rubble from the mountaintop. It was another half-century before the present structure was carved from the vermilion rock, and it took the endeavors of a giant tunneling wang-beetle to create the innermost donjons and chambers of state within the edifice."

"A great many slaves must have died in the process."

"True, though their bones are not interred here or anywhere else. Wang beetles are prodigious and indiscriminate eaters, though I was told that this one expired from gluttony and its carapace remains wedged within a forgotten corridor some hundreds of ells below us."

"You possess a great deal of lore pertaining to this fortress," observed Saloona.

"Hayland made a hobby of learning all he could of this accursed place. Better he had found entertainment elsewhere."

The fire witch's tone suggested that she had forgotten who initiated her lover into the rigors of the Red Dip. Saloona was too despondent to point this out.

"I could remain within the ship and await your return when the festivities are over," she said as the prism ship hovered above a grassy hollow near a drive clotted with other conveyances. "That might expedite our safe return to my farmstead."

"Our safe return is neither assured nor necessarily desirable." the fire witch retorted. "Far nobler it is to bring down a despot's throne! What cost thus are our petty lives, expended to further such a worthy enterprise?"

The ship grounded itself with a bump.

"What cost?" Saloona turned, furious. "I do not share your suicidal impulses, and my presence is certainly unnecessary for you to achieve them. Why did you engage me in this improvident venture?"

Paytim recoiled. She clutched the Black Peal, now disguised as a mottled nosegay, to her breast.

"Why not?" she replied. "You yourself admitted that you needed to get out more. Come, this seat is uncomfortable to the extreme, my leg is badly cramped."

The ship's petals expanded and the fire witch disembarked, hobbling. Saloona followed. The ship trembled beneath her footsteps, and she patted it.

"There, there, don't fret, I will be back. Wait here. I won't be late."

The ship gave a final disconsolate shudder. Its violet plasma-field faded to a metallic gleam. Then the entire vessel retracted into the grass, evident only by a cloudy glister as of a circle of snail-slime.

"Leave your mercurial vessel," commanded the fire witch. "We will have our choice of all these conveyances, if we survive." She gestured at the waiting cabriolets and winged caravans, parked alongside the bridled destriers and sleeping gorgosaurs that lined the long curving drive.

Saloona cast a last, woeful look at her ship, then continued after Paytim.

Her heart felt leaden. She could no longer pretend that her decades-long emotional abeyance had not been undone, perhaps irrevocably, by a few days' exposure to the rod that contained the Black Peal. For the first time in her life, she found herself recalling earlier, more clement times, experiences she had not realized were avatars of happiness. A green sward dappled with hundreds of tiny, milk-white umbrellas, first spore-rich fruits of warm summer rain; the song of thrushes and rosy-breasted hawfinches; a magenta cloud peeling from the surface of the dying sun and disintegrating into violet shreds, harbinger of Earth's final days. All these things Saloona had glimpsed, and thousands more; yet never had she shared a single one with another person.

This is regret, a voice whispered inside her skull. *This is what it means to have lived alone.*

"Quickly now, Saloona Morn —we're late as it is." The fire witch grabbed Saloona's arm. "Here—"

The fire witch thrust a packet into her hand, turned, and hastened toward an immense carven arch that opened onto a hallway larger than any manse Saloona had ever seen. Liveried janissaries leaned against the fortress walls, and several guests milled outside the entry. A bearded wench; an obese man with wattles like the dewlaps of a lichened sloth; glass-skinned gaeants from Thrill whose faces were swathed in a white haze that obscured their features while still suggesting an enigmatic beauty.

In dismay, Saloona examined her own attire—trousers hopelessly rumpled, the absurd curling-toed slippers soaked with dew; shapeless kimono drooping from her shoulders. Only the toxic necklace seemed remotely suitable for an enterance into the Crimson Messuage. She turned to stare resentfully at the fire witch.

Paytim shrugged. "You're with me," she said, and approached the gate.

Saloona clenched her fist, crushing the packet Paytim had given her. Its contents were not damaged, as she discerned when she opened it and found that it contained two yellowish blobs, the beeswax earplugs Paytim had provided against the Black Peal. In her fury, Saloona considered grinding them into the dirt, but was reluctant to further despoil her slippers.

"Your invitation?"

Saloona looked up to see the fire witch confronting a young man costumed as a harlequin.

Paytim raised her hand. "My invitation?"

One serpentine wristlet raised itself as if to strike, then opened its mouth. Out spat a glowing ruby bead that hung in the air as a ghostly, high-pitched voice began to recite.

Paytim Noringal, Incendiary and Recusant! You exile has been revoked, following the abrupt and unfortunate death of Her Majesty Paeolina the Twenty-Eighth. His Majesty Paeolina the Twenty-Ninth hereby requests your attendance at the after-ball following his coronation.

The fire witch dropped her hand. The serpent retracted, the apparition disappeared in a sparkle of gold flame.

The harlequin inclined his head. "Paytim Noringal. Forgive me."

"My guest, Saloona Morn, a renowned Cobalt Mountain witch," said Paytim, and brandished her false nosegay. "Now bid us enter."

They walked down a narrow corridor carved from the soft red stone. Antic music beckoned them, and the scents of burning hyssop, sweet clistre, tangerine peel. A short distance away, within the atrium, Saloona glimpsed revelers in sumptuous dress, garlanded with salya-blossom and ropes of garnet. As they drew near the entry, the fire witch abruptly stopped and grasped Saloona's arm.

"I find your garb increasingly inadequate for a celebration of this magnificence—I fear your presence will draw undue attention to the both of us and prevent the implementation of our implacable charm."

Saloona nodded, and, with precipitate steps, turned to depart. "I could not agree more, I will await you outside."

"There is no need of that. A simple cantrap will ensure your modishness. Shut your eyes lest a disarming glitter blinds you."

Saloona paused, disappointed, but agreed. Behind closed eyelids, she detected a subtle evocation of fireworks, then felt her clothes ruffled into slight disarray before arranging themselves into a pleasing texture.

"There," said Paytim with satisfaction.

Saloona opened her eyes to find her inadequate garments replaced by folds of ice-colored silk and her hair enclosed by a stiff taffeta net in the shape of a chambered nautilus. Instead of the absurd tasseled slippers, her feet were shod in silver-toed mules trimmed with living gleamants—equally ridiculous, but far more modish. The toxic necklace, at last, seemed well-partnered with the rest of her wardrobe. Instinctively, her hand reached for her waist. She was reassured by the touch of her pharmacopoeia pouch, now disguised as an eeftskin reticule, and her fingers traced the familiar outline of the crystal vial within that contained the Ubiquitous Antidote.

"Come now," said Paytim. "Perhaps the King himself will desire you as a partner in the gavot."

Saloona paled at this suggestion, but her companion had already swept into the atrium. As Saloona followed, she was assailed by additional fragrant odors and a raunchier, underlying smell of sweat, along with strains of laughter and genial music. Overhead, a heaven's-worth of lumieres shone in crepuscular eddies of violet and firefly green. Dancers engaged in the complex turns of Spur-Your-Master, or coupled recklessly in recessed alcoves where they were observed by crapulous onlookers sipping canisters of nettlefish liqueur and crimson lager.

"Is the King in evidence?" inquired Saloona.

Paytim gestured diffidently at a gilded platform. "He disports himself there, clad in the Punctilious Trousers that are his mark of office. As Earth has declined into senescence and valetudinarian decay, so too have the Paeolinas. Last of a debauched line: none will mourn his death."

Saloona observed an urceolate figure who held a jeroboam of frothing liquor. Bedraggled yellow feathers clung to his distended torso. The remnants of a lacy filibeg clung to the twisted circlets of the Crimson Crown, its garnets glinting dully, and the Punctilious Trousers bore unpleasant stains.

Still the King capered and shrieked with laughter. He staggered between equally bibulous guests who shoved him back and forth as though he were a dandle-ball.

"It is not an impressive sight," Saloona concurred. "Yet surely not all of these assembled are without virtue, and deserving of destruction?"

"You think not? See there! Lalula Lindinii, as debased as she is lovely behind that wimple—she skewered her entire family as they slept, then fed their corpses to the grues. And there, milky-faced Wanfredo della Ruiz, who shares his bed with a gloth. And there, the conjoined twins Dil and Dorla Klaxen-Haw, whose erotic contortions involve mewling infants and a plasmatic whipsaw. There is not a one here whom Zandoggith the Just would not condemn to ceaseless torment, if She were among us now."

"How then will we escape punishment?" asked Saloona. "You have yet to reveal your stratagem for our escape."

"Fortunate indeed are we that Zandoggith is not in evidence." The fire witch ran her fingers across the false bijoux at Saloona's throat, glancing at the malign nosegay in her other hand. She then gave Saloona a crafty look, and pointed across the crowded room. "I believe you will find refreshment at that banquette. Fortify yourself with nettlefish froth, then sow your fungal confusions amongst this swaggering crowd. I will perform an appraisal of this space and its egress; after that, the Black Peal will ring, and you and I can manage a hasty departure."

Before Saloona could protest, Paytim darted into the crowd and disappeared from sight. Saloona wasted several minutes searching for her in vain, before deciding to avail herself of the Paeolinas' noted gastronomy.

This she found to be disappointing. The black-backed porpoise infused with essence of quince-apple and juniper was cloying, the matalusk-hooves insipid, and a locust blancmange grossly inferior to Paytim Noringal's jelly.

Only the nettlefish froth exceeded her expectations, a pinkish liqueur of wonderful clarity and astringent flavor. Three glasses eased her anxiety to the extent that Saloona momentarily forgot the reason for her presence at the celebration: she wandered listlessly among the throng, enjoying glimpses

of her own silk-clad form in the highly polished walls, and the occasional admiring glance she received from an inebriated courtier or dame.

It was after one such had made excessively libidinous suggestions to her that Saloona, aggrieved, unclasped the necklace, muttered an activating charm, and crushed the first of the toxic vesicles beneath his nostrils.

"A sumptuous odor," the courtier leered. Immediately, he loosed a disarming squeal and fell onto his back, wriggling arms and legs agitatedly before expiring into a sudden, deep slumber.

Saloona regarded her handiwork, then began to make her way across the crowded atrium. Every few steps, she would remove another vesicle, invoke the appropriate incantation, and crush the gemlike receptable between her fingertips. She did not pause to look back until she had made a circuit of the room and deployed every fungal poison. Only then did she turn and, with a self-satisfied smile, note the startling perturbation in the crowd.

First one and then another merrymaker leapt into the air, thrashing and whirling as with St. Vitus Dance, and as quickly dropped to the floor, insensible. Others froze in place like costumed statuary. Still others began to laugh with rash hilarity, then, with maddened eyes, tore off their garments and raced through the atrium, crowing like cockerels and gargle-doves.

"Sweet Bentha's hips, the King's lunacy has contaged them!" a courtier exclaimed.

Saloona stood on tiptoe, and observed a tall figure racing toward the royal dais. The fire witch dashed onto the platform, flinging aside dancers and musicians and janissaries until she stood before the King, who screamed with laughter when he saw her.

"Here's a cormorant to be caught by tickling!" he cried, and attempted to grasp her by the waist. "Long have I awaited your return to our jolly company! Come, dance with me, sweet sot!"

"*Cymbolus Paeolina!*"

The fire witch's voice rang through the atrium. Gasps could be heard at the sound of the King's given name, and a few improvident guffaws. But the King only swayed back and forth, laughter burbling from his flaccid lips as the fire witch raised her arm.

"Witness now the destruction of your witless lineage!" she cried. "Let bones and sinews be the harmonium upon which your last gavot is played!"

Dreadful light candled Paytim Noringal's eyes. Her wristlets melted into strands of hissing gold; the basilisk comb bared its teeth. She lifted her hand, displaying a wand of glaring adamant, aflicker with abstruse numerals and unknown symbols. A fiery line traversed its length, and the rod split in two parts, each ablaze with clefs and breves and mediants, forking clews and fabrudans; every one an eidolon of some arcane note or tongue or hymn.

Saloona blinked, too stunned to flee or even move, as with a piercing cry the fire witch raised the wands above her head and struck one against the other. Silence, save for the ragged breathing of the King.

It is a fraud, thought Saloona, and from within the crowd heard similar sighs and expressions of relief.

Quickly, she turned to go, deeming this an expeditious time to return to her ship, when from somewhere high above sounded a single note of penetrating sweetness.

Saloona froze, enraptured. Such a note might Estragal have blown upon his yellow reed when he first played morning to the Earth, and roused dawn from deep within the dreaming sea. She began to weep, recalling a girlhood afternoon when she fell asleep among a field of coral fungus and fairy clubs, and woke to a sky painted with shooting stars.

Never had she heard such music! The lingering note suffused her with benevolence, a taste as of hydromel upon her tongue; and every face she saw reflected her own, mingling rapture and regret, desire and satiation; transport and pensive yearning.

All save Paytim Noringal's. With acrobatic intensity, she dismounted from the dais, paused to imbibe the contents of a small vial, and fled toward the door.

Saloona frowned. Her rapture faded into a dim memory of something less pleasant, a more astringent flavor upon her tongue…

The Ubiquitous Antidote.

Frantically, she sought within the folds of her silken gown for the reticule containing her pharmacopoeia. Her fingers tore at its ribands, dug inside to retrieve the crystal vial. Saloona unstoppered it and brought it to her mouth.

Only a droplet touched her tongue. In disbelief, she tapped it against her lips, then inspected it more closely.

The vial had been emptied.

Perfidious fire witch!

Too late, Paytim's betrayal grew plain: she had insisted that Saloona come along solely to make use of her prism ship and steal her share of the Antidote, doubling her own protection. At this moment, she would be

stealing another conveyance outside, while her naive neighbor perished from Paytim's treachery. Desperately, Saloona sucked at the crystal tube, attempting to absorb some particle of resistance before she succumbed to the Black Peal.

But even now a new and haunting tune replaced the melancholy note. Fairy horns and tambours, flutes and sonorous oblelloes joined a bolero that swelled and quickened then died away, only to resume in a frenzied, even brutal, cadence. Saloona stumbled toward the room's perimeter, as around her dazed revelers batted fretfully at the air and stumbled past each other, like children playing Find Your Lady.

"*Variana! Oh fair Variana, what betrayal is this?*"

"*Never shall I part from you, Capiloso, you have my heart.*"

"*Essik Longstar, oh my poor sweet child…*"

The air rang with wrenching cries: all mistook the living for those long dead. The music dissolved, only to return, with renewed and clamorous vigor. Mothers lamented slain children; betrayed lovers gouged their own cheeks and breasts. Janissaries rent their livery and grappled, mistaking colleagues for adulterous sweethearts, and Saloona paused in her ill-timed departure.

She knew this wild lullaby—surely it had been sung to her in her cradle? She hesitated, and her feet began to pick out a series of complex steps upon the tiled floor.

Yet some speck of the Ubiquitous Antidote still moved within her. She kicked the unwieldy silver-toed mules from her feet and fought her way to the wall. There she paused for breath, and gazed about the atrium for sign of Paytim Noringal.

The fire witch had disappeared. On the royal dais, groping masquers surrounded the King, who stood with mouth agape as though to catch the cascading notes upon his tongue. Trills and subtle drumbeats, a twanging volley of zithers and bandores, sweet mandols and violones—all swelled to a deafening roar, as the savage rhapsody employed the bewitched guests as its orchestra.

The King's gaping mouth unhinged. Strands of pliant flesh unfurled from his sallow face to form a crimson lyre. Ribs sprang from his chest like tines and commenced to play a mesmerizing glissando. With an echo of kettle-drums, his skull toppled from its gory spindle and cracked, and the garnet-studded Crimson Crown rolled across the tiles.

So it was that every guest in that company became an instrument upon which Blase's notturno played—all save Saloona Morn. Sanguine piccolos shrilled, accompanied by lyres strung with sinew and hair, the clatter of skull castanets and sternum manichords tapped by fleshless fingers. An audience of one heard this macabre symphony, sustained by the power of even the small amount of the Ubiquitous Antidote she had been able to consume; though gladly would she have missed the performance.

The infernal symphony swelled to a crescendo. With each note, a fragment of the fortress toppled, a rain of crimson stone and painted tiles crashing around Saloona's motionless form. Overwrought as she was, she could not move; only watch as the fortress was reduced to a vast ruin of cinnabar and garnet, slick with blood, where the gleam-ants fed. So ended the rancorous line of Paeolina, which had begun with a gavot.

The Black Peal ebbed. The sanguine orchestra fell silent. Saloona Morn started, her ears throbbing, and with alarm noted what remained of the edifice crumbling behind her. The wall fell away, to reveal a violet turbulence.

"RUINATION CATACLYSM DOOM DOOM DOOM."

With a cry, Saloona recognized her prism ship, petals unfolding as it hovered in the dust-choked air. She lunged into it with a gasp.

"Thank you!"

The ship's plasma field surrounded her. Saloona pressed her hand upon its membrane to impart the proper coordinates.

But the ship had already banked. Silently, Saloona stared down at the wreckage of the Crimson Messuage. Cabrielots and destriers lay buried beneath smoking heaps of stone. Of the fortress, nothing remained save a glowering wreck of vermilion rock wreathed in somber flame. Despite the fire witch's perfidy, Saloona sighed in remorse.

"I told you so," said the prism ship, vexed, and bore her home.

THE SHIP returned just as magenta dawn stained the sky above the foothills, and the last mal-de-mutes roosted, whispering and fluttering, among the topmost branches of the evergreens.

"You may sleep now." Saloona touched the ship's membrane. It whirred softly, then settled into a quiescent state.

Saloona hopped out. The mossy ground felt deliciously cool beneath her bare feet. She lifted the hem of her silken gown, hastening toward her cottage, then wrinkled her nose.

A short distance from the front door, the ground was charred. Moss and lichen had been burned away in a circle an ell in diameter. Saloona looked around, confused, until she spotted a small sinuous form crouching behind a blackened rock.

The basilisk.

Saloona bit her lip, then held out her hand and made reassuring chuffing sounds. The basilisk hissed weakly, tail erect with distrust, turned and slunk toward the forest, a trail of singed bracken in its wake.

In the days that followed, Saloona attempted to lure it with tidbits she thought might be enticing—spruce planks, knots of hardwood, the rails of a broken chair. The basilisk only stared at her reproachfully from the edge of the trees, and sometimes scorched her spore nets for spite.

I'm surprised it hasn't starved by now, she thought one chilly afternoon, and began to assemble another desultory meal for herself. Moments later, a commotion rose from the prism ship's paddock.

"HALLOO! BEWARE! EN GARDE!"

Saloona peered out the window. A tall, black-clad figure strode through the mossy field, the basilisk in its arms.

Saloona met her at the door. "Mother's sister's favored child," she said, and watched in trepidation as Paytim stooped to let the basilisk run free inside the cottage. "Your arrival comes as a surprise."

Paytim ignored her. She straightened to gaze with disapproval at the usual farrago of unwashed dishes and dried fungus scattered around the kitchen. Her clothing was disheveled, her black robes smirched with ash and rust-colored stains. There were several unhealed scars upon her arms and face. After a moment, she turned to Saloona.

"You have a wholesome look," she observed coolly. A second, garnet placebit now winked beside the one formed of the lutist's fingerbone. "Your antidote is indeed more powerful than I imagined."

Saloona said nothing. The basilisk nosed at a basket of dried tree-ears, sending up a plume of smoke. When Saloona tried to shoo it off, it yawped at her. Yellow flames emerged from its mouth and she quickly retreated.

Paytim shot Saloona an imperious look, then marched across the kitchen to the hearth.

"Well then." With a flick of her hand the fire witch ignited the cookstove, then grabbed a saucepan. "Who's ready for lunch?"

AFTERWORD:

WHEN I was fourteen, my family rented a lakefront cottage in Maine. This was 1971, the summer before high school. Most of my days and nights were spent swimming, or playing endless games of Monopoly on screened porches with my younger brothers and sisters and other kids vacationing nearby.

But for years—decades—I was haunted by the memory of a rainy Saturday when I was alone in the house for much of the day. (This in itself was a miracle.) Very early that morning, I'd accompanied my father to the local general store for breakfast provisions, eggs and bacon, a bag of freshly-made doughnuts. The doughnuts were the real thing, molasses-heavy and fried in lard.

Now, alone at the cottage, I was scrounging around for something to read.

Back in Pound Ridge, my mother had bought a carton of books at the library book sale. I'd gone through most of them already, but near the bottom of the box I found a paperback with its cover stripped. I sank into an ancient camp chair by the window, rain beating down outside and the bag of doughnuts in my lap. I opened the book and began to read.

It was the single most intense reading experience of my life. A few years earlier, *The Lord of the Rings* had captivated me, but that was over weeks. This was more like a drug (not that I knew that yet)—disorienting, enthralling, disturbing, and slightly sickening. The sickening part was enhanced by the doughnuts. I couldn't stop eating them, any more than I could stop turning pages. For years afterward, I associated the overwhelming, sensual, slightly nauseating sensation of reading that book with the taste of those doughnuts, along with the flickering green reflection of rain on the lake and the sound of wind in the trees. It was my madeleine.

The one thing I couldn't remember was its title, or author. For years, all I could recall was the taste of that book. I couldn't even look for it in used bookstores—the cover had been stripped. Still, somewhere along the road to becoming a writer myself, I heard of Jack Vance, and a classic novel he'd written called *The Dying Earth*. One day—this would have been

around 1985—I was in Wayward Books, a used bookstore near where I lived on Capitol Hill. There was a tiny shelf upstairs for science fiction, and as I glanced at the titles, I spied *The Dying Earth*. I pulled it out, started to read; and tasted molasses and scorched sugar.

It was *that book*.

I took it home and read it straight through. No doughnuts this time. Until then, I hadn't realized what a huge impact *The Dying Earth* had on my own writing, but I do now. My first three novels, bits and pieces of much that came after—none of them would have happened without that book. And I'm writing this now, in a rainswept cottage on a lake in Maine, with *The Dying Earth* in front of me. So maybe I wouldn't have happened, either.

—Elizabeth Hand

BYRON TETRICK

The Collegeum of Mauge

HERE A young boy sets out in search of the infamous father he's never known, and finds a *lot* more than he bargained for…

Byron Tetrick lives with his wife, Carol, in Fishers Indiana. He is a graduate of the Clarion West Science Fiction and Fantasy Writer's Workshop. His short fiction, including a Sherlock Holmes adventure, has appeared in various themed anthologies, as well as *In the Shadow of the Wall*, a collection of fictional Vietnam War stories which he co-edited with Martin H. Greenberg. A retired Air Force fighter pilot and retired International airline Captain, he has also written a non-fiction book on careers in aviation. He is currently working on a homage set in Jack Vance's "Alastor Cluster" universe, and a non-fiction book on book collecting. Byron is honored to be able to call Jack Vance a dear friend of many years.

The Collegeum of Mauge

BYRON TETRICK

Dringo crested the last tired hills of The Mombac Ambit just as the evening flickered into night with a pulse of dim purple light. Below him, teasingly close, the meager glow of a small village cast umber shadows upward through silhouetted branches. So near, yet so far. The shrieks and moans of night creatures seemed to approach him with alarming speed. A sudden amplified roar followed by a piercing howl shredded the last vestige of his nerves. *They're fighting over me*, thought Dringo as he quickened his pace, knowing now he had little chance to reach safety. He drew his small dagger. At an angle between him and the village ahead, a night-jar's mournful *oooeeahh* promised further menace.

"I suppose it would be best to increase our stride, don't you think?" spoke a voice at his side, its suddenness elevating Dringo's banging heart beyond what he thought possible.

A young man, elaborately dressed as though he planned meeting other distinguished nabobs, joined Dringo's trotting gait without further introduction. Voluminous robes of opalescent fabric trailed the stranger like pennants fluttering in a strong gale. An elaborate spiked hat jostled atop his head despite the stranger gripping silver-corded tassels with one hand.

"I cast a Spell of Convenient Disregard earlier," he puffed in staccato, "but it seems to be losing potency."

Dringo could make little more of the man who strode beside him in the gloom of the rapidly darkening night other than he appeared about his own age and similar height. He put his mistrust of magicians momentarily aside; better an unknown ally than a known death in the jaws of a visp or deodand. "Do you know any additional magic that could aid us?" asked Dringo, with similar breathlessness.

"None that I can conjure in our present predicament, other than an admonition that whoever of us lags, most likely will suffice as dinner for our pursuers, allowing the other to reach safety." With that he laughed and surged forward, his pearl-colored garment becoming ghost-like as his distance lengthened.

Though the village lights appeared closer, they were yet some distance away when suddenly the young magician halted and bent over, hands resting on his knees. Still gasping, he spoke: "We're safe now within the boundaries of a protective spell surrounding the village."

Dringo slowed but did not stop. "How can you be certain?"

"I see it," the stranger huffed. "Like a kalychrome it shimmers just beyond the visible spectrum. I doubt you see it."

Not satisfied with such a vague—and invisible to him—assurance, Dringo kept his pace and soon passed him. *He struggles for breath as if he might collapse; perhaps he sees the flashing lights one experiences just prior to passing out*, thought Dringo. *Better to leave him to occupy the hunger of the night creatures.*

"Wait! Slow! A moment only and then we can continue," pleaded the man. He laughed again as he stood upright and started walking. "I'll buy the first gill. Slow, and keep me company."

"Hardly incentive enough to risk my life," replied Dringo

"True, but I promise we are safe within the magical barrier that protects the town." He spoke a few unintelligible words and waved a hand. "Perhaps you can now see the faint aura of that which shields us?"

Dringo looked about. There did seem to be a faint, noctilucent shimmer to the air that quickly faded from his vision. "Well, it's gone now."

"No. No. I just don't have powers enough to hold it within your sight any longer. But you did see it, yes? So slow, and we will build our thirst at a more leisurely pace."

With misgivings, Dringo stopped and waited.

"I've traveled far this day with only the scrape of my soles as comfort, and caws and screeches to distress me." He held out a hand. "Gasterlo. We've outdistanced death and surely we are meant to be friends."

Dringo reciprocated. "Dringo, a lonely traveler myself. I'm curious that you are so versed in magic and yet so young. I doubt we'd have made it otherwise."

Gasterlo lifted a hand in modesty. "My earlier spell could not hold the creatures at bay a moment longer and the power to guard our environs is well beyond my paltry abilities. In fact, it is to become a Master Magician that I left the comforts of an indolent life and venture forth. What entices you? You don't have the look of a vagabond nor the errant."

Dringo hesitated a moment only. What harm can come from openness? "I seek my father. I have—at least so said my mother—only his looks and nothing else that connects me to the man who sired me."

"A noble cause, Dringo! We will ponder our futures over that ale I promised. We draw near the periphery of the town and already I can smell the roasting of meats, and my throat yearns for something other than the fusty water I carry."

As they approached, the town exhibited a liveliness surprising for the lack of nyctophobia so common in the folk that dared to live within the Ambit. Shutters were open on many of the small cottages that abutted the road creating a warm lambency to their path. Cries of greetings and well wishes were generously spoken by those who happened to peer out as the two strangers passed. One would think that they had just heard that the dying sun was to be invigorated on the morrow and that they expected to wake to a dawn of renewed brilliance, such was their obvious mood of sanguinity.

The road led to a small area of shops. Gasterlo pointed to the only two-story building. A weathered plank hung from an equally feeble gibbet. A flickering lantern shared the crossbeam throwing shadowy light on the crudely lettered sign: **Grippo's Hostelry.** "Our destination, it would seem. I see nothing ahead more promising." Gasterlo held the wooden door open and the travelers entered the inn.

Inside, the bonhomie was even more in evidence. Every table and chair was taken by smiling, red faced men. An elevated side room seemed to be the center of attention to all within, though many turned to look as Dringo and Gasterlo entered. From the raised alcove a young man stood up and shouted: "Gasterlo! We had all but given up. Come have a seat."

He roughly pushed the shoulders of an old man sitting nearby. "Make room for our friend." The man rose with a subservient nod. Several others moved to the side allowing Dringo to glimpse the speaker's companions. Four additional young men, two dressed in elaborate doublets of brocatelle and two clad in flowing robes similar to those worn by Gasterlo, were seated on benches that flanked a table of knurled deobado. Succulent food was spread across its surface, and Dringo's stomach lurched in an attack of envy.

Gasterlo stepped up, turned back to Dringo who had hesitated and said, "My cohorts. Join us."

Just then an officious innkeeper bustled up, shoving several local patrons out of the way. "Make room! Don't hinder their path, you uncouth rogues. Let these high goombahs join their friends." He guided them through the crowd to the table. "I assume you'll be wanting a gill, or do you wish something stronger? An absynthea? A green croate? I am Grippo and I'm at your service."

"Beer is fine," replied Gasterlo without glancing at the innkeeper. He clasped his friend with a hearty embrace. "Cavour Senthgorr, you look well. Are you ready to start training?"

"Indeed," he replied. "For too long have we been dogwadled by our powerful fathers. They perch in their manses content to watch the dying sun sink deeper into morbidity while they use their maugism to taunt their rivals and play games of spite with the small folk."

"Precisely!" agreed Gasterlo. "If nothing else, let the Twenty-first Eon, if this be our last, be marked by a renewed thrust of triumphant vibrancy—but here, let me introduce Dringo. We two barely escaped the maw of a visp—or some other equally horrible death— not moments ago." Gasterlo named his friends around the table: Cavour Senthgorr; Tryllo Makshaw; Zimmy Garke; Luppie Fross and Popo Killraye. All were sons of magicians of greater or lesser renown and were to be fellow students at the collegeum. Dringo felt diminished and uncomfortable; the young men were noticeably of higher status and breeding.

Room was made at the table and they took seats. The beer arrived delivered by a lass of sturdy stock who smiled shyly at Dringo. Gasterlo pulled out his purse, but Cavour halted him, "Our expenses are covered. The school has set up an account. However, you might add a few tercels into the common pot."

"The munificence of our fathers surprises me," said Gasterlo.

Dringo ventured into the conversation: "Was it you who lofted the encirclement around the town?"

"Hah," snorted Popo Killraye. "We have many weeks of study before we'll be able to repel an insect. No, Lord Lychenbarr has protected this town for our benefit." He waved an arm in a gesture encompassing the crowd. "Thus, the gratitude of those around us."

"I wondered about the festive mood of the people. The Ambit is not known for folk who dare stroll beneath the shadow of a mowood tree, much less cavort openly along gloamy streets."

Tryllo Makshaw chuckled. "It seems that Lord Lychenbarr wants us to have a place away from the collegeum to do the things young men do without disturbing his symmetry. He is a fusspot and a querulous magician who has been pressed into service to instruct us reprobates." He nodded towards another buxomly server jiggling towards the adjoining table. "I look forward to our time here. We shall see exactly how grateful the townspeople are when it comes to surrendering their daughters' virtues."

Cavour pushed a plate of fried trotfish towards Dringo and spoke to Popo, "Hand over that red-looking fungie. You both must be starved. Grippo! Another gill for all at the table."

Dringo had forgotten the food but was now ravenous. Gasterlo and he filled plates, and more beer was brought to the table. The evening seemed to progress as a moment in time quickly come and gone. There had been much laughter and good-natured ribbing as only young men lacking attachments can perfect without rancor. Though still crowded, the inn began to quiet with small groups wandering towards the door, usually after stopping by their table, doffing hats and speaking a few ingratiating words. Dringo felt quite above himself surrounded by these sons of powerful magicians. They seemed to enjoy his comradeship, though, as he did their boastful banter. The innkeeper had arranged for their rooms upstairs and by unanimous decision they decided on one last drink before retiring.

Luppie Fross leaned over to Dringo. "Where does your journey take you next?" he asked.

"Good question, Luppie. I'll brood over that tomorrow with a clearer head. I'm searching for my father." In a moment of braggadocio, he added, "He was a magician himself, you know?"

"What?" shouted Luppie. He turned to the rest of the table. "Dringo tells me his father is a magician."

Embarrassed, he held up his hand. "Hold on! I base that only from some stories I heard from my mother. She only had a short time with him but he did tell her he was a magician of minor rank—of course, according to her, he also claimed many things of which he was not. I don't even know if he yet lives."

"Dringo told me he goes on a quest in search of his father," remarked Gasterlo.

"Tell us more," said Zimmie.

"Indeed!" added Popo.

"There is little more to tell," said Dringo. "Though I don't know where to begin or whether I can survive the task, I seek my father. Without the aid of Gasterlo tonight, my journey would have ended with only my gnawed bones marking the failure of my mission. But it is a deathbed promise I made to my mother." Dringo made a gesture with his hand. "You all have spoken disparagingly of your fathers this evening, and I well understand why. Yet, you have someone to measure yourself to. I do not."

The table fell silent for a moment. But then Cavour leaned forward in a conspiratorial manner. "I have an outrageous idea, Dringo. Join us at the collegeum. What better way to prepare yourself for the rigors ahead than to have a quiver of spells at your call?"

At once everyone spoke: "Yes!" cried Tryllo. "Splendid!" said Zimmie. "Bravo!" agreed Popo. Luppie raised his beer in a salute, and he and Gasterlo clanked their tankards.

Dringo was bewildered, dizzy with drink and the onslaught of thoughts racing through his mind. It *was* an outrageous idea. "How can that happen? I have only a meager purse. I have no father who has provided a stipend. I know nothing of magic, and obviously you all have some basic skills." He proceeded to give a litany of other arguments, his voice becoming ever more plaintive as he realized that suddenly he *did* want this, more than anything.

"Fiddlefaddle," said Cavour. "The collegeum has been funded by the Magicians Guild. One more scholar will hardly matter. We will help cover any incidentals. Won't we, fellows? As for thaumaturgical abilities, we are all fledglings. Gasterlo here is the only one that has more than rudimentary skills."

"I am honored, my fine new friends," said Dringo earnestly. "But you hold a station high above me. It will be obvious to this Lord Lychenbarr of whom you speak that I don't belong."

He hesitated a moment and then added in a somber tone, "I am a bastard."

They all looked at each other, and then suddenly the entire table broke out in raucous laughter.

Finally, Gasterlo spoke, though haltingly, unable to contain his amusement: "We're *all* bastards, Dringo. You don't imagine that magicians take wives, do you? They live in their manses surrounded by poinctures, sandestins and other entities. Their energies flow in directions that at times seem not even human. They are capricious at best and unreliable always. I suppose my father has sired many bastards; and why he chose me is as mysterious as the most complex spells are to my untutored mind."

"Makes me wonder if I want that for myself," joked Tryllo. "Dringo can assume my place."

Cavour placed a hand on the table, palm down. "Oh, we will be different. Let us make a pact now, that one: We will remain friends and not become factious old men; and two: We will use our skills in a light-hearted manner."

One by one the young men laid a hand on another. They all turned to Dringo.

With a smile, he added his hand to the stack.

LORD LYCHENBARR frowned down at the assemblage from a raised platform. He paced the dais, his robes swishing the air in the muted chamber like the sound of rustling leaves. "I am tasked," he finally began in a voice both powerful and resonant, "with transforming you nescient novices into wizards. It would be easier—much easier, in fact—to change a grub into an eagle."

Dringo heard Tryllo whisper something to Popo and they both laughed.

Lord Lychenbarr's lean face, elongated further by a thin, grey wisp of a beard, darkened with annoyance. He murmured a series of inaudible words.

As if all sound had been banished, the audarium fell silent. The shifting of feet, the rustle of paper, even the slight wheeze of Zimmie's breathing ceased instantaneously. Dringo could not move. He tried to look to his side but his sight was as constrained as his body. A burning prickle began to build within his bowels and quickly bloomed in intensity.

Lord Lychenbarr glared at them. "To say I require absolute obedience and submission to my will in all things can be assumed." He smiled, but it was more a look of malice. "Let me add, I also demand quietude and attentiveness. Are there any questions?"

They all remained motionless, of course.

"Good, then we will proceed." he said.

"I just activated three somewhat minor spells in rapid succession." He raised a finger. "The first was the Spell of Unbending Rigiditosity." He added a second upraised finger. "The second was just a tincture of Lugwiler's Dismal Itch—you *would* not want to experience it in its undiluted grandeur. And the third ..."

By this time a fire burned vertically through Dringo's entrails. So great was the pruritus that he would have torn into his body to reach the source.

Lord Lychenbarr paused as if he had forgotten his train of thought. "Ahh ... yes, I neglected to verbalize the third." He laughed, and then spoke a complex chain of strange syllables.

At once, the room was filled with groans of relief. Dringo looked about the room and could see that they all had suffered as greatly as he.

Lord Lychenbarr continued without notice. "The third was Triskole's Fundamental Reversal that removed the two previous spells. The ability to hold even one such spell in one's mind requires much study and meticulous execution. To utter one mistaken pervulsion will cause unanticipated results. With that in mind we will begin with Amberlin's Warning of Infinite Consequences, a precept critical to the structure of all spells."

Their first day was a day of humiliation and mortification. Even Gasterlo, who all agreed was at least initially more skilled, was inept. Surprisingly, Dringo found Lord Lychenbarr's lecture on theory comprehensible, although his first attempt at effecting a primary spell spectacularly futile. Yet, he didn't feel overwhelmed, and a real glimmer of confidence began to form. As they filed from the room with Lord Lychenbarr's exceedingly crude derision keeping pace with them, Dringo's high spirits, however, were shattered.

"Dringo, I'll see you in my chamber before your dinner," Lord Lychenbarr commanded.

Well, he knew it was coming. The morning they departed the inn for the collegeum, the seven of them had planned how they might pull off the ruse. To better look the part of a young aristocrat, his friends had each donated a few pieces of fine clothing. Tryllo offered to vouch for

Dringo. "You will be a distant relative whose family is highly regarded by my father," suggested Tryllo. "The worse that will happen is that Lord Lychenbarr will place his boot up my arse right after he does the same to Dringo." The story would be that Dringo's father, a mighty magician, was delayed in hearing word of the formation of the school and had sent Dringo on while he would make arrangements with the Guild.

Entering Lord Lychenbarr's chamber, Dringo stiffened his shoulders and tried to appear assured. "Lord Lychenbarr, you wished to speak to me?"

Lord Lychenbarr stroked his wiry chin-whiskers and stared at Dringo. Finally he spoke: "Dringo, I have no authoritative documentation enrolling you into the collegeum. Nor have the appropriate funds arrived."

Dringo held his gaze and answered with as much boldness as he dared. "I'm certain my credentials are enroute, Lord Lychenbarr. I traveled from lands west of the Flattened Sea. I must have outraced the messenger with the documents."

"I'm afraid that explanation will not suffice," said Lord Lychenbarr, shaking his head.

His friends had suggested that Dringo should use bombast and threaten Lord Lychenbarr with the wrath of a powerful father if necessary; however, Dringo was now certain that approach would not work. It was obvious that Lord Lychenbarr could not be intimidated, and it would only open the door to questions for which he had no answers. "I plead for your indulgence, Lord Lychenbarr. This first day has humbled me, but I eagerly await your instruction tomorrow. I will do better. I urge you not to dismiss me."

Lord Lychenbarr regarded him with a look of contemplation, but then surprised Dringo by saying, "I'll wait a few days. Go to your dinner and out of my sight."

Dringo left determined to think no more on the matter. There was nothing else he could do, in any event. After all, the sun might neglect to rise tomorrow leaving that difficulty in obscurity.

The next day, Lord Lychenbarr drove them with relentless energy, demanding exactitude in all things and punishing errors with zest. Dringo, in particular, received painful attention. Late in the day, Lord Lychenbarr departed the room without a word and did not return, leaving them to debate whether they, too, could depart for dinner. Lugwiler's Itch was very much on their minds.

The following day saw little improvement; nor the day after. On the fifth day, Dringo and Gasterlo managed a momentary Spell of Refulgent

Luminosity. Their excitement spurred the others, and within two more days the entire class could duplicate the feat.

The following weeks saw a transformation in Lord Lychenbarr that was as magical as anything Dringo could have imagined. Their mentor had become a patient and enthusiastic teacher, now as quick with praise and encouragement as he had previously been cynical and invective. One evening, following a day of tedious dissection of Killiclaw"s Primer of Practical Magic, he asked them all to join him on his balustraded aerie for a drink. The speckled sun doddered on rays of pale, lavender beams as it fell below the rounded hills of the Ambit and the evening air was cool and fragrant with the sweet aroma of dymphny and telanxis.

"Initially, I resented having to leave my own manse," began Lord Lychenbarr. "You have won me over with your youthful energy and enthusiasm." He paused to refill their glasses with a rich, yellow wine. "I am so satisfied with your progress that I've decided you are ready for your first practical test tonight."

This was greeted with loud moans and mumbled complaints.

Lord Lychenbarr laughed. "Here is your task: You are free to make the journey to Grippo's this evening. I warn you, the dangers are plenitude: visps; erbs; fermines; asms; all the hideous creations of magic gone awry." He waited a moment, and then added, "Of course, if you don't feel ready ..."

Dringo was the first to voice: "NO! We're ready."

A chorus of loud agreement echoed into the purple twilight.

The young mages returned the next evening, blurry-eyed and unsteady, but in a carefree and relaxed demeanor. Dringo also felt a renewed self-assurance. It was one thing to mouth a few words from memory, and quite another to come forth with precision the exact pervulsions necessary when under duress. He and Gasterlo had had a good laugh after arriving at Grippo's the previous night as they recalled their first fearful meeting, now seemingly so long ago.

Lord Lychenbarr began joining them for dinner in the small common room laid out for that purpose. The evenings became as much a time for learning as any daytime lecture. The pragmatic aspects of thaumaturgy just seemed to make more sense following a fine meal lubricated with even finer wine.

The months progressed rapidly. The winter was mild in spite of little assistance from the sun that seemed to labor every morn to rise above the frosted edge of the horizon. Tryllo Makshaw, though not at all insufficient in ability, decided to leave the Collegeum of Mauge. "We labor while the dying earth exults in its release. We should be exuberant in joined celebration while this glorious planet gives forth its fruits and wines, its nymphs frolic in unabashed nakedness and the songs of the dying earth still echo in our ears."

Though Tryllo was missed, especially during their occasional sojourns to Grippo's, the demands of Lord Lychenbarr were unceasing, leaving them little time to think on the matter. Dringo continued to excel, but he still worried that Lord Lychenbarr might renew his investigation into the lack of his enrollment documents. He took solace in that at least he was much better prepared to meet the unknown challenges once he resumed the search for his father.

Lord Lychenbarr never allowed the young magicians to progress beyond the use of madlings, a lesser and thus more controllable form of sandestin. To attempt encodement of the working instructions of a spell into the unpredictable mind of a higher entity had caused misadventure to many wizards. He pointedly emphasized caution every day the lessons entailed practical employment.

Disaster struck, as is usually the case in all things subject to the hubris of young men.

Cavour Senthgorr was attempting a derivation of the Spell of Hastening Profundity. Failure to recite the pervulsion correctly triggered a lesser entity to enlist the aid of a demon of known irritability and vengeful retribution.

The demon stood swathed in the gases and stenches of his sub-world. He loomed above them turning his head back and forth with malevolent smaragdine-colored eyes. A ridged crest fanned the length of his back like the dorsal fin of a sea creature. Below a pouched gut that gave the appearance of a large, living meal just eaten, swayed a pendulous sex organ. It looked at Cavour and spoke: "Your beckoning is inconvenient. However, I subjugate my own desires to your will." Its voice was surprisingly human-sounding and serene, made ghastly by his next words: "I will require an assistant." He again looked around the room and returned his eyes on Cavour. "None of you will suffice. I will make a golem using the eyes of ..." he looked at Gasterlo, "you." He turned to Popo Killraye. "I will use your legs. They look sturdy enough. And I think ..."

Cavour's voice croaked as he yelled, "Halt! I discharge you from your task. You may return to your abode."

The demon chortled. "One instruction at a time. Precedence requires me to forgo that option." He turned back to his inspection of body parts with what may have been a grin splitting its maw.

Dringo looked over to Lord Lychenbarr who appeared deep in thought as he chuntered a spell in sotto voice. His brow was furrowed in worry. Dringo tried to deduce what type of spell Lord Lychenbarr would attempt: Probably the Agency of Far Dispatch. Whatever … it didn't seem to be effective. What could fortify his spell?

On impulse he uttered Jonko's Gentle Aswaggment of Imperious Desires.

With wonder and relief, they all looked at each other in silence. The creature had vanished.

Lord Lychenbarr, visibly shaken, said to Dringo, "Well done. What made you think that spell would work?"

"The demon seemed so obdurate in its intentions that it occurred to me that your spell couldn't work without a mollifying additive. We've used Jonko's Gentle Aswaggment to calm small forest animals before." He shrugged and splayed out his arms. "It's all I could contrive at the moment."

Lord Lychenbarr approached Dringo and put a boney arm around his shoulders. It was the first physical contact any one of them had ever had with this enigmatic man. "I say again, well done. I would not have thought to co-join those spells. I can see now where the two used in conjunction could have many useful applications. I believe we shall have an extra ration of spirits with our dinner tonight. Certainly, I will." He turned and departed the room.

Dringo could still feel lingering warmth on his shoulder. *"Why, he is nothing but a frail, old man beneath those flowing robes,"* he thought with a surge of affection.

Following dinner that evening Lord Lychenbarr asked Dringo to see him in his chambers. Dringo had no reason to be uneasy following an amiable meal where Lord Lychenbarr once more praised Dringo's resourcefulness. That changed as he entered the chambers.

Lord Lychenbarr began sternly, "I have been instructed that without a sponsor you are to be dismissed."

Dringo paled. "Surely, given some more time …."

Lord Lychenbarr's raised a hand in a stopping motion. "You have done well here, Dringo; and I am not one who takes commands from my peers. His features softened and then a smile. "You have a sponsor, Dringo. I will be your benefactor."

Lord Lychenbarr became cautionary at the Collegeum of Mauge. "I realize now that I have imposed too much of my own brashness in your tutorage. After that near disaster with the demon, we will again concentrate more on theory and put more emphasis on the usage of activans and potions. Even the dominant magicians of the Grand Motholam eventually undid themselves through impetuosity and lack of rigor."

Powerful magicians began to visit the collegeum as rumor spread that Lychenbarr was developing potential rivals. Dringo thought them all uniformly haughty, boastful, arrogant, supercilious, and pompous. These powerful pandalects, without fail, immediately attempted to impose their own distorted imprimatur; and it was obvious to Dringo that Lord Lychenbarr realized that he had made a mistake in allowing such visits. None alarmed him more than when he announced that a communication arrived stating that Iucounu the Laughing Magician would honor the collegeum with an assessment.

Iucounu chose to use a whirl-away of grandiose design. Dringo and his fellow students watched from an upper window as the corpulent wizard bounded from the conveyance, crossed a short expanse of swaying grasses on his stubby legs and called into the manse commandingly, "It is Iucounu. Present yourself before my felicitous thoughts are overtaken by irritation and vex."

A servant greeted Iucounu and led him inside and up the stairs to the audarium where they all awaited.

Lord Lychenbarr welcomed Iucounu. "Was your journey without trial?"

Iucounu, in his notably squeaky voice, giggled. "One minor annoyance that was quickly dispatched. Nothing of consequence to one such as myself."

He wore an ill-fitting gown of pale gentian with maroon abstract designs. It did little to mask his rotundity. His large head rode above the silken mass like a boulder perpetually out of balance. "So these are the young mages I hear so much about," he said, looking about the room. Suddenly, Iucounu screamed a high-pitched invective that tested the upper range of the audible spectrum. He held out an arm with his finger rigid in accusation.

"Cugel. It is you!"

Lord Lychenbarr followed the line of Iucounu's venomous stare. He turned to him. "You are mistaken. This is Dringo."

Iucounu squinted. He accessed a pair of gold-rimmed spectacles from some hidden reservoir of fabric and walked a few steps closer. "Ahh .... The resemblance is uncanny. The same slender stature. Hair the color of a crow's wing. The visage of a fox." Iucounu frowned but seemed to calm.

A stunned Dringo stepped forward. “Then you know my father?” he asked without guile or premonition. “My quest is to seek him out.”

Iucounu squealed, “Do I know your father? Do I know your father? A thief and a trickster. He irritates me worse than a canker on my scrotum.” He raised an arm and rushed forward as if to strike Dringo.

Lord Lychenbarr raced forward and placed himself between the two. “Stop, at once! Iucounu, I will not allow you to disrupt the harmony of this collegeum. Whatever your annoyance, Dringo has done you no mischief. He is —”

Iucounu chanted a spell of spatial transposition hurling Lord Lychenbarr across the room and against the wall with such force that stones loosened and fell, ribbons of dust drifted from the rafters covering Lord Lychenbarr who lay slumped on the floor.

Dringo rushed to his side.

Lord Lychenbarr tried to raise his head but failed. Dringo knelt and cupped the back of his head.

“I’m sorry, Dringo …” Lord Lychenbarr managed in an old man’s voice. His hand searched for Dringo’s and placed an object the size and weight of a glass marble firmly into his palm. “My legacy to you, my dear friend,” he whispered.

Iucounu towered over them. “Dringo, you are too much in your father’s image. You want your father? You shall have him!” He invoked the Agency of Far Dispatch followed by an infliction of the Spell of Forlorn Encystment.

Dringo could hear the sound of Iucounu’s girlish whinny as reality shifted in a dizzying swirl of sky and stars and awareness.

DRINGO LOOKED at himself through an ocher err-light, his image distorted further by a strange opaqueness, as if looking through amber. His eyes were open but unblinking. No movement was discernable. Nor was there a trace of sound. He tried to move. It was a sensation beyond the scope of anything he could imagine. Null. Nothingness. An absolute disconnect between mind and body. He sensed no beat of his heart, and he realized at that moment that he did not breathe. There was no pain. There was no cold. There was no heat. Was there life, even? So this was the Spell of Forlorn Encystment. This was worse than being buried alive. Wait! He *was* buried alive. Forty-five miles beneath the surface of the earth to be exact. But there was no hope even for death to bring a cessation of this perpetual nullity. He turned his mind towards Iucounu. There was hate, at least. But he couldn't even hold on to that because if it was possible to still "feel" anything, he did still feel the fragility of Lord Lychenbarr's head as he cradled it in his hand. Was Lord Lychenbarr yet alive? Dringo cried. But he didn't cry.

Time passed. Or he assumed it passed. His universe now ran on a different clock. He didn't seem to sleep, but at times awareness of his own thoughts would recede without volition and then coalesce like a dream suddenly coming into focus. It occurred to him that madness would be the adjunct to his situation. He began to discipline his mind by recalling the entirety of every spell he had learned with each pervulsion recited in exactitude. A mistake required him to start from the beginning. Later, the slightest hesitation was cause enough to start all over again. More time passed.

Dringo was in one of his less cognitive states, his mind meandering as he gazed at himself in the strange reflection of his encystment, when suddenly he noticed a minor imperfection in his countenance that had gone unnoticed. Like passing a painting on a wall, day in and day out, while being unaware of the actual image until one actually *looks* at it. For the first time he concentrated on the image. Although indistinct and vague, there were other minor differences that suddenly seemed obvious. Now he understood what Iucounu meant when he told Dringo he could have his father!

He was looking at his father, not himself. Iucounu had placed him facing Cugel. The irony and the cruelty were manifold and magnified.

The reality shift was almost physical. Where before there didn't seem to be perception of depth, now he could see that Cugel was no more than an arm's reach away. What might be going through his mind? He didn't even know he had a son. Would he think that Iucounu had created a doppelganger as a further perverted punishment? Maybe Cugel's sanity had already departed his body and his thoughts would be inconsequential. *My father*. Now that was something to contemplate.

Time progressed. Dringo existed in what he now thought of more and more as a dreamlike state, vacillating at various levels of awareness. His initial claustrophobic fears of insanity receded. At times he looked into his father's eyes and had imaginary conversations in his head. He found other matters to dwell upon. Would he even be aware of the sun's final struggle when it came?

It was during one such contemplative moment when he became aware of a sensation. It was infinitesimally slight. But when there is nothing, then *anything* seems immense. Some time passed before he could even place the locale on his body; so long it seemed that he had been disassociated from it. It was the orb that Lord Lychenbarr had given him. It moved.

Physical awareness grew. First his hand began to tingle, and then it felt like an animal was running up and down his arm. Next he became aware of heat and odors, and his lungs filled with a gasp of hot, stale air. He blinked. Realized he blinked, and blinked again.

Perched on a rock shelf of only a few inches width and approximately a foot away, there sat a miniature halfling with a smug look on its impish face. "My indenture is complete," it said. "Release me—as I have released you—so that I may return to the sub-world."

Dringo moved his head about. He *was* free. He need only say a spell to return to the surface. "I am indebted to you, little friend," spoke Dringo. His words sounded strange to his ears.

The creature sneered, baring needle-sharp canines. "I am not your friend and I am not small. I only assume this size because crushing you would negate a satisfactory fulfillment of my obligation. How do you think I fit into Lord Lychenbarr's orb? Now release me."

"Of course, you are relea—"

The entity disappeared.

"—sed."

Dringo's encystment was gone but the hollow in the earth created by its removal was barely large enough to turn his shoulders. Cugel's encystment was as before. The features of his father were easier discernable now. He reached out and touched its surface. Though his hand could not penetrate it, neither could he feel it. Was Cugel aware? He was soon to be very surprised if he was not. Dringo rehearsed the required six lines to expel himself to the surface. It was increasingly more difficult to breath and the heat was unbearable. He confidently recited the words.

Dringo was ousted like a living magma. He lay on wet grass too weak to move other than to suck in the cool air. It was night; or had the sun gone out? At the moment it did not concern him. Eventually, he stood on his unstable legs and slowly paced in the darkness. Before he lost his nerve, he uttered the identical pervulsions with the addition of three critical words.

The ground shivered, then quaked, then erupted as Cugel was ejected to a spot not three feet away from where Dringo stood. Cugel lay motionless for a disheartening length of time. In the gloom Dringo could see that his chest did rise and fall; but was there a sane man in the body?

Abruptly, Cugel sat up. "I'm thirsty," were the first words Dringo heard spoken by his father.

"Can you stand?" asked Dringo. "We will have to go in search of water."

Cugel tried to lift himself using an arm to lever himself up but failed. "A moment, first. I think my time beneath the earth is longer than I supposed." He lifted his head towards the sky. "Is it night or has the sun cast its last shadow on the dying earth?"

Dringo looked heavenward also. "I think it is night only. We have twilight enough to dimly see each other and the ground beneath us, but we will know in a few hours."

Cugel laughed. "Just so!" He squinted at Dringo. "Are you a cruel joke played on me by Iucounu? You appear to be a replica of me, though not so dashing." Without waiting for an answer, he slowly turned on his side and rolled to a crouch, then rose up to a standing position. "Well, if you are a demon sent to mimic me and raise false hope, at least lead me to some water before you inter me again."

Dringo answered, "I assure you I am of flesh and blood. But you are astute in suspecting the malicious frolic of Iucounu. More than you can imagine, Cugel."

"You know me by name! More reason to suspect a foul hand at play."

Dringo ignored the comment and turned to face the downward slope of the hillock upon which they had found themselves expelled. "Come, let us seek some water. We have much to talk about."

They stumbled down the small hill in the darkness. Twice Cugel stopped and sat, the second time saying, "I will wait here while you search. You seem more sprightly than I. You may even find a suitable container for returning the refreshment, thus eliminating the need for both of us to traverse these difficult slopes." Dringo disregarded Cugel's complaints and continued on. The terrain kept leading lower to eventually funnel them into a line of fragrant Myrhadian trees that flanked a small arroyo from which they could hear the gurgle of a brook. Both of them cupped hand after hand of the sweet water until their stomachs were distended gourds.

They sat together on a broad, flat rock above the water line.

Cugel, in a much improved humor, smiled and said to Dringo, "Your resemblance to my own is remarkable. Who are you, if not a minion of Iucounu?"

Dringo shook his head at Cugel's opacity. "You can't fathom another possibility?"

Cugel sat mutely with thin, pursed lips.

Dringo realized that his impatience with his father was more a matter of anxiety than frustration. "I am your son!" he blurted.

He watched Cugel's face closely for a reaction. It was not what he expected.

Cugel laughed uncontrollably. "That is an impossibility. You are too close to my own age. Iucounu, show yourself. Your trickery lacks coherency." He leaned forward to study Dringo's features. Suddenly, he raged: "Clarity has reasserted itself. Iucounu, you have robbed me of more years than I ever imagined! The Spell of Forlorn Encystment has maddened me! I thought myself buried a year or perhaps two, but this? It is too much. The Law of Equipoise has been tilted to an extreme that demands equally severe punition."

Finally he calmed. He looked again towards Dringo. "So I have a son. Who is your mother? Perhaps you can refresh my memory?"

"My mother's name was Ammadine. Sadly, she is gone now."

Cugel shook is head. "No, I don't remember. However, it is an appealing name. Was she pretty?"

"She was one of the Seventeen Virgins of Symnathis. They are chosen for their beauty and purity, and their arrival at the Grand Pageant is the signal event of the gala. The caravan that was to deliver the young virgins was one year guarded by a young man calling himself Cugel the Clever. Only two arrived as maidens. My mother was not one of them."

A smile or a smirk crossed Cugel's face. Dringo couldn't tell in the faint light. "Yes, I remember. A misunderstanding of responsibility. I was not given an opportunity to enlighten the Grand Thearch. The caravan arrived without incident, and I would rate my conduct at a value well above the remuneration agreed upon, which I might add was never forthcoming." He paused and reflected. "Was your mother light of hair with amber-grey eyes?"

Dringo answered, "No."

"Ahh. Was she short with dark hair and breasts that swelled—"

"My mother," Dringo interrupted, "was a young girl who lost her high station and gave birth to a bastard son who grew up without a father ..." His voice faltered.

Cugel nodded. "This I regret. You should consider that during this time Iucounu was exacting harsh punishments upon me for motives both unreasonable in their pettiness, and lack of proportionality, considering the absence of ill will on my part." His tone lost its flippancy. "I had thought myself finally free of Iucounu, but he found a way to return from his dissolution. Whether from the Overworld, the Underworld or the Demonworld, I know not. But that fact remains. And his revenge was the Spell of Forlorn Encystment."

Dringo couldn't help but look at his father somewhat differently, "I too, know first-hand the brutality of Iucounu, father."

Cugel relaxed back on the rock. "Tell me your story."

When Dringo had finished, Cugel said to him, "We have much more to tell each other, and I think you have a great deal to teach me of magic. It is settled then. We will join forces to plan the ultimate prank on the Laughing Magician."

They clasped hands in their oath. The dawn light had brightened the sky and the red orb crested the very hill they had earlier descended.

"I see the sun still rises," said Cugel to his son. "It appears that this tired old earth has one more day in it. Let us get started."

THE END

AFTERWORD:

I DISCOVERED Jack Vance at the very beginning of my love affair with fantasy and science fiction. His *Vandals of the Void*, published by the John C. Winston Company, was either the second or the third hardcover book I ever bought; but it was primarily through the Ace Doubles, with their unique branding element of two novels published back-to-back and their imaginative cover art by such greats as Jack Gaughan, Ed Emshwiller, and Ed Valigursky, that I started developing a true appreciation of Jack's remarkable skills. Having already worked my way through the Winston juveniles and the Robert Heinlein young adult novels at the local library, I hungered for more sophisticated reading. The Ace Doubles at thirty-five cents each were the perfect affordable next step. *Big Planet* and *Slaves of the Klau*; *The Dragon Masters* and *The Five Gold Bands*—now that was more what I was looking for!

For a young teen boy, though, his books were a challenge. I found myself using the dictionary much more often than normal. It took a couple of his books for me to realize that he even made up words, for cripes sake! His characters had weird names and often they were not very admirable. I was a DC comic guy and I was used to my Superheroes being, well, Superheroes. Still, there was something about this Jack Vance that appealed to me. It was the publication of *The Eyes of the Overworld* that made Jack Vance one of my favorite authors. It is the second of the four Dying Earth novels, and the first that introduces the character, Cugel the Clever. I mark that moment as the first time I read a book and actually savored the *words* that made up the story. Jack Vance's novels had always transported me to strange worlds full of colors and languages and customs, but now for the first time I realized *how* he did it. There was a reason I had to occasionally look up a word. There was a purpose in Jack Vance making up a word.

Mark Twain wrote: "The difference between the almost right word & the right word is really a large matter—it's the difference between the lightning bug and the lightning."

Jack Vance was asked once at a SF convention how he came up with the name "Cugel," or, for that matter, any of his character's names. He answered, "I come up with a name and roll it around on my tongue to see how it sounds." Jack Vance has been called the Shakespeare of science fiction. I roll that around with my tongue and it sounds just right.

—Byron Tetrick

TANITH LEE

Evillo the Uncunning

TANITH LEE is one of the best-known and most prolific of modern fantasists, with more than a hundred books to her credit, including (among many others) *The Birthgrave*, *Drinking Sapphire Wine*, *Don't Bite The Sun*, *Night's Master*, *The Storm Lord*, *Sung In Shadow*, *Volkhavaar*, *Anackire*. *Night's Sorceries*, *Black Unicorn*, *Days of Grass*, *The Blood of Roses*, *Vivia*, *Reigning Cats and Dogs*, *When the Lights Go Out*, *Elephantasm*, *The Gods Are Thirsty*, *Cast a Bright Shadow*, *Here In Cold Hell*, *Faces Under Water*, *White As Snow*, *Mortal Suns*, *Death of the Day*, *Metallic Love*, *No Flame But Mine*, *Piratica: Singular Girl's Adventure Upon the High Seas*, and a sequel to *Piratica*, called *Piratica 2: Return to Parrot Island*. Her numerous short stories have been collected in *Red As Blood*, *Tamastara*, *The Gorgon*, *Dreams of Dark and Light*, *Nightshades*, and *The Forests of the Night*. Her short story "The Gorgon" won her a World Fantasy Award in 1983, and her short story "Elle Est Trois (La Mort)" won her another World Fantasy Award in 1984. Her most recent books are *The Secret Books of Paradys* and a new collection, *Tempting the Gods*. She lives with her husband in the south of England.

Filling your head with stories of wild adventure and heroic deeds is a tempting way to pass the time when you live in a place as boring as the tiny charmless village of Ratgrad, but as Evillo the Uncunning is about to learn, trying to *duplicate* those adventures can get you into more trouble than you're really prepared to handle…

Evillo the Uncunning

TANITH LEE

1: Above Derna

Some way up behind the steep forested canyon wherethrough flows the slender River Derna, lies a depressing landscape dotted with small villages. One evening, a male child of less than two years was found wandering in the vicinity. Smothered by the dim red dying of the light, among tall clumps of spite-grass and blackly spreading thorn-willow, the infant might easily have gone unnoticed. But it is possible his gleaming golden hair may have been mistaken for something valuable in the metallic way.

The fellow who did so, by name Swind, having learned his error, still carried the infant to the adjacent village of Ratgrad.

"Ho, Swind: Could you not have left that thing where it was? Where is your charity? No doubt some passing hungry gib or ghoul would have welcomed it."

"Tush," said Swind sullenly, dumping the crying boy in the dirt. "In the era of sun's death, life is ever valuable and must be preserved—so that it may also be punished for the insolence of persisting."

Accordingly Swind and his wife, Slannt, were given the child to raise, which they did following the village tradition. They starved the boy and rained constant blows upon him, these actions ornamented by witty verbal abuse in the village mode. Despite such care, he grew to the age of eighteen. He was well-made and handsome, with a tawny skin, large dark eyes, and his hair still golden under the filth Slannt and others diligently rubbed in it.

His given name was Blurkel. But by the time of his seventh year, he thought nevertheless that he had recalled his *real* name, which was, he believed, Evillo. Nothing else could he remember of his former life.

Ratgrad was married to another local village, the equally charmless Plodge. Once every month, the denizens of both villages would meet on a bare rock, known either as Ratplod or Plodrat Spike. There they would sit about a large fire and drink fermented erb berries, next singing various unharmonious songs, and telling stories of the most uninspiring kind.

Fell the day of the festival.

To the Spike trooped all Ratgrad, Evillo perforce going with them.

The celebration proceeded as it always did, becoming more loathesome by the minute. By the hour that the old sun began to crawl to its lair in the west, the Spike and its surrounding shrubland rang to uncouth carroling and eructations.

Evillo, to escape the attentions of certain unpalatable village maidens, had climbed up a tall lone daobado that spread its bronzy limbs behind the rock. From here, suddenly he beheld a solitary figure walking towards the Spike. Evillo stared with all the power of his dark eyes, thinking perhaps that he imagined what he saw; visitors were infrequent thereabouts. But curiously, as a sunfall red as an over-aged wine of Tanvilkat obscured the scene, the figure grew ever more apparent. It had the shape of a man, but was closely robed and hooded.

Something thundered in Evillo's ears: his heart.

Just then, the village look-out, who was that evening the master-hacker Fawp, also noted an arrival and let out a yowl.

Startled silence beset the revellers. Many jumped drunkenly to their feet, and every eye fixed upon the grey-cloaked stranger.

"Stay,'" bellowed Fawp, who had drawn his cleaver. "Proclaim your type and intention."

"Also be aware," added Glak, the carcass-heaver, "while we slay enemies instanter, friends who visit us are required to present a gift."

The mysterious figure had drawn near and now spoke in a low and sonorous tone.

"I am neither enemy nor friend. But I will present a gift."

Stupid greed overcame the stupid bravado of the villagers. They pressed forward and now clustered about the stranger as he entered the sphere of firelight.

Up in the tree, Evillo watched, half waiting for some magic sloughing of disguise, revealing the man to be a frit or other fiend. But the hooded figure did not metamorph into anything else. He came to the fireside and rested himself on a large flat stone. And precisely then, through the mesh of the hood which concealed his face, Evillo fancied that he glimpsed two human eyes that glowed with a mental ability far beyond the average. For a moment, they met his own, and then passed on.

"Be seated," said the stranger to the villagers, and such was his authority that each of them at once obeyed. "The gift I offer is modest, but you shall have it. Know then, I am Canja Veck the Fabler. He who is compelled, by a nameless but omnipotent force, to travel the dying earth, and there to recount its stories to any that will hear."

It was as if the mindless, drunken clamour had never been. As if the sinking sun had wiped all trace of it away with the last swipe of a wine-soaked sponge. In utter stillness, eyes wide and lips parted, the village folk sat waiting like ensorcelled children. And Evillo with them; he more than all.

For every hour of that night of ever-unmooned nights, the Fabler told his tales.

They were by turns swift and fearful, glamorous and enmarvelled, mystic, ribald, hilarious, and of a shocking horror. Canja Veck so controlled his captive audience that none moved more than a muscle, gave no sign of life beyond a blink, a gasp, a sigh or flash of laughter. Drink untasted, fire smouldering low, so they sat. While for Evillo, it was as if at last he had found true reality, the world itself, and it was nothing like the cramped cell he had, from two years old, been forced to occupy.

As he outlined the histories of his heroes and heroines, Canja Veck described also the varieties of place that formed a backdrop. Of Ascolais he spoke, and the white, half-ruined city of Kaiin, of Saponid lands, whose golden-eyed peoples dwelled beyond high Fer Aquila. He suggested the oblique Land of the Falling Wall, and wild Kauchique, and such antique metropoli as doomed Olek'hnit, and such occluded and occult regions as the Cobalt Mountains, and that fearsome forest the Lig Thig or Great Erm. He indicated the demonic realm of Jeldred, created only to house evil, which surely it did; Embelyon too, an alter-world the unseeable magician Pandelume had made to conceal himself, whose skies were fluctuant rainbows. And he told of Almery in the south,from whence stalked—less a hero than the transverse of all heroism—Cugel, the self-styled Clever, an arresting person, long of leg, deft of hand, light of finger, blessed by the luck of fiends—and the *un*luck of one cursed, which two states constantly cancelled each other out. Cugel was, besides, a perfect genius of cunning and razor wit, and also, on ocassion, an utter numbskull.

At last, the black of night grew threadbare in the east. The red sun pulled itself from sleep and glared upon the world that it must still serve, though itself of more than pensionable age.

The spellbound villagers slipped from their enchantment.

They stared eastward to gauge, in the manner of the time, how the solar disc fared. Seeing that it still burned, they looked around again to the rock where Canja Veck had been seated. But he was gone.

Only Evillo, who had not bothered with the sun, had seen him rise up, shake the dew from his robe, and move silently away. Only Evillo, sliding down the daobado, had dared pursue this mage among story-tellers away from the rock, the villages, and, without a backward glance, down into the cliffy forests above the Derna.

ABOUT MIDDAY, Evillo caught up to Canja Veck, who had paused on a wooded spur. Far below, the river was now visible, splashing like a hurried serpent through the ravine.

"Mighty sir—"

Canja Veck did not turn.

"Sir—great magician—"

To this, Canja Veck responded. "My title is Fabler."

"Mighty Fabler—" but here Evillo, steeped so long in village concepts, could think of no means to convey his wants. Instead, in embarrassed banality he asked, "But are you not hungry, sir? Have you eaten today?"

"No," replied Canja Veck gravely, "but I have eaten tomorrow, that tomorrow when the sun goes black. Eaten it entire."

Evillo waited in great awe.

"By which I mean," Canja Veck amended gently, "as any story-maker will, that I see the future as well as the past. I think you have not," he added, "drunk their vile brew of fermented erb berry. Good. It is named, like the similarly styled tea, less for its stimulous than for the sting included in over-imbibition. Since an actual erb, as you may know, is a combination of man, bear, lank-lizard, and demon. Or so certain sorces report."

"Phandaal's Purple Book?" hazarded Evillo, referring back to the Fabler's tales.

Canja Veck shook his head. Mildly, he inquired, "What do you wish from me?"

Evillo felt that he could not speak. He spread his arms and gazed in desperation. "I wish—to live—the life of such a hero as Guyal—or Turjan—or Cugel! Cugel the most."

"Callous and manipulative Cugel? Clever Cugel the fool?"

Evillo deemed himself incapable of constructing sentences. He put his hands into his filthy hair and tore it in frustration.

"Peace," said Canja Veck. "Look how far already you have come from your beginnings. If you will be the hero of a story, that fate is yours to conjur. There lies the river, and there the ancient broken road that will lead you to Porphiron Scar, and thence to white-walled Kaiin."

"And Almery—" whispered Evillo.

"A journey of long months," said Canja Veck, cool as distant stars. "Unless your transport should be super-normal."

Evillo, in a sort of exultant panic, stared out across the river to the road, which, when seen from this height, was narrow as a thread of woven flint. A shadow shifted, noiseless, sudden. Looking about, Evillo saw that Canja Veck had once more serenely vanished. The young man stood alone upon the brink of his destiny, and of the cliff. And in that second, a ghastly and insane shriek sounded from the air. Down swept a gaunt black bird, one third the size of a full-grown man, its scarlet beak levelled squarely at Evillo's newly-woken heart. Whether it were self-determined or the misstep of terror, Evillo sprang straight off the spur, and, in another moment, was hurtling towards the river far beneath.

2: Khiss

THREE WINDS slapped Evillo's face as he fell. Then he was dashed into the river, which, possibly irritated by his unanounced advent, beat him as severely as any Ratgradian. Plunged through silver water to black, Evillo grew unaware for an indeterminate duration.

This trance ended however when an opposite propulsion seized him. He was borne again upward and crashed back through the surface of the Derna, as if through a plate of exploding glass.

Evillo, fighting for breath, found himself held high in the air by the brawny arms of a blue-scaled and blackly scowling man-creature of considerable girth.

"By Pizca Escaleron, incomparable god of my race, how darest thou violate the sacred deeps of the river?"

"I—" attempted Evillo, as he choked forth a percentage of said deeps from his lungs.

"Cease thy verminous squeaks, thou minuscule! Whence camest thou, with such impertinent rush? Didst even knock, thou rustical? Nay, thou didst in no sort. Know, thou intruding inculco, that I, a mighty lord among the river Fiscians, was just then in exquisite dalliance with a fair lady of my realm, which delicious process thou, by thy foul and uninvited entrance, hath disrupted. Had I not sworn upon the eternal fins of peerless Pizca Escaleron, to take no more than three lives in any morning, and having already availed myself early of today's quota, I would tear thee, limbs from torso, devour thine unworthy liver before thy degraded eyes, and cast thy remains into the realms of dreadful Kalu."

"I—" attempted Evillo once more.

"Pearl-button thy lips, thou failed oyster. I am done with thee. Go forth and suffer!"

And with these and similar sentiments, the creature flung Evillo all across the Derna and into some bushes of stinging leaves beyond the road.

Evillo crawled from the bushes and presently sat by the highway.

In fact, the road was often broken up by the ingress of the river. The traveller would be forced to detour here and there among banks of thorn and tubegrass, from which fluted the usual inane whistling. Leagues off, so Evillo thought, the land seemed to check. This was perhaps Porphiron Scar? As shock abated, Evillo felt his eagerness return. And not long after, he noted a tall male figure striding over the terrain towards him.

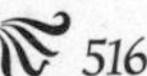

When the man drew level, Evillo got to his feet.

"Pardon an ignorant nobody," he cautiously began, "but does the city lie in that direction?"

The man was indeed very tall; his height was well above one and three quarter ells. Long black hair coursed to his waist, and his garments were the indigo and ebony shades of day sky and night. With dark blue eyes, he regarded Evillo. "My name," said this man, "is Kaiine. What do you deduce therefrom?"

"That you are a citizen of the city of Kaiin?" immoderatly supplied Evillo.

"Which may, naturally," said the man "be a false deduction. All of which you should certainly avoid. On the other hand, you are correct in my case. Be wary however, when you resume your trek, of the large and beautiful snail that lies in the grass at your feet."

In surprise, Evillo glanced down and beheld the snail. The tall gallant had already disappeared around a bend in the road, but Evillo had been most impressed by the care the man had taken over the fate of a snail. Unwarned, Evillo might well have trodden upon it. How very sensitive and civilized therefore must be all Kaiinians!

Evillo prepared to step carefully over the snail, which was indeed attractive, with a jade tinge to its body, its shell a crystalline whorl. The snail spoke: "Forgive me, my friend, I could not but overhear your exchange with the Darkographer Kaiine. Are you en route to the city?" Evillo exalted. A snail which spoke! And was also urbane! This surely was the very stuff of fable, magic, and sophistication!

"I am."

"Might I then trouble you to permit my accompanying you? I fear that you will need to port me, or I shall lag sadly behind. But I weigh little, and the occasional wholesome leaf or lactuca will sustain my existence. Nor do I crave any expensive alocholic beverages."

Evillo conceded this, and raised the snail. He placed it on his left shoulder, from which vantage, as the snail explained, it could see the road as well as he.

For a while then, they progressed in silence. Evillo was shyly tongue-tied, if the truth were told.

Eventually, the snail inaugurated a brief conversation. "The man with whom you formerly spoke is, as I mentioned, a darkographer. You ask, what then is a darkographer? He is one who maps the world, before the sun goes dark and melds everything with shadow.

"But it may be that you are curious too as to the circumstances of my being here, so far from my house at Kaiin. It chanced, during pursuit of my livlihood,which is to cure burns by silkenly crawling across the afflicted area, that a rogue subdued me with a drugged lettuce and bore me off. He intended, he shamelessly confessed, to boil me with garlic to tempt his desired mistress, a vile frog-eating harridan of Thamber Meadow, who is known to send men regularly to their deaths. My abductor meanwhile ranted that he had avoided someone unavoidable, by the simple expedient of not going near him, despite some inducement to do with a tapestry of gold, or some such yarn. Fortunately, another of the rogue's fellowship, being displeased with him, came after, and slew my persecutor on the road. Unnoted during the proceedings, I escaped. Since then, I have spent six days and nights on my return journey.

"Yet enough of me. Let us discuss you. What do you seek in white-walled Kaiin?"

Evillo was nervous that he might bore his eloquent companion. Modestly, he replied, "I am only a peasant of no account. But even I have heard of the wonders of the city."

"And your name?"

"I—call myself Evillo."

The snail seemed to cogitate. "That is a name unfamiliar to me. I myself am known as Khiss."

A couple more miles passed in quietness.

Then Khiss spoke again. "Tell me, friend Evillo, what trade or abilities do you bring to the city?"

Evillo sighed. "None that I know of."

"To succeed therein," Khiss continued in its musical, faintly tinkling voice, "you will require at least the skills of reading, numeracy, and fighting, not essentially in that order."

"I possess none of them."

"Alas," said Khiss. "Let us pause."

Dejectedly, Evillo, and so, the snail, once more sat down. They were by now on a long sweep of land, and saw the hyacinthine brink of the Scar directly before them. But what use was that? Plainly, Evillo was unfit to continue.

"What shall I do? Must I go back to the wedded despondancy of Ratgrad and Plodge?"

"Do not contemplate such a tragedy," advised Khiss fastidiously. "Attend now. I myself am willing to teach you the three abilities I have listed, plus several others. I will even teach you to cure burns, and a little magic, for example, perhaps, Phandaal's geas of the Unputdownable Tome, if not the indespensible but alarming Locative Selfulsion, this last being, I consider, a double-edged sword. In return for these lessons, however, due to the unmitagable Laws of Equivalence, you must in turn perform some slight corresponding services for myself. You will barely note these. Are you agreeable then to engage in such barter?"

Evillo's head whirled. He stared into the emerald eyes of the snail Khiss which, mounted on their tender jade stalks, gazed beadily into his.

"But how long will it take you to educate me? I am an ignoramus:"

"All the more swiftly then shall we go on. Erroneous old knowledge often impedes the entry of new. Be aware that my kind, being slow of motion, are flame-swift of thought and tutor accordingly. Had men only realized as much, their empires of stars had never floundered, nor would the expiring sun now pant and swoon, but, regenerated, have reinvented the entire earth."

Evillo sat astounded, as well he might.

Khiss eyed him a moment more, then spoke certain uncannily soporific phrases, which included the mellifluous words *Twylura Phlaim*, *Phurn*, and *Undimmoril*.

As the young man sprawled senseless yet again among the tubegrass, Khiss climbed to the top of a flowering blush-hyssop, and began the hypnotic schooling.

The sun meanwhile, which seemed to have picked up Khiss' boast, fretfully veiled itself in mauve vapour. This phenomenon, understandably, caused fright and pandemonium throughout the land, since humanity naturally expected possible eternal dark at any moment. But the vapour passed within three minutes; leaving all as before.

When Evillo awoke, he at once knew that he was possessed of many handy knacks, not the least being martial art. Later that day, directly against Porphiron Scar, he was enabled to test this when a leucomorph sidled from a covert.

No sooner seen than recognized from the tales of Canja Veck, Evillo leapt feet first against the monster and brought it down. Then, reaching instinctively for his sword, Evillo impaled the leucomorph's pallor on a solitary tree.

"But how," Evillo wondered, "do I come to have sword belt and sword? It was instantly there to hand, and I was aware of a curious blue sheen upon it as I wielded the blade."

"That is because it is well polished. While you slept, I came upon the assemblage in the grass. Given your new talents, I assumed it should be yours," Khiss answered, with the utmost reasonableness.

Below the Scar lay Kaiin, and beyond the city, the smalt-blue waters of Sanreale Bay. Evillo descended quickly, and passing by the elevated arena of Mad King Shin, sight-saw the preposterously enhanced palace of the present ruler, Kandive, sometimes nicknamed the golden.

The streets were full of interesting people, black-skinned and pale, and scented women in long-stemmed gowns. Khiss, with 'a few discreet murmurs, directed Evillo presently away through a grid of complex streets decked firstly with tall houses, and then with houses less tall, and at last with the lowest of houses. So they moved along the scabrous bank of a canal, reeking of components best left undescribed. Here rose a crumbling hostelry, the Inn of the Tired Sun.

"Enter, and seek a room," commanded Khiss.

"I? How will I know what to say—"

"Trust in the superior tutelage lavished on you." Evillo, having already been thrilled by his prowess with the lurking, now skewered, leucomorph, strode manfully into the inn. At once, words sprang to his tongue.

"A room, I pray you," he announced to the landlord. "And meantime, a meal with alcoholic additions."

The landlord, a brooding man of no teeth, frowned unencouragement.

"Expand initially upon why you enter clad in rags, and with dirt in your hair. Besides why you carry a snail on your shoulder? Do you wish it cooked for your repast? Be enlightened: we serve only our own viands, and never stoop to prepare take-in. Nor do we serve paupers. Payment is anticipated. I doubt if you have ever seen a terce, let alone been awarded one."

Again and at once, dialogue leapt from Evillo's mind to his lips.

Ringingly, he declared, "Know, unworthy innkeep, I am the noble Lord Evillo, sent in disguise to inspect the taverns of Kaiin, and by no less exalted a personage than Prince Kandive himself. The prince wishes to learn how business is conducted in his city, and especially what politenesses and kindnesses are extended to strangers. Already I perceive, and hearken to, your bent for rudeness and sulk. Had I not heard better formerly of you from my cousin—" here Evillo hesitated, unable in fact to coin a name—"who shall be nameless, that he thought you both charitable and courteous, I would even now have reported your conduct to his highness. But I will grant a second chance."

The landlord hurried from behind his counter. "Good sir, forgive my joke—which was, of course, but too easy to misinterpret. I saw at once that you are who you say you are. I will myself show you to the nicest room, and arrange a fine dinner. It will be my personal delight to cook the snail for you myself—"

"Pish! The snail is not for cooking. It is a sorcerous brooch of incredible value, bestowed upon me by a descendant of the magician Phandaal. Say nothing else lest you offend me further."

In the room above, Evillo bathed and barbered himself, then found in a closet some clean garments and linen of an unusual richness, including a long-billed hat of a claret hue. These donned, he was prompted to regard himself in the mirror also unexpectedly found in the closet. While doing this, his pleasure was distracted. A blue-green image suddenly misted the glass. It conveyed a landscape of opalescent beauty, with waters, woods, and mountains, all folded in turquoise luminescence. Next instant, it was gone. While Khiss had seemed to notice nothing, Evillo blamed the mirage on his over-stimulated nerves.

They went down to supper, and so passed the evening. Never in his days had Evillo known such luxuries, for although the inn was not of the best, by comparisom with Ratgrad, it seemed a very-heaven of the Overworld. Khiss dined on a lettuce.

All around, the other patrons nudged each other. "See, see, there is Prince Kandive's courtier, no doubt related to the ruler also, for note his silk jacket and behold the colour of his hair!"

About this time, Evillo conceived the notion that Khiss had grown a little larger, due no doubt to the nourishment of his salad.

When Evillo and Khiss made to retire, an alluring young woman with amethyst hair and fine eyes, if dressed rather to extremes, approached Evillo in the upper corridor.

She inquired if he might be uncomfortable on his own during the night in an unfamiliar building, and offered to keep him company. She would only charge him, she assured him, for the cost of her own chamber at the inn, which obviously, through being with him, she would not use. This room was somewhat sumptuous and accordingly highly-priced, she regretted to say. But she was always prepared to give it up, she said, if needed elsewhere. Evillo was touched, and taken with her, and so about to concur, when Khiss sternly murmured, reminding him that in actuality he had no money at all. With sorrow then, Evillo declined the lady's offer.

At this, her manner inexplicably altered. She shouted vigorously in several octaves. Finally, she called on a demon, whom she named Cardamoq, demanding that it chastise whoever so insulted a poor working girl. In haste, Evillo and Khiss withdrew.

Quiet returned. Outside, the tired sun sank behind the Tired Sun, and unspeakable things playfully splashed into the canal.

3: The Old Town

DURING THE night, the leucomorph, having with some difficulty detached itself from the branches of the tree, bounded through the inn window. It had followed Evillo's scent trail and entered the city—an act unusual for its kind—next clambering up the inn's rickety wall.

A deal of noise resulted. Yells and curses, sounds of blows and counter-blows, the crash of furniture, augmented by warbling growls.

Next, the chamber door burst wide. Evillo and the leucomorph erupted forth, to the elaborate consternation of other guests. Within minutes, many of these rushed screaming from the inn and down the street, wrapped only in bed-sheets. Others hid below tables in the main hall where, in the general distress, a lamp was inevitably knocked from a low rafter, causing a fire. At last, Evillo and the leucomorph, still locked in combat, retired once more into the upper room, where the young man succeeded in braining the thing with the night-pot, then casting it back from the window into the canal. Here it sank amid a cloud of white bubbles. Below, the fire was extinguished. Evillo lay down, ignoring his bruises, and returned exhaustedly to sleep. Sleep was of short duration however.

No sooner did dawn tip the sky than the door of his room once more crashed open.

"Arise, villain!" roared the muscle-girt captain of a band of city militia, each man brandishing sword and club. "You are to accompany us to jail."

Evillo, yet somnolent, still felt his mouth sparkle with words. "You mistake your man!" he cried.

"No, not we. You are a wretch who lured a filthy monster into this inn, wherewith to wreck the establishment. Worse even than this, as was earlier reported by the landlord, you have impersonated a member of the royal household." Eloquently plead as he would, Evillo found himself disarmed of his sword and briskly conducted into the street. He was then marched away into the pillar-fallen and ruinous Old Town of Kaiin, where stood the fearsome, seven-storey dungeon errected aeons before by Gbile the Intolerant. Only when cast upon a vast and stenchful floor in semi-darkness, did he discover that Khiss had accompanied him, and still sat on his left shoulder.

There passed then an unpleasant compendium of hours. The large room was already well stocked with criminals. Some groaned, and some uttered maledictions against various persons, amulets, and gods which had failed them. Some, more energetic, brawled and rolled across the space. Some crept about and attempted unneighbourly acts on the rest. One of these even essayed the theft of Khiss, thinking it to be a jewel. Evillo dissuaded the man, telling him that the gem was worthless, and besides carried a malwill, being the very cause of Evillo's imprisonment.

At noon, a panel was undone in the iron barrier, and a communal cauldron of lumpy, steaming gruel pushed through. On this, most flung themselves, slavering and hooting. Only those too weak, or in such despair as to be beyond nurture, desisted. Evillo numbered himself among the latter.

However, with noon some little drips of maroon light had also penetrated the prison, through an assortment of cracks. By these miserable rays, Evillo noticed a tall and well-dressed older man with sable hair, who sat to one side. Neither eating or grieving, nor complaining, he had fixed Evillo with a piercing grey gaze.

"Behold," whispered Khiss, as if to itself, "it is the sorcerer Pendatas Baard."

Evillo racked his now burnished wits. He did not identify the name, although, for a fleeting moment it had seemed familiar. But the man's gaze disconcerted him, and, presently, lacking the guidance of Khiss, Evillo rose and went towards him.

The cold eyes lifted. "And do you know me?" inquired the mage.

"You are Pendatas Baard, the sorcerer. Why therefore are you in a dungeon? Do your powers desert you?"

This was perhaps too bold; the man grimaced, then smiled in superior fashion.

"My powers are formidable. I was well taught by my father, the lamented Ultra-Mage Kateraspex. Know then, I am here due to an experiment on my part, extrapolated from Phandaal's empurpled theorem of Locative Selfulsion."

Evillo recalled that Khiss, at their first meeting, had mentioned this particular magic.

"What does the theorem entail?" he asked.

"Surely," said the mage, "so much is evident?"

Evillo temporized. "You will pardon me, I hope, but it seemed to me that you stared at me a while. Maybe you have some task for me to perform? Even decidedly, such a necessary task as will cause my swift liberation from this jail?"

"No, nothing like that," replied the mage. "It seemed to me for a moment that I recognized something about you. Have you travelled much?"

Evillo must admit he had not. But then he became animated, thinking of his much-travelled hero, Cugel, and added, "But I have journeyed in my mind. My *mind* has visited so many spots. The sombre north—the Ocean of Sighs—Almery of dim bare hills, the heaving river Xzan, sometimes called the Twish…the glass-turreted manse of the Laughing—"

"Quite," interposed Pendatas Baard concludingly.

Just then, a loud clang shook the dungeon, followed by screeching. In their shoving anxiety to feed, the food vehicle had been toppled among the diners, and a man received burned legs and feet. As the unfortunate lay flapping on the floor, a curious compunction overcame Evillo. Leaving the mage, he hastened to the scalded man. Lying on the floor, Evillo commenced to crawl over his wounded legs. Cries of affronted mockery resulted, then fell still as Evillo completed his progress. The burned man bounced to his feet. "I am cured! The pain is laved from me! My skin is whole!" So much might be witnessed as a fact.

The other prisoners promptly crowded about Evillo. "You are a mighty sorcerer. Save us, great master! We are all innocent as new-born elds. Only free us, and we will be your slaves. Refuse—and mage or not, you shall die!"

Evillo stood aghast, and neither the teaching of Khiss. nor any memories of Cugel's wit, provided him at this point with eloquence.

"Khiss! Instruct me—what now?"

Khiss murmured.

"The great master whispers a spell," surmised the prisoners. "Let us hope it summons our release—for our sakes and his!"

"It is as you desire," Evillo confirmed hastily. "But stand further off, or the force of the freeing mantra may smash us all to pieces." The prisoners withdrew. Khiss then muttered again. Directed by the mutter, Evillo spun about in time to see the real magician, Pendatas Baard, wavering in and out of visibility.

Faithful to Khiss' next injunction, Evillo raced to the mage, and flung himself upon him, grasping him vigorously with both arms and legs.

Pendatas Baard uttered a strangled roar of rage and pain, but the vacillating waver, now unstoppable, had swiftly involved Evillo also. In another second, the full trio, mage, young man, and snail, vanished from the dungeon.

4: The Sembling

THERE WAS a form of bad weather in Almery that day. The three travellers fell amid the tempest, as simultaneously on the hard eastern banks of the Xzan or Twish.

Evillo found that, rather than brush water drops from his face, he brushed off small flexible animalcules of a bluish type which, hitting him here and elsewhere, bit him.

For a short time, Pendatas Baard and Evillo were united in a frenzied dance, beating away this vicious insectile rain. Presently, the mage thought to erect by sorcery a canopy of steel that, no doubt inadvertantly, sheltered Evillo also. Here they huddled, while without the sky fell and the river popped and sizzled.

"You will accept my heartiest curse for this, you felon, a curse too vile even to detail but lasting your life long," stormed Pendatas Baard. "Render your name, that I may fix the bane more thoroughly."

"If I should modestly decline such honour?"

"I shall blast you to syrop here and now."

"Blurkel," offered Evillo.

"My thanks. Consider yourself, Blurkel, accursed to the sorry limit of your days. I will not trouble to curse your brooch. Such an exertion is beneath me. Did you not know that your idiotic attempt to wrap me in an embrace of farewell, however understandable, must dislodge the architecture of the Selfulsion? Behold where you have landed me!"

"Where?" asked Evillo, for he had not yet identified the geography.

"The Selfulsion, which I, like my father Kateraspex, have almost perfected from Phandaal's theorem, having permitted me to enter

the ancient jail and verify certain opinions I hold on the vile nature of humanity, was due to return me to my domicile in the Old Town. Your solipsistic intercession has instead dashed both of us across the landscape and into the environ of Almery, in which country I must assume that you, if not I, take an obsessive interest."

"Almery:"

"Just so. The fanged beetle-pour has lessened: regard, above the slopes, the manse of that pest, Iucounu the Laughing Magician. He has already sensed me and sent a storm of biting mites. He was the mortal foe of my father. And now, quite preposterously, is mine."

From the tales of Cugel, Evillo had already learned of the malice of Iucounu, but also of other events which might be expected to have curtailed it. "But is Iucounu not dead? I had heard—"

"Bah: Such criminals never die, they are ineradicable."

"Can you not then at once avail yourself of the Selfulsion, and vacate the spot?"

"That is the one flaw in my calculus. In the prison, I learned that I was unable immediately to reactivate the spell. Two hours must elapse before I found myself in a position to depart. At which juncture, you befoulled the locomotion. Normally, the practitioner—myself—may, via the Selfulsion, physically manifest in an instant at any place on the earth of which he knows, and which he may at least partially envisage. But your image of *this* place, the purlieus of Iucounu, proved stronger than my own merely formulaic memory of my house. A second time I curse you, Blurkel, and a third!"

Dejected, Evillo left the shelter of the steel canopy. The rain of beetles had ceased, although clouds yet blew across the dark blue sky, revealing the sun only in ruby winks.

Nevertheless he saw—up the hill, nor so far off—the manse that Canja Veck had so aptly described. Its steep gables and lace-work of sky-walks and balconies glittered in the racing interrupted light, while the green glass domes flashed now peridot, now carnelian, reminding him of the flickering tongues of snakes.

"What shall I do?" he inquired of Khiss.

"What men must do. You are here. You must go on."

It seemed to Evillo then that Khiss had grown far heavier, and even perhaps rather larger. As if the snail symbolized the weight of the mage's projected curses—which presumably had missed Evillo himself.

As he climbed the hill, Evillo glanced back once, and noted Pendatas Baard digging for himself, by means of magic, a deep hidey-hole in the ground.

THE MANSE lay along a road paved by brown tiles. These showed some symptoms of wear. Evillo had also spotted a deserted village overwhelmed by trees. Several disconcerting ruins of seemingly great age also lay around. In short, nothing but the magician's home was at all in repair.

Evillo had deduced from the tales the Fabler recounted that Iucounu, even he, had finally met his match—less in the person of Cugel than through the energies of the alarming god-being Sadlark, and the terrible Spatterlight. Yet surely the touchy mage Pendatas should have known the truth.

An air of desuetude and disconsolation nevertheless hung over the building. Reaching it, and cautious as Cugel himself had once been, the young man peered in at a number of windows. Through one, he viewed a chamber hung with crimson papers, where something whirled vaguely along the floor. Through another was a large hall laid with an intricately woven rug of forest green, fusk, fruslian mauve, and orange. On this stood a slender tantalum pedestal atop which, slowly and gracefully, there danced the skeleton of a rodent. In a third window, he spied a beautiful sylph with silver hair$_s$ but she faded even as he looked. Within the fourth window, nothing at all was visible—which is to say, *nothing*, since the entire room was a disturbing void from which Evillo quickly averted his eyes.

He had, in fact, no wish to risk entry. Star-struck curiosity alone impelled him to circle the fatal house. Nor did his teacher Khiss remonstrate, despite once or twice making a tsking noise.

Evillo then found a side-door in the stone-work, hanging ajar.

Beyond lay a courtyard where grew a single spindly mulgoon tree of purple leaves. At that moment, the clouds left the sun. Magenta light flooded the area, and from under the tree came gliding a person whom Evillo might have met only yesterday, he knew him so infallibly. Small and pearshaped, his upper body was bundled in a black tunic with a collar of tall quills. His bird-thin legs were clad in many-coloured pantaloons. His bald head and face had the form and yellow shade of a perch-pumpkin; his eyes were miniatures of dead wood. His mouth curved in an eternal grin. Who else could it be but the Laughing One?

"What have we here?" asked Iucounu, mirthful and merciless. "Yet one more visitor? Ah, to be so popular is indeed a boon! Pray enter and witness my treasures. Never stint your imaginative ambitions with regard to stealing anything you may see. Do pray indulge your most venal fantasies! You will not be the first to do so, nor, I suspect, the last. Until the sun goes out, no doubt, callers will arrive on similar missions."

Khiss offered nothing. Evillo's brain sent a message to his tongue.

"I am glad to see you well, sir," he said, offering a low bow.

"Had you heard I was not?"

Evillo checked, sensing his blunder.

Iucolunu added, leering with apparent glee, "Some story of my perishment in a fountain, I judge, consumed by the Spatterlight, which Cugel the Unclever tricked me into pressing home upon my forehead?"

"Clearly greatly exaggerated…" stammered Evillo.

"Not necessarily. Or perhaps. Which would you say? Do you believe I am dead? More to the point, do *I* believe I am?"

Evillo now prudently kept quiet.

"I will say this," the magician continued, "whether Iucounu lives or has died, whether he *has* died but has since rebecome *living*, if he is perhaps secreted in study elsewhere about the manse, or even should he be away from home merely visiting some other, *I* remain, and currently shall do so always. Grasp, if you are able: I am a sembling which Iucounu made in his own likeness. And now I am caretaker of his castle. In me you will, should you wish to make a test of me, find all his formidable and eclectically amusing powers, for I have been invested with them in perpetuity. Therefore, abandon shyness and step within."

"Your generosity overmatches, alas, my available time. I am due at the manse of my employer, who sent me out solely to locate his pet vowl, which had strayed from the garden," Evillo dissembled.

"Ah, a pet." said Iucounu's sembling. "Iucounu too did or does have one such. See, there it bounds! Ettis, my pretty, to me! To me!" A shrill bark at once responded from above.

Evillo recalled Ettis also. Cugel's gambits to avoid poison offered him by the magician, had resulted in the animal's death. This self-same creature now soared down from the air, conceivably having sprung from a handy parapet. Although still round and long furred, with circular black eyes, Evillo was aware of two extra characteristics missing from the Ettis of the story. Firstly, the daylight shone through its body, Secondly, its teeth and claws had grown to abnormal length and acuity. Ettis, it seemed, had become an undead vampiric salk.

"Pardon me—I hear my master's impatient shout and must be gone," cried Evillo, and took to his heels.

His intention was to charge at once downhill, in the direction of the River Xzan. If needful, he would jump right into it, even should he discompose thereby another Fiscian lover.

Nevertheless, a spell of the magician, or of the guardian sembling, had already been activated. To his despair, Evillo found that he could run only around the manse, here and there leaping over obstacles, such as steps or small statues. In doing this, he passed by the windows through which he had previously stared. He noted inadvertantly that the rodent bones now danced a tarantella, but the whirl in the red paper room, like the sylph, was gone. Rushing by the void, however, a perturbing thought assailed him, even in the midst of his own concern. It seemed to him he had caught a faint echo of converse inside the nothingness: "Let tonight last forever!" said one. "My own sentiment;" averred another. "There is never more to experience than this single 'now'."

Had Cugel, in his triumph, uttered some guileless sophistry and thus himself activated a dormant but deadly domestic safeguard, involving petrified time?

But there was no margin to ponder. Evillo ran, swordless since the jail, and unable to break away from the magician's walls. While behind him galloped Ettis, now on terra firma, now in the air, its joyous canine screams splintering the ears.

"Khiss:" gasped Evillo, as he entered his second circuit of the enormous building, "do you indeed youself know the spell of Selfulsion? It seemed to me you might. If so—can you not release said knack and send us hence?"

Khiss answered, "I will do my best, despite the jolting I presently receive. But you yourself must visualize some place of charm and safety. I cannot work alone."

How heavy in that moment seemed the snail that Evillo carried.

"I know so little, and yet my skull is packed with the scenes of Cugel's journeys—but anywhere other than here will serve."

No sooner had Evillo panted out the words than he stumbled over a low wall inlaid with glossold. He fell into a bush of flowering casperine, from which some of the left-over blue beetlecules lifted to bite him. At the same instant, Ettis came flying from the air like a furry pancake, claws akimbo.

Evillo gave himself up for lost. Then he experienced once more the sensation of fog and vertigo that had attended his ejection from the prison with Pendatas Baard. Rather than Ettis, another country slammed into his spine. He lay staring up into a swimming hallucination of sea-green hills scarfed in a soft blue mist. This lasted less than a heartbeat. Thereafter, he was glaring through the foliage of a gigantic thamber oak to the blood-red sky of sunfall. Stars were already visible, their constellations set in unfamiliar patterns. The diamond mask of Lyraleth bemused him.

He came gradually to see he was in a forest glade, and all alone. If he had sloughed the intolerable Ettis, so he had also sloughed his mentor, Khiss.

Primed to lament, Evillo rose. And learned that he was not quite alone after all.

He had dropped on this occasion into the vernal labyrinth of the Lig Thig, or Great Erm, that stupendous and ominous forest of the far north. Here Cugel had undergone certain trials and tribulations.

About the glade, the trees clustered close, towering deodars and capacious amberquers, limned with cochineal high-lights. Northern mandouars loured like priests attired in smoke. Contrastingly, a pleasing scent of vanilla drifted on an evening Fader, or west wind. The aroma wafted from a long clay pipe that three sabre-toothed, man-eating Deodands passed to and fro between them. They were the impossibly unhuman black of burned skeel. They smoked, and smiled to welcome Evillo to dinner, he being the food.

5: In the Lig Thig and At the Blue Lamped Inn

AS THE daylight ebbed, the tallest Deodand approached Evillo. The Deodand spoke.

"What a pleasure that you have entered the glade. My friends and I have not eaten a morsel for several days. The last of our—shall I say—patrons did however leave us this pipe and pouch of pods and herbs. A selfless thought. We have much enjoyed it."

Evillo glanced at the Deodand. "A tonic to hear you speak of friendship. I fear that my own friend, a very fat fellow named Huge, has lagged behind. Already I miss him painfully, he is such fine company, and though hardly the height of that tree, is at least three times its girth."

The Deodand paused, appearing interested.

"Is he so? Why then is he so disappointingly late?"

"Initially, I believe, in order to persuade two other grand fellows of our acquaintance, by name Gargantuan and Likewise, to come with us on our jaunt."

"Well, then," said the Deodand, with a winning grin, "while we await such excellent extra confreres, we may partake of a starter dish before the feast. Come! We insist that you participate; indeed, it is essential. That seen to, we will greet your friends when they arrive with equal gladness."

"This causes embarrassment," grieved Evillo. "Without a certain act, Huge, Gargantuan, and Likewise will not appear. Let me elucidate. You will have noted my supernatural method of arrival? I can translocate from any one place to any other at the blink of an eye. Huge, inevitably, can do the same. However he has recently become prey to a silly habit of wishing me always, when once I reach any destination, to observe a fussy ritual. Without this, which infallibly he detects from afar, he refuses to follow me. Nor obviously, therefore, will our hefty friends."

By now, the two other Deodands had approached. They sat elegantly on nearby tree-stumps, the pipe stowed. One sang a little ditty.

"*A passing pelgrane called good-day,*
But good for whom it did not say." [1]

"What then does the ritual entail?" another asked at length.

"It is so tiresome," replied Evillo, " I feel I should omit it. Let us simply proceed to the food. After all, three such enormous gentlemen as my friends will surely deplete your stores."

"Not precisely," the first Deodand reassured him. "No, no, we long to meet with them. I urge you to enact the ritual. We will patiently stand by."

"Alas, I must ask you to assist. But no—it is beneath you! Let us make do with the starter dish, of whatever sort it is."

"Not at all. Be assured. We are more than willing to help you."

The other two Deodands concurred with enthusiasm. "Very well then, I must bind your eyes with these strips torn from my shirt, as so—yes, indeed, they must come from my own garments or Huge will know, and withhold his company. There. I trust they are not too tight. Now each of us must lie face down on the ground and count, one after the other, to

1 This truncated doggeral works to better effect in the untranslated original.

the number one hundred. You, sir, the first. Then you, sir, and lastly, sir, you. I must do the counting last of all, for so my foolish friend Huge *will* have it."

The Deodands lay down and pressed their faces to the soil.

By now, the forest was darkening through impressive tints of Kauchique Ale and Violet Mendolence. Evillo, bolt upright by the oak, made pretence that he too had lain down.

"We are all now in position," he informed the Deodands. "Some final advice. Do not begin your counting until I give the signal—Huge is most touchy. After that, and when you are done, do not stir, let alone look about until I have concluded my own count, during which Huge and the others will join us. Be aware that Huge, owing to his extreme bulk, so disturbs the equilibrium of anywhere that he translocates himself to, let alone if in company, that you will be vastly endangered by precipitate motion, especially of the eyes—for just this cause, I have blindfolded you. Hold tight to the ground. Await my signals. And for such inconvenience, accept a thousand apologies."

Evillo paused. The sky was black as ink and only Lyraleth remained visible.

"Commence!" he ordered, and hastily, on silent feet, sought the avenues of the forest.

He had been running for less than a count of fifty however, when he detected sounds of pursuit.

Above him in the dark, Evillo also heard a small and plaintive call. Seizing the trunk of a massive tree, he climbed at speed to an elevated bough.

The owner of the little calling voice squinted at him with tiny luminous eyes. He was a Twk man, and nearby, his dragonfly sat preening its wings among the leaves.

"To repay this favour," said the Twk, "I require salt."

"I have none. Which favour?"

"I am owed," said the Twk. "Know that flights of my kind were recently lured toward the northern limits, with a promise of endless salination, by the unsympathetic mage Pendatas Baard, in his relentless search for the usufructdom of Undimmoril. He claimed of us many and various deeds. When wages came due, he directed us to the sea's edge, and recommended we pan the tideless waves for our reward."

"I am sorry to hear this," whispered Evillo, "but hush a moment, if you will. My hunters prowl below."

The Twk gazed over at the three Deodands, who, illumined by the single large star, sniffed about the tree roots beneath, now and then glancing thoughtfully up into the branches.

"Perhaps I shall betray you to them," mused the Twk. "Sometimes Deodands carry salt, to season less tasty kills."

Evillo felt an eerie coolth on his arm. Looking distractedly, he found Khiss. But Khiss had grown startlingly during their separation, to the size of a cat.

From below came the discouraging sound of agile feet attempting the tree.

"Contain your amazement," instructed Khiss, in a new and testy tone. "We must depart at once. Due to your inanity, not only did we once more miss the target, but were segregated during the transmission. We shall now again try the Selfulsion. On this occasion, by all five demons of Lumarth, think *only* of some terminus secure, and, preferably, *blue*."

Evillo's mind became a perfect blank. But already, Khiss and he were pulsing as their bodily atoms disbanded. From nowhere, a sourceless memory of blueness filled his thoughts. He interpretted this as another of Cugel's temporary haunts, and conjured the Inn of Blue Lamps, southward, in Saskervoy.

Such had been the delay and confusion none the less, that the two wayfarers entered the inn by a high closed window, and so descended in a hail of glass upon several dissatisfied diners.

EVILLO AND Khiss extricated themselves from a roast fowl and a large platter of stewed callow with roseberry. The Twk and dragonfly, involved in the Selfulsion owing to proximity, dived into the salt-dish.

A landlord loomed. Evillo assumed that he was Krasnark, the very same who had waited on Cugel in the Fabler's tale. Black-browed and tall, he glowered. On his forehead, a faint scar boded ill.

"Am I never to free my premises of these surreal incursions? Ever since the fateful night when those two wretches played their gambler's tricks, the villainy of which only later were revealed to me, bad cess has plagued this inn!"

"It is true," confided a buxom dame in cerise plast, beaming upon Evillo despite his antisocial entrance. "Poor Krasnark was brained by

an unseen force and fell into the still-room below, spilling and breaking items to the value of nineteen florins! Besides, a worthy worminger was wounded in the foot by a crustaceous sphigale let go from its tank, the lighting was damaged, beards were sliced, and gentlemen harried at the trough of convenience."

"And *now*," snarled Krasnark, "the ghoul-goat Cleenisz has taken up residence in the cellar, where it lies in wait for my potboys!"

On this cue, a malevolent bleating of inappropriate volume resounded from below. The floor shook.

"If you have stirred up the thing," threatened Krasnark, "by your louche flop into my hall, I will charge you the sum of two hundred terces. The probity of Saskervoy is at stake."

Most of the patrons were now evacuating the inn, even the lady in cerise. Seemingly, they did not take to the voice of Cleenisz.

"I regret, landlord," said Evillo, "I have not a copper shaving to my name."

"But," hissed Khiss, its whisper loudly audible due to its current size, which was now more approximate to that of a small lion, "hand him this ring gleaming there in the spilled salt. It will pay for all."

Evillo took the ring. It was worth more than the entire inn, very likely, a great smouldering gem of bluish-green set in blue tantalum, and chased with blue gold.

Krasnark's manner altered. "That will tally to a nicety, sir. Let me entreat you to finish the dinner you have already sampled…or should you wish to follow me to the urinal?"

Evillo did not attend. A turquoise radiance was flaring from the jewel's heart. It seemed to fill the inn, fading the blue lucifer lamplight to ashes.

There again appeared to him then the mysterious misty woods, hills, valleys, and mountains, the lakes like moire silk, which he had glimpsed so many times before. Evillo, dazzled by the sheen, wondered if this vision, as had the violet eye cusps of the Overworld, at least in Cugel's experience, so effected the organ of sight as to influence also all other senses. For Evillo seemed to smell the fragrance of trees, flowers, and water, and he almost felt the brush of satin leaves against his face.

And then a woman appeared at the heart of the wonder. Her figure was slender, but with exquisite accentuations. Her skin resembled the palest and most clear nacre. Long lustrous hair, in colour the spice pink of a cold dawn, streamed about her. Her eyes were like emeralds in a lavender dusk. She was beauty incarnate, and instantly Evillo found he knew her name, which in ecstasy he breathed aloud: "Twylura Phlaim!"

"Never decant your curses on me:" thundered Krasnark. "Know that I am protected by amulets. Douse the witchlight and hand over the gewgaw. On reflection, I see it will barely cover the cost of dinner, let alone the broken window and lost custom. And still I must pay for eviction of the goat."

Two things thereafter occurred as one. Khiss spoke in a penetrating and masculine tone, rendering to Krasnark an uncensored direction. At this, the landlord bellowed in affront. While from beneath came the noise of smashing pilasters, and out of the collapsing floor shouldered the ghoul-goat Cleenisz.

"We apply the Selfulsion," ordered Khiss, with the utmost authority. "Evillo, fix your eyes upon the image in the ring, and summon no other of your ridiculous Cugelesque venues."

The lucifer, by which the inn lamps were powered, blew up in a furl of royal blue fire. All else was fog and spinning.

6: Undimmoril

ON EVERY side, and to each horizon, stretched the fair, liberally-laked land of Undimmoril. It was as already Evillo had partially viewed it, landscaped enchantingly by unknown gods, and coloured with irridescent blues and greens and every ethereal shade between. Above, the sky was also a composition of jade and azure, and lit sourcelessly, not in the way of sunlight, but more a vivid twilight under a full and incandescent moon.

Presently, Evillo looked about for Khiss. But the snail was again absent. Instead, beside him on the lake shore sat a princely young man, of about Evillo's own age. The newcomer was both tall and strong, with long hair the tint of verdigris and eyes like the darkest malachite. He was clad in velvet dyed cyanide and yu-sapphire, and a wide brimmed hat sporting seven peaks, trimmed with carmine effulgence.

"Gawp, if you must," he said, in off-hand condenscension. "I should guess I am, as in the past, a sight to ravish all eyes."

"Where is Khiss?" Evillo asked.

"Ha! Where do you think?"

"You are—it."

"Indeed. I am Prince Khiss. I know you are a simpleton. There is no demand that you should labour the point."

"And this place?"

"The lovely usufructdom of Undimmoril, where never can shine a sun nor ever can a sun die. This is my realm, from which I was ousted, by the plots of the magician Kasteraspex. And here, I believe, is my clariot."

Certainly a powerful and well-groomed clariot, ready caparisoned, a riding animal of the crossed breed of wheriot and claris, and, in this instance, peacock blue, was stepping tidily along the shore, tossing its four-horned head and chartreuse mane.

Rising, the prince who had been a snail vaulted lightly into the saddle. Graciously, he invited Evillo: "Run beside me if you wish. I am bound for my home, the incomparable palace of Phurn."

Evillo, seeing nothing else to be done, did as Prince Khiss suggested.

As they advanced then, prince and steed galloping nimbly, Evillo stumbling breathless and groaning alongside, Khiss related his story, and Evillo's part in it.

"Kateraspex entered the usufructdom of my domain by means of Phandaal's theoretic Locative Selfulsion, which he, the unworthy Kateraspex, had somehow—and doubtless by accident—realized. Kateraspex then annexed the territory of Undimmoril. I, of course, opposed him. Although myself well-versed in thaumaturgic art, the devil overcame me by a ploy too complex to explain. Since to explain it would exceed our time together, and decidedly your intellect. Suffice it to say, Kateraspex exiled me to the paltry alter-world of the earth, and robbed me, once there, of the ability to reveal my plight. However, owing to the Laws of Equivalence, the villian was yet compelled to allow me to retain certain benefits. These comprised my knowledge and skill in various fields, and those formulas I had mastered of magery. Also he must permit me, albeit haphazardly, to recoup my royal sword, one set of princely clothing, and a ring that marked my status as ruler.

"However again, such was the magician's vile cunning that he made sure I might not put to use any of these elements. He decreed that, my feet once touching the ground of Earth, I should become a more attractive copy of the first creature I beheld there. Which was, as even you may fathom, a snail.

"My only hope then, which Kateraspex failed to foresee, was that I might find some gullible dunce. For if I could but imbue his noddle with some of my own talents, currently useless to me, he and I would together

make up a source of power. Meanwhile, every piece of fair fortune my pupil might expect to encounter would instantly magnetize to my own self, he then suffering a counterbalance of lucklessness. As this happened, my reserves of energy would be recharged.

"Generously, I shall not chide you with the long wait I had, due to your tardy arrival. For though I met many dunderheads, they were too fly to trust me. While the gullible were already so mentally crammed with idiocies my tuition found no room. You, however, were perfection. An imbecile, empty as the night of moon.

"Soon enough you gained my sword, then the garments, and, at length the ring. With each acquisition too you obtained a fleeting glimpse of Undimmoril. Finally, a vision of my land was established in your imagination. Thus primed, the Selfulsions needed lesser and then no intervals between them. Only your intransigent Cugeline fad caused difficulty. In the end, even that did not avail. We achieved Undimmoril. Where, once more on hallowed ground, I reverted to my true persona and emptied your brain of my wisdom. All is now mine. Notice, even the sword has come back to me."

Khiss laughed with joy. Evillo sensed that his own mind was hollow and confused. Khiss was prompted to one more admission:

"By the by, it was not you at whom that farlock, Pendatas Baard, sat staring at in the prison. He stared at *me*. He had never seen me, either as prince or snail, yet he sensed some remnant about me of his accursed father. Who, you may be entertained to know, Pendatas himself dispatched, on a rare paternal visit, with a venom of the Saponids. Ever after, Pendatas has sought for Undimmoril himself. With slight success, as we note."

Exhausted by this far from terse account, as much as by enforced exercise, Evillo plunged face forward in the grass. From this vantage, he grew aware of the palace of Phurn standing close by. It was supplied with pillars of turquoise and many thin towers like sticks of angelica. Gardens garlanded all, crowded with terebinth and myhrhadion, eluent teff and gentians.

In the gateway was the wonderful woman with pink hair. Khiss cried aloud in delight and reined in the clariot. "Behold, my wife, Twylura Phlaim, the only female worthy to partner my splendour!" Glancing back, Khiss added, "Evillo, you may depart. In a moment, I will open a portal, and you will then be propelled back to the fount of your useless and unaesthetic existence."

Before this was done however, the beautiful Twylura Phlaim mounted a cat-headed chariot, which leapt on hare's legs up the hill.

"Art thou home so soon?" she exclaimed to her husband, in a peculiarly raucous tone. "Be cautioned, Khiss, in thy long absence, Twylura Phlaim grew bored and ran away with an untypically handsome gleft. Instead I have taken her place."

"Who then are you?" demanded Prince Khiss.

"The demon Cardamoq. Come thou now and embrace me." Khiss had grown white. The clariot reared and unseated him. Khiss landed by Evillo.

"Oh, Evillo, dear friend, despite my restored powers, the demon's strength overwhelms me! Let us therefore at once return to our beloved dying earth—"

"Nay, husband. Thou shalt stay with thy beloved Cardomoq!" screeched the demon unmusically. She had grown two heads, and smoke billowed from the six nostrils of each. "To be sure of it, I shall transfer some of thy powers to the yellow-haired human there. He may keep them as a momento of this happy reunion."

A blow fell on Evillo's head. He sensed the portal open in the alter-world of Undimmoril, and wisely knew no more.

IN FACT, he fell to earth in the red sunlight of Kaiin. A multitude of hands were assisting him to rise, and the air rang with voices detailing how he had been searched for everywhere. Next came the militia and ringed him round.

Tiredly, Evillo anticipated the prison, but instead the throng, cheering and rejoicing, bore him to the palace of Kandive the golden.

"How pleasing that we have refound you, dear boy," declaimed Kandive. "I am already bereft of sons and nephews; they have such a propensity for extended voyages whereon they vanish. It seems to me, when we have consulted the proper sages, that you will be my direct heir, in default of all the others. For you are the child of my half-sister who, sixteen years before and when visiting an obscure fane above the Derna, mislaid you, through sheer carelessness, near the village of Ratgrad."

Evillo stood nonplussed. Had his good luck returned? He grasped also that certain powers belonging to the arrogant Khiss had indeed been given to him. Released from Khiss' personalized Equivalence, Evillo might surely now enjoy them. And not least as heir to white-walled Kaiin.

While he was considering these prospects, he saw amid the crowd the Darkographer Kaiine. Evillo recalled how he had misunderstood the gallant's warning—not to avoid stepping upon the snail, but simply to avoid the snail altogether.

So easily might one topple into folly. One must have things straight.

He therefore at once asked Kandive, "And is my name Evillo, as I have thought from the age of seven?"

"Not at all," replied the puzzled Kandive. "By the cyclopaedia, whatever put such an idea in your head?

"What then, sir, is my name?"

"Why, my boy, hear, and thereafter bear with pride your true cognomen, written in the archives of Ascolais. It is Blurkel."

Evillo staggered. Supposing this due to rapture, Kandive clapped him on the back.

But it was the full weight of the strident three-fold curse of Pendatas Baard, coming home to roost. Vented upon him in the name of Blurkel, the young man felt it attach itself like a swarm of stones.

That very night, as all feasted in the lavish courts of Kandive, the recurrent leucomorph uncharacteristically dropped from a chandelier upon Blurkel. Its attack had been much refined by practice.

AFTERWORD:

FOR ME, Jack Vance is one of the literary gods.

In the earliest '70's, when I was in a very unhappy and depressed condition, my magical, wise mother, (who had already turned me on to mythology, history, and SF), bought me Jack Vance's *The Dying Earth.* At once I escaped my leaden state and entered the teeming and ironically shining landscape of Vance's extraordinary, decadently future world.

I still possess this volume—the English *Mayflower* edition—treasured and often read, though by now its pages are pale brown and many are loose inside the cover. (The spine seems to have been nibbled by a pelgrane).

The Dying Earth novels and stories are picaresque adventures in the truest sense, peripatetic, and express-paced. They carry echoes not only of the *Thousand Nights and a Night*, but of such other witty sombre epics as *Gulliver's Travels*, not to mention the visions of Milton and Blake. Vance seems genuinely, within the fantasy-SF envelope, to access the Mediaeval mind: here the world may end at any moment and fabulous beasts and monsters co-exist with sinful, selfish, and (rarely) spiritual man. The narratives range from the screamingly hilarious to the seductively beautiful, to the shockingly—if fastidiously presented—violent. As for black humour, Vance might have invented it.

Such masterworks have fired and—I hope—taught my imagination, ever since the first plunge. Influence is too small a word. What I owe to Vance's genius, as avid fan and compulsive writer; is beyond calculation.

Every book reasserts its peerless magic on every one of the uncountable times I re-re-read it. In fact, I don't quite believe Jack Vance invented the Dying Earth. Part of me *knows* he's been there. Often.

But then. He takes *us* there too, doesn't he?

—Tanith Lee

DAN SIMMONS

The Guiding Nose of Ulfänt Banderōz

A WRITER of considerable power, range, and ambition, an eclectic talent not willing to be restricted to any one genre, Dan Simmons sold his first story to *The Twilight Zone Magazine* in 1982. By the end of that decade, he had become one of the most popular and bestselling authors in both the horror *and* the science fiction genres, winning, for instance, both the Hugo Award for his epic science fiction novel *Hyperion* and the Bram Stoker Award for his huge horror novel *Carrion Comfort* in the *same year*, 1990. He's gone on to win two more Bram Stoker Awards and two World Fantasy Awards (for *Song of Kali* and "This Year's Class Picture"). He has continued to split his output since between science fiction (*The Fall of Hyperion*, *The Hollow Man*, *Endymion*, *The Rise of Endymion*, *Ilium*, *Olympos*) and horror (*Song of Kali*, *Summer of Night*, *Children of the Night*...although a few of his novels are downright unclassifiable (*Phases of Gravity*, for instance, which is a straight literary novel, although it was *published* as part of a science fiction line), and some (like *Children of the Night*) could be legitimately considered to be *either* science fiction or horror, depending on how you squint at them. Similarly, his first collection, *Prayers to Broken Stones*, contains a mix of science fiction, fantasy, horror, and "mainstream" stories, as do his more recent collections, *Lovedeath* and *Worlds Enough and Time: Five Tales of Speculative Fiction*. Many of his recent books confirm his reputation for unpredictability, including *The Crook Factory*, a spy thriller set in World War II and starring Ernest Hemingway, *Darwin's Blade*, a "statistical thriller" halfway between mystery and dark comedy, *Hardcase*, *Hard Freeze*, and *Hard As Nails*, hardboiled detective novels, and, *A Winter Haunting*, a ghost story. His most recent books are the bestselling novel, halfway between historical and horror, *The Terror*, the chapbook novella, *Muse of Fire*, and a major new novel about Charles Dickens, *Drood*. Born in Peoria, Illinois, Simmons now lives with his family in Colorado.

In the complex and richly imagined story that follows, he takes us on a race across unknown territory to the very ends of the Dying Earth, with terrible enemies in close pursuit and the fate of all who live at stake, and everything depending on the guidance of...a nose?

The Guiding Nose of Ulfänt Banderōz

DAN SIMMONS

In the waning millennia of the 21st Aeon, during one of the countless unnamed and chaotic latter eras of the Dying Earth, all the usual signs of imminent doom suddenly went from bad to worse.

The great red sun, always slow to rise, became more sluggish than ever. Like an old man loathe to get out of bed, the bloated sun on some mornings shook, quivered, staggered, and rippled forth earthquakes of protesting rumbles that radiated west from the eastern horizons across the ancient continents, shaking even the low mountain ranges worn down by time and gravity until they resembled old molars. Black spots poxed and repoxed the slowly rising sun's dim face until entire days were all but lost to a dull, maroon twilight.

During the usually self-indulgent and festival-filled month of Spoorn, there were five days of near total darkness, and crops failed from Ascolais through Almery to the far fen borders of the Ide of Kauchique. River Scaum in Ascolais turned to ice on the morn of MidSummer's Eve, freezing the holy aspirations off thousands who had immersed themselves for the Scaumish Rites of Multiple Erotic Connections. What few ancient upright

stones and wall-slabs that were still standing at the Land of the Falling Wall rattled like bones in a cup and fell, killing countless lazy peasants who had foolishly built their hovels in its lee over the millennia just to save the cost of a fourth wall. In the holy city of Erze Damath, thousands of pelgranes—arriving in flocks the size of which had never been seen before in the memory of man and non-men—circled for three days and then swooped down, carrying off more than six hundred of the most pious pilgrims and befouling the Black Obelisk with their bone-filled droppings.

In the west, the setting sun appeared to pulse larger and closer until the forests of the Great Erm burned. Tidal waves washed away all cities and vestiges of life from the Cape of Sad Remembrance, and the ancient market town of Xeexees, only forty leagues south of the city of Azenomei, disappeared completely one night at three minutes after midnight during the height of its crowded Summer Fair; some say the town was swallowed whole in a great earthly convulsion, some say it shifted in an eyeblink to one of the unbreathable-air worlds of the dodge-star Achernar, but whichever was the case, the many residents of the metropolis of nearby Azenomei huddled in their homes in fear. And during all these individual tragedies, more than half the surrounding region once known in better days as the Grand Motholam suffered floods, droughts, pestilence, devaluation of the terce, and frequent darknesses.

The people, both human and otherwise, reacted as people always have during such hard times in the immemorial history of the Dying Earth and the Earth of the Yellow Sun before it; they sought out scapegoats to hound and pound and kill. In this case, the heaviest opprobrium fell upon magicians, sorcerers, wizards, warlocks, the few witches still suffered to live by the smug male majority, and other practitioners of the thaumaturgical trade. Mobs attacked the magicians' manses and conclaves; the servants of sorcerers were torn limb from limb when they went into town to buy vegetables or wine; to utter a spell in public brought instant pursuit by peasants armed with torches, pitchforks, and charmless swords and pikes left over from old wars and earlier pogroms.

Such a downturn in popularity was nothing new for the weary world's makers of magic, all of whom had managed to exist for many normal human lifetimes and longer, so at first they reacted much as they had in earlier times of persecution: they shielded their manses with spells and walls and moats, replaced their murdered servants with less-fragile demons and entities from the Overworld and Underworld, brought up jarred foods from their vast basement stores and catacombs (while having their servants plant vegetable gardens within their spell-walled grounds), and generally laid low, some laying so low as to become literally invisible.

But this time the prejudice did not quickly fade. The sun continued to flicker, vibrate, cause convulsions below, and generally offer almost as many dark days as light. The scores of human species on the Dying Earth made common cause with the thousands of no-longer-human sort—the ubiquitous pelgranes and Deodands and prowling erbs and lizard folk and ghosts and stone-ghouls and Saponids and necrophages and visps and burrowing dolorants who were merely the tip of this truly terrible non-human icespike—and that common cause was to kill magicians.

When the unpleasant realities of this particular wizard-pogrom began to sink in, the various magicians of Almery and Ascolais (and other lands west of the Falling Wall) who had once belonged to the now-defunct "Fellowship of the Blue Principles" or its successor-organization, the so-called "Renewed Green and Purple College of Grand Motholam," reacted in ways consistent with their character: some fled the Dying Earth by unbinding the twelve dimensional knots and slipping sideways to Archeron or Janck or one of the other co-existing worlds discovered by the old Aumoklopelastianic Cabal; a few fled backward in time to more felicitous Aeons; more than a few took their motile manses or self-contained glebe-globes and made a run for it through the galaxy and beyond. (Teutch, a recognized Elder of the Hub, brought along his entire private infinity.)

A very few of the magicians who were more self-confident or curious or hoping to prosper through others' misfortune or simply bold (or perhaps merely much more prone to melancholy) took the risk of remaining on the Dying Earth to see what transpired.

SHRUE THE diabolist was more sanguine than most. Perhaps this was due to his age—he was older than any of his fellow thaumaturgs could have surmised. Or perhaps it was due to his magical specialty—most professional binders of demons and devils from the Overworld, Underworld, foreign stars, and other Aeons died young and in great pain. Or perhaps it was due to a rumored broken relationship and broken heart many millennia in his past. (Some whispered that Shrue had once loved and bedded and wedded and lost Iallai, she who had been the entity Pandelume's favorite dancer and the originator of the Dance of the Fourteen Silken Movements. Others whispered—even more softly—that Shrue had tumbled in thrall to one of his male apprentices back when the Mountains of Magntaz were still sharp, and had retired from magical life for centuries when the beautiful young man had stolen Shrue's most powerful runes and run away with a leather-bound Saponid from the night-town of Saponce.)

Shrue had heard all of these rumors and smiled—albeit sadly—at them all.

When the Great Panic came this time, Shrue the diabolist closed up Way Weather, his lovely manse of many rooms and sculpted towers in the hills above the north edge of Were Woods, and, using a less stressful variation on the ancient Spell of Forlorn Encystment, sank his manse, his beautiful gardens, and twelve of his thirteen servants some forty-five miles beneath the surface of the Dying Earth. Shrue's diabolic equipment, mementos, the bulk of his library, and the curios and ancillary demons he'd collected over the many centuries would be safe there underground, unless—of course—the great red sun actually swallowed the Dying Earth this time around. As for the truly amazing collection of flowers, trees, and exotiterra plants and animals from his garden (not to mention his twelve stored human and near-human servants), they were wrapped in miniature Omnipotent Eggs, each egg wrapped in turn in its own Field of Temporal Stasis, so Shrue was confident that if the Earth and he survived, so would his domestic staff, awakening months or years or centuries or millennia hence as if rising from a restorative sleep.

Shrue kept only Old Blind Bommps, his man-servant and irreplaceable chef, to travel north with him to his remote summer cottage on the shores of the Lesser Polar Sea. Bommps knew his way around the polar cottage and its protected grounds there as well as he'd memorized the many rooms, turrets, tunnels, secret passages, stairways, guest houses, kitchens, gardens, and grounds of Way Weather itself.

As for the scores of minor devils, demons, sandestins, stone-ghouls, elementals, archvaults, daihaks, and (a few) rune-ghosts that Shrue kept at his beck and call, all of these save one sank below with Way Weather manse in the Modified Spell of Forlorn Encystment—yet each remained capable of being summoned in an instant by the briefest incantation.

The only otherish entity that Shrue the diabolist took with him to the cottage on the shores of the Lesser Polar Sea was KirdriK.

KirdriK was an odd hybrid of forces—part mutant sandestin from the 14th Aeon, part full-formed daihak in the order of Undra-Hadra. Only the greatest arch-magicians in the history of the post-Yellow Sun Dying Earth dared to attempt to control a mature daihak-sandestin hybrid. Shrue the diabolist kept three such terrifying creatures in his employ at once. Two now rested forty-five miles beneath the surface of the earth, but KirdriK jinkered north along with Shrue and Old Blind Bommp, cushioned atop one of the larger rugs from Way Weather's grand hall. The jinkered carpet traveled at night, never rising above five thousand feet, and was protected by Shrue's Omnipotent Sphere as well as by the ancient carpet's own Cloud of Concealment, generated by the warp and woof of its softly singing incantatorial threads.

It had taken Shrue thirty-five years to summon KirdriK, another sixty-nine years to fully bind him, ten years to teach the monster a language other than its native curses and snarls, and more than twice a hundred years to make the halfbreed daihak superficially civil enough to take his place among Shrue's staff of loyal domestics. Shrue thought that it was time the creature began earning his keep.

SHRUE'S FIRST few weeks at his polar cottage were as quiet and uneventful as even the most retiring diabolist might have wished.

Early each morning, Shrue would rise, exercise his personal combat skills for an hour with a private avatar bound during the days of Ranfitz's War, and then retire to his garden for a long session of meditation. None of Shrue's former colleagues or competitors had known it, but the diabolist had long been adept in the Slow Discipline of Derh Shuhr, and Shrue exercised those demanding mental abilities every day.

The garden itself, while modest in comparison with that of Way Weather and also mostly sunken below the level of the surrounding lawns and low tundra growth, was still impressive. Shrue's tastes ran contrary to most magi's love of the wildly exotic—feathered parasol trees, silver and blue tantalum foil leaves, air-anenome trifoliata, transparent trunks and the like—and tended, as Shrue himself did, toward the more restrained and visually pleasing: tri-aspen imported from such old worlds as Yperio and Grauge, night-blooming rockwort and windchime sage, and self-topiarying Kingreen.

In late morning, when the huge red sun had finally freed itself from the southern horizon, Shrue would walk down the long dock, unfold the masts and sails of his sleek quintfoil catamaran, and sail the limpid seas of the Lesser Polar Sea, exploring coves and bays as he went. There were seamonsters even beneath the surface of the tideless, shallow polar seas, of course—codorfins and forty-foot water shadows the most common—but even such aquatic predators had long-since learned not to attempt to molest an arch-mage of Shrue the diabolist's reputation.

Then, after an hour or two of calm sailing, he would return and enjoy the abstemious lunch of pears, fresh-baked pita, Bernish pasta, and cold gold wine that Bummp had prepared for him.

In the afternoon, Shrue would work in one of his workshops (usually the Green Cabal) for several hours, and then emerge for a late afternoon cordial in the library and to hear KirdriK's daily patrol report and finally to open his mail.

This day, KirdriK shuffled into the library bowlegged and naked except for an orange breachclout that did nothing to hide either the monster's gender or his odd build. The smallest the daihak could contract his physical shape still left him almost twice as tall as any average human. With his blue scales, yellow eyes, six fingers, gill slits along neck and abdomen, multiple rows of incisors, and purple feathers flowing down from his chest and erupting along the red crestbones of his skull—not to mention the five-foot long dorsal flanges that vented wide and razor-sharp whenever KirdriK became agitated or simply wanted to impress his foes—Shrue had to dress his servant in the loose, flowing blue robes and veil-mesh of a Firschnian monk whenever he took him out in public.

Today, as mentioned, the daihak wore only the obscene orange breachclout. After he'd shuffled before the diabolist and knuckled his forehead in a parody of a salute—or perhaps just to preen the white feather-floss that grew from his barnacle-sharp brow—KirdriK went through his inevitable rumbling, growling, and spitting sounds before being able to speak. (Shrue had long since spell-banished and pain-conditioned the cursing and roaring out of the daihak—at least in the magician's presence—but KirdriK still tried.)

"What have you seen today?" asked Shrue.

(rumble, spit) "A grizzpol, a man's hour's walk east along the shore," rumbled KirdriK in tones that approached the subsonic, but which Shrue had modified his ears to pick up.

"Hmmm," murmured the diabolist. Grizzpols were rare. The huge tan bears, recreated by a polar-dwelling magician named Hrestrk-Grk in the 19th Aeon, were reported, by legend at least, to have originated from the crossbreeding of fabled white bears that had lived here millions of years earlier when the poles were cold and huge, with vicious brown bears from the steppes further south. "What did you do with the grizzpol?" asked Shrue.

"Ate it for lunch."

"Anything else?" asked the diabolist.

"I came across five Deodands lurking about five miles into the Final Forest," rumbled KirdriK.

Shrue's always-arched eyebrow raised a scintilla higher. Deodands were not native to the polar forests or gorse steppes. "Oh," he said mildly. "Why do you think they were this far north?"

"Trying to claim the magus-bounty," growled KirdriK and showed all three or four hundred of his serriated and serrated teeth.

Shrue smiled. "And what did you do with these five, KirdriK?"

Still showing his teeth, the daihak lifted a fist over Shrue's tea table, opened his hand, and let sixty or so Deodane fangs rattle onto the parqueted wood.

Shrue sighed. "Collect those," he ordered. "Have Bommp grind them into the usual powder and store them in the usual apothecam jars in the Blue Diadem workshop."

KirdriK growled and shifted from one huge, taloned foot to the other, his hands twitching and jerking like a strangler's. Shrue knew that the daihak tested his restraint bonds and spells every hour of every day.

"That's all," said the diabolist. "You are dismissed."

KirdriK departed by the tallest of the five doorways that opened into the library, and Shrue opened the window that looked into his courtyard eyrie and called in the day's batch of newly arrived sparlings.

There were nine of the small, gray, songless birds this day and they lined up on the arm of Shrue's chair. As each approached the magus's hand, Shrue made a pass, opened the bird's tiny chest, and drew out its second heart, dropping each in turn into an empty teacup with a soft splat. Shrue then conjured a new and preprogrammed blank recording heart for each sparling and set it in place. When he was finished, the nine birds flew out the window, rose out of the courtyard, and went about their business to the south.

Shrue rang for Old Bommp and when the tiny man padded silently into the room, said, "There are only nine today. Please add some green tea to bring the flavor up." Bommp nodded, unerringly found the teacup that sat in its usual place, and padded away with the same blind but barefoot stealth by which he'd entered. Five minutes later, he was back with Shrue's steaming tea. When the servant was gone, the diabolist sipped and then closed his eyes to read and see his mail.

It seemed that Ildefonse the Preceptor had returned from wherever he had fled off the Dying Earth because he had forgotten some of his velvet formal suits. While decloaking his pretentious manse, the pompous magician had been set upon by a mob of more than two thousand local peasants and pelgranes and Deodands working in unison—very strange—and they had Ildefonse's mouth taped, eyes covered, and fingers immobilized before the foolish old magician could waggle a finger or mutter a curse, much less cast a spell. They stripped the old fool of his clothes, amulets, talismen, and charms. As soon as they touched his body with their bare hands, Ildefonse's defensive Egg shimmered into place, but the mob simply carried that into town and buried it in a mound of dung piled to the ceiling of the one-room stone gaol in the center of the Commons, placing twenty-four guards and five hungry Deodands around the gaol and dungheap.

Shrue chuckled and went on to the rest of the sparling-heart news.

Ulfänt Banderōz was dead.

Shrue sat bolt upright in his chair, sending the teacup flying and shattering.

Ulfänt Banderōz was dead.

Shrue the diabolist leaped to his feet, clasped his hands behind his back, and began rapidly pacing the confines of his great library, eyes still closed, as blind as old Bummp, but, like Bummp, so familiar with the perimeter and carpet and hardwood and shelves and tables and other furniture in his great library that he never jostled a curio or open volume. Shrue, whose nature it was never to cease concentrating, was concentrating more fiercely and single-mindedly than he had in some time.

Ulfänt Banderōz was dead.

Other magicians had suspected Ulfänt Banderōz of being the oldest among them—truly the oldest magus on the Dying Earth. But for millennia stacked upon millennia, as long as any living wizard could remember and longer, Ulfänt Banderōz's only contribution to their field was his maintenance of the legendary Ultimate Library and Final Compendium of Thaumaturgical Lore from the Grand Motholam and Earlier. The tens of thousands of huge, ancient books and lesser collections of magical tapestries, deep-viewers, talking discs, and other ancient media constituted the single greatest gathering of magical lore left in the lesser world of the Dying Earth. Ulfänt Banderōz allowed other magi to visit only rarely and upon his own whim, but over the countless centuries, most living wizards had visited the Ultimate Library and walked in wonder through its many corridors of shelved books.

To no avail.

There was some sort of curse or spell on every item in the Ultimate Library so that only Ulfänt Banderōz—and perhaps a few of his apprentices working there—could cull any meaning from the books and other devices. Letters shifted and scurried and melted on each page, defying translation. Verbal artifacts slurred and skipped and lapsed into frequent silences. Ancient drawings and tapestries and pictures blurred and faded even as one began to study them.

And Ulfänt Banderōz—a broad, heavy, bejowled, beady-eyed, ill-smelling ancient—would laugh at the frustrated magicians and have his servants show them out.

Shrue had gone to the Ultimate Library three times over the millennia, twice prewarned of the arbitrariness of the letters and words, and thus prepared with fixating counterspells, magical solutions, enchanted viewing lenses, and other plans, but each time the letters shifted, the sentences began and then faded away, the long, arcane written incantations and spells and numerical cabalistic formulae fled from both his eye and memory.

Ulfänt Banderōz had laughed his croaking, choking, cackle of a laugh, and Shrue had departed, defeated once again.

Some wizards had followed the easiest route and shown up secretly armed with demons and attack spells, their plan simplicity itself—kill Ulfänt Banderōz and either force his odd apprentices (all recombinated from animals and creatures from earlier Aeons) into revealing the secret of fixing the books in time, or, failing that, simply taking over the Ultimate Library until they, the wizards, could solve the puzzle in their own time.

No one ever succeeded. Ulfänt Banderōz could not be intimidated, nor could he be out-magicked in his own Library. The bones of the thousands who had been foolish enough to try such tactics had been ground into

white pebbles that paved the attractive white walkway to the front door of the Ultimate Library.

But now Ulfänt Banderōz was dead. The sparling's heart revealed that the ancient magus's body had, upon the point of death, turned to stone and was currently laid out in his bedroom high in the tallest tower of the huge stone Library keep. The heart-news also told Shrue that it was rumored that only one of the scores of apprentices had survived but that he was a prisoner inside the Ultimate Library since—immediately upon Ulfänt Banderōz's death and turning to stone—at least a dozen terrible spell-barriers had sealed off the Library from the world around it.

Shrue the diabolist did not have to open his eyes or consult a globe or atlas to know where the Ultimate Library and Final Compendium of Thaumaturgical Lore from the Grand Motholam and Earlier lay. Ulfänt Banderōz's library was a mere five thousand leagues southeast of Shrike's cottage and then two leagues up Mount Moriat, high above the Dirindian River, just above the crossroads caravan city of Dirind Hopz, some two hundred leagues southwest of the southernmost limit of the Falling Wall. It was wild country, its dangers and wildness ameliorated only by the fact that Dirind Hopz lay on one of the Nine Major Caravan Routes to the holy city of Erze Damath.

Shrue opened his eyes and rubbed his long fingers and smooth palms together. He had a plan.

First he called down a Gyre from its nest of bones in his eyrie, immobilized the terrible raptor with a magical pass, and prepared a second message heart for it. The message was for Dame Derwe Coreme, formerly of the House of Domber but now War Maven of the Cillian Myrmazons. Derwe Coreme, Shrue knew, was, with her Maven Myrmazons, currently protecting and traveling with just such a caravan of pilgrims headed for Erze Damath and a mere hundred leagues north of his destination of Dirind Hopz.

The Gyre wriggled and protested as much as the inhibitatory spell allowed it to. The megaraptor's red eyes tried to burn its hatred into Shrue the diabolist. Shrue ignored it; he'd been hate-stared by better men and beasts. "Go supersonic," he commanded as he released the Gyre and watched it flap out of the courtyard and south on its preprogrammed course.

Then Shrue touched the pulsing green gem that called in KirdriK. The bowlegged daihak shuffled and strained out of old habit, but it also listened as Shrue gave his commands.

"Go to the pasture and fetch in one of the stronger and smarter horxbrids. Lenurd will do. Then get the larger wares wagon out of the stable, harness Lenurd, and load a week's food and wine in the back as well as eight or ten of our least valuable rugs from the vault. When you finish with that, come up to fetch my traveling chest. Oh, and carefully pour a full lentra of ossip phlogista from the vat into a container and pack it as well."

"A lead container?" growled KirdriK.

"Unless you want to be last seen floating north over the Lesser Polar Sea," Shrue said dryly. "And wear your robe. We're going five thousand leagues south to a place called Dirind Hopz, beyond the Falling Wall."

Shrue usually saw no reason in revealing his plans or reasons—or anything else—to his servants, but he knew that long before he'd first summoned the demon, KirdriK had spent an unpleasant twelve hundred years imprisoned in a cell a mile underground, and still had unpleasant associations with being buried alive; Shrue wanted the creature to prepare himself for the coming voyage.

KirdriK expelled his obligatory snarling and spitting noises and said, "You plan to drive the wares wagon five thousand leagues south, Magus-Master?"

Shrue knew that the daihak had attempted a drollery. With no roads within fifteen hundred leagues of the shores of the Lesser Polar Sea, the wagon would not make it through the sedge barrier almost within sight of the cottage. "No," said Shrue, "I'll be using the Constantly Expanding and Contracting Tunnel Apothegm. We shall ride in the wagon while it rides within the traveling burrow-space."

Now KirdriK actively writhed in his effort to break the unbreakable binding spells, his massive brow, flexible snout, and many rows of teeth gnashing and rippling and flexing. Then he subsided. "Master…" began the daihak, "I humbly submit that it would be faster to jinker the large unicorn carpet, roll the wagon onto it, and fly the…"

"Silence!" said Shrue the diabolist. "This is a bad time for wizards to be arriving anywhere by jinkered anything. Prepare the horxbrid and wagon, fetch my trunk, dress yourself in the dark blue Firschnian monk robes, and meet me on the lawn in forty-five minutes. We depart this very afternoon."

THE LAST few leagues rumbling along with the pilgrims' caravan were much more pleasant—even for Shrue—than the hours spent hurtling underground through rock and magma. KirdriK had been commanded to silence once above ground, but for these last miles and leagues he expressed his dissatisfaction by hissing and belching at every opportunity.

In happier days, such a caravan passing through hostile lands—the primary assailants here were wind-stick wraiths, rock goblins, and human bandits—would have been protected by a minor wizard utilizing his various protective spells in exchange for pay. But since the rise of murderous prejudice against the magi, the pilgrims to holy shrines, merchants, and other caravaners had to make do with mercenary soldiers. The leader of this band of eighteen Myrmazon mercenaries was War Maven Dame Derwe Coreme.

Derwe Coreme and Shrue the diabolist had known each other for a bilbo tree's age, but the magician's true identity was safe with the woman warrior. It's true that she laughed out loud when she first abandoned her megilla to ride in Shrue's canvas-covered wagon; the diabolist sat at the reins shrouded in a common merchant's shapeless tan robes, his lined and almost frighteningly saturnine face largely hidden by the shadows thrown by his soft-crowned, wide- and floppy-brimmed green-velvet Azenomei-Guild rugseller's hat. The two chatted comfortably as Shrue's wood-wheeled wagon rolled along in the rear of a caravan of more than forty similar wagons while KirdriK hawked, spat, and hissed in the rear amongst the carpets and Derwe Coreme's fanged and clawed two-legged megilla bounded alongside in a state of extreme reptilian agitation at the scent of the daihak.

Dame War Maven Derwe Coreme's past was shadowy and largely lost to legend, but Shrue knew that once this beautiful but scarred elder warrior had been a soft, innocent and sullen girl, as well as a largely useless princess fifth in line to the throne of Cil's now-defunct House of Domber. Then one day a thief and a vagabond sent on a useless odyssey imposed as punishment by Iucounu the Laughing Magician had kidnapped young Derwe Coreme, despoiled her for his pleasure, and eventually traded her to a small band of the vile sump-swamp river Busiacoes in exchange for travel advice of very dubious value. The Busiacoes had used her roughly for more than a year. Eventually, her character and heart hardening like tempered steel, Derwe Coreme killed the six Busiacoes who'd kept her as a pleasure slave, wandered the swamp Wegs and Mountains of Magnatz for several years with a barbarian warrior named Conawrd (learning more about blade-and-spear warfare than any former princess in the history of the Dying Earth and, many say, more than the dull-witted Conawrd himself), and then struck out on her own to earn a living as a mercenary while wreaking her revenge on all those who had ever slighted her. The thief and vagabond who had first abducted her—although Derwe Coreme by this time considered that abduction a boon—was eventually tracked down in Almery. Although Derwe Coreme had originally planned for the splay-footed lout to suffer indignities that no male of any species would wish to contemplate, much less experience, she eventually contrived for him to escape with all of his members and appendages intact. (He had not been very good, but he had—after all—been her first. And far more than her parents or early palace tutors, his particular brand of selfish indifference had helped make Derwe Coreme what she was today.)

In recent decades, Dame War Maven Derwe Coreme had personally trained and hired out her Three Hundred Myrmazons—women warriors each with a story and attitude as ferocious as their leader's—for lucrative mercenary work. For this caravan duty, eighteen Myrmazons had come along (although four or five would have sufficed for the few hundred wind-stick wraiths, rock goblins, and human bandits waiting to waylay this caravan) and each young woman warrior was megilla-mounted and dressed in skintight dragonscale armor that left her left breast bare. Even the Myrmazons' adversaries—in their last seconds of life—found this ritual form of dress distracting.

As they chatted, Derwe Coreme laughed and said, "You are as droll and witty and private as ever, Shrue. I've often wondered what might

have been our relationship if you'd been younger and I'd been more kindly disposed toward the male of our species."

"I've often wondered what our relationship might have been had you been older and I had been a female of our species," said Shrue the diabolist.

"You have the magic," laughed War Maven Derwe Coreme. "Make it so!" And with that she whistled shrilly, her megilla ran up alongside the wagon and lowered its scaly neck, and she leaped across to the saddle and spurred the beast away.

THE CARAVAN town of Dirind Hopz was overflowing with displaced pilgrims, merchants, and wayfarers. Bandit activity and general mayhem were so rampant in all directions south that even the most pious worshipers bound for Erze Damath found themselves halted in Dirind Hopz until private armies could clear the roads. There was a huge temporary encampment on the plains just to the northeast of the town and most of the pilgrims in Shrue's caravan camped there, living in their wagons, and Derwe Coreme and her Myrmazons set up their own city of tall red tents. Shrue, however, in his guise as rugseller—and because he wanted to get as close as he could to the mountain along the river that had the Ultimate Library and Final Compendium at its summit—brought KirdriK and sought out an inn.

All the finer establishments were on the bluffs high above the Dirindian River, where they received cool breezes, offered expansive views, and kept their distance from the many sewers that opened into the Dirindian; but all the finer establishments were full. Shrue finally found a tiny room and tinier cot up under the eaves in the ancient, leaning, ramshackle Inn of the Six Blue Lanterns but had to pay an outrageous twenty terces for it.

Schmoltz, the one-eyed innkeeper whose forearms were thicker than Shrue's thighs, nodded at KirdriK and said, "An extra twelve terces if your monk sleeps on the floor or stands in the room while you sleep."

"Followers of the Firschnian Eye seek only mortification and physical discomfort," said Shrue. "The monk, who never sleeps, shall be satisfied to take shelter in your barn amidst the dung heaps and foul-smelling brids and mermelants."

"That'll be ten terces for use of the barn," growled Schmoltz.

After securing KirdriK in the barn, Shrue went up to his room and set one of his own rugs on the floor—it filled the small space between the bed and the wall—and then laid his own clean sheets and blankets on the dubious cot, burning the old ones in a flameless blue vortex. Then the diabolist went down to the common room to eat his late dinner. Rug merchants of Azenomei Guild never removed their hats in public, so Shrue felt moderately comfortable with his disguise under the low-hanging velvet brim, silk straps, half-veil, and floppy ear coverings.

He'd finished only half of his stew and drained just one glass from his flagon of indifferent Blue Ruin when a short, balding man slipped into the empty chair opposite him and said, "I beg your pardon for the intrusion, but do I not find myself in the company of Shrue the diabolist?"

"You do not," murmured Shrue, touching his merchant's hat with his bony fingers. "Surely you recognize the sign of the Azenomei Guild?"

"Ahh, yes," said the short, heavy, beady-eyed man. "But I apologize for any effrontery if I add that I also recognize the long, strong features of an arch-magus named Shrue. I had the pleasure of seeing the famous diabolist long ago in a thaumaturgical wares-fair in Almery."

"You are mistaken," said Shrue with an inaudible sigh. "I am Disko Fernschüm, rugseller and calendar-tapestry menologist from Septh Shrimunq in Province Wunk in south Ascolais."

"My mistake then," said Faucelme, "but please allow me to explain to the honorable merchant Disko Fernschüm the pressing business that I, Faucelme, would have had with the magician named Shrue. It will, I promise, be worth your while, sir." And Faucelme signaled the serving person, Schmoltze's ample-bosomed young wife, over to order a better flagon of wine.

Shrue knew of Faucelme, although the two had never conversed nor been introduced. Faucelme lived a life of some obscurity in the forest-wastes far north of Port Perdusz, living in a modest (for a magus) manse and pretending to be a most minor magician, all the while terrorizing his entire region, murdering and robbing wayfarers, and slowly building his magical powers through the acquisition of curios and talismans. The man himself looked harmless enough—short, bald, stooped, with a nose like a Gyre's hooked beak and tiny, close-set eyes. A fringe of unkempt gray hair straggled down over Faucelme's equally hairy ears. The old magician wore a black velvet suit, shiny and thin with age, and only the rich rings he sported on every finger gave any sense of his wealth and mendacity.

"You see," said Faucelme, pouring Shrue a fresh goblet of Schmoltz's best red, "just to the southeast of this weary—and smelly!—little caravan

town, upon the summit of Mount Moriat, there lies the Ultimate Library of…"

"What has this to do with me?" interrupted Shrue. He'd gone back to drinking his lesser Blue Ruin. "Does the library need rugs?"

Faucelme showed ancient yellow teeth in a rodent's smile. "You and I are not the first wizards here since Ulfänt Banderōz's death," hissed the little guest-killer. "At least a score have left their carcasses on Mount Moriat's summit, just outside the spell-shield wall the master of the Library left behind."

Shrue radiated indifference and ate his stew.

"Ulfänt Banderōz left a dozen layers of defense," whispered Faucelme. "There is a Layer of Excruciating Breathlessness. Another Layer of Internal Conflagration. Then an inert layer, but one stocked with starving stone-ghouls and vampire necrophages. Then a Layer of Total Forgetfulness to the Defiler, followed by…"

"You mistake me for another," said Shrue. "You mistake my silence at your boorishness for interest."

Faucelme flushed and Shrue saw the hatred in the old magus's eyes, but the killer's expression slid back into a simulacrum of generous friendship. "Surely, Shrue the diabolist, it would be better—and wiser and safer—for the two of us to pool our resources…mine infinitely more modest than yours, of course, but surely stronger in combination than in separate attempts—as we both try to pass through the Twelve Defensive Layers after the dawn…"

"Why wait for morning if you are so eager?" asked Shrue.

Real fear flickered across Faucelme's features. "Mount Moriat is renowned for its ghouls, goblins, ghosts, wolves, and albino Deodands, even outside of Ulfänt Banderōz's magical defenses. And you can hear the storm pounding upon the inn's shingles even as we…"

"I do hear the storm," said Shrue as he rose and signaled for Schmoltz's daughter to clear away his things. He took the last of the Blue Ruin with him. "It makes me sleepy. I hope to join a caravan headed south in the morning, so I wish you a pleasant night's sleep Ser…Faulcoom?"

He left Faucelme smiling and flexing his hands the way KirdriK was wont to do when he most wanted to strangle his master.

SHRUE WOKE at exactly two bells in the morning, just as he had hypnotically instructed himself to do, but for a few seconds he was confused by the warmth of another body in bed with him. Then he remembered.

Derwe Coreme had been waiting in his tiny room when he'd come upstairs and watched him coyly from where she lay naked under the covers. She held the covers low enough that Shrue had seen that the cold river air coming in through the open window was affecting her. "I'm sorry," he'd said, hiding his surprise. "I haven't had time to do the gender-changing spell."

"Then I'll have to show you how a woman-version of Shrue might begin to pleasure me," said Derwe Coreme. As it turned out, Shrue now remembered, the former princess to the House of Domber had not been as averse to men as she might have thought.

Now he slipped out from under the covers, careful not to wake the softly snoring warrior, got rid of his rug merchant clothes and cap in a silent flash of blue vortex, and dressed himself silently in his most elegant dark-gray tunic, pantaloons, and flowing robe made of the rarest spider-silk. Then he jinkered the carpet to life, brought it to a hover four feet above the floor, and climbed aboard with his shoulder valise.

"Did you just plan to leave me a note?" whispered Derwe Coreme.

Shrue the diabolist had not stuttered since his youth—a youth lost in the tides of time—but he came close to doing so at that moment. "On the contrary, I planned to be back before dawn and to commence where we left off," he said softly.

"Pawsh," said the war maven and slipped out of the covers, dressing quickly in her dragonscale armor.

"I had no idea that Myrmazons and their leader wore nothing under their scales," said Shrue.

"If blade or beam cuts through those scales," said Derwe Coreme as she buckled up her high boots, "it's best not to have any underlayers with foreign matter that might infect the wound. A clean wound is the best wound."

"My approach to life exactly," whispered Shrue as his carpet floated at the level of the war maven's bare left breast. "May I drop you somewhere on my way?"

Derwe Coreme slipped on two daggers, a belt dirk, a throwing star, a hollow iberk's horn for signaling, and her full sword and scabbard, slid them aside, and climbed on the floating rug just behind him. "I'm coming with you."

"But I assure you, there is no need for…" began Shrue.

"There was no need for the three hours until we fell asleep," said Derwe Coreme, "but they worked out all right. I'd like to see this so-called Ultimate Library and Final Compendium of Thaumaturgical Lore from the Grand Motholam and Earlier. For that matter, I'd like to meet this Ulfänt Banderōz I've heard so much about over the years."

"Him…you might find disappointing," said Shrue.

"So many men are," said War Maven Derwe Coreme and put her arms around Shrue's ribs as he tapped flight threads and maneuvered the jinkered carpet forward, out sixty feet above the river, and then up and east toward the dark mass of Mount Moriat.

THE ULTIMATE Library had been carved into the very rock of Mount Moriat, but rose from the summit in a series of thick but gleaming towers, gables, bulges, cupolas, and turrets. The keep was blind—that is, the many windows were mere slits, none broader than Derwe Coreme's slender (but powerful) hand. The layers of protection spells caused the entire structure to gleam milkily and Shrue thought that countless castles lost to memory must have looked like that in the full moonlight in aeons long past. Then Shrue's incipient melancholy grew deeper at the realization that no one else alive he knew would think of anything on the Dying Earth in moonlight; the Earth's moon had wandered away into deep space millions of years ago, beyond even the reach of most legend. Most of the night sky above them now was dark save for a few dim stars marking the merest hint of where a progression of proud constellations had once burned.

Shrue tried to shake away the debilitating melancholy and concentrate on the task ahead, but—as he was also too prone to do—he wondered, not for the first or ten-thousandth time, what his real motive was in entering the Ultimate Library and reading Ulfänt Banderōz's books. *Knowledge* said part of his mind. *Power* whispered a more honest part. *Curiosity* argued an equally honest part. *Control of the Dying Earth* said the deepest and least-dissimulating core of the diabolist's weary and melancholy brain.

"Are you going to land this rag?" asked Derwe Coreme over his shoulder. "Or are we just going to circle a thousand feet above the Dirindian until the sun comes up?"

Shrue brought the carpet down to a three-foot hover and dejinkered it as they stepped off. KirdriK was waiting just outside the phase fields as ordered. Either he had shed his monk's robes or the beasties on his way up had clawed and chewed them off in their dying seconds.

"Great Krem," whispered the war maven Myrmazon leader, hand going reflexively to her sword. "You choose ugly servants, Shrue."

"You should see Old Blind Bommp," said KirdriK through his rasp and gargle and growl.

"Silence," commanded Shrue. "I have to study Ulfänt Banderōz's layers of defensive fields."

Within a moment, he knew that the vile Faucelme had been essentially correct: there were a dozen layers to the Library's defenses, eight of them active spells, four of them—counting the ghost—physical. As he probed and countered, Shrue felt something like disappointment fill him. Ulfänt Banderōz had been one of the arch-maguses of all magi still living on the Dying Earth, but these defenses—while deadly enough to the average magician or would-be barbarian vandal—were easy enough to foil and countermand. Shrue had to spend less than five minutes on the first eight, and as for the spellbound circling (and starving) wolves, stone-ghouls, and vampire necrophages, KirdriK put them out of their misery within seconds.

They stepped across the massive old drawbridge—the Library's moat was more decorative than serviceable, although Shrue saw croc-men swimming in the black water—and were confronted by the equally massive door sporting a surprisingly heavy lock.

"Are you going to blast that off?" asked Derwe Coreme. "Or would you prefer me to use my blade?"

"Neither you nor your blade would survive, I fear," Shrue said softly. "Civilized people use a key." He pulled one from his robes, fit it, clicked it, and opened the heavy door. Answering the Myrmazon's quick, sharply questioning gaze, Shrue added, "I was a guest here long ago and took the liberty of studying the lock then."

The inside of the Ultimate Library was dark and silent, the air dead, as in a room or crypt that had been closed up for centuries rather than weeks. Wary of boobytraps, Shrue had KirdriK emit a soft but bright glow from his chest that illuminated everything for twenty paces in front of the three of them. Shrue also allowed the daihak to lead the way, although always while under the diabolist's guidance. They moved from room to room, then from floor to floor, up stairways rimned with dust. Here and there on the floor lay what they first took to be stone statues—short, nonhuman shapes—until finally Shrue said, "These are Ulfänt Banderōz's servants or apprentices. It seems they also turned to stone when he died."

On each level of the darkened library, there were racks and shelves and stacks of books, most of the volumes a third to half as tall as Shrue himself. When they had progressed far enough that Shrue was moderately certain that there would be no goblin attack or sudden, deadly efulsion of dark forces, he lifted a dusty volume off its shelf and set it down heavily on an ancient, high, and slanted wooden reading table.

"I'm interested to read whatever this is," whispered Derwe Coreme. It was hard to speak at normal volume in the echoing spaces.

"Be my guest," said Shrue and opened the large book. He read—or rather, looked—over the war maven's dragonscaled shoulder. The yellowish light from KirdriK's chest was more than ample.

Derwe Coreme's head snapped back as if she had been slapped. Shrue himself tried to focus, but the sentences and words and very letters shimmered in and out of focus and visibility as if they were written in quicksilver.

"Ah," cried the woman warrior. "That gives me a blinding headache just trying to bring a word into focus."

"Men have gone blind staring at these books," whispered Shrue.

"Magicians, you mean," said Derwe Coreme.

"Yes."

"Can your monster read it?" she asked.

"No," croaked KirdriK. "I am literate in more than nine hundred phonetic and glyphic alphabets and more than eleven thousand written languages, living and dead, but these symbols scatter like cockroaches when a light is turned on."

Shrue smiled dryly and applauded in the direction of Derwe Coreme and his daihak. "Congratulations," he said to the woman. "You've just elicited the first simile I've heard from KirdriK in more than a hundred…"

There came a sound from the darkness behind them.

Derwe Coreme whirled and her long blade glittered in KirdriK's chestlight. The daihak balled his huge six-fingered fists and showed a wall of teeth. Shrue raised three long fingers, more in restraint of his companions than in defense.

A short—no more than four feet tall—form stepped from the shadows and a genderless voice squeaked, "Do not harm me! I am a friend."

"Who are you?" demanded Shrue.

"*What* are you?" asked the Myrmazon leader.

"I am called Mauz Meriwolt," squeaked the little form. "I was—have always been, since birth—Ulfänt Banderōz's servant boy."

"Boy?" repeated Derwe Coreme and lowered her sword.

Shrue had his Expansible Egg incantation ready to surround them at the utterance of a final syllable, not to mention his Excellent Prismatic Spray spell ready to slice this newcomer to ribbons in an instant, but even the diabolist—who judged few things or people upon their appearance—sensed no threat from the tiny form. Mauz Meriwolt was pibald in hue, with arms and legs thinner and more rubbery than Shrue's old wrists, tiny three-fingered hands, an oversized head with oversized ears placed too far back, a long proboscis with only a few whiskers protruding, and enormous black eyes.

"*What* are you?" repeated Derwe Coreme.

The little person seemed befuddled by the question, so Shrue answered for him. "Ulfänt Banderōz had the affectation of recreating lost life forms from the dim past to fill his staff," he said softly. "I believe that our short friend Mauz Meriwolt came from some long-forgotten line of rodents."

"You can call me Meriwolt," squeaked the shy little form. "The 'Mauz' was some sort of honorific…I think."

"Well, then, Meriwolt," said Shrue, his voice carrying an edge, "perhaps you can explain why you survived here when all of Ulfänt Banderōz's other servants appear to have been turned into stone like their master." The magus gestured toward a stone figure on the floor—what might have been a humanoid attempt at the ancient life form called a feline.

"That's Gernisavien, the Master's neo-cat and tutor to all of us lesser servants," said Meriwolt. "She…changed…at the instant of the Master's death, as did all the others."

"Then we ask again," said Shrue. "Why not you?"

The little figure shrugged and Shrue noticed for the first time that Meriwolt had a skinny but short whip of a tail. "Perhaps I was not important enough to turn to stone," he said, his voice squeaking with misery. "Or perhaps I was spared because—despite my unimportance—the Master seemed to feel some affection for me. Master Ulfänt Banderōz was not widely known for his sentimental side, but it may be the reason I was spared when all the others died when he did. I can think of no other."

"Perhaps," said Shrue. "In the meantime, Meriwolt, take us to your Master."

Derwe Coreme, Shrue, and KirdriK followed the little creature up stairways, through hidden doorways, and through more huge rooms filled from floor to ceiling with racks and shelves of books.

"Did you ever shelve these books for your master?" Shrue asked the little figure as they climbed to yet another level and entered a turrent staircase.

"Oh, yes, sire. Yes."

"So you could read the titles?"

"Oh, no, sire," said Meriwolt. "No one in the Library could read the titles or any part of the books. I simply knew *where* the book should go on the shelves or in the stacks."

"How?" asked Derwe Coreme.

"I don't know, sire," squeaked Meriwolt. He gestured to a low door. "Here is the Master's bedchamber. And within is…well…the Master."

"Have you been inside since your master died?" asked Shrue.

"No, sire. I was…afraid."

"Then how do you know your master is dead within?" asked Shrue. The diabolist knew that Ulfänt Banderōz was dead and turned to stone on the bed within because he had looked through the eyes of his spy sparling perched on the narrow slit of window above, but he was open to catching this Mauz Meriwolt in a lie if there was a lie.

"I peeked through the keyhole," squeaked the little assistant.

Shrue nodded. To KirdriK he said, "Stand guard on the drawbridge outside." To Derwe Coreme and the trembling Meriwolt he said, "Please go stand behind those thick columns. Thank you."

Shrue touched the latch—the door to Ulfänt Banderōz's chamber was unlocked—and then he opened the door and stepped within.

In an instant, Phandaal's Excellent Prismatic Spray sent a thousand shards of frozen colors, each as terrible as a bolt of barbed crystal, hurtling into the space that Shrue the diabolist occupied. Shrue's modified Expansible Egg froze them in midair, and a gesture by the diabolist banished them.

An efulsion of green fog—instantly fatal to human or magician's lungs—erupted from the ceiling and floorboards and from the stone corpse of Ulfänt Banderōz himself. Shrue raised both palms, transformed the efulsion into a harmless, colorless fog, and then waved it away. He waited.

Nothing more erupted, exploded, slouched forth, or efulged.

"You may come in now," Shrue said to the war maven and Mauzman.

The three stood next to the bed that held the stone corpse of the Master of the Ultimate Library and Final Compendium of Thaumaturgical Lore from the Grand Motholam and Earlier. The petrified remains of Ulfänt Banderōz looked ancient but dignified as he lay there fully dressed with his eyes closed, feet together, hands calmly clasped over his lower belly.

"He seems to have known that death was coming," whispered Derwe Coreme.

"The Master had been suffering bouts of ill health for several years before...before...this," squeaked Meriwolt in his softest voice.

"Was your master frequently absent from the Library?" Shrue asked the assistant.

"For a week of every month for as long as I can remember, and I have been the Master's faithful assistant for many centuries," piped the Mauzman.

"As I thought," mused Shrue. "There is a second Library."

"What?" cried the Myrmazon chief.

Shrue opened his hands. "Actually it is the same Library, my dear, but phase-displaced in space—by many hundreds or thousands of miles and leagues, no doubt—and in time by at least a few fractions of a second. This is why the books cannot be read here."

"But they can be read in the other Library?" asked Derwe Coreme.

"No," smiled Shrue, "but in the other Library there must be the means to bring the two libraries back in phase." He turned to Meriwolt. "Did you have a twin by any chance?"

The pibald little figure was so startled that his three-fingered hands flew up and his odd ears went back. "Yes—a sister who died at birth—or rather, when we were devatted. The Master has told me many times that it was a shame that she did not live—he had named her Mindriwolt. How did you know, sire?"

"She did not die at birth," said Shrue. "All these centuries, your twin has been an assistant at Ulfänt Banderōz's phase-shifted second Library. This is how you sometimes 'just know' where to shelve the books your Master ordered you to shelve."

"She did not...was not...turned to stone when the Master died?" asked Meriwolt in a trembling squeak.

Shrue absently shook his head. "I suspect not. We will know when we go there."

"Where is this place?" asked Derwe Coreme, an aggressive explorer's—or perhaps plunderer's—smile on her face. "And what treasures may it hold?"

Shrue opened his hands and arms again, gesturing toward the Library beneath and around them. "The treasures of the secrets of ten thousand-thousand ages of power and science and magic," he said softly. "The great Phandaal's long-lost mysteries. Panguire's Prime Commandments. The secrets of Clamhart and Tinkler and Xarfaggio and a hundred other magi of ancient days—men who make today's magicians, myself included, look like children playing witlessly with colored blocks."

"How do we find it?" asked the war maven.

Shrue crossed the modest room to a recessed closet shielded by a simple rood screen, checked for boobytraps, and rolled back the screen. Atop a single primitive dresser was a glass case, and, within the case, gleaming softly, was a perfectly smooth crystal the size and shape of a merg's egg. Inside the gently pulsing crystal, what looked like the vertical slash of a crimson cat's eye glowed.

"What is it?" breathed Meriwolt.

"A Finding Crystal," said Shrue. "Enchanted to lead the bearer to something important…such as the second Library." He tapped his thin lower lip while he studied the crystal case that contained the treasure. "Now to find a way to open this without…"

Derwe Coreme removed her sword, reversed it—her dragonscaled gauntlet protecting her hand from the blade's razor sharpness—and smashed the heavy hilt down on the priceless crystal case. It shattered into a thousand shards and the warrior maven sheathed her sword, lifted the cat's-eye crystal egg out, and presented it to Shrue, who pondered it a moment and then set it somewhere within the folds of his robe.

"We must begin our odyssey at once!" cried Dame War Maven Derwe Coreme. "Activate your jinker or jinker your carpet or wake up your rug or whatever the hell you must do. Treasures and booty await!"

"I think that we should…" began Shrue but was interupted by KirdriK flicking back into existence next to them.

"We have company," rumbled the daihak. "And one of them is a Red."

THE FIRST pre-dawn light was lighting the crags and scragtrees around the summit and Library keep. Faucelme was there with his small army—eleven pelgranes, each larger than any Shrue had ever seen, each saddled as if to carry a man or demon—and then a tall, blond, handsome male human apprentice, also dressed in black, and the nine demons themselves. These last were the huge surprise to Shrue—not that the foul little magician would show up with demons in tow, that was a given, but that he could muster *these* terrible entities. Arrayed behind the apprentice and Faucelme (who was still dressed in black, the rings on his fingers glowing from more than reflected morning twilight) were nine Elementals—three Yellows (to be expected), three Greens (very impressive for any magus from the 21st Aeon), two Purples (rather astounding and not a small bit terrifying), and a Red.

The presence of the Red, Shrue knew, changed everything. *How has this little homunculus ever managed to summon and bind a Red—or survive the process?* wondered the diabolist. Aloud he said, "Welcome, Faucelme. I came for our dawn meeting, as you requested."

The thief-magus grimaced a smile. "Oh, yes…*rug merchant?* If the best you can do is that simpering daihak, then perhaps you truly are only a carpet peddler."

Shrue shrugged. He could feel Derwe Coreme's poised readiness next to him, but the Myrmazon leader had little chance even with a Yellow, none with a Green or Purple, and less than none with Faucelme and his apprentice, much less with a Red. KirdriK's attention was focused—through and across twelve dimensions of perception—totally on the Red. Shrue could feel the daihak strain against a century's worth of invisible bindings like a wolf on a leash. KirdriK's sublimated snarls were not on any frequency that human ears could hear, but both the two Purples and the single terrible Red were showing row upon row of what would be called fangs on lesser entities as *they* heard KirdriK's challenge .

"I've already had my insects peer in at the rock that used to be Ulfänt Banderōz," continued Faucelme. "Since I already have an adequate paperweight for the desk in my study, I have no use for the dead librarian. But I do want his…ho!…who is this *rat* that's joined your ranks, diabolist?"

Meriwolt had been cowering behind Derwe Coreme but now poked his long snout and wide eyes around her armored hip. The diminutive Mauzman's mouth hung open in awe or horror or terror or all three.

"Merely a possible new servant I am interviewing," said Shrue. "You started to say that you wanted…to go down to the village with us to have breakfast? Or would you and your entourage rather enter the Library and pay your last respects to Ulfänt Banderōz while we return to Dirind Hopz?" Still smiling, Shrue jinkered the little carpet to life and floated it close.

The Red twitched his six onyx-taloned hands, and Shrue's rug—a family heirloom from a time when the sun burned yellow—exploded in heatless crimson flames. The ash scattered in a rising breeze as the red sun struggled to rise across the river in the east.

"Thus to any attempts to jinker skyward," hissed Faucelme. "Your wares wagon and other carpets are already ash, Shrue. I want the Finding Crystal and I want it *now*. "

Shrue's left eyebrow arched almost imperceptibly. "Finding Crystal?"

Faucelme laughed and held his hand out as if ready to release the Red. "Shrue, you're a fool. You've just figured out that Ulfänt Banderōz kept the volumes here unreadable by phase-shifting them in spacetime…but you still think there is a *second* library. There is only this one, the Ultimate Library, displaced in space and time. When I collapse that phase-shift, the magical lore of a million years will be mine. Now give me the Finding Crystal."

Shrue reluctantly removed the crystal from his robe with both hands, but kept his long, gnarled fingers around it as it glowed in his palms. Beneath them, the granite of Mount Moriat shook as the sun struggled to rise, its bloated red face flickering and spotted.

"Faucelme, it is you who've not thought this through," Shrue said softly. "Don't you understand? It's Ulfänt Banderōz's careless tampering with time-space, this very Ultimate Library, that is unstable. *This…*" He took one hand off the mesmeric Finding Crystal and gestured toward the vibrating stone of the Library behind him. "…is what is causing the Dying Earth to die even before its short allotted final days have come to pass."

Faucelme laughed again. "You must think I was born yesterday, diabolist. Ulfänt Banderōz has kept this library stable but time-space separated longer than you—or even I—have been alive. Hand me the crystal at once."

"You must understand, Faucelme," said Shrue. "It was not until I came here that I understood the true cause of the world's current instability. For whatever reason, Ulfänt Banderōz lost control of the two Libraries' phase shift in the months before he died. The closer the Libraries come in time, the greater the space-time damage to the red sun and the Dying Earth itself. If you bring the two Library realities together, as you and your Red propose to do, it will bring about the end of everything…"

"Nonsense!" laughed Faucelme.

"Please listen..." began Shrue but saw the madness flickering in the other magician's eyes. It was not, he now understood, a question of whether Faucelme would release the Red. Faucelme was more the Red's puppet than vice versa, and the Elemental cared not a terce whether the millions upon the Dying Earth survived another day. In desperation, Shrue said, "There is no guarantee that your Red—even with the Purples in support—can defeat a sandestin-daihak hybrid from the 14th Aeron."

Faucelme's eyes *were* flickering red. It was not an illusion or a reflection of the shaking sunrise. Something ancient and inhuman had taken possession of the small human shell and was literally burning to get out. "You are correct, Shrue the diabolist," said Faucelme. "There is no guarantee that my Red shall prevail—only overwhelming odds. But you know as well as I what the outcome will be in thirty seconds if we both unleash our entities—you your daihak, I my Elementals. You might even survive—it's conceivable. But the whore and the rodent will be dead before five of those thirty seconds have passed, as will be all eight thousand people in the valley below. Decide, Shrue. I demand the Finding Crystal...*now*."

Shrue the diabolist tossed the crystal to Faucelme. Suddenly, Shrue seemed to shrink, to become little more than a tall but thin and frail old man in spidersilk robes, his spine curved under the burden of age and a terrible weariness.

"I'd kill you all now," said Faucelme, "but it would be a waste of energy I need for the voyage." Barking in a language older than the mountain upon which they stood, Faucelme commanded the two Purples to remain behind and to keep Shrue and his entourage from leaving the Library. Then Faucelme, his apprentice, the vibrating Red, and the three Yellows and three Greens mounted their mutated pelgranes and rose into the sky.

Even from a distance, Shrue could see Faucelme in the saddle, bending over his glowing Finding Crystal as the eleven giant pelgranes flapped their way southeast until they were lost in the soft red glare of the sunrise.

"Come," Shrue said wearily. "The Purples may allow us to live a little longer and we might as well find something to eat in the Library."

Derwe Coreme opened her mouth as if to speak angrily, looked sharply at the stooped old man who had been her energetic lover just hours earlier, and disgustedly followed Shrue into the Library. Mauz Meriwolt and then KirdriK—the daihak moving reluctantly and jerkily and not under his own volition—followed. The demon's multidimensional gaze never left the two Purples.

ONCE INSIDE, Shrue's demeanor changed completely. The magus loped through the library stacks and bounded up stairs as if he were a boy. Meriwolt's black bare feet slapped on stone and Derwe Coreme had to run to keep up, her right hand holding her scabbard and iberk's horn in place to keep them from clanking. "Did you think of something?" she called to Shrue as the diabolist burst into Ulfänt Banderōz's death chamber again. Derwe Coreme was panting only slightly from the exertion but she noticed with some small vexation that Shrue was not breathing heavily at all.

"I didn't just think of it," said Shrue. "I knew it all along. That beautiful Finding Crystal was mere bait. It will lead Faucelme and his Elementals nowhere—or at least nowhere they want to be. My hope is that it will take them to the open jaws of a Lanternmouth Leviathan in the South Polar Sea."

"I don't understand," squeaked Meriwolt, looking at the shards of shattered glass cover where the Finding Crystal had been so prominently displayed. "Why would the Master leave…" The little Mauzman looked at Shrue and stopped.

"Precisely," said Shrue. He reached into his shoulder bag and pulled out a stone chisel, a hammer, and an elaborate little wooden box with a glass front. Leaning over the remains of Ulfänt Banderōz like a doctor come too late, Shrue chipped off the dead magician's not-insignificant nose with three hard taps on the chisel. The glass panel on the small box slid open at a gesture, Shrue set the nose in place, the panel closed, and there was an audible hiss and sigh as the box pumped all air out of the small space. Shrue held the box out absolutely flat, glass face up, while the other two huddled close and KirdriK remained in the doorway, staring down through wood, iron, and stone at the two Purples outside.

The nose in the box quivered like a compass needle and turned slowly until the nostrils faced south-southeast.

"Wonderful!" cried Derwe Coreme. "Now all you have to do is jinker one of these carpets into flight and we'll find the other Ultimate Library before the sun sets!"

Shrue smiled ruefully. "Alas, Faucelme was telling the truth when he said that he had destroyed all of my jinkerable rugs."

"You're a magician," said the Myrmazon leader. "Won't any carpet turn into a flying carpet at your command?"

"No, my dear," said Shrue. "There was something called science behind the magic in those wonderful jinkered bits of cloth and wire. Faucelme's vandalism this morning has been profound. Those rugs alone were worth more than all the fabled treasure in the catacombs beneath Erze Damath. Also, Faucelme was telling the truth—his Red's spell will bring down any jinkered flying device in all of the Dying Earth—that is how powerful a Red Elemental can be."

KirdriK growled and Shrue realized the daihak had said, "The Tunnel Apothegm?"

"No, the guiding nose will not work beneath all that stone," Shrue said softly.

"We can take the megillas, we bring extras along," said Derwe Coreme, "but if the other Ultimate Library is on the other side of the world, it might take..."

"Forever," chuckled Shrue. "Especially since, the last time I checked, your megillas were not enthusiastic swimmers. There may be several seas and oceans in the way."

"We're foiled then?" asked Meriwolt. The little servant sounded relieved.

Shrue glanced at the little figure and his stare was cold and appraising. "I guess you *are* a member of this expedition now, Mauz Meriwolt. That is, if you want to be."

"If my twin sister really *is* in the Other Library, I would like to meet her," came the squeak.

"Very well then," said Shrue, setting the case with Ulfänt Banderōz's nose carefully in his shoulder bag, nestled amidst an extra set of underlinens. "There are ways to fly other than magic. The caravan transit hub of Mothmane Junction is only fifty leagues south and east from here along the River Dirindian, and, unless I am mistaken, the old sky galleon towers and the ships themselves are still intact."

"Intact," said Derwe Coreme, "but lacking their vital lifting fluid since the trade routes to the far north closed. No sky galleon has flown from Mothmane Junction in the last two years."

Shrue smiled again. "We can take your megillas," he said softly. "If we're willing to ride them half to death—which means saddle sores for this old magus's bum—we can be in Mothmane Junction by midday tomorrow. But we shall have to stop at my wares wagon below to fetch my traveling trunk."

"Faucelme said that he'd burned your ware wagon and all its contents," reminded Derwe Coreme.

"So he did," said Shrue. "But my trunk is hard to steal and harder to burn. We shall find it intact in the ashes. The sky galleon owners of Mothmane Junction will welcome some of the things that KirdriK packed in it...which reminds me. KirdriK?"

The daihak, the purple feathers rising from the red crestbones of his skull to touch the doorframe twelve feet above the ground, his huge six-fingered hands twitching and opening and closing, growled a response.

"Would you be so kind," said Shrue, "as to kill the two Purples waiting below?"

KirdriK showed a fanged smile so broad that it literally went from one pointy ear to the other. Another few inches and the top of his head would have fallen off.

"But take them to the tenth level of the Overworld to do the deed," added Shrue. Turning to Meriwolt and Derwe Coreme he explained, "It reduces the number of collateral casualties considerably. At least in *this* world." Turning to KirdriK again, he said, "Rejoin us as soon as you are finished in the Overworld."

KirdriK winked out of sight and a few seconds later there came an astonishing thunderclap, rattling the Library, as the daihak dragged the two Purples out of one reality and into another. The stone corpse of Ulfänt Banderōz jiggled on its high bed and books and nostrums tumbled from shelves and dressertops.

"To the damned megillas," said Shrue. Derwe Coreme was loosening the iberk's horn from her belt as they left the room.

Mauz Meriwolt lagged behind a moment. Standing over the noseless stone corpse, the little figure clasped his hands in front of him and bowed his head. His huge black eyes filled with tears. "Goodbye, Master," he said.

Then Meriwolt hurried down to join the other two. Dame War Maven Derwe Coreme's shattering hornblast was already echoing from the mountainside while the blare of answering iberk horns rose from the valley below.

THERE WERE three tall steel-and-iron towers rising over the caravan city of Mothmane Junction like metal markers on a sundial. The tower tops ranged from three hundred to six hundred feet above the town and river. Each tower was made of open girders, skeletal and functional yet still ornamental in some forgotten age's style, and the top of each tower was an acre or two of flatness broken only by the necessary cranes, dock-cradles, ramps, shacks, passenger waiting areas, and cargo conveyors necessary to service the almost constant flow of sky galleons that had once filled the skies here. Now as Shrue and his companions, including the seventeen Myrmazons who'd accompanied their leader, rode down the wide main avenue of Mothmane Junction—residents and stranded pilgrims and others scurrying to get out of the way of the exhausted and angry megillas—the diabolist could see that only three galleons remained. For centuries, the sky galleon trade had withered as the quantities of ossip sap and its phlogista extract became more and more scarce. Most of the ancient sky galleons that had called Mothmane their primary port had long since been grounded elsewhere or stolen by pirates and put to more practical uses on the Dying Earth's seas or rivers.

But three remained—grounded atop their respective departure towers but relatively intact. Before they reached the shadows of those towers, Shrue took out his telescope and studied their choices.

The first tower rising into the dark blue midday sky, that of the *Most Excellent Marthusian Comfort Cruise Line*, was little more than girders of rust holding up crossbeams of wooden decay. The outside stairway had collapsed and the broad-bucketed elevator had long since plummeted to the bottom of its shaft. Shrue could see rough rope ladders spiderwebbing the structure and men moving on the sagging platform three hundred feet above the river, but they appeared to be dismantling the once-proud galleon that nestled in its dockstays. The ship's masts were minus their sails and most of the deck structures—and some of the hull—had already been stripped of the priceless ironwood.

The second tower, its ancient signs and banners still proclaiming *Lumarthian Luxury Travel! Cruises and Transits to Anywhere on the Dying Earth! Sky Galleons of Ultimate Comfort and Total Safety and Most Decadent Luxury! Pilgrims Welcome!! Worshipers of Yaunt, Jastenave, Phampoun, Aldemar, and Suul—Praised Be Their Names!—10% Discount!*, was hardly more intact than the first tower and ship. There was no one visible atop the tower—even the cargo-handlers' shacks had fallen down. The sky galleon docked there was larger than the first, but looked as if it had been in a battle—the length of its hull had been scorched and breached and riddled with ten-foot-long iron harpoons that gave the old galleon a porcupined look.

Shrue sighed and studied the third and tallest tower. The stairway—all sixty zigzagging flights of it—looked shaky but complete. The lift platform was still at the bottom of its shaft but Shrue could see that all of the levitation equipment had been removed and the remaining metal cables—looking too old and far too thin to support much weight—were connected to a manual crank at the bottom. The banner here was more modest—*Shiolko and Sons. Sky Galleon Transit to Pholgus Valley, Boumergarth, and the Cape of Sad Remembrance (Ossip Supplies Permitting).*

Well, thought Shrue, no one would be paying to fly to the Cape of Sad Remembrance after the recent tsunamis. He focused his glass on the flat top of the tower.

There were tents and people there—scores of both—which was both reassuring and dismaying. Whoever these potential passengers were, it looked as if they had been waiting a long time. Laundry hung from ropes tied between old tents. The sky galleon, however, looked more promising. Nestled in its tall cradle-stays, this ship—smaller than the other two—looked not only intact but ready to fly. The square-rigged sails were tidily shrouded along spars on the foremast and mainmast while lateen-rigged canvas was tied up along the two after-masts. A bold red pennant flew from the foremast some sixty or seventy feet above the galleon's deck and Shrue could make out brightly painted gunports, although they were closed so he could not tell if there were any actual guns or hurlers behind them. At the bottom of the cradle, sunlight glinted on the great ovals and squares of crystallex set in as windows along the bottom of the hull. Young men—Shiolko's sons was Shrue's wild guess—were busy running up ramps and clambering expertly through the masts, lines, and stays.

"Come," said Shrue, spurring his panting and sulky megilla. "We have our galleon of choice."

"I'm not climbing sixty flights of rusting, rotting stairs," said Derwe Coreme.

"Of course not," said Shrue. "There is a lift."

"The lift platform itself must weigh a ton," said Derwe Coreme. "It has only a cable and a crank."

"And you have seventeen marvelously muscled Myrmazons," said Shrue.

THE OWNER and captain of the sky galleon, Shambe Shiolko, was a short, heavily muscled, white-bearded beetle-nut of a man and he drove a hard bargain.

"As I've explained, Master Shrue," said Shiolko, "there are some forty-six passengers ahead of you—" Shiolko gestured toward the muddle of sagging tents and shacks on the windswept platform where they all stood six hundred feet above the river. "And most of them have been waiting the two years and more that I've lacked the extract of ossip and atmospheric emulsifier which allow our beautiful galleon to fly..."

Shrue sighed. "Captain Shiolko, as *I* I have tried to explain to *you*, I have the ossip phlogista for you..." Shrue nodded to Derwe Coreme, who lifted the heavy sealed vat out of his trunk and carried it over, setting it on the boards of the platform with a heavy thunk. And from his robes, Shrue produced a smaller lead box which still glowed a mild green. "And I also have the crygon crystals for the atmospheric emulsifier you require. Both are yours without cost as long as you book us passage on this voyage."

Captain Shiolko scratched at his short beard. "There are the expenses of the trip to consider," he mumbled. "The salaries for my eight sons—they serve as crew, y'know. Food and water and grog and wine and other provisions for the sixty passengers."

"Sixty passengers?" said Shrue. "There need only be provisions for myself and this servant..." He gestured toward Mauz Meriwolt who was largely disguised within a diminutive Firschnian monk's robe. "With the possible addition of another member of my party who might join us later."

"And me," said War Maven Derwe Coreme. "And six of my Myrmazons. The rest can return to our camp."

Shrue raised an eyebrow. "Certainly, my dear, you have other more... profitable...undertakings to pursue? This voyage will be of an undetermined length, and, indeed, might take us all the way to the opposite sides of the Dying Earth, and that by a circuitious route..."

"Nine of you then," grumbled Captain Shiolko. "Plus the forty-six who have waited so long. That will be provisions for fifty-five passengers, and nine crew of course, counting myself, so sixty-four mouths to feed. The *Steresa's Dream* has always set a fine table, sir. Mere provisions, not including our salaries, will come to...mmmm...five thousand, three hundred terces for the vittles and a mere two thousand four hundred terces above that for our labors and skills...."

"Outrageous!" laughed Shrue. "Your sky galleon will sit here forever unless I provide the ossip extract and emulsifier. I should be charging *you* seven thousand five hundred terces, Captain Shiolko."

"That is always your privilege to do so, Master Shrue," grunted the old sky sailor. "But then the cost of your passage would rise to more than fourteen thousand terces. I thought it easier the first way."

"But certainly," said Shrue, gesturing to the crowd, "these good people do not want to take such a long and…I confess…dangerous voyage, since I would insist that our destination, which is not yet even fixed, will be the first one to which we sail. You can return for them. This amount of ossip phlogista alone should levitate your beautiful galleon…"

"The *Steresa's Dream,*" said Captain Shiolko.

"Yes, lovely name," said Shrue.

"Named after my late wife and the mother of the eight crewmen," murmured the old captain.

"Which makes it even more lovely," said Shrue. "But, as I was saying, even if we were to meet your exorbitant demand for recompense, these good people should not wish to endanger their lives in such a dangerous voyage when they desire simple transit to less problematic destinations."

"With all due respect, Master magus," said Shiolko, "look at them what's waited here so patient for two years and more and understand why they will insist they be aboard whenever *Steresa's Dream* departs its cradle. The three there in blue finery—that is Reverend Ceprecs and his two wives and they booked passage on our fine galleon for their honeymoon cruise, and that was twenty-six *months* ago, sir. The Reverend's religion forbids him to consummate the happy trio's marriage vows until they are officially *on* their honeymoon, you see, so they have waited these two years and more in that leaking old burlap tent you see over near the comfort shack…"

Shrue made an indecipherable noise in his throat.

"And the seven persons there in working brown," continued Shiolko. "They be the Brothers Vromarak who wish nothing more than to bring the ashes of their dead father home to their ancestral sod hut on the Steppes of Shwang in the distant east Pompodouros so they can return to Mothmane and resume work at the stone quarry…"

"But the east Pompodouros almost certainly will not be on our way," said Shrue.

"Aye, Master," said Shiolko, "but as you say, if you won't be wanting transport back to here, we can drop the Brothers on their way—and only

for an additional eight hundred terces from each of them for my inconvenience. And that tall, tall fellow there, that is Arch-Docent Huæ from Cosmopolis University…he's been waiting nineteen months now in that cardboard shack you see there…and he cannot complete his thesis on the effect of antique effectuations on working-glass gloam-mine gnomes unless he visits the city of fallen pylons across the Melantine Gulf. I will charge him only a modest surcharge of fifteen hundred terces for that detour. And then, near the back of that group of orphans, there is Sister Yoenalla, formerly of Bglanet, who must…"

"Enough!" cried Shrue, throwing up his hands. "You shall have your seven thousand five hundred terces and your ossip and your emulsifier and you may load the paying menagerie as well. How long until we can sail?"

"It will take my sons only the afternoon and night to load the necessary viands and water flasks for the first weeks of our voyage, Master Magus," grunted Shiolko, showing only the slightest flush of pride at his success. "We can sail at dawn, should the treacherous sun choose to favor us with one more sunrise."

"At dawn then," said Shrue. He turned to reason with Derwe Coreme but the woman was already choosing the six Myrmazons to accompany her and giving the others instructions about their return to the Myrmazon camp.

AND THUS began what Shrue would later realize were—incredibly, almost incomprehensibly—the happiest three weeks of his life.

Captain Shiolko was true to his word and *Steresa's Dream* lifted away from its docking cradle just as the red sun began its own tortured ascent into the deep blue sky. The galleon hovered for a moment like a massive wood-and-crystal balloon some thousand feet above what looked to be the entire population of Mothmane Junction turned out to watch its departure, and then Shiolko's eight "sons" (Shrue had already noticed that three of them were young women) shook out the canvas sails, the captain engaged the atmospheric emulsifier at the stern—which thickened the air beneath the sky galleon's hull and rudder sufficiently to allow it to make way and to tack against the wind—and, following Shrue's directions after the diabolist had consulted his little box holding Ulfänt Banderōz's nose, set the ship's course south-southeast.

All forty-six of Shiolko's original customers as well as Derwe Coreme and her Myrmazons, Meriwolt (still in his robes), and Shrue himself then pressed to the railings of the mid-deck or their private stateroom terraces and waved to the shouting crowds below. At first, Shrue thought that the thousands of Mothmane Junction residents, peasants, shopkeepers, and rival sky galleon workers were roaring their approval and best wishes up to the voyagers, but then he saw the low morning sunlight glinting off arrows, crossbow bolts, rocks, and a variety of other things flung up at *Steresa's Dream* and he realized that the first departure of a sky galleon in more than two years was not an occasion held in unalloyed affection and approval. But in a few moments, the galleon had gained several thousand feet in altitude and, after first following the River Dirindian south for a few leagues, banked off southwest above the wooded Kumelzian Hills and left Mothmane Junction and its muted roars far behind.

For the next several days and then weeks, Shrue's and the ship's routine blended into one.

At sunrise each morning, the diabolist would rise from his place in the double hammock he shared in the comfortable suite with Derwe Coreme and—even before meditating according to the Slow Discipline of Derh Shuhr—Shrue would scramble up the manropes to the Gyre's nest near the top of the mainmast and there use Ulfänt Banderōz's guiding nose to take a new course reading. That course would be checked via the nose box several times during the day—Captain Shiolko was a master at making the slightest adjustments—and for the final time, by the light of the binnacle (when one of Shiolko's male or female sons was at the wheel), just at midnight.

Steresa's Dream itself was one of those rarest of avas in the later Aeons of the Dying Earth—a machine with complicated machinery inside it—and on the first day of the voyage, Captain Shiolko proudly showed off his beautiful ship to Shrue, Derwe Coreme, robed Meriwolt, and many of the other interested passengers and pilgrims. Shrue immediately then understood that the tiny crew of eight "sons" could manage such a complicated craft not due to the usual reason—magic—but because the huge sky galleon was largely automated. Controls on the quarterdeck at the rear of the ship (which was Shiolko's private preserve unless the captain specifically invited a passenger to come up) or other controls down in the aft engine and steering compartment helped reef and furl the sails, shift and shorten the countless ropes and lines, move ballast as needed, and even calculate wind and drag and mass so as best to move the ossip phlogista through the maze of pipes that honeycombed the hull, masts, spars, and sails themselves. The emulsifier machine so fascinated Shrue with its magickless glows and throbs and safety devices and arcane gauges and bone-felt spell-less vibrations that often, when he could not sleep, he came down to the engine and steering compartment to watch it all work.

The sky galleons had been built for passenger comfort and even those paying the fewest terces found themselves in comfortable surroundings. For Shrue and the other high-paying passengers, it was sheer luxury. The diabolist's and Derwe Coreme's stateroom at the third level near the stern had a wall of crystal windows that looked out and down. Their double-sized hammock rocked softly and securely in even the worst night storms. After Shrue had checked their course and done his Discipline rites in the morning, he would wake his warrior roommate and the two would shower together in their own private bath. Then they would step out onto their private balcony to breathe the cool morning air and would go forward along the central corridor to the passenger dining area near the bow where there were crystal windows looking ahead and underfoot. The sense of vertigo in these glass-bottomed lower rooms faded with familiarity.

On the fifth day, the *Steresa's Dream* passed east out of known territory. Even Captain Shiolko admitted that he was excited to learn what lay ahead of them. Over wine with Shrue and Derwe Coreme late that night, the captain explained that although his sky galleon was built as a world-traveler, Shiolko's wife Steresa, while she lived, so worried about dangers to her husband and children that, in his love and deference to her, the captain had stowed away his impatience to see the farthest lands and satisfied himself with transiting passengers to known (and relatively safe) destinations such as Pholgus Valley, Boumergarth, the former cities on the Cape of Sad Remembrance, and towns and ports in between. Now, said the captain, he and his sons and the brave passengers and the fine ship that Steresa had loved and feared so much were outward bound on the sort of voyage for which *Steresa's Dream* had been designed and built centuries before Shiolko or his late wife had been born.

AFTER THE first week, Shrue had become impatient, eager to rush to the Second Ultimate Library, sure that KirdriK had been bested and eviscerated somewhere in the Overworld and that even now the Purples were

returning to Faucelme's evil band, and he'd urged Captain Shiolko to take the galleon high up into what was left of the Dying Earth's jet stream—up where the wind howled and threatened to tear the white sails to ribbons, where ice accumulated on the spars and masts and ropes, and where the passengers had to retreat, wrapped in furs and blankets, to sealed compartments to let the ship pressurize their rooms with icy air.

But he'd seen the folly in this even before Derwe Coreme said softly to him, "Can Faucelme's false Finding Crystal lead him to the other Library?"

"No," said Shrue. "But sooner or later he—or more likely, the Red—will understand that they've been tricked. And then they'll come seeking us."

"Would you rather they find us frozen and blue from lack of breath?" said the warrior maven.

Shrue had shaken his head then, apologized to the captain and passengers for his haste, and allowed Shiolko to bring the *Steresa's Dream* down—in a slow, dreamlike descent—to her lower, warmer altitudes and more leisurely breeze-driven pace.

During the second week of their voyage, there were some memorable moments for Shrue the diabolist:

For a full day, *Steresa's Dream* wove slowly between massive stratocumulus clouds that rose nine leagues and more before anvilling out high in the stratosphere. When the sky galleon had to go through one of these cloud giants, the ship's lanterns came on automatically, one of Shiolko's sons activated a mournful fog horn on the bow, and moisture dripped from the spars and rigging.

For two days, they flew above a massive forest fire that had already devoured millions of hectares of ancient woodland. *Steresa's Dream* bucked and rolled to the violent thermal updrafts. The smoke became so heavy that Shiolko took the ship as high as she could go without incurring icing, and still Shrue and the passengers had to wear scarves over their noses and mouths when they went on deck. That night, the fifty-four passengers—including Derwe Coreme's Myrmazons and Mauz Meriwolt, who no longer bothered wearing the monk's robes—dined in awed silence, staring down through the dining room's crystal hull-floor as the inferno raged and roared less than a mile below them.

As they neared a coastline, the sky galleon flew low over the last stages of a war, where a besieging army was attacking an iron-walled fortress city. Several of the ancient, rusted walls had already been breeched, and reptile-mounted cavalry and armored infantry were pouring in like ants while the defenders blocked streets and plazas in a last, desperate stand. Derwe Coreme's experienced eye announced that there were more than a hundred thousand besiegers set against fewer than ten thousand defenders of the doomed city. "I wish they could have hired my three hundred and me," Derwe Coreme said softly as the galleon passed above the carnage and burning port and floated southeast out to sea.

"Why?" said Shrue. "You would certainly be doomed. No three hundred warriors in the history of the Earth could save that city."

The war maven smiled. "Ah, but the glory, Shrue! The glory. My Myrmazons would have extended the fight for weeks, perhaps months, and our war prowess and glory would be sung until the red sun goes dark."

Shrue nodded, even though he did not understand at all, and touched her arm and said, "But that could be mere weeks or days from now, my friend. At any rate, I am glad you and your three hundred are not down there."

The *Steresa's Dream* sailed due east across a green, shallow sea and then they were above what both Captain Shiolko and Shrue believed was the legendary Equatorial Archipelago. The passengers lunched on their terraces and looked down as Shiolko brought the galleon low to less than a thousand feet above the tropical-foliaged isles and green lagoons. The islands themselves seemed uninhabited, but the inter-island waterways, bays, and countless lagoons were filled with hundreds upon hundreds of elaborate houseboats, some almost as large as the sky galleon, and all a mass of baroque wood designs, bright brass festoons, crenellated towers and arching cabins, and each carrying more flags, banners, and colorful silks than the last.

They left the archipelago behind and crossed further south and east into deeper waters—the sea went from green to light blue to a blue so dark as to rival the Dying Earth's sky—and the only moving things now spied below were the great, shadowy shapes of whales and the sea monsters who ate the whales. In the dining room that night, the ocean below was alive with a surface phosphorescence underlaid by the more brilliant and slow-moving biological arc lamps of the Lampmouth Leviathans. Realizing that one of those beasts could swallow the *Steresa's Dream* whole, Shrue was as relieved as the other passengers when Captain Shiolko took the galleon higher to find more favorable winds.

The next morning, one of Captain Shiolko's sons showed Derwe Corme and Shrue how to hook their small webbing hammocks to clasps set high

in the crosstrees of the mainmast above the Geyre's nest. It was a gusty day and the sails and tops of the masts were often tilted thirty to forty degrees from vertical as the great ship first tacked and then ran before the wind. The magus's and war maven's tiny hammocks swung sixty feet above the deck and then, in an instant of roll, were thousands of feet above a solid floor of stormclouds miles and leagues below. It was sun-dark day and the primary light came from the lightning that rolled and rippled through the bellies of the clouds beneath them.

"That's odd," said Derwe Corme as she rolled out of her hammock and into Shrue's. The cheap clasps and thin webbing strings on Shrue's hammock groaned and stretched but held as Derwe sat up and straddled him. "I never knew I was afraid of heights until today."

ON SIXTHDAY Night of the second week, Shiolko and his sons opened the beautiful Grand Ballroom—its crystal floor took up almost a third of the hull bottom—and the passengers and sons staged a Mid-Voyage Festival, even though no one had the slightest idea if the voyage was at its midpoint or not. By midnight, Shrue cared no more than the others about such niggling fine points.

Even after two weeks, Shrue was surprised at his fellow passengers' festive skills. Shiolko's sons, it turned out, each played an instrument—and played it well. The side-windows were open in the Grand Ballroom and out into the interocean night went the complex bell-chimes of tiancoes, the string music of violins, serpis, and sphere-fiddles, the clear notes from flutes, claxophone, harp, and trumpet, and the bass of tamdrums and woebeons. Captain Shiolko, it turned out, was as much a master of the three-tiered piano as he was of his ship, and thus the dancing began.

Reverend Cepres and his two wives—Wilva and Cophrane—had not been seen out of their cabin since the voyage commenced, but they appeared in brilliant blue silks this night and showed the interested celebrants how to dance the wild and uninhibited Devian Tarantula. The Brothers Vromarak put aside their mourning for the night and led everyone in a hopping, leaping tango-conga line that concluded with two-thirds of the dancers collapsing in a wriggling, laughing heap. Then Arch-Docent Huǽ—the same tall, silent, solemn form with whom Shrue had played chess every evening on the foredeck—who had left his dark docent robes behind in his booklined stateroom, appeared barechested in gold slippers and silver pantaloons to dance a wild solo Quostry to the pounding piano and tamdrums. The dance was so gravity-defying and amazing to watch that the sixty-some passengers and crew applauded to the beat until Huǽ concluded by literally leaping to the ceiling, tapdancing there for an impossible three minutes, and then lowering himself like a spider to the crystal dancefloor below and bowing.

Little Maus Meriwolt wheeled out an instrument that he'd cobbled together. The thing appeared to be a mixture of organ, calliope, and fog horn, and Meriwolt—dressed now in his fanciest yellow shirt, white gloves, and red shorts—tapdanced in oversized wooden clogs as he sang in his falsetto and pulled ropes to activate the various horns, pipes, and steam sirens. The effect was so comical that the round of applause Meriwolt received rivaled Arch-Docent Huǽ's reception.

But perhaps the most amazing part of the long night to Shrue was the transformation of Dame War Maven Derwe Coreme and her six Myrmazons.

Shrue had never seen Derwe Coreme or her fighters out of their formfitting dragonscale armor, but this night they appeared in thin, floating, incredibly erotic gowns of shimmeringly translucent silk of soft red, orange, yellow, green, blue, indigo, and violet. Everyone in the ballroom gasped when the Myrmazons floated in like a rainbow. And—like the bands of color in a rainbow—the intensity and hues shifted and changed from one to another as the women moved and as one moved in relation to them. Derwe Coreme, who had entered in a red dress, had her thin gauze's color shift to violet as Shrue approached to ask her to dance. Each of the young women's gowns shifted color as they moved and as their bodies moved beneath the fabric, but the full rainbow was always present with all seven of its colors.

"Astounding," whispered Shrue much, much later as he held Derwe Coreme close as they danced. The orchestra, apparently exhausted from its own exertions during the wild dances, was playing a slow waltz half as old as time. The ball was almost over. There was a pre-dawn grayness to the light outside the crystal windows. Shrue could feel Derwe Coreme's breasts against him as they slowly moved together across the crystal hullfloor. "Your gown—all your gowns—are astounding," he said again.

"What? This old thing?" said Derwe Coreme, tossing aside a floating ribbon of the nearly transparent and seemingly gravity-free fabric—it was

now green. "Just something the girls and I picked up after sacking the city of Moy." She was obviously amused—and perhaps pleased—by Shrue's amazement. "Why, diabolist? Does this sort of garb on a warrior not fit into your magician's philosophy?"

Shrue recited softly—

> "*Do not all charms fly*
> *At the mere touch of cold philosophy?*
> *There was an awful rainbow once in heaven:*
> *We know her woof, her texture; she is given*
> *In the dull catalogue of common things.*
> *Philosophy will clip an Angel's wings,*
> *Conquer all mysteries by rule and line,*
> *Empty the haunted air, and gnomed mine—*
> *Unweave a rainbow*"

"*That* is astounding," whispered Derwe Coreme. "Who wrote it? Where did you find it?"

"No one knows who wrote it," said Shrue, pulling her closer and whispering against her cheek. "I was thinking a moment ago that this waltz is half as old as time…well, that verse, the name of its author lost to us, *is* as old as time. And older than all our memories—save my mother's, who used to put me to sleep with ancient poetry."

Derwe Coreme pulled back suddenly to study Shrue's face. "You? Shrue the diabolist? With a mother? It is hard to imagine."

Shrue sighed.

Suddenly Arch-Docent Huǽ cut in—not to dance with Derwe Coreme, but to talk excitedly to Shrue.

"Did I hear you just say something about gnome mines? I am doing my thesis on gnomes in gloam-mines, you know!"

Shrue nodded, took Derwe Coreme's hand, and said, "Fascinating. But I fear the lady and I must turn in now. I shall talk to you about gnome mines another time—perhaps over chess tomorrow."

Arch-Docent Huǽ, appearing somewhat less professorial than usual with his bare chest, red cumberbund, silver pantaloons, and gold slippers, looked crestfallen.

As they went up the grand stairway out of the ballroom, Derwe Coreme whispered, "My leaving will ruin the rainbow."

Shrue laughed. "Five of your other six colors left with gentlemen hours ago."

"Well," said the war maven, "I cannot say that I am leaving with a gentleman."

Shrue glanced at her sharply. Although his expression had not changed, he was amazed to find that his feelings were deeply hurt.

As if sensing this, Derwe Coreme squeezed his hand. "I am leaving with *the* gentleman," she said softly. "Of this voyage. Of all the males I've known in my not-insignificant lifetime. Perhaps in all of the Dying Earth. A gentleman *and* a magician—not a common combination, that."

Shrue did not argue. He said nothing as they went up to their stateroom.

TWO DAYS later the *Steresa's Dream* crossed the western coastline of another continent just after dawn. Ulfänt Banderōz's nose shifted at least ten degrees northeast in its little box and the sky galleon altered its course to follow.

"Captain," Shrue said as he stood on the otherwise empty quarterdeck near Shiolko at the great wheel, "I noticed the gunports along the hull…"

Shiolko rumbled his sailor's laugh. "Paint only, Master magus. Paint only. For appearance sake come sky pirates or angry husbands after a port call."

"Then you have no weapons?"

"Three crossbows and my grandfather's cutlass in the weapons' locker," said Shiolko. "Oh, and the harpoon gun down in the for'ard hold."

"Harpoon gun?"

"A great awkward thing that runs off compressed air," said the captain. "Fires an eight-foot long barbed bolt of a harpoon trailing a mile or three of thin steel cable. Originally meant to hunt whales or baby Lanternmouths or some such. My sons and I have never had reason nor opportunity to use it."

"You might want to bring it up on deck and see if it works," said Shrue. "Practice with it a bit."

Late that afternoon, the galleon crossed an expanse of ochre and vermillion desert glinting with crystals. The *Steresa's Dream* was flying low enough that everyone could see the huge, blue creatures—rather like soft-shelled chambered nautiluses, Shrue thought from where he watched

from the railing—which had evolved a single great wheel by which they rolled singularly and in groups across the red desert floor, leaving tracks ten leagues long.

"We could practice on one of them!" called one of Shiolko's sons to Shrue. He and two others had assembled and hooked up the air-harpoon gun nearby on the deck but had yet to fire one of the barbed harpoons.

"I wouldn't," said Shrue.

"Why not?" asked the goodnatured young man.

Shrue pointed. "Those tracks the blue-wheelers are leaving in the sand? They're ancient glyphs. The creatures are wishing us fair winds and a pleasant voyage."

As they passed beyond the desert, Derwe Coreme joined him at the rail. "Shrue, tell me the truth. You never had any plans to flee the Dying Earth when its last days came, did you?"

"No," said Shrue. He showed a quick, uncharacteristic grin. "It's all just too damned interesting to miss, isn't it?"

EARLY THE next morning they had entered a higher, sharper range of mountains than any of them had ever seen before—the peaks were high enough that real snow remained on the summits—when suddenly the low clouds ahead parted and the *Steresa's Dream* was floating above tall, thin metal-and-glass towers that were lit from within by something brighter than lanterns.

A dozen ancient air cars flew into the air like hornets from those towers and swept toward the galleon.

Captain Shiolko sounded the alarm—he'd had to retrieve several of the klaxons and sirens from Meriwolt's cobbled-together musical instrument—and the passengers went to their stations belowdeck as rehearsed. The captain's sons took their places in the rigging or at fire-fighting stations and Shrue saw all three ancient crossbows in use. Shiolko himself, at the wheel, had buckled on the cutlass that one of his female sons had brought him. Derwe Coreme and her six Myrmazons deployed themselves with their shorter crossbows and edged weapons—two of the women on the port side rail, two on the starboard, one in the bow, one in the stern at the quarterdeck behind the captain, and Drew Coreme herself roaming. Shrue remained where he'd been at the port railing.

Three of the air cars swept in closer. Shiolko was having one of his sons run up the white and blue universal flag of parley when the three air cars fired narrow, intense beams of light at the *Steresa's Dream*. Two sails and narrow circles of decking burst into flame, but Shiolko's sons put out the fires with buckets of water in half a minute.

Four more air cars joined the first three, and they swept in closer on the port side, choosing to unleash their heat beams from only a hundred yards out.

"Fire," said Derwe Corme. All seven of the Myrmazons triggered their blunt but powerful crossbows. They reloaded so quickly from their belt-quivers that Shrue could not see the actual motions. Together, the seven got off eleven volleys in less than a minute.

Bolts pierced the yellowed, brittle canopies of the ancient air cars and six of the seven, their pilots dead, plummeted down through the clouds to crash on the snowy peaks below. The seventh air car wobbled away, no longer under its pilot's control.

The remaining five began to circle the *Steresa's Dream* from half a league out, attempting to ignite the galleon's wide, white sails with their attenuated beams.

Shrue glanced at the compressed-air harpoon gun, but Shiolko's sons were too busy cooling the white-circled hot spots on the sails to man the clumsy weapon. Closing his eyes, Shrue raised both arms, turned his fingers into quickly moving summoning claws, and chanted a spell taught him a century earlier by a misogynist fellow-magus named Tchamast.

Out of the clouds to the northeast emerged a half-mile-long crimson dragon, its wings longer than the galleon, its eyes blazing yellow, its long teeth glinting in the sunlight, its maw wide enough to swallow all five air cars at once. Everyone on the *Steresa's Dream* ceased their cries and motion until the only audible sounds were the flapping of the sails in their stays and the much louder *flap-flap-flap* of the giant dragon's leathery wings.

The air cars turned clumsily and fled back toward the distant tower-city.

The dragon ceased its pursuit of the metal and plastic vehicles and turned its interest toward the *Steresa's Dream*, its long, sinuous body undulating like a sea serpent's as it flew between the clouds. Its yellow eyes looked hungry.

"The harpoon gun!" cried Captain Shiolko to his sons. "Man the harpoon gun."

Shrue shook his head and held up one hand to stop the young men. Checking to make sure that the last of the air cars was out of sight, Shrue raised both arms again—the gray spidersilk of his robe sleeves sliding back—and made motions as if directing an invisible orchestra, and the dragon disappeared with a thunderclap implosion. The passengers applauded.

Later that evening, Shrue came up on deck to another round of applause. The passengers were watching a smaller, greener, but angrier version of his dragon trying to keep up with the sky galleon but falling behind as the wind came strong straight from the southwest, propelling *Steresa's Dream* over and away from the last of the mountain peaks and their attendant clouds. Belching fire in the direction of the galleon, the smaller dragon turned back toward the clouds and high peaks.

"I think your first dragon was more convincing," said Captain Shiolko as the passengers on deck again applauded the magician.

"So do I," said Derwe Coreme. "This one seemed a tad…less solid. Almost transparent in spots."

Shrue shrugged modestly. He saw no reason to tell them that the second dragon had been real.

THEY SPOTTED their followers just after dawn. Shrue and Derwe Coreme were awakened by a son and—after receiving permission from Captain Shiolko—hurried up onto the quarterdeck to the aft railing. The captain, several of his sons, Arch-Docent Huǽ, Meriwolt, and several of the other passengers were sharing Shiolko's telescope to study the dots flitting above the western horizon. The morning air was free of clouds and absolutely clear. Shrue's own tiny telescope folded as flat as a monocle but it was the most powerful instrument aboard the *Steresa's Dream*. The diabolist unfolded it and looked toward the horizon for a long moment, then handed the better telescope to the captain. "It's the eleven pelgranes," he said softly. "Faucelme has found us."

"There's one saddle empty," said Derwe Coreme when it was her turn to look through the telescope.

"The apprentice seems to have gone missing," said Shrue. "But you'll notice that the two Purples are back and in their respective saddles."

Derwe Coreme's pale face lifted toward Shrue. "Then your daihak—KirdriK—has failed. If that is true…"

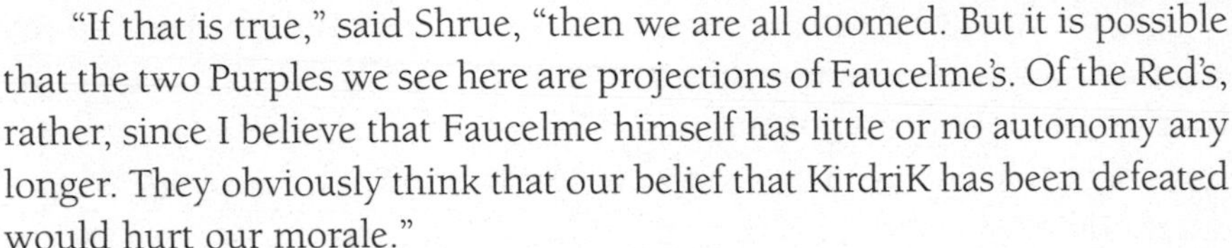

"If that is true," said Shrue, "then we are all doomed. But it is possible that the two Purples we see here are projections of Faucelme's. Of the Red's, rather, since I believe that Faucelme himself has little or no autonomy any longer. They obviously think that our belief that KirdriK has been defeated would hurt our morale."

"It certainly hurts mine," squeaked Meriwolt.

Shrue put his long finger to his lips. "No one else need know about KirdriK's battle with the Purples. Then, projection or no, the morale of our small band will not suffer."

"Until Faucelme and his Red and Purples kill us," said Derwe Coreme very softly. But she was smiling and there was a gleam in her eye.

"Yes," said Shrue.

Captain Shiolko walked over to their group. He and the other crew and passengers knew only what Shrue had felt it necessary to tell them earlier—that there was a possibility of pursuit by another magician and his minions.

"They're closing," said Shiolko. "And unless *Steresa's Dream* is blessed by stronger winds from the southwest, they'll continue to close. Will they attack?"

"I think not," said Shrue. "I have something they want, but what they want most is to reach the place to which Ulfänt Banderōz's nose is guiding us. But as they get closer, I believe I can add a disincentive to any impulsive behavior on their part." Shrue turned to the seven-foot-tall Arch-Docent Huǽ and the diminutive Mauz Meriwolt. "Would you two gentlemen be kind enough to accompany me below?"

Ten minutes later, Shrue reappeared on deck leading an eleven-foot-tall figure by the hand. The form was completely shrouded within the blue robes and black veil of a Firschnian monk. Shrue led the towering, if slightly unsteady, figure aft and set the monk's hands on the railing.

"What if I have to move?" came Arch-Docent Huǽ's muffled voice from approximately the chest of the tall monk.

"You shouldn't have to unless they attack," said Shrue. "And if it comes to that, our little guise will have already been found out. Oh…but if either of you need to use the head, Meriwolt can guide you while one of us holds your hand, Arch-Docent."

"Wonderful," came a frustrated squeak from behind the veil.

Descending to their cabin, Derwe Coreme whispered, "What are the chances that the real KirdriK will be victorious and return in time to help us?"

Shrue shrugged and showed his long hands. "As I've said before, my dear, a battle such as this in the Overworld may go on for anything from ten minutes to ten centuries of our time. But KirdriK knows the importance of returning as soon as he is victorious—*if* he prevailed and survived."

"Is there any chance that the daihak simply fled?" she whispered.

"No," said Shrue. "None. KirdriK is still well and truly bound. If he survives—and either he or the two Purples must die—he shall return immediately."

ALL THAT day the pelgranes and their saddled passengers grew closer, until the black flapping forms held station a little less than two leagues behind the sky galleon. Shrue urged Captain Shiolko to have his sons practice with the air-powered harpoon gun, which they did diligently through the long, hot day, firing and reeling in the long barbed bolt time after time. A little after noon, the guiding nose of Ulfänt Banderōz swiveled due east and the galleon and following pelgranes changed course accordingly.

"I've never seen pelgranes that large," Shiolko said to Shrue late that afternoon as both men studied their pursuers through telescopes. "They're almost twice the size of the normal monsters."

It was true. Pelgranes fed on humans—they liked nothing better for their diet—but it would be all a regular pelgrane could do to carry off one adult man or woman in its talons. These creatures looked as if they could carry a man in each taloned claw while feeding on a third in its mouth-beak.

"Some magical breeding of the species thanks to Faucelme and the Red," murmured Shrue. From the middledeck came a flat explosion of compressed air as three of the sons fired off the harpoon gun yet again. Then the screech-and-whine as they began laboriously cranking back the bolt on its quarter-mile of steel cable.

THE ELEVEN flying forms were backlit by the huge setting sun as one of the pelgranes broke formation and began closing the gap to the galleon.

"The saddleless one," said Derwe Coreme, who was watching through Shrue's telescope. She and her Myrmazons had all of their weapons strapped to their dragonscaled backs and belts. "Damn!"

"What?" said Captain Shiolko and Shrue together.

"It's carrying a white and blue flag."

So it was. Shiolko's sons did their best to train the ungainly harpoon gun on the approaching pelgrane—and Derwe Coreme's Myrmazons found it much easier to bring their short but powerful crossbows to bear—but the pelgrane was indeed carrying a white and blue flag of truce in one of its fleshy, pink little wing hands. They allowed it to flap closer and land on the portside railing.

Most of the passengers made a huge semicircle on deck, then half a semi-circle as they tried to get upwind of the stinking pelgrane, as some of the Myrmazons and Shiolko's sons kept an eye on the other ten pelgranes behind them, making sure this visit was not just a distraction.

Shrue and the captain stepped closer, moving into the sphere of carrion stench that hung around the creature. The diabolist noticed that the pelgrane was wearing smoked goggles—they hated flying in daylight.

"What do you want?" demanded Captain Shiolko. And then, as an afterthought, added, "If you crap on my railing or deck, you die."

The pelgrane smiled a foul pelgranish smile. "Your magician knows what we want."

"I'm fresh out of Finding Crystals," said Shrue. "What happened to Faucelme's apprentice?"

"He became too…ambitious," wheezed the pelgrane. "As all apprentices do, sooner or later. Faucelme was forced to…punish…him. But do not change the subject, diabolist. Hand over the nose."

Something about the phrasing of that demand made both Shrue and Derwe Coreme laugh. The others in the mass of passengers and crew looked at them as if they'd gone mad.

"Tell the Red and his puppet Faucelme that their projection of the Purples is a sad failure," said Shrue. He nodded toward the silent, tall monk's figure at their stern rail. At least Meriwolt had managed to turn Arch-Docent Huǽ around so that the black veil under the hood was aimed in the general direction of the pelgrane. "We know how the battle in the Overworld *really* went."

The pelgrane looked bored. "Are you going to give me the nose or make Faucelme take it from you?"

Shrue sighed. "Let me show you something, my friend," he said softly. "Young Shiolko—Arven—could you give me that extra bit of block and tackle? Yes, set it on the deck in front of me. Thank you. Are you watching, pelgrane?"

The oversized pelgrane's yellow eyes were shifting—hungrily—every way but toward the heavy block and bit of rope on the deck. It licked its foul chops while looking at the passengers, but said, "Oh, is there a birthday party underway here? Did you all hire a village magic-maker? Is the old man going to show us that there's nothing up his sleeves and then make the big, bad block and tackle disappear? *That* will deeply impress one of the seventeen Elemental Reds in all of the universe!"

Shrue smiled and snapped his fingers.

The heavy block disappeared.

The pelgrane screamed in pain and horror. Its talons and both of its tiny fleshy hands clutched at its own belly.

"You looked hungry," said Shrue. "I know that Faucelme and Faucelme's owner are watching and listening through you. Let them know that they could never seize the nose of Ulfänt Banderōz before I send it elsewhere—and to an elsewhere infinitely less retrievable than your foul belly, pelgrane."

Still shrieking, the pelgrane flapped into the air, writhing and rolling, and then screamed, "I'll have my dinner from you yet, mortals." It feinted in Shrue's direction, but banked suddenly, seized Reverend Cepres's younger wife Wilva in its talons, and flapped away toward the south, still screeching and shrieking in pain even as Wilva screamed.

"Quick!" cried Shrue, gesturing the frozen Shiolko sons toward the compressed-air harpoon gun.

The Myrmazons needed no impetus. The pelgrane was no more than thirty yards away when six crossbow bolts slammed into the monster's shoulders, back, and upper hairy thorax—the women warriors were trying to avoid hitting the woman hanging from its talons. The Myrmazons reloaded in an instant and Derwe Coreme raised her hand, ready to signal a second volley.

"No!" cried Shrue. "If it dies, it will release Wilva." He gestured toward the Shiolko boys to fire, even as his lips chanted a spell and his fingers played the air as if it were the captain's three-tiered piano.

Guided by the efulsion, the harpoon flew impossibly true, smashing through the pelgrane's thick thorax. Yellow ichor flew everywhere. The pelgrane's scream reached into the ultrasonic.

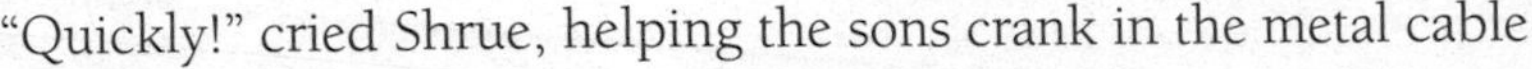

"Quickly!" cried Shrue, helping the sons crank in the metal cable.

"I'll drop her!" screamed the raging pelgrane. "Let me go, or by Highest Gods you worship, I'll bite her head off now and drop her!"

"Drop her and you die now," shouted Shrue, still cranking the pelgrane in. The six Myrmazons had their crossbows aimed unshakingly at its head. "Return her safely and you have a chance to live," he said. "I promise you your freedom."

The pelgrane screamed in frustration and pain. They cranked it aboard like some huge, stoop-shouldered, carrion-stinking, feathered fish, and the pelgrane flopped and writhed and bellowed and vomited yellow and green ichor everywhere. But Wilva flew free and Reverend Cepres gathered her up, weeping but alive, in his arms.

"You promised me my freedom!!" screamed the pelgrane.

"So I did," said Shrue and nodded to Derwe Coreme, who instantly used her longest and sharpest sword to strike the giant pelgrane just above the thorax, severing that hairy body part—larger than Meriwolt, who had to leap and scramble to avoid its thrusting stinger—and sending the thorax flopping on the deck, still pierced by the long barbed harpoon. Shrue gestured again, a backhand dismissal, and the rest of the shrieking pelgrane was thrown overboard as if by a huge, invisible hand. It plummeted a thousand screaming, cursing, ichor-venting feet or more before it remembered it still had wings.

IT WAS a long night and neither Shrue nor Derwe Coreme slept a moment of it. The clouds had closed in and by midnight *Steresa's Dream* was enveloped in cloud-fog so thick that the sons had reduced all canvas so that the sky galleon was barely making way. Huddled in the slight glow of the binnacle near Captain Shiolko at the wheel, Shrue and the Myrmazon chief could see the bright lanterns on the mainmast only as the dimmest and most distant of spherical glows. The only sound aboard the ship, besides the quarter-hour calling of the time by one of Shiolko's sons, was the drip-drip-drip of droplets from the masts and rigging. But from beyond the ship, growing closer by the hour, was the leathery flap of wings from ten pelgranes closing their circle.

"Do you think they will come aboard tonight?" whispered Derwe Coreme. Shrue was interested that he could hear no fear or concern whatsoever in her voice, only mild curiosity. Her six Myrmazons were wrapped in blankets on the damp deck, sleeping like children. And, Shrue knew, unlike children, they could and would come fully awake in a fraction of a second when the alarum was called. What must it be like, he wondered, to have trained and disciplined yourself to the point where fear could be banished?

He said, "It depends on whether the Red controlling Faucelme thinks he has a real chance of stealing the nose." Shrue patted his robes where the small box was pocketed next to his heart.

"Does he…it?" whispered Derwe Coreme. "Have a real chance, I mean. By magic?"

Shrue smiled at her in the soft glow of the binnacle. "No magic that I cannot counter, my dear. At least in so obvious an attempt."

"So you're an equal to the Red and Faucelme in a fight?" The woman's soft whisper may have had the slightest edge to it.

"I doubt it," said Shrue. "I can keep them from snatching the nose, but odds are very much against me in a stand-up fight."

"Even," whispered Derwe Coreme as she patted the short crossbow slung across her shoulder, " if Faucelme were to die suddenly?"

"Even then," whispered Shrue. "But even without the Red, the ancient magus known as Faucelme would not be so simple to kill. But that isn't what's worrying me tonight."

"What is worrying you tonight, Shrue?" said Derwe Coreme and slipped her calloused fingers inside his robe to touch his bare chest.

Shrue smiled but pulled away and removed the tiny box from his robes. Holding it near the binnacle light, he whispered, "This."

The guiding nose of Ulfänt Banderōz was levitating in its box, rattling at the glass cover. Shrue turned the box on end and the nose slid to the top as if magnetized, the nostrils pointing up and only a little to their left in the night and fog.

"Above us?" hissed Derwe Coreme. "That's impossible."

Shrue shook his head. "You see that dial on the post near Captain Shiolko between the wheel and capstan? The small device in the ossip engine room below sends out pulses from the atmospheric emulsifier in the hull by the keel and those return to a receiver, telling the captain the true altitude of the ship even in darkness and fog. You notice that it now reads just above the numeral five—five thousand feet above sea level."

"So?"

"We are in a valley," whispered Shrue. "We've been following its contours for hours. The Ultimate Library is on one of the peaks above us and to the east—probably at about nine thousand feet of altitude."

"Why haven't we struck the cliffs around us and died?" asked Derwe Coreme. Once again, Shrue noticed, the only overlay was of mild curiosity.

"We are going dead slow, floating with the breezes," whispered Shrue. "Also, I devised a little instrument—there, you may notice our good captain playing close attention to those four dials I jury-rigged from Meriwolt's calliope."

The warrior chief looked at the wires running from the device toward something in a box set near the binnacle, chuckled and shook her head. "Boys and their toys. But what's to keep Faucelme and his pelgranes from striking the surrounding rocks in the dark?"

"Ahh," breathed Shrue. " They know where they and where we are to a much finer degree than we do, I'm afraid. Pelgranes are nightflyers. They navigate by sound waves bouncing back from objects. That's what my 'little instrument' is connected to—our unfortunate pelgrane visitor's vibrating thorax. The creatures also 'hear' through their thoraxes…it's why I let our friend come so close and behave true to pelgrane form earlier."

"You needed his thorax."

"Yes." He squeezed her hand. Her skin was very cold and damp but her hand was not shaking in the least. "You can sleep if you want, my dear," he whispered. "I have nothing to base it on but a hunch, but I don't think the Red and Faucelme and the three Yellows and three Greens and their pelgranes will make their move tonight, in the dark."

"Sleep?" whispered Derwe Coreme, former princess of the House of Domber. "And miss all this? You must be joking." Spreading a blanket, she slid under Shrue's outer robe and pulled him down next to her.

Captain Shiolko glanced over in their direction once, grunted softly, and then returned his attention to the emulsifier and thorax dials.

THE NOSE began spinning at first light, when the clouds first showed a milky pre-dawn glow and then parted as the red sun struggled to rise. Captain Shiolko brought the galleon to full stop and then allowed it to rise more than three thousand feet.

The Second Ultimate Library was on a rocky promontory overhanging a vertical drop four thousand feet or more to the wooded valley below it. There was no moat at this version of the library, but wooded wilderness stretched away between high peaks for uncounted miles to its west.

"You can set down in that glade near the front door," Shrue said to the captain. "Then let us out and go on to deliver the rest of your passengers."

Shiolko grinned. "I know better than that, Master Magician. That Faucelme devil and the red thing what pulls his strings won't let us go, no matter what. We'll drop you off if you want, then we'll moor nearby to that huge old tree near the waterfall where we can refill our casks, but we'll watch and help if we can. Our fate is your fate. We know that."

"I am sorry it has come to that," Shrue said sincerely.

Captain Shiolko shrugged. "Somehow I think I'm speaking for everyone on the ship and perhaps for everyone on the Dying Earth. How it come to this, I don't know…and don't especially care. But we could have done worse than have you as our standard-bearer, I think, Master Magician Shrue. I don't see no stinking kid's birthday party anywhere near."

THE TEN pelgranes landed in the glade even as *Steresa's Dream* hovered and let down its gangplank. Derwe Coreme went down first, followed by her six Myrmazons leading sluggish and sleepy megillas just wakened from their sorcery-induced, three-week-long naps, straw from the livestock pens on the middle deck still clinging to their scales.

Faucelme laughed as Shrue descended the gangplank, leading the tall robed and veiled figure by his hand. "Your daihak looks a little wobbly there, diabolist!" called Faucelme as the robed form felt gingerly with his foot before stepping to the soil.

"Well," said Shrue. "He's been through a tough fight. At least he's more solid than your pathetic Purples."

Faucelme's laughter stopped but his broad grin remained. "You'll soon see how solid my Purples are, dead man."

All of the Elementals had dismounted by now—the three Yellows, three Greens, two Purples, and the towering Red. The ten pelgranes began bellowing and surging—they'd obviously not been fed fresh meat or blood all through the long chase.

"Silence!" bellowed the Faucelme puppet and froze the pelgranes into an icy block of steaming Temporary Stasis with a single wave of his upraised palm.

Shrue blinked at the ease with which Faucelme—or, in truth, the Red—had effectuated such a difficult spell.

Faucelme stepped closer. Indeed, his clumsy, bowlegged steps did resemble those of a poorly handled puppet—although, thought Shrue, three weeks in a pelgrane saddle would create the same effect.

"Faucelme," said Shrue. "Where is your apprentice?"

"Apprentices," growled the little magus. "Bah! You know apprentices, Shrue. They always overreach…always. It's why you've never had one of your own."

"True," said Shrue.

"Give me the nose," demanded Faucelme, "and I may let your pet soldier-whore live. I might even allow the sky galleon to depart in one piece. But for you, Shrue, there is no hope."

"So my mother often told me," said Shrue. He reached into his robes and withdrew the nose box. "Do you give me your word, Faucelme…and *your* word, Elemental Red of the True Overworld's Eleventh Realm?"

"You have our word," said Faucelme and the Red in perfect unison.

"Well," said Shrue, holding the box with the nose's nostrils toward them, "then it saddens me a little to know that both your words combined aren't worth a steaming pile of pelgrane shit. KirdriK!"

The tall figure in the blue monk's robes pulled back its hood and veil with its huge, six-fingered hands revealing its red crest and purple feathers, then ripped the robes to shreds and stepped free. KirdriK's dorsal flanges flared ten feet wide and glowed orange from internal heat. There were new, raw scars running across the daihak's white-fuzzed brow and chest and upper thigh, but the creature seemed taller, stronger, more muscled, meaner, and more confident.

"He followed me home during the night," said Shrue. "I decided to keep him."

"My Purples," said the Red even as the two projections winked out.

"Your Purples were good to the last drop of ichor," rumbled KirdriK. "Their energy is in me now, along with their bones and viscera. Perhaps you can tell, Elemental."

Faucelme only stared as the Red moved forward quickly in three huge strides. "No sandestin-daihak half-breed ever decanted can stand up

to an Elemental Red of the True Overworld's Eleventh Realm!" roared the huge shape.

Before the daihak could speak, Shrue said softly, "KirdriK is daihak-bred from the order of Undra-Hadra. Do you really want to gamble your actual *existence* on the hope you can best him? Is the Ultimate Library so important to you?"

"Pah!!" roared the Red. "The Ultimate Library means *nothing* to me. All the spells in all the books in all the lost Aeons of the Dying Earth cannot equal the inbred knowledge of a Red fresh out of its egg!"

"Shut up, salamander," rumbled KirdriK. "And fight. And *die*...."

Both the daihak and Elemental blurred around their extended edges as they prepared to flash to any of a dozen dimensions.

"Pah!" cried the Red again. "You and your library and your Dying Earth have less than twenty-four hours of existence anyway, diabolist. *Enjoy it if you can!*" The Elemental made a dismissive gesture and imploded out of existence on the plane of the Dying Earth. The Yellows and Greens followed in less than a second. The pelgranes remained frozen in their block of solidified Temporal Stasis.

Alone, twitching and staggering from the withdrawal of the Red from his nerves and brain and guts and muscles and sinews, Faucelme took a confused step backward.

Shrue allowed himself to grow until he was twenty feet tall. The morning wind rippled his spidersilk robe like a gray banner. "Now," rumbled the giant, "do you still have business with me, Faucelme, waylayer of vagabonds, murderer of night-guests and cows and old women?"

The short magus shook his bald head and looked around like a man who had mislaid his teeth.

"Go away then," said Shrue. He waved his arm and Faucelme flew into the air, and in less than five seconds had become a speck disappearing over the western horizon. Shrue resumed his normal size.

Meriwolt had descended the gangplank. His already rubbery-looking legs seemed especially wobbly after the three weeks of sky-galleon flight. Shrue pocketed the nose box, removed a heavy key from his pocket, and turned to KirdriK, Derwe Coreme, and Meriwolt. "Shall we look inside this library now? KirdriK! Bring my traveling chest. "

EVERYTHING LOOKED precisely as it had in the first Library: the same benches, shelves, and thin windows, the same indecipherable books in the same places.

There was a scurry and scuttling in the shadows and the female twin of Mauz Meriwolt—Mauz Mindriwolt—came hurrying forward with a shriek to embrace her brother. The two hugged and kissed and passionately embraced with a duration and intensity not totally proper for a brother and sister, at least—if judging by the glance flashing between them—in the opinion of Derwe Coreme and Shrue the diabolist. KirdriK, still carrying his master's huge trunk, showed no opinion.

After a moment, Shrue cleared his throat repeatedly until the two untangled themselves.

"Oh!" cried Mindriwolt in a squeaky voice only an octave or so higher than that of her brother's, "I am so glad to see all of you! It has been so terrible—first the Master, Ulfänt Banderōz, turning to stone, and then the earthquakes and the fires and the red sun with its poxed face each morning—oh, I've been terrified!"

"I am sure you have, my dear, and as the Red Elemental outside reminded us, there's nothing we can do to stop the reconvergence in time and space of your Library and the first Library within a day or less. The Dying Earth may truly meet its end before tomorrow's sunset. But we are still alive and should celebrate small victories while we can."

"We should indeed," squeaked Meriwolt. "But first we should go up and pay our respects to *this* stone body of Ulfänt Banderōz, Master Shrue. May I borrow the nose box for a moment? Our Master—Mindriwolt's and mine—should not lie there without a nose."

"You are correct, my little friend," Shrue said somberly. "And if I'd not needed to find this place, I never would have used the chisel in the way I did." He removed the nose box but hesitated and then pocketed it again. "But at this moment, Meriwolt, my old bones ache from the voyage and my nerves quiver from the terror of the near-showdown with the Elementals. Is there any place in this stone keep where we can step outside into sunlight for a moment of relaxation and refreshment before paying our respects?"

"The terrace at the end of the hallway outside our Master's bedroom?" said Mindriwolt in her tiny, sweet, uncertain voice.

"That will do nicely," said Shrue. "Come along, KirdriK. Do not jostle the refreshments."

THE DYING Earth was alive with earthquake tremors. Boulders crashed down avalanche chutes and trees vibrated in the thick forest. The sun was laboring harder than ever to climb toward the zenith and even the flickering sunlight felt uncertain. Still, the morning air was bracing as the Mauz twins, the warrior maid, the daihak, and the diabolist stepped out onto the open terrace. In the clearing and orchard below, the six Myrmazons had set up tents for an overnight stay and were exercising the megillas. Shiolko had moored the galleon to the huge tree near the waterfall and his sons were rolling giant water casks up and down the gangplank as the passengers stretched their legs in the meadow.

"It's a good day to be alive," said Shrue.

"*Every* day is a good day to be alive," said Derwe Coreme.

"Let's drink to that," said the diabolist. Despite Meriwolt's and Mindriwolt's impatience, he took his time removing a deep bucket of ice from the large trunk KirdriK had set down. From the ice, he slowly removed a magnum of sparkling goldwine. Then he removed four crystal flutes from their careful padding.

"We should look in on the Master's body…" began Meriwolt.

"All in good time," said Shrue. He handed the brother and sister and then Derwe Coreme their flutes, filled theirs with bubbling wine, and then filled his own. "This is the best of my cellars," he said proudly. "Three hundred years old and just reached its prime. There's no finer sparkling goldwine in or on all the Dying Earth."

He raised his flute in a toast and the others raised theirs. "To knowing that every day is a good day to be alive," he said and drank. The others drank. KirdriK watched without interest. Shrue refilled all of their glasses.

"My dear," he said to Derwe Coreme, "I'll be staying here at the Second Library, no matter what happens. Do you have plans?"

"If the world doesn't end in a day, do you mean?" she asked, sipping her wine.

"Yes," said Shrue.

Derwe Coreme shrugged slightly and smiled. "The girls and I have discussed it. Our guess is that we're about as far away from Ascolais and Almery and Kauchique and the Land of the Falling Wall as we could be, without coming closer to home by continuing on eastward, I mean, so we thought it might be fun to ride the megillas home."

"Fun?" repeated Shrue, refilling everyone's flute. "It might take years for you to get home...if any of you survived the adventure, which would be highly doubtful."

Derwe Coreme smiled and sipped her sparkling goldwine. Meriwolt and his sister frowned and downed their third flute in an impatient gulp.

"Well," Shrue said to the Myrmazon chief, "I hope your megillas can swim, my dear. But then again...if we survive this current crisis...as you said, your adventures would be sung of for a thousand years or longer."

"Oh, I think..." began Derwe Coreme.

"I really think we need to go inside and visit the Master's corpse," interrupted Meriwolt. "May I at least *look* at the nose of our Master, Ulfänt Banderōz? Perhaps there is some way we could reattach it."

"Of course," Shrue said apologetically, setting his flute down on the stone balustrade and fumbling in his robes for the box. He handed it to Meriwolt.

The Mauz twins both clutched the box at once and a change came over their features. Meriwolt struck the box against stone, smashing the glass, and lifted the nose out. Both brother and sister held the nose high and a radiance poured from the stone chard and surrounded both of them. Then the two opened their mouths and a fog flowed forth, surrounding Shrue, Derwe Coreme, and KirdriK.

Shrue recognized the Moving Miasma of Temporal Stasis by its perfume-stink, but before he could react, his body and muscles were frozen in place. Even the daihak stood frozen over the open trunk.

Meriwolt and Mindriwolt cackled and writhed and rubbed against one another. "Oh, Shrue, you old fool!" squeaked Meriwolt. "How my darling and I feared that you'd figure things out before this moment! How much useless anxiety we had that you were smarter than you actually are...we sent the Red to Faucelme to distract you, but now I doubt if we needed to have bothered."

The two separated and danced around the frozen trio. Mindriwolt squeaked at them, "My darling brother, my darling lover, was never just a clerk, you foolish magus. He was Ulfänt Banderōz's trusted apprentice in the First Ultimate Library...as was I here in the Second. Ulfänt Banderōz trusted each of us...needed us, since only through our womb-joined minds and twinned perceptions could even he unscramble the time-twisted titles and contents of his many books...and so he *taught* us a few paltry tricks, but all the time we were *learning, learning...*"

"Learning!" roared Mauz Meriwolt. The radiance of power around him had turned from silver to red as he spoke. Pirouetting much as he had when he'd danced to his own calliope, the little figure mumbled a spell, called up a sphere of blue flame, and pitched it at the moored sky galleon. The ship's reefed mainsail burst into flame. Meriwolt threw another blue-flame sphere and then Mindriwolt joined him.

Captain Shiolko threw down the gangplank and cast off the mooring lines, but it was too late—the *Steresa's Dream* was burning in a dozen places. Meriwolt and his sister danced and capered and laughed as the burning sky galleon listed to one side and lost altitude, trailing smoke behind it, smashing through trees as Shiolko attempted to guide it into the waterfall.

Meriwolt turned, stalked up to Shrue, stood on the railing, and tweaked the time-frozen diabolist's long nose even as he held up the stone nose of his former Master.

"This…" the pibald rodent cried, holding high the stone nose, "was our last worry. But that worry's past, as are your lives, my helpful fools. Thank you for reuniting my darling and me. Thank you for insuring the end of the Dying Earth as you knew it." Meriwolt danced to the oversized hour glass near the door. "Twenty-two hours and the Libraries converge…"

"…and this world ends…" squeaked Mindriwolt.

"…and the new age begins…" piped Meriwolt.

"…and the Red and other Elementals join us, their Masters in…" squeaked Meriwolt.

"…in a new age where…"

"…where…a new age where…"

"…where…why does my belly ache?" squeaked Mindriwolt.

"…a new age where…mine does as well," squeaked Meriwolt. He rushed at the frozen Shrue. "What have you done, diabolist? What… where…what have…speak! But try a spell and…die. Speak!" He waved his white-gloved, three-fingered hand.

Shrue licked his lips. "Apprentices always overreach," he said softly.

Meriwolt cried out in pain, fell to the ground, and doubled over with cramps. Mindriwolt fell atop him, also writhing and screaming, their short tails twitching. In fifteen seconds, the writhing and screaming ceased. The pibald bodies were totally entangled but absolutely still.

The Temporal Stasis fog began to disperse and Shrue banished the last of it with a murmur. KirdriK rumbled into consciousness. Derwe Coreme half-staggered and touched her pale brow as Shrue supported her.

"Something in the sparkling goldwine?" she said.

"Oh, yes," said Shrue. "You may feel a little unsettled for a few hours, but there will be no serious side effects for us. The potion in the wine was quite specific as to its target…an ancient but very effective form of rat poison."

MERIWOLT HAD bragged that they only had twenty-two hours left until the end of the world: Shrue and Derwe Coreme used ninety minutes of that remaining time helping Shiolko and his sons and passengers douse the last of the flames and attend to the superficial burns of the firefighters. Most of the damage to *Steresa's Dream* had been limited to its sails—for which it had replacements—but there would be days if not weeks of labor finding, cutting, replacing, sanding, and varnishing new planks for its deck and hull.

Then the diabolist and warrior and daihak used another two of their few remaining hours hunting through Ulfänt Banderōz's cluttered workshops and personal rooms looking for a tube or jar of epoxy. Shrue knew more than fifty binding and joining incantations, but none that would work as well with stone as simple epoxy.

It was KirdriK who found the tube, tucked away with some suspicious erotic paraphernalia in the lowest drawer of a seventy-drawer cluttered desk.

Shrue joined the nose to the noseless stone corpse's face with great care, wiping away the traces of excess epoxy when he was done. Derwe Coreme had been wanting to ask why this corpse of Ulfänt Banderōz was also noseless—since Shrue had done nothing here with his chisel and hammer—but she decided that the mysteries of conjoined but separate time and space with their twelve dimensional knots and twelve-times-twelve coexistent potentials could wait until a less time-critical juncture. The reality was that this corpse of Ulfänt Banderōz had also turned to stone and—at least since Shrue's chiseling three weeks and more than half a world away—was indeed noseless. The reality of now was a concept that Derwe Coreme had never failed to grasp—or at least not since she was kidnapped from Cil and the House of Domber when she was a teenager.

The gray-slate corpse of Ulfänt Banderōz turned to pink granite, the pink granite slowly fading to pink flesh.

The Master of the Ultimate Library and Final Compendium of Thaumaturgical Lore from the Grand Motholam and Earlier sat up, looked around, and felt on his nightstand for his spectacles. Setting them on his nose, he peered at the two humans and daihak peering at him and said, "You, Shrue. I thought it would be you…unless of course it was to be Ildefonse or Rhialto the self-proclaimed Marvellous."

"Ildefonse is buried alive in a dungheap and Rhialto has fled the planet," Shrue said dryly.

"Well, then…" smiled Ulfänt Banderōz. "There you have it. How much time do we have until the Libraries converge and the world ends?"

"Well…eighteen hours, give or take a half hour," said Shrue.

"Mmmm," murmured Ulfänt Banderōz with a scowl. "Cutting it a little close here, weren't we? Trying to impress the lady, perhaps? Mmmm?"

Shrue did not dignify that question with an answer but something about Derwe Coreme's grin seemed to please the resurrected old Library Master.

"How long will it take you to set the time-space separation of the two Libraries to rights?" asked Shrue. "And can I help in any way?"

"Time?" repeated Ulfänt Banderōz as if he'd already forgotten the question. "The time to repair my so-called apprentices' little vandalism? Oh, about four days of constant work, I would imagine. Give or take, as you like to say, a half hour."

Shrue and Derwe Coreme exchanged glances. Each realized that they'd lost their race with time and each was thinking of how they would like to spend the last eighteen hours of his or her life—give or take thirty minutes—and the answer in both their eyes was visible not only to each other but to Ulfänt Banderōz.

"Oh, good gracious no," laughed the Librarian. "I shan't let the world end while I'm saving it. We'll establish a Temporal Stasis for the entire Dying Earth, I'll exempt myself from it to do my repair work outside of time, and that, as they say, will be that."

"You can do that?" asked Shrue. "*You can set the whole world in Stasis?*" His voice, he realized, had sounded oddly like Meriwolt's squeak.

"Of course, of course," said Ulfänt Banderōz, hopping off the bed and heading for the stairs to his workshop. "Done it many a time. Haven't you?"

At the top of the stairway, the Librarian stopped suddenly and seized Shrue's arm. "Oh, I don't want to play the arch-magus of arch-maji or anything, dear boy, but I do have a bit of important advice. Do you mind?"

"Not at all," said Shrue. The mysteries of a million years and more of lost lore were at this magus's beck and call.

"Never hire a mouse as your apprentice," whispered Ulfänt Banderōz. "Goddamned untrustworthy, those vermin. No exceptions."

TO SHRUE'S and every other human being on the Dying Earth's way of perceiving it, the time-space crack—which no one else (except the still flying and fleeing Faucelme) even knew about—was fixed in an eyeblink.

The earthquakes ceased. The tsunamis stopped coming. The days of full darkness dropped to a reasonable number. The elderly red sun still struggled to rise in the morning and showed its occasional pox of darkness, but that was the way things had always been—or at least as long as anyone living could remember it being. The Dying Earth was still dying, but it resumed its dying at its own pace. One assumed that the pogroms against magicians would go on for months or years longer—such outbursts have their own logic and timelines—but Derwe Coreme suggested that in a year or two, there would be a general *rapprochement*.

"Perhaps it would be better if there's not a total *rapprochement*," said Shrue.

When the Myrmazon leader looked sharply at him, Shrue explained. "Things have been out of balance on our dear Dying Earth for far too long," he said softly. "Millions of years ago, the imbalance benefited political tyrants or merchants or the purveyors of the earliest form of real magic called science. For a long time now, wealth and power have been preserved for those willing to isolate themselves from real humanity for long enough to become a true sorcerer. For too long now, perhaps, those of us who are—let us say—least human in how we spend our time and with whom we associate, have owned too much of the world's literature and fine food and art and wealth. Perhaps the Dying Earth has enough years and centuries left to it that we can move into another, healthier, phase before the end."

"What are you suggesting?" asked the war maven with a smile. "Peasants of the world, unite?"

Shrue shook his head and smiled ruefully, embarrassed by his speech.

"But no matter what comes, you want to wait and see it all," said Derwe Coreme. "Everything. Including the end."

"Of course," said Shrue the diabolist. "Don't you?"

There came several weeks as the galleon and people were being repaired when life was easy and merry—even self-indulgent—and then, too suddenly (as all such departing times always seem to be) it was over and time for everyone to go. Ulfänt Banderōz announced that he had to go visit himself—his dead stone other self—at the First Library and to repair that oversight of death.

"How can you do that?" asked Derwe Coreme. "When you need the stone nose and there was only one of those and Shrue here used it on you already?"

The old Librarian smiled distractedly. "I'll think of something along the way," he said. He gave Derwe Coreme a hug—an overlong and far too enthusiastic hug, to Shrue's way of thinking—and then she handed the Librarian the half-full tube of epoxy and he winked out of existence.

"I'm not sure," mused Shrue, stroking his long chin, "how instantaneous travel allows one to figure anything out along the way."

"Is that how you're going home?" asked Derwe Coreme. "Instantaneous travel?"

"I haven't decided yet," Shrue said brusquely.

Captain Shiolko and his passengers had voted and had decided—not quite unanimously, but overwhelmingly—that they would return home the long way, continuing to travel east around the Dying Earth.

"Think of it," called down Captain Shiolko as the gangplank was being drawn up. "*Steresa's Dream* may be the first sky galleon of the modern era to circumnavigate the globe—if globe it really is. My dear wife Steresa would have been so proud of the boys and me. We might be back at Mothmane Junction in a month—or two or three months—or perhaps four—six at the most."

Or you might all be eaten by a dragon larger than the one I conjured, thought Shrue. Aloud, he shouted his wishes for a safe and happy voyage.

Then there were only the eight of them, nine of them counting KirdriK, and before Shrue could say farewell to the Myrmazons, the daihak cleared his throat—a sound only slightly softer than a major boulder avalanche—and said, "Master Magus, binder, foul human scum, I humbly ask that I might stay."

"What?" said Shrue. For the first time in a very, very long time, he was truly and totally nonplussed. "What are you talking about? Stay *where*? You can't *stay* anywhere. You're *bound*."

"Yes, Master," rumbled KirdriK. The daihak's hands were clenching and unclenching, but more as if he were running the brim of an invisible hat through them than as if he were rehearsing a strangulation. "But Master Ulfänt Banderōz has asked me to stay and be his apprentice here at the Library, and if you would release me—or loan me to him, at least temporarily—I would like to do that... Master."

Shrue stared for a long minute and then threw his head back and laughed. "KirdriK, KirdriK...you know, do you not, that this will mean that you will be *double-bound.* By me and then by Ulfänt Banderōz, whose binding spells are probably stronger than mine."

"Yes," rumbled KirdriK. The rumble had the sullen but hopeful undertones of a child's pleading.

"Oh, for the sake of All Gods," sputtered Shrue. "Very well then. Stay here at this Library at the east ass-end of nowhere. Shelve books... a daihak shelving books and learning basic conjuring spells. What a waste."

"Thank you, Master Magus."

"I'll reclaim you in a century or less," snapped Shrue.

"Yes, Master Magus."

Shrue gave one last whispered command to the daihak and then strolled over to where the Myrmazons had finished collapsing their tents and packing them onto the megillas. He squinted at the disagreeable, spitting, venomous, treacherous reptiles and their high, small, infinitely uncomfortable-looking saddles set ahead of the packs and weapons. To Derwe Coreme, who was tightening the last of what looked to be a thousand straps, he said, "You're really serious about this epic seven-riding-home nonsense."

She looked at him coldly.

"You do remember," he said equally as coldly, "those seas and oceans we crossed coming here?"

"Yes," she said, hitching a final strap so tightly that the huge megilla gasped out its breath in a foul-smelling *whoosh*. "And perhaps you remember, in all your centuries of bookish studies—or maybe just because you brag about having a *cottage* there—that there are land bridges around the Greater and Lesser Polar Seas. That's why they're called *seas*, Shrue, instead of *oceans*."

"Hmmm," said Shrue noncommittally, still frowning up at the restless, wriggling, spitting megillas.

Derwe Coreme stood before him. She was wearing her highest riding boots and held a riding shock-crop which she slapped against her calloused palm from time to time. Shrue the diabolist admitted to himself that he found something about that vaguely exciting.

"Make up your mind if you want to come with us," she said harshly. "We don't have an extra megilla or extra saddle, but you're skinny and light enough that you could ride behind me. If you hang on to me tight enough, you won't fall off too *many* times."

"*That* will be the day," said Shrue the diabolist.

Derwe Coreme started to say something else, stopped herself, grabbed a loose scale, and swung herself easily up over the packs and scabbarded crossbows and swords to the tiny saddle. She kicked her boots into the stirrups with the absent ease of infinite experience, waved her hand to the Myrmazons, and the seven megillas leapt away toward the west.

Shrue watched them go until they were less than a dust cloud on the furthest ridge to the west. "The chances of any of you surviving this voyage," he said to the distant dust cloud, "are nil minus one. The Dying Earth simply has too many sharp teeth."

KirdriK came out of the Library carrying the things Shrue had requested. He laid the carpet out on the pine needles first—a good size, Shrue thought as he sat crosslegged in its center, five feet wide by nine feet long. Enough room to stretch out and take a nap on. Or to do other things on.

Then KirdriK set out the wicker hamper with Shrue's warm lunch, a bucket holding three bottles of good wine set to chill, a sweater-cape should the day turn chilly, a book, and a larger chest. "It would have been a mixed metaphor of the worst sort," said Shrue to no one in particular.

"Yes, Master Magus," said KirdriK.

Shrue shook his head ruefully. "KirdriK," he said softly. "I am a fool's fool."

"Yes, Master Magus," said the daihak.

Without another word, Shrue extended his fingers, jinkered the old carpet's flight threads into life, lifted it eight feet off the ground in a hover, turned to look sideways directly into the daihak's disinterested—or at least noncommittal—yellow eyes, shook his head a final time, and commanded the carpet west, rising quickly over the trees, pursuing the disappearing dust cloud.

KirdriK watched the speck dwindle for a moment and then shambled bowleggedly into the Library to find something to do—or at least something interesting to read—until his new Master, Ulfänt Banderōz, returned, either alone or with his other self.

AFTERWORD:

THE SUMMER of 1960—I was 12 years old and visiting my much-older brother Ted and my Uncle Wally in Wally's third-floor apartment on North Kildare Avenue just off Madison Street in Chicago. Most of the daylight was spent taking the El to museums or the Loop or North Avenue beach or to the beach near the planetarium or to movies, but some days—and many of the evenings—were spent with me sprawled on the daybed in Wally's little dining room, under the open windows with the heat and street noises of Chicago coming in, reading Jack Vance.

Actually, I was reading a tall stack of my brother's Ace Double Novels, old issues of *The Magazine of Fantasy & Science Fiction*, and other paperbacks, but it was the Jack Vance that I remember most vividly. I remember the expansive, odyssiad power of *Big Planet* and the the narrative energy of *The Rapparee* (later known as *Five Gold Bands*) and my introduction to semantics through *The Languages of Pao* and the brooding fantasy brilliance of *Marizian the Magician* (later to be *The Dying Earth*) and the literary style that saturated *To Live Forever*.

Mostly, it was the style. My reading even then had already moved beyond a steady diet of SF and other genres, but as my tastes sharpened and my appetite for literature grew—as I encountered not just the stylistic power of the best in genre but also that of Proust and Hemingway and Faulkner and Steinbeck and Fitzgerald and Malcolm Lowry and all the others—what stayed with me was the memory of Jack Vance's expansive, easy, powerful, dry, *generous* style, the cascades of indelible images leavened by the drollest of dialogue, all combined with the sure and certain lilt of language used to the limits of its imaginative powers.

When I finally returned to SF in the mid-1980's, not only as a reader but as a writer working on my first SF novel *Hyperion*, it was to celebrate SF styles old and new, from space opera to cyberpunk, but most of all to acknowledge my love of SF and fantasy in an *homage* to Jack Vance's work. Please note that I didn't say in an attempt *to imitate* the style of Jack Vance; it's no more possible to imitate the unique Vancean style than it is to reproduce the voice of his friend Poul Anderson or of my friend Harlan

Ellison or any of the other true stylistic giants in our field or from literature in general.

Reading Jack Vance's work today, I am transported back forty-eight years to the sounds and smells of Chicago coming in through that third-floor window on Kildare Avenue and I remember what it is like to be truly and totally and indelibly transported into a master magician's mind and world.

—Dan Simmons

HOWARD WALDROP

Frogskin Cap

HOWARD WALDROP is widely considered to be one of the best short-story writers in the business, having been called "the resident Weird Mind of our generation" and an author "who writes like a honkytonk angel." His famous story "The Ugly Chickens" won both the Nebula and the World Fantasy Awards in 1981. His work has been gathered in the collections: *Howard Who?*, *All About Strange Monsters Of The Recent Past: Neat Stories By Howard Waldrop*, *Night of the Cooters: More Neat Stories By Howard Waldrop*, *Going Home Again*, the print version of his collection *Dream Factories and Radio Pictures* (formerly available only as in downloadable form online), and a collection of his stories written in collaboration with various other authors, *Custer's Last Jump and Other Collaborations*. Waldrop is also the author of the novel *The Texas-Israeli War: 1999*, in collaboration with Jake Saunders, and of two solo novels, *Them Bones* and *A Dozen Tough Jobs*, as well as the chapbook *A Better World's in Birth!*. He is at work on a new novel, tentatively entitled *The Moone World*. His most recent book is a big retrospective collection, *Things Will Never Be the Same: Selected Short Fiction 1980-2005*. Having lived in Washington state for a number of years, Waldrop recently moved back to his former home town of Austin, Texas, something which caused celebrations and loud hurrahs to rise up from the rest of the population.

Here he takes us to a Dying Earth very near at last to the end of its span, to show us that the one thing that never ceases is the quest for knowledge.

Frogskin Cap

HOWARD WALDROP

The sun was having one of its good days.

It came up golden and buttery as if it were made of egg yolk.

The dawn air was light blue and clear as water. The world seemed made new and fresh, like it must have seemed in previous times.

The man in the frogskin cap (whose given name was Tybalt) watched the freshened sun as it rose. He turned to the west and took a sighting on a minor star with his astrolabe. He tickled the womb of the mother with the spider, looked away from the finger and read off the figures to himself.

A change in light behind him gained his attention. He turned—no, not a cloud or a passing bird, something larger.

Something for which men had sometimes taken dangerous journeys of years' duration, to the farthest places of this once green and blue planet, to see and record. Now it was just a matter of looking up.

The apparent size of a big copper coin held at arm's length, a round dot was coming into, then crossing, the face of the morning sun.

He watched the planet Venus seemingly touch, then be illuminated by the light, which suffused all around it in an instant. So it was true, then: there was still an atmosphere on the planet, even so close to the Sun as it had become (there was once an inner planet called Mercury, swallowed

up long ago.) This Venus had once been covered with dense clouds; its atmosphere now looked clear and plangent, though no doubt the sunlight beat down unmercifully on its surface.

He wished he had brought his spectacle-glass with him instead of leaving it up in his tower. But he knew of tales of others, who, looking directly into the Sun with them, had become blind or sun-dazzled for years, so he sat on the wall and watched, out of the corner of his eyes, the transit of Venus til the big dot crossed the face of the sun and disappeared, to become another bright point of light on its far side.

HE HAD found his frogskin cap while exploring some ruins in search of books many years ago. The skin was thin and papery, as living frogs had not been seen within the memory of the oldest living being, or his grandfather. The cap, then, was of an earlier time, when there still had been frogs to skin, probably while there still had been a Moon in the sky.

The first time he had put it on, it seemed made for him. Another sign from an earlier age to his times. From that day forward, his given name, Tybalt, was forgotten and people only knew him as "the man in the frogskin cap."

This morning he was fishing where a stream rose full-blown from a cave in a cliff-face. He had a slim withey pole and a 6-horsehair line. On the end of his line was a fine hook cunningly covered with feathers and fur to resemble an insect. He was angling for fish to take to town to trade to some innkeep for lodging (and a fine meal.) He was bound for Joytown, where they would be celebrating the Festival of Mud, after the return of the seasonal rains, delayed by a full month this year (due no doubt to strong fluctuations in the Sun).

The fish in the stream at the cave mouth were eyeless of course, which did not make them lesser eating. That they had come out of the darkness was testament to the usual dimness of light from the Sun.

His artificial fly landed on the water near a rock. He twitched the line several times, setting off rings of ripples from the fly.

With a great splash, a large blind fish swallowed the fly and dove for the bottom. Tybalt used the litheness of his pole to fight the fish's run. In a moment, he had it flopping on the bank. He put it in the wet canvas fishbag with the three others he'd already caught, and decided he had more than enough for barter.

He wrapped his line around his pole and stuck the fly into the butt of the rod. Carrying the heavy bag over his shoulder, he continued on to Joytown.

THE FESTIVAL was at full peak. People were in their holiday clothes, dancing to the music of many instruments, or standing swaying in place.

Those really in the spirit were in loincloths and a covering of mud, or just in mud, returned from the wet-hill slide and the mud-pit below.

Tybalt was heartened to see that primitive sluice-machinery kept the slide wet. Perhaps the spirit of Rogol Domedonfors had never died through all the long centuries of Time. Not all was left to magic and sorcery in this closing down of the ages. The quest for science and knowledge still simmered below the swamps of sorcery.

"KI-YI-YI!" yelled someone at the top of the wet-hill slide, and plunging down its curving length, became an ever-accelerating, ever-browner object before shooting off the end of the slide and landing with great commotion and impressive noise in the muddy pit beyond.

Polite applause drifted across the watching crowd.

Tybalt had already traded the fine mess of fish (less one for his own meal.) for lodging at inn. At first, the publican, a small stout man with a gray-red beard had said "Full -up, like all other places in this town." But as Tybalt emptied his bag on the table, the man's eyes widened. ."A fine catch," he said, "and supplies being somewhat short, what with the crowd eating anything that slows a little all week…" He stroked his chin. "We have a maid's room; she can go home and sleep with her sisters. This mess of fish should be enough for—what?—two nights let's say. Agreed?"

They put hands together like sawing wood. "Agreed!" said Tybalt.

SHE WAS a pretty girl in less than a costume. "Kind Ladies. Strong Gentlemen," she said, in a voice that carried incredibly well, "Tonight for the first time, you will see before your very eyes, the True History of the Sun!"

She stepped to one side in the cleared space before the milling crowd, now beginning to settle down. "To present this wonder to you, the greatest Mage of the age, Rogol Domedonfors, Jr."

The audacity of the nom du stage took Tybalt aback. The one true Rogol Domedonfors had lived ages ago, the last person dedicated to preserving science and-machinery before mankind waned into its magics and superstitions.

The man appeared in a puff of flame and billowing smoke.

"I come to you with wonders," he said, "things I learned at the green porcelain palace which is the Museum of Man."

"All wonders are known there," he continued, "though most are studied but once, then forgotten. If you but know where to look, the answers to all questions may be found."

"Behold," he said "the Sun." A warm golden glow filled the air above the makeshift stage. The glow drew down into a ball and the simulacrum of a yellow star appeared in the wings. It moved from the east, arced overhead, and settled westward. A smaller silver ball circled around it.

"For centuries untold, the Sun circled the earth," he said. "And it had a companion called the Moon, which gave light at night after the Sun had set."

Wrong, thought Tybalt, but let's catch his drift.

The sun-ball had dropped below the leftward stage-horizon while the Moon-ball moved slowly overhead. Then the Moon-ball swam westward while the sun began to glow and came up in dawn on the eastward of the stage.

"Oooh," said the crowd. "Ahhhh."

"Til," said Rogol Domedonfors Jr, "Men, practicing their magick arts, conjured up a fierce dragon which ate up that Moon,"'

A swirling serpentine shape formed in the air between the Moon-and-Sun balls, coalescing into an ophidiaform dragon of purest black. The dragon swallowed the Moon-ball, and the Sun-ball was left alone in the stage-sky.

Wrong, thought Tybalt again, and I get your drift.

"Not satisfied," said Rogol Domedonfors Jr, "Men, practicing their magic arts, pulled the Sun closer to the earth, even though they had to dim its light. Hence, the Sun we behold today."

The Sun-ball was larger and its surface redder, great prominences curled out from it, and it was freckled like the fabled Irishman of old.

"So man in his wisdom and age has given himself a Sun to match his mood. Long may the Spirit of Man and his magicks last, long may that glorious Sun hold sway in the sky."

There was polite applause. From far away, on the slide-hill, another moron dashed himself into the mud-pit.

IT HAD begun to rain. They were inside the inn where Rogol Domedonfors Jr. and his companion, whose name was T'silla, lodged. T'silla placed before her a silver ball and three silvered cowbells.

"Ah!" said Tybalt, "The old game of the bells and the ball." He turned back to Rogol Domedonfors Jr,

"Great showmanship," he said, "But you know it be not true. The Moon was swallowed when Bode's inexorable law met with the unstoppable Roche's Limit!"

"True physics makes poor show," said the Mage.

T'silla moved the cowbells around in a quick blur.

Tybalt pointed to the center one.

She lifted the bell to reveal the ball, quickly replaced it, moved the bells again.

Tybalt pointed to the leftward one.

She lifted that bell and frowned a little when the ball was revealed.

"Listen to the rain," said Rogol Domedonfors Jr. "The crops will virtually spring up this year. There will be fairs, festivals, excitements all growing season. And then the Harvest dinners! "

"Aye," said Tybalt. "There was some indication that wind patterns were shifting. That the traditional seasons would be abated. Changes in the heat from the Sun. Glad to see these forebodings to be proven false. Surely you ran across them when you were Curator of the Museum of Man?"

"Mostly old books," said the mage. "Not very many dealing with Magick, those mostly scholarly."

"But surely…"

"I am certain there are many books of thought and science there," said Rogol Domedonfors Jr. "Those I leave to people of a lesser beat of mind."

T'silla let the blurred bells come to rest. She looked up at Tybalt questioningly.

"Nowhere," he said. "The ball is in your hand."

With no sign of irritation, she dropped the ball on the table and covered it with a bell, then brought the two others around.

"Then do you not return to the Museum of Man?" asked Tybalt, adjusting his frogskin cap.

"Perhaps after this harvest season is over, many months from now. Perhaps not."

T'silla moved the bells again.

From far away on the slide-hill, an idiot screamed and belly-flopped into the cloaca at its bottom.

"Give the people what they want," said Rogol Domedonfors Jr, "and they'll turn out every time."

THE WAY southward had been arduous, though most of the country-people were in an especially good generous mood because of the signs of a bumper harvest. They invited him to sleep in their rude barns and to partake of their meager rations as if it were a feast,

It was at a golden glowing sunset after many months of travel that he came within sight of the green porcelain palace that had to be the Museum of Man.

From this distance, it looked to be intricately carved from a single block of celadon, its turrets and spires glowing softly green in the late afternoon sun. He hurried his steps while the light lasted.

A QUICK inspection revealed it to be everything he'd hoped for. Tome after tome in many languages; charts and maps; plans of cities long fallen to ruin. In the longer halls, exhibit after exhibit of the history of the progress of the animal and vegetal kingdoms, and of Mankind. There were machines designed for flying through the air; others seemingly made for travel beneath the seas. There were men of metal shaped like humans whose purpose he could not fathom. He had time before darkness to discover that the northenmost tower was an observatory with a fine giant spying-glass.

He found a hall of portraits of former Curators of the Museum. Just before he had parted company with Rogol Domedonfors and T'silla months ago, she had handed him a folded and sealed paper.

"What's this?" he had asked.

"There will come a time when you will need it. Open it then," she said. All these months, it had been a comforting weight in his pocket.

He travelled up the hall of portraits, pausing at the one of the original Rogol Domedonfors from long ages past. He came up the hall as if transgressing time itself, noting changes in the styles of costuming in the portraits, from the high winged collars to the off-the-shoulder straps. The last full portrait outside the Curator's door was of Rogol Domedonfors Jr. Tybalt noted the faint resemblance of the features shared by he and the original—the wayward cowlick, the frown-line on one side of the mouth, the long neck. Almost impossible that the same features would skip so many generations, only to show up later in the namesake.

Last outside the door was an empty frame with four pins stuck at its center.

Tybalt reached in his pocket, took out the folded and sealed paper, broke its waxen seal, and unfolded it.

It was a drawing of himself, done in brown pencil, wearing his frogskin cap. The legend below said: "Tybalt the Scientist. "Frogskin Cap" The last Curator of the Museum of Man." It was an excellent likeness, though the words uneased him. When had T'silla had time between the game of the bells and the ball, and early the next rainy morning when they parted, to do such a good drawing

He pinned the drawing within the frame—it fit perfectly. It made him feel at home, as if he had a place there.

He noticed too, that as the night had darkened, the walls of the room it had begun to glow with the faintest of blue lights, which intensified as the outside grew blacker. He looked from the office-room and the whole Museum glowed likewise

He found a writing instrument and pages of foolscap, cleared a space on the desk, and began to write on the topmost sheet:

THE TRUE.AUTHENTIC HISTORY
OF OUR SUN
By Tybalt, "Frogskin Cap"
Curator of the Museum of Man

HE HAD worked through most of the night. The walls were fading as a red glow tainted eastwards.

Tybalt stretched himself. He had barely begun outlining the main sequence of the birth, growth, senescence, and death of stars. Enough for now; there were books to consult; there was food to find. He was famished, having finished some parched corn he'd gotten at the last farmhouse before coming to the woods that led to the Museum of Man, late the afternoon before. Surely there was food somewhere hereabouts.

He went outside the green porcelain Museum and turned to face the East.

The darkened Sun rose lumpy as a cracked egg. Straggly whiskers of fire stood out from the chins of the Sun, growing and shortening as he watched.

A curl of fire swept up out of the top of the sphere, and the surface became pocked and darkened, as if it had a disease.

The Sun was having one of its bad days.

AFTERWORD:

I REMEMBER sitting in a green and white lawn chair under a magnolia tree (at the only house I ever lived in that had one) in the summer of 1962, reading Jack Vance's *The Dying Earth.*

I would read on those unairconditioned summer mornings til it got too hot, then walk two miles to the municipal swimming pool and swim all afternoon, return home, eat something, then go to my seven-day-a-week, 5-hours-a-night job at a service station, being somewhere between a Johannes Factotum and a grease monkey.

The edition I read was the one I have now, "The Lancer Science Fiction Library Limited Edition" second printing of the book from 1962, and the first generally available. (My friend Jake Sanders was a Jack Vance collector, having many of the original appearances of Vance's works in *Thrilling Wonder* and *Startling Stories*: he had a first printing (by Hillman, publisher of Airboy Comics!) of Jack Vance's *The Dying Earth.*

I had remembered the Lancer edition as having rounded corners (a trick of memory; Avon paperbacks had rounded corners in the early 1960s, not Lancer.)

Bibliographic anomalies aside, Lancer had done the world a favor by bringing an ignored classic back into print 12 years after its first printing.

I remember entering that world of magicians, madmen, strange plants, and beautiful unattainable women as if it were happening to my circumscribed life, which I saw as stretching out forward in time, forever, to my 16-year-old mind.

Vance probably started some of the stories that composed *The Dying Earth* while on leaky tubs in the Atlantic or Pacific in the merchant marine during VWII. His imagination found a way of transcending his circumstances—while other SF writers were still reeling from, and writing about, man-made nuclear disasters, Vance looked beyond to a time when the Earth, the Sun, and the Universe had grown old, and mankind found its own ways to deal with it.

Rereading *The Dying Earth*, with one eye full of blood, flat on my back in a VA hospital, was a revelation. It was a different book; it had grown in its implications. (Part of this I attribute to my growth as a person in the intervening 46 years; partly to the depth of writing Vance put into the book.)

The Dying Earth is a fully-thought-out work of pure imagination. It spoke to me again (sad shape that I was in) across the years—it will continue to speak to people as long as books are read.

And every time someone new reads it, it will be a different book.

You can't ask for more than that.

—Howard Waldrop

GEORGE R. R. MARTIN

A Night at the Tarn House

HUGO, NEBULA, and World Fantasy Award-winner George R. R. Martin, *New York Times* best-selling author of the landmark *A Song of Ice and Fire* fantasy series, has been called "the American Tolkien."

Born in Bayonne, New Jersey, George R. R. Martin made his first sale in 1971, and soon established himself as one of the most popular SF writers of the '70s. He quickly became a mainstay of the Ben Bova *Analog* with stories such as "With Morning Comes Mistfall," "And Seven Times Never Kill Man," "The Second Kind of Loneliness," "The Storms of Windhaven" (in collaboration with Lisa Tuttle, and later expanded by them into the novel *Windhaven*), "Override," and others, although he also sold to *Amazing*, *Fantastic*, *Galaxy*, *Orbit*, and other markets. One of his *Analog* stories, the striking novella "A Song for Lya," won him his first Hugo Award, in 1975.

By the end of the '70s, he had reached the height of his influence as a science fiction writer, and was producing his best work in that category with stories such as the famous "Sandkings," his best-known story, which won both the Nebula and the Hugo in 1980 (he'd later win another Nebula in 1985 for his story "Portraits of His Children"), "The Way of Cross and Dragon," which won a Hugo Award in the same year (making Martin the first author ever to receive two Hugo Awards for fiction in the same year) "Bitterblooms," "The Stone City," "Starlady," and others. These stories would be collected in *Sandkings*, one of the strongest collections of the period. By now, he had mostly moved away from *Analog*, although he would have a long sequence of stories about the droll interstellar adventures of Havalend Tuf (later collected in *Tuf Voyaging*) running throughout the '80s in the Stanley Schmidt *Analog*, as well as a few strong individual pieces such as the novella "Nightflyers"—most of his major work of the late '70s and early '80s, though, would appear in *Omni*. The late '70s and '80s also saw the publication of his memorable novel *Dying of the Light*, his only solo SF novel, while his stories were collected in *A Song for Lya*, *Sandkings*, *Songs of Stars and Shadows*, *Songs the Dead Men Sing*, *Nightflyers*, and *Portraits of His Children*. By the beginning of the '80s, he'd moved away from SF and into the horror genre, publishing the big horror novel *Fevre Dream*, and winning the Bram Stoker Award for his horror story "The Pear-Shaped Man" and the World Fantasy Award for his werewolf novella "The Skin Trade." By the end of that decade, though, the crash of the horror market and the commercial failure of his ambitious horror novel *Armageddon Rag* had driven him out of the print world and to a successful career in television instead, where for more than a decade he worked as story editor or producer on such shows as new *Twilight Zone* and *Beauty and the Beast*.

After years away, Martin made a triumphant return to the print world in 1996 with the publication in 1996 of the immensely successful fantasy novel *A Game of Thrones*, the start of his "Song of Ice and Fire" sequence. A free-standing novella taken from that work, "Blood of the Dragon," won Martin another Hugo Award in 1997. Further books in the "Song of Ice and Fire" series. *A Clash of Kings*, *A Storm of Swords*, *A Feast for Crows*, and *A Dance with Dragons* (forthcoming), have made it one of the most popular, acclaimed, and best-selling series in all of modern fantasy. His most recent book are a massive retrospective collection spanning the entire spectrum of his career, *GRRM: A Rretrospective*, a novella collection, *Starlady and Fast-Friend*, a novel written in collaboration with Gardner Dozois and Daniel Abraham, *Hunter's Run*, and, as editor, two new volumes in his long-running *Wild Cards* anthology series, *Wild Cards: Busted Flush* and *Wild Cards: Inside Straight*.

Here he takes us to The Land of the Falling Wall, through a haunted forest and across a bleak and desolate tarn, for a dangerous and surprising night of hospitality at the Tarn House (famous for their Hissing Eels), in company with a strange and varied cast of colorful characters—none of whom are even remotely what they seem.

A Night at the Tarn House

GEORGE R. R. MARTIN

Through the purple gloom came Molloqos the Melancholy, borne upon an iron palanquin by four dead Deodands .

Above them hung a swollen sun where dark continents of black ash were daily spreading across dying seas of dim red fire. Behind and before the forest loomed, steeped in scarlet shadow. Seven feet tall and black as onyx, the Deodands wore ragged skirts and nothing else The right front Deodand, fresher than the others, squished with every step. Gaseous and swollen, his ripening flesh oozed noxious fluid from a thousand pinpricks where the Excellent Prismatic Spray had pierced him through. His passage left damp spots upon the surface of the road, an ancient and much-overgrown track whose stones had been laid during the glory days of Thorsingol, now a fading memory in the minds of men.

The Deodands moved at a steady trot, eating up the leagues. Being dead, they did not feel the chill in the air, nor the cracked and broken stones beneath their heels. The palanquin swayed from side to side, a gentle motion that made Molloqos think back upon his mother rocking him in his cradle. Even he had had a mother once, but that was long ago. The time of mothers and children had passed. The human race was fading, whilst grues and erbs and pelgranes claimed the ruins they left behind.

To dwell on such matters would only invite a deeper melancholy, however. Molloqos preferred to consider the book upon his lap. After three days of fruitless attempts to commit the Excellent Prismatic Spray to memory once again, he had set aside his grimoire, a massive tome bound in cracked vermillion leather with clasps and hinges of black iron, in favor of a slender volume of erotic poetry from the last days of the Sherit Empire, whose songs of lust had gone to dust aeons ago. Of late his gloom ran so deep that even those fervid rhymes seldom stirred him to tumescence, but at least the words did not turn to worms wriggling on the vellum, as those in his grimoire seemed wont to do. The world's long afternoon had given way to evening, and in the dusk even magic had begun to crack and fade.

As the swollen sun sank slowly in the west, the words grew harder to discern. Closing his book, Molloqos pulled his Cloak of Fearsome Mien across his legs, and watched the trees go past. With the dying of the light each seemed more sinister than the last, and he could almost see shapes moving in the underbrush, though when he turned his head for a better look they were gone.

A cracked and blistered wooden sign beside the road read:

TARN HOUSE
Half a League On
Famous for Our Hissing Eels

An inn would not be unwelcome, although Molloqos did not entertain high expectations of any hostelry that might be found along a road so drear and desolate as this. Come dark, grues and erbs and leucomorphs would soon be stirring, some hungry enough to risk an assault even on a sorcerer of fearful mien. Once he would not have feared such creatures; like others of his ilk, it had been his habit to arm himself with half a dozen puissant spells whenever he was called up to leave the safety of his manse. But now the spells ran through his mind like water through his fingers, and even those he still commanded seemed feebler each time he was called upon to employ them. And there were the shadow swords to consider as well. Some claimed they were shapechangers, with faces malleable as candle wax. Molloqos did not know the truth of that, but of their malice he had no doubt.

Soon enough he would be in Kaiin, drinking black wine with Princess Khandelume and his fellow sorcerers, safe behind the city's tall white walls and ancient enchantments, but just now even an inn as dreary as this Tarn House must surely be preferable to another night in his pavilion beneath those sinister pines.

SLUNG BETWEEN two towering wooden wheels, the cart shook and shuddered as it made its way down the rutted road, bouncing over the cracked stones and slamming Chimwazle's teeth together. He clutched his whip tighter. His face was broad, his nose flat, his skin loose and sagging and pebbly, with a greenish cast. From time to time his tongue flickered out to lick an ear.

To the left the forest loomed, thick and dark and sinister; to the right, beyond a few thin trees and a drear grey strand dotted with clumps of salt-grass, stretched the tarn. The sky was violet darkening to indigo, spotted by the light of weary stars.

"Faster!" Chimwazle called to Polymumpho, in the traces. He glanced back over his shoulder. There was no sign of pursuit, but that did not mean the Twk-men were not coming. They were nasty little creatures, however tasty, and clung to their grudges past all reason. "Dusk falls. Soon night will be upon us! Bestir yourself! We must find shelter before evenfall, you great lump."

The hairy-nosed Pooner made no reply but a grunt, so Chimwazle gave him a lick of the whip to encourage his efforts. "Move those feet, you verminious lout." This time Polymumpho put his back into it, legs pumping, belly flopping. The cart bounced, and Chimwazle bit his tongue as one wheel slammed against a rock. The taste of blood filled his mouth, thick and sweet as moldy bread. Chimwazle spat, and a gobbet of greenish plegm and black ichor struck Polymumpho's face and clung to his cheek before dropping off to spatter on the stones. "*Faster!*" Chimwazle roared, and his lash whistled a lively tune to keep the Pooner's feet thumping.

At last the trees widened and the inn appeared ahead of them, perched upon a hummock of stone where three roads came together. Stoutly-built and cheery it seemed, stone below and timber higher up, with many a grand gable and tall turret, and wide windows through which poured a warm, welcoming, ruddy light and the happy sounds of music and laughter, accompanied by a clatter of cup and platters that seemed to say, *Come in, come in. Pull off your boots, put up your feet, enjoy a cup of ale.* Beyond its pointed rooftops the waters of the tarn glittered smooth and red as a sheet of beaten copper, shining in the sun.

The Great Chimwazle had never seen such a welcome sight. "Halt!" he cried, flicking his whip at Polymumpho's ear to command the Pooner's attention. "Stop! Cease! Here is our refuge!"

Polymumpho stumbled, slowed, halted. He looked at the inn dubiously, and sniffed. "I would press on. If I were you."

"You would like that, I am sure." Chimwazle hopped from the cart, his soft boots squishing in the mud. "And when the Twk-men caught us, you would chortle and do nothing as they stabbed at me. Well, they will never find us here."

"Except for that one," said the Pooner.

And there he was: a Twk-man, flying bold as you please around his head. The wings of his dragonfly made a faint buzzing sound as he couched his lance. His skin was a pale green, and his helm was an acorn shell. Chimwazle raised his hands in horror. "Why do you molest me? I have done nothing!"

"You ate the noble Florendal," the Twk-man said. "You swallowed Lady Melescence, and devoured her brothers three."

"Not so! I refute these charges! It was someone else who looked like me. Have you proof? Show me your proof! What, have you none to offer? Begone with you then!"

Instead, the Twk-man flew at him and thrust his lance point at his nose, but quick as he was, Chimwazle was quicker. His tongue darted out, long and sticky, plucked the tiny rider from his mount, pulled him back wailing. His armor was flimsy stuff, and crunched nicely between Chimwazle's sharp green teeth. He tasted of mint and moss and mushroom, very piquant.

Afterward, Chimwazle picked his teeth with the tiny lance. "There was only the one," he decided confidently, when no further Twk-men deigned to appear. "A bowl of hissing eels awaits me. You may remain here, Pooner. See that you guard my cart."

LIRIANNE SKIPPED and spun as on she walked. Lithe and long-legged, boyish and bouncy, clad all in grey and dusky rose, she had a swagger in her step. Her blouse was spun of spider-silk, soft and smooth, its top three buttons undone. Her hat was velvet, wide-brimmed, decorated with a jaunty feather and cocked at a rakish angle. On'her hip, Tickle-Me-Sweet rode in a sheath of soft grey leather that matched her thigh-high boots. Her hair was a mop of auburn curls, her cheeks dusted with freckles across skin as pale as milk. She had lively grey-green eyes, a mouth made for mischievious smiles, and a small upturned nose that twitched as she sniffed the air.

The evening was redolent with pine and sea salt, but faintly, beneath those scents, Lirianne could detect a hint of erb, a dying grue, and the nearby stench of ghouls. She wondered if any would dare come out and play with her once the sun went down. The prospect made her smile. She touched the hilt of Tickle-Me-Sweet and spun in a circle, her boot heels sending up little puffs of dust as she whirled beneath the trees.

"Why do you dance, girl?" a small voice said. "The hour grows late, the shadows long. This is no time for dancing."

A Twk-man hovered by her head, another just behind him. A third appeared, then a fourth. Their spear points glittered redly in the light of the setting sun, and the dragonflies they rode glimmered with a pale green luminescence. Lirianne glimpsed more amongst the trees, tiny lights darting in and out between the branches, small as stars. "The sun is dying," Lirianne told them. "There will be no dances in the darkness. Play with me, friends. Weave bright patterns in the evening air whilst still you can."

"We have no time for play," one Twk-man said.

"We hunt," another said. "Later we will dance."

"Later," the first agreed. And the laughter of the Twk-men filled the trees, as sharp as shards.

"Is there a Twk-town near?" asked Lirianne.

"Not near," one Twk-man said.

"We have flown far," another said.

"Do you have spice for us, dancer?"

"Salt?" said another.

"Pepper?" asked a third.

"Saffron?" sighed a fourth.

"Give us spice, and we will show you secret ways."

"Around the tarn."

"Around the inn."

"Oho." Lirianne grinned. "What inn is this? I think I smell it. A magical place, is it?"

"A dark place," one Twk-man said.

"The sun is going out. All the world is growing dark." Lirianne remembered another inn from another time, a modest place but friendly, with clean rushes on the floor and a dog asleep before the hearth. The world had been dying even then, and the nights were dark and full of terrors, but within those walls it had still been possible to find fellowship, good cheer, even love. Lirianne remembered roasts turning above the crackling fire, the way the fat would spit as it dripped down into the flames. She remembered the beer, dark and heady, smelling of hops. She remembered a girl too, an innkeeper's daughter with bright eyes and a silly smile who'd loved a wandering warfarer. Dead now, poor thing. But what of it? The world was almost dead as well. "I want to see this inn," she said. "How far is it?"

"A league," the Twk-man said.

"Less," a second insisted.

"Where is our salt?" the two of them said, together. Lirianne gave them each a pinch of salt from the pouch at her belt. "Show me," she said, "and you shall have pepper too."

THE TARN House did not lack for custom. Here sat a whitehaired man with a long beard, spooning up some vile purple stew. There lounged a dark-haired slattern, nursing her glass of wine as if it were a newborn babe. Near the wooden casks that lined one wall a ferret-faced man with scruffy whiskers was sucking snails out of their shells. Though his eyes struck Chimwazle as sly and sinister, the buttons on his vest were silver and his hat sported a fan of peacock feathers, suggesting that he did not lack for means. Closer to the hearth fire, a man and wife crowded around a table with their two large and lumpish sons, sharing a huge meat pie. From the look of them, they had wandered here from some land where the only color was brown. The father sported a thick beard; his sons displayed bushy mustaches that covered their mouths. Their mother's mustache was finer, allowing one to see her lips.

The rustics stank of cabbage, so Chimwazle hied to the far side of the room and joined the prosperous fellow with the silver buttons on his vest."How are your snails?" he inquired.

"Slimy and without savor. I do not recommend them."

Chimwazle pulled out a chair. "I am the Great Chimwazle."

"And I Prince Rocallo the Redoubtable."

Chimwazle frowned. "Prince of what?"

"Just so." The prince sucked another snail, and dropped the empty shell onto the floor.

That answer did not please him. "The Great Chimwazle is no man to trifle with," he warned the so-called princeling.

"Yet here you sit, in the Tarn House."

"With you," observed Chimwazle, somewhat peevishly.

The landlord made his appearance, bowing and scraping as was appropriate for one of his station. "How may I serve you?"

"I will try a dish of your famous hissing eels."

The innkeep gave an apologetic cough. "Alas, the eels are…ah…off the bill of fare."

"What? How so? Your sign suggests that hissing eels are the specialty of the house."

"And so they were, in other days. Delicious creatures, but mischievous. One ate a wizard's concubine, and the wizard was so wroth he set the tarn to boiling and extinguished all the rest."

"Perhaps you should change the sign."

"Every day I think the same when I awaken. But then I think, the world may end today, should I spend my final hours perched upon a ladder with a paintbrush in my hand? I pour myself some wine and sit down to cogitate upon the matter, and by evening I find the urge has passed."

"Your urges do not concern me," said Chimwazle. "Since you have no eels, I must settle for a roast fowl, well crisped."

The innkeep looked lachrymose. "Alas, this clime is not salubrious for chicken."

"Fish?"

"From the tarn?" The man shuddered. "I would advise against it. Most unwholesome, those waters."

Chimwazle was growing vexed. His companion leaned across the table and said, "On no account should you attempt a bowl of scrumby. The gristle pies are also to be avoided."

"Begging your pardon," said the landlord, "but meat pies is all we have just now."

"What sort of meat is in these pies?" asked Chimwazle.

"Brown," said the landlord. "And chunks of grey."

"A meat pie, then." There seemed to be no help for it.

The pie was large, admittedly; that was the best that could be said for it. What meat Chimwazle found was chiefly gristle, here and there a chunk of yellow fat, and once something that crunched suspiciously when he bit into it. There was more grey meat than brown, and once a chunk that glistened green. He found a carrot too, or perhaps it was a finger. In either case, it had been overcooked. Of the crust, the less said, the better.

Finally Chimwazle pushed the pie away from him. No more than a quarter had been consumed. "A wiser man might have heeded my warning," said Rocallo.

"A wiser man with a fuller belly, perhaps." That was problem with Twk-men; no matter how many you ate, an hour later you were hungry again. "The earth is old, but the night is young." The Great Chimwazle produced a pack of painted placards from his sleeve. "Have you played peggoty? A jolly game, that goes well with ale. Perhaps you will assay a few rounds with me?"

"The game is unfamiliar to me, but I am quick to learn," said Rocallo. "If you will explain the rudiments, I should be glad to try my hand."

Chimwazle shuffled the placards.

THE INN was grander than Lirianne had expected, and seemed queer and out of place, not at all the sort of establishment she would have expected to find along a forest road in the Land of the Falling Wall. "Famous for Our Hissing Eels," she read aloud, and laughed. Behind the inn a sliver of the setting sun floated red upon the black waters of the tarn.

The Twk-men buzzed around her on their dragonflies. More and more had joined Lirianne as she made her way along the road. Two score, four, a hundred; by now she had lost count. The gauzy wings of their mounts trilled against the evening air. The purple dusk hummed to the sound of small angry voices.

Lirianne pinched her nose and took a sniff. The scent of sorcery was so strong it almost made her sneeze. There was magic here. "Oho," she said. "I smell wizard."

Whistling a spritely tune, she sauntered closer. A ramshackle cart was drawn up near the bottom of the steps. Slumped against one of its wheels was a huge, ugly man, bigbellied and ripe, with coarse dark hair sprouting from his ears and nostrils. He looked up as Lirianne approached. "I would not go up there if I were you. It is a bad place. Men go in. No men come out."

"Well, I am no man as you can plainly see, and I *love* bad places. Who might you be?"

"Polymumpho is my name. I am a Pooner."

"I am not familiar with the Pooners."

"Few are." He shrugged, a massive rippling of his shoulders. "Are those your Twk-men? Tell them my master went inside the inn to hide."

"Master?"

"Three years ago I played at peggoty with Chimwazle. When my coin ran out, I bet myself."

"Is your master a sorcerer?"

Another shrug. "He thinks he is."

Lirianne touched the hilt of Tickle-Me-Sweet. "Then you may consider yourself free. I shall make good your debt for you."

"Truly?" He got to his feet. "Can I have the cart?"

"If you wish."

A wide grin split his face. "Hop on, and I will carry you to Kaiin. You will be safe, I promise you. Pooners only eat the flesh of men when the stars are in alignment."

Lirianne glanced up. Half a dozen stars were visible above the trees, dusty diamonds glimmering in a purple velvet sky. "And who will be the judge of whether the stars are properly aligned for such a feast, or no?"

"On that account you may place your trust in me."

She giggled. "No, I think not. I am for the inn."

"And I for the road." The Pooner lifted the traces of the cart. "If Chimwazle complains of my absence, tell him that my debt is yours."

"I shall." Lirianne watched as Polymumpho rumbled off toward Kaiin, the empty cart bouncing and jouncing behind him. She scampered up the winding stone steps, and pushed her way through the door into the Tarn House.

The common room smelled of mold and smoke and ghouls, and a little leucomorph as well, though none such were presently in evidence. One table was packed with hairy rustics, another occupied by a big-bosomed slattern sipping wine from a dinted silver goblet. An old man attired in the antique fashion of a knight of ancient Thorsingol sat lonely and forlorn, his long white beard spotted with purple soupstains.

Chimwazle was not hard to find. He sat beneath the ale casks with another rogue, each of them appearing more unsavory than the other. The latter had the stink of rat about him; the former smelled of toad. The rattish man wore a grey leather vest with sparking silver buttons over a tight-fitting shirt striped in cream and azure, with large puffy sleeves. On his pointed head perched a wide-brimmed blue hat decorated with a fan of peacock feathers. His toadish companion, beset by drooping jowls, pebbled skin, and greenish flesh that made him look faintly nauseated, favored a floppy cap that resembled a deflated mushroom, a soiled mauve tunic with golden scrollwork at collar, sleeve, and hem, and green shoes turned up at the toe. His lips were full and fat, his mouth so wide it all but touched the pendulous lobes of his ears.

Both vagabonds eyed Lirianne lasciviously as they weighed the possibilities of erotic dalliance. The toad actually dared to venture a small smile. Lirianne knew how that game was played. She removed her hat, bowed to them, and approached their table. A spread of painted placards covered its rough wooden surface, beside the remains of a congealed and singularly unappealing meat pie. "What game is this?" she asked, oh so innocent.

"Peggoty," said the toadish man. "Do you know it?"

"No," she said, "but I love to play. Will you teach me?"

"Gladly. Have a seat. I am Chimwazle, oft called the Gallant. My friend is known as Rocallo the Reluctant."

"Redoubtable," the rat-faced man corrected, "and I am *Prince* Rocallo, if it please you. The landlord is about here somewhere. Will you take a drink, girl?"

"I will," she said. "Are you wizards? You have a sorcerous look about you."

Chimwazle made a dismissive gesture. "Such pretty eyes you have, and sharp as well. I know a spell or two."

"A charm to make milk sour?" suggested Rocallo. "That is a spell that many know, though it takes six days to work."

"That, and many more," boasted Chimwazle, "each more potent than the last."

"Will you show me?" Lirianne asked, in a breathless voice.

"Perhaps when we know each other better."

"Oh, please. I have always wanted to see true magic."

"Magic adds spice to the gristle that is life," proclaimed Chimwazle, leering, "but I do not care to waste my wonderments before such lumpkins and pooners as surround us. Later when we are alone, I shall perform such magics for you as you have never seen, until you cry out in joy and awe. But first some ale, and a hand or three of pegotty to get our juices flowing! What stakes shall we play for?"

"Oh, I am sure you will think of something," said Lirianne.

BY THE time Molloqos the Melancholy caught sight of the Tarn House, the swollen sun was setting, easing itself down in the west like an old fat man lowering himself into his favorite chair.

Muttering softly in a tongue no living man had spoken since the Gray Sorcerers went to the stars, the sorcerer commanded a halt. The inn beside the tarn was most inviting to the casual glance, but Molloqos was of a suspicious cast, and had long ago learned that things were not always as they seemed. He muttered a brief invocation, and lifted up an ebon staff. Atop the shaft was a crystal orb, within which a great golden eye looked this way and that. No spell nor illusion could deceive the True-Seeing Eye.

Stripped of its glamor, the Tarn House stood weathered and grey, three stories tall and oddly narrow. It leaned sideways like a drunken wormiger, a crooked flight of flagstone steps leading upwards to its door. Diamond-shaped panes of green glass gave the light from within a diseased and leprous cast; its roof was overgrown with drooping ropes of fungus. Behind the inn the tarn was black as pitch and redolent of decay, dotted with drowned trees, its dark oily waters stirring ominously. A stable stood off to one side, a structure so decayed that even dead Deodands might balk at entering.

At the foot of the inn's steps was a sign that read:

TARN HOUSE
Famous for Our Hissing Eels

The right front Deodand spoke up. "The earth is dying and soon the sun will fail. Here beneath this rotten roof is a fit abode for Molloqos to spend eternity."

"The earth is dying and soon the sun shall fail," Molloqos agreed, "but if the end should overtake us here, I shall spend eternity seated by a fire savoring a dish of hissing eels, whilst you stand shivering in the dark and cold, watching pieces of your body ripen and rot and tumble to the ground." Adjusting the drape of his Cloak of Fearful Mein, he gathered up his tall ebony staff, descended from the palanquin, stepped into the weed-choked yard, and began to climb the steps up to the inn.

Above, a door banged open. A man emerged, a small and servile creature with gravy spatters on his apron who could only be the innkeeper. As he hurried down, wiping his hands upon his apron, he caught his first good sight of Molloqos, and paled.

As well he might. White as bone was the flesh of Molloqos, beneath his Cloak of Fearful Mien. Deep and dark and full of sadness were his eyes. His nose curved downward in a hook; his lips were thin and rather dour; his hands large, expressive, long-fingered. On his right hand his fingernails were painted black, on his left scarlet. His long legs were clothed in striped pantaloons of those same colors, tucked into calf-high boots of polished grue hide. Black and scarlet was his hair as well, blood and night mixed together; on his head perched a wide-brimmed hat of purple velvet decorated with a green pearl and a white quill.

"Dread sir," the innkeep said, "those…those Deodands…"

"…will not trouble you. Death diminishes even such savage appetites as theirs."

"We…we do not oft see sorcerers at the Tarn House."

Molloqos was unsurprised. Once the dying earth had teemed with such, but in these last days even magic was waning. Spells seemed less potent than before, their very words harder to grasp and hold. The grimoires themselves were crumbling, falling to dust in ancient libraries as their protective charms winked out like guttering candles. And as the magic failed, so too did the magicians. Some fell to their own servants, the demons and sandestins who once obeyed their every whim. Others were hunted down by shadow swords, or torn apart by angry mobs of women. The wisest slipped away to other times and other places, their vast and drafty manses vanishing like mist before the sunrise. Their very names had become the stuff of legend: Mazirian the Magician, Turjan of Miir, Rhialto the Marvelous, the Enigmatic Mumph, Gilgad, Pandelume, Ildefonse the Perceptor.

Yet Molloqos remained, and it was his intent to go on remaining, to live to drink a final cup of wine while he watched the sun go out. "You stand in the presence of Molloqos the Melancholy, poet, philosopher, archmage, and necromancer, a student of forgotten tongues and bane of demonkind," he informed the cringing landlord. "Every corner of this dying earth is known to me. I collect curious artifacts from aeons past, translate crumbling scrolls no other man can read, converse with the dead, delight the living, frighten the meek, and awe the unenlightened. My vengeance is a cold black wind, my affection warm as a yellow sun. The rules and laws that govern lesser men I brush off as a wayfarer might brush the dust from his cloak. This night I will honor you with my custom. No obsequies are necessary. I will require your best room, dry and spacious, with a feather mattress. I shall sup with you as well. A thick slice of wild boar would fill me nicely, with such side dishes as your kitchen may supply."

"We have no boars hereabouts, wild or tame. The grues and the erbs ate most of them, and the rest were dragged down into the tarn. I can serve you a meat pie, or a piping hot bowl of purple scrumby, but I don't think you'd like the one, and I know you'd hate t'other." The innkeep swallowed. "A thousand pardons, dread sir. My humble house is not fit for such as you. No doubt you would find some other inn more comfortable."

Molloqos let his visage darken. "No doubt," said he, "but as no other inn presents itself, I must make do with yours."

The innkeep dabbed at his forehead with his apron. "Dread sir, begging your pardons and meaning no offense, but I've some trouble from sorcerous folk before. Some, not so honest as you, settle their accounts with purses of ensorcelled stones and chunks of dung glamored to look like gold, and others have been known to inflict boils and warts on unhappy serving wenches and innocent innkeepers when the service does not meet their standards."

"The remedy is simple," declared Molloqos the Melancholy. "See that the service is all that it should be, and you will have no difficulties. You have my word, I will perform no sorceries in your common room, inflict no boils nor warts upon your staff, nor settle my account with dung. But now I grow weary of this banter. The day is done, the sun is fled, and I am weary, so here I mean to stay the night. Your choice is simple. Accomodate me, or else I shall pronounce Gargoo's Festering Reek upon you and leave you to choke upon your own stench until the end of your days. Which will not be long in coming, as pelgranes and erbs are drawn to the smell as mice are drawn to a nice ripe cheese."

The innkeep's mouth opened and closed, but no words emerged. After a moment, he shuffled to one side. Molloqos aknowledged the surrender with a nod, ascended the rest of the steps, and shoved through the inn's front door.

The interior of the Tarn House proved to be just as dark, damp, and dismal as the exterior. A queer sour odor hung in the air, though Molloqos would not have ventured to say whether it emanated from the innkeep, the other customers, or whatever was cooking in the kitchen. A hush fell upon the common room at his entrance. All eyes turned toward him, as was only to be expected. In his Cloak of Fearful Mien, he was a dreadful sight.

Molloqos took a seat at the table by the window. Only then did he permit himself to inspect his fellow guests. The group near the fire, growling at each other in low, gutteral voices, reminded the sorcerer of turnips with hair. Over by the ale casks, a pretty young girl was laughing and flirting with a pair of obvious scoundrels, one of whom appeared to be not entirely human. Nearby an old man slept, his head on the table, pillowed atop his folded arms. There was a woman just beyond him, sloshing the dregs of her wine and eying the wizard speculatively across the room. A glance was enough to tell Molloqos that she was a woman of the evening, though in her case evening was edging on toward night. Her visage was not altogether hideous, although there was something odd and unsettling about the look of her ears. Still, she had a pleasing shape, her eyes were large and dark and liquid, and the fire woke red highlights in her long black hair.

Or so it seemed through the eyes that Molloqos had been born with, but he knew better than to put his trust in those. Softly, softly, he whispered an invocation, and looked again through the enchanted golden eye atop his staff. This time he saw true.

For his supper, the sorcerer ordered a meat pie, as the specialty of the house was unavailable. After one bite Molloqos put down his spoon, feeling even more melancholy than he had a moment before. Wisps of steam rose through the pie's broken crust to form hideous faces in the air, their mouths open in torment. When the landlord returned to inquire if the repast was to his liking, Molloqos gave him a reproachful look and said, "You are fortunate that I am not so quick to wroth as most of my brethen."

"I am grateful for your forebearance, dread sir."

"Let us hope that your bedchambers keep to a higher standard than your kitchen."

"For three terces you can share the big bed with Mumpo and his family," the landlord said, indicating the rustics near the hearth. "A private room will cost you twelve."

"None but the best for Molloqos the Melancholy."

"Our best room rents for twenty terces, and is presently occupied by Prince Rocallo."

"Remove his things at once, and have the room readied for me," Molloqos commanded. He might have said a good deal more, but just then the dark-eyed woman woman rose and came over to his table. He nodded toward the chair across from him. "Sit."

She sat. "Why do you look so sad?"

"It is the lot of man. I look at you, and see the child that you were. Once you had a mother who held you to her breast. Once you had a father who dandled you upon his knee. You were their pretty little girl, and through your eyes they saw again the wonders of the world. Now they are dead and the world is dying, and their child sells her sadness to strangers."

"We are strangers now, but we need not remain so," the woman said. "My name is—"

"—no concern of mine. Are you a child still, to speak your true name to a sorcerer?"

"Sage counsel." She put her hand upon his sleeve. "Do you have a room? Let us repair upstairs, and I will make you happy."

"Unlikely. The earth is dying. So too the race of men. No erotic act can change that, no matter how perverse or energetic."

"There is still hope," the woman said. "For you, for me, for all of us. Only last year I lay with a man who said a child had been born to a woman of Saskervoy."

"He lied, or was deceived. At Saskervoy the women weep as elsewhere, and devour their children in the womb. Man dwindles, and soon shall disappear. The earth will become the haunt of Deodands and pelgranes and worse things, until the last light flickers out. There was no child. Nor will there be."

The woman shivered. "Still," she said, "still. So long as men and women endure, we must try. Try with me."

"As you wish." He was Molloqos the Melancholy, and he had seen her for what she was. "When I retire, you may come to my bedchamber, and we shall try the truth of things."

THE PLACARDS were made of dark black wood, sliced paper thin and brightly painted. They made a faint clacking sound when Lirianne turned

them over. The game was simple enough. They played for terces. Lirianne won more than she lost, though she did not fail to note that whenever the wagering was heavy, somehow Chimwazle showed the brightest placards, no matter how promising her own had seemed at first.

"Fortune favors you this evening," Chimwazle announced, after a dozen hands, "but playing for such small stakes grows tiresome." He placed a golden centum on the table. "Who will meet my wager?"

"I," said Rocallo. "The earth is dying, and with it all of us. What do a few coins matter to a corpse?"

Lirianne looked sad. "I have no gold to wager."

"No matter," said Chimwazle. "I have taken a fancy to your hat. Put that in the wager, against our gold."

"Oho. Is that the way of it?" She cocked her head and ran the tip of her tongue across her lip. "Why not?"

Shortly she was hatless, which was no more than she had expected. She handed the prize to Chimwazle with a flourish and shook out her hair, smiling as he stared at her. Lirianne took care never to look directly at the sorcerer seated by the window, but she had been aware of him since the moment he had entered. Gaunt and grim and fearsome, that one, and he stank of sorcery so strongly that it overwhelmed the lesser magics wafting off the odious fraud Chimwazle. Most of the great mages were dead or fled, slain by shadow swords or gone to some underworld or overworld, or perhaps to distant stars. Those few who remained upon the dying earth were gathering in Kaiin, she knew, hoping to find safety there behind the white-walled city's ancient enchantments. This was surely one of them.

Her palm itched, and Tickle-Me-Sweet sang silent by her side. Lirianne had tempered its steel in the blood of the first wizard she had slain, when she was six-and-ten. No protective spell was proof against such a blade, though she herself had no defense but her wits. The hard part of killing wizards was knowing when to do it, since most of them could turn you into dust with a few well-chosen words.

A round of ales arrived, and then another. Lirianne sipped at her first tankard while her second sat untouched by her elbow, but her companions drank deep. When Rocallo called for a third round, Chimwazle excused himself to answer a call of nature, and loped across the common room in search of a privy. He gave the necromancer's table a wide berth, Lirianne did not fail to note. That pale grim creature seemed deeply engrossed in conversation with the inn's resident doxy, oblivious to the wattled pop-eyed rogue scuttling past, but the golden eye atop his wizard's staff had fixed on Chimwazle and watched his every move.

"Chimwazle has been cozening us," she told Rocallo when the toad-faced creature was gone. "I won the last showing, and you the two before that, yet his pile of terces is as large as ever. The coins move whenever we're not looking. Creeping home across the table. And the placards change their faces."

The prince gave a shrug. "What does it matter? The sun grows dark. Who shall count our terces when we're dead?"

His ennui annoyed her. "What sort of prince sits by and lets some feeble wizard make a fool of him?"

"The sort who has experienced Lugwiler's Dismal Itch, and has no desire to experience it again. Chimwazle amuses me."

"It would amuse me to tickle Chimwazle."

"He will laugh and laugh, I have no doubt."

Then a shadow fell across them. Lirianne looked up, to find the grim-visaged necromancer looming over them. "It has been three hundred years since last I played a hand of pegotty," he intoned in a sepulchral tone. "May I sit in?"

THE GREAT Chimwazle's stomach was a-heave. The meat pie might be to blame, all that gristle and suet. Or perhaps it was the Twk-men he had eaten in the woods. Delicious little things, but never easy to digest. They might be in his belly still, stabbing at him with their silly little spears. He should have stopped at a dozen, but once he had started, it was so easy to think, well, one more would be nice, and perhaps another after that one. He wondered if their spears were poisoned. Chimwazle had not considered that. It was a disagreeable thought.

Almost as disagreeable as this inn. He should have paid more heed to the Pooner. The Tarn House had little to recommend it, save perhaps the pretty freckly thing who had joined his little game of peggoty. Already he had won her hat. Her boots would soon follow, and then her stockings. Chimwazle was only waiting for some of the other travellers in the common room to retire to their beds before beginning his assault in earnest. Rocallo was too dull and diffident to interfere, he was certain. Once he'd won her clothes the girl would have nothing to wager but her indenture,

and afterward he could harness her to his cart an arm's length ahead of Polymumpho. Let the Pooner chase after her henceforth, that should serve to keep those hairy legs of his pumping briskly. Chimwazle might not even need to ply the whip.

The inn's privy was cramped and smelly, and offered neither bench nor bar, but only a ragged hole in the floor. Squatting over it with his breeches round his ankles, Chimwazle grunted and groaned as.he voided his bowels. The act was never a pleasant one for him, attended as it was by the risk of waking the imp nested in the fleshier portions of his nether parts, whose second favorite amusement was loudly describing Chimwazle's manhood in terms of withering scorn (its first favorite amusement was something Chimwazle did not wish to think about).

He was spared that ordeal on this occasion, but worse awaited him when he returned to the inn's common room and found that the tall magician with the fearsome face had taken a seat at his own table. Chimwazle had had enough experiences with great sorcerers to know that he did not want any more such experiences. His present appearance was the legacy of a misunderstanding at a crossroads with one such, and the imp with the loquacious mouth hidden in his breeches was a souvenir left him by the witch Eluuna, whose affections he had enjoyed for a fortnight when he was young and slim and handsome. This sorcerer in scarlet and black lacked Eluuna's charms, but might well share her fickle temper. One never knew what small gaffes and innocent omissions a wizard might take for mortal insult.

Still, there was no help for it, unless he meant to flee at once into the night. That course seemed less than advisable. The nights belonged to grues and ghouls and leucomorphs, and there was some small chance more Twk-men might be awaiting him as well. So Chimwazle donned his best smile, resumed his seat, and smacked his lips. "We have another player, I see. Innkeep, run fetch some ale for our new friend. And be quick about it, or you may find a carbuncle growing on the end of your nose!"

"I am Molloqos the Melancholy, and I do not drink ale."

"I perceive you are of the sorcerous persuasion," said Chimwazle. "We have that in common, you and I. How many spells do you carry?"

"That is none of your concern," warned Molloqos.

"There now. It was an innocent inquiry, between colleagues. I myself am armed with six great spells, nine minor enchantments, and a variety of cantraps." Chimwazle shuffled the placards. "My sandestin awaits without, disguised as a Pooner and bound to my cart, yet ready to whisk me off into the sky at my command. But no sorcery at table, please! Here dame fortune rules, and may not be confounded by spells!" And so saying, he placed a golden centum in the center of the table."Come, come, put in your stakes! Pegotty has more savor when gold is glinting in the pot."

"Just so." Prince Rocallo laid his centum atop Chimwazle's.

The girl Lirianne could only pout (which she did very prettily). "I have no gold, and I want my hat back."

"Then you must put your boots into the wager."

"Must I? Oh, very well."

The sorcerer said nothing. Instead of reaching into his own purse, he rapped thrice upon the floor with his ebon staff and pronounced a small cantrap for the dispelling of illusions and concealments. At once, Chimwazle's centum transformed into a fat white spider and walked slowly from the board on eight hairy legs, while the pile of terces in front of him turned into as many cockroaches and scuttled off in all directions.

The girl squealed. The prince chortled. Chimwazle gulped down his dismay and drew himself up, his jowls a-quiver. "Look what you have done! You owe me a golden centum."

"Far be it!" Molloqos said, with outrage. "You aspired to hoodwink us with a cheap conjurer's glamor. Did you truly believe such a feeble ploy would work upon Molloqos the Melancholy?" The great golden eye atop his staff was blinking, as green vapors swirled ominously within its crystal orb.

"Softly, softly," protested Prince Rocallo. "My head is hazy from the ale, and harsh words make it ring."

"Oh, will you fight a wizard's duel?" Lirianne clapped her hands together. "What grand magics shall we see?"

"The innkeep may protest," said Rocallo. "Such contests are the bane of hospitality. When swordsmen duel, the only damage is some broken crockery and perchance a bloodstain on the floorboards. A pail of hot water and a good elbow will set that aright. A wizard's duel is like to leave an inn a smoking ruin."

"Pah," said Chimwazle, jowls quivering. A dozen rejoinders sprang to, his lips, each more withering than the one before, but caution bid him swallow every syllable. Instead he jerked to his feet, so quickly that it sent his chair crashing to the floor. "The innkeep need have no fear on that account. Such spells as I command are far too potent to be deployed

for the idle amusement of hatless trollops and feigned princes. The Great Chimwazle will not be mocked, I warn you." And so saying, he made a hasty retreat, before the scarlet and black sorcerer could take further umbrage. A fat white spider and a line of cockroaches scuttled after him, as fast as their legs would carry them.

THE FIRE had burned down to embers, and the air was growing cold. Darkness gathered in the corners of the common room. The rustics by the hearth huddled closer, muttering at one another through their whiskers. The golden eye atop the staff of Molloqos the Melancholy peered this way and that.

"Do you mean to let the cheat escape?" the girl asked.

Molloqos did not deign to answer. Soon all the veils would fall away, he sensed. The fraud Chimwazle was the least of his concerns. The shadow swords were here, and worst things too. And it seemed to him that he could hear a faint, soft hissing.

The landlord rescued him from further inquiry, appearing suddenly by his elbow to announce that his room was ready, should he wish to retire.

"I do." Molloqos rose to his feet, leaning on his staff. He adjusted his Cloak of Fearful Mien and said, "Show me."

The innkeep took a lantern off the wall, lit the wick, turned up the flame. "If you would follow me, dread sir."

Up three long flights of crooked steps Molloqos climbed, following the landlord with his lantern, until at last they reached the upper story and a heavy wooden door.

The Tarn House's best room was none too grand. The ceiling was too low, and the floorboards creaked alarmingly. A single window looked out across the tarn, where black waters churned and rippled suggestively beneath the dim red light of distant stars. Beside the bed, on a small three-legged table, a tallow candle stood crookedly in a puddle of hardened wax, flickering. A chest and a straightback chair were the only other furnishings. Shadows lay thickly in the corners of the room, black as the belly of a Deodand. The air was damp and chill, and Molloqos could hear wind whistling through gaps in the shutters. "Is that mattress stuffed with feathers?" he asked.

"Nothing but honest straw at the Tarn House." The innkeep hung his lantern from a hook. "See, here are two stout planks that slide in place to

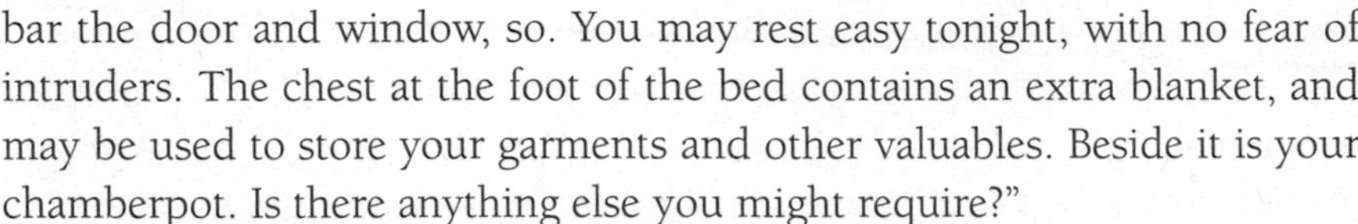

bar the door and window, so. You may rest easy tonight, with no fear of intruders. The chest at the foot of the bed contains an extra blanket, and may be used to store your garments and other valuables. Beside it is your chamberpot. Is there anything else you might require?"

"Only solitude."

"As you command."

Molloqos listened as the innkeep made his descent. When he was satisfied that he was alone, he gave the room a careful inspection, tapping on the walls, checking the door and window, thumping the floorboards with the butt of his staff. The chest at the foot of the bed had a false bottom that could be opened from beneath, to give access to a crawlway. Doubtless that was how the thieves and murderers crept in, to relieve unwary travellers of their goods and lives. As for the bed…

Molloqos gave the mattress a wide berth, seating himself instead in the chair, his staff in hand. His last few spells were singing in his head. It did not take long for the first of his visitors to arrive. Her knock was soft, but insistant. Molloqos opened the door, ushered her into the bedchamber, and slid the bar in place behind her. "So we are not disturbed," he explained.

The dark-haired woman smiled seductively. She pulled the ties that closed her robe, then shrugged it off her shoulders to puddle on the floor. "Will you remove your cloak?"

"As soon remove my skin," said Molloqos the Melancholy.

The woman shivered in his arms. "You talk so strangely. You frighten me." Gooseprickles covered her arms. "What do you have in your hand?"

"Surcease." He stabbed her through the throat. She sank to her knees, hissing. When her mouth opened, her fangs gleamed in the half-light, long and pointed. Her blood ran black down her neck. A leucomorph, he judged, or something stranger still. The wilds were full of queer things now; mongrels fathered by demons on Deodands, spawn of succubi and incubi, mock men grown in vats, bog-born monsters made of rotting flesh.

Bending over her pale corpse, Molloqos the Melancholy brushed her hair back from her cheek and kissed her; once upon the brow, once upon each cheek, deeply on the mouth. Life left her with a shudder and entered him with a gasp, as warm as a summer wind in the days of his youth when the sun burned brighter and laughter could still be heard in the cities of men.

When she was cold, he spoke the words of Cazoul's Indenture, and her corpse opened its eyes again. He bid her rise, to stand sentry while

he slept. A great weariness was on him, but it would not do to be taken unawares. He would have other visitors before the night was done, he did not doubt.

He dreamt of Kaiin, shimmering behind its high white walls.

A CHILL hung in the night air as Chimwazle slipped from the inn through a side door. A grey mist was rising off the tarn, and he could hear the waters stirring down below, as if something were moving in the shallows. Crouching low, he peered this way and that, his bulbous eyes moving beneath his floppy cap, but he saw no sign of Twk-men. Nor did he hear the soft ominous trill of dragonfly wings.

They had not found him, then. That was good. It was time he was away. That there were grues and ghouls and erbs out in the wood he did not doubt, but he would sooner take his chances with them than with the necromancer. A few brisk licks of the whip, and his Pooner would outrace them all. And if not, well, Polymumpho had more meat on him than Chimwazle. Grinning ear to ear, he loped down the rocky hummock, his belly wobbling.

Halfway down, he noticed that his cart was gone. "Infamous Pooner!" he cried, stumbling in shock. "Thief! Thief! Where is my cart, you lice-ridden lump?" No one gave reply. At the foot of the steps, there was nothing to be seen but a sinister iron palaquin and four huge Deodands with flesh as black as night, standing knee deep in the tarn. The waters were rising, Chimwazle realized suddenly. The Tarn House had become an island.

Fury pushed aside his fear. Deodands relished the taste of man flesh, it was known. "Did you eat my Pooner?" he demanded.

"No," said one, showing a mouth full of gleaming ivory teeth, "but come closer, and we will gladly eat you."

"Pah," said Chimwazle. Now that he was closer, he could see that the Deodands were dead. The necromancer's work, he did not doubt. He licked his ear lobe nervously and a cunning ploy occured to him. "Your master Molloqos has commanded you to carry me to Kaiin with all haste."

"Yessss," hissed the Deodand. "Mollogos commands and we obey. Come, clamber on, and we'll away."

Something about the way he said that made Chimwazle pause to reconsider the wisdom of his plan. Or perhaps it was the way all four of the Deodands began to gnash those pointed teeth. He hesitated, and suddenly grew aware of a faint stirring in the air behind him, a whisper of wind at the back of his neck.

Chimwazle whirled. A Twk-man was floating a foot from his face, his lance couched, and a dozen more hovering behind him. His bulging eyes popped out even further as he saw the upper storeys of the Tarn House a-acrawl with them, thick as tasps and twice as veriminous. Their dragonflies were a glowing green cloud, roiling like a thunderhead. "Now you perish," the Twk-man said.

Chimwazle's sticky tongue struck first, flicking out to pull the small green warrior from his mount. But as he crunched and swallowed, the cloud took wing, buzzing angrily. Yelping in dismay, the Great Chimwazle had no choice but to flee back up the steps to the inn, hotly pursued by a swarm of dragonflies and the laughter of a Deodand.

LIRIANNE WAS vexed.

It would have been so much easier if only she could have set the two wizards to fighting over her, so they might exhaust their magic on one another. That the ghastly Molloqos would make short work of the odious Chimwazle she did not doubt, but however many spells that might have required would have left him with that many fewer when the time came for her to tickle him.

Instead, Molloqos had retired to his bed, while Chimwazle had scuttled off into the night, craven as a crab. "Look what he did to my hat," Lirianne complained, snatching it off the floorboards. Chimwazle had trampled on it on his haste to depart, and the feather was broken.

"His hat," said Prince Rocallo. "You lost it."

"Yes, but I meant to win it back. Though I suppose I should be grateful that it did not turn into a cockroach." She jammed the hat back on her head, tilted at a rakish angle. "First they break the world, and then my hat."

"Chimwazle broke the world?"

"Him," Lirianne said darkly, "and his sort. Wizards. Sorcerers and sorceresses, sages and mages and archmages, witches and warlocks, conjurers, illusionists, diabolists. Necromancers, geomancers, aeromancers, pyromancers, thaumaturges, dreamwalkers, dreamweavers, dreameaters. All of them. Their sins are written on the sky, dark as the sun."

"You blame black magic for the world's demise?"

"Bah," said Lirianne. Men were such fools. "White magic and black are two sides of the same terce. The ancient tomes tell the tale, for those who have the wit to read them correctly. Once there was no magic. The sky was bright blue, the sun shone warm and yellow, the woods were full of deer and hare and songbirds, and everywhere the race of man was thriving. Those ancient men built towers of glass and steel taller than mountains, and ships with sails of fire that took them to the stars. Where are these glories now? Gone, lost, forgotten. Instead we have spells, charms, curses. The air grows cold, the woods are full of grue and ghouls, Deodands haunt the ruins of ancient cities, pelgranes rule the skies where men once flew. Whose work is this? *Wizards!* Their magic is a blight on sun and soul. Every time a spell is spoken here on earth, the sun grows that much darker."

She might have revealed even more, had not the pop-eyed Chimwazle chosen that very moment to make a sudden reappearance, stumbling through the door with his long arms wrapped around his head. "Get them off!" he bellowed, as he lurched between the tables. "Ow, ow, ow. Get off me, I am innocent, it was someone else!" Thus shouting, he went crashing to the floor, where he writhed and rolled, slapping himself about the head and shoulders while continuing to implore for assistance against attackers who seemed nowhere in evidence. "Twk," he cried, "twk, twk, wretched twk! Off me, off me!"

Prince Rocallo winced. "Enough! Chimwazle, cease this unmanly caterwauling. Some of us are attempting to drink."

The rogue rolled unto his rump, which was wide and wobbly and amply padded. "The Twk-men—"

"—remain without," said Lirianne. The door remained wide open, but none of the Twk-men had followed Chimwazle inside. Chimwazle blinked his bulbous eyes and peered about from side to side to make certain that was true. Although no Twk-men were to be seen, the back of his neck was covered with festering boils where they had stung him with their lances, and more were sprouting on his cheeks and forehead.

"I do hope you know a healing spell," Rocallo said. "Those look quite nasty. The one on your cheek is leaking blood."

Chimwazle made a noise that was half a groan and half a croak and said, "Vile creatures! They had no cause to abuse me thus. All I did was thin their excess populace. There were plenty left!" Puffing, he climbed back onto his feet and retrieved his cap. "Where is that pestilential innkeep? I require unguent at once. These pin-pricks have begun to itch."

"Itching is only the first symptom," said Lirianne, with a helpful smile. "The lances of the Twk-men are envenomed. By morning, your head will be as large as a pumpkin, your tongue will blacken and burst, your ears will fill with pus, and you may be seized by an irresistable desire to copulate with a hoon."

"A hoon?" croaked Chimwazle, appalled.

"Perhaps a grue. It depends upon the poison."

Chimwazle's face had turned a deeper shade of green. "This affront cannot be borne! Pus? Hoons? Is there no cure, no salve, no antidote?"

Lirianne cocked her head to one side thoughtfully. "Why," she said, "I have heard it said that the blood of a sorcerer is a sure remedy for any bane or toxin."

Chimwazle went creeping up the stairs with his companions padding quietly at his heels. Lirianne had her sword, and Prince Rocallo a dagger. Chimwazle had only his hands, but those hands were damp and soft and hideously strong. Whether they were strong enough to twist a wizard's head off remained to be seen.

The steps were steep and narrow and creaked beneath his weight. Chimwazle panted softly as he climbed, his tongue lolling from his mouth. He wondered if Molloqos would be asleep yet. He wondered if the sorcerer had thought to bar his door. He wondered why it was that he was going first. But there was no turning back. Lirianne was close behind him, blocking his retreat, and Rocallo came after her, smiling with those pointy yellow teeth. And the boils on his face and neck were itching abominably and growing by the moment. One just beneath his ear had swelled up large as an egg. A bit of blood was not too much to ask, a favor from one magician to another. Alas, Molloqos might not see it that way. He did not have Chimwazle's generosity of soul.

At the top of the steps, the three conspirators clustered close together outside the sorcerer's door. "He's in there," said Lirianne, sniffing at the air with her pert little nose. "I can smell his wizard's stink."

Rocallo reached out for the latch. "Gently," Chimwazle cautioned, in a whisper. "Oh, soft goes it, slowly, slowly, it would be discourteous to wake him." He scratched at a boil on his brow, but that only seemed to make the itching worse.

"The door is barred," Rocallo whispered back.

"ALAS," CHIMWAZLE said, relieved. "Our plan is foiled. Back to the common room, then. Let us reconsider over ale." He scratched furiously beneath his chin, groaned.

"Why not break the door down?" asked Lirianne. "A big strong man like you..." She squeezed his arm and smiled. "Unless you would rather give pleasure to a hoon?"

Chimwazle shuddered, though even a hoon might be preferable to this itching. Glancing up, he saw the transom. It was open just a crack, but that might be enough. "Rocallo, friend, lift me up onto your shoulders."

The prince knelt. "As you wish." He was stronger than he looked, and seemed to have no trouble hoisting Chimwazle up into the air, for all his bulk. Nor did the nervous trumpet notes emitted by Chimwazle's nether parts dismay him unduly.

Pressing his nose to the transom, Chimwazle slid his tongue through the gap and down the inside of the doorframe, then curled it thrice around the wooden plank that barred the way. Slowly, slowly, he lifted the bar from its slot...but the weight proved too great for his tongue, and the plank fell clattering to the floor. Chimwazle reeled backwards, Prince Rocallo lost his balance, and the two of them collapsed atop each other with much grunting and cursing while Lirianne skipped nimbly aside.

Then the door swung open.

MOLLOQOS THE Melancholy did not need to speak a word.

Silent he bid them enter and silent they obeyed, Chimwazle scrambling over the threshold on hands on feet as his fellows stepped nimbly around him. When all of them had come inside he closed the door behind them and barred it once again.

The rogue Chimwazle was almost unrecognizable beneath his floppy hat, his toadish face a mass of festering boils and buboes where some Twkmen had kissed him with their lances. "Salve," he croaked, as he climbed unsteadily to his feet. "We came for salve, sorry to disturb you. Dread sir, if you perhance should have some unguent for itching..."

"I am Molloqos the Melancholy. I do not deal in unguents. Come here and grasp my staff."

For a moment, Chimwazle looked as he might bolt the room instead, but in the end he bowed his head and shuffled closer, and wrapped a soft splayed hand around the ebon shaft of the tall sorcerer's staff. Inside the crystal orb the True-Seeing Eye had fixed on Lirianne and Rocallo. When Molloqos thumped the staff upon the floor, the great golden eye blinked once. "Now look again upon your companions, and tell me what you see."

Chimwazle's mouth gaped open, and his bulging eyes looked as though they might pop out of his skull. "The girl is cloaked in shadows," he gasped, "and under her freckly face I see a skull."

"And your prince…"

"…is a demon."

The thing called Prince Rocallo laughed, and let all his enchantments dissolve. His flesh was red and raw, glowing like the surface of the sun, and like the sun half-covered by a creeping black leprosy. Smoke rose stinking from his nostrils, the floorboards began to smoulder beneath his taloned feet, and black claws sprang from his hands as long as knives.

Then Molloqos spoke a word and stamped his staff hard against the floor, and from the shadows in a corner of the room a woman's corpse came bursting to leap upon the demon's back. As the two of them lurched and staggered about the room, tearing at each other, Lirianne danced aside and Chimwazle fell backwards onto his ample rump. The stench of burning flesh filled the air. The demon ripped one of the corpse's arms off and flung it smoking at the head of Molloqos, but the dead feel no pain, and her other arm was wrapped about its throat. Black blood ran down her cheeks like tears as she pulled him backward onto the bed.

Molloqos stamped his staff again. The floor beneath the bed yawned open, the mattress tilted, and demon and corpse together tumbled down into a gaping black abyss. A moment later, there came a loud splash from below, followed by a furious cacophony, demonic shrieking mingled with a terrible whistling and hissing, as if a thousand kettles had all come to a boil at once. When the bed righted itself the sound diminished, but it was a long while before it ended. "W-what was that?" asked Chimwazle.

"Hissing eels. The inn is famous for them."

"I distinctly recall the innkeep saying that the eels were off the menu," said Chimwazle.

"The eels are off our menu, but we not off theirs."

LIRIANNE MADE a pouty face and said, "The hospitality of the Tarn House leaves much to be desired."

Chimwazle was edging toward the door. "I mean to speak firmly to the landlord. Some adjustment of our bill would seem to be in order." He scratched angrily at his boils.

"I would advise against returning to the common room," said the necromancer. "No one in the Tarn House is all that he appears. The hirsute family by the hearth are ghouls clad in suits of human skin, here for the meat pies. The greybeard in the faded raiment of a knight of Old Thorsingol is a malign spirit, cursed to an eternity of purple scrumby for the niggardly gratuities he left in life. The demon and the leucomorph are no longer a concern, but our servile host is vilest of all. Your wisest course is flight. I suggest you use the window."

The Great Chimwazle needed no further encouragement. He hurried to the window, threw the shudders open, and gave a cry of dismay. "The tarn! I had forgotten. The tarn has encircled the inn, there's no way out."

Lirianne peered over his shoulder, and saw that it was true. "The waters are higher than before," she said thoughtfully. That was a bother. She had learned to swim before she learned to walk, but the oily waters of the tarn did not look wholesome, and while she did not doubt that Tickle-Me-Sweet would be a match for any hissing eel, it was hard to swim and swordfight at the same time. She turned back to the necromancer. "I suppose we're doomed, then. Unless you save us with a spell."

"Which spell would you have me use?" asked Molloqos, in a mordant tone. "Shall I summon an Agency of Far Dispatch to whisk us three away to the end of the earth? Call down fire from the sky with the Excellent Prismatic Spray to burn this vile hostelry to the ground? Pronounce the words of Phandaal's Shivering Chill to freeze the waters of the tarn as hard as stone, so that we may scamper safely over them?"

Chimwazle looked up hopefully. "Yes, please."

"Which?"

"Any. The Great Chimwazle was not meant to end up in a meat pie." He scratched a boil underneath his chin.

"Surely you know those spells yourself," said Molloqos.

"I did," said Chimwazle, "but some knave stole my grimoire."

Molloqos chuckled. It was the saddest sound that Lirianne had ever heard. "It makes no matter. All things die, even magic. Enchantments fade,

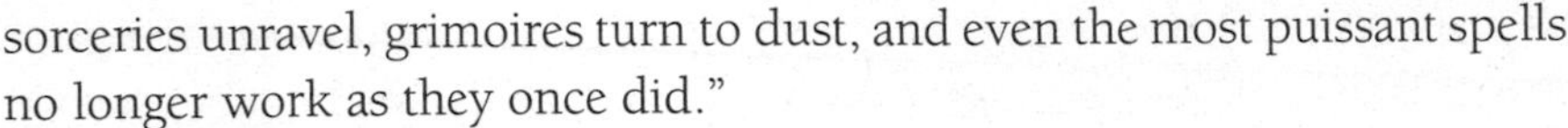

sorceries unravel, grimoires turn to dust, and even the most puissant spells no longer work as they once did."

Lirianne cocked her head. "Truly?"

"Truly."

"Oho." She drew her sword and gave his heart a tickle.

THE NECROMANCER died without a sound, his legs folding slowly under him as if he were kneeling down to pray. When the girl slipped her sword out of his chest, a wisp of scarlet smoke rose from the wound. It smelled of summer nights and maiden's breath, sweet as a first kiss.

Chimwazle was aghast. "Why did you do that?"

"He was a necromancer."

"He was our only hope."

"You have no hope." She wiped her blade against her sleeve. "When I was fifteen a young adventurer was wounded outside my father's inn. My father was too gentle to let him die there in the dust, so we carried him upstairs and I nursed him back to health. Soon after he departed I found I was with child. For seven months my belly swelled, and I dreamed of a babe with his blue eyes. In my eighth month the swelling ceased. Thereafter I grew slimmer with every passing day. The midwife explained it all to me. What use to bring new life into a dying world? My womb was wiser than my heart, she said. And when I asked her why the world was dying, she leaned close and whispered '*wizard's work*.'"

"Not my work." Chimwazle scratched at his cheeks with both hands, half mad with the itching. "*What if she was wrong?*"

"Then you'll have died for nought." Lirianne could smell his fear. The scent of sorcery was on him, but faintly, faintly, drowning beneath the green stink of his terror. Truly, this one was a feeble sort of magician. "Do you hear the eels?" she asked him. "They're still hungry. Would you like a tickle?"

"No." He backed away from her, his bloody fingers splayed.

"Quicker than being eaten alive by eels." Tickle-Me-Sweet waved in the air, glimmering in the candlelight.

"Stay back," Chimwazle warned her, "or I will call down the Excellent Prismatic Spray upon you."

"You might. If you knew it. Which you don't. Or if it worked. Which it won't, if our late friend can be believed."

Chimwazle backed away another step, and stumbled over the necromancer's corpse. As he reached out to break his fall, his fingers brushed against the sorcerer's staff. Grasping it, he popped back to his feet. "Stay away. There's still power in his staff, I warn you. I can feel it."

"That may be, but it is no power you can use." Lirianne was certain of that. He was hardly half a wizard, this one. Most likely he had stolen those placards, and paid to have the roaches glamored for him. Poor sad wicked thing. She resolved to make a quick end to his misery. "Stand still. Tickle-Me-Sweet will cure your itch. I promise you, this will not hurt."

"This will." Chimwazle grasped the wizard's staff with both hands, and smashed the crystal orb down on her head.

CHIMWAZLE STRIPPED both corpses clean before tossing them down the chute behind the bed, in hopes of quieting the hissing eels. The girl was even prettier naked than she had been clothed, and stirred feebly he was dragging her across the room. "Such a waste," Chimwazle muttered as he heaved her down into the abyss. Her hat was much too small for him and had a broken feather, but her sword was forged of fine strong springy steel, her purse was fat with terces, and the leather of her boots was soft and supple. Too small for his feet, but perhaps one day he'd find another pretty freckly girl to wear them for him.

Even in death the necromancer presented such a frightful countenance that Chimwazle was almost afraid to touch him, but the eels were still hissing hungrily down below, and he knew his chances of escape would be much improved if they were sated. So he steeled himself, knelt, and undid the clasp that fastened the dread wizard's cloak. When he rolled his body over to pull the garment off, the sorcerer's features ran like black wax, melting away to puddle on the floor. Chimwazle found himself kneeling over a wizened toothless corpse with dim white eyes and parchment skin, his bald pate covered by a spiderweb of dark blue veins. He weighed no more than a bag of leaves, but he had a little smile on his lips when Chimwazle tossed him down to the hissing eels.

By then the itching seemed to be subsiding. Chimwazle gave himself a few last scratches and fastened the necromancer's cloak about his shoulders. All at once, he felt taller, harder, sterner. Why should he fear the things down in the common room? Let them go in fear of him!

He swept down the steps without a backward glance. The ghost and ghouls took one look at him and moved aside. Even creatures such as they knew better than to trouble a wizard of such fearsome mien. Only the innkeep dared accost him. "Dread sir," he murmurred, "how will you settle your account?"

"With this." He drew his sword and gave the thing a tickle. "I will not be recommending the Tarn House to other travellers."

Black waters still encircled the inn, but they were no more than waist deep, and he found it easy enough to wade to solid ground. The Twk-men had vanished in the night and the hissing eels had grown quiescent, but the Deodands still stood where he had seen them last, waiting by the iron palanquin. One greeted him. "The earth is dying and soon the sun shall fail," it said. "When the last light fades, all spells shall fail, and we shall feast upon the firm white flesh of Mollogos."

"The earth is dying, but you are dead," replied Chimwazle, marvelling at the deep and gloomy timbre of his voice. "When the sun goes out, all spells shall fail, and you shall decay back into the primeval ooze." He climbed into the palanquin and bid the Deodands to lift him up. "To Kaiin." Perhaps somewhere in the white-walled city, he would find a lissome maid to dance naked for him in the freckly girl's high boots. Or failingthat, a hoon.

Off into purple gloom rode Molloqos the Melancholy, borne upon an iron palanquin by four dead Deodands.

AFTERWORD:

I EXPECT I was about ten or eleven years old the first time I encountered the work of Jack Vance, when I grabbed one of those Ace Doubles with the colorful red-and-blue spines off the spinner rack in the candy store at First Street and Kelly Parkway in Bayonne, New Jersey. Most of the Doubles featured "two complete novels" (today we would call them novellas) by two different writers, published back-to-back, but this one had the same byline on both sides, pairing *Slaves of the Klau* with an abridged version of *Big Planet*.

Slaves of the Klau was pretty good, my eleven year old self decided after reading it. *Big Planet* blew me away, even in its abridged state. Thereafter

I looked for Vance's name whenever I set one of those spinner racks to spinning. And so it was that a few years later, I stumbled on the Lancer paperback of *The Dying Earth*.

Half a century has passed since then, and that slim little collection remains one of my all-time favorites. Scarcely a year goes by that I do not take it down and dip into it again. The world that Vance created ranks with Tolkien's Middle Earth and Robert E. Howard's Hyborian Age as one of fantasy's most unforgettable and influential settings. The poetry of Vance's language also moved me (not to mention expanding my vocabulary!). His dialogue in particular was so arch and dry and witty that I could not read enough of it, then or now. But it was the characters that I loved best. T'sain and T'sais, Guyal of Sfere, Turjan of Miir…and of course Liane the Wayfarer, whose encounter with Chun the Unavoidable remains perhaps my single favorite fantasy short story.

Vance made us wait sixteen years between the first Dying Earth book and the second, but by the time *Eyes of the Overworld* was published, I was accustomed to snatching up every book that had his name on it as soon as it hit the bookshops. To my surprise, this new one was nothing at all like the original. This time, Jack showed us an entirely different side of the world he had created, while introducing us to Cugel the Clever, a rogue so venal and unscrupulous that he makes Harry Flashman look like Dudley Doright. How could you not love a guy like that? Other readers shared my enthusiasm, plainly, to judge from the number of times that Cugel has come back. You can't keep a bad man down.

By now I have read every book Jack Vance ever wrote; the science fiction, the fantasies, the mystery novels (yes, even the ones he wrote as Ellery Queen). All of them are good, but of course, I have my favorites. The *Demon Princes* series, the *Planet of Adventure* quartet, *Emphyrio*, the *Lyonesse* trilogy, the Hugo-winning novellas "The Dragon Masters" and "The Last Castle," the unforgettable "Moon Moth"…but *The Dying Earth* and its three sequels still rank up at the top.

It has been a real privilege for me to co-edit this tribute anthology with my friend Gardner Dozois, and (even more so) to write a Dying Earth story of my own. No one writes like Jack Vance but Jack Vance, of course, but I cherish the hope that Molloqos, Lirianne, and Chimwazle may prove not entirely unworthy companions for Rhialto, T'sais, Liane, Cugel, and the rest of Jack's unforgettable cast, and that all Jack's myriad readers will have enjoyed their brief stay at the Tarn House, famous for its hissing eels.

—George R.R. Martin

NEIL GAIMAN

An Invocation of Incuriosity

AT SOME point, no matter how many millions of years from now it is, the Last Day will arrive, and the sun will go out, cold and dead as a burnt-out ember.

What happens *then*...?

One of the hottest stars in science fiction, fantasy, and horror today, Neil Gaiman has won three Hugo Awards, two Nebula Awards, one World Fantasy Award, six Locus Awards, four Stoker Awards, three Geffens, and one Mythopoeic Fantasy Award. Gaiman first came to wide public attention as the creator of the graphic novel series *The Sandman*, still one of the most acclaimed graphic novel series of all time. Gaiman remains a superstar in the graphic novel field; his graphic novels include *Breakthrough*, *Death Talks About Life*, *Legend of the Green Flame*, *The Last Temptation*, *Only the End of the World Again*, *Mirrormask*, and a slew of books in collaboration with Dave McKean, including *Black Orchid*, *Violent Cases*, *Signal To Noise*, *The Tragical Comedy or Comical Tragedy of Mr. Punch*, *The Wolves in the Walls*, and *The Day I Swapped My Dad For Two Goldfish*.

In recent years he's enjoyed equal success in the science fiction and fantasy fields as well, with his best-selling novel *American Gods* winning the 2002 Hugo, Nebula, and Bram Stoker Awards, *Coraline* winning both Hugo and Nebula in 2003, and his story "A Study in Emerald" winning the Hugo in 2004. He also won the World Fantasy Award for his story with Charles Vess, "A Midsummer Night's Dream," and won the International Horror Critics Guild Award for his collection *Angels & Visitations: A Miscellany*. Gaiman's other novels include *Good Omens* (written with Terry Prachett), *Neverwhere*, *Stardust*, and, most recently, *Anansi Boys*. In addition to *Angels & Visitations*, his short fiction has been collected in *Smoke & Mirrors: Short Fictions & Illusions*, *Midnight Days*, *Warning: Contains Language*, *Creatures of the Night*, *Two Plays For Voices*, and *Adventures in the Dream Trade*, and *Fragile Things* He's also written *Don't Panic: The Official Hitchikers Guide to the Galaxy Companion*, *A Walking Tour of the Shambles* (with Gene Wolfe), *Batman* and *Babylon 5* novelizations, and edited *Ghastly Beyond Belief* (with Kim Newman), *Book of Dreams* (with Edward Kramer), and *Now We Are Sick: An Anthology of Nasty Verse* (with Stephen Jones). His most recent books are a new novel, *The Graveyard Book*, and two YA novels, *Odd and the Frost Giants*, and, with Gris Grimly, *The Dangerous Alphabet*. A movie based on his novel *Stardust* was in theaters worldwide in 2007.

An Invocation of Incuriosity

NEIL GAIMAN

There are flea-markets all across Florida, and this was not the worst of them. It had once been an aircraft hangar, but the local airport had closed. There were a hundred traders there, behind their metal tables, most of them selling counterfeit merchandise: sunglasses or watches or bags or belts. There was an African family selling carved wooden animals and behind them a loud, blowsy woman named (I cannot forget the name) Charity Parrot sold coverless paperback books, and old pulp magazines, the paper browned and crumbling, and beside her, in the corner, a Mexican woman whose name I never knew sold film posters and curling film stills.

I bought books from Charity Parrot, sometimes.

Soon enough the woman with the film posters went away and was replaced by a small man in sunglasses, his grey tablecloth spread over the metal table and covered with small carvings. I stopped and examined them—a strange set of creatures, made of grey bone and stone and dark wood—and then I examined him. I wondered if he had been in a ghastly accident, the kind it takes plastic surgery to repair: his face was wrong, the way it sloped, the shape of it. His skin was too pale. His dark hair looked like it had to be a wig, made, perhaps of dog-fur. His glasses were so dark as to hide his eyes completely. He did not look in any way out of place in

a Florida flea market: the tables were all manned by strange people, and strange people shopped there.

I bought nothing from him.

The next time I was there Charity Parrot had, in her turn, moved on, her place taken by an Indian family who sold hookahs and smoking paraphernalia, but the little man in the dark glasses was still in his corner at the back of the flea market, with his grey cloth. On it were more carvings of creatures.

"I do not recognise any of these animals," I told him.

"No."

"Do you make them yourself?"

He shook his head. You cannot ask anyone in a flea market where they get their stuff from. There are few things that are taboo in a flea market, but that is: sources are inviolate.

"Do you sell a lot?"

"Enough to feed myself," he said. "Keep a roof over my head." Then, "They are worth more than I ask for them."

I picked up something that reminded me a little of what a deer might look like if deer were carnivorous, and said, "What is this?"

He glanced down. "I think it is a primitive thawn. It's hard to tell." And then, "It was my father's."

There was a chiming noise, then, to signal that soon enough the flea market would close.

"Would you like food?" I asked.

He looked at me, warily.

"My treat," I said. "No obligations. There's a Denny's over the road. Or there's the bar."

He thought for a moment. "Denny's will be fine," he said. "I will meet you over there."

I waited at Denny's. After half an hour I no longer expected him to come, but he surprised me, and he arrived fifty minutes after I got there, carrying a brown leather bag tied to his wrist with a long piece of twine. I imagined it had to contain money, for it hung as if empty, and could not have held his stock. Soon enough he was eating his way through a plate piled with pancakes, and, over coffee, he began to talk.

THE SUN began to go out a little after midday. A flicker, first, and then a rapid darkening that began on one side of the sun and then crept across its crimson face until the sun went black, like a coal knocked from a fire, and night returned to the world.

Balthasar the Tardy hurried down from the hill, leaving his nets in the trees, uninspected and unemptied. He uttered no words, conserving his breath, moving as fast as befitted his remarkable bulk, until he reached the bottom of the hill and the front door of his one-room cottage.

"Oaf! It is time!" he called. Then he knelt and lit a fish-oil lamp, which sputtered and stank and burned with a fitful orange flame.

The door of the cottage opened and Balthasar's son emerged. The son was a little taller than his father, and much thinner, and was beardless. The youth had been named after his grandfather, and while his grandfather had lived the boy had been known as Farfal the Younger; now he was referred to, even to his face, as Farfal the Unfortunate. If he brought home a laying-fowl it would cease to give eggs, if he took an axe to a tree it would fall in a place that would cause the greatest inconvenience and the least possible good; if he found a trove of ancient treasure, half-buried in a locked box at the edge of a field, the key to the box would break off as he turned it, leaving only a faint echo of song on the air, as if of a distant choir, and the box would dissolve to sand. Young women upon whom he fastened his affections would fall in love with other men, or be transformed into grues or carried off by deodands. It was the way of things.

"Sun's gone out," said Balthasar the Tardy to his son.

Farfal said, "So this is it, then. This is the end."

It was chillier, now the sun had gone out.

Balthasar said only, "It soon will be. We have only a handful of minutes left. It is well that I have made provision for this day." He held the fish-oil lamp up high, and walked back into the cottage.

Farfal followed his father into the tiny dwelling, which consisted of one large room and, at the far end of the dwelling, a locked door. It was to this door that Balthasar walked. He put down the lamp in front of it, took a key from around his neck and unlocked the door.

Farfal's mouth fell open.

He said only, "The colours". Then, "I dare not go through."

"Idiot boy," said his father. "Go through, and tread carefully as you do." And then, when Farfal made no move to walk, his father pushed him through the door, and closed it behind them.

Farfal stood there, blinking at the unaccustomed light.

"As you apprehend," said his father, resting his hands on his capacious stomach and surveying the room they found themselves in, "this room does not exist temporally in the world you know. It exists, instead, over a million years before our time, in the days of the last Remoran Empire, a period marked by the excellence of its lute music, its fine cuisine, and also the beauty and compliance of its slave class."

Farfal rubbed his eyes, and then looked at the wooden casement standing in the middle of the room, a casement through which they had just walked, as if it were a door. "I begin to perceive," he said, "Why it is that you were so often unavailable. For it seems to me that I have seen you walk through that door into this room many times and never wondered about it, merely resigned myself to the time that would pass until you returned."

Balthasar the Tardy began then to remove his clothes of dark sacking until he was naked, a fat man with a long white beard and cropped white hair, and then to cover himself with brightly-coloured silken robes.

"The sun!" exclaimed Farfal, peering out of the room's small window. "Look at it! It is the orange-red of a fresh-stirred fire! Feel the heat it gives!" And then he said, "Father. Why has it never occurred to me to ask you why you spent so much time in the second room of our one-room cottage? Nor to remark upon the existence of such a room, even to myself?"

Balthasar twisted the last of the fastenings, covering his capacious stomach with a silken covering that crawled with embroideries of elegant monsters. "That might," he admitted, "have been due in part to Empusa's Invocation of Incuriosity." He produced a small black box from around his neck, barely large enough to hold a beetle. "This, when properly primed and invoked, keeps us from being remarked upon. Just as you were not able to wonder at my comings and goings, so neither do the folk in this time and place marvel at me, nor at anything I do that is in any wise contrary to the mores and customs of the Eighteenth and Last Greater Ramoran Empire."

"Astonishing," said Farfal.

"It matters not that the Sun has gone out, that in a matter of hours, or at most weeks, all life on Earth will be dead, for here and at this time I am Balthasar the Canny, merchant to the sky-ships, dealer in antiquities, magical objects and marvels—and here you, my son, will stay. You will be, to all who wonder about your provenance, simply and purely my servant."

"Your servant?" said Farfal the Unfortunate. "Why can I not be your son?"

"For various reasons," stated his father, "too trivial and minor even to warrant discussion at this this time." He hung the black box from a nail in the corner of the room. Farfal thought he saw a leg or head, as if of some beetle-like creature, waving from inside the little box, but he did not pause to inspect it. "Also because I have a number of sons in this time, that I have fathered upon my concubines, and they might not be pleased to learn of another. Although, given the disparity in the dates of your birth, it would be over a million years before you could inherit any wealth."

"There is wealth?" asked Farfal, looking at the room he was in with fresh eyes. He had spent his life in a one-roomed cottage at the end of time, at the bottom of a small hill, surviving on the food his father could net in the air—usually only seabirds or flying lizards, although on occasion other things had been caught in them: creatures who claimed to be angels, or great self-important cockroach-like creatures with high metal crowns, or huge bronze-coloured jellies. They would be taken from the netting, and then either thrown back into the air, or eaten, or traded with the few folk that passed that way.

His father smirked and stroked his impressive white beard like a man petting an animal. "Wealth indeed," he said. "There is much call in these times for pebbles and small rocks from the End of the Earth: there are spells, cantrips and magical instruments for which they are almost irreplaceable. And I deal in such things."

Farfal the Unfortunate nodded. "And if I do not wish to be a servant," he said, "but simply request to be returned to where we came from, through that casement, why, what then?"

Balthasar the Tardy said only, "I have little patience for such questions. The sun has gone out. In hours, perhaps minutes, the world will have ended. Perhaps the universe also has ended. Think no more on these matters. Instead, I shall procure a locking-spell-creature for the casement, down at the ship-market. And while I go to do that, you can order and polish all the objects you can see in this cabinet, taking care not to put your fingers directly upon the green flute (for it will give you music, but replace contentment in your soul with an insatiable longing) nor get the onyx bogadil wet." He patted his son's hand affectionately, a glorious, resplendent creature in his many-coloured silks. "I have spared you from death, my boy," he said. "I have brought you back in time to a new life. What should it matter that in this life you are not son but servant? Life is life, and it is infinitely better than the alternative, or so we presume, for nobody returns to dispute it. Such is my motto."

So saying he fumbled beneath the casement, and produced a grey rag, which he handed to Farfal. "Here. To work! Do a good job and I shall show you by how much the sumptuous feasts of antiquity are an improvement over smoked sea-bird and pickled ossaker-root. Do not, under any circumstances or provocation, move the casement. Its position is precisely calibrated. Move it, and it could open to anywhere."

He covered the casement with a piece of woven cloth, which made it less remarkable that a large wooden casement was standing, unsupported, in the centre of a room.

Balthasar the Tardy left that room through a door that Farfal had not previously observed. Bolts were slammed closed. Farfal picked up his rag, and began, wanly, to dust and to polish.

After several hours he observed a light coming through the casement, so brightly as to penetrate the cloth covering, but it soon faded once more.

Farfal was introduced to the household of Balthasar the Canny as a new servant. He observed Balthasar's five sons and his seven concubines (although he was not permitted to speak to them), was introduced to the House-Carl, who held the keys, and the maidmen who hurried and scurried thence and hither at the House-Carl's command, and than whom there was nothing lower in that place, save for Farfal himself.

The maidmen resented Farfal, with his pale skin, for he was the only one apart from their master permitted in the Sanctum Sanctorum, Master Balthasar's room of wonders, a place to which Master Balthasar had hitherto only repaired alone.

And so the days went by, and the weeks, and Farfal ceased to marvel at the bright orange-red sun, so huge and remarkable, or at the colours of the daytime sky (predominantly salmon and mauve), or at the ships that would arrive in the ship-market from distant worlds bearing their cargo of wonders.

Farfal was miserable, even when surrounded by marvels, even in a forgotten age, even in a world filled with miracles. He said as much to Balthasar the next time the merchant came in the door to the sanctum. "This is unfair."

"Unfair?"

"That I clean and polish the wonders and precious things, while you and your other sons attend feasts and parties and banquets and meet people and otherwise and altogether enjoy living here at the dawn of time."

Balthasar said, "The youngest son may not always enjoy the privileges of his elder brothers, and they are all older than you."

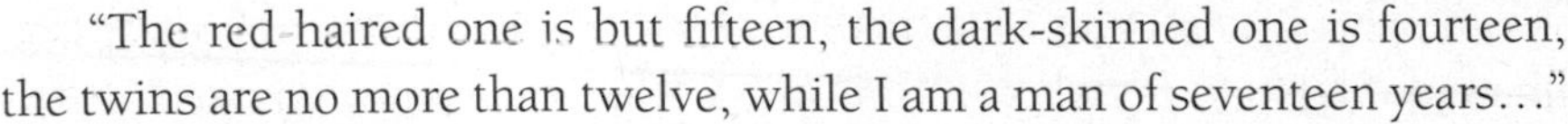

"The red-haired one is but fifteen, the dark-skinned one is fourteen, the twins are no more than twelve, while I am a man of seventeen years..."

"They are older than you by more than a million years," said his father. "I will hear no more of this nonsense."

Farfal the Unfortunate bit his lower lip to keep from replying.

It was at that moment that there was a commotion in the courtyard, as if a great door had been broken open, and the cries of animals and house-birds arose. Farfal ran to the tiny window and looked out. "There are men," he said. "I can see the light glinting on their weapons."

His father seemed unsurprised. "Of course," he said. "Now, I have a task for you Farfal. Due to some erroneous optimism on my part, we are almost out of the stones upon which my wealth is founded, and I have the indignity of discovering myself to be overcommitted at present. Thus it is necessary for you and I to return to our old home and gather what we can. It will be safer if there are two of us. And time is of the essence."

"I will help you," said Farfal, "if you will agree to treat me better in the future."

From the courtyard there came a cry. "Balthasar? Wretch! Cheat! Liar! Where are my thirty stones?" The voice was deep and penetrating.

"I shall treat you much better in the future," said his father. "I swear it." He walked to the casement, pulled off the cloth. There was no light to be seen through it, nothing inside the wooden casing but a deep and formless blackness.

"Perhaps the world has entirely ended," said Farfal, "and now there is nothing but nothing."

"Only a handful of seconds have passed there since we came through it," his father told him. "That is the nature of time. It flows faster when it is younger and the course is narrower: at the end of all things time has spread and slowed, like oil spilled on a still pond."

Then he removed the sluggish spell-creature he had placed on the casement as a lock, and he pushed against the inner casing, which opened slowly. A chill wind came through it which made Farfal shiver. "You send us to our deaths, father," he said.

"We all go to our deaths," said his father. "And yet, here you are, a million years before your birth, still alive. Truly we are all composed of miracles. Now, son, here is a bag, which, as you will soon discover, has been imbued with Swann's Imbuement of Remarkable Capacity, and will hold all that you place inside it, regardless of weight or mass or volume.

When we get there, you must take as many stones as you can and place them in the bag. I myself will run up the hill to the nets and check them for treasures—or for things that would be regarded as treasures if I were to bring them back to the now and the here."

"Do I go first?" asked Farfal, clutching the bag.

"Of course."

"It's so cold."

In reply his father prodded him in the back with a hard finger. Farfal clambered, grumbling, through the casement, and his father followed.

"This is too bad," said Farfal. They walked out of the cottage at the end of time and Farfal bent to pick up pebbles. He placed the first in the bag, where it glinted greenly. He picked up another. The sky was dark but it seemed as if something filled the sky, something without shape.

There was a flash of something not unlike lightning, and in it he could see his father hauling in nets from the trees at the top of the hill.

A crackling. The nets flamed and were gone. Balthasar ran down the hill gracelessly and breathlessly. He pointed at the sky. "It is Nothing!" he said. "Nothing has swallowed the hilltop. Nothing has taken over."

There was a powerful wind then, and Farfal watched his father crackle, and then raise into the air, and then vanish. He backed away from the Nothing, a darkness within the darkness with tiny lightnings playing at its edges, and then he turned and ran, into the house, and through the door into the second room. But he did not go through into the second room. He stood there in the doorway, and then turned back to the Dying Earth. Farfal the Unfortunate watched as the Nothing took the outer walls and the distant hills and the skies, and then he watched, unblinking as Nothing swallowed the cold sun, watched until there was nothing left but a dark formlessness that pulled at him, as if restless to be done with it all.

Only then did Farfal walk into the inner room in the cottage, into his father's inner sanctum a million years before.

A bang on the outer door.

"Balthasar?" It was the voice from the courtyard. "I gave you the day you begged for, wretch. Now give me my thirty stones. Give me my stones or I shall be as good as my word—your sons will be taken off-world, to labour in the Bdellium Mines of Telb, and the women shall be set to work as musicians in the pleasure palace of Luthius Limn, where they will have the honour of making sweet music while I, Luthius Limn, dance and sing and make passionate and athletic love to my catamites. I shall not waste breath in describing the fate I would have in store for your servants. Your spell of hiding is futile, for see, I have found this room with relative ease. Now, give me my thirty stones before I open the door and render down your obese frame for fat and throw your bones to the dogs and the deodands."

Farfal trembled with fear. Time, he thought. I need Time. He made his voice as deep as he could, and he called out, "One moment, Luthius Limn. I am engaged in a complex magical operation to purge your stones of their negative energies. If I am disturbed in this, the consequences will be catastrophic."

Farfal glanced around the room. The only window was too small to permit him to climb out, while the room's only door had Luthius Limn on the other side of it. "Unfortunate indeed," he sighed. Then he took the bag his father had given to him and swept into it all the trinkets, oddments and gewgaws he could reach, still taking care not to touch the green flute with his bare flesh. They vanished into the bag, which weighed no more and seemed no more full than it had ever done.

He stared at the casement in the centre of the room. The only way out, and it led to Nothing, to the end of everything.

"Enough!" came the voice from beyond the door. "My patience is at an end, Balthasar. My cooks shall fry your internal organs tonight." There came a loud crunching against the door, as if of something hard and heavy being slammed against it.

Then there was a scream, and then silence.

Luthius Limn's voice: "Is he dead?"

Another voice—Farfal thought it sounded like one of his half-brothers—said, "I suspect that the door is magically protected and warded."

"Then," boomed Luthius Limn, decisively, "we shall go through the wall."

Farfal was unfortunate, but not stupid. He lifted down the black lacquer box from the nail upon which his father had hung it. He heard something scuttle and move inside it.

"My father told me not to move the casement," he said to himself. Then he put his shoulder against it and heaved violently, pushing the heavy thing almost half an inch. The darkness that filled the casement began to change, and it filled with a pearl-grey light.

He hung the box about his neck. "It is good enough," said Farfal the Unfortunate, and, as something slammed against the wall of the room he took a strip of cloth and tied the bag that contained all the remaining

treasures of Balthasar the Canny about his left wrist, and he pushed himself through.

And there was light, so bright that he closed his eyes, and walked through the casement.

Farfal began to fall.

He flailed in the air, eyes tightly closed against the blinding light, felt the wind whip past him.

Something smacked and engulfed him: water, brackish, warm, and Farfal floundered, too surprised to breathe. Then he surfaced, his head breaking water, and he gulped air. And then he pushed himself through the water, until his hands grasped some kind of plant, and he pulled himself, on hands and feet, out of the green water, and up onto a spongy dry land, trailing and trickling water as he went.

"THE LIGHT," said the man at Denny's. "The light was blinding. And the sun was not yet up. But I obtained these," he tapped the frame of his sunglasses, "and I stay out of the sunlight, so my skin does not burn too badly."

"And now?" I asked.

"I sell the carvings," he said. "And I seek another casement."

"You want to go back to your own time?"

He shook his head. "It's dead," he said. "And all I knew, and everything like me. It's dead. I will not return to the darkness at the end of time."

"What then?"

He scratched at his neck. Through the opening is his shirt I could see a small, black box, hanging about his neck, no bigger than a locket, and inside the box something moved: a beetle, I thought. But there are big beetles in Florida. They are not uncommon.

"I want to go back to the beginning," he said. "When it started. I want to stand there in the light of the universe waking to itself, the dawn of everything. If I am going to blinded, let it be by that. I want to be there when the suns are a-borning. This ancient light is not bright enough for me."

He took the napkin in his hand then, and reached into the leather bag with it. Taking care to touch it only through the cloth, he pulled out a flute-like instrument, about a foot long, made of green jade or something similar, and placed it on the table in front of me. "For the food," he said. "A thank you."

He got up, then, and walked away, and I sat and stared at the green flute for so long a time; eventually I reached out and felt the coldness of it with my fingertips, and then gently, without daring to blow, or to try to make music from the end of time, I touched the mouthpiece to my lips.

AFTERWORD:

I WOULD have been thirteen. The anthology was called *Flashing Swords*, the story was called "Morreion," and it started me dreaming. I found a British paperback copy of *The Dying Earth*, filled with strange misprints, but the stories were there and they were as magical as "Morreion" had been. In a dark second-hand bookshop where men in overcoats bought used pornography, I found a copy of *The Eyes of the Overworld* and then tiny dusty books of short stories—"The Moon Moth" is, I felt then and feel now, the most perfectly built SF short story that anyone has ever written—and around that point Jack Vance books began to be published in the UK and suddenly all I had to do to read Jack Vance books was buy them. And I did: *The Demon Princes*, the Alastor trilogy and the rest. I loved the way he would digress, I loved the way he would imagine, and most of all I loved the way he wrote it all down: wryly, gently, amused, like a god would be amused, but never in a way that made less of what he wrote, like James Branch Cabell but with a heart as well as a brain.

Every now and again I've noticed myself crafting a Vance sentence, and it always makes me happy when I do—but he's not a writer I'd ever dare to imitate. I don't think he's imitable.

There are few enough of the writers I loved when I was 13 I can see myself going back to in twenty years from now. Jack Vance I will reread for ever.

—Neil Gaiman